Nereid

The Narun – Book Three

G. M. Worboys

Published by G. M. Worboys
Website: gmworboys.com

Print Edition 1.0 (March-2014)
First published Mar-2014

ISBN 978-0-9874583-4-6

Cover image and design by G. M. Worboys

For my pre-readers. I would name names, but if I accidentally left anyone out I'd be mortified. Thank you, your help has been invaluable.

...

But I must add a special thanks to Paul. For your time and patience, thank you.

Contents

What Has Gone Before   *1*

Prologue   7

Falling   *15*

1. Isolation   17

2. Control   32

3. Darkness   46

4. Angel   69

5. Hunted   85

6. Zakti   105

7. Meeting   123

8. Samudraka   137

9. Caged   164

10. Peren   181

Reaching   *197*

11. Confinement   199

12. Mermaid   219

13. Trust   249

14. Connection   268

15. Breakout   301

16. Choosing   325

17. Violation   351

18. Legion   376

19. Preparations   398

20. Battle   410

Touching   *429*

21. Revelation   431

22. Attack   449

23. Tactics   466

24. Tonight   483

25. Storm   502

26. Touched   524

27. Rage   544

28. Departure   568

Epilogue   577

Appendix   *585*

Glossary   587

What Has Gone Before

(From *Dryad*, The Narun – Book One)

John Caldor, grief stricken by the loss of his wife and daughter, believes that the beautiful woman he sees emerge from the forest must be his daughter's imaginary friend, reinvented by his own broken mind. The woman, Asha, tries to explain that she is real, a being made of prana, the stuff of life.

Humans cannot normally see her kind – the narun – they have no material, flesh-and-blood body. They can only be seen by those with vedana, the sense of life, a sense that has woken in John through the agonies of his grief. Asha's people are the aaranya, forest dwellers, dryads. There are other narun peoples: naiads, nereids and others.

While he is with Asha, John can only believe her, and believe in her, but when she is gone his doubts assail him – she cannot be real. One night it comes to a head and Asha leaves in tears.

John finds it is not so easy to ignore his heart. Despite his words to Asha, he is not willing to let her go. He takes time off work to search for her in the forest, and there he finds another of her kind, Andrei. This cheeky young man agrees to lead John to the Glade, the home of the aaranya.

Asha had returned to John's house while he was at work but she is captured by two humans, Ian O'Dwyer and Darren Davies, with equipment that lets them detect and disable the narun. The humans are aided by a strange narun, Sando, who remains hidden within his protective silver suit. Asha is taken to the city and imprisoned in a laboratory beneath a large facility called the Forest Conservation Research Centre. In this laboratory she meets Dr Henry Karlin, a human that can see her. Karlin, always accompanied by Sando, performs experiments on Asha, as he has others of her kind, in an attempt to discover the secrets of prana and the narun.

At the Glade, John hears some of the history of Asha's people and learns that they fear she has been abducted by narun working with humans – a repeat of an ancient war that had devastated the narun.

An epiphany on the journey home, the discovery that narun speech is a limited form of telepathy, finally convinces John that Asha and her people are real. John is accompanied by aaranya from the Glade: Andrei, Barma, Tilvy, Darnu and Garjae. He is also given a small creature from the Glade, a brevi named Casseta.

John and his aaranya friends overpower Ian, who was waiting for them at John's house, and they drive to the city. Ian escapes from them and they are forced to try and hide in the unfamiliar city.

Asha meets other narun prisoners. She is eventually shown some strange, small and distorted narun beings that, at first, she cannot identify. She opens her senses to one of the beings and discovers it is Ellie, John's daughter. The being is the life from Ellie's human body that had been pushed violently from the flesh, becoming what the narun call a preta – a hungry ghost. The young girl's mind is lost or hiding behind the insatiable hunger of the tiny being. Asha discovers that she has an unsuspected talent for healing, and the doctor hopes that Asha may eventually be able to heal the preta.

Waldron Stephenson, a human, and another narun called Jaimee, visit the laboratory briefly. Stephenson, Jaimee and Sando appear to be the ones truly behind what has been happening. These are aided by the dhumraka, a strange narun people with a dull grey skin.

John and the others are shown around the city by Senna, a young aaranya woman of the city that has taken a fancy to Andrei. They meet Senna's father, Taiza, an aaranya with unusual interests for a narun, and Guyen (Uncle), an old aaranya man that shows them how to hide from the detectors used to find the narun.

During an attempt to rescue Asha and the other prisoners, Darnu, Garjae, Barma and Tilvy are captured and taken hostage.

Guyen, Taiza and some other city aaranya come to John and offer their help. John is befriended by a young human woman, Tracey, and she is present in the confusion after John receives a call from Karlin saying that John must come to the Research Centre or the hostages will die. John introduces Tracey to the aaranya.

John presents himself at the Research Centre where Karlin tries to convince him that he should help their efforts to study the narun. While they are distracted, Tracey and the aaranya begin to rescue the prisoners, mostly aaranya but there are also two jalaja – naiads.

When Sando discovers what is happening he reveals himself to be a different sort of narun, neither dhumraka nor aaranya. He also reveals the ability to influence minds. John frees himself of Sando's influence by punching him, and some dhumraka try to take Sando to safety. On the way out Sando recovers enough to command three of the dhumraka to make certain that everyone else is trapped. Using his control over their minds, he insists that "all must burn".

Guyen is killed protecting Tracey from the dhumraka, but the fire is started and many remain trapped. Sando is injured by Barma but escapes. Karlin and most of the preta are killed in the fire, but Ellie is saved. John breaks through a wall to release the rest of his friends from the fire. They make it out of the Research Centre and return to a refuge in a distant park. Asha has to heal Barma after he was seriously injured when hit by a car.

Asha and John acknowledge their love for each other. It may or may not work out between an aaranya and a human but, if it didn't, there would be time to be unhappy later.

(From *Naiad*, The Narun – Book Two)

John's daughter, Ellie, remains a preta – a small grey being, with her mind hidden or lost. Asha takes Ellie to the Glade, where the power of life there will sustain the child for perhaps a year. John, Asha, Andrei, Senna, Darnu and Garjae, then depart to try and trace rumours of a powerful healer that might be able to help Ellie. Tracey remains behind with Barma and Tilvy, to mind John's house.

Hidden from view, the mysterious narun, Sando and Jaimee, have their own plans.

John and his friends meet aaranya from Myanmar (Burma) that have come to northern Australia to warn that Glades to the north and east of their home are going mysteriously silent. Travelling with these aaranya is a human, Dengali, that knows of the narun – he can sense them but not see them. This apparently serendipitous meeting provides John and the others with a ship ride to Myanmar.

John gets very seasick, and when they arrive in Myanmar he is treated by a doctor, a human woman named Jia. John's illness gets worse and begins to affect his vedana (his life sense), threatening his link to Asha. Jia and Dengali take them into northern Myanmar where they meet Ben – a strange man of primitive appearance and a strong life presence, like that of the narun.

Ben and Jia, and some others of widely mixed heritage, form a community called the Samgha, a human-like people that can all see the narun. The Samgha dwell inside a large complex of tunnels and caverns within and beneath a plateau deep in the lush forests of the area. The Samgha are served by the people of the surrounding villages. Dengali, and his adult son Reyndani, are from the village just below the cliffs of the Samgha.

Asha and the others visit Glades of aaranya in the surrounding forest, while John remains in the Samgha to be treated for his illness. Supposedly as part of his cure, John goes through a dangerous procedure that allows him to pull his prana free of his human body – an ability that all those of the Samgha possess. Divided this way, his praanin form is known as saarvaya. In this new form, smaller but otherwise identical to his physical body, John is now much like the narun. While separated, his physical body remains dormant and must be protected.

Tracey's boyfriend, Mike Asquith, is getting jealous of all the time she spends at John's house – where she goes to spend time with her best friend, Tilvy. Tracey has also been catching glimpses of a man that she thinks she should recognise.

Asha and the others find the Glades of the area are not very cooperative. Only when Andrei and Senna are led away by Litak, an elder of one of the Glades, do they discover the healer they seek is a jalaja, a naiad. If she still lives she is a long way to the north.

Ben is surprisingly cooperative and agrees to arrange everything John and the others need to fly north to Siberia, to Lake Baikal in search of the healer. John separates from his human body so that he can join this new search.

Tracey and Tilvy spend time together in the city. Tracey meets the man that has been following her, it is Ian O'Dwyer, a man she saw briefly the night the Research Centre was burned. He warns her that she is being watched, and that there is a war starting back near John's house. Tracey and Tilvy rush back to try and warn the others.

4

Barma watches as the Glade is surrounded by humans and dhumraka. Most of the stand retreat into the Glade. Kaia, an elder, closes the Glade just before Sando sets fire to the forest, leaving the aaranya trapped inside – and with them the still fading preta of Ellie. Sando leaves, intending to return as often as necessary to make sure the Glade never opens again. Tracey and Tilvy arrive at John's house just as a fire is started there too. With Beenae (a youth from the Glade) they seek unreliable refuge in Tracey's car.

Beneath the ice of Lake Baikal, John finds a new world. He discovers that he can let the water pass through his body, like the narun do, and this allows him to swim to great depths. The group are led by some jalaja to the zarana (Glade) of this lake, and for the first time John enters an other-world home of the narun.

In this world within the lake, John and Asha and the others meet Ulvanya – the now ancient jalaja healer. She tells them that to heal Ellie they will need the help of someone that can see the connections between life, and to bring Ellie's mind back to her body they need someone able to find where her mind is hiding. Asha spends time with Ulvanya, refining her already powerful talent for healing. To Asha's great distress, Ulvanya tells John that he must be Asha's shield, that he must be prepared to sacrifice all to protect Asha.

In the jungles of Asia, three pale and powerful narun siblings sit on a branch and discuss the problems of taking over a particularly troublesome Glade. These are Jaimee, Sando and their beautiful sister, Helix – Queen of the Dhumraka. With them is the presence of a fourth, unseen sibling, their sister Peren.

Tracey wakes in hospital. She is questioned by a man called Raymond Cleaver, and is later taken into custody and imprisoned as a terrorist. She is confronted with photos proving she and John were at the Forest Conservation Research Centre when it was burned down, and she learns that similar fires have happened elsewhere in the world. Cleaver and his partner, Paul Aldercott, want answers, but Tracey has none that they would believe.

Tilvy and Beenae journey to the city. Tilvy wants to find Tracey and make sure that her friend is okay.

Asha feels the shadow of doom falling over her. On the last stage of their journey back to the Samgha, Jia warns Asha that Jaimee and Sando are waiting for the group. Asha agrees to depart with Jia and leave the others behind. Garjae discovers her leaving and is in time to cling to the helicopter. The others are stranded and decide to try and run the final distance. They encounter a young man, Leavek, who was sent to find them by Litak. Leavek leads them along the fastest ways through the jungle.

Asha confronts Jaimee, Sando, and Helix. She will cooperate if they let John and her friends live. They reluctantly agree. After a lengthy preparation Asha gets into a helicopter with the siblings, leaving Garjae behind to guard John's human body. Sometime later, Asha feels a rending of her heart and she believes that John must have been killed, that the doom she had been dreading had fallen.

John wakes in the jungle. With them is Asha's twin brother, Sarva, who had left the home Glade many years previously. He is one of the few survivors of the Glade that was destroyed by Jaimee, Sando and Helix. Sarva had done something that helped John when he unexpectedly collapsed in pain. They continue on to the Samgha and find that John's human body has been mutilated, his throat cut.

Garjae is there, alive, but saying strange things. Garjae causes bombs to go off, sealing them inside the tunnels. Sarva brings Garjae back to himself, and explains that Helix can control others and force them to do what she wants even at great distances. It was Garjae that had killed John, but at Helix's behest.

They find Saarvaya Ben, his flesh-and-blood body has been shot, and he is waiting to die, as all must die when their material half is killed. He tells them that he has been working with Jaimee and Sando for years. It is Jaimee, Sando and Helix that are taking over the Glades. Jaimee wanted Asha to find the old healer, he wanted her to learn all she could, so she would be better skilled to help the siblings' mother, and this had all been arranged through Ben. Once Jaimee had Asha, he decided that Ben and the Samgha were no more use, so Ben and most of the others there had been killed.

They leave Ben lying there, waiting for death, and search the tunnels. They find the bodies of Jia and many others. John remembers the river cavern where he had exercised with Reyndani, so he takes the others down there, hoping it may offer a way out.

Prologue

Three Years Ago

Sarva loved her as much as he had ever loved anyone, even his precious sister so far away. He reached forward and stroked the glossy black hair away from the side of her round face. After all he and Karya had shared, she knew his most shameful secret but had loved him anyway, to see the look of doubt so clear on her face was heartbreaking.

He could change that. He knew he could. He could release her from the Glade. That was all it would take to get his beloved back again. But he couldn't do it. It wouldn't be right.

The change had started when the strangers had arrived and began meeting with the elders. One after another the elders had gone with the strangers to meet their emissary, and as each elder returned the change was clear – to Sarva. No one else saw it, and he knew why. His attachment was to Karya, the Glade had not fully accepted him. He knew why that was too. A large piece of his heart still belonged to his twin sister. He was a man torn apart. Homeless. The only sanctuary he had found was his place beside Karya.

"Come with me," he said softly. "Tytha is the last one. She is our last chance to find out what is happening. We *must* follow her."

"No," Karya replied. "It would be wrong to interfere."

The words were wrong, even the tone was wrong.

"Then I'll go alone," he said, and stepped away from her.

He saw the panic in her eyes. He had to stop himself from rushing back to her side and proclaiming what he knew to be true, he could never leave her. If she didn't come with him he wouldn't go. But he had to discover the true cause of the changes he had seen. Perhaps, if there was no other choice, he really would free Karya from the Glade, and together they would escape this madness.

Or was the madness only in himself? Was it only his strangely distorted vision?

It was why he had waited so long before taking this step. He didn't trust himself. He knew himself to be capable of great wrongs. Could he be wrong about this? He didn't think so, but how to be certain?

"Sarva?" Karya whispered.

"Come with me." Sarva took another step away, and then another.

Karya stumbled forward. "Wait."

"No, Karya, we must go now."

And then Karya was by his side, her hands grasping at him. Sarva didn't stop. Karya had found the strength to resist the power over her, he wouldn't delay and risk having that resolve eroded away.

Together, always touching, Sarva and Karya made their way quickly but silently through the forest. It was springtime, the forest was lush and colourful around them. It was a hurried spring here, too short after the long white winter.

The strangers escorting Tytha were easy to follow, they weren't looking around, they weren't expecting trouble. They looked and felt like aaranya, but they were different somehow. Tytha was travelling slowly, perhaps reluctantly. Sarva suspected that she, too, had her doubts about what was happening to their Glade. As an elder, how could she not sense it?

They travelled a long way. The sun sank in the west and evening descended. At last the group assembled close to a large tree and waited. Sarva and Karya drew as close as they could, using the abundant life of the forest as cover.

A figure emerged from the tree. Her skin was pale, almost white, almost glowing. Long white-blond hair rose up and then cascaded down past her shoulders like a waterfall. She wore a long pure-white dress. She was beautiful. She looked young, barely an adult, but something about her spoke of greater maturity, perhaps it was the confidence that radiated from her like sunshine. And she was compelling. It was only when Karya tugged at his arm that Sarva realised he had been about to stand up and approach the woman.

Tytha and the young woman spoke softly to one another, Sarva couldn't make out the words. Tytha looked to be getting impatient. She started to turn away.

"Wait!" the young woman called, and Tytha paused.

The young woman reached out and touched Tytha gently on the side of the head, as if stroking her hair. An almost loving touch.

But the damage was done. Sarva could see it. His strange sight, the thing that was wrong with him, let him see what had happened. With his normal sight he saw Tytha straighten and turn back to the young woman. For just a moment Sarva thought he could see some resistance in the elder, the way she stood, the way she stared back into the young woman's eyes. And then it was gone. Tytha's shoulders relaxed, and she knelt before the young woman and lowered her head. There were more words too soft for Sarva to hear.

Now he knew. And he knew what had to be done. When they got back to the Glade he had to see each of the elders, if they would let him. Perhaps Karya could help. He turned to look at his beloved. She was utterly still.

The last of the elders had been taken. He should have realised. He would have to release Karya after all. They would escape together and find a new home. He reached out and touched her face. But it was such a cruel thing to do. He hesitated. "Karya," he whispered, but she didn't respond.

"Perhaps you'd like to join us?" A voice as seductive and compelling as the speaker.

Sarva looked up. The young woman was looking right at where he thought they had been so well hidden. Tytha was standing beside her, arm still raised and pointing in their direction. Tytha must have known they had been there all along. Something else Sarva should have considered.

Karya stood and began to move forward. Sarva tried to hold her back, but Karya was determined. Sarva followed, reluctantly at first, and then accepting the inevitable, he walked at Karya's side.

Karya stopped a few feet from the young woman.

"My name is Helix," the young woman introduced herself, "and these are my dhumraka."

Sarva looked around. The aaranya that they had followed no longer looked like normal aaranya. Now they were all a deep grey, shadows against the life of the forest. The polite, reassuring expressions were gone now too. Some grinned at him, pleased to have something new to entertain them, others merely looked on with distaste. Tytha had stepped back, apparently finding nothing of interest in the events.

"You are not a member of this Glade," Helix said, looking at Sarva with curiosity.

The young woman had been beautiful and compelling even from a distance, up this close Sarva had trouble stopping himself from reaching out to touch her.

"I have not been here that long," Sarva said. It wasn't the complete truth, he had been here long enough that he should have been part of the Glade by now, but it hadn't happened. "My name is Sarva."

"And your lady love?"

"This is Karya."

"She is mine already, I see," Helix said.

There was a smugness in her tone that angered Sarva. He reached across Karya, his hand stopping a few inches from her heart. He concentrated for a moment until he felt the tension against his fingers. He rubbed his thumb over that tension and it vanished.

Karya gasped in pain and turned to Sarva in shock.

But Sarva was looking at Helix. "Not any more."

"Sarva?" Karya pleaded, bewildered by what was happening to her.

Sarva put his arm around Karya and squeezed her against his side. "It's all right, my love." He turned and kissed the side of her head. "We're going to be fine."

As Sarva turned back there was movement. A light brush of fingers across his face. While his attention was diverted, Helix had reached out and touched him. He felt a wave of love for the beautiful pale woman before him. He wanted to abase himself before her and plead for her forgiveness. He let go of Karya, and his knees started to bend. But another part of him rebelled, appalled at what was being asked of him. A moment later the feelings broke and he straightened up. His body had rejected the woman's touch.

He glared back at her. "Not me."

Helix stared at him in surprise, and then glanced at her hand as if

10

looking for the fault there.

Sarva turned, looking for a way out, but he was surrounded by dhumraka. He turned back to Karya, hoping to find some way to protect her, but when he tried to pull her close, her body resisted. Helix had touched her.

He reached out and rubbed his fingers a few inches from Karya's head and she sagged against him.

"No!" Helix said loudly. "That is not possible!"

Sarva held Karya close and didn't try to respond to Helix.

"Sarva?" Karya pleaded again. Such helpless tones sounded unnatural. The woman he loved was strong and exuberant, but what he had done to her, twice now, had set her adrift. He didn't know how much of this she would be able to take. He had to find a way to escape, but he couldn't afford to take his eyes off Helix.

A dhumraka man appeared at Helix's side. In his hand was a long slender blade, metal with a wooden handle. The point of the sword plunged toward Sarva's chest and he was too surprised to try and evade it. At the last moment it stopped. Helix had reached out and restrained the dhumraka's arm.

"No. Not yet." Helix had regained her equilibrium and confidence. "Karya," she said softly. "Come here, Karya."

Karya clung to Sarva and shook her head.

"Come here, Karya, or watch your lover die."

Karya looked up tearfully at Sarva, squeezed him tightly and then released him. Sarva watched on helplessly, the tip of the sword hovering at his chest, as Karya approached Helix.

"That's right, sweet child." The words Helix spoke seemed incongruous, Helix looked younger than Karya. Helix pulled Karya into an embrace, resting her head against the side of Karya's. A moment later Karya's previously slack and reluctant body animated and she hugged Helix fiercely. Helix smiled at Sarva over Karya's shoulder, and then she turned her head and the two women kissed passionately. Karya's hands moved up and her fingers explored Helix's face, then ran back through her hair, trying to hold the kiss longer and harder.

Helix broke the embrace.

"No," Karya pleaded.

"Go back to your lover, sweet child," Helix told her softly.

Karya turned. There were tears streaming down her face. She looked at Sarva without affection, as if he was a stranger, an unwanted intruder. Her return was as slow and reluctant as her departure had been. She stood at Sarva's side and stared back at Helix with a longing that Sarva recognised though it was no longer directed at himself.

"Now break it," Helix told him.

Sarva stared at her in disbelief.

"Break it," Helix insisted. "If you can."

This was no ordinary connection, but he could break it. Unlike Helix, he had no doubts. And he wanted to break it, he couldn't bear to see Karya like this. But Karya had already been through too much. "No," he said. "It's not safe."

"You have a choice." Helix reached across to the dhumraka and pulled on his arm until the tip of the blade was pointing at Karya. "Break it, or watch her die."

Karya didn't react to this threat. She stood still, watching Helix with adoring eyes.

Sarva looked back and forth between the two women. Then he looked around hoping for some way out of his dilemma. The dhumraka were all watching eagerly. Tytha was no longer visible, Sarva hadn't seen her leave.

"Break it," Helix repeated.

Sarva didn't know what would happen if he obeyed. He didn't know how much damage it might cause. He looked down. The blade had been pressed closer, its tip was now touching Karya's breast. Maybe there was a chance. It was the only chance left open to him.

He reached out and lifted the tip of the blade carefully away. Then he reached up and grasped at a place a few inches from Karya's head. The tension was stronger this time, he had to press harder with his thumb. He rubbed twice and the tension was still there, so he pressed down harder and rubbed a third time.

Karya screamed.

The desolate cry echoed through Sarva's head. And then silence.

Sarva reached out and turned Karya to him. Those beautiful brown eyes that had looked at him with such love were empty now. No recognition. No sign that they saw anything at all.

"Karya?" he called quietly.

He pulled Karya close but she didn't respond. He released her and held her at arm's length, studying her, hoping to find some sign that she would recover. She stayed standing, but that seemed the limit of her abilities. What had he done?

He was still standing there, staring at his beloved in despair, when there was a flash of silver from one side. He glanced down in time to see the blade of the sword pass into Karya's chest and through her heart. It withdrew with a gush of golden prana that splashed out over Sarva.

Karya made no sound. Sarva caught her as she collapsed, lowering her gently onto his knees as he sat down. Sarva watched as her eyes went dull. He was silent. In shock. He still couldn't believe what had happened. None of it.

"That was interesting," Helix said flatly, "but I don't think you're someone we want around."

Sarva looked up. Helix was already turning away from him.

"See to it," she told the dhumraka with the sword, and then she walked away.

Sarva still couldn't believe it, refused to believe it, but he wasn't going to let that woman get away. He laid Karya gently on the ground, and touched her lips one last time before standing up.

The dhumraka with the sword was standing between Sarva and the disappearing back of Helix. Sarva rushed at the man. The speed and abandon of his attack took the dhumraka by surprise. The sword was raised clumsily and Sarva brushed it aside with his left hand, receiving a deep cut that he didn't feel. He snatched out with his right hand, close to the dhumraka's head, but never touching it, and gave a savage tug. The dhumraka screamed and collapsed.

Sarva would have kept going then, kept chasing after Helix, but the other dhumraka were on him. As he fell to the ground his hand touched the hilt of the sword. He grabbed it and lashed out. More screams and the dhumraka fell back.

There was a wary pause, and then one of the dhumraka found a small branch and picked it up. Others began to follow his lead.

Sarva's chances of following Helix evaporated. The sword was a better weapon but there were too many dhumraka. He couldn't win. He ran at a dhumraka reaching down for a branch, and skewered him. Now beyond the circle of his attackers, Sarva dropped the sword and ran.

He fled from his attackers. He fled from the beautiful pale woman that could control a person with a touch. But – most of all – he fled from the body of his love and the memory of what he had done.

Falling

1. *Isolation*

The swirling wet voice of the underground river filled the space around them, its tones, muted against the rock, were like standing in a crowded room with everyone speaking in whispers. There was no light down here in the depths below the Samgha, but John's vedana, his sense of life, allowed him to sense – to clearly see – the cavern to which he had led his friends. The rock itself, extending across from the valley of Gayatri, was imbued with life, and the dark and cold water of the underground river carried its own life swiftly past them.

On a rise to one side John could see a shadow against the rock that he knew to be a pile of towels. John wondered what had become of Reyndani, whose task it had been to keep that pile of towels stocked. John could only hope Reyndani and his family had escaped the massacre. There was no other sign that anyone had been to this cavern recently.

They had come down here, away from the devastation and the death that filled the corridors above them, seeking to escape their isolation. This was their way out, if they had the courage to take it.

"Nice morning for a dip," said Andrei brightly.

John glanced at him. Was it really morning?

"The current is very strong," said Darnu, "it will be easier if we can follow it downstream, but how are we going to get you past that, John?" He pointed to the metal grid that stretched across the river and down below its surface. It was there to protect those that came down here to swim from being swept away.

"I think we should find another way," said Leavek. There was an unfamiliar tone of fear in his voice.

"Can't you swim?" asked Andrei.

Leavek ignored that. "There are stories," he started, and then stopped.

"What is it?" Senna asked him.

Leavek glanced at Senna, then back down to the dark water. "They speak of spirit-beings, soul-suckers."

"Someone's a sucker, anyway," John heard Andrei mutter. Then a muffled, "Ow!" after a jab from Senna's elbow.

"They live off the lives that get dragged below ground," Leavek continued, oblivious to Andrei's commentary. "No one who goes down there ever returns."

John watched Leavek carefully as he spoke. The confident young tracker was gone, replaced by this frightened youth. Whatever those stories were, they had obviously gone deep.

"I don't know any other way," John said quietly.

"We could look," answered Leavek, "we have time."

John looked calmly back into Leavek's eyes. The others may have time, but John? His time was already overdrawn. His human body was decomposing on a bed far above them, all he had left was this praanin body and however long he could make it last. He could not draw life from the water or trees as his friends could. Without Asha to feed him John would fade; perhaps quickly, perhaps slowly, but according to everything he had been told his end was not far away. There might yet be ways to stave off the inevitable, but whatever time he had left he had dedicated to finding Asha. Without that driving force he would still be sitting next to his corpse, waiting for death to catch up.

Leavek turned away from him.

"Garjae?" Darnu called.

John looked up to see Garjae walking into the river.

"Might as well find out if John can get out this way," Garjae called back, and then disappeared into the water.

John looked to Darnu. "What does he mean?"

"The rest of us can get through that grid without a problem," Darnu explained. "We just merge with the water and flow through with it. But you can't merge, so the grid will remain a barrier to you."

John stared at the river, remembering how it had chilled his human body. In this body he could let the water flow through him, and he through it, but he could not merge fully as the narun could, he could not become part of the flow. His body would remain tangible and solid to everything except the water, and this body was too large to squeeze through the metal grid.

A few moments later Garjae surfaced on the other side of the grid, holding on to stop the water sweeping him away. "It doesn't go all the way to the bottom," he called, "you can go under it."

"I can't," Leavek said.

Leavek was shaking his head back and forth, fighting some internal battle. "It's not safe," he muttered. "No one returns. Unfriendly spirits."

"There's nothing friendly left upstairs," Andrei reminded him.

Leavek continued shaking his head, not looking at any of them. Senna went to him and put her hands on his arm, trying to comfort him. John looked to Asha's brother in question. Sarva had been quiet since they had left the bodies in the tunnels above.

"I heard some of those stories when I first came north, years ago," Sarva admitted. "I don't know what they really mean. I don't know what the dangers are. No one does, because no one returns."

Leavek looked up gratefully at Sarva.

"Someone must have returned if they know there are unfriendly spirits to be had," Andrei argued.

Sarva shrugged.

"I don't have a choice," said John. He looked around at the others. "But you do. You don't have to come with me if you want to try and find another way."

"I prefer spirits to corpses," said Andrei. "I'm coming with you."

"I think we should stay together," said Darnu.

"Are you coming?" Garjae yelled, still clinging to the other side of the grate.

"Still a patient soul," observed Andrei, "it's good to see his recent experiences haven't changed him too much."

John walked into the shallows at the edge of the river, feeling the cold water swirl around his legs. He looked back to the others. "I have to go. I have to keep moving. The rest of you should stick together, whatever you choose to do. I don't have a choice." He turned back to the river and pushed out into it. The main stream quickly caught at his body. He concentrated and felt the wash of cold as the water began to flow through the prana of his body. Much of the pressure from the current dropped away, but some remained. Darnu was right, even like this it would be hard work to swim far upstream.

Swimming gently against the current, John let the water carry him back slowly to the grate. He grasped at the metal and looked through at Garjae.

"What's the hold up?" Garjae asked.

"It may not be safe," John told him. "Perhaps you should go back to them, they may decide to stay and look for another way out."

"And you?"

"I'm going on."

Garjae nodded. "I'll come with you."

"You don't owe me anything, Garjae."

"There's nothing left up there," he answered. "Any exits we're likely to find will already be closed. It's this or nothing."

John descended beneath the water, holding onto the grate and following it down until he found the gap at the bottom. He came up on the other side and held on beside Garjae.

Darnu and Sarva were already in the water, making their way downstream. On the bank it appeared that Andrei and Senna had persuaded Leavek to come with them, however reluctantly.

As soon as Darnu and Sarva surfaced on this side of the grid, Garjae let go and let the water take him. John gave a brief glance back to the three on the far side. They were still coming, so John released his hold too. On one side he could feel Darnu's presence, on the other was that half-familiar presence of Sarva, enough like his twin sister that John had to look across to remind himself that Asha was truly gone.

- - -

Asha felt a hand push her hair to one side and stroke her shoulder. It wasn't John. She woke properly. John! She thrust out one fist as hard as she could. There was a grunt as she connected.

"What did you do to him!" she yelled. She pushed herself up and out of the chair.

Jaimee put his arms up to block her next blows. "Whoo, girl."

Asha kept hitting, and when her fists failed to get through she

20

pulled back for a moment and then reached out and ran her fingers across his arm.

"Ow! Fucking hell!"

Jaimee's arm came down and he clutched at the wound now spilling golden prana. Asha punched out again, connecting hard with Jaimee's mouth and nose, and his head snapped back. She pushed forward to hit him again, but stopped suddenly, clutching at her head. Invisible sharp spikes stabbed into her temples and she cried out in pain.

"No, Sando!" Jaimee called out. "I'm all right. Don't damage her."

The pain in her head receded, but so did her momentum. John used to laugh at how quick her temper was to come and then to go again. Used to.

Jaimee was stepping back away from her and Sando came up beside him. The brothers were identical in appearance, but Asha would always tell them apart. Of the two, it was Jaimee that scared her the most, though she didn't know why.

"What did you do?" she asked, her tone pleading and desperate. "You did something to John. I know you did. I felt it."

"We did nothing," Jaimee answered. "As we promised."

Asha stared back at this strange narun. All confidence and elegance expressed in pale shades. Even the almost colourless eyes, just the slightest hint of an ice-blue iris surrounded his pupils, carried that sense of assurance. His entire stance and presence proclaimed that lies were anathema to his existence, that he would not deign to be stained by such ugliness. Asha began to question herself.

The pain that had swamped her, that had carried her into darkness and nightmares for so many long hours, had seemed so real. Every instinct told her that the pain had come from John. Ulvanya had spoken of connections between living things, including between lovers, and Asha was convinced that she had felt the pain of John's death through such a connection. It had felt so real. It was real. She knew it was. But she had to admit that she didn't know, couldn't know, what that sharp pain had really meant. And it was gone now, leaving just a dull ache echoing through her chest. Surely, if John were truly dead, that pain would still be there? It could not heal so quickly. Or was she now, as Ulvanya had once been, in denial of an impossible loss?

"It was not a promise we gave easily. My brother had other plans, but he gave them up for you." Jaimee now wore an expression of patient sympathy. "Are you even certain of this harm? Would you like us to go back and check?"

She turned her face away from his disturbing gaze. She couldn't ask them to go back. As much as she might crave a last glimpse of John, any further confrontation just increased the chances that he would be hurt. Was that an admission that she thought he may still be alive? That harm was still possible? Was the thought just a desperate hope or did she truly believe it? She couldn't tell. She wanted to believe. She ached to believe. If John was still alive then her sacrifice meant something. She needed it to be true, but that didn't make it true. There was no acceptable way to break this circle.

"We have to move, Asha." Jaimee spoke the words softly, almost as if he cared about her distress.

Asha turned back to him. He even looked concerned. A lie. It was enough to spark her anger again, but then she noticed something strange. She stared at his arm. The last of the prana was evaporating and the wound she had made was almost invisible now. So fast? She looked up into his face.

"You're a healer?"

Jaimee glanced down at his arm and shrugged. "It is not an appellation that really suits," he said. "I have other, more useful, talents." He flicked the index finger of one hand.

Asha's eyes went to the pain on her own arm. There was a scratch. It wasn't deep, but it was real, and it hadn't been there a moment before. Jaimee was still a body length or more away from her, and yet he had cut her even from there.

"That's just a sample. I can go much deeper. Remember that next time your temper tries to get the better of you."

"Come on," said Sando, "they'll want to close up soon."

They were inside a plane that Asha didn't remember entering. She didn't remember it taking off. She didn't remember it landing. She followed Sando numbly down the steps, Jaimee came behind. The small jet was inside a hanger. There were a few humans around, doing whatever it was they did in these places.

"What happened to the other one?" Asha asked, looking around,

22

remembering that Helix had been with them before.

"My dear sister had pressing matters to attend to," Jaimee answered.

Sando continued walking, giving the humans a wide berth, and led the way through a door into a long corridor.

"It's a roundabout route," Jaimee apologised from behind Asha. "Some idiot blew up some buildings and now we're forced to walk around the pointless security measures. If they only knew," he finished enigmatically.

At one point they passed into an open area teeming with humans, many walking, others waiting in lines. Asha was tempted to rush off through them and try to lose herself in the crowd, but where would she go? The chance, if it had ever existed, had gone before she could find an answer.

It was more difficult once they reached the outside of the main buildings. There were humans everywhere and keeping out of their way took concentration. But they didn't have far to go. Asha recognised Stephenson, Jaimee's human servant: sparse red hair, heavily built, expensively dressed. He saw them coming, opened the door of a long black limousine, and then made a point of looking for something in his pockets while Sando, Asha and Jaimee climbed into the car. Stephenson climbed in after them. As he settled into his seat he nodded at Asha, perhaps as a reminder that he could see her.

The car moved off into the slow traffic.

The men talked, but Asha wasn't listening. She was still trying to find some point of stability in her mind. Some point of reference she could hold onto as her own. She had placed herself under the control of these two brothers, but she hadn't really understood what that would mean, just how complete that control would be. They had taken her away from everyone and everything she knew and left her with no basis for making choices. At the centre of the turmoil was John. She had done all this for the man she loved, a man she could never see again. She couldn't even be certain he still lived. She could still feel the ache in her chest, was that her pain or his? Her uncertainties left her mind in a tormented limbo.

- - -

Kaia had survived. Her unconscious body had fallen where Barma

23

now stood and the other elders had taken her away to care for her. She still hadn't regained consciousness.

Barma was thinking about Tilvy. He did that a lot. There didn't seem much else to do since the Way had closed and the Glade had been isolated. Thinking about Tilvy also meant thinking about Tracey. He hoped they were together, friends should be together in times of trouble. And this made him think about Andrei. He wondered where his childhood friend was now. Could he be outside? Perhaps looking in where Barma was looking out – or trying to look out.

Barma was standing before a large oval of exposed wood, deadwood it appeared, framed by a curl of living bark. This was where the shimmering surface of the Way had been stretched before it closed. The exposed wood was finely grained and beautifully patterned. Swirls of deep browns and blacks marked the surface, testimony to the flames that had destroyed the trees outside. None of them had seen those flames but they had all felt them, they had all felt the pain of their forest burning.

Tilvy and Barma had tried to describe the Glade to Tracey. Perhaps if they had been younger they might have had more success. As children this had all been new and wondrous. Andrei had led Barma into every nook and crevice, there was no part of the Glade that wasn't as familiar to them as each other's face – or so it seemed at the time. But they had grown and that familiarity had led to a certain blindness. Barma felt he should remedy that, so that when the Way opened again he could offer a description worthy of the Glade.

He took a few steps back and looked up along the massive trunk. His eyes reached further and further up, finally reaching the canopy. The tree wasn't dead, he reminded himself when the brown of the leaves shocked him. It was only damaged, it would recover. It had to recover, or the Way would never open. He held his eyes to that great height and understood that the first thing any description needed was some common point of reference, some way to describe the scale of things inside the Glade.

Outside the Glade was – had been – a forest of huge trees. Barma had come to learn that the trees of their forest were much larger than those of many other places. Hundreds of feet high, huge by any human scale, and the two great supports of the Way had been the most substantial of them all. And yet even those trees were dwarfed by the trees inside the Glade.

This tree was the baijika, the source of the Glade; the core, the centre, the heart. From here the Glade stretched out in all directions to distances that Andrei and Barma had pretended to conquer. The baijika sat on a base that would have covered John's house and rose in a single great stem until the limb on which Barma stood, a height greater than the height of the trees outside. When you walked in at ground level from the outside, this was where you came out, hundreds of feet above the ground of this world.

Yes, thought Barma to himself, that's a good start. Now we have set the scale.

In front of Barma was the deadwood wall, where once the Way had rippled and glistened in subtle tones of tan and gold, like naked timber seen through the surface of a frolicking stream.

Barma grinned to himself, pleased. He was almost poetic.

The deadwood imposed itself and turned his thoughts sombre. That deadwood wall was like the injured trees you sometimes saw outside, where the internal timber had died but the insistent growth of the bark pushed its way over and around the injury. The bark formed a moulded oval frame, as if waiting for a picture like the photo-frames Barma had seen on John's mantelpiece. But this was much larger, a dozen people had once been able to walk side by side through the Way.

One of the things that marked the baijika out from the other trees of the Glade was that you couldn't merge with it. The life in it was too strong, even now when it was so obviously under stress. Only this oval wall in front of him felt devoid of life. He pressed his hand against it. His palm submerged to not much more than skin deep before it hit the barrier of life beyond. It was reassuring that the damage was not deep.

Enough, Barma warned himself, or he'd lose his audience.

He turned and looked out, pretending he had just come through the Way. This is what they would see.

He shook his head. That was too much. He'd have to work up to it, so he looked down at the limb on which he stood. It was almost as wide as the trunk and the top was almost flat. He could assure his

25

friends that they needn't worry about falling off – not that anyone able to enter the Glade would be hurt by the fall.

A few paces out from the trunk, the limb forked and stretched its mighty arms out to the nearest trees on either side. Each arm twined with a limb from the companion to form a bridge. Let your eyes follow the line of that bridge to the trees beyond. As your view expands into the forest you see that all the trees were linked, like a crowd of people reaching out to one another in joyous greeting. The higher branches reached gently upwards toward the distant sun, forming dense bowers of leaves.

Even with the abundant growth of the foliage this wasn't a dark place. The sun shone down through and between the widely spaced trees so that during the day the entire forest at this level was light, and felt airy and open. Far beneath where Barma stood, there lay an understorey of much smaller trees, most less than a hundred feet high, and those shaded a final, darker layer of ferns and shrubs that covered much of the ground beneath the forest.

Barma let his eyes come back again to the view that you met as you came out from the Way.

Barma tried to think of some human experience that might give comparison to this. Perhaps a cathedral like those he'd seen in the city would provide a suitable, if still inadequate, example. Huge trees formed a broad avenue that reached down a gentle slope into the distance. At intervals the trees on each side reached branches across this avenue in delicate arching bridges. Down the centre of this open avenue ran a clear blue river. It wandered slightly from side to side as it flowed into the distance. The understorey trees did not encroach on this avenue, though the ferns and shrubs did spill out from beneath that understorey in places. Between those areas were expanses of lush green grass. He could see the tiny figures of people relaxing near the river.

He closed his eyes and re-opened them to see if his explanation was enough. If he was an artist like John, then he would draw sketches for his audience. But he wasn't, his words would have to do. Barma grinned, thinking that John would say all this was impossible, that these long branch-bridges should break under their own weight. Barma would explain that life in the Glade made its own rules.

There was more, not all the Glade was covered in this way. There were galleries, sculpted and filled by artists, and beyond this large central forest were open areas and other forests of lesser trees, but he would think about those another time.

He sat down against the deadwood wall. There was another huge limb on the other side of the tree, opposite this wall, where people sometimes went for secluded meditation – near the heart, but hidden from the busy thoroughfare of the Way. But it wasn't busy now. Barma had this space to himself. He sat quietly and brooded.

- - -

The breeze off the river whispered through Tracey's hair. After her weeks of confinement it felt very good. Not clean exactly, the river here in the middle of the city was never really clean, but the breeze felt fresh. Tracey had grown up in this city, the constant smells of traffic and modern humanity were something she only ever noticed at a time and place like this, where the scents would come and go with the air blowing off the water.

She could feel the eyes of the two men, Cleaver and Aldercott, watching her from behind the darkened windows of their car. She knew them well enough now to know that they were both nervous. Cleaver in particular was concerned about the danger this meeting posed to Tracey. But Tracey wasn't worried, not about the sorts of danger that Cleaver was imagining. She watched the river and waited, and while she waited she tried to work out if she was doing the right thing.

She remembered the moment when her interrogations had turned. Cleaver had slid one more dreaded photograph across the table. Tracey had stared down at the photo, anticipating the horror she would see, but still not really prepared. The photograph showed just the head and shoulders of a man. He was obviously dead. There was a bullet hole in the centre of the man's forehead. At least she assumed that it must have been a bullet that made that surreal dark cavity, so much like a cigarette burn in the photograph that Tracey had almost reached out to touch it. On the floor beneath the head she could see a dark brown stain, the pattern of the carpet showed through in places. The man's face was pale, almost a glossy white, and the expression made it certain that this man had seen his death coming.

After everything that Cleaver had already shown Tracey, in the hope of shocking her into cooperating, even such details as these would have meant little. But this photo was different. Tracey had cringed and tried to turn her head away, but her eyes stayed locked on the face. She had pushed the photo away, but her traitor eyes had helplessly followed. She put her hands over her eyes and pulled her face down. Her eyes were wet. It was only then that she heard the sobs that were shaking her body. She knew that man. It was Ian. The man had delayed his own escape to warn Tracey she was in danger. A warning she had ignored.

Cleaver hadn't pushed her then. Tracey had sensed the surprise from the others in the room, she had been surprised herself. Cleaver had called an end to the day's interrogations and let Tracey return to her cell.

The next morning Tracey hadn't waited for Cleaver to start. After a sleepless night, her mind constantly flashing up images of Ian as he had been, and then Ian as he was in that photo, Tracey had no strength left to argue or resist. "I'm going to tell you everything," she had told them, "but you won't believe me."

Tracey was right, they hadn't believed her. The interrogations were more brutal for a time. Cleaver was angry with her for spinning such wild tales, he thought Tracey was being frivolous. When Tracey didn't move from her story a psychologist was called in. Tracey heard them talk about her delusions and how real they were to her. It was then that Cleaver offered Tracey protective custody. Tracey had readily agreed.

The questions had continued, but gently now, and in the more relaxed atmosphere of an apartment in the city. They were trying to piece together facts from the small pieces of her statement that they found believable. Tracey was not free, there were always at least two guards, but she could fool herself into thinking she was no longer a prisoner as such. And if her treatment bore the hallmarks of one thought to be mentally ill, at least her captors no longer treated her with the harsh judgement that she was a terrorist.

Two days ago, Cleaver had come in and shown her a short text message: "Where are you!!! T." They had been monitoring Tracey's old mobile telephone number though the telephone itself no longer worked. That message had led them here, to the park by the river, waiting for Tilvy.

Tracey brought her focus back from the tall buildings across the river, and her mind back to the present. Was she betraying her friend? It only now occurred to Tracey that there were probably more people watching her than just the two men in the car. They wouldn't have brought Tracey out here in the open without backup of some sort. Tracey peered around at the other people she could see, but she couldn't detect anything out of place.

Tracey's justification to herself for going along with this meeting, what her captors thought was a trap, was that she wanted to warn Tilvy about how much she had told these people. It was only right that Tilvy, and all her people, should know what Tracey had done. But, when lying awake at night, a more personal reason forced itself on her. With their careful condescension, at times even speaking loudly and slowly as if she were deaf rather than delusional, Cleaver and the others had almost convinced Tracey that she really was mentally ill, that her experiences had all been some trick of her mind. Tracey desperately needed confirmation that it had been real, she needed the touch of her best friend.

There was movement to her left. Tracy turned her head, and despite expecting it, jumped when a hand touched her arm. "Tilvy!"

Warm arms enveloped Tracey and hugged her tightly. She closed her arms around her friend and tears of relief ran down her face. "Tilvy," she repeated quietly. "I've missed you so much."

Tracey remembered she was being watched and pulled back out of Tilvy's arms. Cleaver was out of the car, the door was still open. He was watching her but not moving. "I'm being watched," Tracey explained to Tilvy. "I picked this spot so you could escape to the river, or to one of the trees, if anyone comes close."

Still holding one of Tilvy's hands, unwilling to let her friend go, Tracey tried to think what she should do, what she should say. "Let's sit," she said. "I'll tell you what happened."

Tracey and Tilvy sat together beneath the nearest of the trees. Tracey could see that Cleaver was leaning against the car, talking on his mobile. She decided she could ignore him for now. With Tilvy's shoulder touching Tracey's, one hand resting lightly on Tracey's arm, Tracey began to tell her friend what had happened, and how much Tracey had told her human captors.

"And so they had me respond to your message and arrange this meeting. It's supposed to be a trap, they're waiting for the mysterious T to show her face."

Tilvy rubbed Tracey's arm gently.

"They still don't believe me," Tracey finished. "Obviously, or there would be people swarming around us already, so perhaps it doesn't matter. But I thought you should know."

Tilvy's hand squeezed Tracey's arm in reassurance, and then drew squiggles lightly along the arm.

"Pen and paper? I did bring some, but people will see you writing."

They huddled together with the small pad resting on Tracey's knees, and Tracey's arms on either side to obscure the view of anyone trying to watch. It was an awkward position but Tilvy managed to write out her brief message.

"I MISSED YOU TOO!!!" was the first thing Tilvy wrote.

Tracey smiled sadly.

"I could knock them out. We could leave together," was the next message.

Tracey shook her head. "I thought about that. There's got to be others watching. Anyway, where could I go? I can't go home. Cleaver says there's probably others looking for me. I'm probably safer where I am, even if they think I'm loony."

The page of the small pad was flicked over, and Tilvy wrote, "Where are they keeping you? I can visit!!"

"It's too dangerous. I'm in an apartment in the city."

"I've used elevators before." This was followed by a little smiley face.

"I know, but you could get trapped."

Tracey heard a car door and looked around. "They're coming. You'd better go."

The pen made a brief squiggle on the pad before both slid down into Tracey's lap. There was a last squeeze of her hand and then Tilvy's presence was gone.

In a rising panic Tracey realised that they'd made no plans for the future. She stood quickly and called out, "I'll send you a message."

A moment later a small cluster of leaves dropped to the ground, brushing Tracey's shoulder as they fell.

Tracey looked up into the tree and grinned. "I love you too!"

The two men arrived. Aldercott was staring up into the tree, but Cleaver was looking at Tracey, his eyes showing open concern – and pity. He thinks I've just had an *episode*, she realised. Tracey smiled back at him happily. She didn't care. She knew she was okay, her friend had been there for her.

2. Control

They swam facing upstream to control their speed against the swift current. They had to watch over their shoulders to see what was coming. The river followed a gentle bend and soon John could no longer see the grid, nor the three that had not yet come through.

The next bend was sharper and the roof began to descend. They were forced to sink beneath the surface to avoid knocking their heads on protrusions from the rocky ceiling. John had to remind himself that this body didn't need to breathe, and that narun telepathy didn't need air to speak.

"The river is getting faster," said Sarva, pointing to the side.

The walls of the river had been slowly closing in, and Sarva was right, they were passing much more quickly now.

Sarva peered ahead. "The others haven't caught up, we should stop and wait for them."

John nodded and looked over his shoulder to where Darnu had allowed the current to take him closer to Garjae. He could see the curve in the river as it dropped even more steeply.

"We need to stop," he called to them.

As he spoke they seemed to recede from him. A protrusion from the wall went past and the rough currents buffeted him. Sarva helped John to steady himself back into the centre of the rushing river. The water was roaring angrily now. He looked across to Sarva, hoping he had some idea what they should do.

Sarva reached out to the wall of the river on his side. "It's too smooth," he spoke loudly over the roar of the water.

Garjae and Darnu were swimming hard against the current and their efforts managed to slowly close the distance. The group came together and swam forward strongly. They could slow their descent, but they couldn't stop and they couldn't gain purchase on the sides. At Sarva's suggestion they relaxed their efforts to conserve their strength.

The walls faded to black as they descended below the vein of living rock. John's vedana could still see through the water to his friends, but the rock tube that encased them was now just an ominous dark shadow.

An empty lurching sensation and the river became a vertical tube of relentless water. A swirling side current caught at John and twisted him around. Sarva grabbed his wrist and John did his best to return the hold. There was no fighting this current, they had ceased trying.

"Thanks," John managed to say before they were caught in a stronger side current. He lost all sense of direction as they were swirled in a wide circle.

John had time to realise that the walls had receded, that they had entered a large bulge at the bottom of the tube. He heard Darnu yell out for Sarva. Sarva reached out with his free hand and grabbed Darnu's ankle. Beyond Darnu, John could see Garjae and then the dark floor of this cavern where two areas, made pale by the whirling currents, were like eyes staring back at him – holes where the water was escaping from this flooded, whirling bulb.

The currents of the whirlpool had them, they couldn't fight their way out. The four were swept helplessly down to the gaping holes. Garjae, Darnu and Sarva were dragged inexorably to one side, but John was caught in a current that tried to pull him to the other. His arm was wrenched as the current tried to break his hold on Sarva. John felt their fingers begin to slip. Their hold was on the verge of breaking when the pressure vanished and John was swept out with the others.

This new tunnel was narrower than the tube leading into the cavern, time and again John felt his shoulder or leg bang painfully against the side. Sarva clung tenaciously to John's wrist and drew him closer.

A momentary quiet as the tunnel walls vanished, and then the torrent crashed into a pool of water. The boiling currents tore Sarva and John apart. For a time John could make nothing out through the swirling water. He fought his way to the surface but was quickly washed under again.

He thought he heard Garjae call and tried to fight his way in that direction. The swirling currents kept turning him. At last he broached the surface beyond the waterfall and could hear Garjae more clearly. The currents were still strong, but they were confused and it was possible to force his way across them.

Garjae appeared to be standing in darkness above the water. Only as John got closer did the film of water over the rock allow him to see that Garjae was standing on a ledge. Darnu was lying at his feet, not moving. John took a moment to search the water and was relieved to see Sarva just a small distance behind, swimming strongly.

They gathered on the rocky ledge with Garjae. Darnu was starting to come around, groaning.

"He banged his head as we came through," Garjae explained.

They rested for a time, not moving or speaking.

John was breathing heavily after the excitement and exertion of their ride, though the breaths were redundant to this form. At first he supposed it was a hangover from being human, then he noticed the others were doing the same. Something built-in then. More evidence, perhaps, that the stories old Nayati had told him, suggesting a common heritage for humans and narun, might be true.

He looked around their weary group and then out across the water. There was something peculiar about what he was seeing, he had trouble making sense of it. In the forest at night his vedana could sense life in almost everything around him, even plants and creatures that died soon have living inhabitants move in. His mind translated this sensory input from his vedana into vision, and so he could "see" in the forest on even the darkest nights, just as his friends the aaranya did. It was much the same back in the Samgha, where the living rock allowed them to navigate the tunnels without light. But down here they had left the living rock behind. If this rock held any life the amount was too small to be detected by John's senses.

That left just the life of the water. Water was that special substance that both carried prana, the substance of life, and also

34

spare nadis, spaces for life; a trait that made it possible for praanin creatures like John and the narun to pass through it. This also meant that the water was both visible and mostly transparent. It didn't glow, it didn't impart any light or visibility on the rock except by its presence as a thin film trickling over the surface, and as a fog in the air from the constant mist raised by the waterfall. It was this that gave the scene of the cavern such a strange appearance. Their small group looked to be floating in a void, and the mist that swirled about them would sometimes clear enough to reveal only darkness streaked with faint lines, rivulets of water on the walls of the cavern.

The pool of water in front of them, that would have been crystal clear to normal vision, was deep enough that the life it carried, and the currents that kept it in constant motion, prevented John from seeing to the bottom. The effect on his senses was one of a translucent silver. Not shiny as it might have been under light, but neutral and darkening the deeper you tried to look into it. Like looking into infinity, John thought.

Eventually John noticed that Sarva was staring at the waterfall. Apparently sensing John's gaze, Sarva glanced at him briefly before returning his attention to the roaring water.

"Andrei and the others shouldn't have been far behind us," he said.

"They should have been here by now," agreed Garjae.

"I almost got dragged into the other tunnel when we came out of that whirlpool," John said. "Maybe they went the other way."

"Give them more time yet," said Sarva. "Leavek may have held them up."

"And I'm not ready to go anywhere yet," added Darnu in a groggy voice.

They agreed to rest and wait, taking it in turns to watch for their friends.

John woke to see Darnu and Garjae entering the water, Sarva was again watching the waterfall. "It should be my turn," John told him.

"You need to rest, conserve your strength," Sarva replied.

John did feel weaker, and tired, though considering what they'd been through that was not surprising. He decided not to argue the point. "What are they up to?" he asked, pointing to the water where Darnu and Garjae had disappeared.

"They're going to try and find where the water is leaving this cavern, and hopefully avoid being swept away in the process."

John sat back. After a moment he observed, "I can dimly remember a man that thought he had finally gotten his life under control. I find it impossible to believe that man was me."

"Control is only an illusion," Sarva said flatly. "A trick of the mind. Something fleeting that we fool ourselves into believing so we can feel safe for a time."

"I remember it felt good."

"That's why we're so happy to accept that, *this* time, it might last. But it never does," Sarva finished unhappily.

The roaring of the waterfall filled the space between them for a time.

"They could be a while," Sarva said into the space. "Why don't you tell me how my sister became involved with someone like you?"

"A human?" John asked. He looked carefully at Sarva, trying to sense if there was disapproval in his tone.

"I guess you were. I'm not sure what you are now."

"Saarvaya is what they called me in the Samgha."

Sarva nodded without looking away from the waterfall. "But you're not just half any more, are you? You're all there is. ... Go on. I got the short version from Andrei when we met in the forest, but I'm guessing there's a lot more to it."

"It all seems a lifetime ago now. Maybe that's exactly what it is."

After some time to gather his thoughts, John proceeded to tell Sarva how he'd lost his wife and, he thought at the time, his daughter. How something had changed in his head that allowed him to see the narun. He described his first meetings with Asha, of finding his daughter as a preta – a hungry ghost. Her praanin body had been forced from her human body to produce a creature much like himself, but in a process that had left her withered, small and grey, with her mind gone. And, as John was now, Ellie was slowly dying. The familiarity of Sarva's presence, and the knowledge that he was Asha's twin, made it easier for John to be as open and honest as if he were speaking with Asha.

"So you came all this way in the hope of saving your daughter?" Sarva asked when John had finished.

"And failed," agreed John. "And lost Asha. And brought death to my friends. It's some track record."

Sarva turned to John, reached out and squeezed his hand firmly. "We're not dead yet, and my sister is only lost, she may yet be found."

"And my daughter?"

Sarva turned back to the waterfall. "I can't say. We can only hope that the ancient healer you met was right, that there may still be a way – if we can find it soon enough."

A short while later Darnu and Garjae returned to the ledge.

"There's no way through," Darnu told them. "It's a mass of jagged cracks and small holes down there. The floor is a great plate of shattered quartz or something. Even if we found a gap to try and squeeze into, there's no guarantee it would stay large enough, and there's no telling how far it goes like that. You could get stuck in the current and not be able to get back."

"There's no way back, anyway," John pointed out. He thought about it for a moment. "But you can get through, can't you? Without me, I mean."

Darnu shook his head. "It would probably be suicide for us too." Seeing that John didn't understand, he continued, "We can merge with the water and safely flow with it as long as we can keep ourselves together – all in one connected flow. If the water starts to spray and separate, and that seems likely through some of those cracks, then it would kill us. We're vulnerable when we're merged. With the strength of the currents fighting their way through those cracks we might not even make it out of the cavern before we were torn apart."

"No sign of the others?" Garjae asked.

Sarva shook his head.

"So either they stayed up there, or they got washed a different way."

"Andrei said he was coming," said John.

"He might not, not if Senna decided to stay."

John shook his head. He couldn't see it working out that way, at least the two of them would have tried to come.

Darnu made a noise suspiciously like a chuckle.

"What?" John asked.

"I was just laughing at myself for missing Andrei, and wondering what he would be saying."

"Probably something like: now we know why no one ever returns," said Sarva.

John laughed.

- - -

Unable to think clearly, Asha watched the heavy traffic. The sun glared on the windshields. Their car moved onto a highway and picked up speed. The country was surprisingly open, low scrub and a few gentle hills. For a long stretch there was water visible to her right.

"The City by the Bay," Jaimee said.

The statement had been intended for Asha, but she ignored it. It didn't matter where it was. It wasn't home. It wasn't near John.

Views of the ocean dwindled and their surroundings turned into concrete and low buildings. Roads merged and split around them, occasional patches of trees and bushes tried unsuccessfully to break up the monotony. It could be any city. The buildings grew more substantial and a cluster of tall buildings seemed to rise out of the ground as they got nearer.

They branched onto a narrower road and the traffic slowed and banked up. The buildings grew taller. Wires appeared overhead. The footpaths were wide, and thin trees struggled to grow in their concrete surrounds. Somewhere in this jungle of concrete, steel and glass, the limousine turned to pull in under one of the buildings.

The car was forced to stop by a cluster of people holding up banners. "Save the forests," one read. "Don't cut down our heritage," read another. There was a clamour of voices and one of the banners was thrust in front of the driver, "Trees not timber," it proclaimed.

"What did we do this time?" Sando asked.

Jaimee shrugged.

"There was a piece in Saturday's paper," Stephenson said, "it wasn't complimentary."

Some protesters were pressing their hands around their faces, trying to see through the heavily tinted windows. Jaimee looked past them and studied the crowd.

"How about that one?" he asked his brother.

"You or me?" Sando asked

"Me first, then you." Jaimee leaned forward and touched Asha's

38

arm. "Watch."

Asha looked out where Jaimee was pointing. Just a few feet from the car was a young blond man holding up one side of the large banner that read, "Save the forests." She glanced back at Jaimee.

"Just watch."

A pause, as if Jaimee was waiting for something, and then he moved one hand in a slicing motion. The young human man suddenly dropped his side of the banner and clutched at his arm. The banner collapsed over the man's partner, a young woman, and she was lost in its folds.

"Now," Jaimee said.

The young man looked up from his arm and peered across the street as if something had caught his eye. He turned and started to walk. He stepped out onto the street just as a truck was coming past. There was a brief screech of tyres and a dull thud.

The truck hadn't been going fast, it didn't need to be. The young man bounced off the front and fell to the ground in front of it. He wasn't dead. Asha saw him try to get up, though there was blood streaming down his face and something was horribly wrong with one leg. The young woman started screaming, dropped the tangled banner, and ran after her friend. The young man fell and struggled again to get up. Jaimee flicked out his hand again and the young man collapsed and lay still.

Asha stared in disbelief. She tried to push her senses out to see if the young man was still alive, but the people that had been protesting around the car now crowded toward the man and her view was blocked.

She turned to Jaimee. "You?" She glanced at Sando, he smiled back at her. She looked back at Jaimee. "Why?"

"It's a sure way to clear the driveway," Jaimee said. His smile replicated Sando's.

"Let's go in," Jaimee told Stephenson. "You'd better get someone to come out and help them. Can't have them thinking we don't care."

Stephenson instructed the driver and then pulled out his mobile telephone.

Asha watched the scene disappear behind them as the car moved beneath the building. The young man remained hidden behind a growing crowd of onlookers.

"That may add to the press coverage," Stephenson said. "It could make things worse."

"Send the family some money," Jaimee said. "Discreetly, but not too discreetly, if you get my meaning. It'll be good PR."

Stephenson lifted his telephone again.

From the echoing car park Asha was taken up in a lift to a level of quiet corridors. The carpet was pure wool, most of the doors were solid timber, and all the door handles were wooden. An environment made for the comfort and convenience of the narun.

Jaimee opened a door and gestured for Asha to go in. It was a large room, furnished with luxurious leather lounge chairs, a small wooden coffee table, and wooden cabinets carrying expensive looking ornaments. Windows spanned the far wall and there was a large television screen mounted on the wall to her right.

"Make yourself comfortable," Jaimee said. "We have to get ready for a press conference. I'd put it off, but the timing's right so we have to move now."

Sando picked up a remote control off the coffee table and turned on the television. He flicked around a few channels until he found the one he wanted.

"Keep watching," Sando said. "See if you can pick us out of the crowd."

Asha looked at the two of them and identical smiles stared back at her. She didn't understand what they were talking about, and it was obvious they were waiting for her to ask. She turned away and walked to the windows. She looked out over the city.

"There will be someone outside your door if you need anything," Jaimee told her.

Asha didn't turn until she heard the door close. On the television there were two people sitting at a desk, talking. She didn't try to listen. She found the remote control, even that was mounted in a wooden box, and pressed the mute button. She had expected to hear the noise of the city outside, but there was only the low hum of the air conditioning.

She picked out a lounge chair and curled up on the leather. Her eyes watched the pair of humans on the screen, but she wasn't really seeing them. Her mind felt numb. And perhaps that was best. The world was going on around her, but she wasn't part of it. She had become a disinterested observer in her own life. She had no control over what happened, not to herself, not to anyone.

- - -

Sando picked up a pink glob in his hands, it ran over his fingers and hung there like some strange pink slime. "We're supposed to wear this stuff?"

Jaimee looked back at him. "It's not so bad once it's on, it just looks disgusting like that."

"What's wrong with your usual hoody?"

"We're entering the realm of the paranoid, anyone they can't see clearly is a threat. Young punks in a hoody will make them nervous. Anyway, the projection system isn't good enough for close company."

"How long have you been using this stuff?"

"Years now. It's been a long time since you've come out with me, brother."

"Politics really isn't my thing," Sando replied. He rolled back the fine surface of the material, the inside of it felt sticky. He'd never felt anything quite like it, usually anything manufactured was slippery to the point of being difficult to hold. He looked to Jaimee in question.

"The inside is painted with some compound that retains a fine film of water, that way it can adhere to our skin, not well, but enough when combined with how tightly it fits. The outer layer stops the water evaporating while you're wearing it. When it dries out it's useless, so you only get one use out of it."

"And that's why they're stored in water," finished Sando, poking at the globs still floating in the containers on the bench.

"They're heaps better than those rubber things we used to use. Remember them?"

Sando pulled a face. "Vividly. Humans used to think we were burn victims and give us pitying looks."

Jaimee nodded. "But this stuff is so good even Helix is using it."

Sando tried to imagine Helix soiling herself with this pink slime. "What for?"

"She likes to put in the occasional appearance with the human troops, she says they respond better. I think she enjoys having them ogle her."

"I didn't think her troops would be that interested in a pretty face."

Jaimee grinned. "She had me get full upper-torso versions made so she can show off her bust too."

Sando shook his head. "I sometimes worry about our sister."

"You may as well throw that one out," Jaimee told him, pointing to the pink glob in Sando's hands. "It will have dried out too much already. The trick is to put them on quickly. While they're fresh out of the water they stretch well, but let them dry too much and they tear. Here, let me show you."

Jaimee put his hands in and pulled out another pick glob from the container marked "Heads" and quickly turned it inside-out. He concentrated for a moment until the hair on his head disappeared, then he pulled the pink film over his head and rolled it down. The elastic material pulled back in beneath Jaimee's chin and rolled smoothly down to cover his neck. A few adjustments at the ears, mouth, eyes and nose and the job was complete.

Sando was impressed, it still looked odd, but he assumed Jaimee must have answers for the remaining details. He pulled out his own glob and tried to duplicate his brother's actions. Moments later Jaimee was laughing at him. Sando glared out at him from the one eye-hole he'd managed to get lined up close to an eye. "Very fucking funny, brother," he muttered through the stretchy material, his mouth was not lined up either. Jaimee laughed harder.

Sando tore the mask from his head and Jaimee took another from the container and showed Sando the trick for getting all the holes lined up before he started. When it was on, properly aligned this time, Jaimee showed him how to tuck up the pieces that went into his mouth, nose and ears so that the face looked close to complete.

"Try not to blow air through your nose too much, otherwise those tags will dry out and hang loose, and everyone thinks you've got great goobers up your nose."

"Thanks for that picturesque description. I promise not to breathe." Sando flexed his face and his mouth trying to get used to the clingy material. "This stuff is bloody horrible," he said.

"Just keep reminding yourself how bad the rubber was." Jaimee handed Sando an elaborate but flimsy set of dentures that covered his teeth and tongue. "With these you can afford to open your mouth without drawing attention."

"And avoid people staring into your mouth and wondering what was missing," Sando said. "I remember that too. Soon learned to keep my mouth shut."

"Still best not to open too wide," Jaimee warned him. "We're mutes as far as the humans are concerned, so there's generally no need to do more than show them your teeth."

Sando slid the dentures over his tongue and teeth and moved his jaw around to try and get comfortable. "Are you sure this is all worth it?" he asked, thankful that he could speak without needing a functional mouth or tongue.

"Hold still," Jaimee told him, ignoring the question. He held up what looked like artificial eye sockets. "Close your eyes."

Sando did, and Jaimee fitted them over his eyes.

"How's that?"

Sando opened his eyes and looked through the tinted film. "Crap," he said, still not moving his mouth. Talking normally wouldn't be practical, or at least not comfortable, until he could remove the dentures. "But then you know that." The view was clear enough that he wouldn't fall over anything, but it was not comfortable. The view blinked as the artificial socket blinked its eyelids.

Jaimee lifted up a small pair of spectacles. "Remember to keep these on. It helps to hide the fact that your eyes protrude too much."

"What happened to the dark glasses and playing blind-mutes?"

"Too hard to remember not to duck. I know it's not great, but after that silver suit you used to wear, this stuff is luxurious."

Sando grunted. The old silver suits weren't great, the lack of peripheral vision and the muffled senses were annoying problems, but at least they had offered some protection, this stuff wouldn't. He supposed he would probably get used to this too, eventually.

Next came similar material from containers marked "Left Hand" and "Right Hand". These gloves rolled most of the way up the forearm.

Jaimee then took Sando through the make-up routine. Eyebrows and lips and so on. Then the wigs and formal clothing, specially made so it wouldn't slip around too much or fall off them.

"And you do this by choice?" Sando said, moving about trying to get used to everything.

"Only when I have to," Jaimee admitted. "Today the security is going to be tight, and it could get crowded, so trying to get through while we're not visible could be risky."

"So let's visit him at home or something like we usually do."

Jaimee shook his head. "I want this to happen in public."

- - -

Asha stirred when the door opened.

A dhumraka looked through. "Jaimee said to let you know when they were due to come on." He pointed to the television screen, then pulled back and closed the door behind him.

On the screen the camera was panning over a crowd seated in an auditorium of some sort. All were dressed in suits, some chatted with one another. Occasionally the camera would zoom in to highlight some particular group, and after hovering for a few moments would move on. Asha wondered what she was supposed to see.

The camera suddenly changed point of view and she was staring at the stage at the front of the audience. A man was walking to the microphone at centre stage. He was obviously quite old, thin and slightly frail looking, but he walked with an erect and confident bearing. He lifted one hand and waved to the crowd. The camera changed perspective again and Asha was shown an appreciative audience standing and applauding. The view changed back to the man as he was smoothing back his neat silver and grey hair. He started to speak.

Asha hadn't been that interested to start with and watching the man speak with the sound turned off wasn't adding to the experience. She sat forward, intending to find the off button, but when she looked up the camera was again panning over the crowd, and this time zoomed in on a face she recognised. Sitting near the front was the hulking figure of Stephenson. Seated next to him were two small suited figures, similar in stature but otherwise very different. One had dark hair and thick rimmed glasses, the other brown hair with wire rimmed glasses. Both looked well tanned.

As she watched, one of them nudged the other and pointed up at the camera. They both lifted their hands and waved, glossy white

44

teeth showing in their smiles. Jaimee and Sando. The smiles gave them away. They were waving to her, she knew it. They were hamming it up especially for her.

Rather than turn it off, Asha pressed the button to restore the sound.

At that moment the camera returned to the old man on the stage.

"I know you've all heard rumours that I was intending to retire," the man's voice came over the television speakers. "Well, I'm here today to tell you ..." he started. He looked very happy, and sounded cheerful and optimistic, it seemed obvious that he was about to deny those rumours. A few people in the audience even started to clap, but when the man stayed quiet the clapping died out.

The old man now looked dazed, staring over the heads of his audience as if seeing something beyond them. Murmuring rose from the audience.

"I'm here today to tell you," the old man repeated, he looked alert now, his expression determined, "that those rumours are true."

The camera drew back enough to reveal the surprised expressions of the people sitting behind the man on the stage. The murmuring of the audience grew louder.

"I know this will come as a surprise to many," the old man continued, "not least to my staff." He turned to acknowledge them. "But I don't think I'm up to it, and I don't want to let the people down that way. My health has been getting worse ..."

The noise of the audience had increased further, and the camera changed perspectives to pan over the crowd again. Asha caught a brief glimpse of the brothers, but they were apparently of little interest to the camera and it didn't pause on them again.

Asha switched off the screen. She had seen what she was supposed to have seen. She didn't understand the details, but it was obvious that the brothers were demonstrating that they had power even in the human world. What they intended to do with that power she didn't know. She knew she should care. If there was anything she could do about it then maybe she would. But there wasn't. She curled up in the chair and listened to the air conditioning.

3. Darkness

When the brothers returned they came into the room still dressed as they had been at the press conference.

"What do you think?" Jaimee asked. He turned around in front of the television, showing off his attire.

"Did you spot us?" Sando asked.

Asha blinked slowly. She hadn't been asleep, but she hadn't been fully awake either. It was strange seeing the brothers without their usual pale colouring. Jaimee with dark hair just looked wrong.

"You didn't miss us, did you?" Jaimee asked. His voice sounded genuinely disappointed.

Asha shook her head. "I saw you."

Sando pulled his teeth out, or that's what it looked like, but these turned into flimsy pieces of plastic film.

"Phht," he said, moving his mouth this time. "That's better."

He loosened his tie and reached inside his shirt. The plastic slipped up, and as he started to stretch it over his head the plastic tore and fell away, drawn by the weight of the wig. His usual pale features reappeared as if he'd peeled off a rich tan.

Jaimee repeated the procedure, but turned away first, as if coy about revealing himself this way in front of Asha. When he turned back he had restored his short white-blond hair. Seeing this, Sando remembered to restore his own.

"I thought you'd be impressed," Jaimee said.

"With what?" Asha asked, not sure why she was bothering.

"I wouldn't worry about the human. His career was almost over anyway, we just hurried it along. It's not like he's going to suffer. A politician like that will never go hungry."

"It was a bit flat though," Sando said. "Just retirement. I thought you'd ask me to get an admission of paedophilia or something juicy?"

"Not this time. The man has been considering retirement anyway, but his popularity is at an all-time high and his staff had convinced him to keep going for another term. We just made sure he won't."

"I gave him a good push," Sando said, "but he could still change his mind."

"No one would trust him again now if he tried to retract," Jaimee said, "not with it having gone live country wide. There's no respectable way to back out of it now."

Sando looked at his brother curiously. "You haven't always been this subtle. You're not going soft, are you?"

"I've learned the value of doing only what's necessary," Jaimee said, slightly defensively. "If too much of a stir happens around our political enemies every time we're close by, then awkward questions could start."

"So? We can deal with that."

"And we have, but it's better this way. Trust me."

The brothers disappeared for a time to finish getting out of their material clothes. When they returned they escorted Asha back down to the car park, but instead of the limousine they climbed into a large black four-wheel drive vehicle. It was luxurious inside, spacious and the upholstery was all natural fibres. The back of the front seats each held a small screen and keyboard, even the individual keys had been carved from some pale timber.

Asha didn't recognised the driver, and Stephenson wasn't with them. Jaimee and Sando sat either side of her in the back. "You'll like where we're going next," Jaimee assured her, and patted her on the arm. He reached out and typed something on the keyboard in front of him and the driver started the car.

- - -

<Do you think you might have damaged her?> Jaimee asked directly into his brother's mind.

All narun speech was telepathic, and whether they moved their mouths or not, all narun within range could hear. The siblings also shared a special connection that allowed them to speak directly into each other's minds, and to feel what the other was feeling. Often

47

speech of any sort was unnecessary, each knew the others so well, but it was a difficult habit to break. For Jaimee, Sando and Helix this private connection only worked when they were close to one another, it was Peren that kept them in touch when they were apart.

Sando looked at Asha sitting between him and his brother. She was staring at the back of the seat in front of her, as she had since the journey had started. *<Sulking,>* was Sando's appraisal.

<It looks like more than that to me,> Jaimee said.

<I didn't damage her, brother. It takes more than a little push like the one in the plane to cause anything permanent.>

<Maybe she's more fragile than most.>

<Not from what I saw when we had her at the Research Centre,> Sando said. *<She's stronger than she looks.>*

<There's something else too. Something drawing on her. I can't tell what it is.>

<Maybe Peren can.>

<What?> Peren interrupted, her voice and presence entering their minds.

<Jaimee's worried that I may have damaged the healer,> Sando answered.

<Is it serious?>

Jaimee shook his head, Peren wouldn't see it but she would feel it. *<I don't think so, or not yet anyway. Maybe she just needs time. We've had her a few days now, we don't know when she last merged.>*

<Mama's just fed, and it seemed to go well today.>

<So we can give Asha some time to recover.> Jaimee finished his sister's thought.

<Do you think she will cooperate anyway?> Peren asked.

Sando observed, *<I don't think she can help herself. It's built-in.>*

Peren didn't respond, and Jaimee felt her presence leave. She could be touchy sometimes.

They had left the city far behind, and now they were travelling on a narrow road that led them on a twisting path through the hills. Patches of forest grew thicker and the trees more substantial.

Asha's head came up and her pale green eyes looked past Jaimee to watch the forest go past. Light from the late afternoon sun flickered across her soft face and her light brown hair. She didn't seem to notice that Jaimee was watching her.

The siblings had been brought up to despise the aaranya, but Jaimee thought he could probably make an exception for this one. She was special. Beautiful, gentle but strong in a way he had rarely seen, and powerfully talented. She could fit in with his family as no one else he'd ever met.

Jaimee reached across and lifted Asha's hand, placing it in his own.

Asha turned and looked at him briefly, and then looked back out at the forest. Her fingers didn't so much as twitch in his hand.

<Brother?> Sando queried.

<She is beautiful. You said so yourself.>

<She is aaranya.>

<Talent trumps the accidents of birth, my brother, we of all people know that.>

The contempt came from Sando without words, but there was something else in there too.

<I do believe you're jealous, Sando. Beat you to her, did I?>

<I had plenty of opportunity – if I had wanted it.>

<And you're kicking yourself now, aren't you?>

Sando closed himself off.

- - -

Deep in the shadows of the forest, at the end of a long narrow lane, the car stopped at an elaborate gateway. Words were spoken between the driver and a human guard that emerged from a small building beside the road. Dhumraka emerged from the forest on either side of the car, they bowed with reverence to Jaimee and Sando. The gates opened and the car moved through to a second set of gates. After a moment, these opened.

Jaimee typed something on the keyboard in front of him and the car pulled to a stop again after it had passed through the second set of gates.

"Asha and I will walk from here," he said. "Did you want to come with us, brother?"

Sando waved his hand.

"Your loss," Jaimee said amiably.

Jaimee had not released her hand since he first took it. He grasped it more firmly now and pulled Asha from the car.

The car quickly disappeared as it continued up the slope, the driveway winding its way between the trees. Jaimee turned to appraise Asha. She could feel his gaze piercing her, and wondered what he could see. Just how powerful was this man?

"You aren't well," Jaimee told her.

Asha didn't answer.

"We need you to be well. You need to be in top form."

For what? Asha almost asked – perhaps her resignation from life wasn't quite complete, but she quelled the response.

"So we decided to give you the run of our front yard." Jaimee waived his hand over the forest around them. "For tonight, anyway."

Jaimee pulled on her hand and led her back closer to the gates they had just been driven through. The double lines of fencing followed a broad line that had been cleared of trees and low shrubs.

"A few things you should know, to save you finding out the hard way." He smiled at her. "The outer fence is just a fence, it's intended to keep humans out. Only eight feet high, simple chain link with barbed wire on the top. Beyond that fence are some of our friends." Jaimee waved to the dhumraka still standing beside the road beyond the gates. They bowed in return.

"You won't see much of them, except at the regular shift changes. They're not fond of the forest, but they put up with it for us." Jaimee touched Asha's chin, turning her face so she was forced to meet his eyes. "They're a sort of insurance. They keep watch against external intruders and for anyone from the inside that should want to leave early. Am I making myself clear?"

Asha met those piecing eyes and didn't flinch – resigned enough perhaps. The hand that had held her chin, now reached up and stroked her cheek tenderly.

After a few moments Jaimee turned back to the fences. "The inner fence you will recognise. Nasty stuff. It's higher, obviously, and the taller trees are all cleared back away from it, so jumping over it will not be an option."

Asha looked along the line of the fences. The outer fence had grass growing right up against it and through the mesh. The inner fence was just wire to the bare ground. The grass didn't start for several inches either side, and anything hanging closer had gone brown.

"The front yard is yours for the night, and perhaps more if you promise to be good. But behind the house is off limits. There can be no confusion where the backyard starts, more of this fencing keeps it separate."

Jaimee pulled on her hand again. "Come on. It's getting late and I'd like you to see more of your new home before the sun is completely gone."

Asha followed, she didn't see any point in resistance.

"We've had this place a long time," Jaimee told her, "so we've had time to add a bit of variety to what's in the park. You can see we went with these spreading pines along the roadway, it almost creates a tunnel. A bit gloomy to my mind, but our mother likes them."

He tugged her further into the forest, pointing out more trees. "You probably know what they are better than I do," he admitted, "but I thought you might like these, perhaps they remind you of home."

Asha gazed up at the immense pine trees. Aside from their immense height, they had little in common with the trees of her home. The smell of the pines was rich and fragrant, but nothing like eucalyptus.

"The humans call them Douglas firs," Jaimee told her.

Despite their unfamiliarity, the life in them still called strongly to her. Asha resisted, unwilling to open anything of herself while this man was so close.

She tasted a hint of salt in the air, the ocean could not be far away. She wished it was closer, she would have liked to be able to hear it, though she couldn't have said why.

It was getting dark quickly now, and Jaimee pulled her on, working their way up the slope. It was easy going through the forest. "The front is quite large, you should be comfortable enough," he assured her.

They emerged from the trees to a wide green lawn, beyond which stood a large house. Three storeys high and very wide. Close to the house, the road from the gates did a small circle, and around it was a border of flowers. In the centre of the circle was a fountain and small rock garden. Floodlights lit the entire front of the house.

"Impressive, isn't it?" Jaimee asked her.

Asha didn't respond.

"Our mother likes it, and that was always the point."

Unexpectedly, Jaimee pulled Asha back into the trees. He stepped close to her and Asha stepped back until the bole of a tree pressed against her back. Jaimee pressed himself lightly against her.

"You're lonely," he said quietly.

How far would it go? Asha wondered. If I don't do anything, how far would he take this? She didn't want to know. She pushed him away with both hands.

Jaimee didn't seem offended or upset by that. "You're tired," he said. "I'll leave you to get acquainted with the trees."

He walked away a few steps, almost reaching the lawn, and then turned back. "Don't forget that you agreed to cooperate with us. Don't make us come looking for you."

Asha watched as he crossed the lawn and entered the house. Only when the door had closed did she turn away and look back into the forest again. It was full dark now, and the darkness suited her mood, but the life of the forest was clear to her senses. It beckoned to her, and she responded.

She walked for a long time, not knowing what else to do. She wasn't thinking, that wasn't an option. When she could feel the fence-line getting close she would alter her course and keep walking.

When she finally stopped, she thought it must have been about midnight, she was in a grove of immense pine trees. She pressed her back to one and wrapped her arms protectively over her stomach. She peered up through the branches and was able to glimpse the occasional star shining so far above. It glimmered unnaturally and she realised she had been crying.

A sensation of warmth travelled along her arm and Asha looked down at it in surprise. She raised her forearm and a small ginger nose emerged from her skin and twitched.

"Cassey?"

The brevi pulled itself clear of Asha's arm, its tiny black eyes staring up at her face. The deeper ginger stripes that ran along its back highlighted the glow from the white stripes and the paler ginger fur of the body. The brevi was pleased to be out at last.

"Oh, Casseta. I'm so sorry." Asha had forgotten the brevi was there, hadn't given it a thought. She should never have brought it

52

with her into this captivity. She tried to remember when Casseta had merged with her. She could remember the two brevi rejoining them when they'd left the zarana back at the lake. And she could remember playing with Cassey while they waited at the cabin for their ride back to the Samgha. But she couldn't remember exactly when Cassey had decided to merge with Asha rather than John.

"You should have stayed with John, my darling girl," Asha murmured to the brevi. "He might need you. And Nuttachen. What will your boyfriend do without you?"

Cassey ran up her arm and twittered quietly in her ear, as if answering her, and then it reached across Asha's face and nuzzled at her tears.

"You can't let these men find you. You know that, don't you?"

More quiet twittering.

"If you think you can make it home, you should go."

The brevi didn't respond to that.

"If you have to stay then you should hide in these trees. I'll come to you when I can."

There was a brief sound, Asha thought it was almost a word, and then Cassey leapt from her shoulder onto the tree behind her. Asha turned and watched the small glowing figure disappear into the branches. How much did it understand? She didn't know. But since Cassey had remained hidden all this time, perhaps that meant the creature understood the need to stay hidden from the brothers. Asha could only hope so.

Asha pressed her hands into the tree in front of her and felt the warm life of it tugging at her. As much as she regretted bringing Cassey into all this, Asha did feel better. Stronger somehow. It didn't make sense, but it was enough. She pushed the rest of her body into the welcoming life of the tree. She would build her strength now and try to prepare herself for whatever was still to come.

- - -

They rested and waited, John couldn't tell how long. His mind kept returning to Asha, wondering where she was now, and how she was being treated. He had no idea where to find her, but he would keep looking until his time ran out. That was assuming they could get out of here. Restless, John got up and decided to try and explore

53

the cavern.

"Want company?" Sarva asked.

"Sure."

They made their way slowly around the edge of the cavern. Sometimes the ledges they tried to follow ran out and they had to enter the water and fight the currents until they found the next place where they could climb out.

Here and there they found chinks in the rock wall, visible only because it was a darker shadow against the wet black of the rock. Anything that looked promising they climbed into, to see if they went anywhere, but each quickly ran out or broke into smaller jagged tunnels that they could not enter.

They had gone away from the waterfall at first, but eventually found themselves approaching it from the other side. The great cascade of water was falling well away from the wall, but the impact of the torrent into the pool threw back a wash of roiling currents against the rock, so descending into the pool there would be dangerous. By careful climbing, each boosting or lifting the other where necessary, they managed to find a ledge that carried them behind the fall, well above the level of the pool.

When they were behind the fall, John stopped and looked out at the falling column of water. It made him think of some huge garden hose turned on full, the mass of water twitching and stirring and slopping according to whatever rules it was that water followed. The surface of the pool looked to be boiling madly. There was the bucket that the garden hose was filling, but a bucket full of tiny holes. John grinned, some part of him was still human if he could come up with analogies like that for such a magnificent spectacle.

Sarva touched his arm. "Coming?"

John started to turn away, and then looked back. There was something odd about the currents and splashes that came back from the wall beneath them. He lay down on the ledge and pushed his head and shoulders out to get a better look. Sarva grabbed his legs to steady him. There, beneath the ledge, was a large hole in the wall, and some water looked to be leaving that way. It had to be a large cave, perhaps a tunnel that led somewhere.

John showed Sarva. It looked promising so they went back to tell Darnu and Garjae. They discussed the possibilities and decided to give Andrei and the others more time.

Finally, reluctantly, they gave up waiting. It looked like the others were not coming this way.

Back behind the waterfall, Darnu and Garjae went first and then Sarva lowered John from the ledge until he found a foothold in the rock. John took a precarious step down and to one side. He helped Sarva to find a hold and then concentrated on moving out of his way. Another step and he felt the reassuring touch of Garjae's hand there to steady him. Another few steps and John was standing inside the cave next to Garjae. He looked back for Sarva, only to see him slip and fall the short distance into the swirling currents. But Darnu was there ready, and he thrust one hand out and grasped Sarva by the arm before the currents could drag him away.

The four of them stood in the mouth of the cave behind the waterfall, and looked around. It wasn't just a cave, as John had feared it might be, it was the entrance to a tunnel. The floor was almost flat, and though it was partly submerged in a constant wash of water, the water was less than ankle deep. If they reached up they could touch the highest part of the curved ceiling; it was all very smooth, as if sometimes the water had been much deeper and flooded even this tunnel.

"We going?" asked Garjae. He started forward without waiting for a response.

The first part was easy going. The walls and ceiling were wet from the mist of the waterfall, so it was possible to see their way forward for a small distance. But further in the walls were dry. John could see his friends and the thin sheet of water over the floor, everything else was totally black.

Despite the dark they made good progress. The path remained smooth, worn that way by the swift currents. The tunnel descended, sometimes gently, sometimes more steeply, and always curving slowly to one side or the other. John gave up trying to keep track of what direction they were headed, for all he knew they might have been doing spirals. The roar of the waterfall faded behind them, but there remained the constant trickling sounds of the water on the floor, and their own splashing as they walked. John found the sounds comforting.

"Do you think we might be missing useful side tunnels in the dark?" Sarva asked.

"What's a useful tunnel look like?" Garjae wanted to know.

Black, like everything else, John thought, but kept it to himself.

"I don't know," Sarva answered, "maybe one that leads up instead of down."

"The water has to come out somewhere," said Darnu. "I think it's better to follow it."

John agreed with this sentiment, but didn't say anything. It wasn't so much that he had any faith in where the water might lead them, it was mainly that its presence was reassuring, something for them to stand on. Without it they would seem to be standing in a void, and he wasn't sure he was ready to cope with that.

"If we start trying to look for side tunnels it'll take us forever to get anywhere," Garjae added.

"I guess—" Sarva began, but he was interrupted by a loud curse from Garjae.

"The ceiling is getting lower," he reported.

John put his hands up and found the ceiling only just above his head. They were all forced to walk in an awkward crouch. Soon after that the path looked to be narrowing, but this was only because the water had made its own deeper channel, one that they couldn't walk in, so they were forced to walk beside the water. Now it really did feel like walking in a void, though they still had the line of the narrow river to guide them. Whenever they paused, John would lean down and splash water over the rock where he was standing. He knew it was silly, but it made him feel better.

Sometime later – John found it impossible to guess how long – Garjae broke into more determined curses and everyone stopped. It took considerable, and very careful, probing in the dark to discover that the river was sinking more deeply into its already narrow channel, and now that channel had drifted to the side. Just a short distance ahead the water disappeared as it dropped still further below them. Garjae tried squeezing himself down to see if it was possible to try and follow the water, but returned to say that there wasn't room.

John turned his head to look around them. The only frame of reference he had was the presence of the other three, everything else was absolutely black. He thought they looked like cartoon characters waiting for the artist to come back and draw in the background, all the more comical because each was leaning over to avoid cracking their head on the ceiling. John crept carefully to the side so he could glimpse the water disappearing down the narrow channel, but it no longer reassured him.

"What do we do now?" he asked. In his fear John was a little surprised that his voice didn't echo back at him, it was as if the blackness was a true void, swallowing even his voice. But of course his voice wasn't really sound, it was only telepathy, and that didn't echo – which led to another stupid thought: they couldn't even try to be like bats and use echo location.

"We keep going forward," Darnu said.

"How will you even tell which way is forward?" John asked, he could feel the panic edging into his voice.

"I think ..." Sarva started, and then hesitated.

"I think so too," said Darnu. "There's water somewhere ahead of us. I mean something much bigger than this stream. I'm almost sure of it. We just keep moving toward that."

John couldn't tell what they were sensing, but he wasn't going to argue.

"What do you suggest?" asked Garjae. "Do you think Nuttachen could lead us?"

Darnu shook his head. "I'd rather not risk it."

"So, what? Are we going to crawl, or do we walk forward boldly and all fall down the first hole we hit?"

"Single-file, holding hands," said Darnu. "I'll go first if you like."

Garjae declined. "Just let me know if you think I'm going off course."

It was awkward. They had to remain crouched below the low ceiling, and they needed to face in alternating directions, each holding another wrist-to-wrist, so that if one fell the hold would be strong enough to catch them. This also meant that only Garjae at the front, and Sarva at the end, had a free hand to check the space around them. But, as awkward as it was, it was still easier and faster than crawling.

Faster, but still not fast. At first Garjae tried to keep up a good pace, but after he crashed into the wall as the tunnel turned, he slowed and felt his way more carefully. More than once they entered

57

dead-ends and had to back out and try a new path. After a while they changed positions to give Darnu the lead. John insisted on taking his turn in the lead, but acknowledged that it was better he didn't take the all-important second place; he knew he didn't have the strength and resilience of the others to be certain of catching the lead when they fell – it wasn't a matter of if.

Some indeterminate time later they stopped in the blackness to rest. Despite being exhausted, John had trouble sleeping. It was almost silent, but only almost. Obscure sounds would come to them from different directions, subtle groaning and breathing sounds, so faint it was hard to be sure they were real, and impossible to tell whether the source was wind or water or rock ... or something else. Thoughts of Leavek's unfriendly spirits broke through and John tried to push them away, there was enough to worry about. Eventually John found a position where, with his eyes open, he could see Sarva to one side. This allowed him to tell whether his eyes were open or closed, and that was enough to let him settle.

Some time during the next day, if day it was, John began to get the occasional smell or sense of something that the others had spoken of. Some moisture in the air, or scent of something more than just water, he wasn't sure. It wasn't until well into the following day that he became certain, the smell of moisture in the air was constantly with them. But their progress remained very slow and they were forced to rest again before they reached whatever it must be.

John had taken the lead again. The ceiling had been higher for a while, but a short time later he found out painfully that it had lowered. Crouched over, he had his left hand out, reaching ahead to feel for obstructions. Garjae held his right wrist, and John clung tightly back to Garjae's wrist – John suspected that his grasp probably felt like that of a desperate man. Reach out, find nothing in his way and step, and then repeat, and again. John felt that he should be getting used to the dark by now, but his mind wouldn't adjust. Reach out, step. Reach out, step. And then he was falling.

His arm wrenched and his face slammed into the rock face. He heard, vaguely through his own pain, Garjae grunt and gasp above him. John peered up and saw a line of gold marking out the edge of the rock, and next to that was Garjae's arm still gripping tightly to his own.

"Thanks," said John. "Sorry about your arm."

But there was no response, nor from the others. John dangled there in the dark wondering how far he would drop if Garjae let go. In theory, in this body he could fall great distances and land safely, but that depended what you landed on and it wasn't an experiment he was in a hurry to try in the dark. "Thanks," he said again, trying to gain their attention.

"That's incredible," came Darnu's voice in a tone of quiet awe.

"I knew it must be something big, but ...," trailed off Sarva.

Garjae remained quiet, but from the stillness of his hold it was apparent that his attention was elsewhere.

All John could see was blackness, though he knew from painful experience that there was rock just in front of him. He didn't want to try and twist around in case he loosened Garjae's hold.

"Ah ... guys?" John tried again. Then, finally, "Guys!"

Garjae's grip tightened and John was lifted. He used his free hand to help guide his body over the edge and lay there flat, trying to hug the rock. After a time John looked up at the others, their attention was once more out beyond him. John sat up, careful not to tip himself over the edge, and looked out.

At first he couldn't understand their excitement, but then he lowered his gaze and saw an immense expanse of water reaching into the distance. Their tunnel had come out somewhere close to the ceiling on one side of a huge cave, and it was only when you looked down and saw how far above this ocean they were that the scale began to sink in. The life of this huge underground lake, an ocean it seemed to John, came to his senses as a deep grey against the pitch black. He could see the pattern of shallow waves on the surface. He looked further out but couldn't find a far edge, the surface slowly darkened until it faded into total blackness.

The ceiling was wet and visible a dozen or so feet above where their tunnel opened out into this cave. It curved upwards into the distance, but quickly joined the black void. He thought he could detect some patches of the ceiling that might be glowing faintly, but it was difficult to be sure.

"Almost worth the trip just to see this," Sarva said quietly.

John glanced at him, he looked to be serious. "I'd have been happy with a postcard," he said.

Sarva raised an eyebrow.

"Someone to come back and tell me about it," John finished lamely, the aaranya didn't get mail.

"I'm with John," agreed Garjae.

"I'm glad your arm was up to holding me," John said by way of thanks.

"Just be glad I was holding you with my good arm." Garjae held up the other and flexed it, "This one would have dropped you." The arm had been badly injured weeks before and he had refused Asha's offer of further help.

John shuddered at the thought and looked back at the water, it was a long way down. "How do we get down there?" he asked.

Darnu edged forward and looked down. "I was going to suggest the fast way."

"Jump?" John asked in disbelief.

Darnu nodded and smiled. "Sure."

"The water doesn't come all the way below us," Garjae observed. "I can't tell if the wall slopes out or if there's a beach. We'd have to jump out a long way."

"It might be safer to climb," agreed Darnu.

"But not nearly as much fun," added Sarva, as much to watch John's expression as anything else.

John leaned forward and looked down at the black void that stood between them and the water far below. Maybe jumping had something going for it after all, trying to climb down that wall without being able to see where you were going didn't seem such a great idea, and no one could hold his hand while he climbed.

"Could we do it?" he asked at last. "Could we jump far enough out, do you think?"

"With a run-up, sure," said Darnu.

"But how do you see where the edge is to jump from?"

"I'll stand here so you can see," said Garjae.

"And how will you manage?" Darnu asked him.

"Thanks to John, I can mark it." Garjae held up his arm and showed them where it had been torn on the rock. It had already mostly closed, the injury was now just a fine golden line. "I'll just open it up a bit more and paint myself a line, it should last long enough for me to make the jump."

John grimaced and Darnu looked doubtful.

Sarva lay down at the edge and felt below it with this hands. Then he turned and lowered himself down. Darnu quickly rushed to him and lay down too, grabbing Sarva's wrists.

"What are you doing?" he asked gruffly.

There was no answer for a time. John could see that Sarva was wriggling around, and then slowly, and with Darnu's help, he climbed back up. Still without saying anything, Sarva made his way to one side of their tunnel and reached out and down.

Eventually he turned back to them. "I was just trying to see if climbing was an option. It's rough there just below the edge for a few feet, I think a chunk of it must have broken away in recent times."

John looked at the edge nervously.

Sarva continued, "But further down it gets smooth again, and the same on the sides. I'm guessing that water will have worn away most of the useful holds a long time ago. I think climbing might be out." He looked to Garjae. "If you're up for it, I think your idea might be best."

Garjae nodded. "Let's get on with it before this heals over and I have to start again."

After feeling their way around they worked out the best path for the run-up, the smoothest straight path to the edge. Darnu and Garjae lay down and stretched their arms out to define the line from which Sarva and John were to jump.

From their starting position, John took a few deep breaths to try and build up his courage.

Sarva patted his shoulder. "I'll lead the way, shall I?"

John nodded.

"Don't leave me hanging out there on my own, and don't land on me when we hit the water." Sarva smiled to show he was joking.

John tried to grin back, but wasn't sure how it came out.

Then Sarva was running. He leapt out in an elegant dive, shouting, "Whoo ... hoooo!" He seemed to hang in the blackness for a long time before disappearing below the edge.

John was still standing, apparently fixed to the rock. He cursed himself for being a coward and pushed himself into a run. He felt the ceiling of the tunnel touch his hair as he straightened up, and then those last few paces to the outstretched arms. He pushed himself off as strongly as he could.

This is madness, was John's first thought as he looked down at the grey ocean they wanted to reach and the line of blackness that they hoped to pass over. The outline of Sarva's body was below and ahead of him. Sarva had his arms and legs outstretched. Jumping without a parachute, thought John. Then he reconsidered this thought and tried to emulate Sarva's example, maybe it would help to slow them down, it might even help them move forward to the water.

There seemed to be plenty of time. If it wasn't for the wind against his face and body, John might have thought he wasn't really falling. And then, suddenly, as if everything had sped up, he could tell the surface of the water was rushing at him. He saw Sarva reorient himself to land feet first and tried to do the same.

There was a stinging sensation as his feet hit the water and then he was under. Water swirled around him and he tried to hold his breath. Then he remembered that he didn't need to breathe and tried to relax. Slowly he rose to the surface in a mass of bubbles. He'd made it!

He turned to the sound of splashing and saw Sarva.

"Ready to climb back up?" Sarva asked.

John stared at him.

"Don't you want to do it again?"

John splashed him with water.

Sarva laughed and drew closer. They tread water where they were and looked up into the dark, watching for Darnu and Garjae.

"Don't suppose they've changed their minds," John said.

"No. Here comes Darnu now."

John saw the figure quickly growing. He hadn't come out as far as Sarva and John but it looked like he would be fine. When he hit the water John started to swim forward, but Sarva held him back.

"Wait," Sarva said. "You don't want to be under Garjae when he lands."

John looked up and saw the second figure falling.

"Oh no," Sarva said under his breath, and started to swim.

John stared for another long moment. Garjae was falling further away from them – closer to the edge of the lake. He bounced off something and fell the last distance tumbling. John started after Sarva.

When John got there, Darnu was checking Garjae over for himself, not taking Garjae's word that he was fine.

"It worked fine," Garjae was explaining. "I just misjudged the last step and didn't get a very good kick off. I hit a bulge in the wall, but it was smooth, it didn't do any real damage."

There was no beach. There was no shallow water near them. They swam a long way before they came to a mound of smooth rock extending out from the wall. It didn't come out far, only a few metres. It was wet and slippery looking, but it formed a level enough surface that John could lie back with reasonable comfort to try and sleep.

After the others had vanished into the water, merging to rest and rebuild their strength, John lay down and stared up into the blackness. He wasn't feeling very good. He hoped it was just because he was tired from all the worry and exertion, but he thought it went beyond that. All the posturing to himself that he was going to do all he could to find Asha seemed likely to come to nothing. If he didn't find some way to feed himself, as the others were doing now, he was going to get progressively worse until he was no use to anyone. He thought about Ben's words before they'd left him back there in the Samgha. "Taking the life of animals, or people for that matter," he'd said, "may keep you going longer – if you want that."

John did want that, but not enough to take the life of another human. Could he consider doing it to an animal? He didn't even know how it was done. His daughter was a preta, there was something about her that dragged the prana up from any human she touched, and perhaps animals too, though he'd never seen that happen. But John wasn't like that – at least not yet. He supposed it was possible that he might turn into something like that if he lasted long enough, if that was how it worked. He just didn't know.

There were fish in the water here, he'd seen a few: strange pale eyeless things. Back in the depths of Lake Baikal, beyond the reach of the sunlight, his vedana had created its own colours for the living creatures that they encountered, but so far there had been little or no colour in anything he had seen down here. The fish here were nervous rather than curious, as if they distrusted the aaranya, which seemed very strange to John. They were also quite small and very fast. He doubted if he could catch one, and even if he could he still wouldn't know what to do with it.

His thoughts were all pointless and self-defeating. He tried to distract himself by focusing on his surroundings. From close by came the occasional sounds of water trickling down the wall or dripping into the lake. Behind that was a faint roaring noise. After his experiences getting here, John guessed that sound must come from rivers pouring into the lake, though it sounded more like static from a poorly tuned radio or television. The static came from all around him as it echoed off the rock walls, there was no picking the direction, or directions, of the source.

In the blackness far above him, John thought he could see small patches glowing, like the dusting of faint stars that you sometimes saw on the darkest nights. He wondered if it was real, or if his vedana was playing tricks on him.

Real or not, the thought of lying under the stars was comforting. It made him think of the times he had spent with Asha, staring up at the night sky. That memory brought a smile to his face and he drifted off to sleep.

John woke, groaning at the stiffness in his back. What had felt comfortable when he lay down, now felt like a bed of rock – and, of course, it was. The others weren't back yet. John had no idea how long he'd slept, only that it didn't feel like long enough. He tried to get comfortable again, but couldn't, and ended up just staring at the wet rock that was his bed.

He thought it might be the same sort of stuff that stalactites and stalagmites were made of – though he'd not seen any of that sort of formation elsewhere on this journey. He got up and made his way to the wall where he could see that a wet line of similar rock extended down from some place lost in the darkness above. He guessed this stuff might have been washing or dripping slowly down the wall for thousands of years. If he lay here long enough it might form an elegant sort of casket over him. More morbid thoughts.

"Something interesting enough to keep you from sleep?" came

Sarva's voice.

John turned and smiled at him, pleased to have company again. "It's more interesting to look at than it is to lie on."

"The others have gone off to explore. They want to see if they can work out which direction we should be going," Sarva answered before John could ask. "I thought you might like some company."

"I'm flattered."

Sarva gave him a doubtful look. "You may not be soon. I wanted to talk to you away from the others."

John wasn't sure what to make of that. He pointed down. "My rock is your rock, make yourself comfortable."

They sat down together and stared out across the water.

Sarva said nothing at first, so John asked, "Do you suppose Andrei and the others could be down here somewhere?"

Sarva shrugged. "I guess it's possible, though I don't know how we go about finding them, it's a big lake."

"Or they could still be up there somewhere, perhaps finding their own way out."

"That's possible too," agreed Sarva.

John carefully avoided the other possibility. He sent a quick glance at Sarva, who appeared to be content to stare out over the water. John figured he'd probably stated enough of the obvious and turned to look off in the same direction while he waited for what Sarva wanted to say.

"I can see why Asha likes you," Sarva said after a long silence. "I don't disapprove, in case you've been wondering."

"Um, thanks," was all John could think to say. At least this explained why Sarva wanted this conversation away from Garjae.

"Not that it's up to me to approve or not. My sister's a big girl now, she can make her own choices. Anyway, I'm hardly in a position to pass judgement. You must think I've been a bad brother."

John glanced at him again, but Sarva's gaze hadn't shifted.

"You must have wondered why I left my sister all those years ago," Sarva continued.

"I know that Asha has."

Sarva nodded. "My dear sister has found her talent now, I'm pleased. Everyone expected something great from us – being twins."

65

Now he looked at John. "Asha explained about twins? How it is with our people, that twins often have special capabilities, like Asha's ability to heal?"

John nodded and Sarva returned his gaze to the water.

"More than a few were disappointed when we showed no signs of talent by the time we reached maturity. They didn't know I already had my talent. I didn't know either, at least I didn't understand it. I thought there was something wrong with me ... I grew to be sure of it."

Sarva turned and faced John. "You told me how hard it was for you to accept that Asha was real. When you knew that no other human could see what you could see, you thought your mind was broken."

John nodded.

"I know what that feels like. I see things too. Things that no one else I've ever met, or even heard of, can see. At least no one I'd heard of until your story. I can see the connections that Ulvanya told you about, the connections of life. Between twins, between the aaranya and their stand, between lovers, and even between friends. I saw the connection between you and your human body break when your human body was killed."

"You're the one we're looking for?" John asked, astounded.

Sarva nodded. "But now you're missing Asha, and we can't achieve what you want without her."

John stared at Sarva in silence, not quite believing what he'd heard. And then the unfairness of it all started to crowd in and he wanted to scream. He got up and walked to the rock wall and hit it. It hurt his hand, but he felt better for it anyway. He came back and sat next to Sarva. "Sorry."

"I understand. But even if Asha were here, you would still not have everything you needed," Sarva reminded him.

John nodded. They also needed someone to help them recover Ellie's mind. Asha was confident that Ellie was still there somewhere, hiding from the torments of her existence, and John had to believe her. Ulvanya had told them they would need help to find Ellie, but there had been no hint where they might find such help.

To distract himself from the hopelessness, he asked, "What do you see? What does it look like?"

"You've heard humans talk of auras?"

John nodded.

"I don't know if humans can really see these connections, but what I see is something like that, I think. There's like a field that surrounds a living body, human or narun, animal or praanin. Yes, it is sometimes coloured, like humans say, but it's not different colours for different people, it's more a mood and health thing. Some people may be predominantly one colour, but that's just because some people have particular moods that dominate their existence. I can't really explain it any better than that."

"Garjae comes to mind," suggested John.

Sarva smiled faintly, and then continued, "Tendrils extend from the aura."

"Like the corona that shows around objects in Kirlian photography?"

Sarva gave him a blank look.

"Don't worry about it, I was thinking out loud."

"Most of the tendrils are fine and vanish almost before you can see them. But the larger, more important ones remain visible, tangible, further out from the body."

"Doesn't it get crowded?" asked John. "Seeing all these connections floating through space joining everything?"

Sarva shook his head. "Even the largest tendrils quickly disappear into the ether. It's only when the two ends are close together that I can see the entire connection. I can see the one that joins us." Sarva waved his hand along a curved line between them. "I've rarely seen a connection grow so strong so quickly as this one between us. I think you trust me more than you should. I may feel much like my sister, but I'm not her."

John looked into the space between them, but could see nothing. "What does all this have to do with why you left Asha?"

Sarva stared at John in silence for a while before answering, "I thought, with your past, you might understand what it's like. To think you are broken, to think there is something wrong. You don't act rationally. You can't, because you don't understand what it really means."

John remembered that period of his life, of believing that Asha was merely a figment of his imagination. He nodded.

Sarva looked back across the water, as if he could see across time. "I didn't think that what I could see could be real. I didn't think such insubstantial things could matter. I was wrong."

John listened with horror verging on disbelief as Sarva detailed the events that made him want to leave his home Glade, that forced him to leave his twin.

4. Angel

"You look very good this morning," Jaimee greeted Asha cheerfully.

Asha returned his gaze, but didn't respond.

He had called for her from the edge of the lawn and she came out from the trees to meet him. Not happily, but not as reluctantly as he might have expected. She was feeling much better. They had left her among the trees for two days. She had seen the brothers depart on some errand early on the first morning, and they only returned late last night.

"Time to see the Palace," Jaimee said. "The rest of us call it the Estate, but Mother still calls it her Palace."

Asha had spent a day crying for Ellie, John's daughter, the young girl that felt like her own. She thought that Ellie was probably still alive, might even live a few months yet, but Asha knew – in her heart and in her head – that Ellie was dying. There was nothing more Asha could do for Ellie, even if Asha could leave this place. She would have preferred to be with her, to do what she could to comfort the preta that had once been a beautiful human girl, but admitted to herself that Ellie probably wouldn't even notice Asha's absence. Perhaps John ...

"I feel like a human taking his girlfriend home for the first time," Jaimee remarked as he reached for Asha's hand. "Ready to meet our mother?"

Nothing had changed for her, and yet Asha felt that everything had changed. She had broken the circle of doubts. Her heart told her that John must be alive, so she would follow her heart. John would return to his home and be able to visit with his daughter, to be there at the end, and that was more important than anything Asha wanted. She would believe that John was alive because any other possibility was simply unbearable. And there was something else, though Asha hadn't worked out what it was yet. There was something ...

"Asha?"

She blinked slowly, coming back to the morning. "What?"

"Are you ready?"

Asha nodded, and allowed herself to be led across the lawn. There were two human gardeners working at the flower bed along the edge of the roadway.

Noticing her gaze, Jaimee explained, "We have several human servants here. Most know there's something odd about the place, and a few carefully chosen ones know that we exist, they can be more useful that way."

"Don't you worry that they will talk to others?" Asha asked him.

"We're in a unique position to watch them. Most have grown into their jobs, any new-comers are carefully monitored, and everyone is checked regularly. We make sure they know that we know everything about them. Most come to treat us as omniscient gods, or in a few cases their God Himself. We encourage that, it's a useful way to ensure their compliance and to keep their tongues in their heads."

They climbed the carved granite stairs to the wide verandah. Before them stood a large and ornate wooden doorway. Asha's first surprise came when Jaimee knocked on the door instead of just opening it. The second surprise came when she was greeted by a young human girl.

"Hello," the girl said. She nodded to Asha and then bowed to Jaimee. "Won't you come in?"

Jaimee laughed at the surprise on Asha's face. "I thought you'd like that. We run a very exclusive orphanage – though not officially, of course. Just a few children like Tonia here. They make useful personal servants."

"Servants?" Asha thought the pretty girl looked to be around eight years old.

"They live much better than many human children in this country. We see they are educated and get everything they need.

And when their vedana fades they have the option of working for us in other ways. It works out well all round."

"You don't—" Asha started. "Karlin?"

Jaimee laughed again. "No. There's nothing like that here. We like to keep our little operations separate as much as possible. Humans are so unreliable, don't you find? It's best if none of them know too much about what's going on."

Asha followed Jaimee into the large entry hall, and the girl closed the door behind them. The house was filled with many scents, but unusually these were all natural. Timber and the oil used to polish and maintain it dominated at the moment. Asha soon saw the reason for this, two adult humans knelt on a broad staircase, polishing the balustrade.

Jaimee turned to the girl. "Tell them to finish up quickly, they should have been done before now."

Tonia nodded meekly to Jaimee, but when she addressed the adults her voice was confident and commanding.

Jaimee nodded his approval. "This way," he told Asha, and led her past the staircase.

Asha caught brief glimpses of richly appointed rooms on either side of the corridors they followed, but Jaimee kept walking briskly, leaving little time to take it in. She did notice that there were many indoor plants here, large and well cared for. Combined with the natural timbers and materials of the furnishings, it gave the house a more natural feel than most human residences.

They walked through a large room at the back of the house and came to glass doors that opened out to a broad courtyard. The area was filled with an apparently random collection of small gardens, fountains, and ponds. Small streams and granite pavements wove their way amid the maze.

Beyond this area, well away from the house, were three magnificent oak trees. The intensity of their life presented an imposing presence. Wide, low sweeping branches with rich evergreen foliage cast deep shadows beneath the trees, and the higher branches reached out so that the outline was a perfect oval. In the centre of the triangle of trees the branches twined together so neatly that the triumvirate appeared to form one huge living thing.

Asha was captivated. She barely noticed when Jaimee opened the glass door and walked her outside with his hand at the small of her back. "It's beautiful," she said quietly.

Jaimee chuckled. "My sister will be pleased."

Asha glanced at him. "These must be centuries old."

He shook his head. "The oldest is not much more than seventy years. My sister is very talented. She'd have made a good aaranya, don't you think?"

"They're incredible."

"One of our fathers would have been very disappointed at how well they've come on." Jaimee shrugged, as if to say that such disappointment wasn't Jaimee's problem.

Asha willingly followed Jaimee past the low growing gardens of the courtyard. Brightly coloured fish swam in the ponds and in the streams that flowed between them. The sound of the running water was comforting and calming. But most of her attention was still held by the majestic oaks.

They walked beneath the trees and Asha reached out and caressed the glossy, dark green leaves, the life of them thrummed beneath her fingers. Inside the triangle, Asha looked up at the complex forms of the branches stretching out and winding their way back and forth above her. To think that Jaimee's sister could have helped to create such a natural living beauty was barely believable, Helix seemed a woman obsessed with only herself.

"I can't let you merge," Jaimee said, "my sister wouldn't approve, but you can touch. Go on. I can see you want to."

Asha went to the tree at the back of the trio, and placed her hands gently on the grey bark. It felt smoother than it looked. The life beneath the bark was vibrant. Asha was tempted to plunge her hands into that life and experience this wonder from the inside.

Jaimee's hand gently closed over hers and lifted it away. "No cheating," he said quietly.

He turned Asha around. She pressed her back against the tree as Jaimee stepped closer. He reached up and stroked the side of her face.

"There's no need to panic," he said. "I'm not going to hurt you."

"This isn't why you brought me here." Asha tried to sound confident.

"Isn't it?"

72

Jaimee's pale eyes pierced Asha's. She couldn't move.

His face moved closer to hers. "Are you sure?"

Before Asha could respond she felt something brush at her hair. It felt like a hand, but it wasn't Jaimee, she was very conscious of his fingers on her face, and his hold on her wrist.

Something changed. She couldn't tell what it was. Like a blink, or like something had dropped across her vision and then vanished. She turned her head to try and see what had touched her, but there was nothing there. Had there been anything?

When she turned back to Jaimee he stepped away from her, though he retained hold of her hand. "You're ready," he told her, and pulled her away from the tree.

Still feeling dazed from whatever had happened, it was a few steps before Asha thought to ask, "Ready for what?"

"My mother," Jaimee said.

Beyond the trees was a lush green lawn. This was surrounded by a dense hedge, and beyond that Asha could see the taller trees of the forest. In the centre of the lawn, resting on a soft reclining chair surrounded by lush foliage, was a small woman.

Asha didn't know what she had expected, she hadn't given it much thought, but this wasn't it. The mother of the siblings should have been proud, confident and imposing. This woman didn't appear to be any of those things.

The woman was small and thin. Though obviously old, her form and presence spoke of youth. Asha could readily envisage the woman as a willowy girl with blond hair and pale skin, not the porcelain paleness of her children, but something softer, warmer and gentler. Age had greyed and wrinkled the skin, and the straight blond hair was now mostly white, and yet still the sense of an insecure young girl clung to her.

"Mother," Jaimee began, "this is the healer we've been telling you about. This is Asha."

The woman had already been staring at Asha. Her gaze moved to Jaimee while he was speaking and her face softened, but tightened again when her eyes return to Asha.

There was nothing threatening or intimidating about the woman, yet Asha almost fell back under the scrutiny. Distrust and disapproval dominated, but there was fear and hatred mixed in as well.

Asha was at a loss to understand why the woman should react this way.

"Asha," Jaime said, "this is our dear mother."

"Hello," Asha said. She bowed her head, but when she lifted her eyes again the same look of disapproval was centred on her.

The silence drew out.

"We talked about this, Mother," Jaimee said.

"And none of that changes what she is," the woman replied. Though the words were spoken firmly, the woman's voice was soft, sounding more apt for apology than argument.

"Asha is not like that. She can help you."

"My children are all the help I need."

"We've tried, Mama," Jaimee said.

Asha glanced at him, surprised at his young sounding tone.

"I know you have, my darling boy, but this ...?" The woman waved at Asha.

Asha studied the woman again. There was something vaguely unnatural about her, but also something familiar. The siblings had always been a mystery, they felt like no other narun that Asha had ever met, but this woman was familiar. There was nothing of the dhumraka about her, they too remained a mystery, but there was something ... almost human. That was it. The woman felt human, as John did even when he was separated from his human body.

"Saarvaya?" Asha asked Jaimee quietly.

Jaimee ignored her.

"Mother," Jaimee said, "Asha can help you, I'm sure she can. You've got to give her a chance."

"What is it you want me to do?" Asha asked. There was nothing obviously wrong with the woman, she was simply old.

Jaimee watched his mother for long moments before answering, "Just sit." He indicated the lawn in front of his mother's seat.

Asha hesitated, then decided there were worse things, like time alone with Jaimee. So she sat on the thick grass of the lawn. From here she could tell that it wasn't a constructed chair that the woman was sitting on, it was a living bush. The vines had been woven into a seat and a padded material had been laid over it.

Jaimee fidgeted for a few moments, he seemed unsure what to do. Then he nodded, as if to some interior voice, and said, "I'll leave you two to get acquainted."

"Jaimee?" His mother sounded genuinely fearful.

"Don't worry, Mama," he reassured her, "we won't be far away. Give Asha a chance, you'll soon see that she won't harm you." He hesitated for a moment longer and then walked back to the house.

The woman leaned back in her seat and closed her eyes, apparently intent on ignoring Asha.

Asha decided not to push the issue. She made herself as comfortable as she could on the grass and watched the small creatures that lived within it. In the quiet, Asha could hear the birds and squirrels out in the forest. She thought she could hear human voices too, coming from out beyond the hedge somewhere.

Movement caught her eye and Asha turned to watch a pair of quail wander out from beneath the hedge and make their round-about way toward her. She smiled at them. The strutting male was brown and grey with striking white highlights and a black face. He also had a cute little black feather crest that reached out in front of his face as if leading him forward. The female was more demure, her topknot smaller and standing upright. They came closer and Asha reached out, letting them peck lightly at her hand. It only lasted a few moments, the quail caught sight of movement overhead and scuttled rapidly under the bush where the woman was resting.

Other birds came to investigate, birds that Asha recognised from the two days she had spent out in the forest at the front. A pair of flycatchers made a brief visit and then flew off again. A humming bird hovered near Asha before seeking protection closer to the bush beneath the woman. And more.

"They come for my children too," the woman said.

Asha looked up in surprise.

"Even more than this," the woman told her.

"The birds are always curious about the narun," Asha replied.

The woman pursed her lips. "Many come to my children."

"And the animals too?"

"Not so much, though Helix has a way with them."

The silence threatened to draw out again, so Asha asked, "What do I call you?"

At first Asha thought the woman wasn't going to answer, then she heard faint mumbling, it sounded something like, "All right, my darling." There was another pause before the woman told Asha, "You can call me Angel."

"Hello, Angel, you can call me Asha."

"I know."

Uh-huh. So exchanging names wasn't an opening to get too friendly. Asha wasn't sure why she was even trying. Curiosity, she supposed.

After a while the woman spoke up again. "What can you do for me that my children can't?"

"I don't know," Asha admitted. "I came because Jaimee ... asked me to." Asha wondered what the mother knew of her children's activities.

A brown bird with a pale underbelly and speckled front swooped in and alighted on Asha's shoulder. Some sort of thrush, Asha thought. It sang out a delicate tone that was quickly followed with a series of descending calls.

"Hello," Asha greeted it softly.

The bird repeated its musical calls with some subtle variation.

"Now you're just showing off."

The bird ruffled its feathers.

"Jaimee will lose interest in you, you know," Angel said loudly. "Just as he has with all the others."

Asha was still trying to work out how to react to that when a shrill scream rang through the air. The thrush flew off, striking the side of Asha's head with its wings as it went. The other birds that had been crowding in also flew off or scuttled for cover.

By the time Asha had stood up the scream had been cut short. It had sounded like a human woman, and had come from somewhere out beyond the hedge.

"What was it?" Asha asked.

"It happens sometimes. It's a nuisance, but someone will take care of it." Angel had barely reacted to the sound.

"Nothing to worry about," Jaimee called.

Asha turned to watch him approach across the lawn.

"Just one of our guests. Someone will see to it."

Jaimee leant down and grasped his mother's hand.

"I'm all right, Jaimee darling," Angel assured him. "You were right, she hasn't tried to hurt me. ... But I still don't like her much."

Jaimee smiled at his mother. "We'll take it slow, Mama. You'll see, it will come out all right."

He straightened up and addressed Asha. "Let's leave Mother to rest for a while. Come on, I'll show you around."

Jaimee led Asha through the house, from lavish room to lavish room. The few adults that Asha saw moved slowly, as if wary of sudden movements. The few children all stopped what they were doing and bowed to Jaimee as he walked past.

"What's wrong with your mother?" Asha asked him when Jaimee failed to offer any explanations.

"Want to go for a drive?" Jaimee asked, ignoring her question. "Sure you do, it'll be fun." He grabbed her hand and led her back downstairs. In a corridor that they hadn't visited previously, Jaimee stopped and entered a code into a keypad beside a door.

This room was different to the others, more of a laboratory than a living space. There were few obvious luxuries and there were no indoor plants or aquariums, though most of the furniture was timber and the various equipment had been adapted for narun use.

Jaimee opened some cupboard doors, inside were a set of glass jars filled with water and floating pink globs.

"Time to dress up," Jaimee said. "They don't like it when they can't see the driver."

"You're going to drive?"

Jaimee grinned and nodded. "Of course. Been driving for years."

He pulled the lid off a jar and pulled out a handful of what looked like pink slime. He fiddled with it for a few moments and then slipped it over his head. A few adjustments and suddenly Jaimee was bald but with a tan over his face and neck.

"Pretty neat, yeah?"

Asha didn't respond.

"You want to try it?" He pointed to another cupboard. "We've got some of Helix's torso skin in there if you wanted. She's a bit more ... full-figured than you – no offence meant. I think you're beautiful, but my sister is something special. Anyway, the stuff is very stretchy, I'm sure it would work okay."

Asha shook her head.

"You sure? You could dress up and we could get photos taken."

Asha shook her head again and stepped back. For once Jaimee

was acting as young as he looked. She didn't know if that was a good thing or a bad thing.

Jaimee continued to pull on more of the artificial skin and then started on the make-up. Asha watched. She found that she was interested, perhaps even curious to try it for herself, but she refused to admit that to Jaimee.

He was now only dressed in brief shorts, like human underwear. His hands were tanned to the elbow, his legs to just below the knee, and his bald head was tanned down to where his neck joined his body. It was a strange look.

"I'll skip the torso for today, the skin is a pain to put on." Jaimee told her. "We've got people working on a spray on version to make it easier."

He went to a tall cupboard and looked in. "Casual, I think." He pulled out a shirt of soft material and slacks to match. These were followed by a pair of light shoes, no socks. He opened another door, hanging from it was a large selection of wigs. "What do you think?" he asked. "Dark hair again, or would you prefer blond?"

"Not dark," Asha answered without thinking. What did she care?

"Okay, blond it is. I've got a red one here, but I mainly use that when I want to play up the Jamie, son of Stephenson role."

Jaimee pulled on the wig. The hair was wavy and longer than Jaimee usually styled his own. He turned to Asha. "What do you think?"

"Your eyes—"

"Right. Thanks." He went back to the cupboard with the jars and pulled out his false eye sockets. After that he chose a pair of fine gold rimmed glasses and slid them on. "Better?"

Asha nodded.

"Nothing missing?" Jaimee checked out each of his limbs. "Wouldn't be the first time I've gone out missing a hand or something. Walt generally checks me out."

"What happened to your other outfit?" Asha asked him. "The one you were wearing when I first saw you." Asha was pleased to remind Jaimee, and herself, of their first meeting – Jaimee staring at Asha in her cell. Amid all this casual conversation it was too easy to let Jaimee pretend this was some sort of friendly outing.

"The old hoody is easier and more comfortable, but you saw for yourself that it's not much good up close. If a cop pulls us over I want to look the part."

In a garage under one side of the house Jaimee led Asha to a sleek, deep blue sports car. "Ferrari," he told her. "The Americans make some nice cars, but you can't beat the Italians for style."

He opened the door and waited for Asha to step in. He closed it and went around to the driver's side. "Beautiful, isn't she?" He ran his hand over the leather interior. "Had a few modifications made, can't have my foot slipping off the brake at the wrong time." He glanced across at Asha, and explained, "Sometimes I drive without all this get-up, but mostly at night."

As the gates of the property closed behind them, Jaimee accelerated quickly, and kept pushing hard around every bend. Asha clung to her seat and cringed each time they rushed at a twist in the road.

"Don't worry," he assured her, speeding out of another tight corner.

"Watch the road!" Asha told him.

Jaimee gave her an insolent grin before obeying.

Despite his showing off, it was obvious that Jaimee was concentrating, there was little conversation during the drive. It was also obvious that he was having fun.

Asha tried to watch the scenery, rather than the road, in an effort not to worry about the constant threat of crashing, but the trees were close and they rushed past so fast that it made her feel unwell. She tried closing her eyes but that seemed to make it worse.

When they did finally stop, it was beside the road at the top of some low hills. Beyond the rough green slopes to the west was the deep grey-blue of the ocean.

Jaimee got out of the car. "Come and take a look."

Asha sat quietly for a few moments, waiting for her world to settle again, before getting out and following Jaimee over a fence to the crest of the grassy slope. A cool sea breeze was blowing in gently.

"Is my home out there somewhere?" Asha asked.

Jaimee pointed to the south-west. "About eight thousand miles that way."

So far. Asha slumped. She knew she could never go back – but so far away!

"That's not why I brought you here."

Asha didn't look away from that distant horizon.

"We were born not far from here," Jaimee said.

Now Asha looked. Jaimee was pointing to the north.

"I could take you there. It's a tourist spot now. Fat humans go huffing and puffing along trails made just for them to get back to nature. It's a beautiful spot. We all loved it, even my mother." Jaimee turned back to Asha. "But the aaranya drove us away."

"What do you mean?" Asha asked.

"I mean that they would have killed us if we hadn't moved." Jaimee's voice was almost savage. "We were driven into the city. The city where my mother was born." Jaimee pointed to the south. "We almost died there too, and we had to leave for a time. And everywhere we went the aaranya drove us away."

"Why?"

"We were children, we didn't ask." Jaimee paused. "So you see, we do have reason to hate the aaranya. My mother has reason to fear you. Your people threatened her and her children. It's not something she's going to forget in a hurry."

"But ..." Asha started, but didn't know how to continue.

"I'm not blaming you personally. We know you better. With powers like yours we would never have let you near our mother if you were like those others. You are not. You are a gentle creature." Jaimee stepped closer to Asha. "Gentle and beautiful."

Asha stepped back from him.

Jaimee didn't press. "I wanted you to understand our mother's reaction to you. She's not going to trust you easily. You need to show her what you truly are."

"I truly am aaranya."

"You're a healer now. Something different, something like us. Aaranya is just what you were when you were born. Don't you see? My mother was born human, but she's not human any longer. Even Pheyton saw that. She needs to see that the same is true of you."

Who was Pheyton? She pushed it away as irrelevant. Asha knew she was different, she could recognise that, accept that, but she was still an aaranya too. And she wasn't like Jaimee and the others. She would *not* accept that.

Jaimee paid no attention to Asha's shaking head. "You need to be patient. Work with her. Earn her trust so that you can help her."

"Help her how? I don't even know what's wrong."

"Our mother is aging prematurely," Jaimee said, "and it's getting worse."

"How old is she?"

"A hundred and thirty-three years."

"And you?"

"A hundred and thirteen." Jaimee laughed when he saw Asha's surprise. "We wear it well, don't we?"

She had known that the brothers had to be older than they appeared, they looked like they were barely out of their youth, but over a hundred years old?

"Something about us keeps us young." Jaimee looked Asha up and down. "Your powers probably do the same for you, but you came into them later. Not that I mind, I think you look very good as you are."

"You said your mother was born human." Asha asked, ignoring Jaimee's penetrating gaze. "Really human, or something like those in the Samgha?"

"Not like those," Jaimee said firmly. "Until we found Ben and the Samgha, we thought of Mother only as a preta that had survived."

"That can't be. How could she survive it?"

Jaimee shrugged. "It's complicated. She was human, like your pet, but without his advantages. She separated as her human body was dying. She was all alone at the start. She had to learn how to survive on her own. She almost died. But our mother is very special."

Asha tried to take all this in. It was contrary to everything she had learned about preta. "Have others ...?"

Jaimee shook his head. "That was part of why we took over the Samgha, and why Sando spent so many years down in your country with that doctor. If we could somehow reproduce what happened to our mother we might be able to find out how to help her now. But it all came to nothing. Your human managed to separate at the Samgha and live for a time, and contrary to what Ben ever knew, he wasn't the first human to do so. But no one ever survives after their material body has died. No one, except our mother."

"For over a hundred years," Asha said quietly.

81

"Yes."

"That may be all the time she has," Asha said. "The aaranya in the city now live less than that. Our lives are governed by the environment. You must know that."

Jaimee shook his head in frustration. "Of course we know that. We've done everything we can to make her environment as perfect as possible. You've seen where she lives. We would set up something for her in the ocean, but she doesn't like living in the water.

"That's not the problem. You haven't known her long enough to see it. She's aging now because she can't feed properly. She drinks, but most of it just disappears."

"Like with the preta, with Ellie?"

Jaimee nodded. "I watched you with that child. I could see that most of what you gave was going to waste, but still you tried. I knew then that we had to have you here."

"So—?"

Jaimee talked over Asha's question. "We weren't worried about losing that centre, there wasn't much new coming from it any more. Sando was pissed off because of the way it happened, very, but it was losing you that really hurt. We were never going to let you just disappear again."

"So how—?" Asha tried again.

Jaimee kept talking. "When we heard you hadn't given up, that you wanted to learn how to heal a preta, we did everything we could to help you."

"How does your mother feed?" Asha managed to ask when Jaime paused. She thought she knew, but wanted to hear Jaimee say it.

He waived that away. "I know that you didn't learn everything you wanted, but you did learn something. What was it? The emails we picked up weren't clear."

Asha explained what Ulvanya had told them about the connections between life, and how breaking those connections allowed the life of the body to leak into the invisible ether. A leak that can only be healed with the aid of one that can see them. She also explained that, to heal Ellie, they had to find someone that could call Ellie's mind back from wherever it was hiding.

"My mother's mind is fine," Jaimee dismissed the second requirement. "But a leak from the broken connection to her human body, that could explain it. Maybe with Mother it started small or closed but has opened as she got older ..." Jaimee trailed off, thinking it over.

"Not everyone believed Ulvanya," Asha said, "not about connections that none of us can see."

"Of course they exist."

Asha was surprised at Jaimee's confident response.

"You've barely met Helix, or you wouldn't doubt it," Jaimee said.

"I don't understand."

"What you and I can do is direct. We have to be near or touching. It's a prana to prana thing."

"Life attracts life," Asha said.

Jaimee nodded. "Sando's power operates in much the same way. His power is strong and precise, like mine and yours, but it works against the mind rather than the substance. He can push a few minds at a time, and release them mostly undamaged, or he can push hard at one and lock the mind forever to a particular task. But as strong as he is, like us, his power has to be specifically targeted at close range.

"Helix is different. When she touches you she can establish a connection that works over any distance. It is less precise, but it is difficult to resist – so I'm told. You want to please her. You want to do whatever it is that will make her happy. She can't tell you exactly what to do, as Sando can, but it's enough. And her power just keeps growing. The more connections she makes the stronger her influence becomes."

Asha's mind whirled with this new information. The implications were too much to take in. She asked the first question that rose to the top, "So why didn't you get Helix to touch me and be done with it?"

"Power over the mind comes at a price," Jaimee explained. "You can't keep pushing at a mind and expect it to work the way it did before. Sando can get away with it for a while, but eventually his power begins to damage the mind that it influences, and the harder he pushes the faster damage is done. Helix's power is more insidious. There's no damage as such, or not that we know of, but it can't be reversed. She can establish the connections, but she can't release them again. Once you're hers, you're hers forever."

"So?"

"So, what might that do to someone like you? If your mind is locked on Helix, might that stop you from being able to do what you do? It wasn't a risk we were willing to take."

"Can Helix see these connections?" Asha asked, not knowing what answer to hope for.

Jaimee shook his head. "No. But she can feel them. We can all feel them through our connection with her."

"You know what this means?" Asha asked.

Jaimee went very still, his gaze piercing hers.

<What?>

The question appeared inside Asha's mind, like the memory of hearing a young woman's voice. Asha shook her head to try and shake the strange sensation.

"What?" Jaimee echoed the question.

Asha answered slowly, carefully. Jaimee looked dangerous now, she couldn't predict how he might react to her words. "If this is right. If your mother's problem is the same as Ellie's, then I can't heal your mother. Just as I can't heal Ellie. Not without help. Not without someone that can see these connections, someone that can direct my healing."

Jaimee turned abruptly and walked off. He stopped where the hill began to drop away and stood quietly for some time. Eventually, he turned and came back with confidence in his step.

"We knew this," he said. "Or we knew it was possible. But you can still help."

Asha waited for him to go on.

"We've seen you feed a preta. You kept your human alive while he was separated by feeding his praanin body directly. Even if you can't heal our mother, you can still feed her more effectively than she can feed herself, and that's a start. I'm sure that's what she needs to keep her going. You can give us more time."

"And if I can't? If it doesn't work?"

"It will work," Jaimee said firmly. "You must *make* it work."

5. *Hunted*

Sarva finished quietly, "I've tried to wish my vision away. I've even contemplated trying to blind myself, but feared that I would still be left with the vision of the connections. They're always there. I can't *not* see them. I can't turn them off."

"But you could have told Asha, she would have understood," insisted John.

"I couldn't, not then. I didn't know how – I still don't. What I had done, what I had caused … I couldn't bear to have someone else know, not even – *especially* not even – my precious twin.

"She was the main reason why I had to get away, and stay away. From everyone else I could have hidden my shame, but every moment trying to hide anything from my sister was an eternity of torment. You can't know what it's like trying to hide from someone that is so close to you, someone that knows you so well because they are part of you. She is attached to me as no other being can ever be, and I *know* this as no one else can. To part from her still remains, despite everything else that I've been through, the most difficult thing that I have ever done."

"So how did you do it?"

"By pretending to myself, at the start, that I was coming back. I couldn't stay still. To be still was to let it all overwhelm me. Everyone thought it was just the restlessness of youth, and that gave me the excuse I needed to leave for a time. I could leave, everyone expected it."

John tried to imagine the apparently calm and collected man sitting next to him as a nervous and restless youth. It wasn't easy.

Sarva was saying, "Almost everyone. Asha didn't. She didn't see it coming because she knew it was impossible. And she wouldn't understand. I knew she wouldn't, but I couldn't explain it to her. Better the pain of separation, for her, than the pain of knowing what her brother had done – or so I thought then. I may still have been right."

John shook his head.

Sarva ignored him and continued, "So I took off with a few friends and headed north. In a few months I left the others behind, they were happy taking it slow, but I knew I had to get right away or I would weaken and return, so I kept on moving.

"I found a band of yaayaavara for a time and wandered with them. It's a hard life that they lead, surviving without a home, but it suited me well. It seemed fair and right. Then they started moving south and I couldn't do that, so I moved away to the north and eventually crossed into the sea. I tried settling on one of the islands, but the pull to turn back was still too strong. I thought when I got to this continent, and away from the temptations of the coast, I might find some sort of peace.

"But I didn't. Even in those Glades where I found welcome, where I was made and felt comfortable, I couldn't stop looking south. And my sight. Always my sight. I could see things that I didn't want to see, understand things in a way that no one else could, but I couldn't explain. I never tried. I feared what they would think of me. So I would quietly move on and try again somewhere further north.

"I was growing desperate. Another band of yaayaavara, other Glades, but none could hold me. Sometimes my journeying led me west, sometimes far to the west, but always something dragged me back, as if I could only find the strength to pull one way, north, always north.

"But, finally, I did find a new home – in a land to the east of where you found Ulvanya in Lake Baikal. It is a land of deep winters but beautiful springs. There I found a Glade in a deep forest off the coast of what humans call the Sea of Okhotsk.

"And there was another reason." Sarva broke off and looked shy, perhaps embarrassed. He also looked forlorn. It was the youngest and most vulnerable that John had seen him.

John waited, not saying anything, not wanting to interrupt, wanting to know but not wanting to press. He'd already been given such secrets as he had never expected to hold. Perhaps Sarva thought his secrets were safe with John, not because John could hope to keep them from Asha, but because he was not likely to live long enough for it to be a problem.

"A woman," Sarva admitted finally. "Perceptive and patient, gentle but spirited. Determined." He smiled sadly. "A dark haired beauty that stole my heart the moment I saw her. Karya tied me to her with a bond of such strength that I finally felt I could resist the constant tug to turn home. The pull to return to my sister was still there, still strong, but now it was balanced by another bond that pulled me the other way. I could stay. I could rest. I told Karya my secrets and found a sort of peace. At last I could settle. I could trust myself not to turn back."

John waited again, wondering if Sarva would continue, but the silence drew out.

Eventually Sarva sighed. "The rest I should tell to the others as well. They need to know what brought me back here, it is not a journey I made willingly." He turned to look into John's eyes. "I don't know how to tell them about my sight. I'd hoped that by telling you first, by explaining to one that can see what others of his kind cannot, that I'd find some insight." He shrugged. "But, in that way at least, I remain blind."

"Do you have to tell them?" John asked gently.

Sarva nodded. "They have already been asking about my past, and about how I came to be where you found me – and they *need* to know. When we get out of here, whatever happens to you – I don't mean to sound callous – they need to be prepared. They need to believe me. They need to believe that what I can see, and what I can do, is real. Only then will they understand the power that is descending over the aaranya, and perhaps all the narun."

\- - -

Darnu and Garjae had swum a long way, and there was still no sign of the other end of the lake. Even the bottom of the lake had dropped away from them, and in places they had felt warm currents drifting up from some heat source far below. They had come past a couple of waterfalls, vast heavy sprays of water after falling from the distant ceiling, and Darnu had insisted that they look around each carefully.

Garjae knew that Darnu had been hoping to find Andrei and Senna, but there had been no sign, and Garjae didn't expect there to be. The odds were that they'd been killed in the currents of the underground river.

At last Darnu had sensed something in the distance ahead of them. Garjae couldn't feel it, but Darnu had always been the more sensitive of the two of them. When Garjae asked if it was the end of the lake, Darnu had shaken his head. He hadn't explained what it was he was sensing, saying only that they should probably head back and get the others. But they were tired, so they descended below the surface and stopped to rest.

Darnu merged with the water, but Garjae wasn't ready to sleep yet. Too much had happened in the last few days. He had so much to sort through, not least what he'd been forced to do to John's human body. He would never forget the spraying blood that coated him, wetting him as only blood and water could. He would never forget hearing the last stuttering heartbeats as the body died. It was a horrible and terrifying memory. And yet, at the time, he'd felt victorious. An overwhelming sense of triumph and satisfaction. He'd never admit it to anyone, but not all those feelings had come from the outside. He had wanted John out of the way for a long time. He would never have done anything like that on his own, and he was sorry that it had happened, but ... he couldn't finish that thought, not even to himself.

Garjae looked down at the gash on his forearm. He'd done a very good job opening it up to paint a line on the rock, and all this swimming had slowed the healing. He could still see the occasional wisp of golden prana leak out and disappear into the water. It would stop soon, it was almost closed over. He had caught John when he fell. He need not have, the gash could have explained it away. But he'd caught him. It was a reflex. Or was it guilt? Garjae didn't know.

He looked up in surprise. There were praanin creatures swimming toward them. Strange bulbous forms, pale and trans-lucent, like large jellyfish, with a long outer membrane that undulated behind them. Six of them. As they got closer they began to change shape, slowly spreading the membrane into a broad sheet. They were calling to one another softly in high-pitched tones. They came to a stop not far from Garjae, and he watched in fascination as the creatures drew together at their edges until they formed a globe in the water. The creatures fell silent. The surface of the globe rolled in long shallow waves, slowly at first, but quickening.

Garjae was mesmerised. He had no idea what these things could be. Perhaps Darnu had heard of something like them. He tried to sense for Darnu's presence in the water and couldn't find him. He looked back at that translucent globe, its surface now rippling in tight, complex patterns. A part of the globe bulged out, making a half-formed hand shape as if someone was trying to get out, and Garjae realised that Darnu was right there, still merged with the water inside that globe.

He swam closer and grasped at the surface of the globe. It felt slimy and sticky to his touch, and there was pain, as if he had touched something hot. He held on and pulled at the skin, but it wouldn't come away. With his other hand he grabbed at another patch and tried to pull the creatures apart. At first there was nothing but the pain in his hands, and then slowly a small gap opened as the seam joining two of the creatures began to come apart.

One of the creatures broke away from the globe, issuing a single high note. It began to roll itself over Garjae's hand, the membrane creeping up his arm like an oil slick. Then a second came away and started spreading over his other arm. He shook his arms to little effect. The slippery, sticky substance of the creature's translucent membrane waved freely in the water, as if he were wearing it. The main part of the creature's body continued to crowd in on him.

There was a touch on one shoulder and Garjae found a third creature coming up behind him. He tried to swim away from it, but it had already latched on. He tried to pull the creature from one arm using his other hand, but it was like he was wearing a slippery glove, he couldn't get a grip through the membrane that coated his hand. The pain was increasing and making it hard to concentrate. He tried again to swim away from them, but the drag of the three creatures kept him from being able to move fast enough.

And then Darnu was there. He grabbed at the body of the creature on Garjae's shoulder, planted his feet against Garjae and pushed away, pulling the creature with him.

"Merge," Darnu yelled at him, "and come out wet!"

It took Garjae a few moments to understand what Darnu had

said. At the moment, he was letting the water run through his body and the water didn't wet him. By merging fully he could come back out without letting the water flow through – and like a human he would get wet. As Andrei always put it, he would put a hole in the water.

Darnu was back again, trying to drag Garjae further away from the other creatures that were coming at them, and trying to drag one of the creatures off Garjae's arms. "They don't stick so much when you're wet," he explained.

Garjae finally responded. When he came out of the water he could feel the uncomfortable pressure of it against his body.

"Come on!" Darnu called to him.

Two of the creatures had immediately tried to attach themselves as Garjae emerged, but he found that now he could, with difficulty, shake them off. He followed Darnu's lead, swimming close to the surface, they couldn't go much deeper swimming like this.

When they had a little distance between themselves and the creatures, they let the water back through their bodies so they could swim faster. They headed back to where they'd left John and Sarva. Darnu was lagging, so Garjae slowed his pace.

Darnu looked pale and weak.

"What's wrong?" Garjae asked. "What did they do to you?"

"They were sucking my life right out of the water," said Darnu, his voice had gone husky. "I couldn't get it together enough to try and draw myself out. I'm glad you came when you did."

"Are you going to—?"

"That's not good," Darnu interrupted, looking ahead.

More of the creatures. Dozens of them. Spaced out, forming a wall between Darnu and Garjae and where they wanted to go.

- - -

Sarva jumped up. "Something's coming!"

John stood and followed his gaze. Something in the distance, coming out of the dark from the unexplored end of the lake. At first his hopes rose that it might be Andrei, Senna and Leavek, but there were too many figures.

As the strange jellyfish-like creatures came closer it was obvious these were not people. "What are they?"

Sarva shrugged. "I don't know. Some sort of spret, or matsya, I suppose the jalaja would call them. I've never seen anything like them before. I wonder if these are Leavek's soul-suckers, they don't look friendly."

Soon the smooth rock promontory on which they stood was surrounded by these pale, billowing beings. There was something insubstantial, almost ghost-like about them. They did indeed look like spirit beings. They had no eyes, as far as John could tell, but sometimes a pair of shadows would pass beneath the smooth central bulb of their bodies, the part that was most stable and substantial, and those shadows seemed to stare back at him. The peripheral membrane extended in pale, almost transparent sheet-like arms that moved around the body in waves.

John watched as the creatures tried to slide up the rock, but they didn't have much strength out of water. Limbs, for want of a better word, formed from their membrane and extended onto the rock. They looked more like wet plastic that had been scrunched up than anything living.

Sarva pulled John back, further from the water. "I don't think we should touch them."

John looked at him in question.

"They're too keen to get to us, I doubt if they only want a hug."

The creatures were calling to one another, a soft, but high-pitched and eerie, siren song. Several creatures joined to extend their combined limbs further up the rock. After a few moments the limbs slid back into the water with a muffled sucking sound.

More of the creatures were arriving, and as more joined the heaving mass at the edge of the water their calls grew more excited and their efforts to push out onto the rock became more urgent.

Sarva and John backed up to the wall.

"Great," muttered John. "After everything else I've been through, I'm going to get slimed to death by a mass of wet Glad-Wrap."

Sarva looked at him.

"Thin plastic stuff you stretch over leftover food," John tried. "Cling-film." If he lived long enough, John was going to have to find new analogies to deal with his new life.

Sarva nodded slowly. "I think I know what you mean. Somehow I think slime is going to be the least of our worries."

Some of the creatures were completely out of the water now, lying on the rock, held there by the others pushing up from the water. The nearest of them was spreading its membrane, parts of it reached forward in flat fingers, oozing closer to their feet.

John checked the wall behind them, but it was too smooth to try and climb.

"I think we'll have to swim for it," said Sarva.

"Swim for what?" John wanted to know. There didn't seem anywhere to go.

"Good point. I say we go that way," Sarva pointed.

"That's where these have been coming from."

"It's also the direction that Darnu and Garjae went."

John nodded. If Darnu and Garjae were still okay, and that was in doubt now, then they had to stop them coming back to this swarm of ... whatever they were. "You want me to walk over these things and just dive in?"

"I'd suggest you run."

"Ow!" John pulled his foot back from where the encroaching membrane had touched it. "That hurt."

"Run fast."

"Okay."

"I'll lead the way again, shall I?" Sarva asked, smiling. John was starting to wonder about Sarva's sense of humour.

John nodded grimly. They were out of time and options.

Sarva leapt forward, but as his foot came down it slipped from under him and he slithered helplessly over the creatures and into the writhing mass of them in the water. John heard a yell of pain and Sarva disappeared under a churning confusion of water and creatures. The creatures around Sarva had gone silent, but on the other side their calls became louder and more strident.

"Bloody hell, I was relying on you to show me how," John muttered. "You can't have him!" he yelled at the creatures, and instead of trying to run over them he dived straight for the swirling water where he thought Sarva must be.

John's hand hooked around what he hoped was Sarva's armpit, and he used the momentum of his dive to drag them both down.

Still trying to swim deeper, John looked across at what he hoped was Sarva. One of the things had completely encompassed Sarva's head, like some bizarre hat. John could only vaguely make out

Sarva's face beneath the translucent body of the creature. Sarva's hands came up to try and tug at the creature, but became embedded in the membrane. Another creature was spreading its membrane over one of Sarva's legs, and this one was slowing them down the most.

In the confusion above them the creatures were slow to respond and give chase, so John spent precious seconds pulling the creature off Sarva's leg. It was like touching something too hot for comfort. The creature came free of Sarva's leg and tried to attach itself to John's hand, but he shook it loose.

The creatures above them worked out that their prey had slipped through and began to follow, calling stridently as they descended. John ignored the creature that still enveloped Sarva's head and pulled him deeper. The pressure of the water began to get uncomfortable so John moved in the direction he thought Sarva had wanted to go.

As he kicked with his feet to keep their movement going, John struggled with the creature around Sarva's head. At last he got one of Sarva's hands free, but as the hand reached back up it was quickly trapped in the membrane again. John couldn't tell why it was giving Sarva so much trouble.

There was a touch against his feet. John glanced back. The other creatures had almost caught up. He swam harder for a minute, wishing he could go faster. In frustration he leaned in and bit the main body of the creature that still enclosed Sarva. The creature emitted a loud screech that rang inside John's head. The pain inside his mouth overrode his revulsion at the slimy, sticky consistency, and he bit down harder. To his surprise the membrane burst open and warm prana flowed into his mouth. In reflex, he swallowed this and soon after felt it glowing in his stomach. Encouraged, he lunged in again and bit down as savagely as he could. Another gush of prana and John drank at it greedily.

He had stopped swimming as the warm fluid running down his throat absorbed his attention. He lunged again, hoping for another drink. Something grabbed at his leg. He felt the painful heat of a creature's membrane, and kicked out savagely against the distraction. There was a tug on his arm and John lashed out.

"It's me!" Sarva shouted at him. "Come on."

Sarva drew him on and John watched the creature that he'd injured fall away behind them. He wanted to go back and feed some more. The other creatures closed around it and there was a surge as a struggle broke out. Many creatures stopped to join the battle amid a confusion of high-pitched calls, but others were still closing in on Sarva and John, skirting around the battle.

"Swim!" Sarva demanded. "Let the water through."

Now John understood why he was so slow, and why he had been unable to swim deeper. It took him long moments to remember how to do it, but at last the water flooded through his body and he could swim more freely.

"Thanks, by the way," Sarva said, after they'd gained some distance from the creatures. There was a strange expression on his face when he glanced at John. "It let go pretty quickly once you started biting it."

"I wasn't going to get far on my own," John answered.

"I don't think it expected that. I know I didn't. Not sure what scared me the most, the creature, or the sight of you lunging at my face with your teeth bared."

"Sorry."

"I was joking. You were much more frightening." Sarva grinned at him.

They swam on, looking back regularly to make sure they were still keeping well ahead.

"So you're able to drink prana," said Sarva eventually. "Like a preta," he added.

"What do you mean?"

"I saw you drinking it."

"Yes," John said hesitantly. "It was sort of compulsive."

"It seems to have done you some good," Sarva noted.

John nodded. He wasn't sure if he saw Sarva actually shudder. John did feel better, not great maybe, but less tired. He wanted more, though he wasn't about to admit it.

"It doesn't work for most narun," Sarva said after a while.

"What?"

"Drinking prana. We can't absorb it that way."

"Oh."

"We may have found a way to keep you going."

94

"What? Keep a herd of those things around?"

Sarva shook his head. "Probably best to stay away from them. But it must be what Ben was saying to you. If you can find a way to pull the prana from other creatures ..." he trailed off, and then restarted, "You'll find narun, and most normal praanin creatures a much tougher prospect than that thing was, but maybe with animals it might be possible. If ..."

"If what?"

"I'll think about it," was all Sarva would say.

They were forced to slow down. John might have felt stronger, but he still couldn't keep up this pace forever. They couldn't see the creatures behind, but it was a reasonable bet they were still following.

A while later Sarva pointed and started to swim deeper.

"What is it?" John asked.

"Not sure ... oh." Sarva stopped.

Below them was a small group of the creatures, huddling around something.

"We should move on," Sarva said. Then he looked more carefully. "Darnu and Garjae are down there. Are you ready to try that thing with your teeth again?"

John nodded.

"Try not to drink it this time," Sarva advised. "You get too distracted, and you'll probably upset Garjae."

John nodded again, though he wasn't sure it was a promise he could keep.

They swam down quickly. As they got nearer, John could sense the presence of their two friends inside the mass of creatures somewhere.

Sarva got there first. He didn't try to pull the creatures away, just lunged in with his teeth and started trying to make as many holes in as many creatures as he could reach. High-pitched screeches rose from the mass.

John tried to follow his example. Even against the pain of biting into the membranes he found it hard to resist the compulsion to drink deeply of the fluid. He did swallow some, but he tried not to dwell on it, forcing himself to move on and attack another creature.

The battle was over quickly. The creatures that were unhurt

95

immediately turned on their injured companions. From within the swirling mass of their distracted captors, Garjae emerged dragging Darnu behind him. Neither looked in great shape.

Sarva did what he could to help Darnu, who looked very weak. Garjae looked more shaken than injured, and refused any offer of aid. They moved away from the creatures that were still feasting on one another.

Darnu pointed. "That way, I think."

As they swam, Garjae explained what happened. He finished, "They forced us to swim deep, so we couldn't come out of the water. It was a choice between getting crushed by the pressure or letting those things close around us."

"We never thought of your solution," Darnu said to Sarva, his voice low, as if speaking was an effort.

"It probably only works if you get in early," said Sarva. He explained what had happened to him and John, though John noted that he glossed over the details of John's drinking problem – as John was starting to think of it.

They slowed a few times, but more of the creatures would appear from one direction or another and they were forced to move on quickly.

"There it is," said Darnu. "A tiirtha. There's a zarana here." He pointed ahead and down.

John peered into the distance. There was a faint glistening in the darkness. It took him a moment to remember the words he'd first learned when visiting Lake Baikal. What the aaranya called simply the Way into their Glade, other narun people called the tiirtha into their zarana.

As they got closer the tiirtha revealed itself as a glistening black surface, like a satin sheet seen in candlelight. It was supported by two great spires of rock reaching up from the unseen bottom of the lake. There was a noise like rain coming from a falling cascade of water splashing into the surface far above them.

"But what people live here?" Sarva asked. "We've only seen those creatures."

"Could it be theirs?" John asked.

Darnu turned and stared at John, his face a mask of horror. "I didn't think," he said. "I just felt the presence of a zarana and thought it must offer help."

"You mean it might really be theirs?"

Darnu nodded.

"We should move on," said Sarva.

"Too late," said Garjae quietly.

Creatures were swimming at them from one side. John turned and saw others behind. There were more on the other side. And above them.

"There are more coming from there too," said Sarva, who had swum out to look around the side of the tiirtha.

There were two directions open to them. One led down into the depths, but it couldn't be that much deeper, reasoned John, those rock spires couldn't be that tall. The only other way was through the tiirtha and into the home of the creatures.

"My mouth's still sore from the last batch," said Sarva, swimming back to them. "I don't fancy chewing on any more. Do you?" He looked at John as he said this, a slight twitch at the corner of his mouth.

John shook his head.

"Then I suggest we go in and find out if there's anyone home," Sarva said.

"And hope the place is big enough to get lost in?" Garjae asked.

"You'd rather play hide and seek out here?"

Garjae didn't answer. He cast one more look around at the creatures still closing in and then swam into the tiirtha.

"I only get to lead the way when it's just you and me," Sarva complained to John.

"Garjae has a thing about going first," said Darnu, "always has."

They followed Garjae.

The sensation of passing into nothingness, and then emerging back out again, was something John had felt before, but he wouldn't call it familiar, and this time he didn't have Asha to reassure him. He felt the same trepidation as he had the first time. The fear of entering a new, alien world, and the contradictory fear that the zarana would sense his human-ness, and reject him as something that didn't belong. But this new world did accept him.

Large rock columns were scattered around them, visible to his vedana, but the depths of the water still faded into blackness in all

97

directions. The dark columns had a glossy finish, and tapered and bulged in apparently random forms. There was no floor or ceiling visible, the extent of the great columns hidden in darkness. All of it came to an impossibility that confirmed this as an alien world, separate to the one they'd just left.

"Not the place to sit and stare," Sarva reminded him.

Garjae had moved ahead. Sarva followed, assisting Darnu as much as he could. John looked nervously behind him, but so far none of the creatures had followed them through. He swam quickly after the others.

In places the columns grouped together so tightly that they joined, and their round bulges and tapers created small tunnels. In a few of these spaces John caught glimpses of small creatures. None came out of their hidey holes, so it was difficult to get a clear view. A few were very peculiar, almost incomprehensible shapes, but after John spied a few that looked like small versions of the creatures outside, he decided it was better to stay well away. Garjae kept to the wider spacings as much as he could, tending upward as he continued to move away from the tiirtha.

Out of the darkness above them emerged the roof of this strange world, or that's what John first thought. As they got closer it looked more like the columns had melted at the top and all collapsed and twisted in on themselves, forming a labyrinth of strangely shaped hollows and tunnels. Some of the spaces were small, but others were very large, like gaping and distorted mouths that could have swallowed a truck. The whole mass looked something like a writhing mass of bloated worms or, even less comforting, the intestines of some huge animal. And they had still not found a surface to the water.

"I don't suppose their mother lives in one of those caves," said Sarva.

"I really wish you hadn't said that," muttered Darnu.

"Mother?" John asked nervously.

"Joke," Sarva explained.

Sarva definitely needed lessons on humour, John decided. "Do you think those things will have followed us?" he asked. "Maybe we could sneak back another way and get out while they look for us in here."

"If it was our own Glade I might be tempted," Darnu said. "But here I'm not even sure I could find our way back the way we came. Garjae?"

Garjae shrugged. "Maybe."

John felt strangely good about this. For a change it wasn't just himself that was lost without a clue. It mightn't be a good thing, but at least he didn't feel quite so useless in comparison.

Sarva was staring up at the caves.

"You want to go in there?" John asked him.

"Darnu needs some time to rest and recover before we can go much further. Up in there somewhere we might be able to hide for a while."

Darnu tried to protest, but Garjae interrupted. "Sarva's right. We could all do with some time to rest."

John didn't offer an opinion. None of the options appealed.

"Time to go," Darnu said.

John pulled his eyes from the caves and looked down. Creatures were rising out of the darkness below, and even as he watched, more emerged from between the columns. He could hear them calling softly to one another. Making plans, he thought uncomfortably.

Garjae led the way into one of the larger openings. The spaces between the melted columns formed strangely inverted tunnel shapes that made it difficult to choose a direction or to keep up a good speed. The spaces kept twisting and turning, and choices presented themselves unexpectedly as columns parted. As far as John could tell, Garjae kept trying to ascend, but the twisted mass often turned in unexpected directions.

They reached a space that seemed to clear and they picked up speed, only to stop quickly when the columns folded together and closed it over. They backtracked hurriedly and found a creature squeezing between columns that opened from a parallel space. Garjae didn't hesitate. He swam straight for it and began biting into it. John suspected there was more than a little vengeance in his ferocity.

The creature pulled itself away and they rushed on. They encountered two more creatures coming at them, but they managed to squeeze through a gap and find a new path. They swam on through more twisting spaces. Sometimes they could hear the creatures calling to one another and were able to avoid them. But then there was another dead-end. And then another space was blocked by creatures coming the other way. Each time they were forced to retreat and find a new way, and each time there were more creatures coming at them from some new direction.

It felt like the chase had been going on forever. All of them were exhausted and Darnu was getting steadily weaker. Many times John was certain the creatures must have them surrounded, but each time a space appeared that allowed them to ascend through to another level. But the spaces between the twisting columns were getting progressively tighter. Soon they would be caught with no way out.

They squeezed through another tight space. Sarva and Garjae had to haul John painfully through the gap because he couldn't reduce his size as much as they could. They found themselves in a vast open space. To either side of them the water faded into empty darkness. Below them was the dark granite floor, that confusion of dark, twisting, melted columns. Several metres above them was a ceiling of white rock, mottled with shades of grey. John stared at it in wonder, it looked like clouds that had turned to stone. It was pockmarked here and there with darker shadows – the mouths of small round tunnels.

Creatures began to rise around them from the tangled floor, each calling out a single high tone as they floated gently upward. More creatures emerged through the spaces below them, and John and the others were forced to approach the ceiling.

There didn't seem to be a choice. Garjae led them into one of the tunnels in the white rock. It was only a few feet across and they had to swim in single-file. The tunnel was a simple cylindrical shape, its interior was hard and smooth, and shiny like polished glass. They swam past several intersections, Garjae kept leading them upward, though the way was confusing. To John it felt like their path must be following some sort of convoluted cork-screw shape. The constant twisting of the tunnel meant that they couldn't see far behind and they couldn't see far ahead. Sometimes they could still hear the creatures calling, so they knew they were still being followed or perhaps even overtaken, but they couldn't see their pursuers.

The small tunnel ended, and one after another they emerged into a tunnel that was much larger, five or six metres in diameter. This new tunnel turned upward on either side of them, as if they had come out at the bottom of a giant U-bend. Garjae hesitated, at a loss to decide which direction to take. They had been unable to help Darnu much through the narrow tunnel getting here and the effort had taken most of his remaining strength.

John looked back at the tunnel they'd just left. A creature appeared. He was about to shout a warning when he saw that it had stopped. Part of its bulbous body protruded into the tunnel, and tendrils of its membrane drifted forward as if sensing the water. The creature looked nervous.

"Wait here," Garjae said, and swam to one side to get a look at where the tunnel might lead.

John looked along the base of this larger tunnel. There were more small tunnels descending from here, and more creatures appeared, each stopped and hovered at the entrance. "What do you think they're waiting for?"

A moaning sound resonated inside John's head, and he saw all the creatures suddenly pull their membranes back within the small tunnels.

"You and your big mouth, Sarva!" Garjae shouted, swimming rapidly back to them. "Go!"

John and Sarva each grabbed one of Darnu's arms and started swimming to the other side of the tunnel.

"What is it?" Sarva called back.

"You said something about a mother?"

John looked over his shoulder. Descending from the other side was the end of a huge bulbous body. From what little he could see, it was a sickly jaundice yellow version of the creatures that had been following them, but this one was huge. It almost filled the tunnel. And it was coming fast.

Garjae caught up and took the lead, searching for a way out, but all the smaller tunnels were still blocked by the creatures that had chased them this way.

The large tunnel divided and Garjae followed the smaller branch, but it wasn't small enough. The monster continued to gain on them.

At last Garjae spied a small side tunnel that was empty and led them into it. It didn't go far before it joined another large tunnel, so they stopped where they were to see what the monster would do. The huge thing came to a halt at the end of the tunnel. John thought he saw a pair of shadows flash across the entrance and then the creature's membrane began to press into the tunnel.

"Anybody want to argue with it?" Sarva asked.

"Do you think it'll do any good?" was Garjae's response.

No one did.

The ugly yellow membrane continued to force its way into their small tunnel. John began to get the idea that the huge thing could probably squash its malleable form enough to come right through. Garjae apparently had the same thought.

"Let's go," he said.

They entered the large tunnel on the other side and picked a direction. They hadn't gone far when they saw another of the huge creatures coming the other way.

"Is that Dad, do you think?" Sarva asked. "Or might there be even more of these things."

"You can stop and ask, if you want," Garjae said hurriedly. "I'm going the other way."

The creature they had been fleeing was already starting to emerge from the small tunnel where they'd left it. It was oozing out like a noxious yellow sludge from a drainpipe. They made their way carefully past the exposed membrane as it waved toward them, and swam on as fast as they could. Darnu hung between Sarva and John, barely aware of what was happening.

Inexplicably, Garjae slowed. And then John saw it. Coming from the other direction was another of the huge creatures.

"There!" Sarva shouted, pointing to the top of the tunnel ahead of them. There was an opening. Smaller than this tunnel. A way out if they could get to it in time.

Garjae, impatient with their lack of speed, came back and took John's place holding Darnu. They raced toward the tunnel.

The huge creature reached the mouth of the tunnel just before them, its great bulk about to block off their only exit. John was ahead of the others and swam into the ugly yellow membrane, biting into it as he hit. The pain was no worse than with the smaller creatures, but his teeth couldn't penetrate the skin. The mouthful of the creature felt greasy in his mouth, and seemed to give off a horrible smell. It made him want to gag. He bit down harder and jerked his jaws from side to side. He felt his teeth meet. There might have been prana flow from the wound, he couldn't tell past his mouthful of the creature's skin, and he didn't dare swallow.

The creature flinched and pulled back slightly. John felt the others slip past him into the tunnel. John tried to follow them, but he couldn't pull free from the creature's membrane. Then Sarva had a hold of him, and managed to tug him free by pushing against the tunnel wall.

John spat out his ghastly mouthful and swam after the others. A quick glance behind showed the creature was already starting to force its great body into this smaller tunnel.

They hadn't gone far when the tunnel opened into a wide vertical tube. There was something strange about what John could see above him. It wasn't until he burst into the air that he realised they had finally found the surface of the water.

Sarva kept hold of Darnu while Garjae scanned their surroundings. Below them, in the water, there was only one way in or out of this wide tube, and that tunnel was now filled with the creature pushing its way in after them. A few meters above the water, on one side, was a ledge, and behind that might be a tunnel or cave, it was hard to tell from where they were. The rest of the tube was just smooth white rock. No ledges, no holds.

Another low moan resonated from the monster below them.

Garjae swam to the side beneath the ledge and tried to thrust himself out of the water. When that failed he descended and then swam up fast. But as hard as he tried, he never came closer than about a metre from the ledge. His fingers would grasp at the glassy surface of the rock, but uselessly and helplessly, he would slide back into the water again.

"Fuck you all!" Garjae screamed in frustration.

John was surprised. He'd heard Garjae curse before, but such an abandoned outburst was something new.

"We'll have company soon," Sarva observed, looking down through the water. "Maybe he'll give us a leg-up."

"Sarva!" Garjae called. "Let's try it together."

John took Darnu's limp body while Sarva went over. Darnu was muttering softly under his breath, but John couldn't make out what he was saying. Working together, Sarva and Garjae managed to get within a foot or so of the ledge, but it wasn't enough. John stuck his head under the water. The creature was starting to spill out from the tunnel. They didn't have long.

"John, come here," Garjae called.

John swam over, pulling Darnu.

"Leave Darnu for a minute," Garjae said. "We'll try to lift you up."

The first attempt achieved little. On the second attempt John felt the ledge graze the tips of his fingers, but not enough to grab on, and then he was falling back into the water.

"One more try," said Sarva. "Then I suggest we see if we can get back out past that thing as it comes out."

"There are others coming behind it," Garjae reminded him.

"I didn't say it was a good idea."

Darnu was floating motionless near the surface as the three descended. John glanced down, he thought the creature looked to be freeing the last of itself from the tunnel. Then he was moving up through the water, Sarva pushing against one ankle, Garjae the other. John did what he could with his hands to try and build their speed.

John felt a burst of exhilaration, this was it, they'd pushed him far enough. He reached out with this fingers and felt nothing. They were too far out from the rock! He tried to lean in but already he was starting to fall. It was too late.

A hand grasped his wrist and John gasped in surprise. His face hit the rock as he fell forward and hung suspended over the water.

"Whoops," came a familiar voice. "Sorry about that."

6. Zakti

John tried to make sense of what had happened. He turned his face up.

"About time you guys showed up," Andrei told him.

"You want to hurry it up a bit?" Sarva called.

Senna reached over Andrei and helped John make it up onto the ledge. There was time for a brief smile before they turned to help the others. They sat on Andrei's legs as he slid further out, his torso hanging down to extend his reach.

"John, you'll have to help me," Andrei grunted. John leaned over Andrei and grasped at Darnu as Andrei tried to pass him up. For a moment John was sure that he and Darnu were both going to fall, but Senna pulled back on John's hips and he was able to draw Darnu onto the ledge.

Sarva followed quickly. "Garjae wanted the hero's spot," he muttered as he climbed over Andrei.

"He's in trouble," Andrei called up to them. "Lower me down further."

John and Sarva eased Andrei down, dangling him by his ankles, while Senna sat across their legs to help stabilise them.

Garjae descended below the water, John thought they'd lost him, there didn't look to be any room down there beside the creature. Garjae surged forward. He left the water well, reaching up to Andrei's outstretched hands. The membrane swept out and caught one of Garjae's legs. Andrei and Garjae's hands met. On one side their hands slapped together but slid apart, on the other side they held by their finger tips. It was just enough to let them bring their other hands together again. They struggled and stretched to improve their grip. Now it was a tug of war with the great bulk of the creature.

The creature extended another part of its membrane and Garjae's other leg was caught. John could see Garjae gritting his teeth. Andrei, stretched out between them, groaned. They seemed to hang that way for an eternity.

"Don't you dare!" Andrei yelled. "You're not letting go!"

"Try to pull them up," Sarva told John.

"I thought I was," muttered John, but he closed his eyes and strained harder.

There was a shudder, and something gave way.

John opened his eyes, Garjae was climbing over Andrei. After clambering over Sarva and John, Garjae turned and helped them to pull Andrei back up. John saw him spit a chunk of the creature back down at it. John shuddered, remembering what such a mouthful was like.

John had trouble believing they were all safely on the ledge. He couldn't quite believe that his arms were still attached to his body, although the pain was probably a giveaway. He started to sit down.

"No!" Andrei warned. "Those things have a long reach."

As if to accentuate the warning, there was a wet splash as part of the membrane slapped against the ledge and then fell away again. Another moan came up from the creature.

They quickly gathered up Darnu and moved into the tunnel.

"We really weren't that far behind you," Andrei was explaining.

John, Sarva, Andrei and Senna were sitting by another pool of water in the complex system of caves and tunnels that made up this part of the zarana. Darnu had been coaxed into merging with the water in the pool. Garjae was in there with him, not merged, but resting and keeping watch on the two small tunnels in the side of the pool in case another of those monsters should find them. This was about as safe as it ever got here, Andrei told them.

"Leavek had stopped again after we came under the grid. He found steps in the rock at the side and told us we should see where they went."

"We should have let him go," murmured Senna. She had been very quiet. She seemed depressed, and now John was starting to guess why.

Andrei put his arm around her and squeezed. "We couldn't know," he told her softly. He looked up at John. "We told him we were going to follow you and we thought he should come with us."

"And he did," said Senna flatly.

"We found the first part of the trip much the same as you, but I'm guessing we must have picked a different way out of the whirlpool."

"I don't recall picking which way we wanted to go," John said.

"No," Andrei agreed. "It went pretty smoothly for us after that. The river turned more horizontal than vertical, and it widened out again. It was actually kind of fun for a while. Then we heard a noise, and found out what it was. The bottom fell out of the river and dropped us into that huge underground lake.

"We looked around for you guys, and that's when Senna sensed the tiirtha below us. We went down to take a look. There was no one around, so we figured you must have already gone through. I remember thinking it was a bit rude not to have waited for us, I didn't realise you'd taken the scenic route. So we came through.

"We hadn't gone far when those big jellyfish things started showing up – at least I thought they were big, that was before we met their big brothers up here. You could tell just by looking at them that they weren't coming to welcome us. We tried to get out but they wouldn't let us."

"Didn't they attack you?" Sarva asked.

"Not until we tried to leave. Senna got caught up in one, but when Leavek and I pulled her back, it let go. They crowded in on us and we were forced to retreat. They herded us up through that maze of columns and then forced us into these tunnels. I'm not sure if we're sacrifices to their gods, a delivery to their elders, or maybe it's just feeding time at the zoo. Whatever, this is where they wanted us."

"So you don't think they were trying to get us?" John asked.

Andrei shrugged. "Who knows what they were doing to you. They might have thought the three of us enough to give away and wanted the rest of you for themselves."

"Or maybe the rules change when you enter the zarana," said Sarva.

"Could be," agreed Andrei. "Anyway, unlike you, we struck lucky. When one of the big ones started chasing us we managed to find a pool that we could get out of easily."

"So ..." John started.

"What happened to Leavek?" Sarva finished.

"You saw the reach of those big ones. We got out of the water and thought we were safe. Like idiots we stood there watching the creature, wondering what it would do. It thrust that sticky membrane out of the water and flapped it over us. It was huge and we didn't expect it, but we still should have been fine. The creatures aren't that fast, but Leavek slipped on the rock and got caught up in the membrane. There was nothing we could do for him. Nothing."

Senna shuddered and Andrei turned to hold her.

Silence reigned for a long time. John spent much of it wishing he had not been so dismissive of Leavek's fears. Maybe there was another way out of the Samgha they could have found. But John had been insistent, and now Leavek was dead – and John was still no closer to being free to search for Asha. It had all been for nothing. He felt Sarva's hand on his arm and looked up. Sarva looked at him with the same compassionate eyes that John knew so well from Asha. Sarva shook his head. The message was clear.

"So you've been here for a while now," Garjae spoke up from the water. "Any guesses on how we might get out of this place?"

"We've been looking. There's tunnels here that go places." Andrei looked across to John and explained, "Like I was telling you back with the jalaja. Inside zarana and Glades there are strange tunnels that end up in unexpected places, often a long way from where you started."

"The ones you think once connected Glades to one another?" John asked.

Andrei nodded. "There are some tunnels here like that, and probably more down in the water, but we've not been game to try and explore those." He looked back at Garjae. "We've been searching those out, hoping for one that might take us out of this system of caves and away from those things. If we can get away from these monsters then perhaps we can make our way back out again."

"No luck yet, I take it?" Garjae said.

Andrei shook his head. "But I don't think we were the first ones here."

"What do you mean?" Sarva asked.

"I'll show you." Andrei pulled away from Senna and stood up. "Hang on a minute." He disappeared back into the tunnel. He was gone for only a short time and returned carrying something that looked to John like a sword, except that it wasn't metal. It looked crystalline. It was blue, rich and vibrant like a sapphire. A little more than a metre long, it had a straight and slender blade that came to a fine point. The hilt looked to be just a thickening of the blade, the guard and pommel were bulges in the crystal.

"A zakti," said Sarva in surprise.

Andrei almost dropped it. "This is a zakti?"

"I think so. I've never seen one before, but I've heard of them."

"I've heard of them too, but how can you tell this is one?"

Sarva shrugged.

"You sure?" Andrei asked. He ran his thumb over the edges. "It's not very sharp."

John interrupted, "I didn't know the narun used swords."

"In the Aeonian War all the narun people were forced to learn such skills," Sarva explained. "But these days only the samudraka continue to use them, and that," he pointed to the blade in Andrei's hand, "is almost certainly a samudraka weapon. Probably someone very important."

"Maybe it's been down here since the War," Senna suggested.

"No," Darnu spoke from the edge of the pool, he was pulling himself weakly from the water. He still didn't look well, but getting around without aid was a big improvement.

Darnu looked at Sarva. "I didn't know the samudraka still used such things?"

"They do," Sarva responded with a shrug.

Darnu continued, "That sword must have been dropped much more recently than the War."

"Why?" Andrei asked.

"Because it still exists. It must be still alive. May I see it?"

John looked at Darnu and then turned to Sarva for confirmation. He nodded.

"How can a sword be alive?" Senna spoke the question that John hadn't been able to get out.

"Stormbringer," John muttered quietly.

"What?" Sarva asked.

109

John shook his head, and then explained, "Back in my youth I read fantasy tales of an odd hero, his name was Elric and he carried a black sword that drank the souls of those it killed. The sword was named Stormbringer."

"No," Darnu said absently. He was frowning down at the blade. "Nothing like that. Although this blade probably did have a name, most did. The zakti were grown inside the Glade – or a samudraka zarana in this case, I guess. It's a complicated and very long process. Maybe the elders at home remember how, but it's not something the aaranya do any more."

"What makes the blades so special," Sarva added, "is the life they carry in them. It allows the blade to be carried through the tiirtha. It can be used both inside and outside the zarana." Seeing John's puzzled expression, Sarva continued, "Material weapons can't be carried into the zarana or Glade, and most weapons created inside cannot be carried out, or, if they can, are too weak outside to be much use against material weapons. The zakti are different. And because they are so rare and so special, only the most important people carry them."

"So is John right?" Andrei asked. "If it contains life it must have to feed. Does it drink the life of those it kills?"

Darnu shook his head. He was still frowning down at the blade. "It's strange." He held the blade out to Garjae. "What can you make of it?"

Andrei, still looking for an answer, turned to Sarva. "So how does it feed?"

"From the person that possesses it," Sarva told him.

"Anyone want a sword?" Andrei asked, looking around at the others. "Going cheap. What about you, Garjae, you seem to be admiring that fine specimen?"

Garjae tried a few experimental swings of the blade. "This could have been handy when you came to get us."

"We didn't have it with us. You'd rather I'd gone to fetch it first?"

Garjae looked up at Andrei briefly, grimaced and shook his head, then turned back to the sword. He tried a few more swings but, like Darnu, ended up frowning at the blade in puzzlement. "I don't think it likes me," he said at last. He passed it over to Sarva.

Sarva turned it over in his hands a few times, touched one edge lightly, and then handed it to John.

The blade was light, it felt too light to be all that effective. Carefully, he checked the edges, both sides felt very sharp to him. He tapped the hilt lightly against the rock floor and the sword rang loudly with a singing sound that reminded John of fine crystal glasses, though this tone was deeper. He grasped the hilt and tried to swing the blade, but it was uncomfortable in his hand, as if the balance was wrong.

"I think it's yours, Andrei," Sarva said.

"What do you mean?" Andrei asked, eyeing the blade in John's hands with suspicion.

"Was the blade that bright when you found it?"

Andrei shook his head. "It was dark and dull when I first picked it up, but the handle felt warm."

"I think it decided you must be the new owner."

"*It* decided? *It?* Who's possessing who in this deal?"

"You found it when it needed someone," Sarva said, "and that made you the one."

John was watching Sarva, wondering if his understanding of this came from his mysterious additional sight. Sarva glanced at John and gave a slight nod.

John handed the sword back to Andrei. "What are you going to call it?"

Andrei took the sword gingerly, as if expecting it to burn him. "I don't know that I want to call it anything." He looked at Sarva, "Can I give it away?"

"If you left it untouched for long enough it might select someone new, I don't know."

"Remember your legends, Andrei" Garjae put in, "there was a more traditional way that these swords changed hands."

Andrei nodded glumly. "Kill the owner and the sword becomes yours. Is there a good side to having a sword like this?"

"Sure," said Sarva. "They have to get past the sword first."

"Perhaps the more interesting question," Darnu said, "is how it got here. I didn't think we were anywhere near the ocean."

"I doubt whether its owner left it behind on purpose," said Garjae, "and we can probably guess what happened to him, so he's not likely to be any help. We still have to find our own way out."

They stopped for the night – or the time they had chosen to sleep, there was no night and day here – and John moved away from the others. He could feel himself growing weaker again. It was several days since he had consumed the prana from the creatures in the lake and any benefit from that was long gone.

He found himself a niche in the tunnel and curled up, staring at the wall. He wondered why he was trying to go on. Was there really any point? He had failed everyone. Perhaps the others would have a better chance if they left him here. He could sit and stare at the patterns of the rock until he faded away, or if his own company got too much for him, the monsters of this place would surely oblige.

There was a touch on his arm and John jerked back in surprise. He relaxed again when he saw who it was. "Is it time to move already?"

Sarva shook his head. "I came to see how you were."

"Depressed."

Sarva nodded. "You're not the only one."

"Hmm?"

"Senna's still too quiet. She's feeling guilty about Leavek."

"That's silly," John said. "I was the one that insisted we had to move on without looking for other ways out."

"And Darnu is kicking himself for not leading us upstream when we entered the river. In retrospect that probably would have been safer."

"He wasn't to know," John argued.

Sarva raised an eyebrow. "And you were?"

"I pushed."

"And Garjae led, and I followed without argument. We did this together, John. It's no one's fault or it's everyone's fault. You can't have it both ways."

John looked back at Sarva. He wanted to be angry with Sarva for interfering in his misery, but couldn't bring himself to it.

"It doesn't help to wander off contemplating suicide," Sarva told him.

"You read minds now too, do you?" John asked in surprise.

Sarva shook his head and smiled sadly. "No."

John looked away. "I'm not really the suicidal type. I've had plenty of chances, plenty of incentive."

"I know," said Sarva, answering both observations.

"I've always managed to find reasons to go on," John continued, staring at the wall. "But they're getting pretty thin on the ground right now."

John felt Sarva's hand on his arm again, and turned back.

"What about your friends, John," Sarva told him, pointing back to the cave where the others were resting. "None of them want to lose you."

"I don't imagine Garjae would lose too much sleep."

Sarva shrugged.

"Yeah, I know. You can't please all of the people all of the time," John mumbled, looking down. "My friends are going to lose me soon anyway. I'm dead already, I just haven't laid down yet."

"Part of your depression comes from getting weaker," Sarva said, ignoring John's self-pitying turn of phrase. "You need to feed."

John laughed out loud, without much humour, but the sound of it surprised him.

"What?"

"It's become the story of my life," John said, "people worrying about how much I eat."

Sarva studied him for a moment, then shrugged and continued, "If one of these tunnels takes us near those smaller creatures then I think we should try to grab one for you to feed from."

John looked up in surprise. "And what will Garjae think? Or the others for that matter?"

"Do you care? You need something, you're running out of time."

There was no denying the logic. John nodded.

"And something else," Sarva said, his voice almost a whisper.

"Yes?"

"I think you should talk to Senna. Try to make her realise that it's not her fault."

"Why me?" John asked, not really feeling up to the task, though niggling in the background was the thought that it was John's job because it was his fault, no one else's.

"Because you're closer to her than anyone here other than Andrei," said Sarva, "and Andrei is too involved in the guilt she's feeling for it to come from him. They persuaded Leavek together, in her mind they are both responsible for what happened."

"You can see all that?"

"I can see the bond of friendship between you, the rest ..." Sarva shrugged and left the sentence dangling.

- - -

Senna sat leaning against Andrei as the others chatted about people back in their home Glade. Some she had met, some she hadn't, but she wasn't really listening. In her mind she was playing back Leavek's final moments.

That huge, sickly yellow membrane had raised itself out of the water, what seemed an impossible distance into the air, and they'd all stared at it, mesmerised. And then it started to fall and Andrei was pushing her back out of the way. They heard Leavek yell, and saw him scrambling on the rock where he'd slipped and fallen. The membrane fell over the lower half of his body and began to wrap itself around him. They rushed back and grabbed his arms. Together they should have been able to pull him free, but more of the membrane flowed up in a wave behind them and folded itself around Andrei's legs. Senna had reached across with one hand to grab Andrei, and the three of them had been dragged into the water.

Beneath the water, the membrane began to undulate and she watched in horror as Leavek was pulled deeper inside the creature. Still she had clung on. She was surprised when Leavek released his hold on her, now it was just the inadequate strength of her fingers clutching at his wrist. It wasn't going to be enough, but she had refused to give up. She couldn't believe it when Leavek reached forward with his other hand and prised her fingers away. She had screamed at him then, or thought she had. She saw Leavek smile sadly at her before his face disappeared beneath another fold of the membrane.

Senna had turned, expecting to see the same thing happening to Andrei. The creature had moved them down toward the bottom of the pool and, miraculously, Andrei had found a ridge in the floor and was pulling hard against it. It had kept him from being pulled further into the pulsing membrane. Working together they managed to pull Andrei free and work their way up and out of the pool, alternately fending off the creature and pulling each other from its sticky embrace. Even when they were free of the water they were still not safe, having to scramble further up the rock to escape wave after wave of the membrane reaching out to pull them back.

There was movement beside her and Senna screamed in fright.

"Senna," John said quickly. "It's just me. I'm sorry."

"It's all right my paurakanya," Andrei whispered at her from the other side.

Pulling herself back to the present she tried to smile at John.

"I must have been daydreaming," she said.

"Some dream."

Senna could see John searching her face, and wondered how much he could see. Could he see her and Andrei persuading Leavek to come with them into the river? Literally pulling on his arms, not forcing him, just lending force to their words, "This is the only way out." Was it? It hadn't been a way out for Leavek, it mightn't be for any of them.

"I wanted to apologise," John was saying to her.

"What?" Senna had barely heard the words.

"To apologise," John repeated. "If I could take it back, I would."

Senna shook her head, still not understanding.

"It was me that insisted on ignoring Leavek's warnings. It was me that insisted on moving straight away. I'm so sorry for what you had to go through. What we're all still going through."

Senna shook her head again. "We had to come."

"And I knew that. I depended on it. I expected it. I pushed you all into following me. What sort of friend does that make me?"

Still shaking her head, Senna insisted, "It wasn't like that. We agreed."

"But I didn't give Leavek much of a choice, did I? Either be left back there alone, or follow us down into everything he feared. And he came. He was incredibly brave. He had done so much for us, for me, and that was how I repaid him."

Senna stared back at John. It was obvious he believed what he was saying, she could see it hurting him, so why was he putting himself through it? It was also obvious that he was getting weaker day by day. "You didn't have a choice. You don't have much time."

Strangely, he didn't react to that. He said only, "But I don't have to drag all my friends down with me, and I don't want to."

"You're not. You are not responsible for us, John. We made our choices."

He smiled at her sadly. It reminded her of Leavek as he smiled his goodbye, despite the pain he must have been in. She didn't want another friend to sacrifice himself.

Senna reached forward and hugged John tightly. "Don't give up," she whispered to him.

"Thank you," he said, and squeezed her tightly in return. When he turned away she saw tears in his eyes. She wasn't sure what put them there, there were too many choices.

Senna trudged along beside Andrei. Andrei kept lifting the zakti to examine the blade as they walked, and Senna kept reaching over and pushing his arm down. "You'll end up stabbing someone," she warned him, John and Sarva were not far in front of them. It was another day searching for a way out of this maze of tunnels.

Senna might be aaranya, but having grown up in the city, without a Glade, the impossibility of these places – Glades and zarana – was still something she had difficulty accepting. Like the fact that they could see here, because the zarana itself was visible to their sense of life, vedana, not because there was any light in these tunnels. Even so, it was like walking in moonlight, the distances all faded quickly into darkness. And since they couldn't see far ahead, they were often forced to backtrack and try other paths when they reached dead-ends, or entered one of the many tunnels that led into the unsafe water.

They entered a large cavern with several exits. One of the tunnels sloped down, but since they'd already climbed a considerable distance to find this cavern, they thought it was worth investigating. The tunnel branched at random intervals and they had to explore each one. None led back into the water, but each stopped, either abruptly or gradually shrinking until it became impassable. Forced to return from yet another tunnel that went nowhere, they paused where it met the main tunnel. Garjae moved past Senna and Andrei so he could take the lead again.

"Ah ... Garjae?" Andrei called.

Garjae paused and looked back, an eyebrow raised in question.

Andrei pointed down with his sword.

There was a trickle of water running down the floor of the main

116

tunnel. Not much, but it had been dry before.

"That's interesting," said Sarva, looking over Senna's shoulder.

"We'd better find out where that's coming from," said Darnu, peering up into the dark.

They hadn't gone far when the trickle became a stream, and soon it was gushing past them, making it difficult to walk. They came to the joining of a tunnel that they had already explored. They stopped there, holding onto each other to form a knot of bodies over the crotch of the tunnel junction, bracing themselves against the current.

The water kept getting stronger. None of them spoke. They held tightly and waited, hoping for it to stop.

It did stop, but not the way they hoped. The water rose over them in a swirl of bubbles. The currents slowed and the bubbles rose higher, leaving them submerged in a confusion of minor eddies. The tunnel was filling up.

"That saved us some walking," said Andrei, "obviously there's no way out down below."

"But where did it come from?" Garjae asked.

"We'd better find out," Sarva said, pulling himself free of their huddle, "before we get company."

The water kept rising ahead of them, and after a while they reached their starting point, coming out into the cavern with its multiple exits. Senna swept her eyes around, trying to remember where they had come in.

"You had to say it, didn't you, Sarva," Garjae called out and pointed.

One of the ghastly yellow monsters was entering the cavern, moving slowly as it forced itself through a tunnel too narrow for its bulk. Senna looked around and could make out another one oozing its way through an even smaller tunnel.

"That way," Darnu said, pointing up. The rising water had brought them within reach of a small tunnel that might offer a way out.

The first monster was already pulling itself into the cavern. They swam as fast as they could. Garjae reached the tunnel first and climbed out, the water was lapping at the edge. He pulled Darnu after him and then turned to try and find a way through.

"It's going to be a tight fit," Garjae's voice came back.

Darnu pulled John out of the water, but the others were forced to wait while Garjae tried to force his way further in.

Senna looked back down. The monstrous creature was swimming up to them, its membrane already spreading out.

Andrei pushed Senna behind him. "Come on, Zak," he said, waving the sword. "Time to do your thing."

"Andrei, no!" Senna cried. She tried to pull him back.

"Just tell me when there's room to leave," Andrei called.

Senna looked up, she couldn't see John any more, and Darnu was pulling Sarva out of the water.

"Take that, foul beast!" Andrei yelled dramatically, and flourished the sword.

Senna couldn't tell if he hit anything or not. "Don't be an idiot," she called to him.

"I thought that's what you loved about me," he called back. He took another swipe as part of the membrane closed in on him.

A small spurt of gold stained the water and the membrane flinched back.

"Yes!" Andrei cried out, and moved down closer to the creature.

"Andrei, come back!"

The membrane swirled up in a great spiral that closed around Andrei, swallowing him whole.

"Andrei!"

The membrane continued to tighten.

"Andrei!"

The ugly yellow membrane stiffened and was unnaturally still for what seemed the longest time. Then it jerked and quivered, and finally burst open in a violent spasm, ejecting a cloud of golden prana that coloured the water like spilled ink. Andrei emerged through the cloud, the zakti glowing in his hand.

Hands grabbed Senna's arms and she yelped in fright.

"Come on," Sarva said as he pulled her up into the tunnel. "Time to get out."

Senna took a last look down. The creature was descending, falling away, and Andrei was still swimming upward, a wide grin on his face. "You scared me, you idiot!" she screamed down at him, and then she turned and clambered up past Sarva.

There wasn't much space in this short stretch of tunnel, but Garjae had found a way for them to squirm through. Senna pushed herself into the gap and Darnu pulled her through from the other side. Sarva and Andrei followed quickly behind.

"Watch where you're waving that thing," Sarva warned when the blade appeared through the gap before Andrei.

The water was still rising, but more slowly now, finding other places to fill first. They kept working their way upward for a while, but eventually they had to stop and rest. They found the best place they could and tried to settle down.

Senna had already made sure Andrei knew what she thought of his heroics. His grin turned embarrassed and apologetic for a while, but it didn't hold for very long. Now they were sitting next to each other, trying to settle, but Andrei was still worked up.

She watched as he compulsively turned the zakti over and over in his hands. There had been some of this from the start, but now it was worse than ever. It was like the blade had some sort of hold over his attention. The only reason they didn't have it with them when they'd first found John and the others was because she'd insisted that he leave it behind while they found somewhere to rest. She had wanted to be somewhere away from it, but even then Andrei had kept turning his head as if wanting to go back for it.

After discovering that the sword was somehow using him, using his life, Senna had thought she might convince Andrei to leave it behind for good – she didn't like it. But first Sarva, and then Garjae and Darnu, had said that a weapon might be useful. So Andrei had taken it up, both repulsed and captivated by the blade, and he fidgeted with it almost constantly. Now that he had used it to such good effect, Senna imagined it was here to stay.

"You'll cut yourself with it," she warned him.

"It's not that sharp." Andrei didn't look up from the blade. He ran a thumb over the edge to emphasise his words. "Though it did cut through that creature okay."

"It's only not sharp to you," Sarva said from the other side of John.

That got Andrei's attention.

"The blade is attuned to you," Sarva explained. "It tries not to cut you. But if you keep waving it around, you'll cut one of us. It's sharp enough to us."

"You keep finding such reassuring things to tell me," replied Andrei sarcastically. "Now you say it knows who to cut and who not to cut? What if it changes its mind?"

Sarva shook his head. "It's not sentient. It's just you. It's your life animating that blade now, of course it recognises your touch."

Andrei didn't look reassured, and Senna wasn't any happier about the thing.

"You need a scabbard for it," suggested John.

"A sheath might be enough," said Sarva.

Andrei fiddled for a while, forming and reforming his clothing until he had a belt and sheath that held the blade at his side without cutting him – or anyone else. Senna still didn't like it, but it did stop him fiddling with the thing quite so much.

They were forced to move on again, the water was still rising. They knew they had to keep well ahead of it so that they had time to backtrack out of the inevitable dead-ends. They also wanted to get a good distance from the water so they could rest for longer, but distances were difficult to judge here. It wasn't always possible to tell when a tunnel was one that could land them almost anywhere.

They entered a long straight tunnel. It started mostly level, and for a long distance there were no side tunnels. When the tunnel started to slope gently down they considered turning back, not wanting to get trapped, but decided to try going a bit further.

"Damn!" came Garjae's voice from ahead of them.

A few more steps and Senna could see what he was cursing.

Another impossibility of the zarana faced them. The tunnel ahead was filled with water, the vertical wall of it was rippling gently. It wasn't the first time they'd seen something like this, though as Senna drew closer she thought there was something different about this one.

"Hey, Garjae, you're right," said Andrei. "It is a dam."

"Ha ha," Garjae replied sarcastically. He looked to Darnu. "What do you want to do?"

Darnu looked down and said, "Time to go back." There was a thin wash of water flowing down from the direction they'd come from.

Garjae started back and most of the others followed.

Senna stood where she was, staring into the wall of water, trying to sense beyond it. There was something strange here, but she couldn't decide what it was.

She looked to the retreating backs of the others. Andrei turned to see what she was doing.

"Better hurry, Sen'," he said.

Senna ignored him and tried to sense further into the dark tunnel past him, then she turned back to look through the wall of water. It was different and she was sure it wasn't just the presence of the water.

She walked up next to the wall and stuck her hand into the water. It passed in easily, it didn't feel any different to what she expected.

"Hey, guys!" Andrei yelled out, "Wait up a minute." He came up next to Senna. "What is it?"

"I don't know," she admitted, "but I think we should look."

The water flowing down from behind her was already pooling at her feet, but it wasn't mixing with the wall of water in front of her. She pulled her hand back out of the wall and smelt her skin. She put her hand to Andrei's nose.

He took a deep sniff. "Lovely, as usual," he told her.

"Be serious for a minute."

He smelt her hand again. "Salt?"

"I think so."

"What's the problem?" Garjae asked impatiently, the others had returned to see what they were doing.

"Senna thinks we should take a look."

"You're the one with the sword," Garjae replied, "be my guest. We'll keep watch here, but don't take long."

Senna pushed herself in through the water, feeling the cool pressure of it close in around her. She let the water through her body and pushed up gently, swimming forward. Andrei was beside her and she felt John and Sarva not far behind.

They hadn't gone far when the taste of salt grew stronger, and there was a flavour or smell to it like some sort of vegetation, something there had been no sign of anywhere else in the zarana.

"Even the rock's changing," said Sarva from behind them. "I'll go back and get Garjae and Darnu."

Senna kept swimming slowly, but she glanced to the side and saw that Sarva was right. The rock was getting darker and rougher, no longer the smooth glassy finish they had been exploring. A short distance further and the rock was like any other long exposed granite, though there was no sign yet of any growth to explain the smell of vegetation in the water.

The tunnel curved to one side and then straightened again. It looked lighter ahead. Senna picked up speed.

"Slow down, Sen'," Andrei said. "We don't know what we're going to meet."

"This is the ocean, Andrei," she told him.

"I know. Bizarre isn't it. Who'd have thunk it?"

"Do you suppose those creatures mind the salt water?" Garjae asked.

Senna turned in surprise, she had been too busy looking forward to notice him catch up.

"What's the matter, Garjae?" Andrei asked. "Think we might get lost?"

Garjae didn't answer, just swam a little faster until he was in front.

The tunnel grew wider but continued going straight. It was definitely getting lighter ahead, and they could see that the tunnel turned to the right in the distance. Garjae reached the bend, he started to make the turn but suddenly stopped, his body rigid.

Andrei reached the turn next and he, too, suddenly went still, his momentum carrying him mostly behind Garjae. Senna heard him say quietly, "I don't think we're in Kansas any more, Toto."

Senna swam up beside Andrei, and bumped into him as her eyes took in the scene before them. The first thing she noticed were the sharp points of the spears. She followed the line of the four long shafts back to the people holding them. The four men were arrayed around the mouth of the tunnel, and they did not look friendly.

"Samudraka," Sarva noted softly as he joined them.

7. Meeting

Cleaver let Tracey keep the page of her notepad on which Tilvy's last hurriedly scrawled message read, "I'll find you!!!" Tracey would bring it out and stare at it before she went to sleep at night, and at times through the day when she was feeling down. She worried about it, she was concerned that Tilvy would get herself into trouble, but it was also comforting. Tracey carried it around the apartment like a talisman, patting her pocket to feel its presence.

At first, after the cell of her early interrogations, this apartment had felt luxurious and open, but now it was just small and confined, and familiar without being at all friendly. Within a few days Tracey knew every stain in the carpet, every chip in the paintwork and every detail of the few framed prints on the walls. And today had been another long boring day, like so many others.

Night had fallen and her late-shift chaperones had arrived: a surly, thickset woman named Sonja, and a young, weedy man who had not been introduced, Sonja called him "kid." Their arrival meant that it was time for another movie, just like every other night; a way to fill the time without talking to people you barely knew.

This movie was a soppy and predictable love story. Tracey's mind wandered. Probably provoked by the uninspiring movie, she remembered meeting Mike in the video shop and his observation that watching a movie when you were alone was always unsatisfying. What a mistake he had turned out to be, she should have picked a movie and gone home to watch it alone. Tracey would have preferred to be alone now. Sonja kept snorting at inappropriate times, seeing some unintended humour in the story, and Tracey thought she'd spotted the young man surreptitiously wiping the corners of his eyes during the most soppy parts.

Sonja's mobile rang.

Sonja quickly pressed the pause button on the remote control and answered the call. "Uh-ha," was all she uttered before hanging up. She turned to the young man. "Dry your eyes, kid, and get the door. Cleaver and co are on their way up."

Tracey didn't wait to be told, she was familiar with the routine, and Sonja was always careful with the routine when Cleaver called. Tracey got the impression that Cleaver was more protective of her than most of the others expected – or approved, perhaps. Tracey got up and retreated to her bedroom. Sonja followed closely behind and stood in the doorway while the young man went to the door. Moments later Tracey heard Cleaver's voice.

Sonja and Tracey returned to the lounge where Cleaver was looking at the television screen. The couple on the screen were either just about to kiss, or had just finished, Tracey couldn't remember which.

"I hope I didn't interrupt at the best part," he said.

Sonja snorted.

Aldercott reached down and switched the television off.

"This is a late one, Ray," Sonja commented. And it was. Question time with Cleaver was generally in the mornings, or at least in daylight. Tracey had come to welcome their visits, they helped to break up the time, but there had been no sign of the pair for several days.

Cleaver didn't respond.

"We'll play cards in the other room," said Sonja, turning to go. It was the usual routine.

"Take a break," Cleaver said. "Go get a coffee somewhere. Give us an hour."

"But ...?"

"Change of routine," The words seemed innocuous but Cleaver's tone was abrupt.

Sonja received this as some sort of reprimand, pulled herself straighter and wiped the questioning expression from her face. She nodded to Cleaver, turned and pulled at the young man's shoulder. "Come on, kid, time to go."

The young man's eyes flicked from Cleaver to Aldercott to Tracey.

Sonja pulled him harder and he stumbled and had to turn. Aldercott followed them to the door, to see them out and lock it.

Cleaver indicated the chair. "You'd better sit."

Tracey felt for the slip of paper in her pocket, seeking reassurance, and then sat and looked at Cleaver. "What is it? What's happening?"

Cleaver sat slowly. He looked tired and unhappy. He stayed silent for a long time before asking, "In all this ... were any of the people you met American?"

"Boss—" Aldercott started, but Cleaver held up his hand.

Tracey could see Aldercott's slim figure standing quietly at the start of the short hall. His face retained that constant careful neutrality as he returned her look. She found that imperturbable gaze annoying. The disinterested appearance looked studied, as if he was purposefully hiding unflattering judgements.

"Anyone with what might have been an American accent?" Cleaver pressed.

Tracey shook her head. "I didn't meet many humans."

Cleaver winced at her answer, and his shoulders slumped further.

"John talked about the doctor."

"We know about him. Karlin was from the UK. He was bailed out of an institution back in '96."

"Steven said—" Aldercott started again.

"I know what our boss said," Cleaver retorted, "but there's nothing wrong with asking the question."

Something sparked in Tracey's mind.

Cleaver saw her expression change and pressed again, "What? Was there someone else?"

"Stephenson," Tracey said quietly. "Something like Walter Stephenson, but that wasn't it."

"Waldron?" Cleaver prompted.

"Maybe. You remember I said that John had spoken about believing that there was someone else behind all that stuff at the Research Centre?"

Cleaver nodded. "But you hadn't given me a name."

"I hadn't remembered it. I wasn't even sure that John had told me, he never said much to me about that part of it. It came back just now. I never met the man, but John said he was a rich American. He visited John at his home, long before the fire at the Centre."

"You're sure that was the same man? You're sure that was the name?"

"About the Stephenson part, yes, and his being rich and American. You know him?"

Cleaver nodded slowly and gave a slight smile, the first of the evening. He collected himself and added, "But not in a way that helps you."

"What do you mean?"

"Waldron Stephenson owns the parent company behind the Research Centre," Aldercott said.

"So I didn't tell you anything new?"

"We had no reason to suspect he knew what went on there," said Cleaver. "Now we do."

"Maybe," said Aldercott.

"So ... why are you asking about Americans now?" Tracey asked, puzzled. Usually the questions they put to her were just going over the same old ground.

"Someone's blabbed," Cleaver started. He saw the shock on Tracey's face and quickly added, "Nothing like that. I just mean that now the Yanks know about you, and they want in. What that actually means is that they want to take over, and my bosses are all too pleased to oblige. Someone else to carry the cost, that's what they care about most."

"I don't understand," Tracey said.

"There's no reason you should. The Yanks have started taking a big interest in you, and I don't trust their reasons. It's not like you've given us that much."

"I've told you all I know."

"I know you have." Cleaver looked sympathetic, the now familiar *the poor dear is unbalanced* look that Tracey hated to see but could do nothing about. He probably thinks I belong in the institution where Karlin had come from, Tracey thought to herself.

Cleaver opened his mouth, stopped, and then said, "If you could persuade your friend T to come in—"

"Tilvy," Tracey corrected him.

Cleaver nodded impatiently. "I could give you a phone, maybe you could get her chatting."

"I told you, she can't talk over the phone."

"She can only send text messages?"

Tracey nodded.

"We know approximately where she calls from, but she never leaves the phone on long enough to narrow it down. We only want to talk to her. We can offer her the same deal that you have."

Some deal, Tracey thought, but asked, "You've been tracking her?"

Cleaver shrugged. "If she would come in then maybe I can persuade my bosses to stay interested, keep you here."

"She won't come in, and I won't ask her to." Tracey slid her hand to her pocket and felt for the slip of paper, her talisman.

Tilvy walked up the footpath, then stepped to one side and tried to look in the window, but the glare of the sun made it impossible. She went to the other side, where the shade of a tree touched the glass, and looked in. It looked to be empty. It felt empty. Good. She climbed over the tall wooden gate at the side, stepped around the clutter and ducked under a wide cobweb, making her way around the back. The back door was solid timber and easy to slide through.

The inside of the house was dark and cold and a little stuffy. It was almost winter, and even a warm autumn day like this had not been enough to heat the inside. The house was fully furnished, and there was tinned food in the kitchen cupboards. Someone must be planning to return here eventually. But there was no one here now.

Tilvy went upstairs to a bedroom that, judging from the furnishings, must belong to a young girl. Tilvy reached behind the dressing table where she'd stashed the phone and its charger – hidden in case the human occupants returned.

She had carried this phone all the way back from Tracey's house in the dark, hiding it when she had to pass any humans on the footpath. The cars were never any trouble, even if any had seen anything they never stopped. But the phone had been useless. The charge had run out and she hadn't seen the charger in the drawer with the phone. It was Taiza, Senna's father, that had found a compatible charger, and Taiza that had found this house for Tilvy, only one street over from the beach. And he got the power back on. It was what she needed, she couldn't carry the mobile telephone around in daylight. She needed somewhere safe to keep it, and to charge it. Not that it needed charging very often, she kept it switched off most of the time to make sure.

After meeting with Tracey the first time, Tilvy had convinced Taiza and Beenae to help her search for Tracey in the city, but it had been useless. They had been forced to give up after a few days. Instead, on most days, sometimes twice a day, Tilvy kept coming back here to check the phone – hoping for news. She had sent two more messages of her own, but so far there had been no responses.

She fumbled, her fingers slipping over the plastic of the phone, before managing to get it turned on. She waited for it to do its thing. The house was mostly silent, just the occasional creak as the roof warmed in the afternoon sun, and distant sounds of traffic.

The phone beeped ... and then beeped again. Tilvy looked down. There was a message!

"Meet me at the river. Same place. Tonight. Tr."

"Yes!" Tilvy called out, a smile spreading across her face. Another meeting. She'd get Taiza and Beenae to come with her, maybe they could convince Tracey to make a break for it. They had a house for her right here that she could live in, and if the occupants came home they would find another.

She looked back down at the phone. "Tonight," it said. That was a bit odd. Maybe Tracey was already out. It didn't matter. A meeting was a meeting. Maybe they could have longer this time. Tilvy started to think about smuggling in a piece of paper with questions and stuff already written out, save some time that way.

She keyed in, "OK," and sent it, and then carefully turned the phone off and returned it to its hiding place. Next, she went hunting around the house for paper and a pencil. She found what looked like someone's study desk in another room. There was a pad of paper and lots of pens, but she couldn't find a wooden pencil. She tried writing with a pen but couldn't hold it, her fingers kept slipping on the plastic, and eventually she gave up. They'd have to make do without it.

Tilvy left the house and made her way back to the beach. A main road ran along the beach and traffic was building up as the afternoon moved on. She checked that no one was looking and pressed the pedestrian walk button at the traffic lights. She waited impatiently. Tonight! The cars all drew to a stop at the lights. Tilvy had learned to be cautious, sometimes one would try to sneak through when they didn't see anyone, so she didn't waste any time getting across.

There were always a few humans down on this broad beach, even the occasional one that went swimming, though the weather wasn't really warm enough for them. Tilvy quickly found Taiza and Beenae, but frowned when she saw they had company. She hoped they wouldn't spoil her plans for tonight.

It was Ceeda and Nacee. Poor legless, listless Nacee was curled under Ceeda's arm. Whatever had been done to her in that awful prison appeared to be permanent. She was totally dependent on Ceeda and panicked if he left her field of vision. She and Ceeda had stayed in the city rather than return to the Glade because Nacee refused to get into a car, she didn't even like to get too close to one, which must make getting around this city pretty difficult.

There was a stranger too. A jalaja. That was different.

Ceeda smiled at Tilvy as she drew close. "This is Pasith," he said, pointing to the jalaja. "He wanted to meet you."

Tilvy looked at the stranger curiously. He was small, like most jalaja. The hair smoothed back on his head was dark and his skin was pale. He had a wide face with deep set eyes, small nose and thin lips. Tilvy thought he looked sneaky, slippery.

"Do I know you?" Tilvy asked. She didn't mean to sound unfriendly, but she was feeling impatient, wishing the sun would hurry up and set.

Pasith shook his head. "I have seen you once. When you were hiding beside the cage of that strange aaranya woman. The powerful one. You call her Asha?"

"You were in the prison?"

Pasith nodded. "I saw you talk with her."

"I didn't notice you. Sorry."

Pasith shrugged.

"Pasith was looking for Andrei," Ceeda said. "He wanted to thank him properly."

"We were rude," Pasith said. "Neso and I couldn't believe it was real. We thought it must be just another trick."

"Neso?" Tilvy asked.

"My mate. She –" Pasith paused, looking uncomfortable. "She doesn't think I need to do this. But I feel bad. Andrei was ... he was patient with us when he didn't need to be. I understand how urgent it was, but Andrei took the time to make sure we got out. I wanted to thank him."

Tilvy smiled, maybe the jalaja wasn't so bad. "I'm sure Andrei would like that."

"And thank you too. I know you were part of it."

"I didn't do much."

"But you were there. It must have taken a lot of courage."

A human woman walked past them and they waited for her to get clear. Tilvy was grateful for the interruption, she didn't know how to respond to Pasith.

They sat in a circle and talked about the prison and the escape for a while. Then the sun was sinking low and Tilvy was getting impatient to be on her way. She told the others about her meeting with Tracey tonight.

"Ah," commented Ceeda.

"What?"

"We're going back to the Glade. I thought I'd see if you wanted to come with us," Ceeda said.

Tilvy was silent for a moment, trying to work out her response. "You're going to walk all that way?" she said at last.

Ceeda nodded and his arm tightened around Nacee. "There's a group of us, some of the younger city folk are interested in coming with me."

"There's nothing there," Tilvy reminded him, "just ashes."

"I know, but I can help the recovery. I know what to do, I wasn't always on the outer."

Tilvy nodded. Ceeda was from her Glade, as young as he looked, he was actually of the same generation as Garjae and Darnu – over a century old. He grew up with them, spent time with the elders as they had. He would know things that Tilvy had not yet learned.

"Did you want to come?" he asked again.

"No. Not yet." Tilvy looked to Beenae. "You can go with them if you want."

Beenae shook his head.

Tilvy was relieved, she liked having him around. They had been spending most of their time around Taiza, and while she liked Taiza well enough, she was uneasy in his company; he never sat quietly and such restlessness was unsettling. Whereas Beenae was reassuringly familiar, like an easygoing younger brother. That Beenae and Taiza got along so well also made things easier on that front.

"All right," said Ceeda. "If you change your mind, we aren't leaving until the morning. You know where to find us."

Ceeda moved forward until he was crouched in front of Nacee. She crawled onto his back and wrapped her arms around his neck. Ceeda stood and put his arms beneath what was left of Nacee's legs to help support her. Nacee rested her head against his shoulder on one side. Tilvy couldn't help but stare at the strange flattened ends of Nacee's legs. The cut – or whatever had done this – had been made a few inches above where her knees should have been. When Tilvy looked up she saw that Ceeda was watching her unhappily, he didn't like people staring at Nacee's deformity.

They all stood to say goodbye.

"Be careful," Tilvy said. "It's a long way."

"We will. If we stick together we should be fine." Ceeda started to walk away, and then stopped and turned back. "I guess I'll see you there, when you're ready to come home."

"We might even beat you there," Beenae put in, grinning. He had enjoyed hitching the ride to the city in the back of a truck, something Ceeda couldn't consider with Nacee.

Ceeda smiled at him. "I guess so." Then he turned and walked away, Nacee still clinging silently to his back.

"If you're going to the river anyway, I'll walk with you," Pasith said to Tilvy.

"Sure. You can point out where we can find you. When Andrei gets back I'll get him to come and see you." *If* Andrei comes back, Tilvy added to herself in unhappy silence.

- - -

Today's guards were Larry and Hal – Hal's real name was something unpronounceable that Tracey had heard only the once when the two men had first been introduced, and she had subsequently forgotten it. Both men were tall and slender, but otherwise looked nothing alike. Larry was pale to the point of looking sickly, with sandy hair and a long face that hid a comedic nature. Hal was dark skinned, dark haired, and with a kind, friendly face that always looked happy to meet you and talk with you. Days with these two tended to be more fun than most.

Larry was a board game nut, and today he'd brought along something that he said was a classic. It was called *Trouble*. The square plastic board had a clear bubble in the middle that you pressed on to roll the dice inside it, then you moved your pieces around the board, trying to get all your pieces home while opportunistically sending your opponents' pieces back to the start if you landed on them. For such a simple game it took a surprisingly long time to finish a round of play.

Tracey pressed hard on the central bubble and released it to a resoundingly loud popping sound.

"Oh!" cried Larry. "What's it gunna be, girl? You can get one home with that, or you can send the scoundrel back to India."

"Sydney," Hal repeated. "I was born in Sydney."

"Huh, and that explains your accent does it?"

Tracey laughed. Hal didn't have much of an accent, what little there was sounded more British than anything else. The constant gibes between the two went on all the time, they both seemed to enjoy it. Tracey saw an alternative move, grinned, and took it.

Larry groaned.

"Yes!" approved Hal. "Put the pale bastard back under the rock where he came from. My turn." He pushed the bubble to another loud pop.

Larry's mobile rang. As he pulled it from his pocket he said accusingly to Tracey, "See? Now you've done it, he got that one home." Then into his phone, "Yup? ... Just in the nick of time, Sonja my darling, got loads of *trouble*. ... You'll see." He hung up.

"Cop-out," Hal told him as Larry stood.

"Time to change the guards at the palace. We can't disappoint our queen." Larry bowed to Tracey.

Tracey smiled regally and waggled one hand back and forth as a royal wave.

"You just don't want to sit out a game you're losing," Hal told him.

"Places, kiddies," Larry instructed.

"What happened to *queen*?" Tracey asked as she got up, still smiling.

"Big Brother is watching," Larry reminded her, pointing to the camera in the corner of the room. It covered most of the main living area and down the entrance hall. Tracey had been concerned about it at the start, but they assured her that her bedroom was not monitored.

Tracey went into her bedroom and Hal took up his position, leaning against the door frame waiting. She heard the knock on the door and Larry's response.

"Come in, come in, oh watchers of the night. ... And lock up behind you, I have a point of honour to contest."

By this time Larry was back near the bedroom door. He addressed Hal, "So, you want to finish this battle for the favour of our fair queen, do you, dark knight?"

"What's the trouble?" Sonja asked as she joined them.

Larry pointed to the board.

Sonja stared for a moment and gave a groan.

"Go home, guys," Tracey said.

"What? Pack up my *Trouble* in my old kit bag?" Larry asked, one eyebrow raised.

"What's up, kid?" Sonja called out loudly. They all turned.

"I think someone—" The kid's eyes went dull and he started to fall.

Tracey had seen that dazed expression before. "Tilvy?" It couldn't be. Her hand went to her pocket to feel for the slip of paper, and she felt someone or something slip past her. She turned her head, saw nothing, and turned back again.

Sonja had her hand under her jacket as she stepped toward her fallen partner, and then she was falling. Larry and Hal both had their guns out. Hal reached out with his free hand and pulled Tracey behind him. His grip went limp and he fell back, pushing her into the frame of the door to her bedroom. She tried to grab him as he fell, but it all happened too fast and he slipped from her hands.

Half-crouched over Hal, Tracey looked up to see Larry waving his gun wildly, looking for the enemy. Tracey didn't know what to wish for. This couldn't be Tilvy. She wouldn't do this.

Larry's gun suddenly fell, and he stared at his hand in surprise. A moment later his face went slack and he collapsed where he was.

Tracey stood up and pressed her back against the door frame.

What should she do? "Tilvy?" she called out. Hoping that it could be her friend, but not really believing it.

- - -

Pasith was full of questions about Asha. He'd watched what she had done with the trees in her cell. "I wondered if it was something the doctor had done to her," he said.

Tilvy shook her head. "She's a twin."

"A twin," Pasith repeated, his voice a mixture of awe and surprise. "So she's always been able to do that?"

"No. It came as a surprise to Asha too."

"I didn't see her sister in the prison ... they didn't ...?"

"Her twin is a brother. He went north a long time ago."

"Why?"

Tilvy shrugged. She didn't want to go into it, so she tried to divert the conversation, asking Pasith about his life in the river, and how many jalaja were still around.

Taiza and Beenae were walking ahead of them. Tilvy watched with fond amusement as Taiza pointed things out to Beenae. Taiza talked with his hands a lot and Beenae followed every gesture with avid interest. It looked like Senna's father had found a keen protégé.

Night had fallen and with it the temperature. The roads were all choked with traffic, their headlights glaring and the cold still air was full of fumes. There weren't many people on the footpaths they were using, and what few there were paced out determinedly with their heads down, in a hurry to get where they were going.

They weren't far from the river now. Just ahead was the park where Tilvy would wait for Tracey. They drew closer and conversation stopped as they looked ahead. If Tracey was around, and if it was like last time, then there would presumably be other humans watching.

Tilvy couldn't see Tracey in the park yet. There were four vehicles in the parking area, two vans and two cars. Tilvy thought she could sense a few humans in them, but couldn't tell if any of them was Tracey. There were also a few humans in the park, which was a little surprising considering the frosty cold that had descended with the night, so some must be here to watch Tracey. A man with a dog on a lead was leaving – good; dogs couldn't sense the narun, but they were harder to avoid as they bounded around chasing other things.

There were also two couples with prams, one at either end. Tilvy thought they were a bit irresponsible having their babies out in the cold.

Taiza stopped abruptly, reaching out one hand to grab at Beenae. Tilvy and Pasith caught up.

"What is it?" Tilvy asked.

"Did y' feel it?" Taiza responded.

"What?"

"A buzz ... like the sensor thing the grey 'ns used."

The others shook their heads.

"Jus' faint. Sort o' faded in 'n' then out 'gain."

"It can't be," argued Tilvy, "the people with Tracey don't know about any of that. They don't even believe we exist."

Taiza shrugged. Beenae didn't say anything, but he looked nervous and excited.

"I've got to get to the river, whatever," said Pasith.

"I don't sense any other narun," said Tilvy.

"Go careful," Taiza warned.

They started forward again, unconsciously keeping close together. They entered the park and paused near one of the large trees at the edge. None of the humans were paying attention to them. There was still no sign of Tracey.

"The trees are no good to me," said Pasith, his voice startling Tilvy. "I say we get closer to the river." She hadn't thought about that, the jalaja couldn't merge with the trees.

Pasith started walking across the open grass, the most direct path to the water. The others followed closely behind.

They were walking past a park bench when Taiza stopped suddenly. "'s not 'uman!"

One of the people at the pram near the river threw back his cloak. Taiza was right, it wasn't human after all. It was a dhumraka. The detector came on. There was nothing faint about it this time. The uncomfortable buzzing sensation made Tilvy shiver and she froze in fear with the sudden recognition.

"Sh't" muttered Taiza.

There was a sound from one of the vans behind them and Tilvy turned to look. The side door was opening and she could see a dhumraka climbing out. Movement caught her eye and she saw another human-turned-dhumraka next to the other pram, he was lifting something from inside it. She watched with dread as the odd antenna shape glinted dully in the street lighting. She knew what that was.

"That's one of those ray-g—" Beenae started.

"Come on!" Pasith yelled and pulled at Tilvy's arm.

They ran for the river, but the dhumraka on that side was already sweeping his antenna over them.

Pasith collapsed in front of her, as if his legs had suddenly given out, and then Tilvy's world filled with pain and chaos. Everything seemed to be spinning around her while fire and knives tried to rip her apart. She heard screaming but didn't know whether it came from her or one of the others. The ground rushed up to meet her.

8. Samudraka

"Mermen," John translated for himself. He tried to remember what he'd been told. The samudraka were narun of the sea, as the jalaja were narun of fresh water. He'd also heard them called nereids and oceanids, names from human mythology, but these weren't myths. They were floating there in front of him. Men with strangely flattened faces, broad and strongly muscled chests, and narrow but powerful hips that flowed down to broad flukes, like a dolphin's tail but the curves were wrong.

Where the tail met the torso the tough leathery skin grew thinner and softened, colour and texture merging smoothly into what John could only think of as the normal human skin of their torso. The skin of the tail came well up in front, covering the stomach like a shield, but it swept back low over their backs.

Each of the men had dark hair pulled back in a long loose braid that floated out behind them, and each had a neat beard. Two of them had olive-green skin, their tails were similarly coloured but with a smooth silvery cast. The other two men – John turned his head to try and see them more clearly, they were floating upside down from the top of the mouth of the tunnel – were much darker than their companions, their skin a deep jade green and their tails a shiny black. One of the dark men was huge, half as large again as any of his companions, and none of them were small.

"Who are you?" one of the paler men asked.

There was something oddly accented about the voice. John couldn't quite make out what it was, his mind kept coming up with the strange idea that the accent was in flavour rather than in sound – and, of course, narun telepathy should have neither. Then he thought of Taiza, whose very thoughts must be truncated to affect his speech as it did.

Sarva placed a hand on Garjae to stop him from speaking, and moved himself in front of the group. The spear of the pale man that had spoken centred itself over Sarva's face. "My name is Sarva," he told the man.

Watching Sarva speak down the length of the spear made John think of a man talking into a boom microphone, except such things didn't usually end in a savage barbed point.

"We seek refuge from those creatures of the far zarana," Sarva continued.

"The nirarkta," the man responded. It wasn't a question, they obviously knew what lay beyond this tunnel.

Sarva shrugged. "We have no name for them."

"We do not welcome aaranya," the man told him.

"I know," Sarva said, "and we apologise for intruding, but we are lost and unable to return the way we came. Will you give us passage to the outside?"

"Did you see Holitto?" asked the larger of the two dark men, interrupting whatever the paler guard had been about to say. "A samudraka like myself?" referring to his dark skin.

Andrei, almost directly behind Sarva, started to say something but Sarva reached back and squeezed his arm.

"No," Sarva responded. "We saw no samudraka, no other narun at all."

"Better you had fed the nirarkta than force us to soil our spears with your lives," said the second of the pale men.

Sarva considered this, perhaps uncertain how to proceed, though his expression remained carefully blank. Eventually he said, "We will, of course, seek the company of the nirarkta, rather than trespass on the will of the samudraka."

This was news to John, though staring the wrong way down the shaft of a sharp spear did colour things a bit. John also wondered about Sarva's formal manner of speaking with these people. John noticed that Darnu, too, was paying close attention, surprised at Sarva's familiarity with the samudraka.

Sarva started to turn around. It seemed he was serious about going back.

"Too late for that, videzaka," said the man that had first spoken. His spear reached forward and touched Sarva lightly on the back before withdrawing again.

Sarva's shoulders slumped and he turned back.

"We do not wish to stain your water with our prana. If you permit, we will return to the nirarkta."

"It is upapaurnamasi for the nirarkta," noted the man, "they would welcome you, but our waters are wide, your stain will soon fade."

"Why risk it?" returned Sarva. "And think of your weapons," Sarva acknowledged the second of the pale men. "A spear spoiled with the life of an aaranya could not be carried into battle with honour."

"It is my brother's spear," answered the man, the grin on his face was widening, though John didn't see any comfort in it. "He has another."

"And whose spear would you borrow then?" Sarva asked.

The man laughed. "I did not know videzaka could argue so eloquently."

"The sharp end of your brother's spear is a great teacher."

"All right—"

The smaller of the dark men interrupted. "What is he?" The end of his spear had moved and pointed directly at John's head.

John held himself still, all he could see of the spear was the deadly point of it. He flicked his eyes to Sarva.

Sarva didn't turn around, he didn't need to, to know where the question had been directed. "He is saarvaya."

"I have not heard of such a people," the dark man said.

Sarva shrugged in deprecation. "They are videzaka."

"Satisfied?" asked the man that had been enjoying his conversation with Sarva.

John stared past the point of the spear into the eyes of the dark man. His eyes were also dark, and they seemed to bore into John. Finally the dark man tilted his head and his spear drew back a few inches.

"You may leave," the pale man said. "I do not like to take the life of one so able with his tongue. You shall have your chance, however small. The nirarkta will enjoy their feed."

"And your brother will thank you," added Sarva.

The pale man laughed and made a shooing motion with one hand.

Sarva turned around. "Come on," he said quietly, "while we still can." He grabbed Andrei by his shoulders and turned him around, pushing and holding him so that Sarva remained between Andrei and the guards.

John turned to follow. He was unhappy about turning his back on the spears, he could almost feel the points coming at his back.

It was only a short distance before they would be out of sight of the guards, but it was to the side, following the turn of the tunnel, and that was enough.

"Stop!" John recognised it as the deep voice of the large dark man.

The group paused, trying to hold themselves still in the water. They all looked to Sarva to see what he wanted. Sarva hesitated, torn between obeying and fleeing.

"You cannot outswim *us*, videzaka," warned the same voice.

Sarva turned, still trying to place himself in front of Andrei, and swam back to face the spears.

"Your friend," the large dark man demanded, his spear pointed over Sarva's shoulder at Andrei, "what is he carrying?"

"We found it in the tunnels of the nirarkta," said Sarva.

"Show us."

Reluctantly Sarva moved to the side. "Show them, Andrei. But slowly. No sudden moves."

Andrei looked nervously at Sarva and then pulled the zakti slowly from its sheath at his side.

"Zamayitar!" exclaimed the smaller of the dark men.

Suddenly all the spear points were much closer, the points of three of them hovering in front of Andrei, but the one held by the large man remained directed at Sarva, its point touching his chest.

"Holitto?" he demanded.

"We saw no one," Sarva answered. "My friend found the zakti lying in one of the tunnels."

"Liar!" said the small dark man.

"You can have it if you want," Andrei offered. He held the blade out to them.

The spears all fell back. John couldn't make out the expressions on the four guards. There was anger there, and definitely shock, confusion too, but could there also be a touch of fear?

"No one wants the bloody thing," murmured Andrei under his breath.

"It doesn't work like that," said Sarva, "not for the samudraka."

"So what happens now?"

"I have no idea."

* * *

John tried to find himself a comfortable corner of the cave, and sat down resting his arms on his knees and his head on his arms. He was exhausted. Now that he was no longer looking down the length of a spear from the wrong end his weariness had returned redoubled.

Their group had been escorted from the tunnel leading back to the nirarkta, and were shown, with remarkable politeness considering what had gone before, down another tunnel and into a small cave filled with water. So far they had seen nothing of the zarana outside these tunnels, which made it feel like an extension of the system they had left behind. John felt as if the only real change was that the monsters in the water now bore human faces.

Low in one wall of that water filled cave had been a hole just large enough to swim through. They had been asked to go through. John was pleased he wasn't first. When he swam through he was caught by Sarva as he fell out of the water.

"They could have warned us," Andrei complained.

The cave was similar to the one they had left, but this one was dry. The small hole back to the previous cave showed water rippling from the effects of their passage but, impossibly, the water itself did not flow through the hole and this cave remained dry. The samudraka rolled a boulder over the hole and the water that had been visible pulled itself back as if sucked away by a vacuum.

John, head down between his arms, stared at the floor without seeing it and listened to the conversation going on around him.

"Nice of them to find us a dry spot, I suppose," Andrei said, "probably not too many of them in a samudraka zarana."

"I don't think this is dry for our convenience," Sarva said. John could hear the amusement in his voice.

"Huh?" Andrei queried.

"I think this is probably some sort of punishment cell. Intended to isolate a samudraka from the water."

"Oh."

"So we are prisoners?" Senna asked.

Silly question, thought John, didn't you notice the rock over the doorway?

"Yes," said Sarva, "but that's better than what I thought might happen."

"Why didn't they take Zak?" Andrei asked.

John heard Andrei pulling the sword from its sheath.

"Put it away, Andrei," Senna told him.

"Couldn't you come up with something a bit more inventive to call it?" John asked without lifting his head.

"I don't know," said Sarva, "I think it's sort of cute. Better than its original name. Did you hear what they called it?"

John shook his head on his arms.

"Zamayitar. I'm not sure exactly what emphasis the samudraka put on the word, but it means something like killer or destroyer."

"You're just brimming with good news," said Andrei.

John noticed that Sarva hadn't explained why the samudraka hadn't taken the sword, but decided to leave it alone. Instead he asked, "What did they mean by upapa-whatever for the nirarkta?"

"Upapaurnamasi is the time of the full moon," said Sarva. "That probably explains why the water was rising in those caverns."

"Okay, smarty," said Andrei, "then what's this thing about videzaka?"

"It means foreigner," said Darnu.

"I know what it means," responded Andrei, "but they say it like a swear word."

"It is," said Sarva, "to them. It means people of a foreign land, emphasis on land. The samudraka use it as a sort of double insult. We are not only foreign, but we come from the land. To the samudraka there's not much worse they can call someone."

"How do you know so much about the samudraka?" Darnu asked.

"Can that wait? We don't know how long before they come back, and there are some things you should know before they question us further."

"What makes you think they want to question us?" Andrei interrupted.

"If they didn't want something like that, we'd be dead already."

"Go on," said Darnu.

"You and Garjae already know some of this," Sarva began, "though what you learned from the elders of our Glade is very old. But we all need to understand what we are facing."

John lifted his head and nodded wearily to Sarva to indicate that he was paying attention, and then rested his head in his arms again.

"After the Aeonian War the narun peoples grew apart, distrustful of one another. Each blaming the other for their part in the conflict.

"The aaranya were devastated, almost annihilated. The lessons we aaranya drew from that war were an aversion to conflict and a distrust of collaboration. We became, and remain, a people of passive and isolated communities, each held deliberately separate from the other."

"I wouldn't say it has been deliberate," Darnu argued. "Our Glades have never formed the connections that existed before the War. Our isolation has been forced."

"But the Glades form around us – for us. Isn't it possible that the connections have not reformed because of what we have become?"

"There are other explanations, reasons that the elders have always held to be true: the distances between most Glades."

"Not between all Glades. And we have just come through a connection between disparate and distant zarana," Sarva pointed out. "You said yourself that you thought we were nowhere near the ocean, and yet we are now inside a new zarana, that of the samudraka. Its tiirtha must open into the ocean. Doesn't this argue that distance has little to do with it?"

"There may be other reasons for what we experienced here," Darnu said doubtfully.

"Or I could be right. I believe the aaranya are isolated because, as a people, we distrust hierarchies and collusion. We don't want the connections to re-establish, and so they don't."

"This is all very fascinating," interrupted Andrei, "but if you really want John to hear it, you'd better move on."

"I'm all right," John said, lifting his head briefly. "I'm not asleep."

"Yet," said Andrei.

"I'm sorry, John," apologised Sarva. "I'll get on with what you need to know.

"The samudraka drew different lessons from the War. Where we aaranya remember the War as involving all the narun people, the samudraka blame the aaranya almost exclusively, but humans too because they also joined the conflict, usually on the wrong side. So, John, it's best if they don't learn of your true origins."

John nodded into his arms. He thought about his drinking problem, it didn't look like being a problem now they were away from the nirarkta. What was he going to do? How was he going to gain more time? He raised his head and looked at Sarva.

Sarva returned his look. "I don't know," he said. "We'll just have to hope they don't hang on to us too long."

John could see Andrei looking at him in question, but put his head back down on his arms, he didn't feel up to talking about it right now.

Sarva continued, some of his explanation intended specifically for John, "The samudraka had once made their homes in the shallows near the shore, but after the War they moved out into the deep waters of the ocean. They wanted nothing further to do with the land. Away from the land and other narun, they have changed a great deal. They had suffered huge losses in the War, but they were still the most numerous of the narun and they have flourished in the ocean deeps since that time.

"The samudraka blamed their losses on not being prepared when the War started. So rather than become passive, like the aaranya, they went the other way. They have kept the weapons that they learned to create during the War, and they have maintained their skills at combat."

"Isn't that a bit ... ?" Andrei stopped, unable to find the word.

"Ironic?" John suggested.

"I was thinking perverse. They think the best way to stop another war is to keep on fighting?"

"I don't think they see it quite that way," Sarva said.

"Who do they fight?" Senna asked.

"Each other, mostly," Sarva answered. "Their ocean communities are made up of loose affiliations between zarana, affiliations that change as the strength of each grows or declines. In theory each of the major oceans is ruled by one king, but in practice the king's power, and his influence over his dominion, varies a lot."

"All right," said Garjae, "so we know they don't like us—"

"It's more than that," Sarva interrupted. "Besides blaming us for the War, they also despise our now passive communities. They see us as primitive, ignorant and weak, an inferior people – hence that talk about staining their weapons. And yet they still retain a certain amount of fear of us. It's that fear, that idea that we may still be dangerous, that puts us at risk. They will reluctantly accept a jalaja, though probably not a yaayaavara, but the aaranya they tend to kill first and ask questions later."

"What? Like: Are you dead yet?" Andrei said.

"Something like that," Sarva answered. "I've only known one Glade with any links to the samudraka, and there it was a personal friendship thing, not any wider acceptance. That's where I learned most of what I'm telling you now."

"But you haven't really told us much we hadn't already worked out for ourselves," said Garjae. "Just that now we know not to tell them about John."

John thought he could hear the unspoken, "Big deal," finish to Garjae's statement.

"There is something else," Sarva said.

There was something odd in Sarva's tone. John lifted his head.

Speaking quietly, as if concerned about being overheard, Sarva continued, "The samudraka took to heart another lesson from the War. All narun believe the War started because some narun gained unusual powers, and we all know where those powers most often appear."

"In twins," said Darnu.

Sarva nodded. "The samudraka see twin births as perversions of nature. They call us papayamala – which, roughly translated, means a-pair-of-all-things-bad. The samudraka kill twins the moment they are born. In most zarana the mother will also be killed, blamed for producing such aberrant offspring. In some places the slaughter goes wider, to the father and siblings. Some of their most fierce conflicts have taken place over the mere suspicion that a zarana was harbouring twins. I think that's the reason why they still have any fear of the obviously passive aaranya. They believe that a new conflict could arise from aaranya twins."

"So …" Andrei started.

Sarva nodded. "So I'd appreciate it if you didn't mention anything about my being a twin. We'll have to be lucky to get out of here anyway, without adding that to the mix."

There was silence for a while as they took this in.

"It gets worse," Sarva said eventually. "Any talent or power that they don't understand, or that they think is in any way abnormal, they look on with deep suspicion. So if we speak of Asha do *not* mention that she is a healer."

- - -

Andrei could feel the eyes on their group as they swam within the loose circle of guards. With one hand he brushed at the sword at his side.

They had been released from their cell and led outside the tunnel system into the open water of the zarana. It was bright, a sort of luminous sea green, like swimming in the shallows of the ocean on a sunny day – though to Andrei it looked like there was a lot of water between their group and the sun of this zarana.

Their guard included the two dark samudraka they'd first met. They had learned through the conversation around them that the large man was called Polyphemo, and his smaller companion was Beluso. There was also the paler, olive-green, man that had so enjoyed speaking with Sarva, his name was Stepolous. There were three other olive-green samudraka, their names as yet unknown. Each of them carried spears, shorter than the ones that had been used to threaten Andrei and the others earlier, but these shorter weapons had savage looking blades at both ends. With such powerful tails the samudraka didn't need their hands for swimming.

Andrei glanced around again, then concentrated on following behind Sarva and John, his hand reaching briefly to the sword.

"Something wrong?" Senna asked from beside him.

"The people are staring at us."

"I thought you liked an audience," John called back. A full day's rest had helped him. Though still weak, John was managing to keep up, and apparently still had the energy for quips.

"I think this one might be a tough gig," Andrei replied. He tried to remember where he'd first heard that phrase. John laughed, so Andrei figured he must have got it right.

146

As far as Andrei could tell the samudraka weren't into clothes. The main distinguishing feature between the men and the women was that, on most of the women, the skin of their tail reached higher in front, covering the lower parts of their breasts, and most kept their hair flowing freely about their shoulders, or longer. Some women had floral or other decorations in their hair. Many men and women showed decorative patterns in bands about their arms, upper and lower. Some had the appearance of human tattoos, others were raised as if they were wearing a cloth band. The few younger samudraka he saw looked to be emulating the older ones.

Senna touched Andrei's shoulder and pointed. Another of the islands floating in the water, connected to nothing. There were many of these islands scattered through the water at different levels. Island was probably not the right word, the structure was too organic. Some parts looked like a coral reef that had broken away from the seabed, other parts looked like deliberately constructed spires. Large areas of greenery sprouted in drifting fronds, and all of it was riddled with openings from which more samudraka watched as their small group swim past.

"I wish they'd learn which way was up," grumbled Andrei.

There was nothing about the structure of the islands that suggested any particular direction was considered up or down, and the samudraka that watched them did so from whatever position they currently held in the water. Even their guards swam with blithe disregard for the seabed. Only John and the aaranya consistently swam with their bellies to the ground, to the samudraka it seemed to have little significance.

They had seen few creatures other than samudraka since emerging from the tunnels. A few small dolphin-like things, and the occasional small school of fish. Andrei thought there was probably more hidden in the vegetation of the islands and the seabed. It would have been good to feel welcome enough to explore, or at least to ask about it, but by unspoken agreement they left it to Sarva to do most of the talking. It left Andrei feeling fidgety and restless.

They approached a large island and the guards led them up into a wide cavern in its base. The cavern slowly narrowed and then began to twist its way up through the island.

After a while, Andrei asked, "Is it just me, or should we have run out of island by now?"

Stepolous looked across. "You have left the hospitality of my people, the Andama," with one hand he tapped his chest. "You are now in the realm of the Marr," he pointed to Polyphemo, swimming at the front. "You may have found the nirarkta better company." Stepolous grinned, but as always there was no comfort or reassurance in it.

The smaller dark guard, Beluso, flashed an angry look at Stepolous.

"You don't have to come with us, Stepolous," the deep voice of Polyphemo called back. "This is no longer your concern."

"It concerns us all," Stepolous answered. "I imagine the Marr will have a great many guests as the news spreads."

The group swam out of the tunnel and into the open water again, but this was obviously a different place, a different zarana to the one they had just left. The water here was a deep blue, though it was still bright and clear enough to see a considerable distance. There were no floating islands visible, but ahead of them was a huge wall, a midnight blue barrier. Andrei couldn't see the ocean floor, the wall disappeared into the depths and stretched up and to the sides, further than he cared to guess.

As they approached the wall it was possible to see that it wasn't solid, nor completely straight. The side facing them looked like a frozen pattern of large overlapping waves.

They swam through an opening in this first wall and passed into a short tunnel, other tunnels branched off theirs, reaching up inside the wall. There was no sign of vegetation or creatures, not even samudraka. They came out the other side and swam a short distance to another wall, this one identical to the first, except that now there were areas of sparse vegetation and some small creatures, odd looking things, like turtles with a soft carapace. They swam on through the second wall and found yet another, and then another. Andrei stopped trying to keep track. With each new wall the amount of vegetation increased and the creatures that inhabited it became more varied.

When they reached what turned out to be the last wall it was no longer possible to see the midnight blue strata of the rock beneath the lush and colourful growths, and the swarms of fish and shrimplike creatures.

By this time John was lagging. Sarva called Darnu back and they took John's arms and pulled him forward with them. Garjae remained near the front, not far behind Polyphemo. Garjae had said little since coming under the eye of the samudraka, but he watched everything that happened with his usual grim expression.

Andrei looked past them to the peak of the mountain that now loomed ahead. Between their group and the mountain were dozens of narun, maybe hundreds. Almost all of them dark like Polyphemo and Beluso, and all of them going about whatever it was that they were doing. All, that is, except those close enough to have noticed Andrei's group. Those samudraka stopped where they were and watched as the group swam past.

It might help, thought Andrei, if a few of them looked even a little bit friendly.

"Not more tunnels," Senna groaned as it became obvious they were heading directly to the mountain.

"Not really, no," Stepolous told her.

As they got closer his meaning became apparent. This was no solid mountain with a few tunnels. This was a filigree mountain, more spaces than rock. It looked solid from the distance because of the wild abandonment of plants and flowers that crowded over it and, as they were soon to discover, through it. What tunnels there were existed as well travelled spaces through this verdant growth.

Though the plants were insubstantial compared to real trees, it was still a moment of great joy to Andrei when their group entered this immense mountain of greenery. The peaceful forest of his real home felt an eternity away, even the rainforest outside the Samgha was a distant memory cut off by horror. To be finally back amid real plant life after their ordeal was an unexpected and unlooked for ecstasy. He sent his senses out through the life that surrounded him and revelled in it.

When he started paying attention to his immediate surroundings he saw that Senna was laughing at him. "What?"

"Nothing," she said, still laughing.

Andrei didn't know what had sparked her laughter, but it was contagious and he joined in. Soon after he saw Darnu and Sarva laughing too. John was smiling, even Garjae's face looked less unhappy than usual. They had stopped moving, all of them simply happy to have found themselves somewhere like this, whatever the circumstances.

The guards had stopped, it was either that or leave their prisoners behind. They looked on with puzzled expressions.

"Can't you feel it?" Andrei asked Stepolous.

Stepolous raised his eyebrows in question.

Trying a different tack, Andrei swam toward him, still laughing. "Do you have any idea how long it's been since we've been anywhere like this?"

Stepolous backed off a little and shook his head.

"No? Neither do I. But it feels like forever."

Andrei stopped when he realised that Stepolous was still backing away, his eyes not on Andrei's but looking lower. Abruptly Andrei remembered the sword at his waist. For some reason Stepolous was afraid of it. The laughter died from Andrei's lips and one hand dropped to the hilt. He turned back to his friends. As he turned he realised that their group had gathered an audience of the dark samudraka, many peering through the fronds of greenery.

The laughter of the others quickly dropped away as they saw Andrei's expression.

"This way!" Polyphemo called to them, and the group started swimming again. The watching samudraka drew back to let them pass.

Andrei was surprised and disappointed that they were swimming down deeper into this mountain. For no particular reason he expected to be taken up to meet someone important. This going down felt too much like being taken to the dungeons he'd seen in human movies, and experienced firsthand when they had gone to rescue Asha.

Eventually Polyphemo drew to a halt and turned to face his captives.

"You two," he pointed to Sarva and Andrei. "Come forward."

Andrei squeezed Senna's hand and then went up next to Sarva.

"You two will remain at the front. You will speak only when spoken to. You will remain a respectful distance from his Lordship. And you," he pointed directly at Andrei, "will keep Zamayitar sheathed and your hand away from the hilt. Do otherwise and you will feel the point of my spear – to the serpent with the consequences. Do you understand me?"

Sarva and Andrei both nodded.

"You." Polyphemo pointed to John. "You'd better come to the front too. He will no doubt want to see you for himself."

Andrei glanced around. So far it wasn't obvious who they were supposed to be respectful to. But he supposed this was a promising development, it didn't sound like there were any dungeons involved. He glanced at John, who smiled back.

"Do you think you can manage to speak only when spoken to, Andrei?" John asked quietly. It looked like John was still doing okay, not up to getting around in a hurry but still alert and with them.

Andrei grinned back at him. "Sure. If he speaks at the right times."

"Andrei," Sarva warned.

"What?"

Further conversation was halted when Polyphemo called out in a loud voice, "We beg audience with his Lordship."

The dense growth in front of them swept back in two large curtains, pulled away by four young female samudraka, two on each side. Polyphemo led them in, swimming just in front and to the left so that he was near Andrei.

They entered a huge open space. Andrei supposed this might have been called a cavern, if this was an ordinary mountain. But this was far from ordinary. The walls and ceiling were covered in bright, colourful blooms that formed pictures. To the right a bright red serpent figure flowed along the wall, there were dark green figures of samudraka around it, and all of it lay against a background of pale green. To the left were a series of murals that Andrei didn't stop to study. High above them the ceiling was a patchwork of bright sky-blue and white, and in the centre of those blooms was a ball of the brightest yellow flowers that Andrei had ever seen; like the sun itself, it was difficult to look at.

The floor of the cavern was covered in a dense growth of a vine with tiny leaves, some a pale green, others a pale creamy-brown, all short and neat like a manicured lawn. The floor sloped gently down as they first entered, and then curved back up as they got close to the other end.

When Andrei looked forward he realised that this was not just any cavern or open meeting place, it was a throne room. Centred at the front of this huge space was a tangle of green vines of many shades that stretched from floor to ceiling. The greens were mostly muted in tone, no one wanted to distract from the sovereign, was Andrei's guess. Well above the floor level the vines formed a broad couch-like bench that could have seated six comfortably, though Andrei didn't know if the samudraka ever really sat, what with their tails to consider. It seemed more likely that this was simply a delineation, something to say, "this is the throne." There was no way to tell how it was usually used, because the bench, the entire throne area, was currently empty.

Behind, and to either side of the throne were long streams of gold and silver flowers, and behind those could be seen occasional glimpses of the dark green vines from which they blossomed.

In front of the throne was a wide area over which a plant raised huge leaves on strong stems that floated more than a body length off the floor level. Reclining on several of these leaves were men. Most looked old, Andrei thought they were probably true elders, but the man on the highest and most central leaf was young. Probably not a lot older than me, thought Andrei.

"At least they know which way is up in here," he whispered across to John.

Polyphemo turned his head and glared at Andrei.

Since speaking aloud was out, Andrei kept the rest of his thought to himself: that the only way a king could raise himself above the others was to make sure everyone knew which way was up – and that the commoner's way was down.

They came to a stop a few metres away from the young man. Following Polyphemo's lead, Andrei and the others put their feet close to the floor and bowed to the young man.

"My Lord Theseo," Polyphemo said in a loud formal voice. There was no other introduction or explanation offered. Andrei guessed the explanations had been made before they got here.

The young man looked down at the group with apparent interest. He was not as dark as the other samudraka of the Marr, the usual dark jade colour appeared to have been tempered with something

152

lighter. Though obviously young, the man had glistening silver streaks that stretched back along each side of his head, the rest of his hair was jet black. The eyes that swept over them were a luminous deep green.

While the young man gave them the once-over, Andrei checked out each of the elders. They varied widely in everything except expression, none of them looked happy to see aaranya in their throne room. He caught movement out of the corner of his eye and turned his head as much as he dared. Senna nodded to the right side of the throne and Andrei tried to follow her gaze. There was someone looking through the gold and silver blossoms from behind the throne, they were visible because their skin was pale compared to the green vines – one of the Marr would have been effectively invisible.

"What brings aaranya into our domain?" the young man asked, his gaze resting on Sarva.

You do, Andrei wanted to respond, but bit his tongue.

"My Lord King—" Sarva started.

"I am not king!" Theseo interrupted in a loud, angry voice. More mildly he continued, "I am merely regent, awaiting the return of my brother, King Holitto. You may address me as Lord Theseo."

Could be in for a long wait, thought Andrei. And I could have told Sarva that it's possible to overdo obsequious – if I'd been allowed to speak.

"I apologise, my Lord Theseo," Sarva said, bowing his head.

"And I'm not *your* lord!" Theseo snapped back

Sarva hesitated.

Andrei tried hard to send his next thought to Sarva: *don't* try to argue with him!

"Lord Theseo," Sarva said, trying to sound as humble as he could, his head still bowed.

"Answer me! What brings the aaranya to our domain?"

Andrei bit harder on his tongue.

Sarva raised his head slightly but avoided meeting the gaze of the young regent. "We entered the zarana of the nirarkta by mistake. We did not realise that we were trespassing on the samudraka when we sought refuge from those creatures. We ask—"

"Enough! You. Explain how you have Zamayitar."

Andrei had been watching Sarva and it took him a moment to realise the question had been directed at himself.

"Explain yourself!"

Andrei looked up, then quickly dropped his eyes again, but in that glance he thought he saw more fear than anger in Theseo's eyes. There was movement on his left and Andrei saw Polyphemo raising his spear, it was only then that Andrei realised his own hand had dropped to the hilt of the sword and he jerked it away.

"Can this imbecile speak?" Theseo demanded.

"I found it, m— Lord," Andrei managed to stammer out. "In the tunnels of the nirarkta."

"The king? Did you see King Holitto?"

"No, Lord. There was only the sword."

"And a stone? Was there a stone near the zakti?"

Andrei tried to remember a stone. What sort of question was that anyway? They were in tunnels of stone, how was he supposed to remember if there was another rock nearby, or if it was one that mattered. Of course, the tunnels themselves had been mostly bare. Andrei shook his head.

"Speak up!"

"No, m— Lord Theseo. There was no stone."

Muttering came from one of the elders, Andrei couldn't make out the words.

"How bright was the zakti when you found it?" Theseo asked.

"It was dull, Lord. It has become much brighter since."

There was more murmuring among the elders. Andrei risked raising his head to watch. Theseo had turned his back and the elders crowded in to whisper to him.

A few minutes later Theseo turned around again. Andrei met Theseo's gaze for longer this time. What he saw there was almost reassuring. Despite the arrogant tone of the regent's words, this didn't look like a crazy man or even a bad man, merely one in a position he did not want. Andrei dropped his eyes in deference.

"Show me the zakti," Theseo asked, a man resigned to his fate.

Andrei glanced at Polyphemo, who nodded almost imperceptibly, more noticeable was his grip tightening on the spear.

Andrei pulled the sword slowly from its sheath and held it forward like an offering. Something told him he must not say the words, but he held the sword high and met Theseo's gaze, hoping his eyes would convey what he wanted to say: take it, I don't want it.

The sword glowed more brightly here, its sapphire blue turning almost transparent in its brilliance.

Theseo shook his head, as if in answer to Andrei's plea. "There is no doubt. It is Zamayitar. ... Put it away."

As Andrei carefully slid the zakti back into its sheath he realised that silence had descended over the room. The sword carefully stowed, he risked a glance back up at the regent, the young man's eyes were downcast, deep in thought.

"Lord Theseo."

Andrei looked across at Sarva in surprise. Now who was speaking out of turn?

"Yes?" Theseo looked up, his tone more surprised than angry.

"Lord. There is news of the aaranya that I think you and your council should hear," Sarva said. There was a look of determination on Sarva's face, he had made up his mind about something.

"What should we care for news of the videzaka?" Theseo snapped at him.

"There are papayamala taking over our Glades."

Voices raised in an uproar around them. John and the aaranya remained silent, but stared at Sarva wondering what he was doing.

"Quiet!" Theseo said loudly, and the talking among the samudraka subsided.

Theseo stared at Sarva silently for such a long time that Andrei began to worry what may come out when the silence was broken. But, when it came, Theseo's voice was calm, almost mild.

"Speak."

- - -

John was getting tired again. He'd been doing his best to hide how weak he felt, but it was taking more and more effort. He'd been better for a while, having rested during their long session in the Hall of the King, but they had come a long way since then.

Their escort guard, now all the dark jade samudraka of the Marr, led them up through the mountain. It felt like miles to John. Eventually their escort led them outside the verdant paths of the mountain to the open water outside, but still they continued upward.

The blue water grew lighter and the nearby mountain grew narrower until, at last, John could see its peak. Above the mountain was a large circular shadow, its dark grey looking like a tarnished silver coin balanced on the tip of the mountain cone.

The guards led their group to the edge of this shadow. John could hardly believe it when he saw the ripples of the water's surface above him, and then they all broke through into late afternoon sunshine. Before he had a chance to look around him, Polyphemo addressed them loudly and sternly, like he was speaking to naughty children.

"You may use this island if you wish, and you may merge with the water here to sustain yourselves. But do not stray far, there will be guards watching from below. You will not be offered second chances if you try to venture beyond this immediate area." He stared hard at Sarva and Andrei, and received a nod of understanding from each before he and the other guards dropped back below the water.

John was eager for the land. He swam to the sandy beach and walked out of the water on unsteady legs, his body instantly dry as the water fell away from him. The scene was bright, the almost white sand was glaring in the sunlight, so at first he wasn't sure of what he was seeing. He rubbed his eyes, shook his head in disbelief and turned to look back out to sea. It was empty ocean for as far as he could see. He looked back at the island again.

He burst out laughing. Perhaps it was because he was tired. A thousand jokes and allusions flooded through his mind. I should have brought a book, he thought, and that sent him off again. He fell to his hands and knees in the sand, still laughing.

Andrei knelt beside him, "Are you all right?"

Andrei's tone was caring and concerned, but that just made it worse. John laughed even louder.

"John?"

John didn't look up. He'd never be able to get any words out if he looked up. "What do you see?" he asked, gasping for breaths he didn't really need.

"An island," answered Andrei, puzzled.

"Describe it."

"There's not much to describe. It's just a large mound of sand with a palm tree growing out of the middle."

"So I didn't imagine it."

"No ..." Andrei sounded uncertain.

"I guess it's a human thing," John admitted. Or maybe it's a dying man's thing, he added to himself. He had calmed down now, so he looked back up to see the island again. A few more chuckles escaped, but the laughing jag appeared to have run its course.

Eventually he managed to explain that humans had this thing about being stranded on desert islands. All the jokes about it that showed an island almost exactly like this one, a mound of sand with a palm tree in the middle. The uncountable articles about the things you might want with you on such an island.

"A way off?" Andrei suggested.

That almost set John back off again. He shook his head. "No. It's stuff like, if you were stuck on a desert island with only one book, what book would you choose?"

"Oh," Andrei said. Then he looked puzzled. "Why would you want a book?"

John looked around. All his friends were looking at him as if he had gone crazy. Maybe he had. It probably wasn't that funny. Except that it was, to John. After everything he had been through, here he was stuck in a cartoon – yet again, he thought, as he remembered the dark tunnels before the lake – he had to stop himself looking around for the caption. He wondered if he could get his shirt and trousers to emulate the ragged appearance usually depicted, so he would better fit the scene, but decided that was probably not a good idea. But he'd definitely keep his eye out for a message in a bottle floating past.

They made their way up to the lonely palm tree. The small amount of shadow it cast was stretched out to the east. The group settled on the sand looking to the west. The sun was still warm but already low in the sky.

"You want to go through all that again, Sarva?" Darnu spoke up.

"Yeah," added Andrei. "The unexpurgated version this time."

Sarva sighed and looked across at John.

John gave him a sympathetic look.

There was silence for a while as Sarva stared out over the water deciding what to say.

"Garjae," he said at last, "you must already understand what I was

157

trying to describe to the regent. You've met Helix, you've felt what she can do."

"Yes," Garjae answered, not happy to be reminded.

"She can do that to others. Many others. I think her power is similar to that of our elders."

Sarva looked to Andrei, Senna and John, and explained, "The elders of our Glade, most Glades, tend not to make their power obvious. Most members of the stand never feel their power, most don't even realise it exists, but Darnu and Garjae understand. I dare say they have even felt it, had it demonstrated."

Darnu nodded.

Sarva continued, "The elders can require our compliance."

"What? Like what Sando did to those prisoners, even to his own dhumraka?" Andrei asked. His expression made it obvious what he thought of the idea.

"I've not seen Sando," Sarva reminded him, "but that sounds like something different. The elders are part of the Glade, we all are, but the elders have become an integral part of it, an extension of it. Their will is the will of the Glade, that's where their power comes from. If they want something for the Glade then we can be compelled to do what is necessary to fulfil that requirement. But their power is limited. We cannot be forced as such, but to resist we must be prepared to feel as if we are hurting the Glade, and by extension ourselves."

"That is true," Darnu confirmed, though he stared at Sarva, curious about his knowledge of such matters.

"Does that apply to me too?" Senna asked, she didn't like the idea any more than Andrei.

Sarva stared at her for long moments before shaking his head. "I cannot tell whether the Glade has accepted you yet as a member of our stand."

"How—?" Darnu started, but Sarva interrupted.

"Something changed at our Glade. Something happened about a month, maybe a bit more, before I met you in the forest. Did you feel it?" Sarva asked Darnu.

Darnu thought for a while, but it was Senna that reminded them, "That was probably when we were still stuck on the ice of the lake."

"Yes," Darnu agreed. "We weren't noticing much of anything

except our immediate problems at the time."

"But we did share a dream," said Andrei. "Do you remember?"

"Fire," said Garjae. Darnu nodded.

"Did you have that dream?" Sarva asked Senna.

Senna shook her head.

"Then probably you are not yet part of the Glade."

"Do you mean there's really been a fire at home?" Andrei asked.

Sarva shrugged. "I don't know. I just know that something happened. Something changed."

"You were talking about what Helix could do," Garjae said.

"Yes. Helix can control the elders of a Glade. I think it's similar to how elders control members of the stand, but it's much more powerful. I've not met anyone that can resist her."

"If she can control the elders," said Darnu, the horror clear on his face, "then ..."

"Then she can control the entire Glade," finished Sarva. "I think her power reinforces that of the Glade so that even the people she doesn't control directly cannot easily resist her."

"And what makes you think she's a twin, a papayamala, as you told the samudraka?" Garjae asked.

"I've always thought it was likely, from the time I met her."

"You met her?" Senna interrupted.

Sarva nodded, and continued, "And then you, Garjae, described your meeting with the twin brothers, Jaimee and Sando, and I took that as confirmation. I think there must be two sets of twins."

"So there's one we haven't met yet?" Andrei said.

"I suppose so," Sarva agreed.

"Maybe they're triplets," suggested John. He had noticed that Sarva had avoided saying anything of Sarva's own power, his own sight. John wondered if that was one of the reasons why Sarva had decided to bring it up with the samudraka first, perhaps he hoped he could avoid explaining everything if his friends were distracted with other problems.

"Triplets don't happen among the narun," Darnu said.

"How did you meet Helix?" Senna asked.

Sarva stared at Senna for a long time before answering. "I've been running away from her for a long time now. Years. I would get ahead of her and try to prepare a Glade to resist her, but it never worked. Most of the time I couldn't even convince them that the danger was real. I was a stranger, why would they listen to me? I made so little difference that I doubt if Helix even realised I was still alive. Except, perhaps, at the last Glade. It's possible she knew then … perhaps that's why they destroyed it. Burnt it to the ground."

Sarva looked away, out to where the sun was now dropping below the horizon. He continued, "I suppose it's possible she didn't realise it was me even then, I don't know that I was ever that important to her. She may not even remember me. With that Glade I came the closest to success that I'd ever come, but it turned into my worst failure. So many killed. The Glade lost, perhaps forever."

"That was where you'd come from when you found us?" John asked.

Sarva nodded.

"Where did it start?" Senna asked.

"After years of travelling I had settled in a Glade in the far north," Sarva said. He glanced at the others. "Near the coast, east of the lake you visited. I'd fallen in love. I was going to spend the rest of my life there with Karya – we had less than ten years.

"Near the end we noticed that we had not heard from the few Glades to the north of us for a long time, but we didn't pay much attention. It wasn't that unusual. That's what I meant about the aaranya living in isolation. It makes us vulnerable.

"Back then the dhumraka were taking it easy. And it was easy. There were no dramatic confrontations, it was all politeness and courtesy. A group of aaranya arrived at the Glade – they were dhumraka disguised as aaranya, but we didn't know that then – and asked to speak with an elder. One of the elders agreed to go with them to meet someone, we didn't know who. The next day he returned and all seemed normal.

"The following day another elder went to meet this emissary, and a day later he returned. And so on. The life of the Glade went on unchanged for most, but I began to grow uneasy.

"Perhaps it was because I was new to the Glade." Sarva looked across to John, waiting to see if he was going to make any comment.

John didn't know what to do or say, so he gave a tiny shrug.

Sarva continued, "I could feel that something was changing. With each elder that came back there were changes in the way everyone was behaving. I could see it most especially in Karya, but could feel it in the others too. I can't really explain how they changed, it was all very subtle – in the beginning.

"I convinced Karya that we should take a look, that we should find out who they were meeting. She had trouble understanding what I wanted, she was reluctant to agree. And that was one of the most obvious changes. Karya trusted me. There would have been no reluctance before this started.

"But she shouldn't have trusted me this time. I should have left her behind.

"We followed the elder and his dhumraka escort. Some hours away from the Glade they stopped at a large tree. It was early evening. A woman, pale and beautiful and compelling – even just to look at – emerged from that tree."

"Helix?" Senna asked.

Sarva nodded.

"Helix stepped forward and touched the elder – this was a woman, Tytha. I knew immediately that something had changed, even before she moved." Sarva's eyes flickered to John and then away again.

"Tytha turned and pointed to where Karya and I thought we had been well hidden. Tytha must have known we were there all along, but had said nothing, not until she was touched by Helix."

Sarva drew a deep breath and finished quickly. "Karya was caught and killed by one of the dhumraka. I managed to get away. I've been running ever since."

There was silence for a while.

"How could you tell—?" Senna started.

Garjae interrupted, "How can she control a Glade when she's no longer there?"

Sarva looked at him. "I think you explained it best. You said it was like Asha had been replaced by Helix in your affections."

Garjae nodded uncomfortably.

"I think Helix somehow inserts herself in place of the Glade. Everything the stand would do for the Glade, they would now do for Helix. Where the will of the elders had been the will of the Glade, it now becomes *her* will. I don't know whether she can issue specific commands, like you say Sando can – I think that might be something else, something different – but it is enough that a Glade under her control will behave according to her desires."

"More than enough," agreed Darnu in a murmur.

Garjae got up and walked down the sand and into the water. Darnu followed. Senna leaned across and whispered in Andrei's ear. He stared back at her for a moment, then shrugged and stood up.

"Come on, Sarva," he said. "You could probably do with some time out after that."

Sarva looked at him blankly, then nodded. Andrei gave him a hand up and they both went down to the water.

John had a pretty good idea that Senna had engineered this time alone with him, and thought he knew why. But he sat silent and stared to the west where the horizon still glowed as the sunset faded. The scene felt desolate, a true desert island. The only sound came from the quiet lapping of the waves on the beach and the occasional rustle of the palm leaves in the light breeze. There were no birds, no sign of land-life that John could see. Whatever living creatures existed here remained below the water.

"Sarva left a lot out," Senna said eventually.

"Guess so," agreed John. "He's been away a long time."

"Do you know what he left out?"

"What?"

"Everything important."

John glanced at Senna and then looked away again. He shrugged.

"How he helped you when they killed your human body. How he knew Garjae was no longer under the control of Helix. How he could tell what was going on at that Glade. How he escaped when his Karya was killed. Did he tell you that?"

John shook his head. "This was the first time I'd heard about that."

"But you know something, don't you?"

John pondered that for a while, unsure what, if anything, to say. Eventually he said, "If Sarva has anything more to add I'm sure he'll get to it in his own time."

"You trust him."

Though it hadn't been a question, John answered firmly, "Yes I do."

"He's not Asha," Senna said.

John looked at her. Her eyes showed that she was concerned, it hadn't been meant cruelly. John couldn't help remembering that it was Sarva that had reminded him of this last time.

"You treat him like some long lost friend," Senna said, "but we hardly know him."

"I think I do."

"He's been gone a long time. We don't really know what he's become."

"What you see," said John. "What you've just heard. A good man that's had a hard time of it. A man that's been hard on himself."

"I don't like secrets," Senna said. "I don't trust them."

"After what we've been through that's understandable. But whatever secrets Sarva may possess, they harm him, not us."

"You know this?"

John met Senna's eyes calmly. How did he answer? He didn't like being in the middle like this. Sarva's secrets weren't his to share, but he didn't like keeping things from friends that had been through so much with him – for him!

"It's what I believe," he said finally.

Senna held his gaze a moment longer and then nodded. "Good enough."

9. Caged

It was a dream, but it was also real. An almost silent movie played out by her memory of that horrific night. It had all happened so quietly, the only sounds in the dream were Tracey's breathing and her racing heartbeat – and the wet sound of the knife slicing through flesh.

At first there had been nothing. Tracey just standing there, staring at her fallen guards and trying to understand. But then came a metallic sound from the kitchenette of the apartment. When she looked up she saw a large carving knife floating in the air. She stood completely still. Frightened and disbelieving.

She still didn't move, not even when the first cut happened. It couldn't *be* happening.

The kid's head was pulled back and the knife blade ran across his neck. There was a sudden gush of blood that painted the feet and legs of someone that hadn't been there before, and the hand and arm that held the knife. When the being stood she could see where a spray of blood had marked out a face, it looked to be smiling at her.

Tracey had screamed then. She only knew this because Cleaver had played the video recording for her. There wasn't much to be seen on the video. The kid was falling and then the scene blurred as the camera was moved, until all it showed was the pale paint of the ceiling. After that there were only the sounds, and later some splashes of blood. Tracey's scream had been cut short, but her harsh breathing was still there. The recording hadn't picked up her heartbeat, which seemed impossible, it had been so loud to Tracey.

In her dream, as she had that night, she opened her eyes again because there was movement against her legs. She was sitting on the floor, leaning up against the wall. Someone she couldn't see was holding her head so that she couldn't turn away from the horror unfolding before her. She couldn't remember whether she struggled against that hold. In her dream she didn't. She just sat there and watched as if nothing else was possible.

Sonja was on her back, a wide smile had been opened beneath her chin. Closer to Tracey was Larry, blood was still spilling from his neck, but slowly now, oozing rather than gushing. She looked down as Hal was rolled back from her legs by a literally blood-red ghoul. There was a low moan from Hal. The knife came down, so close it almost cut Tracey's leg as it began its journey through Hal's neck. The body jerked and twisted, but it was too late. The cut had been made. And then the blood. It gushed up at her in a hot stream. Tracey took a breath to scream again, but her mouth filled with Hal's blood and she sat forward coughing and trying to spit out the warm copper taste of it, still aware of Hal's body trembling and twitching against her leg.

Incongruously, someone was patting her hard on her back, as if trying to stop her from choking. That same person pushed her back against the wall. Those hands forced her to face the room again. There was blood everywhere she looked. The bright yellow, red and green pieces of the game of Trouble glared at her from where they had spilled on the floor, most of them floating in glistening pools of dark red blood. The blood covered ghoul knelt down in front of her, holding the knife in front of her face.

She remembered his smile, and the way he raised his eyebrow in question, and then the blood began to run off him like water over oil. In moments all that was visible before her was the large blood coated knife. That knife came slowly closer. She remembered expecting the blade to be cold. But it was warm and wet against her cheek. She felt the pressure of it.

Tracey woke screaming, her hands reaching for her face.

Tracey thought she could feel the cuts, gaping open at the sides of her face. Then, slowly, she calmed down enough to feel what was really there. Just tears. It had probably been the back of the knife, Cleaver had told her. Just something to scare her. It had worked.

No one came to try and comfort her. They were used to her night-mares by now. On the first night, a woman's head had poked in the door, presumably to make certain Tracey wasn't really being attacked.

Tracey couldn't remember much of what had happened after she felt the knife. Cleaver said that they had found her unconscious when they arrived. The only sign that there had been anyone else there were a few bare footprints in the blood. Tracey had been cleaned up, and spent the rest of the day back at the interrogation cells where Cleaver and Aldercott tried to get her to tell them what had happened. She told them, but they didn't believe her. Their looks of sympathy made her want to scream at them, but she couldn't find the strength even for that.

She sat up and stared at her pillow, surprised to see that there was no sign of blood staining its clean white surface. She climbed out of the bed and put a warm dressing gown over her nightie. She was still trying to patch together her memories, still trying to distance herself from the nightmare.

She remembered being pulled from her cell by strangers. Cleaver and Aldercott were both there as well, anger and frustration were clear on Cleaver's face. The Americans had taken over. There must have been a leak, they said. The Australian investigation couldn't be trusted, they said. So it had all been taken over. Tracey was to be moved to an American facility – a safe house, they said.

Tracey walked out of her bedroom and headed for the stairs. It was never very dark here in the safe house. Dim lights were kept running all night in most areas.

The house was a huge two-storey thing in one of the more affluent areas of the city. It sat on a large block with high fences that surrounded a meticulously maintained garden. The inside had a very modern feel, spotlessly clean and new looking, and done out in mostly pale colours. Tracey felt self-conscious here. She felt as though anything she did might leave a mark. And her mind kept seeing blood spots that weren't really there. Every time she reached out to touch something she expected her fingers to leave behind trails of blood.

The kitchen light was already on when Tracey walked in.

"I made you a tea," Cleaver said quietly, and pointed to the cup on the other side of the table.

Cleaver and Aldercott had been brought to the house with her.

"For their own safety," was the official explanation, but Cleaver had confided, in one of these shared sleepless night meetings, that he and Aldercott were under suspicion for the leak, so they were being held incommunicado while the investigation continued.

"Thanks," Tracey muttered. She sat down and put her hands around the cup. "I'm sorry if I woke you." She didn't look up, she didn't want to see the sympathy on his face.

"I was already down here."

"But you heard me." Tracey lifted the cup.

"Yes."

Tracey sipped at her tea. It was good. Cleaver knew her tastes in tea and coffee well enough after all this time. She sneaked a peek across the table. It was strange to see Cleaver out of his too tight suits. His greying, close-cropped hair stuck out at odd angles on one side, and pressed flat on the other. If it wasn't for his unhappy expression he would have looked almost cuddly in the thick dressing gown, what the Americans called a bathrobe. It was white and plush, like her own. Their sleepwear had been provided. It felt and smelt like it had come from an expensive hotel.

Cleaver's eyes lifted from the table and saw her watching him. He raised an eyebrow.

"Is there any news?" Tracey asked.

"Word is that they're waiting for another guest, then it sounds like we're all being whisked off to home-sweet-home, Alabama. Well, America somewhere."

"America?"

Cleaver nodded. "Sounds like it."

"Why?"

Cleaver shrugged. "They've taken a shine to you, I think. Paul and I are just the baggage you come with."

Tracey pondered that. She wanted to touch the slip of paper with Tilvy's message, but that had been ruined with blood, and discarded with the clothes she had been wearing. Could it be that the Americans believed her? And if they did, was that good or bad? Cleaver obviously didn't trust them. What should Tracey make of that? Despite everything, or perhaps because of everything, she'd come to like and trust Raymond Cleaver. She hadn't warmed to Aldercott at all, but she was comfortable with Cleaver, she was glad he would be coming with her.

"Will I be able to tell Mum where I'm going?" she asked.

Cleaver shook his head.

"You think she will be safe?" Tracey had asked the question many times. "I mean ... the others that were killed."

"Someone will keep an eye on her, but the fact that she's been okay this long makes it clear they're not interested in your mother."

"They didn't kill me either."

Cleaver shrugged. No one had any idea why that was.

"What do you think they want from me?"

"The Americans started to get interested after we took you to the river. I'm starting to think I've missed something."

Only everything I told you, Tracey thought. Then something occurred to her. "Americans? What happened to Yanks?" she asked, and smiled. It had been one of the few glitches in Cleaver's otherwise carefully chosen words.

"The senior bloke here told me to be polite. I dare say some of them are from the south and got offended with being lumped in with their northern cousins."

"You never say it to their faces."

Cleaver was silent for a moment, then said, "I doubt there's anywhere in this house they can't hear us – if they want. Probably see us too."

Tracey glanced around the room.

"Don't bother," Cleaver said, "the only ones you'll find are those they want you to find."

"The bedrooms?"

Cleaver nodded.

"So I have to get dressed in the dark?"

"Won't help."

Tracey looked at him in panic.

"Look, forget I said anything. There's nothing you can do about it."

"Just pull my stomach in and avoid picking my nose, is that it?"

Cleaver chuckled. It wasn't something Tracey had heard very often.

They hadn't spoken much. Tilvy could only imagine how much

168

Pasith must be regretting his impulse to say thanks. Taiza fidgeted, studying the handles and the mesh of their cage, often muttering to himself. Beenae sat and stared. He didn't respond when Tilvy sat next to him and put her arm around him.

The cage was tall enough that they could stand, but the mesh was only a few inches over their heads; it would have been uncomfortable for someone of more typically human height. There was enough floor space that they could lie down to rest, though the metal flooring was slippery and they had to take care not to slide into the mesh walls that burned when you touched them. There were a number of looped handles welded to the floor, and they'd soon discovered what they were for. The cage was inside the back of a truck. When the truck moved you had to kneel down and hold on to the handles to avoid being thrown against the mesh. It didn't always help.

The truck hadn't moved again after transporting them that first night. Days had passed. They could hear the occasional hum of traffic, sometimes the footsteps of humans not far away, even the murmuring of their voices. And they could observe the passing of the hours in the small amount of light that found its way through cracks in the truck walls. There was nothing they could do but wait.

It was morning. There was a series of loud metallic clangs and then the back of the truck began to roll up. The truck filled with daylight and that much was comforting. There was more loud noise as a ramp was run out.

The pale figure of Sando walked slowly up the ramp. What slim hopes Tilvy had been holding onto quickly faded. She had felt what this man could do.

"I thought it was time to come and see what my friends had collected," Sando said, his voice sounding stronger and more mature than his youthful appearance made you expect.

He stopped about a foot away from the mesh of the cage and peered in. "You, I was expecting," he said nodding to Tilvy. "I've been looking forward to renewing our acquaintance." He looked at Pasith and tilted his head. "You're a surprise. Couldn't get enough of me?"

Pasith stepped forward, angry, but Tilvy put an arm out to hold him away from the mesh.

Sando continued, "I'm sure your mother warned you about keeping bad company. Let this be a lesson to you." Sando's gaze moved onto Taiza and Beenae and his expression turned puzzled. "I don't know you two." His eyes flicked back to Tilvy. "Neither of them is your precious Barma, I think. One too old, the other too young."

"How do you—?" Tilvy started.

"How do I know about Barma? Like Pasith here, you should be wary of the company you keep. Humans don't make very reliable confidantes, not when their phones and computers are so willing to share all. Where is your precious boy, by the way?"

"Safe from you!"

"Ah. So he's locked up with the others in the Glade, is he? I'm almost tempted to wait for it to open just so I can talk to the one that dared strike me. But I guess not. I don't have that much patience. Your home's gone, girl. Get used to it. I won't let it open again."

Tilvy couldn't think of a response, her mind wouldn't think at all.

"So who are you?" Sando asked Taiza. "You're obviously city-folk. Were you part of that night?"

"I had that pleasure," said Taiza.

Tilvy turned to the sound of pain coming from Taiza. He had his hands to his head.

"Stop it!" yelled Beenae and rushed at Sando. When Beenae hit the mesh he screamed and was forced to step back.

"We have a hero in our midst. What's your name, boy?"

"I don't have—" Beenae started, and then he walked into the mesh. He screamed and pulled back.

"Your name, boy?" Sando repeated.

When Beenae didn't respond fast enough, he was again walked into the mesh.

Tilvy pulled Beenae back, wrapping her arms around him to stop him trying to walk forward again. "His name's Beenae!" she cried out to Sando.

Sando watched them both in silence for a time, then his expression softened slightly and Beenae went slack in Tilvy's arms.

"Enough games," Sando said. "Understand that I don't need this mesh or those toy ray-guns to get what I want from you."

"What *do* you want from us?" Tilvy asked.

"I haven't decided yet. But I'm sure I'll come up with something suitable. In the meantime you're all coming home with me. Won't that be fun? Say goodbye to your homeland, you won't be seeing it again."

- - -

"What the hell is he doing here?" Cleaver demanded loudly.

Tracey couldn't do anything but stare.

Mike Asquith stood inside the doorway. Two heavily built American minders stood behind him, Tracey had seen them around the house before. Mike was staring back at her. He looked like he'd found something rotten floating in his breakfast cereal.

A voice came from behind them, "Mr Asquith will be joining us on the flight, Ray." It was Franklin Johnson, the one in charge. He was smaller than most of the other agents that Tracey had seen, but he had a gaunt, cruel-looking face that she found frightening, and Johnson appeared to sense that, and enjoy it.

"He's a criminal," Cleaver said.

"So arrest him."

Cleaver didn't answer.

"In which case he's someone that's had contact with Miss Ryner here, and so he is at risk. He's coming with us."

"Do I get a say?" Mike asked.

Johnson looked across at Mike with amusement. "Certainly. If you'd rather go to jail, I'm sure we can help find the evidence needed to make that happen."

Mike pressed his mouth closed and glared at Tracey.

"Fine," said Johnson. "I hope everyone's packed, the cars will be here soon."

To everyone's displeasure, except his own, Johnson put Mike and Tracey together in the back of one car, Cleaver and Aldercott in another. The trip to the airport was silent and tense.

Tracey didn't have a passport, she'd never needed one, but that didn't cause any problems. They spoke with few people and neither Tracey nor the others were asked any questions as they were hurried through back corridors and then into a small bus that took them out to a building separate from the others. Inside was a jet plane.

As they pulled up, Tracey saw a forklift unloading something out of the back of a truck. From the quick glance she got it looked like a cage of some sort. She frowned, she had seen something like that before.

"What's with the kids?" Mike said.

Tracey looked where Mike was pointing. There were eight or more figures climbing the steps onto the plane. They looked like teenagers or something, not that you could tell much about them, they all wore windcheaters with the hoods pulled up. Some of them moved a little strangely, as if they were uncomfortable or nervous.

"They to do with you too?" Mike asked. He was looking at her now.

Tracey remembered when those brown eyes had looked at her with apparently sincere affection. There was no sign of that now. She shook her head, and then shrugged.

Mike grunted and turned away.

The car doors were opened and Tracey and Mike were ushered out and quickly up into the plane. The interior was more open and luxurious than the few commercial flights that Tracey had ever been on. Franklin Johnson was standing in the aisle not far from where they came in. He smiled at them both as he pointed to a pair of seats.

Mike paused and looked at Johnson. "There are other seats free," Mike said, indicating the mostly empty cabin.

The teenagers were nowhere to be seen. There was a secure door that closed off the back section, Tracey assumed they must have gone through that. Franklin returned Mike's gaze calmly. It looked to be some sort of testosterone battle with staring eyes, so Tracey left them to it and pushed past Mike to take the window seat.

No words passed between Mike and Johnson, but Mike eventually sat down next to her and stared sullenly to the front. Apparently he'd lost.

Cleaver and Aldercott were shown to seats further back on the other side. Cleaver gave Tracey what she supposed was meant to be a reassuring smile, but she wasn't comforted. The pair that had had so much power over her life for so long were now powerless with her. Behind those two came half-a-dozen American agents who took various seats, though none close to her and Mike. Tracey was starting to wonder if she smelled bad.

The plane took off and eventually levelled out. The low drone of the engines and some quiet chatter among the American agents did little to fill the void. Tracey stared out the window at the clouds. How many hours was this going to take?

"So what did you do?"

Tracey turned in surprise. Mike was talking to her. She studied his face. The usual movie-star stubble that he sported was little more than a shadow at the moment, he must have needed to shave recently. She smelt the cologne he used and remembered being immersed in it as they held each other close, and touched each other intimately. She also remembered that it never went further. And that she had wanted it to. His expression hadn't been that unfriendly when she first turned around, but a look of annoyance passed over it now.

"You must have done something to get this bunch involved. What was it?"

Tracey looked down at her knees. "Just something I saw," she answered quietly. And didn't see, she added silently.

"Something to do with that Caldor bloke?"

Tracey nodded.

"I should have known better than to get involved," he muttered.

Tracey looked up but Mike was looking past her, out the window perhaps. Did she dare ask what she had wanted to know since talking to Ian? She looked back down. "Why did you ...?" she started, but couldn't finish.

"I was paid."

Tracey looked up again. He was looking at her in defiance.

When Tracey didn't say anything, Mike continued, "It seemed like easy money. Get you out of the house when they wanted, and ask a few questions that they wanted answers to, not that you were much help there. I was supposed to try and get you to take me to Caldor's place, but by the time it seemed like that might actually happen it all went balls up and I was told to pull out."

She couldn't meet his eyes any more, so turned back to her knees. She could feel tears building up and tried to will them away.

"It's not like I wouldn't have been happy to get you laid if that's what you wanted," Mike said. Tracey thought it sounded like an attempt at consolation, the only good thing was that it made her angry, and that helped her to hold back the tears. Mike continued, "But you were giving out some pretty mixed signals, and I was told not to push it. ... Were you porkin' this Caldor guy?"

"He was just a friend," Tracey said, and then wondered at her use of past tense.

"Oh."

After an extended silence, Mike asked, "So what is it? Why have I been dragged into your mess?"

Tracey shrugged.

- - -

The plane landed and their cage was offloaded into another truck. No one seemed concerned about taking it gently, and several times one or more of them were thrown against the mesh. The air was different here, the traffic sounded different, even the voices they heard were different. It had been mid-morning when they'd left, and now it felt like early morning again. Could it have been that long?

Beenae had recovered from the humiliation and pain of Sando's violation of his mind, and was more talkative now, but Tilvy had no answers for the questions he kept asking. Taiza continued to fidget and mutter, sometimes he made shapes in his hands as if envisaging something moulded in them. Pasith was the biggest surprise. He had been friendly and supportive with all of them. His manner was slowly revealing itself as easygoing and self-deprecating. He reminded her of Barma in that way.

The truck moved inconsistently through traffic for a long time before it finally stopped. There was a beeping sound and the truck began to reverse. It stopped again and Tilvy could hear humans moving, the sound of large doors closing, and then all went silent.

There was nothing more for a while. Eventually there came echoing sounds of a door opening and things being moved around. The rear doors of the truck were opened and Tilvy could see they were parked inside a building. On the floor outside the truck were several dhumraka, two of them standing next to a small trolley, one with a ray-gun antenna in his gloved hands.

There was a set of stairs pushed up against the back of the truck, and another dhumraka wearing gloves came up and unlocked the door to their cage. Before he opened the door he pointed to the ray-gun. "Do I need to explain?" he asked.

174

Tilvy shook her head.

The dhumraka opened the door and swung it back. "Follow me."

He led them down the steps, through a normal, human-sized, door into a corridor. They passed many closed doors without signs. The unexpected sound of bird calls, still muffled at this point, came to them as they approached the door at the other end. The dhumraka pulled open a heavy door and the sound of the birds grew louder, this was joined by the sound of running water and the rustle of leaves. The air was warm and humid. A mesh gate was opened into the last section of the corridor, and just a few metres past that was another mesh gate opening into something like a large courtyard.

Several large tropical trees, draped with vines, grew in the centre, reaching up into almost the full height of the multi-storey building that surrounded them. Around the trees grew an assortment of ferns and ground cover. The ceiling was closed in with glass, the sky beyond was a clear bright blue.

"This is your space for now," the dhumraka told them. "More than you deserve, but convenient."

Tilvy looked around and understood. The walls of the building held up a fine mesh enclosing the trees and the birds of this exotic aviary. This was much the same mesh as their previous cage, it was finer but still untouchable. She could see where a branch reaching out from one of the trees had withered where it came too close to the mesh.

The gate was closed behind them and the dhumraka said, "You should not try to follow the water out from here." He pointed to the deep pool on one side of the enclosure. It was filled from a fountain bubbling up over rocks at one end, and the water overflowed into a stream at the other. The stream flowed a short distance before disappearing into a drain under the building. "You won't like what happens to you."

"We understand," Pasith told him.

"Also," the dhumraka continued, "you will come to this gate when you are called. If you do not then we may need to persuade you. You will not like our methods of persuasion. Is that clear?"

Pasith nodded.

The dhumraka gave them one last disapproving look and then

disappeared back into the building.

More of the space imposed itself on Tilvy's senses: the scent of flowers and of rotting vegetation; the sounds of frogs and scuttling creatures. There were insects here too. The feel of life was strong and familiar, and yet few of the individual elements were. Some of the ferns might be mistaken for plants she had seen at home, but the trees were very different, with strange complicated buttresses as if they were made up of many plants growing together. She could recognise the noisy parrots for what they were, but she had never seen their like before. And there were other, stranger, birds here too.

"Not what I expected," observed Pasith.

"No," Tilvy agreed quietly. When she did pull her eyes away from the scene she saw that Beenae was already making his way to the closest of the trees. Taiza looked bewildered and lost, as though he didn't know where he was. Tilvy could empathise.

"We should merge and rebuild our strength," Pasith said. "We don't know how long we might have." He looked at Tilvy. "Do you agree?"

Tilvy nodded absently.

Pasith hesitated, as if reluctant to leave them, and then made his way to the pool and quickly disappeared.

Tilvy touched Taiza on the shoulder. He jerked as if startled.

"Are you okay?" she asked him.

He nodded. "Jus' not what 'm used t'. ... Wonder if Sen's seen stuff like this?"

Tilvy's thoughts, too, had been turning to their friends that had disappeared into the distant north. What had they seen and where were they now? She had thought her Barma was safe inside the Glade, but not even that was the refuge she had imagined.

"Come on," she said gently.

They found Beenae and all merged into the same tree so they could reach out and touch one another for comfort when they needed it.

\- - -

Tracey opened her eyes with a start. The sensation of movement against her legs, the trembling of Hal's dying body, faded with her dream. Instead of the deep red of a blood soaked room, the light around her was tinged green. Where was she?

She sat up quickly. Out the window were the upper reaches of a lush tree, its leaves glistening in the rain. No, it wasn't rain. Above the tree was a network of sprinklers. Perhaps it was those turning on that had woken her. Sun shone through the immense panels of glass above the trees. The light, filtered by the leaves and water, tinted the pale colours of the room a mottled green.

She remembered the long flight coming to an end and being whisked away to this tall building in the city. San Francisco, Cleaver had told her. They had been escorted up an elevator and shown to their rooms. It was early in the morning when they got here, but Tracey was exhausted. She'd closed the door behind her, pulled off her clothes, taken a long hot shower, and then climbed naked into the bed. Only now did she remember that she was probably being watched. She hurriedly pulled the sheet up over her breasts and stared around her, looking for the cameras. She didn't feel much reassurance in not being able to find them.

The clock beside the bed said it was after three in the afternoon. What day was it? Did it matter?

The clothes she had been wearing before were all on the floor of the en-suite bathroom, and her suitcases were all the way over there, beside the door.

"Oh, stop being a prude," she muttered to herself.

She got up and tried to force herself to walk calmly, but quickly, over to her cases. She hauled one to the bed, there was no way to be elegant about that, and looked through it quickly. Of course her underwear was in the other one. After going through all that, she decided the damage was done and went to have another shower.

Clean and dressed, Tracey opened the door of her room and looked out. It was an open area, it looked like a campus common room: clumps of lounge chairs, a few tables and a kitchen area to one side. To her right was the corridor where they'd been brought in. She vaguely remembered there being a balcony area along there somewhere, it overlooked the mini-rainforest inside the building.

"You want a coffee?" Cleaver lifted a coffee pot and waggled it at her from the kitchen.

"Please," Tracey agreed eagerly.

There was an array of large windows along the wall to her left.

Aldercott was standing there looking out, he didn't acknowledge her presence.

Tracey joined Cleaver at a table near the kitchen. She picked up her coffee and took an eager mouthful. She pulled a face.

"No," agreed Cleaver. "It's not good. But it's still coffee."

Tracey took another sip and put her cup down. Maybe it would grow on her. She looked up at Cleaver.

"God, you look awful. Didn't you get some sleep?"

Cleaver shook his head. "Someone once told me that the best way to beat jet lag was to stay awake, or maybe it was in a movie."

Tracey looked across at Aldercott. He was rocking back and forth on his feet, as if nervous, and from what she could see of the side of his face, the usual blank expression was having trouble holding. "And him?" she asked quietly, nodding.

"Paul tried to get some sleep a while ago but he couldn't settle."

Aldercott turned away and walked down the corridor that went along that side of the building. Tracey lost sight of him, but heard a door click shut.

Tracey looked back at Cleaver. "So is this it? Is this where they're keeping us?"

Cleaver looked down at his cup.

"What?" Tracey asked.

He shook his head.

"Tell me."

"Why don't you come see their rainforest. It's very impressive," Cleaver said getting up.

"It's raining in there."

"You're not scared of a little damp are you?"

Tracey followed him back past her room and along the corridor until they came to a pair of large glass sliding doors on the right. Cleaver slid one open a short distance, gestured Tracey through and then followed and closed the door.

It was a wide balcony and quite deep. The walls to either side reached out a few feet beyond the handrail. Stretched from below the balcony rail to the ceiling above, like a bubble, was a light framework covered with insect screens. The other balconies she could see from here were similarly protected. Beyond the screens was the wire mesh that enclosed the trees like a huge aviary. Apparently it was, Tracey could hear the screech of parrots and a haunting call from a bird she didn't recognise.

The air was moist and warm, Tracey's light shirt was already sticking to her body. The rain from the sprinklers had stopped now, but the sound of water dripping from the leaves continued. Cleaver touched her elbow and indicated they should get closer to the edge. They leaned on the handrail and looked out into the trees. They were on the top floor of the building and their view was of the uppermost foliage of the trees, only in one place could Tracey look down into the larger branches through a tunnel of leaves. Mosquitoes whining in front of her made it obvious why the insect screens were needed.

"Is it safe to talk here?" Tracey asked in a whisper.

"Maybe," Cleaver said quietly, though not actually whispering, "maybe not. I don't know if they're monitoring the rooms here or not, but it's safer to assume they are. The balcony might be safe." He paused and wiped his fingers over the rail. "The constant moisture would make it difficult for hidden cameras and microphones. I looked before and couldn't find anything."

"So what is it? Something is worrying you, or is it just lack of sleep?"

"I don't like this place, Tracey. I don't think it's government."

"What do you mean?"

"The agents that were with us have all peeled off. The people around here don't feel right. They're not in the job." He read the question on Tracey's face. "It's just something you know. When you're in the job you can recognise it in others. And this place ..."

"This place what?"

"After you mentioned Stephenson I did some digging. A place that sounded a lot like this one came up. He's into houses with inside forests, huge aquariums, and that sort of thing."

"Can't you call someone? Find out what's going on?"

"I couldn't do that even if this was kosher. *Officially*, we've been handed over to those that can best protect us, we're supposed to trust them."

"But you don't?" Tracey asked, though the answer was obvious.

Cleaver shook his head.

"But you didn't anyway, not even before."

179

"But those back home, the ones that brought us here, they *were* in the job."

"What does Paul say?"

"He believes me now. He didn't before. That's part of what's got him upset."

"It's good to see something can get that condescending look off his face." Tracey hadn't really meant the bitterness in her tone to come out.

"Paul's good at his job, just ... sometimes he over-compensates."

For what? The stick up his butt, Tracey thought but didn't say. She wasn't sure why she was fixating on Aldercott, maybe it was because she was frightened.

Cleaver seemed to sense her mood. "It'll be okay. We'll work it out."

"It didn't work out so well for Hal and the others," Tracey said quietly. She looked down at her hands, she thought the warm moisture on them felt like blood.

10. Peren

The brothers were standing in a large, plush office. They chatted quietly in the corner near the window while the senator sat behind his desk talking with yet another set of corporate sponsors, or that was Jaimee's description of them. Sando ignored them, but he knew his brother was keeping one ear tuned to the conversation. This was what he did. Sando didn't have the patience for it.

"So, now that you have your *objets de la vengeance*," Jaimee grinned at Sando, "what are you going to do with them?"

"You disapprove?"

Jaimee shrugged. "You know me. I flare and let it out. You're the one that bottles it up and lets it stew."

"Bullshit. You make a game out of everything. You draw it out worse than I do. You like playing with people's heads."

"Ironic really, when you're the one that can actually do it."

Sando grinned back. "Yeah, but I think you enjoy your sort more."

"So what have you got planned?"

"Nothing yet. Maybe take them back to the Estate, think about it there."

Sando's recent trip to Australia had been reluctant, but necessary. The siblings hadn't bothered trying to establish control of the human authorities there, according to Jaimee it wasn't worth the effort, Australia would go where America led. But they did have to tie up the loose ends before too many humans got to hear about things they shouldn't. The main pay off, as far as Sando was concerned, was being able to gather some of those that had escaped his closing of the Glade.

"You'll have to keep them away from Asha," Jaimee reminded

him. "We can't have her learning what you did to her Glade, it won't make her happy."

"There's plenty of room out back."

"Leave them where they are for now. Let's make sure of Asha first."

Sando waited while Jaimee turned his head and listened to the senator's conversation for a few moments. This senator was one of the ones that thought he received messages directly from God, Jaimee's favourite trick. There were others that thought they got their information from deceased relatives, and one or two that thought they heard from long dead presidents. It didn't matter. As long as they acted on the messages Jaimee passed them, he was happy to let them believe what they wanted. Anything but learn the truth.

"You think she'll work out?" Sando asked when Jaimee's attention returned.

"She's got to. We need the time. Time to start a whole new search."

There was more to it than that. Sando knew his brother was smitten with Asha. Sando understood, he was attracted too. Not that it had done Jaimee much good. It had been almost three weeks now. Asha had remained compliant to their demands, but there was no sign of her responding to Jaimee's charm. Such lack of reaction was starting to bother Jaimee, he wasn't used to being ignored.

And there were practical reasons to try and get Asha on side. Even if it turned out the aaranya couldn't help their mother, there were other things they wanted from the healer. Things they avoided talking about. Perhaps that was part of the attraction, a hope that Asha could solve more problems for them than just their mother.

"Remind me why we're here," said Sando. "Haven't we been through all this before?"

"We have. Like so many things to do with humans, you have to keep doing the same things over and over. It's what keeps most of them occupied."

"And us, it seems."

Jaimee nodded ruefully.

"So explain it to me." Sando was bored, and getting his brother started on his favourite subject was one way to fill the time.

"We've got the military already, right? Between myself and Helix we've had them for years," Jaimee started in his best lecturing tones.

"If you say so. You haven't done much with them."

"They're messy and tend to get carried away. More often than not they're overkill."

"So why bother?" Sando prompted.

"Humans may be happy to destroy the world as long as their enemy dies with it. Me, I'd prefer to have somewhere to live after we've won. I first wanted the military because I thought that would give us power, but it's turned out to be mainly about keeping their damn fingers off the buttons."

"And you want the government too."

"It's a tidier way to keep control, but it's a lot of work. The ones in power keep changing every few years, so it's a constant effort to keep a useful level of influence."

"So why not get Helix here? She likes to dress up."

"She prefers playing Queen of the Dhumraka more. Anyway, her sort of control has its place, but sometimes it's a bit much. The humans start acting strange. Obsession in the military is expected and easy to cover up. Politicians are unpredictable, and too public."

Jaimee turned back to the people across the desk from the senator. "There. The one on the right. He's trying to get out of this cheap. Push him."

Sando turned reluctantly and looked. The man was young compared to the other humans in the office, but according to Jaimee he was the one that controlled the purse strings of that particular company. Glossy black hair slicked back, buffed nails and an expensive suit. Everything expected of the corporate highflier.

"With everything else we do for you, Senator," the man was saying, "the offer seems reasonable."

The deep voice of the senator remained mild but authoritative. "Of course, generous even. But it does cost a lot to keep the campaign running, so we're always very happy to welcome those that can do a little extra."

Sando concentrated, trying to find a hook into the young man's mind. Some way to turn the flow of his thoughts without being too obvious. He probably should have been paying more attention earlier.

"You do have others to help you out," the young man said.

<What are you doing?> Jaimee spoke into Sando's mind.

Sando ignored his brother and kept concentrating, feeling the emotions driving that slippery mind.

"I do have many enthusiastic supporters, it's true," the senator agreed, "that's what makes me so valuable to my favoured contributors."

That was it, Sando realised. He shouldn't be looking for a way to make the young man more generous, it wasn't in his nature. It would take too much of a push. But doubt, yes. The man needed this senator, needed to be one of the favoured. Sando gave a nudge.

The young man frowned, and sat silent for a moment. "I suppose, if we—"

Sando didn't bother to listen any more, he knew he'd done enough. When he looked back at his brother, Jaimee was smiling at him.

"It's so much easier having you around. All that time you spent down under I had to do this the hard way."

"Can we go now?"

Jaimee shook his head. "I've had the senator arrange several of these things in a row, so we could get them all out of the way at once."

Sando slumped. This really wasn't his thing. The lumbering humans and their petty games annoyed him.

"You were asking me why I do this," Jaimee reminded him.

Sando nodded. Jaimee's enthusiasm for his project would at least distract from the droning voices of the humans sitting there, the ignorant beasts oblivious to the presence and conversation of their betters.

Jaimee leaned against the wall and returned to lecture mode. "We want to control the humans. As Pheyton taught us, people, any people, are easier to lead if they are used to being led." Jaimee paused, waiting for the leading question.

"So?" Sando obliged.

"So religion fits the bill. It doesn't matter what one. A few may waste time arguing over interpretations, but the rest sit in their congregations and blindly accept what the man in front tells them.

"This is what it means," he says, and they all nod and kneel and pray, and stand and sing praises, grateful that this man in front of them has made it all so clear."

"What's all that got to do with this?" Sando waved his hand toward the senator.

"We'll get to that," Jaimee assured him. "Many of these people have been going to church since they were babes in the arms of their mothers. Only when they get older do they start to get taught logic and independent thought, and for many that's way too hard. They already have the easy answers given to them by their church. Where is the incentive to take the harder road and think for themselves?"

"But they don't all believe."

"Sure, but here we have that wondrous thing called democracy. If the majority believe what they are told, and we control what they are told, then we control everyone."

Movement made Sando look around. The senator had risen to say goodbye to this round of visitors. While he was at the door, Jaimee went to the desk and wrote something on the notepad on the desk. He returned with a grin on his face.

"Just a little something to keep him believing in Me."

Sando pondered what Jaimee had been saying before. "If the majority really believe then how come there's so much crime and cruelty among them."

"You've been listening to too many sermons, religion is the cause of a lot of it. Anyway, just because people don't live by the rules doesn't mean they don't believe. They avoid thinking about the bits they don't like, or they plan to make up for it later. They get told that they only need to be truly penitent before their time comes. The obvious response to that is: Why rush?"

"So what good does it do us?"

"Because they do believe it, and all we need is their belief. Their belief may not make them behave well day to day, but when it comes time to vote they choose those politicians that represent their beliefs, the things they wish were true."

"And so we come to our senator."

"Exactly, *our* senator. It's a system that feeds on itself. He gets votes because the voters think he believes in God and won't let the heathens take over. He adds his support to getting religion taught in schools and so we get more religious voters. These continue to vote for him, and his successors, keeping us in control."

"Neat," Sando said. Sando didn't bring up the various experiments that they had run over the years, Jaimee refining his knowledge and techniques. Little cults they'd set up to test human reactions, and to see how far they could be pushed. Most could be pushed a long way if they were given the right incentives.

"It's even neater than that," Jaimee continued. "We want control over science, especially any science concerning life, and that's the science that religion is most sensitive about. And, to top it all off," Jaimee paused for effect, "the religious are the ones most accessible to my form of influence. If they do find out anything about us their immediate response is ..." Jaimee waited for his brother to fill in the gap.

"Angels." Sando obliged.

"Exactly. Angel's angels."

They both laughed at the old joke.

Jaimee continued, "I've been gradually building up my stock of humans. It could have taken a lot longer, but by using religion I got to use a structure that was already in place."

"No need to be modest, brother."

"I'm serious. I may have made some of the common conspiracy theories true now, but the really crazy thing is that I probably wasn't necessary. A lot of this would have happened anyway, but we wouldn't have been in a position to control it."

The senator was getting up to greet his next visitors. Sando was about to give the newcomers the once-over when Peren's voice cut through their minds.

<Jaimee! Zandy! Mama's hurt!>

Asha sat on a branch high in one of the huge pine trees, leaning back against the trunk. From here, looking past the rows of hills stretched out below the estate, she could catch distant glimpses of the ocean, it glinted faintly in the mid-afternoon sun. There was a strong breeze blowing from the west and it brought the scent and taste of the ocean with it. She looked to the south-west with longing. Could John be home yet?

She frowned. Somehow she didn't think so. She'd been getting

186

increasingly worried about John. It felt like he was in trouble. In a strange way these feelings were almost comforting, they justified her faith that he was still alive. But what was wrong?

Casseta wriggled in Asha's arms, Asha had been squeezing her too tightly.

"Sorry," Asha murmured, and let the brevi run up and settle on her shoulder.

Asha turned her thoughts to Angel, the mother of the siblings. For a few hours every day Asha would sit with the woman out on the lawn, or under the immense oak trees, or up in one of the rooms on the third floor. Not much was said during these times. Questions from Asha were unwelcome, Angel would turn sulky. Sometimes Angel would ask Asha a question about Asha's past, most often it was about John. Asha would answer, but only because she felt obliged. She couldn't risk making the brothers angry, though so far there had been no more reminders of the unspoken threat – her home, and the people she loved.

Over a period of days Asha would watch Angel grow progressively weaker. Then, mysteriously, the following day the woman would be stronger again. Asha knew what must be happening, but pushed the thought away. There was nothing she could do but watch as the cycle kept repeating.

One or other of the brothers were away a lot, sometimes both, and there had been no sign of Helix since Asha got here, but the routine continued regardless. Earn their mother's trust, was the repeated mantra. So Asha continued to sit with Angel each day and patiently wait for the old woman to become more responsive.

Asha's eyes returned to the distant horizon. "What do you think, Cassey? Could I make it?"

She often thought about escape. Not seriously. She rarely went within sight of the fences, and never saw the dhumraka guards. None of those mattered, they could be taken away and still Asha would remain trapped here. She stayed away from them because, in her mind, they were a reminder of the threat that was the true barrier. No, escape was just a fantasy she indulged in during her hours out here alone. She would imagine returning to her place on the edge of her forest, of spending time with John. In her imaginings he would rise up out of his human body as effortlessly as an aaranya emerging from a tree, and together they would dance through the trees, together they would enter the Glade and Asha would show him its wonders.

<Asha!> cried a young woman's voice inside Asha's head.

Asha sat up straight and Cassey leapt into the air and glided away.

<Come now!> came the voice again.

"Who are you?"

<Mama's hurt. My brothers are away. You must come now!> The intensity of the woman's voice was a sharp pain in Asha's mind.

Asha shook her head.

<NOW!>

Asha gasped and clutched at her temples.

<Please.> The pleading voice was softer, sounding like a young girl now.

Asha stood up and ran out along her branch until she saw a clear path to the ground. She jumped. Arms out for balance, she fell slowly and landed softly on the bed of pine needles.

<Quickly!>

Asha ran through the trees as fast as she could.

<Hurry. Please hurry.> The voice urged her on.

Across the lawn. Asha didn't pause to open the door, just pushed herself through it. But in the entrance hall she suddenly stopped. She didn't know which way to go.

<That way,> the voice instructed. Somehow the instruction was clear, Asha knew exactly which way the voice meant. She ran on. *<There.> <Here.>* The instructions continued, keeping Asha on the ground floor and leading her through the corridors. *<In here.>*

Asha pushed at the door. It wasn't timber. She couldn't pass through. It wouldn't move. She stepped back. There was a keypad to one side. She stared at it blankly. The numbers appeared in her mind. She typed hurriedly, but the device beeped at her angrily.

<One. Nine.> The voice repeated the first digits.

Asha tried again. This time the door clicked ajar. She pushed it open, stepped inside, and froze.

There were three people in the room. A tall human man was standing beside a wide, low bed. He held the leg of a broken chair in his hand, blood and prana dripped from the end. A human woman lay sprawled on the bed, one side of her head was a jagged mass of grey and glistening blood, and prana was evaporating from below her throat.

<Help Mama. Please!>

Asha's eyes moved down. On the floor beside the bed lay the old woman, Angel. Golden prana glowed from a deep wound on one arm, more came from a wound on one side below her breast, and yet more from a gash on one side of her head. She wasn't moving.

It was a different voice that Asha heard in her mind now, one from a true memory, Ulvanya insisting, "You must work faster."

Asha glanced at the woman on the bed, there was nothing she could do there, the woman was already dead. The man?

<Don't worry about him,> the young woman urged.

Asha looked anyway. He was uninjured and familiar. She pushed that thought away. Kneeling down beside Angel, Asha evaluated the injuries quickly. The head wound didn't look serious, the arm was but it could wait. She concentrated on the wound in Angel's side. This one was bad, prana was gushing in pulses from the opening.

Pressing her fingers into the wound, Asha let her senses explore the damage.

<What are you doing?> the voice asked. Worried but hesitant.

Asha ignored it. She concentrated on the worst areas first, blocking flows to give her more time to work. The gush of gold over her fingers slowed to a trickle. Now she began to sort out the details, encouraging the strongest parts to bring themselves together, giving of herself only where it was most needed; Ulvanya's lessons were proving their worth. She slowly pulled her fingers out as the wound knitted together beneath them. The skin closed over. It was still weak, but it was done. It would hold until the body could finish the healing.

She started on the arm. More of herself was needed here, a large piece of the arm had been torn away. Asha gave it willingly, without thought or hesitation. This was what she did. When the arm was closed she moved her attention to the gash on the side of the head. It was only shallow. A few swipes of her fingers and the skin closed over. There was bruising, but it would heal on its own.

Still lost in concentration, Asha moved back over each of the wounds and checked them, strengthening each as she went.

There was no more she could do, Asha leaned back. The faint

golden steam of prana still rose from around the wounds, and Asha now saw the splashes of human blood that marked the old woman's body. She wiped at one of them absently with her fingers.

<Will she be okay?> the woman's voice asked.

Asha nodded.

<When will she wake?>

"She should merge," Asha said, "rebuild her strength."

<She can't merge.>

Of course not, Asha acknowledged to herself. That was why the human woman had been here.

<Can you help her? Feed her? Jaimee says you can.>

Movement in the room made Asha look up. The man was standing in a doorway, one that led directly to the outside. Asha could see a path and some trees past the man. She glanced to the bed. The dead woman was gone. Back to the man. He was looking at Asha and Angel, but there was something wrong with his focus.

<Reyndani can't see you, but he knows you're there.>

"Reyndani?" That's why he was familiar. He was John's exercise instructor from the Samgha. A friend? "What's he doing here?"

<My brothers thought he might be useful.>

"But he's got a family."

<He belongs to Helix now.> There was something flat and final in the young woman's tones.

"Who are you?" Asha asked.

<I'm the other one.>

"You're Helix's sister?"

<Yes.>

"Where are you?"

<With my trees.>

"They're *your* trees?"

<Trees aren't really Helix's thing.>

Asha tried to reorganise her thoughts. A jumble of questions came out at once. "Why haven't I met you in person? How do you talk to me like this? What do I call you?" Across the connection Asha could feel the amusement that preceded the woman's response.

<My brothers and sister call me Peren.>

A strange answer.

<Can you feed my mother? Please try.>

Asha rearranged herself on the floor and carefully lifted Angel so that the old woman's head was leaning against Asha's breasts. Remembering Reyndani, Asha looked up, but he was gone and the door was closed.

<I'll get him to come back and clean up later,> Peren told her.

It was very strange, sometimes the girl seemed to be responding to Asha's thoughts.

<Please try,> Peren prompted again.

Asha lifted Angel higher and concentrated. She was looking for a way in. She couldn't put it better than that. She didn't know how it worked. It just did. Sometimes.

Her first probe met with a grey veil that yielded without letting her through. Asha drew back, tried to calm herself, and then tried again. The same veil met her, but this time it started to fade. Asha felt Angel move in her arms, she was waking up. Asha pushed a little harder and the veil gave way to flickering scenes as memories replayed themselves.

A human woman swinging the leg of a broken chair wildly. Unbearable pain. The memory flickered out to be replaced by another.

Facing the same woman, now lying on the bed. Reaching out and drawing the prana up from the skin below her neck. Breaking into that prana with her teeth. The pleasure of drinking the liquid golden life that flowed from the wound.

The scene faded and was replaced by another face, a human man, obviously dead, drained of life. Her fingers were tracing a symbol on his forehead. A faint yellow fog of evaporating prana still hovered over the wound below his neck.

Another memory, another face, another death. And another. And another. An endless line of faces reaching across the years, each one indelibly etched in Angel's mind.

It was too much!

Asha wasn't sure if she threw herself out, rejecting the horror of what she was seeing, or whether it was Angel. The memories closed off abruptly, as if a shutter had fallen, and Asha was being pushed, both mentally and physically.

"Get out! Get away!" Angel shouted at her weakly. She was pushing ineffectually at Asha with her hands.

Asha let Angel go as gently as she could and crawled back from her. She was worried that Angel would tear open her wounds in her distress. Angel's face was distorted with fear – and something more, dread and shame. Her eyes searched Asha's reluctantly, wanting but unable to turn away. Her mouth was moving but no words emerged.

<You'd better go,> Peren told Asha.

Asha stood slowly. Angel huddled against the bed as if Asha were threatening to attack.

<Just leave. Please.>

"She shouldn't be left alone," Asha whispered.

<Just go. She's scared of you.>

Asha turned and left.

- - -

<What happened?> Jaimee asked his sister. She was calmer now that their mother was out of danger, maybe he could get some sense out of her.

<The sedative didn't work,> Peren said.

<Why not? Did Reyndani do something wrong?>

He felt his sister shaking her head. *<I watched him.>*

Jaimee nodded absently. Peren could watch like no other. She watched from inside their heads. *<So what went wrong?>*

<I don't know. It's like the drug sent the woman crazy. Mama had just started feeding when the woman woke up. She pushed Mama away, broke a chair and used it to attack Mama. Reyndani barely got there in time. Then we got Asha. She was amazing to watch.>

<Does she know about you?>

<No. But you were right, Jaimee, she's incredibly powerful.>

<We should have Reyndani stand guard inside the room,> Sando put in.

<Mother will never stand for it,> said Jaimee. *<She likes to be alone when she's feeding.>*

<What do we do?> Peren asked.

Jaimee shrugged. *<Be more careful in the future. Is Mother okay? Was Asha able to feed her?>*

<I got another human for Mama. It helped, but she's still not well,> Peren answered. There was a pause before she continued, *<I don't think it's going to work out with Asha. She frightened Mama.*

Mama is refusing to let Asha near her again.>

Jaimee thumped his leg in frustration. Weeks of slow progress all gone. *<We'll be home tomorrow. I'll talk to Mother then.>*

\- - -

The morning light was growing slowly brighter. Asha lay sprawled along a branch, she had her chin resting on one hand, with the other she had reached forward to stroke the side of Cassey's face with the tips of her fingers. The brevi was sprawled in a similar manner, facing Asha. They had been exchanging meaningless but comforting sounds.

<Asha?> Peren's voice spoke softly into Asha's mind.

Cassey twittered, apparently annoyed with the interruption. The brevi got up and leapt off the branch, gliding into the distance.

"How is your mother?" Asha spoke out loud.

<Still weak, but she is recovering.>

"Unlike the human woman," Asha couldn't keep silent, "and all the others."

<There is no choice. There never has been.>

Asha didn't try to argue.

<Wasn't it like this with your John?>

"His presence doesn't pull the prana out from the body of a human as your mother does. As a preta does."

<That's not the only way to access the prana of a material body. John could do it. Or you could do it for him.>

"Acintya you mean," Asha said, "pushing the life from the body."

<It doesn't have to be much. Not to feed as Mama does.>

"You sound like you have experience."

The pause was a long and loud silence.

Eventually Peren asked, *<If you hadn't been able to feed John yourself, wouldn't you have done everything you could to keep him alive?>*

"Would I have killed another to save him?"

<Yes.>

"It wouldn't have come to that. He wouldn't have stayed separated."

<If he couldn't return to his human body, wouldn't you have done anything you could to keep him alive?>

Asha thought about this for a long time. There had been a time

193

when she had thought it might come to that decision. The first time she tried to feed him she wasn't certain it was going to work, and they had been so far away from his human body.

"No," she answered quietly. "Not anything. Not like you mean. Not killing another person."

<You loved him so little?>

"No. I love him that much."

<I don't understand.>

"For one thing, John wouldn't accept it."

<And you wouldn't offer because it would have disappointed John?>

"No. I mean that love involves both sides. It's a two-way thing. I wouldn't offer because it's wrong. It's part of who I am. John knows that. He knows me. Who we are is an integral part of our love for each other. You can't break one without breaking the other."

<You're saying that trying to save him would have destroyed your love for one another? I can't accept that.>

Asha shook her head. "It's more basic than that. Our love would have prevented the attempt in the first place. Love will live on after death, but it can't survive betrayal."

<No,> said Peren. Her tone suggested something other than a simple rejection of what Asha had said. There was a profound sadness behind it.

"I don't mean that I wouldn't be tempted. A stranger's life in exchange for John's? Of course I would be tempted. But it wouldn't happen." Asha thought a bit longer. "I am tempted. I'd leave here in a moment, leave your mother to take more lives, if I could be sure John and my home would be safe."

<So you would do it. You are doing it.>

"It's not the same," Asha responded loudly, angry at the relief and satisfaction she heard in Peren's voice. Angry at her own weakness. "It's not the same," she repeated. "There's no exchange. I'm not certain I can help your mother, even if she would let me try. And whatever happens, I can't stop you from doing what you're doing."

<But you will still help us?> Peren's tone was suddenly softer, hesitant and doubtful. <Mama needs your help.>

Asha nodded. Despite what she'd said a moment ago, it wasn't so easy to turn her back on what was going on here, not when there was a chance she could do something to stop it.

"When did you want me to come down and sit with her?"

<Not yet. Maybe not for a few days. You scared her. Those memories. Is that—?>

"I don't know. They're not something I want either, especially not from your mother. They just happen."

<You see them too, but that's not part of your power.>

"Like it is yours?"

<No. I only see what's in your mind now. I can't go searching.>

"I don't search. They just happen. They're like obstacles, or a maze that I have to pass through to find the connection. I have to be allowed through."

There was a pause, then Peren continued, *<My brothers are coming back today. Jaimee will talk to Mama and try to persuade her to cooperate.>*

Oh joy, Asha thought sarcastically.

<My brothers like you. Jaimee especially.>

Asha didn't try to express her disgust at that thought, it probably wasn't necessary.

There was another, longer, hesitation. *<I wanted to ask a favour.>*

A favour?

<I wasn't supposed to let you know about me, and especially not that I was watching you.>

"Why not?"

<I think it's a ... a test. Jaimee wants to know whether you're cooperating willingly.>

"Why would he think that might happen?" Asha asked in surprise.

This time the silence was so long that Asha thought Peren might have gone, if it was ever possible to say that.

<I haven't told them about your brevi.>

Asha hadn't even thought about that, though it was obvious now. Angry, she answered, "You may be more subtle than your siblings, but the threats are the same."

<No! I didn't mean it like that.> Peren sounded genuinely contrite. *<I think Cassey is beautiful. I'd love to meet her. I just meant that I ... I don't share everything with my brothers.>*

"And Helix?"

195

Asha got the sense that Peren was shaking her head.

"What do I tell your brothers about yesterday?"

<I told them you were close to the house, and you heard Reyndani calling.>

"And if they ask Reyndani, will he lie too?"

<They won't talk with him. It probably won't even come up, they've no reason to think I would lie to them.>

"You just don't want me to volunteer anything."

Peren agreed, and then said she had to go and help her mother.

Asha stayed lying on the branch, thinking. Not only did she have fences and guards and threats holding her here, now she also had someone inside her head – someone that could see what she saw, feel what she felt. She had been more reassured than she had let on when Jaimee told her that neither Sando nor Helix would be playing with her mind. It never occurred to her that there was another possibility. No wonder they trusted Asha with their mother. The others didn't have to watch, they didn't have to ask, Peren could simply tell them what Asha was thinking.

It was a whole new dimension of imprisonment. Not even her thoughts were her own. Was Peren listening in even now?

There was no response to the question in her mind, but what did that mean? And even if Peren wasn't there all the time, she could be there at any moment.

Asha had found the strength to accept her prison from somewhere. So far. But she could feel the fragile walls of her bravado starting to crumble. She put her face down into her arms. Moments later Cassey returned and squeezed into the gap between the branch and Asha's face. The brevi nuzzled at Asha's tears.

"You should go," Asha told the brevi. "It's not safe here for you. Not any more."

Reaching

11. Confinement

The uncounted days passed and John felt himself getting progressively weaker. The cravings of his body for sustenance, not exactly hunger as he had once known it but no other word really suited, had helped to keep driving him on for a time. So had his determination to be of use. If surviving to find Asha was beyond him now, at least he should do what he could for his friends. But, as more time passed, even that was not enough.

On some days the group were escorted down to be presented again to the regent. Most of these were just so that Andrei could show the zakti to a new set of samudraka, and for Sarva to repeat his tale of the papayamala. As yet they had been given no hint of what the samudraka had planned for them.

On the most recent trip John had to be aided for the entire journey, and Sarva had been questioned about him.

"What is wrong with him?" one of the guests had asked. A young, arrogant, samudraka with skin the colour of diluted blood.

"He swam in a pool corrupted by humans," Sarva said. "Now he is unable to merge to regain his strength."

John almost smiled, it wasn't that far from the truth as how the samudraka might see it.

"He is dying?" asked the regent.

"Unless we can find some way to help him, yes," said Sarva.

Their group had been sent away again to await their fate.

The confinement wasn't helping the others either. Sarva seemed to sink into himself, John couldn't tell if he was thinking about the past or wondering about the future. Garjae kept making futile suggestions about escaping the zarana. Senna was irritable and got into arguments with Garjae. Andrei, always restless, had already managed to run afoul of the guards watching them – several times. He had played to their fear of the zakti until Polyphemo paid a visit and explained he would wear the consequences and see Andrei dead if he pushed any more. They still didn't know what those consequences were. Why didn't the samudraka simply take the sword if that was what they wanted?

Only Darnu seemed normal to John. Darnu would listen to Garjae's ideas as if they had any chance, but when Garjae turned away the sympathy was clear on Darnu's face. Darnu bore Andrei's antics with his usual patience, like a brother enduring the annoyance of a younger sibling.

It had now reached the point that John couldn't walk up onto the island without assistance. Darnu and Andrei sat John down near the palm tree after another few hours spent floating in the water near the shore. Not for the first time, John caught Darnu looking at him with pity.

"You should spend more time in the water," Darnu told him. "You will fade less quickly if you stay in the water."

John closed his eyes and shrugged weakly. He had never gained the knack of resting or sleeping in the water, not without Asha there to hold him, and all he felt like doing now was resting or sleeping. He would close his eyes and try to take himself back to happier times. Sometimes he would go all the way back to when he had a family, a wife and daughter, and his memories of their laughter. But more and more he found himself returning to the all too brief time that he had spent with Asha.

He had failed them all. Samantha lost because she went to see Karlin in secret, concerned that John would tease her if it turned out to be a scam. Ellie would soon be lost, if she wasn't already, because he had failed to find a way to heal her. Asha was lost when John had failed to be the shield he had promised to be. And all his friends here were lost because they had tried to help him. Was there something he could have done differently that would have spared at least some of them?

"Why did you tell the samudraka about Helix and the others?" Garjae asked.

John's eyes flickered open at the loud and argumentative tones.

He could see Darnu frowning at Garjae. It wasn't a new argument.

Garjae continued, "What good can come of it?"

Sarva took a long time to pull himself back from wherever he'd gone in his mind.

Senna took up the argument, "Does it matter, Garjae? It's done."

"It might help if he would explain what he thought he was doing."

"How? We're stuck here. Hasn't that gotten through to you yet?"

"What has gotten through to me is that we're not helping anyone while we sit here doing nothing."

"If—"

"I had a few reasons," Sarva's quiet voice interrupted Senna's angry response.

"Such as?" Garjae demanded.

"You've heard what they think of aaranya. We were lucky not to be killed the moment they saw us, even before they saw the zakti. I don't know what's going on with that, but whatever it is, I doubt it will end well for us. But I do know what they think of twins, or papayamala. They fear them more than almost anything else, it's built into their culture. I'm hoping that I've given them a reason to keep us alive."

"And *how* is that supposed to work?"

"*If* we can convince them to act against Helix then they'll need our help."

"They're more likely to march out and kill every aaranya they meet."

Sarva shook his head. "They rarely go on land at all any more, they won't do that more than they need to. They don't even know what's up there any more. They'll need us to show them the way."

"You hope."

Sarva nodded. "I hope."

"You said a few reasons," Darnu reminded him.

"The other one is what I told the samudraka. I don't think the aaranya can fight this on their own. Too many Glades are already under Helix's control. We need their help."

"Do you really think they will?" Senna asked.

Sarva shrugged. "I don't know. I only know that this was our chance to ask for it, perhaps the only chance the aaranya will ever get."

"Right," Garjae scoffed. He turned away, walked back down to the water and dived in.

"Put it away, Andrei," Senna said impatiently.

John tilted his head so he could see what Andrei was doing. He had the sword out again, turning it over in his hands.

John let his head roll back and closed his eyes again, it was too much effort to keep them open.

"Isn't there anything we can do for John?" Senna asked.

John didn't hear a response. He imagined it was a shake of the head.

After a while he heard footsteps in the sand, fading as they descended to the water. He thought he was alone, left to sleep, so he was surprised when Darnu spoke.

"Is there anything you'd like us – me – to do for you?" Darnu asked quietly. "If the rest of us eventually get out of this."

"Find Asha," John answered, in a whisper. "Protect her."

- - -

Asha was leaning back against the pillows of the large bed, she held Angel in her arms as if she were comforting a child. It had taken two weeks before the old woman had relented and allowed Asha to be alone in the room with her. It had taken only one week more before Angel had permitted Asha to try feeding her again. It hadn't worked. And every attempt had failed each day since, but they both kept trying.

Asha kept trying because she could no longer ignore the people being killed. It had been bad before, but it was worse now. Every second day another human was sacrificed to keep this woman alive. If Asha could put a stop to that she would. It was also a distraction from her increasing worries about John. Every day she grew more convinced that something was terribly wrong. He might be dying, and there was nothing she could do.

Angel was trying because even feeding every second day wasn't enough. Still she was fading. She had confided in Asha that she only now realised how close she was to death, and that she was frightened. That fear had made her compliant.

<Any further this time?> Peren asked into Asha's mind.

No, Asha answered. She had learned that she only needed to express her thoughts as words in her mind and Peren would be able

202

to pick them out. This allowed private conversations in the presence of others.

<I've tried to tell her to relax. That she can trust you.>

She's not doing it intentionally. I think it's a reflex. I get so far and then the memories get too hard for her and she shuts me out.

<Can't you do it without sparking all those memories?>

I don't know why the memories show up, they just do.

Asha could feel Peren shudder. She understood, there were true horrors in Angel's past. Peren had been able to tell Asha about some of them, but most remained a mystery, private to the woman resting in her arms.

<How long do you think?>

I don't know. Not long.

<Do you think you'll be able to get through?>

I'll keep trying.

They sat quietly for a time, and then Peren broke into Asha's thoughts. *<I like your voice. Your mind. It's different to others. Sometimes there are echoes.>*

Echoes?

<I don't know how to explain it better than that. And it's not just that. I can relax when I'm talking to you. You make me feel welcome ... or maybe it's because I don't have to hide from you.>

Asha wasn't sure how to respond to that. She was relieved of the need when Angel began to stir in her arms.

"I'm sorry," Angel murmured.

"It's not your fault," Asha answered. "Sleep now. We'll try again tomorrow."

"I am tired," Angel whispered.

Asha lay the old woman gently back on the pillows and covered her with a sheet. The human remnants in the old woman still liked the comfort of a covering. Angel curled up on her side, looking more like a child than ever.

Asha got up slowly and went to the door.

Peren warned her, *<Sando's waiting for you. I think it's his turn to show off.>*

Asha gave an exaggerated sigh. She felt the expected chuckle from Peren. It was a strange thing, but Asha's early despondence had given way to a liking for the girl/woman that spoke inside her head.

There was none of the arrogance and exalted self-confidence that Asha associated with the other siblings. Peren seemed to be someone real, someone likeable. Her presence in Asha's head no longer felt like the intrusion it had been.

Sando was watching the door as it opened. Asha guessed that Peren had warned him similarly, the girl had a sense of humour – mostly hidden, but it was there when you looked for it.

"Got a hook-up with my sister," Sando said. "I thought you might like to see it."

He doesn't mean you, does he? Asha asked in her mind. Peren didn't answer, she must have gone off somewhere, perhaps back to her mother.

"Come on," Sando said. He reached out for her hand and pulled Asha after him.

They might look the same, but this one was very different from his brother. It was obvious that he was trying to be engaging, but that was part of the problem, it was obvious. Taking Asha's hand was something natural for Jaimee to do, he just did it as part of how he behaved. With Sando it was something he thought about, something he consciously chose to do.

Asha followed him down to the ground floor. They passed a large kitchen and attached dining area. There were four humans in there, a woman and three children.

"The humans have to eat somewhere," Sando waved dismissively at the rooms. "Their upkeep doesn't come cheap."

Further along, a door opened as they were passing, a young man was about to come out. Sando placed a hand on the man's chest. The man's eyes flicked wide in surprise for a moment, then he stepped back and bowed.

"Is he ...?" Asha started.

"One of the ones that used to be able to see us, yes," Sando answered. "Now he does surveillance duties." Sando pointed inside the room. The walls were filled with screens showing various parts of the estate. "Don't worry. We don't turn on the Karlin Field unless we have to, the dhumraka don't like the feel of it. So this is usually just keeping an eye on the fences in case trees fall against them – that sort of thing."

Across the hall from the surveillance room was a staircase going down into a basement. Sando turned to that and started down. Asha hesitated at the top of the steps. She didn't like going underground.

Sando felt her stop and looked back, the question clear on his face.

Didn't this man remember that he used to keep me imprisoned in such a place? Asha wondered.

"What's wrong?" he asked.

Obviously not, Asha answered her own question. "Nothing," she said out loud and reluctantly followed him down.

The first room was a large storage area. The smell of various sorts of vegetables and grain were dominant. Food for the humans of the household, and a lot of it. Sando continued past the racks to a large heavy door. When he opened it a gush of warm air came through, the scents carried out were of machine oil and fuel. He closed the door behind them and they walked through the large, dimly lit room filled with ducts and the echoing sounds of fans and electric motors. There were several large petrol engines sitting still and quiet.

Sando didn't explain any of it, just led on through to an apparently solid brick wall on the far side. There was a hole in the wall where a brick was missing.

"Stick your hand in there," Sando said, smiling.

Asha hesitated.

"It's safe," he assured her.

Reluctantly, she did as she was asked. She was startled by the familiar tingle of a Karlin Field and pulled her hand out quickly.

Sando chuckled. "We incorporated the doctor's tricks into our security. No one but a narun can open this door."

It took a moment for Asha to understand what he meant, and then she saw it. A section of the brick wall was swinging silently out. She took a step back.

When the piece of wall finished swinging back it revealed another door, this one with a keypad on it.

"But we can't have just any narun," said Sando. He stepped forward and typed in a code.

The inner door clicked and Sando pushed it open. Once they were inside, Sando pressed a control on the wall and the two doors closed behind them.

This room was large too, but much quieter now that the doors were closed, just a soft hum from the computer equipment that filled most of the room. The air was cool and had a slightly burnt electrical smell.

Sando waved his arm over the expanse. "My sister is Queen of the Dhumraka. My brother is the power behind the military and political might of this country, and so much of the world. *This* is where I come in. I've put together a team, humans and dhumraka I might add, that puts the entire world at their disposal through IT – that's information technology for newbies like yourself. When Jaimee wants to know what some corporate giant is planning, or maybe he wants to listen in to government chit-chat, this is how he does it. When Helix wants to present herself to one of her human lapdogs, this is what lets her do it."

Asha looked around. It didn't mean much to her. Just a bunch of boxes and a lot of large screens.

Sando must have taken her disinterest as doubt. "You want to see what the authorities have to say about your old human pet?" He walked along one wall until he reached the computer he wanted. He sat down and started typing.

Asha watched over his shoulder, though nothing he was doing meant much to her.

"In we go, past the firewalls as if they weren't there," Sando carried on cheerfully. "Now we dig our way down into their terrorist files. ... Here we are. Now we search."

Asha recognised John's name as Sando typed it. A list appeared on the screen and Sando chose one of the entries. The screen filled up. In one corner was a photo of John's face.

"You see? They think he was some sort of terrorist bent on destroying the world's forests. The file's almost dormant now, which is just as we planned."

Asha wasn't a fast reader, she hadn't had much practise, but just before Sando cleared the screen she did see a short summary. It contained the words, "Missing. Presumed dead." She tried to work out what that must mean. John hadn't returned to his old life. He was still missing. And someone somewhere thought he was a terrorist. What did that mean? ... Was? Sando said, "was."

Sando got up from that screen and tugged Asha over to another.

"She should be online now." He started typing.

Helix's face filled the screen. She was smiling. "Hello, Sando," the face spoke.

Asha was surprised back to attention. The voice wasn't quite right, but the face was almost as she remembered it. "How are you doing that?"

There was a clatter of keys, a delay and then the picture spoke again.

"Hello, Asha. My brothers tell me you've been trying very hard to help our mother. Do you think you might have success soon?"

"I don't know," Asha answered absently. "Sando, how is she doing that?"

"It's a simulation. We created them so we can talk to humans, make it seem like we're human too. It's useful. Here, I'll put my side of the conversation up so you can see it."

Helix's face reduced in size, and beside it appeared Sando's, or it could have been Jaimee's. On the screen it wasn't obvious who it must be.

"Asha says she doesn't know," the screen face of Sando said.

"Keep trying," Helix said. "Our mother is very important to us."

"Are you done there yet?" Sando's image asked.

Helix's head nodded on the screen. "This Glade came over quietly too. There's been no more trouble. I'm just tidying up a few things. I should be home tomorrow."

Asha stepped back and let the siblings talk. Little of this was new, not really. Asha had seen much of what the siblings were doing, but it had all seemed ... small. Discrete and disconnected. But now? She didn't know what to make of it. To believe what Sando was telling her was to accept that these siblings were taking control of everything, human and narun alike. Was such a thing really possible?

"Impressive, yes?" The conversation had finished and Sando was watching her.

"Why?" was all Asha could think to ask.

"Because we can," Sando answered glibly.

Asha shook her head.

"No, that's not all. Jaimee and I saw it years ago, and we started making plans. Humans are dominating this planet. They're taking it over and not thinking about the consequences. They don't even

207

understand the things they can see for themselves. Most of them don't care. Where does that leave the narun?"

Asha didn't try to answer.

"Nowhere. Even if they knew we existed we'd be nothing more than a scientific curiosity. The narun people are being squeezed into the corners of the world, and soon even those will be destroyed. So we're doing something about it."

"But Helix? The Glades?"

"The aaranya were never going to do anything on their own. The jalaja and the yaayaavara are too few to do anything, even if they wanted. If anyone's going to keep the humans in their place it's got to be us. But there's not enough of us on our own, so Helix is recruiting the aaranya. When we need an army she'll have it ready."

"Army?"

"Sure. To be honest, if I'd had my own way, we'd have already pruned the human population. Courtesy of the humans themselves we have access to the biological weapons that can do that for us now, at no cost or risk to the narun. But Jaimee's ambitious. Humans are handy. They can make things." Sando waved his hand around the room. "So we're trying to be selective. Organise things so we get to keep access to all the neat stuff. Humans on tap to build things for us."

"And then?"

- - -

Barma wasn't sure why he'd been brought here. This was a place for elders and their helpers, experienced aaranya like Darnu and Garjae had been. It was normally busy with such people, but now there were just the four of them. Five if you counted Ellie.

Milla had brought Barma with him. Kaia was already here, lying back on a bed of leaves formed from branches that had folded themselves into place to support her. She was holding Ellie. Hovering over them both was Telia, the woman who had been caring for Ellie while Kaia was unconscious.

Kaia didn't look well. What had been a cloud of white hair looked thinner now and it hung about her face in limp strands. Her once brown skin looked bleached, and her face was now gaunt rather than thin. She said something to Telia, and the woman reached down and lifted Ellie.

Barma was surprised when the tall, elegant woman approached him and held Ellie out to him. He hesitated, uncertain what was expected.

"Take her," Telia told him. "Kaia wants you two to get to know each other."

Barma took the child awkwardly. Telia stepped in closer and helped him to rearrange Ellie so they were both more comfortable. Once settled in the crook of his arm the creature – the girl, he reminded himself – barely moved.

Such a strange sight. Tiny, grey, naked and sexless. The white globes of eyes stared past him, through him. A preta. A being of hunger and little else. It was almost impossible to believe that this had once been a beautiful, vibrant, human girl. Barma had never met her, but John had shown him photographs and the snippets of video. And Ellie was dying. She had been dying slowly ever since she was pushed from her human body. Asha had helped her, had given her more time, but Ellie was as small and frail now as she had ever been. Only the intensity of life inside the Glade had kept her going this long. Maybe Asha could help extend life still further, but Asha wasn't here.

He looked up. He had to blink a few times to clear the wetness from his eyes. The other three were watching him. Kaia said something, but it was too soft for him to hear. Telia put her hand around Barma and pressed his back, pushing him closer to Kaia.

"Do you see?" Kaia asked, her voice a whisper.

Barma looked down at the child and then back up at Kaia. "She's dying."

Kaia nodded slowly.

"Can we do anything?"

It didn't seem that Kaia had heard, she was staring off somewhere past him.

Milla spoke. "Kaia thinks it is possible that a connection may open to another Glade."

Barma turned in surprise. "Like in the old days?"

"Like before the War, yes." Milla nodded.

"Why now?"

"Because it is the will of the Glade. Kaia has convinced the rest of us that this is something we can do. Something that, given the right

209

conditions, might happen – if we want it enough, if we believe it enough."

"Right conditions?"

Milla smiled tenderly past Barma to Kaia. "She has not been clear about that."

Barma heard Kaia say something, but didn't catch the words.

"I can't help my questions," Milla answered her.

At a weak movement in his arms, Barma looked down and studied the preta. "What does this have to do with Ellie?" he asked.

"She can't stay here." Kaia spoke more loudly than before.

"But she can't leave the Glade either," Barma argued, then shut his mouth quickly. Arguing with an elder wasn't done. Only Milla ever encouraged that sort of thing.

Kaia smiled at him. "Waiting here, her death is certain. ... Out there, there is a chance. Asha is out there somewhere. I can feel my granddaughter. ... She is not happy, but she is well. I can feel ..." Kaia's voice trailed off as if distracted. She smiled faintly.

Barma watched Kaia staring off again at something he wouldn't see even if he turned to look. Her pale green eyes were so much like Asha's that he couldn't deny her claim.

Milla guided Barma back to Telia, then turned back and bent down in whispered conversation with Kaia.

"I don't understand," Barma told Telia quietly.

Telia was slightly taller than Barma, and next to his stick-figure build she looked stronger too. She smiled kindly at him. "Kaia wants you and me to find the connection when it opens. To go through it and take Ellie with us."

Barma looked down at Ellie and contemplated his new responsibility. "Why me?" he asked of no one in particular.

"You and Andrei have explored this Glade like few others," Telia answered him. "She thinks you may know more of the tunnels here than even the elders."

"That was a long time ago."

Telia laughed. "Anyone would think you were an old man."

Barma looked up and smiled. Telia was older than him, maybe Asha's age or a bit more. He could understand why his comment sounded funny to her, but the truth was that he felt old now. Maybe it was the idea of being responsible for a child.

"Here," Telia said, "let me take her. We can't have you hurting your aging back."

He found himself strangely reluctant to relinquish his hold, but Telia's hands were sure and confident. He didn't argue.

Milla stood as his conversation finished with Kaia.

Barma heard her finish softly, "It might not work so well when they learn more of Australia."

Milla nodded his understanding.

Barma accompanied Milla and Telia away from Kaia's tree. They took the quieter branches, away from the busy central bowers.

"Is she going to be all right?" Barma asked.

"Kaia? Yes, I think so," Milla answered. "She's getting stronger. It may have knocked off a century or two, but I think she will be with us for a while yet."

"What did she mean? About it not working when they learn more of Australia."

Milla glanced at him. "You and Andrei must have been off causing trouble when you should have been paying attention to what your elders were telling you." But he looked more amused than upset. He explained, "The Glades in Australia have more cause to know about closing the Way than some others. Bush fires are common here, and sometimes a Glade will lie in its path."

"What happens if the trees burn while the Way is open?"

"Any violent closure of the Way tears at the Glade and much of its life can be lost. The Glade shrinks and can support fewer people inside. The damage can be so bad that the Glade is unable to survive. It and everyone inside is lost. Fire not only tears at the Way, it burns the life energy and draws it out, though the fire itself cannot enter. So our ancestors learned to minimise the damage by closing the Way as gently as possible, before the trees holding it are burned."

"So why didn't you just close it before Sando arrived?"

"The Way does not close on a whim, not even at the combined will of the elders. It is made from life but it is not conscious, it only reacts. To force it to close we must make the threat apparent."

Milla had stopped, so Barma urged him on, "How?"

"If an elder, appropriately prepared, dies or is badly hurt then the Way will feel that harm and react to protect the Glade. You saw Kaia take part of the Way into herself. In a bush fire she would have walked into the approaching flames and her death would have closed the Way."

"Suicide!"

"We elders refer to it as a sacrifice, the ultimate service we can perform for our stand. A death that serves to protect the life of the Glade."

"So you thought Kaia would die out there?"

"I did. She did. Ironically, it was the ray-gun that allowed her to close the Way around her, it allowed her to survive. Had it been a normal fire she would have had to go out to meet it."

Barma considered this for a while, and then asked, "So what happens now?"

"If Kaia is right then perhaps a connection will open and give some a way out." Barma understood what Milla didn't say, that the elders might be able to leave but they couldn't escape, their fate was tied to the Glade. Milla continued, "Otherwise, we wait. In normal circumstances the Australian bush will restore itself quite quickly, it loves the fire and returns revitalised. New growth takes off, and after a few years—"

"Years!"

"Yes, Barma, years. Though time works differently here in the Glade when the Way is closed."

"Differently how?"

"Unpredictably, but generally time passes more slowly here."

"Or does it just feel like that?" Barma said.

Milla smiled at him.

"A very Andrei comment," noted Telia.

Barma ignored that and asked, "And then what, the Way just opens again when it's ready?"

"We elders will know when the time comes and the Way will open for us."

"So we're safe here, it's those outside that are still in danger, who might have to wait years before they can return."

"Just because Sando did not expect us to close the Way in the manner we did, does not mean he is unaware that the Glade may reopen in the future. What happens outside is beyond our control now, and I assume that Sando has plans to make sure the Glade never reopens."

"He can do that?"

"Easily. He just has to stop the forest from returning, and there are many ways to do that. In the War they simply salted the ground."

"But why? No, I mean, what? There must be something we can do."

"In the distant past, when the Glades were all connected, the people could leave through other Glades, and depending on where they came out, return to help protect the region of their home. In more recent times some of our number would remain outside and try to get clear of the fire. After the danger had passed they would encourage the return of life, of the forest. The trees that anchored our Way were planted in such a recovery."

"So if Telia and I can get out?"

"If Sando is out there it won't be safe. You had better stay away," Milla warned.

"And what happens to the Glade if he does stop the Way returning?"

"Eventually, we die. The Glade will slowly shrink until it is no longer able to sustain the population and we fade – starve as if we had been kept away from the forest for too long."

"Eventually?"

"I think the slowing of time when the Way is closed is the Glade's way of conserving itself. I imagine that time would slow more and more as the Glade becomes weaker."

"So it may take a long time for us to die."

"From an outside perspective, yes. From in here, I think it would seem to happen all too quickly."

"Or all too slowly, if we're starving to death," Telia observed.

Milla nodded.

- - -

They had been left alone for many days, Tilvy was wondering if they'd been forgotten. It had given them time to learn something of their enclosure, though there wasn't a lot to add to the first impressions. Lots of unfamiliar creatures inhabiting many unfamiliar plants, all inside a cage inside a massive building. Despite all that, it wasn't actually unpleasant. The regular afternoon rain from the sprinklers in the roof, and the constant warmth and humidity through the day took some getting used to, but it seemed to suit the life of the environment. Even the large trees were doing surprisingly well, and, Tilvy admitted to Pasith, they were good to merge with. Complex, and vigorous, they were an interesting contrast to the trees of her home.

Pasith was less happy with his small pool and stream. The water was clean, and there were fish, and plants growing in and around, but it was small and dull compared to the river of his home.

The windows of the surrounding building were coated with something that prevented them from seeing in, except at certain times of day when the light was just right. They could sense the presence of humans in the building to a limited degree with vedana, but the mesh interfered even there. Sometimes humans would come out on the balconies that overlooked the enclosure, generally they were carrying drinks and would chatter amongst themselves for a while before going back in.

Tilvy and Pasith sat on some rocks by the pool. There had been plenty of time to talk. Pasith had told her how he and his mate had come to be imprisoned. Tilvy had told Pasith about John and Asha. She told him how much she missed Barma, now locked away in the Glade. And today she had, yet again, been talking about Tracey, wondering where she must be.

Pasith was shaking his head.

"What?"

"You aaranya are a strange people."

"Special, you mean." Tilvy grinned at him.

Pasith smiled at her. "I can see that some of you are, but I was talking about your dealings with humans."

"Some of them are okay."

He shrugged. "I see them every day, but the best I ever think of them is as an inconvenience. Most of the time they're at least annoying, and that's only when they're not downright dangerous."

"That's because they don't know we're here."

"Uh-uh," Pasith disagreed. "It's not just us. You watch them. It's like they don't see anything, even the stuff they're supposed to see."

Tilvy frowned. Her instinct was to try and defend the humans, but that was something new. Was it having a friend like Tracey, or was it

214

having an enemy like Sando?

"They think it's their world now," Pasith continued, "to do with as they please."

"Look around you, Pasith," Tilvy reminded him. "It is."

"It's not the way they should look at it. They don't own it, they share it with everything else."

"I don't think they're good at sharing."

"Maybe that's what Sando's about. Regaining ground for your lot."

"My lot?"

"The aaranya."

"He's not aaranya."

"No," Pasith admitted. "Maybe not. I don't know what he is. But the ones called dhumraka feel like aaranya."

Tilvy told him about the pools of kelp plants she'd seen at the research centre, and the dhumraka sleeping in them.

"They're not samudraka," Pasith said firmly.

"And I don't think they're aaranya, whatever they feel like. Anyway, how do you know?"

"There used to be samudraka visit the bay, back at home. We'd go out and talk with them. They don't think much of the aaranya."

Beenae came up to them through the thick undergrowth.

"Hi, Beeny," Tilvy called to him.

Beenae grinned, he didn't mind Tilvy calling him that. "Taiza says you sh'd come see."

Tilvy smiled, that was probably exactly what Taiza had said. "See what?"

"The mesh." Beenae turned to go.

"We can see it well enough from here," said Pasith.

Beenae shook his head. "Not like this."

Pasith and Tilvy got up reluctantly and followed Beenae through the ferns. On the far side of the cage they found Taiza poking away at something with a stick. He looked up as they arrived and then pointed at something. It was Taiza's stick that Tilvy noticed first. It was a few feet long and fairly straight, the twigs and other roughness had been cleaned from the surface. The end of the stick held a sharp piece of rock, she couldn't tell how it was held in place.

"How did you do that?" Tilvy asked him.

"Tools." Taiza pointed to one side. There, amid a heap of shredded wood, was a small pile of rocks – that's what Tilvy would have called them, Taiza managed to think of them as tools.

"I told you aaranya were strange," Pasith whispered in her ear.

Tilvy pushed him away. "Practical is the word," she replied. But she laughed a little too.

"Look," Beenae insisted.

Tilvy peered into the dim corner where he was pointing. A branch had fallen from somewhere above and one end of it had pushed the mesh out in a bulge. Where the branch had hit the mesh it had gone a different colour, and part of it was now red with rust.

"And there. See?" Beenae said.

Where the mesh was embedded into the concrete there was rust, but above it the wire of the mesh was shiny where the surface coating had been recently worn away by something, and one of the strands looked ready to part.

"Taiza did that," Beenae told her.

"Won't people see?" Pasith asked.

"None t' see" said Taiza.

"We watched," explained Beenae. "No one's using the building just here, so there's no one t' see."

"And you can turn this into a way out?" Pasith asked.

Taiza nodded. "'ll take time, but c'd be."

"We could get in trouble if they discover what you're doing?" Tilvy said cautiously.

"Y'd rather stay?" Taiza asked her.

Tilvy shook her head.

They agreed it was worth a try.

That night, while Taiza, Beenae and Pasith were all merged and resting, Tilvy got restless and climbed high into the trees. She hadn't come up here very often. She wasn't sure what she was looking for, maybe a view of the moon or some other sign of the world outside. It was cooler at night, and not so humid, which was a pleasant relief and a reminder of home.

As she got higher she heard the soft murmuring of voices, so she climbed further. It was two men. She worked her way out along a branch that reached up to one corner, and eventually found a place where she could see them standing on the balcony.

She knew them. They had been the men watching over Tracey. Tilvy pushed her senses out as strongly as she could, hoping to feel past the barriers of the mesh and the building walls. She thought she could feel the existence of two others up there on that top floor, but she couldn't tell who they were.

Though the two men were speaking softly, their voices carried faintly to her through the still air and down the tunnel of leaves.

"You saw it too, Ray. Right there on—"

"Careful. We can't know it's really safe here, keep it as clean as you can. I saw it, but it didn't tell me anything I didn't already guess."

"But you still haven't guessed why they killed the others, have you?"

"Maybe."

"Why?"

"To let the Yanks take over. To get us here."

"That's paranoid, Ray."

"We're here."

"All right then. It's overkill, literally, but it works. But why did they want us here? I think we should go over what she told us again."

"It won't help *us* to get lost in her delusions."

"What if they're not all delusions?"

"Paul."

"You're the one that used to quote Sherlock Holmes to me. However improbable, remember?"

"I don't think he had fantasy worlds in mind when he said it. Look, I agree with you. She's a lovely girl, and she seems perfectly sane in every respect except that one."

"Exactly. So why don't we ask ourselves *why* except that one?"

"What did that analyst say?"

"Forget the analyst, I think they're way off target."

"Paul, you can't—"

"Wait. Here me out. Even if we accept that it can't be real, perhaps we should look at it anyway. Perhaps what she's saying can tell us something."

"We've already tried finding the reality in her fantasy. It didn't help."

"But we kept thinking of it all as a delusion. What if some of it's not? You just said that Tracey seems sane about everything else. More than sane I'd say. Exceptional. Why not give her some credit and try—"

"I need a drink. And then I need to sleep. I'll think about it, okay? And we'll wait and see what more news comes through. We still have some time yet."

The two men returned inside.

Tracey was here. That had to be what that conversation meant. Tilvy studied the rooms. In the right light she might be able to see in, though the angle from here was wrong. The room next to the balcony was dark, and the curtains were pulled. As Tilvy watched, the light came on in the room around the corner, and the younger of the two men came to the window. He stared out for a while, apparently at the curtains of the other room, then he drew his own curtains closed.

12. Mermaid

John didn't know how long he'd been asleep. He woke to the sun in his eyes but couldn't remember whether he had been facing east or west. He pushed his fingers slowly into the sand in front of him and decided it must be morning, the sand was still cool. He seemed to be alone. He had vague memories of someone trying to tell him something, but that could have been a dream.

He tried to push himself into a sitting position but only got as far as resting on one elbow. It couldn't be long now, he thought, sometime soon I'll go to sleep and never wake up. Even Andrei had stopped making jokes about John going to sleep on the job *again* – and that couldn't be a good sign.

There was movement on the water, not far out from the beach. A head surfaced. Long, glossy black hair, parts of it streaked silver in the sun. The person swam toward the beach. A samudraka. The tail splashed in a brief flurry over the last few metres, then the person pulled themselves out onto the sand in clumsy movements with their hands and tail.

A woman. It hadn't just been the sun, her rich black hair contained broad glistening streaks that matched her silver tail, and these shone like polished metal in the sun. The skin of the woman's torso was a smooth cream. For all that her face had the slightly flattened appearance typical of the samudraka, and that she looked to be half-dolphin, she was very beautiful.

John found that he still had enough strength to be surprised. A mermaid on the beach of his desert island. His mind threw up more desert island jokes; wasn't there one where the punch line was something about asking a beautiful woman if she had a set of golf clubs? He started to wonder if maybe he was still asleep, possibly delirious.

"Can you make it down here?" she called to him.

"Golf—" he started, and then tried to shake his head. Maybe it was a dream, one of those where he couldn't get any sensible words out. He tried to pull himself toward her. He couldn't even find the strength to raise himself to his hands and knees. It must be a dream he thought. Only in a dream could such a small distance seem so far. He had gone barely one body length before he had to stop and rest.

The woman watched him for a minute or so, waiting to see if he was going to move again. When he didn't, she turned away. Definitely a dream, thought John, I'm lying here helpless, watching my only possible salvation move away. Exactly why he thought of this stranger as his salvation he didn't know, which made him all the more convinced it was a dream.

But she didn't go away. John didn't see the transformation. From behind all he could see was her thick hair hanging past her shoulders and the smooth cream skin of her lower back. But when she stood, unsteadily at first, the transformation was obvious – she had legs. She turned her naked body around and walked slowly up the sand.

Yes, thought John, tail or no tail, she was very beautiful. It had to be a dream. If he was awake he would be feeling embarrassed, and not just a little guilty, about admiring another woman when he was supposed to be searching for Asha.

The woman reached down and tried to lift John. After a few unsuccessful attempts to get him to stand, she turned him over and dragged him backwards down to the beach.

She put him down just below the waterline, John felt the edge of a wave creep up around his head and shoulders. She came around and knelt down at his side, looking into his face. Her large eyes, a deep blue in her wide face, searched for something, John couldn't tell what. There was none of the distaste in her expression that he had seen in other samudraka, and that much was reassuring.

John opened his mouth to say something, but no words came, so he closed it again.

"I didn't know I was going to have to carry you all the way," she muttered. "I hope you're worth it."

She stood and grabbed one of John's hands, using that to drag him deeper into the water. John's human instincts tried to take over as the water splashed around his mouth, and he spluttered and tried to hold his head up. He was pulled beneath the waves and struggled weakly against her hold.

"Come on," she called impatiently, and tugged at his arm.

You could breathe underwater when you were with a mermaid, John's mind threw up. He stopped struggling and relaxed. He felt the water flow through his body and his slow-moving mind remembered that this was a skill he had acquired before meeting this woman. Appeased by his cooperation, she started pulling him along, trailing from one arm. Her tail thumped against his side and he realised she must have transformed again.

Her tail thumped him a few more times and she stopped. She grumbled something about never getting there like this and pulled him across in front of her, holding him like an oversize child. His head rested against her bare shoulder, her hair brushing softly across his face.

The woman started swimming again. John rocked gently in her arms. The regular motion and the comfort and warmth he felt from being held firmly against her soft body lulled him off to sleep. His last semi-coherent thought was that he was being abducted by a mermaid, it must be a dream.

- - -

Andrei listened to the droning assembly with growing impatience. Every visit to the Hall of the King was effectively the same. There were more people each time, an ever increasing rainbow of colours as more samudraka from distant places joined the throng, but that only meant that these interminable discussions went on longer and longer. But, however much the discussions continued, there was no progress. No change.

But there was one change this time. They had left John back on the island. Polyphemo had assured them that John would come to no harm, and there seemed no point in trying to rouse him for another pointless excursion into the depths of the mountain. Senna had tried to tell John where they were going, but it was doubtful whether he had woken enough to hear properly.

There was nothing they could do for John. Even if they hadn't been stuck here, what could they possibly do?

Senna touched Andrei's arm, and whispered, "She's not there today."

Andrei looked across to one side of the throne where they had usually been able to see a pale face looking out over the crowd. Senna was certain it had been a woman.

"Maybe she got bored with it all too," Andrei muttered. He turned his attention back to the crowd.

Their small group had been pushed off to one side near the front, not far from the large leaves where the elders of the Marr arranged themselves for the convenience of the regent. The floor of the hall angled up steeply near the sides, so they were left with a good view of the crowd, and vice versa. However careless of what was up and what was down the samudraka may be outside, inside the hall they all hovered near the floor. Only when the regent left his position on the highest leaf before the throne did this adherence to protocol relax. And, Andrei noticed, this young regent rarely did that, apparently satisfied that the people should be reminded where the true power currently lay. Andrei couldn't tell whether this was confidence in his position, or if he thought the reminder was necessary.

On their earlier visits Andrei and Senna had amused themselves by trying to determine what they could about the different samtaana, the communities of samudraka, represented by the people in front of them. They hadn't been able to work out if there was any significance to the colours and markings of the different people. It was obvious early on that most samtaana were male-dominated, it was only in later meetings that a few groups turned up with a roughly equal proportion of women.

Another thing they had noticed was that there were no elders among the visitors. The only elders present were those of the Marr, seated with Theseo at the front. And while Theseo sometimes consulted them privately, the elders otherwise took no part in the discussions. The visiting samudraka ignored them.

Andrei spotted an unusual group, one of the rare mixed-sex groups, these ones were a deep yellow-brown, mottled with irregular black stripes. He glanced around before remembering that John wasn't with them. "Garn the Tigers," he said quietly anyway.

"What?" Senna asked.

Andrei pointed. "Wasn't that John's favourite football team, the Tigers?"

Senna smiled weakly.

"Maybe that's what we're waiting for, some sort of grand final game."

"I think you're holding the prize," Sarva reminded him.

Andrei grimaced. Not that he wouldn't be happy to hand over the sword, but he could guess that it wasn't going to be that simple. Not for the first time, he wished he had never picked the damn thing up.

Coming softly up from one of the tiger-women, Andrei heard, "Why doesn't Theseo just take it and be done?"

Good question, Andrei agreed.

The response, if there was one, was too quiet for him to hear, and the group moved away. The entire assembly seemed in constant flux, and the colours of the people made swirling patterns in the crowd. It looked like they were being driven by random currents boiling up around them.

"Kill them without touching it, that's the answer," Andrei heard from a samudraka man, one of the group with skin the colour of human blood mixed with water.

Is that *us* you're talking about? Andrei wanted to ask.

"Let the aaranya suffer their papayamala," came from a lime-green man, "they are of no concern to us."

Later another voice asked, "What if they don't stay on the land?"

"They're cowards, they'll never brave the deeps," another voice said.

"We don't all live as deep as you do," responded another.

Hearing such snippets of conversation only made it all the more frustrating. Sometimes there was enough to tell what subject each group was discussing, but there was never enough to be sure what the participants might conclude.

Andrei realised his hand was creeping back to the hilt of the zakti again and pulled it away. Most of their guard didn't pay much attention to them during these extended sessions, but Polyphemo kept a good eye on Andrei.

"You're the expert," Andrei whispered to Sarva. "Tell us what's going on."

Darnu and Senna leaned in to hear Sarva's response, Garjae stayed scowling at the back.

Sarva was uncomfortable with the request. "I'm not an expert, Andrei. I'm only guessing."

There was a snort from Garjae, intended as a remark on the reliability of Sarva's guesses. Andrei placed his hand on Senna's arm to stop her responding.

Sarva appeared not to notice Garjae's input. "There seems to be something complicating the selection of a new king. I'm guessing it's related to that," Sarva pointed to the sword at Andrei's side. "I think Theseo is the prime candidate, but there is doubt."

Senna intercepted Andrei's hand as it dropped reflexively to the hilt.

"I think there is another candidate with a strong following." Sarva nodded toward a group made up of mainly the blood-red samudraka. "I've been watching the dance, and I think his support has been growing."

Andrei looked out over the assembly, trying to see what Sarva had seen. If it was there, Andrei couldn't tell. It all looked random to him, like minnows mixing in a shallow pool.

"From the few comments I've picked up, there's also a timing issue involved," Sarva continued, "but I don't know what that is. It's like some are not really convinced that Holitto is gone, that he might yet return."

"I'm happy to give the sword to anyone that wants to go and look," Andrei said hopefully.

Sarva shook his head. "That's not going to work. I think most *are* convinced, even if they won't admit it openly, and your Zak is the main reason."

"It's not mine," Andrei insisted.

"It is. Everyone here knows it. They saw it glowing in your hand when you raised it." Sarva paused before adding in defeated tones, "And, for better or worse, I've confused it further by talking about the papayamala."

Another, louder, snort from Garjae. This time Andrei caught Senna as she turned and kissed her hard on the lips. She pushed him away, glared at Garjae, but ended up not saying anything.

"The possibility of battle has excited some of them," Darnu noted.

Sarva nodded. "I think so. But that has put its own imperative on this assembly. You can almost feel the growing impatience for some action to be taken, but I have no idea what they will decide to act on first."

"Choosing a king, surely," Andrei said.

"Maybe."

"If elders can compel the stand – the samtaana," Senna corrected herself, "then why don't they step in and just sort it out, rather than have all ... this."

"Most of the time, the elders of the aaranya choose not to exert their power," Sarva explained, "I can only guess the same must be true here."

The assembly drew to a close with a few non-committal words from the regent, and the samudraka began to leave the hall. The regent and the elders left using some path hidden off to one side behind the throne. Andrei and the others were forced to wait with their guards until the hall had been emptied.

The group remained mostly silent as they ascended through the lush mountain paths. Garjae was always silent on these journeys, but Andrei wondered if the others were caught up in the same thoughts as he – grateful to be leaving yet another pointless assembly of samudraka, but dreading what they would find when they returned to their strange desert island. Would John be awake? Would he ever wake again? To have come all this way with his strange human friend and have it come out like this. It was so unfair. And still they were caught up with the samudraka. Andrei's hand dropped to the hilt of the zakti and gripped it tightly in frustration.

The last part of the journey was outside the mountain, as usual, and as usual the guards stopped below the surface. They preferred to avoid the surface when they could, letting the prisoners continue on their own.

Garjae, also as usual, was the first to break the surface and the first to swim to the island, but Andrei wasn't far behind and Senna swam at his side. Garjae walked up onto the beach and stopped. Andrei strode past him, anxious about his friend.

There was no one there.

Andrei ran up the loose sand to the central, lonely tree, and looked around the small island in disbelief. "John!" he called out loudly. "John!" Andrei scanned the water around the island looking for some sign, but the water was empty. The gentle swell of the ocean was as it always was, they had not yet seen it broken by storm, not even rain. "John!"

"Andrei," Senna called for his attention. She was pointing to the sand on the east side.

He walked to where she indicated. Light drag marks in the sand led down to the beach. Had John dragged himself down to the water? Andrei didn't think so, he was sure John no longer had the strength for that.

There could be only one explanation. Andrei pulled the zakti from its sheath and waded into the water.

"Andrei! Andrei, wait!" he heard Senna call, but he ignored her.

The sword made swimming more difficult, but he didn't put it away.

"Polyphemo!" Andrei yelled as loudly as he could, it was almost a scream. "Polyphemo!"

He saw the dark Marr guards swimming up from the mountain, Polyphemo at the point.

"What did you do with him!" Andrei yelled at Polyphemo. "Where is he?"

As he drew closer, Polyphemo had a look of puzzlement on his face.

"Don't feign stupid with me, fishtail! Where did you take him?"

"Andrei?" Sarva called from behind. Andrei didn't look around, he was too busy glaring at Polyphemo. The other guards had fanned out around their leader, their double-ended spears held at the ready.

"Where is he?" Andrei yelled again. He lifted the zakti and pointed it at Polyphemo. Andrei noted absently that the zakti was glowing brightly, as it had only done before in the Hall of the King.

Polyphemo and the other guards weren't far from Andrei now, and they pulled back slightly, a look of fear and surprise on their faces.

"We want him back!" Andrei yelled. The frustrated and helpless anger wasn't letting him go.

"Who?"

"I said don't play stupid!" Andrei swam forward waving the zakti clumsily in front of him.

The guards began to close in around him, but Polyphemo fell back and shouted harsh commands to his guards. They moved away. Andrei didn't watch them, but he could sense their attention turning to Sarva and the others behind him. He didn't think about that, he concentrated on Polyphemo.

"You'd better not have harmed him!"

"Go back to your island," Polyphemo commanded.

"I'll go when you bring him back." Andrei closed the distance again, the zakti waving wildly.

"Put that away."

"I'll put it somewhere!" Andrei thrust forward.

Polyphemo slid easily out of the way. He swung the flat side of his spear point down against Andrei's shoulder.

The pain burned along Andrei's arm and seemed to reach up into his head too, adding heat to his anger. He curled around, swinging the sword in a savage arc. But Polyphemo wasn't there. Andrei felt a strike on his other arm and lashed back the other way, again finding only water.

"Put the zakti away," Polyphemo called.

Andrei turned to the voice and swam in as hard as he could, thrusting again with the sword. And again he was struck with the flat of the spear. The advantage of not caring which way was up or down in the water was apparent to Andrei now. The fact that he was obviously being played with just made Andrei angrier. He ignored the next strike when it came and tried to slide and turn through the water at the same time, swinging the sword as strongly as he could.

The manoeuvre caught Polyphemo by surprise and he only just manage to drop one end of his spear to block the sword from slicing into his hip.

Andrei felt the blade catch, there was just a moment's hesitation in the movement, and then the end of the spear was carved away and the swing continued. The tip of the sword caught the edge of Polyphemo's tail as he was still twisting away. A line of gold appeared in the water like a contrail.

Andrei stared at the fluid in surprise and horror. The full impact of what he was doing finally came to him.

"Andrei!" Senna screamed.

Before he had any chance to respond he was buffeted by a blow to the side from Polyphemo's tail. Andrei thought his chest might collapse. He raised the sword to protect himself but couldn't even tell where Polyphemo was. Another blow swiped at his legs. Andrei swung the sword down low, and then looked up to see the point of Polyphemo's spear coming right at his face.

I really should have remembered that those things have two sharp ends, Andrei thought.

- - -

John woke to voices. There was black silk across his eyes, he couldn't see anyone. He tried to move his arms. The lower one was caught up somehow and couldn't move, the higher one moved slowly, weakly, and his fingers touched skin. He was lying against someone. He tried to remember where he was.

A woman spoke, something about Lord Theseo. Her voice was familiar and it came back to him. He was still in his dream. He was still in the arms of the mermaid. His hand stroked at the skin beneath his finger tips.

"My Lady," a man spoke with obvious deference.

There was a hard jerk and the hair lifted from his face as the woman moved rapidly on. John caught a brief glimpse of a dark samudraka, one of the Marr, watching as they passed.

"Stop fondling my breast," the woman demanded under her breath. "Men!"

John moved his hand away. He hadn't realised. He wanted to apologise. He started to try and speak, but then they entered a void. A place empty of any sensation except the woman that held him in her arms.

And then out again. It was cold here. And dark, as if he had been carried into the night. The water was slightly murky, not as clear as where they'd come from, and occasionally he caught glimpses of larger things, strange things, that he couldn't identify. Not that he was seeing much as the woman's hair floated back and forth across his face. The steady rocking movement claimed him again and he closed his eyes.

When John opened his eyes again he was looking up into a golden face surrounded by a cloud of black hair with gold highlights. She looked familiar. He had the impression she had just shaken him by the shoulders.

"Can you stay awake?" the woman asked.

It was still his mermaid, but her colour had changed.

"Can you stay awake?" the woman asked again.

"Yes ... maybe," John managed to whisper.

"Remove your clothes."

John wasn't sure he'd heard right.

"Your clothes," the woman insisted. "This will work better in your naked form."

John dropped his eyes and saw that the woman had transformed again, she was floating naked above him. Her legs, her entire body, glowing a soft golden colour.

Her hand moved his face back so that John's eyes met hers. "Yes, I'm exposed. Forget that and listen to me."

John managed to nod his head.

"Now. Your clothes."

He concentrated and eventually felt the change.

The woman's eyes moved down over his body. "Better," she nodded. She made a few light movements with her hands and feet and was soon kneeling beside him. It was only now that John realised that his body, mostly weightless in the water, was resting lightly against something. The woman helped him to bend forward and John was at last able to take in his surroundings.

They had settled on a dark rock platform, and before them lay a sea of deep gold. An aura, like a pale mist, rose from this sea at the bottom of the sea, and it was this that had imparted its sheen to the woman beside him. John's eyes wandered over his own body and saw that it had taken on similar tones.

"Sarasi-jilvana," the woman said. "It is a pool of life. It is where we bring those that are injured or weak, and where lovers come when they want help to spark new life. Perhaps it can serve you too."

She reached across and turned John's face to hers. "But you must stay awake and be ready. There is danger above," she indicated the blackness of the ocean above them, "and below."

"What—?" John managed.

"Never mind. I'll be here, just be ready." She knelt next to him and slid him feet first out from the dark rock.

The surface of the golden pool was warm against his skin. Although the surface felt soft and velvety, he did not sink into it. The woman continued to push him out onto the surface until it felt like he was sitting over a warm air vent.

He felt her touch leave his back and turned his head slowly to watch her. She moved herself lightly off the rock and then, grasping at the edge of it for leverage, forced her legs into the pool. Once she had herself immersed to her waist, she turned back to John and pushed his legs down.

John gasped in surprise. This was a pool of soft mud, or something like it, and the heat of it below the surface was like stepping into a hot bath.

The woman kept pushing at John's body until he was submerged to his neck. Each time she raised her arm from the pool the gold streamed back with barely a ripple, leaving no trace on her skin. John looked at her standing next to him, immersed to her waist in the pool. The golden aura of the pool glowed against the bottom of her breasts and her jaw. She wasn't watching John now, her eyes were scanning the surface of the pool and occasionally glanced up into the darkness of the ocean.

John looked away from the woman and out across the deep gold of the pool, and the pale gold aura above it. With his eyes this close to the surface he couldn't see far through the aura, but looking upward he could see the gold tinged darkness above him. There wasn't much to see, and he wondered what dangers the woman was searching for.

John recognised the heat of the pool as coming from the intensity of the life, the prana that it carried; it wasn't really hot, not as he would have recognised it when he had a human body. Could such a place offer anything for him? Back in the Samgha, Ben had told John that the Initiation Room wouldn't work after his saarvaya body developed its tough outer skin. But this was different. It felt stronger. Like a hot bath, John could feel the heat seeping into him, and he hoped that meant the life of the pool was feeding him, sustaining him, giving him more time.

And also like a hot bath, it was relaxing. John felt his eyes begin to droop. He knew he should stay awake, the woman had told him it was dangerous here, but he was tired. His eyes closed. I'll just rest them for a moment, he thought, half-expecting the woman to shake him or rouse him, but she said nothing. Maybe she wasn't watching.

- - -

The tip of the spear came at him in slow motion, but however slow it came, Andrei couldn't move fast enough to evade it. He was frozen in place by surprise, both at the spear and at his own actions that had led to this moment.

"Hold!" a voice came faintly but distinctly, yelled from a distance.

The command was too late to stop the thrust of the spear, there was no pulling it back, but at the last moment it turned slightly and Andrei felt the flat of it slide along his cheek.

It seemed like only a moment later that Polyphemo was floating calmly in front of Andrei, the remaining blade of his spear held inches above Andrei's arm, the one that still held the zakti – which was almost as much of a surprise to Andrei as everything else.

"Put Zamayitar away," Polyphemo said quietly but firmly, showing no sign that the fight had been any effort. "Slowly and carefully, but do it now."

Andrei did as he was bid and his thoughts finally caught up with him. He had started all this because he wanted to know where John was. There was a chance, he admitted to himself, that he may have overdone it – just a bit.

"Where is John?" Andrei asked. "Where's our friend?"

Polyphemo ignored him.

Andrei looked back and could see that the other guards were holding his friends back at spear point. Darnu and Sarva had hold of Senna.

"What were you doing?" Senna mouthed at him.

Andrei raised his hands in a shrug.

"Stay still," Polyphemo warned.

"Fall back, Polyphemo," the voice came again.

Andrei glanced down. It was Theseo with a phalanx of dark Marr guards arrayed behind him.

"What were you thinking?" Theseo asked Polyphemo as he drew close.

Polyphemo bowed his head but did not answer.

231

"You were Holitto's friend," Theseo continued. "Do you really think he'd want me to have to kill you?"

"No, my Lord," Polyphemo said quietly.

Andrei couldn't quite believe it, but he actually felt sorry for Polyphemo. This huge man, that Andrei had been intent on trying to kill just moments ago, now so submissive before his regent.

"It was my fault, Lord Theseo," Andrei said, looking the young regent in the eye.

"I know that," Theseo replied, "but that wouldn't have changed anything. I would still have had to kill my brother's best friend."

Andrei bowed his head, and in doing so saw the gold of the prana still pooling in the water as it seeped from Polyphemo's injured tail. "I am sorry about that," he said quietly.

"Rejoin your friends," Theseo told Andrei.

Andrei returned to the others. Senna came to him, her expression a mix of anger and concern. She ran her fingers lightly over his cheek. Andrei flinched in pain and pulled back. Her finger tips were coated with prana.

"He got me?" Andrei noted in surprise. He remembered feeling the blade of the spear, but hadn't realised that it had actually cut him.

"He almost killed you, you idiot," Senna whispered to him harshly.

"Yeah, I suppose."

Senna cuffed him on the arm.

"Ow!" Andrei complained, she had struck a place already bruised by Polyphemo's spear.

"If you're going to play warrior, you're going to have to do better than that," Sarva said.

"I just ..." Andrei trailed off. He wasn't sure what he'd been thinking.

"Sarva!" Polyphemo called.

They all turned.

"Lord Theseo would speak with you – privately." Polyphemo didn't look happy as he indicated Theseo swimming away on his own.

Sarva swam out after the regent.

"You others return to the island and wait," Polyphemo demanded.

"What about—?" Andrei started.

"Now!"

Senna grabbed Andrei and started dragging him.

"Ow," Andrei complained again. More and more bits of him were starting to hurt.

"Wimp," Senna said, and pulled him harder.

They sat on the island and watched the sun set. It was unusual because there were clouds gathered on the western horizon, and the sky glowed red for a long time before it went dark. A long time later Sarva finally climbed the beach and joined them.

"Well?" Andrei asked when Sarva appeared reluctant to speak.

"There's some good news and some bad news," Sarva started. "The good news is that John has not been harmed. Lord Theseo tells me that he has been taken somewhere that may help him to survive longer."

"They might have said something," Andrei said.

"Lord Theseo had intended to be here before us but got delayed."

"And almost got Andrei killed as a result," Senna said.

"Andrei almost got Andrei killed," Garjae corrected her.

"Theseo said that, because of what happened," Sarva hurried on to stop an argument, "they would probably keep John as a hostage to our good behaviour. Theseo probably planned that anyway. I think he still has doubts whether John will live, and this way he can pretend to still have John and avoid us getting upset over his loss."

"How do we know they're treating him anyway?" Darnu asked.

"They could have just taken him away to die elsewhere," Garjae added.

"I believe Theseo," Sarva answered.

"Why?" Senna asked.

"That's the other good news. He does want our help, and we're more likely to give it if he can keep John alive and prove it to us when the time comes. He's trying to convince the samudraka to follow him as regent in a fight against the papayamala *before* they decide on a new king. But that's going to be difficult."

"If it's so hard why not do it the other way around?" Andrei asked, dreading the answer.

"That's the bad news," Sarva admitted. "Firstly, it's not clear that Theseo has the support needed to claim the throne. If he tries as things are now then he might start a war among the samudraka of this ocean. That's why they're all so careful of the zakti. If the wrong samudraka gets it, even by accident, it could spark a war. A war that Theseo might not win, and a war that might delay action against the papayamala, perhaps for years."

"And?" Andrei prompted.

"And, secondly, to claim the throne means taking possession of Zamayitar – it is the king's sword. Whoever has it *is* the king, if they can hold on to it."

"He can have it any time he wants it," said Andrei.

Sarva shook his head. "He must take possession of it, and the only way to do that is to fight for it, and *kill* the one who possesses it."

Andrei swallowed and thought that one over.

"But ..." Senna started.

"Yes," Sarva said. "The same will be true even after any battle with the papayamala."

"So I die whichever way it comes out?" Andrei said quietly.

"Sooner or later, yes," agreed Sarva. "Theseo seemed to think you'd prefer later. He hoped that the concession would be enough to convince us to help him anyway."

"Later is good," said Andrei.

"So Andrei is technically the king now?" Darnu said.

"I don't think the samudraka see it that way," said Sarva. "He's merely an inconvenience."

"Thanks," muttered Andrei, though he understood well enough. Even with a sword that could cut through Polyphemo's spear he was no match for the samudraka, probably any samudraka. He simply didn't have the skills or speed and agility in the water to come close. Just seconds after Polyphemo had stopped playing with Andrei, he would have been dead – if it hadn't been for the timely intercession of the regent.

"There's something I still don't understand," said Darnu.

"What?" Sarva asked.

"If they distrust the aaranya so much, why are they willing to accept our story? Why do they believe us at all?"

"Because we are not the first they've heard of these papayamala."

- - -

John knew this dream, it was one of his favourites. He was sitting

234

in the deep bath of his home, it was filled almost to the brim with hot water. Such use was extravagant, but he'd worry about that later. He lay his human body back against Asha and felt her breasts pressing against him as her arms wound themselves around his chest. Her presence was a warmth and comfort that went far beyond that of the hot water. But her arms kept tightening around him, tugging at him, pulling him free of the water. "No!" Asha was shouting. "You are not my shield! I won't let you." John struggled against her hold, he had to protect her. "No! Stop that!" Asha yelled at him, her hold tightening further. "Stop—"

"Stop that!" a woman's voice growled at him. It wasn't Asha. It wasn't Asha's arms around him. It wasn't Asha that he could feel pressing against his back.

It was cold now. John's eyes opened to darkness and confusion. A streak of red coming swiftly out of the darkness above. Rapid rhythmic motion as he was pulled backwards through the water. Large, glowing white teeth in a gaping mouth rushing toward him. A shadow passing over him. His legs knocking against rock. And then stopping. The woman's arms holding him still.

Loud screeching; a ringing, rasping call that rose in volume and echoed in John's head. It was unlike anything he'd heard before, some harsh merging of a bird of prey and he didn't know what. Something huge and red began passing the entrance to their shelter and the sound diminished. The streaking red continued like a long freight train going past, and then vanished.

"Mahasarpa," the woman spoke next to John's ear. She released her hold and explained, "A great serpent. Perhaps the one that took my husband. You have been honoured."

Outside their shelter was the flat rock platform where John had rested sometime earlier. He hadn't seen this cave then, though he supposed it made sense to pick a place like this if you were expecting visitors like that. He turned around. The cave was large, though the opening was, thankfully, quite small. It was formed from an apparently random pile of huge slabs of rock. The interior glowed a faint green, picked out here and there with other colours from small, formless creatures that moved slowly over the rock surfaces.

The woman was half-floating, half-standing in front of him. He didn't know how he could have mistaken this woman for Asha, even in his dream. Asha was finely built, she looked fragile, felt fragile in his arms. This woman was full figured and strongly built. There was nothing fragile in her appearance, nor in the strength he had felt from her as she pulled him into this refuge. He watched as a silver patch appeared low on her belly, it spread out and down. Her legs were pulled tightly together as it bound them inside the tough looking skin of her tail. More slowly, the skin, looking thinner and translucent, stretched up and over the lower part of her breasts, just covering her nipples.

"Is that less distracting?" the woman asked him.

Not a lot, John thought, but said quietly, "Sorry." He met her eyes and saw amusement in them. "Who are you?" he asked.

"Lantea," she replied. "Who are you? Sarva has, conveniently I think, never introduced you."

"John," he answered, and then wondered if that would give away his origins.

Lantea raised her eyebrows. "And what are you?"

"Saarvaya."

"So Sarva said, but I have a feeling that's not really an answer."

"Where are my friends?" John asked, avoiding the question.

"Back where we left them. They haven't been harmed."

"And me?"

"You haven't been harmed either. Don't you feel stronger now?"

John nodded. He did feel much better. Still not strong, but definitely better. "Why are you helping me?"

"I suggested to my son that this might be a good idea."

"I don't understand."

"Come back to the pool. Perhaps talking will help you to stay awake this time."

They returned to the pool. John looked up nervously for any sign of the serpent.

"She's gone for now," Lantea assured him.

"She?"

Lantea nodded. "The females are the largest."

John peered across the pool. He thought he could discern cliffs rising above them in the distant darkness. "Where are we?" he asked. "Is this a zarana, or is it the real world?"

"It's all real." Lantea looked at him sharply, wondering at his choice of words.

"I mean ... is this the outside? Could I swim up there," he pointed up into the darkness, "and find my home?"

"If you could make it," Lantea acknowledged. "We call this andhakara-nitya – the eternal dark ocean. The sun never reaches here."

John shook his head. "Why would you choose to be away from the sun? Isn't it the source of all life?"

"Perhaps, but everything falls, even the life raised by the sun. Everything, eventually, falls into the andhakara-nitya. Everything serves the serpent – and the samudraka."

Lantea paused and indicated the deep golden pool before them. "This pool is just one example of what falls from the sun above. Frail physical bodies were crushed long before they reached this depth, the residue, still full of the life that once animated such a delicate material existence, accumulates and concentrates and provides for the creatures of the andhakara-nitya, both praanin and material. Enter now, and if you stay awake this time, you will see the creatures that come to this pool to draw on its life."

John pushed himself slowly down into the golden mud, the heat of its life as strong and welcoming as before. Lantea joined him in the pool. He was very conscious of her nakedness and tried to keep his eyes averted.

"Why do you enter too?" he asked.

"So I can tell if there are jaluda or kravyada about. Creatures of the pool that may undo all the good we are trying to achieve. Until you are stronger and better acquainted with the hazards it is best if I keep watch with you."

"Thanks." John kept his eyes on the pool, as if searching for the creatures she had mentioned, though he had no idea what they were.

"Do I really make you that uncomfortable?" Lantea asked.

"I love another. I doubt Asha would approve."

"Only if you find me attractive, surely."

John didn't answer that, he didn't think he needed to.

"My kind would not approve either, especially not with a videzaka, which is why I insisted that I do this alone. Normally the samudraka only expose themselves to their lovers. But my legs are hidden within the pool now, is that not acceptable?"

John glanced at her and then away again. "It wasn't just your legs I was noticing," he admitted.

"Oh." Lantea laughed. "My breasts too. At my age I am flattered to find that a man still finds them attractive."

"There are few who wouldn't," John said, and then bit his tongue.

"Among the samudraka it is exposing the legs that is considered private. The breasts are less so, although most well-bred women still show some reserve. ... Is this better?"

John looked back. Lantea had pulled herself lower into the mud so that her breasts were mostly covered, though she remained close. "I suppose it depends on what you mean by better?"

She smiled.

John sought for a more comfortable topic of conversation. "How long was I asleep last time?"

"More than a day, close to two."

"And you watched over me all that time, and didn't wake me."

"There wasn't much point, you would only have drifted off again."

John was surprised to find that he wasn't feeling sleepy. The heat of the pool, while still relaxing, was also invigorating. After a pause, during which they both scanned the dark waters above them, John asked, "Can you explain what's happening? I have trouble understanding the ways of the narun, even when I'm well."

Lantea stared at him and John realised he'd said more than he should. Apparently deciding to ignore it, Lantea began, "You and your friends arrived at a difficult time for Agadharastra – this kingdom."

She picked something small out of the mud and tossed it through the water – it didn't go far before it disappeared back into the pool without a ripple.

"My husband died almost a year ago, he was taken by the serpent," she continued. "He was older than I, but still too young. It should not have happened when it did, Holitto was not ready."

John tried to piece together what she was saying. "Holitto? The king?"

"Poseitto, my husband, was his father."

"You were the queen? Are the queen?"

"There are no queens in Agadharastra, not while the Marr rule. I

238

was merely the king's woman, accorded respect, but that is all. And there is little enough of that now he is gone."

"But you are not of the Marr," John said. That much seemed obvious.

"I am of the Yezova, from the north. I was Poseitto's second wife. Many of the Marr did not approve, but Poseitto was always one to take what he wanted. And I did not mind, he was charismatic and treated me well. I loved him in my fashion.

"Holitto was the son of his first wife. He was big and strong and enthusiastic, and charismatic like his father, but not all that bright. Theseo is my son. He is wiser, but still young. He is the reason I have stayed with the Marr since Poseitto died."

"So Theseo will be king next, now that Holitto is gone?" John asked.

"It's not that simple, especially not now. First the people must accept that Holitto will not return."

"Why was he there? Why would anyone hazard the nirarkta?"

"The king must possess Zamayitar and a nikasa. The zakti is his power, the touchstone his wisdom. The true king must gain each for himself.

"My husband was mortally injured in a struggle with a great serpent. Holitto was there and did what was expected of him; he took what remained of his father's life and gained possession of Zamayitar. Poseitto's body was left for the serpent, and Holitto was king – provisionally. He would only be fully accepted when he had obtained his nikasa."

"Couldn't he take his father's stone?"

"Tradition demands that the old king's stone is left untouched, the new king must seek his own."

"A sort of rite of passage?" John queried, trying to understand.

"Partly. The stones have real value, but they only work for the one that first touches them."

"And the stones come from the zarana of the nirarkta?"

Lantea nodded. "Poseitto told me that you have to get to the surface, above the caves and tunnels where the nirarkta live, and there, on the cold and desolate rock plains, bathed in moonlight, lie countless of the stones. He told me how he was tempted to carry an armful back with him but, in the end, he followed tradition and ventured out across the plains until he found one that drew his gaze. He touched only that one, picking it up to bring back with him."

"And that's what Holitto was trying to do?"

"Yes. It can only be done at upapaurnamasi. Only with the full moon has the water risen enough to make passage to the surface possible."

"And so he also had to face the nirarkta to get there."

Lantea nodded again. Her face twisted into a grimace and she raised herself partly out of the mud. "The jaluda have moved in, we must find another place." She pulled one breast inwards and showed John a small leech-like creature clinging to her side. She grasped it with her fingers and pulled it away, a faint trace of gold stained the water where it had attached itself.

Lantea pulled herself from the pool and turned back to help John pull himself free. They spent a few minutes checking for jaluda. John found one on his inner-thigh and another on his stomach. Pulling them away stung sharply for a moment, but the pain didn't last. Each creature was thrown back down into the pool.

"You check my back, and I'll do yours," Lantea told him and turned her back.

John found one creature low down on one side and pulled it free. Otherwise her back was smooth and perfect.

"What about lower down?" Lantea asked. "It feels like there's something ..." She waved her hand vaguely.

John looked but could see nothing untoward.

"Lower," Lantea said.

"I ..." John wavered, feeling embarrassed.

She turned and lifted his head. "You are fun to tease."

John turned his back without comment. He felt her remove two of the creatures from his back.

They found another place not far from where they had been settled. "The jaluda are slow to move, we should be safe here for a time," Lantea told him.

"Since Holitto hasn't come back, doesn't that make Theseo the new king?" John asked, still trying to work out what they'd come into the middle of, and wanting the conversation to remain away from less appropriate topics.

"It's not that simple. First we must wait the required time. Holitto was already later than expected. He had not returned while the first moon was high, so everyone thought he would return with the next ... but you and your friends showed up instead.

"Tradition would have us wait for the passing of another two upapaurnamasi, but your friend was carrying Zamayitar and now many argue that there is no need to wait."

"And then Theseo would be king," John pressed.

"Perhaps. If he were full-blooded Marr he might have been quickly accepted. But he is very young and untried, and he is my son. His skin is pale, and this is his true liability. Having him nominated as regent by Holitto was acceptable, it was only a formality for the short time Holitto was to be away. But now ... Theseo does not even have the full support of the Marr, let alone their usual allies, and our rivals – the Raktana – are using this to make a bid for the throne."

"But wouldn't the Marr prefer Theseo to losing the throne altogether."

"That is the only reason it has not fallen to the Raktana already."

"And the zakti, Zamayitar?" John asked.

"If any samudraka were to take Zamayitar, other than one already accepted as the rightful king, it could bring war to the samudraka."

"And even when that happens they still have to find a touchstone?"

"A nikasa, yes. And who said videzaka were stupid?"

They remained silent for a long time. John was thinking about what he'd learned, and wondering what it meant for him and his friends. The jaluda found them again and they exited the pool.

Lantea pointed up into the darkness. "Mahasarpa is hunting."

John could just make out a distant red line in the darkness.

They retreated to the cave where Lantea merged with the water to sleep. John tried to cram himself into a niche, first moving a couple of the formless blobs that were roaming over the surface of the rock. Feeling a little less like he might float away, John managed to sleep.

- - -

Andrei faced Polyphemo, both were floating in the water well below the surface. Forming a large sphere around them floated Andrei's friends and the rest of the guard. Polyphemo held the shaft of a spear, the ends shaped roughly like a spear blade, but blunt and the tips rounded. Andrei held a smaller shaft shaped roughly like a sword, but it too was blunt.

"Stop looking for the sky," Polyphemo told him. "It makes you predictable and weak."

Andrei stopped trying to orient himself, but turned, as Polyphemo had shown him, so that he was facing in the direction of his opponent.

This had all been Theseo's bright idea. He had seen enough of the earlier fight between Andrei and Polyphemo to see just how seriously outclassed Andrei had been. When the time came for Theseo to take the Zamayitar, honour demanded that the event bore some resemblance to a fight rather than a slaughter. Andrei bore the bruises that testified to Polyphemo being just as unhappy to be the teacher as Andrei was to be the student.

Polyphemo jabbed forward with his spear and Andrei tried again to swipe across it. He was too slow and the rounded tip of the spear struck his chest. Andrei backed away, rubbing at the bruise.

"I keep telling you, *trail* and then slice," Polyphemo said loudly. "The sword is not an ideal weapon for this sort of combat, you must learn to overcome its deficiencies. Stop trying to swing it out wide, that's too slow. Let the blade trail and *then* slice it down. You need speed of arm and strength of wrist."

"Yeah, yeah," Andrei muttered under his breath. He was getting mighty sick of this. He had bruises on his bruises and seemed to be getting worse rather than better.

"Polyphemo," Sarva called from the side. "Maybe that's enough for now. I think Andrei's too tired to learn much more right now."

Polyphemo studied Andrei for a moment then nodded.

Sarva swam up and reached out for Polyphemo's practice weapon. "May I?" he asked.

"There's no point practising up there," Polyphemo said. "Waving around in the air while he's standing on the ground will just reinforce his bad habits."

"I know. But maybe we can offer something a bit more gentle. Something to warm him up for your next session."

Polyphemo looked doubtful but handed over the shaft. "If you think it might help."

Back on the island they settled on the beach. Andrei looked

himself over. He had fashioned himself a pair of tight fitting shorts for modesty, Polyphemo had pointed out that more complex clothes would only slow down his movement in the water. Wherever Andrei looked there were blotches coming out as bruises.

"I don't see the point of all this," Andrei grumbled. "Theseo wants me trained up so he can feel better about killing me. What's in it for me?"

"Maybe if you get good enough you can win?" Senna said, trying to sound optimistic. She was no happier about Andrei's position than he was.

"Andrei, King of the Samudraka," said Sarva. "Has a nice ring to it."

"That's not how it would go, and you know it," Garjae said.

Sarva glanced across at him and then back to Andrei. He shrugged. "Garjae's right. Even if you do win, there will be another challenger. They will never accept you as king."

"I don't want to be their bloody king anyway." Andrei struck the sand with the practice shaft.

"Can I see that?" Darnu asked. Andrei passed the shaft across. "I wonder what they grow this from," Darnu said, turning it over in his hand.

Andrei got the zakti back from Senna, who had been holding it for him during practice. He felt somehow reassured by its touch. "And I don't particularly want to kill Theseo." He rubbed a spot on his chest. "Though I suppose I might warm up to the idea after a few more of these sessions."

- - -

John and Lantea continued their routine, time in the pool and retreating to the cave for rest and safety as needed. And through it all they talked. John tried to keep the conversation directed at Lantea and the samudraka as much as he could, but guessed that his own ignorance of life as a narun was showing through anyway.

He discovered that the kravyada he had been warned about were a small praanin fish-like creature with a body shaped like the spear blade of the samudraka. They had a nasty bite. They lived mostly in the mud itself and didn't move very quickly through it, so they weren't a big danger unless you got trapped by a school of them. He also saw many creatures come down to the pool, like animals to a

243

waterhole. Some appeared to drink from it, others immersed themselves for periods of time, as if taking a bath.

Most of the material creatures were small simple things, he thought they looked liked bloated amoeba or something. A few looked like simple plants that moved slowly through the debris. Lantea said that some zarana, like her original home, opened to water not so deep as here, and there they saw a greater variety of material creatures. But at this depth the greatest variety was with the praanin creatures. Some moved along the seafloor, John was particularly taken with a large yellow-brown creature that waddled along like a wombat when it was browsing for things in the sediment. Other creatures were obviously designed only for swimming – if they were designed for anything, there were some very peculiar creatures among them.

John caught several glimpses of the great serpent, Mahasarpa. The head, strongly defined and angular, was slightly larger than the body. The jaws projected forward, finishing in a rounded snout. The creature was narrower through the body than it was high and about a third of the way back the body narrowed further. The dorsal fin, not very high, started where the body narrowed and continued in an even line to the tail. The fin looked like a delicate membrane, supported at intervals by spines that extended above the line of the fin, ending in a short, sharp spike. A similar long fin ran beneath the body. The spines of the tail fin projected further, looking like an array of spears. A pair of small pectoral fins protruded a short distance behind the head, low on the body, and these too had sharp spines projecting beyond the fin. The shape put John in mind of pictures he had seen of eels, if eels could grow over a hundred metres in length. But unlike an eel, the skin on the serpent was covered in large scales like those John had always envisaged on dragons in fantasy stories. With its bright red sheen it was a stunning creature, he might have considered it beautiful if it wasn't so intent on eating him.

Days passed and occasionally a small samudraka woman would arrive, always the same one, one of the Marr, and Lantea would go out to speak with her.

After one such visit, as they settled back into the pool, John said, "I'm feeling pretty good now. When do you think I can go back to my friends?"

"Best not to rush it," Lantea said. "Otherwise you'll just have to hurry back, and I don't want to have to carry you all the way again."

John nodded, but with reservations. Getting better was a two-edged sword. The pool was now having the same effect that he felt when Asha would feed him. It hadn't the same fiery intensity, but he spent so much time in the pool that the sensations never got a chance to fade. He was feeling randy and it was getting embarrassing. Without that, he thought, he might have managed to get used to Lantea's often exposed presence, but instead he was finding it more and more difficult to pull his attention away from her. And Lantea knew it. All too often she could see it and she found many ways to tease him. There was no real need for her to enter the pool now, John could fend for himself, but she always did. John presumed that the pool must be having the same effect on her as it was on him, it probably had been from the start, but he'd been too weak to recognise it then.

In the never-ending search for topics to distract himself, John had started talking about Helix and the others. He wanted to know if the samudraka knew anything of them.

"Sarva originally came from the far south, near where you lived," Lantea said, "but he's lived up in the far north for some years?"

John nodded.

"But you've both met with the papayamala?"

"I've only met Sando. He can control minds somehow, force you to do things."

"But you were able to resist."

"Only just, and it wouldn't have been for long," John answered.

The samudraka had been given a carefully edited version of what John and his friends had witnessed. Sarva wanted the samudraka to take the threat seriously, so he told them as much as he could. There had been no mention of Ellie, or of Asha's ability as a healer, but he had explained that the papayamala were using humans. Much of John's side of the conversation with Lantea these past days had been talking about humans and what they could do now, he wasn't sure how much of it she believed.

Lantea asked, "None of you have met the fourth of the siblings?"

"If there is one."

"There is. A girl."

"You mean, because Helix is a girl?"

"No, I mean because I've met them," Lantea answered. She sighed. "It's over a hundred years ago now. I met them as not much more than babies."

"A hundred years? But Sando looked so young?"

"A more honourable man would have said that *I* couldn't possibly be a day over fifty," Lantea said, pretending to be offended.

John opened his mouth, but didn't know what to say, so closed it again.

Lantea laughed. "Never mind. You've missed your opportunity to flatter an old woman."

John just shook his head. Lantea was obviously not old, not in narun terms, and certainly not in appearance.

Lantea smiled at him. "I was very young when I met them. In my youth I decided that I wanted to swim across the ocean without using zarana. It was a very long journey."

"How do you know—?" John started.

"That these are the same people?"

John nodded.

"You described them; so pale of hair and skin. Two sets of twins of such similar ages and appearance, they must be the same. History tells us that such beings may not age the same as the rest of us."

"And where did you see them?"

On the other side of the ocean, far to the east."

"America?"

Lantea paused, and then answered, "I believe that's what the humans call it now."

"And what were they like?" John pushed on.

"Like I said, they weren't much more than babies. The brothers were identical, they were obviously twins. The girls didn't seem quite so much of a match, but I still think they were papayamala.

"The strange thing was that I wasn't appalled by them. I should have been. Everything I was brought up to believe should have been demanding that I kill them, but I was ... enchanted. I think now that that might be exactly what I was: under their power even when they were that young. They called themselves angels."

"Angels?"

Lantea nodded. "That word has special significance to humans I believe."

John nodded absently.

"One of the girls touched me. She spoke directly into my mind and warned me to go."

"She threatened you?"

"No. She said I was in danger from others there, and that I should leave. She said this directly into my mind, I don't think even her siblings heard her.

"It was enough. I left them there on the beach. Later, when I joined with Poseitto, I told him about them. He was angry at first that I didn't act when I could have, should have, but after he settled down he resolved to keep watch and warned the other zarana.

"So much time had passed that most hoped it had come to nothing. But it was not so long ago that it has been forgotten. That's why Theseo agreed to hear Sarva speak, and after hearing his description of the papayamala, why he was believed."

Lantea paused and her expression turned melancholy. "I don't think I could have killed those children anyway, even if I had broken the enchantment. They were beautiful. I just don't think I could have done it."

"It would have been wrong," John agreed.

But Lantea shook her head. "I know your kind believe that, but we samudraka know better. See what has become of leaving those children? Now the aaranya are being overrun and asking for the samudraka to come to their aid. The war we have feared for generations is returning."

John couldn't argue, but he couldn't agree either. He shook his head.

"I learned later," Lantea continued, "that I had entered an area of the ocean considered deadly to the samudraka. Few who have entered it ever return. Had I travelled through the zarana I would have been warned away."

"Do you think that's because of those children?"

"No. That area has been bad for a very long time. It's a line along the coast of that continent, mostly shallow and quite unstable, so it was of little interest to the samudraka. We never pay much attention to it. I think most believe the water there has been poisoned by the land somehow and so we simply avoid it."

John sat quiet for a while, thinking. Could this be what he needed? Could the siblings still be there? Could that be where they took Asha? How could he get Lantea to narrow down where she had seen them? With this pool she had given him back some time, but it would not be enough to search the entire east side of the Pacific Ocean.

Lantea leaned in close to him and John looked up in surprise. The blue of her large eyes seemed impossibly deep, and much too close. She rested one hand lightly on his chest beneath the level of the pool.

She whispered to him, "I have a secret that I have never told anyone, not even Poseitto. If I tell you mine, will you tell me yours?"

13. Trust

Tracey's bedroom was the only one that opened directly to the communal area. Cleaver's bedroom was down the hall across from the balcony. He claimed to be quite happy that his window gave a view over the city rather than the fake forest. The other two had their rooms off the corridor that ran down the side of the building. Tracey discovered that Aldercott's room was visible from her window, if you looked across the corner of the interior space, and presumably that meant he could see hers, so she had learned to pull her curtains. Hidden cameras were something she couldn't control, curtains she could. Mike's room was past Aldercott's.

There were other rooms here too, before you reached doors that wouldn't open. If you knocked on those doors a burly man would open it and ask if there was anything you wanted. Presumably it wasn't always the same man, but Tracey never bothered to try and pick the differences. Some of the other rooms were bedrooms, others were set up as meeting rooms or offices, and still others were empty. One large room, past Cleaver's bedroom, contained an assortment of gym equipment, it had one wall covered in mirrors – so you could watch yourself sweating.

Tracey tried to catch glimpses of the floors below, but rarely saw much. Cleaver said he thought they were mostly offices, they went quiet and dark after hours. The floor immediately below them appeared to be unused.

Their meals and supplies for the kitchen were delivered by dumbwaiter. As was anything else they asked for – within reason. Laundry came and went the same way. There was one telephone in the communal area, but it only connected to some anonymous voice that asked what they wanted. There was a large television in the communal area and a smaller one in each of the bedrooms. The television screens could be used as primitive Internet browsers but the options were limited and prevented them from sending messages.

It could have been very comfortable if it wasn't so obvious you were in a prison, and that you couldn't talk to anyone except your wardens.

Cleaver chafed, and for the first few days he kept badgering the guards at the doors, wanting to speak with whoever was in charge. Franklin Johnson eventually showed up briefly and tried to assure Cleaver that everything was all right. Cleaver wasn't convinced. Aldercott seemed to be avoiding Tracey, she didn't know why, though she sometimes thought he was watching her. And Mike avoided them all at first, sulking in his room or spending time in the gym.

They had been there a few weeks when Franklin Johnson showed up wanting to interview each of them. Aldercott went first. It didn't take long. When he came back he waved to Cleaver that it was his turn, then disappeared into his bedroom. Cleaver's interview took longer. When he came back down the corridor he was red in the face.

"Asquith's next," he told Tracey, waving her back into her seat. He went to tell Mike he was wanted.

When he came back he sat down heavily across from Tracey.

"I need a drink!" he said before Tracey could say anything, and got back up to get one.

"So?" Tracey asked.

"So nothing," Cleaver answered from the kitchen. "Rubbish. A complete waste of everyone's time."

"What did he want?"

"He wanted to know who else I'd told about all this. As if he doesn't know. He's job, even if no one else here is. He knows it all goes into the report, and you give a verbal to the boss. *And that's it.* It doesn't go anywhere else." Cleaver slumped back down, almost spilling his vodka – one of the few things he'd asked for specially. He drank it straight, it made Tracey shudder just to think of it.

"So there's nothing new. Nothing's changed?" Tracey asked,

knowing Cleaver would understand what she meant.

"Nada, nowt, zero, zip, squat," Cleaver answered. "Bupkes," he added as an afterthought.

Tracey wasn't sure what to say, but it didn't turn out to be a problem. Cleaver picked up the remote control and started flicking around the stations until he found an American football match. "Padded pansies," he muttered, and took a mouthful of his drink.

Obviously he didn't want to talk, so Tracey got up and went out to the balcony overlooking the rainforest. The afternoon was getting late already, and the birds were all chattering loudly, but it was better than listening to football. In a way it was almost peaceful.

A large green parrot with a blue head flew up out of the tree, it made a strange high squeaking call. Tracey watched as it tried to land against the mesh not far from her. It gave a deafening screech, as if in pain, and fell away before catching itself and flying back into the branches. Tracey peered after it, wondering if it was okay.

Something rattled the mesh not far below her balcony, and Tracey glanced down. The stick that must have caused it was still falling. Where had it come from? Then she heard a tapping noise. In past the leaves she thought she could make out some movement. The tapping was regular, like a slow drumbeat. Hadn't she seen something about parrots that tapped out messages or something with sticks. The tapping stopped and Tracey pushed back from the rail. The tapping started again. This time there was a rhythm to it, something vaguely familiar.

"Tracey?"

She turned. Mike was standing in the door to the corridor. He looked sad and lonely. She supposed it was his own fault for being such a ... she couldn't come up with a suitable word. But even so, she felt sorry for him. He was the odd man out here. "What is it?"

"Johnson's ready to see you now."

"Oh. Okay." Tracey pushed away from the rail.

"And Tracey?" Mike asked.

She was close to him now, he hadn't moved from the doorway. "Yes?"

"Can we talk sometime. I'd like to apologise. I know I was rude to you on the plane. I was angry ... and a little scared, I guess. I didn't know what it was all about."

251

The expression on his face now was familiar to Tracey. Soft, although that wasn't quite the right word. He looked like he cared. Was it possible that he still did? She would like that to be true.

"It's okay," he said quietly, backing away. "I understand."

"No." Tracey reached out and caught his arm. "We can talk. After dinner maybe. I don't think Cleaver will be sitting up late tonight." Not with the way he was drinking when she'd left him before, and if Cleaver wasn't around she knew Aldercott would make himself scarce.

"Thanks." Mike touched her hand gently. "That will be nice. And don't worry about Franklin Johnson, he's not as mean as he looks."

Tracey pondered that as she walked down the corridor, trying to prepare herself. Had the two men bonded as part of Mike's recent change of heart?

"Come in, Tracey." Johnson waved her to a seat. "I won't keep you long. There's just a few things I wanted to go over."

Though the man's tone was friendly, there was something mean and hungry about the way he looked at her. She suddenly had a vision of him watching her through the cameras in the bedroom, and for all she knew, the bathroom. She shuddered at the thought. It seemed too real, too likely, for her to easily dismiss.

"Are you cold? Did you want to get something dry, before we talk?"

Tracey realised that she was damp from her time on the balcony, her light shirt was wet and sticking to her skin. She tried to shake it loose. "No," she answered. "Let's get this done."

"As you want."

It went much as Cleaver had described. Questions about who she had told about the events. How much she'd told her mother. How much she thought John's friend Jason might know. It occurred to Tracey that it was strange that Jason wasn't here with them.

Johnson began to pull his papers together, apparently the interview was over.

"I can go now?" Tracey asked.

"Certainly. Dinner must be arriving soon, we don't want you to miss that."

Tracey stood and started to turn around.

"Mike seems like a nice boy," Johnson observed. "What do you

252

suppose Cleaver's got against him?"

Tracey turned back. "Drugs, I think."

"Oh, I wouldn't take too much notice of that. A lot of young men experiment for a while, they usually grow out of it."

"I think it was more than that."

"Phht," Johnson scoffed. His eyes travelled down Tracey's body. "I think you're losing weight. People will say we're not taking care of you." He smiled at her.

Tracey had wanted to ask questions, like how long they would be here? But she couldn't stand being under the man's gaze any longer and quickly left the room.

Cleaver was already less than his usual sturdy self before dinner arrived, and he made his excuses quickly after eating and left for his room. Aldercott stayed longer than Tracey had expected. He didn't say much, none of them did, but Tracey thought that he gave her and Mike some strange looks, as if he sensed there was something going on. When he caught Tracey watching him, he smiled a small sad smile. It was a vulnerable expression, and more real than she had seen on his face before. And then it was gone again.

"I'm tired," he said. "If you two are okay, I think I'll have an early night too."

Tracey watched him go, wondering at the changes she was seeing in him.

"I thought he was going to hang around all night," said Mike. It was usually Mike that escaped to his room as soon as he finished eating, not comfortable in the company of three people that obviously didn't like him.

Tracey watched Mike as he flicked around the channels. He found a music video show and left it on that with the sound turned low. At Mike's suggestion they moved to a sofa, but Tracey kept her distance. She wasn't ready to just forget everything she had learned about this man. She still wasn't sure which was the real Mike.

"Thanks for agreeing to talk to me," Mike said. "It means a lot."

"How could it? You were paid to talk to me before."

"Look ... I know that's what I said."

"Weren't you?"

"Yes. But that doesn't mean it was all a put-on." Mike turned to the television, and then to the empty space between them. "I did enjoy going out with you." He glanced up. "We had a good time, didn't we?"

Tracey nodded warily. She had, but then she had also thought it was real.

"It must have been obvious I was attracted to you." Mike looked down again and said quietly, "I didn't fake the erections I had when we cuddled." He lifted his eyes. "And I know you enjoyed it when I touched you, that wasn't fake either."

Tracey didn't want to go there. She looked away. On the television some almost naked white woman was wrapping herself around an almost naked black man. Neither seemed that interested in the other. It was all just a dance.

"What about the drugs?" Tracey asked. "Ray says you're involved in drugs."

"I suppose that's true." The admission was slow and hesitant. "But it's more bad company than anything else. The people I got caught up with. It's hard to get out once you're in."

Tracey nodded. She could see that might be true. She shook her head and turned back to look at Mike. "But you were paid to go out with me!"

"I was. I admit that. But does it matter what brought us together? If it works now I mean. Does all that really matter? I like you, Tracey. I think it could grow to be more than that. I'd like you to give me another chance." Mike slid closer on the sofa. He reached out and placed one hand on her shoulder.

Tracey stood up quickly, took a few paces, and then turned back. "And how do I know you're not being paid now?"

Mike gave her a pained look. "As if I would. If I was still being paid I'd never have told you what happened before." He stood up and held out his hand. "Please, Tracey. We were good together. We could be again."

She stared at his hand. This wasn't what she expected at all. He had said he wanted to apologise for being an arsehole, she could handle that much. But all this?

"I'm going to bed," she said. When she glanced up she saw something strange in his expression. Surprise? Hope? "That's not an invite," she told him.

She went to her room and closed the door firmly behind her. She wasn't sure what she was feeling. She went to the window to pull the curtains, Aldercott's light was on. She pulled the curtains closed and went for another shower.

She lay awake much later, still trying to sort through her emotions. She really had liked Mike, back when she thought it was real. A lot. She thought there had been a chance it might mean something. She had wanted it to. Could Mike be serious now? She couldn't reconcile the apparently sincere expressions she saw now with what she had seen and heard on the plane. If only there was someone she could talk to. Her mother was on the other side of the world, her father wasn't any closer, and he was never someone that Tracey could talk to like that. Tilvy. If only Tilvy was here.

Tracey sat up. That rhythm on the branch earlier? That was one of Tilvy's favourite songs. Something off one of Tracey's CDs, she tried to remember what it was called. Tracey got up and pulled back the curtain to look out. Aldercott's light was out now, but there were a few dim lights from the windows of lower floors that cast the leaves and branches into obscure silhouettes. Could Tilvy be out there? And if she was, what did that mean? Tracey had to know.

She felt around the edges of the window, there didn't seem to be any way to open the glass. She thought about grabbing her bathrobe to go over her nightie, but it was too warm and heavy to wear for long. As far as she could tell it was quiet outside, so she cracked open the door. The television was off, only one dim light lit the room. No one was out there.

Tracey crept out and down the hall to the balcony. The large glass door sounded loud in the quiet of the night. She squeezed through into the humid air, closed the door, and crept over to the handrail. She could hear insects and other noises, she hoped they were frogs or something.

"Tilvy?" she called out in a loud whisper.

Some of the closer noise makers fell silent, but there was no other response. Tracey recalled that she could barely hear what went on out here from inside her room, everything was carefully sound proofed. So she tried again, louder. "Tilvy?"

Another brief silence was broken by a few tentative croaks from a frog or something, then the chorus picked up again. Tracey stared into the darkness wondering what she could do. She shivered.

Maybe the bathrobe would have been a good idea after all, it wasn't so warm out here at night. A strange haunting call echoed through the space. It made Tracey jump. When it came again Tracey remembered hearing it previously. A bird maybe. She didn't know what they had in this place.

She wrapped her arms around herself. She was being silly, she might as well go inside. She turned to go.

Tap, tap. It was a dull noise, not loud, but distinct.

Tracey turned back. "Tilvy?"

Tap.

"Is that really you?"

Tap.

Tracey didn't get much sleep. Despite knowing how bad it was that Tilvy was prisoner, there was comfort in knowing that her friend was so close, and that Tracy now had confirmation of all that Cleaver only suspected. They had been sold out. There was probably lots more to know, but it was difficult to hold a conversation when one side was limited to saying yes or no. She had to talk to Cleaver.

Aldercott was up before her, he nodded to her when she came out of her room.

"Have you seen Ray yet?" she asked him.

He shook his head and dropped his eyes down to his bowl of cereal.

"Do you know if he's been up?"

Aldercott shook his head again.

"I need to talk to him."

"About Asquith?"

"What? No. It's ... something else."

"Asquith's not good enough for you, Tracey."

At first Tracey wasn't sure she'd heard right. Aldercott had spoken quietly, Tracey wasn't sure she was supposed to have heard it. She was still trying to make up her mind whether to ask what he meant, or to tell him to mind his own business, when Mike appeared.

"Good morning," he said.

Aldercott made a show of chewing his cereal and raised one hand in acknowledgement.

Tracey smiled at Mike doubtfully. Since finding Tilvy, Tracey hadn't given much thought to Mike's proposals. To look at him now, well groomed and cheerful, you'd think they'd already set a date. Should she be flattered?

"Want to join me in the gym?" Mike asked her.

Tracey glanced at Aldercott, he was still looking down at his breakfast. He could be there for a while. "Sure," she agreed.

Once she got there she realised it was probably a mistake. She wasn't really into all this stuff anyway, she wasn't dressed for it, and she'd probably given Mike the idea that he was winning – whatever the game was. She had only wanted to get away from Aldercott.

Mike noticed her reticence. "It's okay. You can sit, or use the other treadmill or something if you want. It's just nice to have some company for a change."

He pulled off his lightweight tracksuit, underneath he wore loose shorts and a sleeveless T-shirt. Getting on a treadmill, he started a slow jog. "Was Aldercott trying to warn you away from me?" he asked.

Tracey glanced at him in surprise. "Why should he?"

"Monkey see, monkey do. I don't think Cleaver likes me much."

Tracey looked over the other treadmill, and decided it was too much effort this early in the morning. She sat down on a weight lifting bench. They watched each other in the mirrors.

"I don't think Ray likes anyone that deals in drugs."

"It's not hard stuff or anything." Mike picked up speed. "Strictly recreational. Stuff to brighten up a party."

"I thought you said it was just the company you kept."

Mike smiled. "It is. But the company's not so bad that they'd push smack on kids or anything."

"I don't think—" Tracey started.

"Cleaver's not happy here," Mike interrupted. "You don't think he's going to upset things, do you? You know, do a number and spoil it for all of us?"

Tracey paused, trying to make her mind change tracks. "Spoil what exactly?"

"All this." Mike waved his hand around. "Nice place, no work, everything delivered. I could get used to this."

"It's still a prison."

"Is that what Cleaver thinks?"

Tracey shook her head. "He just ..."

Mike slowed the treadmill and then stopped. He turned to look directly at her. "Just what?"

"I think he wonders if everything is what it seems."

"He's the one that ought to know. He got us all into this, don't forget."

Tracey nodded slowly. Mike was standing over her now. There was warmth coming off him. His skin, flushed with the exercise, showing faint signs of perspiration, but that was all. The muscles on his body were well defined but not exaggerated. Even his natural scent was pleasant. He was a hard man not to be attracted to. When her eyes reached his face, she saw that he was looking to one side. She followed his gaze and he smiled at her in the floor-to-ceiling mirror.

"You don't want to believe everything Cleaver tells you," Mike said, "and you don't want to let him get us all into trouble."

Tracey frowned at that. She did trust Cleaver.

Mike grasped Tracey's arms just below her shoulders and lifted her to stand in front of him. They were very close now, Tracey could feel his breath on her cheek, and smell the peppermint of his toothpaste. It was familiar. She had been here before. And liked it.

"All those photos of dead people that Cleaver showed us," Mike whispered in her ear. "We don't know how they died. *Who* killed them? Look out for yourself. Remember that what Cleaver wants is not necessarily what is best for *you*."

Tracey was confused. Her body was telling her what it wanted while her mind battled with the contradictions. What it felt like to be this close to Mike again fought against what she had experienced on the plane. The trust she had developed for Cleaver struggled against the doubts that Mike had just whispered to her. And her friend. She needed to help Tilvy, and she needed Tilvy to help her. Tracey pushed herself back and almost fell over the bench. Mike grasped her arms firmly and pushed her to the side.

"I need that bench. I want to lift some weights. You can spot for me if you like."

Tracey shook her head. She needed to get out of here. "I'd better go."

He held her a moment longer than she felt comfortable with, and when he let go, she stumbled at his sudden release.

"Don't forget what I said," he called after her as she was closing the door.

Tracey reached the communal area and saw that Cleaver was sitting at the table. He looked surprisingly good for a man that had drunk so much the night before. There was no sign of Aldercott.

"Paul said you had something to tell me," Cleaver said.

Tracey stared at him for a moment, confused. "It was nothing," she said at last.

Cleaver looked doubtful, but Tracey ignored that and turned for her room.

"Tracey."

She turned back to him.

"Paul also said you were with Michael Asquith. That you two have been talking."

"What is this? The bloody schoolyard? Who's going out with who. Who's got the shits with who. I'm sick of it!"

"I just—" Cleaver started, but Tracey didn't wait to hear any more, she stormed into her room and slammed the door.

She lay on the bed with tears streaming down her face, and she couldn't even have said why. She had wanted to tell Cleaver what she'd learned from Tilvy, but what was the point? Cleaver didn't believe her invisible friends existed. And what if what Mike had said was true? Telling Cleaver might be exactly the wrong thing to do. Should she trust anything Mike said? He was a drug dealer according to Cleaver. But she wanted to trust Mike. Needed to. It couldn't all have been a lie back then. If it was, what did that make her?

- - -

"You could keep them as pets," Jaimee suggested, "or give the video feeds over to one of the human television networks."

Sando laughed while he turned the sound down. "I don't think it would rate well, it's not normally that exciting. I think that's the first time I've seen her throw a tantrum."

Jaimee made a show of looking around the room. The brothers were the only ones in this quiet and secure room, though there were half-a-dozen big screens and comfortable seating for ten. "Where is everyone?"

"Johnson's agents took less than a week to decide it was a waste of time. They all left, none-the-wiser for their experience."

"No chance our guests will abscond?"

Sando leaned forward and hit a button. The view on the screen changed from Tracey crying on her bed to Mike lifting weights. "Thanks to Johnson's forward thinking, we'll soon know if they start getting restless. This one comes a lot cheaper than paying people to sit here watching the screens all day."

"Nothing's cheap."

"Nothing is exactly what he will end up getting."

Jaimee smiled at that. "How much longer do we have to keep them here?"

"Not long. Mother can have them soon."

"Anyone else we can have? The stocks are getting low."

"Talk to Johnson," Sando said. "I said he was devious."

"Greedy is the word," Jaimee corrected. "He's not cheap."

Sando ignored that. "He thinks he can get the agency to outsource their entire protection scheme to us, give us a constant supply."

"A service happy to help people really disappear?" Jaimee considered this, the smile on his face showed that the thought appealed. Then he shook his head. "Too much paperwork, too close to home. We're not there yet."

"So we do another round-up of Mother's usuals, runaways and street people."

Jaimee offered his trademark shrug. "Tried and true. There's no shortage, and no one misses them."

"For most of them the accommodation and food is a big step up on their usual fare. It's funny to watch how grateful they are – while it lasts."

"We can't have Mother feeding straight from the gutter. She had enough of that at the start."

Sando nodded, he remembered all too well.

A message flipped up on one of the screens. Sando grinned and looked across at his brother. "Ready to see our other pets?"

Sando led the way from the monitoring room to a balcony on the third floor. They spoke mind to mind.

<It's odd to think we learned of this cloaking technique from

them,> Jaimee noted. He tugged his more firmly around him.

<What's odd is that they don't even think about it being used against them. Even after being caught that way they're still not on the lookout for it. I'm not sure if they're trusting or stupid.>

<Or both. But is it still effective this close?>

<Maybe not if they look around properly, but they won't. The mesh obscures their senses and,> Sando grinned, *<today they're going to have other distractions.>* He pointed down to a place just outside the mesh. He was gratified to see surprise on his brother's face.

<You allowed this?>

<Sure. The more someone has, the more you get to take away – you taught me that.>

- - -

"They're coming!" Pasith gave a shouted whisper.

Tilvy leapt up and ran into the undergrowth. They had been here long enough that it was all familiar. They had almost worn a path through to where Taiza and Beenae were working.

"They're coming," Tilvy repeated the warning as she pushed through the hanging vines that obscured the work site. Then she stopped short. Beenae was outside the mesh!

He grinned at her and waved. "I was just going to come around and show you," he said. "We did it."

Tilvy put her fingers to her lips. "Shush. There are dhumraka coming."

Beenae hurried back to the gap and Taiza was waiting there with a stick that he used to lever the mesh out from the base. Beenae squirmed back up through the space and then the two of them quickly moved still living vines across the area to hide what they'd been doing, careful to keep the leaves off the mesh itself.

It had taken them many days to get to this point. The mesh wasn't that thick, but they had only their primitive handmade tools; they couldn't cut the mesh, they had to wear it away. It didn't help that they were trying to make as little noise as possible, the entire mesh wall would vibrate loudly if they worked at it too hard. Tilvy didn't know where they got the patience to keep at it. Taiza had explained that he was cutting more of the mesh than they really needed so that it could be flexed out when they were ready, but would spring back

261

in and look like it was still intact the rest of the time. And now it was done. It was ready when they were, but Tilvy wasn't sure if she was. What should she do about Tracey?

When the area was as natural in appearance as they could make it, they split up to pretend that they weren't expecting visitors. The dhumraka didn't come often, hopefully this was just another check to make sure they were all still accounted for.

Tilvy hurriedly climbed up into one of the trees to wait for the expected call. She only just found a place to stop when she heard Pasith call out.

"They want to see you all here."

Tilvy made her way back to where she'd been just a few minutes before, trying hard to look bored and depressed.

Today's visitors were a dhumraka woman, small with a narrow pointed face, and two tall thin men. All of them the dull monotones of the dhumraka. This trio had visited them before.

The woman was staring at Beenae. Tilvy glanced across and could see that he was fidgeting. It was partly a habit he was picking up from spending so much time with Taiza, but today it was exacerbated by excitement.

The dhumraka woman gestured to the gate and one of the men unlocked it. The woman entered and closed the gate behind her. "Keep watch," she ordered her companions.

Tilvy stepped closer to Taiza and Beenae. Pasith stayed where he was at the water's edge, watching, he was puzzled but Tilvy couldn't try to explain now.

The dhumraka woman approached Beenae. When she was a few feet away she stopped and studied him. "You're cute – for an aaranya." She walked around him for a few steps. "What's got you so excited, eh, boy?"

"Nothing," Beenae replied defensively.

"Nothing? Aaranya get like this over nothing? What would you be like if I showed you a really good time?"

The woman didn't wait for an answer. She eyed each of the others and then turned and looked around the cage. "I guess this place is nicer than your home. Is that what's got you worked up, eh, boy?"

"No it's—" Beenae started, but stopped when Taiza touched one arm and shook his head.

"I doubt if you're the cause, eh, old man," the woman said with scorn.

When she failed to get a rise from Taiza, she eyed Tilvy speculatively, then shrugged and turned away. "You four stay here. I'm going to see if this place is any more interesting than the last time I was in here."

Beenae gave Taiza a panicky look. They could do nothing but watch helplessly as the woman disappeared into the undergrowth.

"Should we—?" Beenae started.

Taiza shook his head. "Jus' wait. Be calm, B'nae." The advice was incongruous coming from someone like Taiza, who only ever looked calm when he was working at something.

Tilvy went to Pasith.

"Do you think she will find it?" Pasith whispered without moving his lips.

Tilvy gave a helpless shrug. "It's obvious where we've been going, we've worn tracks."

"Obvious to you maybe, it still looks the same to me. Maybe it will to her too."

"They've done it," Tilvy whispered. "Beenae was outside the mesh when I got there."

Pasith looked at her, his eyes wide in surprise. "We can go?"

Taiza and Beenae had approached, the two dhumraka men outside the fence were watching them closely, but said nothing.

"C'n get o'side the mesh," Taiza answered Pasith's question.

"But where do we go from there?" Tilvy finished his thought.

Taiza nodded. "'s the question."

"'m really sorry," Beenae said. "I didn't mean t'—"

Tilvy reached across and squeezed his arm. "It's not your fault. We're all excited about what you two have done. It was just bad luck that these showed up when they did."

Pasith touched Tilvy's shoulder and nodded his head.

Tilvy turned to see the dhumraka woman emerge through the undergrowth and walk along the bank of the artificial stream. She walked up close to their group, studied them for a few moments, and then shook her head and went to the gate.

As the dhumraka were leaving it was on the tip of Tilvy's tongue to ask if the woman had found it. How could she have missed it?

"What do we do now?" Pasith asked, drawing Tilvy's attention back from the door where the dhumraka had disappeared. "When can we leave?"

"Til'?" Taiza asked. Tilvy kind of liked the way he said her name.

"One of us needs to explore outside the mesh, find out if there's a way through the building where we won't be seen."

"Bes' at night" Taiza said.

Tilvy nodded. "And I want to talk to Tracey. I don't want to leave her behind."

Pasith didn't look happy about that, but didn't say anything.

"I'll start looking tonight," Beenae volunteered.

- - -

When Tracey was out of her room, Mike made a point of sitting close to her. He made light conversation and reminisced about movies they had seen together or restaurants they had gone to, as if defying the other two men to make something of it. And yet, though she wasn't certain of Mike's motives, Tracey did find the conversations comforting. Remembering back to when her life was her own, and when her time with Mike felt special, made it possible to believe those times might return.

Both Cleaver and Aldercott adopted the carefully neutral expression that Tracey had found so annoying even when it was just Aldercott. It was obvious that they must disapprove, but they were so damn careful not to show it.

The result was that Tracey found herself spending more time with Mike, and avoiding the others. This made Mike happy, and he pressed his advantage whenever he could. But Tracey wasn't ready to let that go further yet either, so she spent a lot of time in her room alone.

She was sleeping in late most mornings now, after talking with Tilvy from the balcony in the early hours of the morning. But even that was frustrating. There seemed to be no good way to overcome the small distance that separated them. Tracey wondered if she could get Cleaver to teach her Morse Code or something, but she would have to withstand that carefully neutral but oh-so obviously disapproving gaze, so she dismissed the idea.

The change to her sleeping habits wasn't all bad. Though she was only sleeping lightly, waking often and getting up feeling tired, at least when the sun was up she rarely dreamed those dreams of blood that came so often in the dark of the night.

After dinner, Tracey retreated to her room and stared blankly at the television screen. She waited, as she did most nights now, for about an hour after everyone else had gone to bed. She got up, put on her robe, and made her way quietly out to the balcony.

"What am I going to do, Tilvy?" Tracey cried out in frustration. A question she had asked many times, to herself and to Tilvy, though she knew it was a question Tilvy wasn't able to answer.

There was a scraping sound that Tracey understood was the equivalent of, "I don't know."

"Should I trust Mike?" Another repeated question.

Another scraping sound.

"And what about Cleaver?"

There was a rapid light tapping sound that Tracey didn't understand. "Wh—?"

"What about Cleaver?" asked Cleaver quietly from behind her.

Tracey spun quickly and fell back against the handrail. She almost tipped back over it.

Cleaver rushed forward, but stopped suddenly when Tracey cringed away from him. "It's okay. It's all right." he tried to reassure her.

"You scared me," Tracey gasped, clutching at the rail.

"You scared me too. I thought you were going over. It's a long way down."

Tracey turned away from him and pulled her bathrobe tighter around her. She was shivering, but not from the cold.

"What is it, Tracey? I wouldn't hurt you. You must know that."

She stared out into the blackness of the leaves and branches, resenting his intrusion into her private time with Tilvy.

"Won't you talk to me? Tell me what has changed. Has Michael said something?"

"I don't want to talk about Mike." Tracey hated the way she sounded, so defensive and childish, but she couldn't seem to help it.

"All right. But can't you tell me what is wrong?" Cleaver asked.

"There's nothing wrong."

"There is. You're not eating properly. You're not sleeping. You come out here most nights for hours on end. Is it your dreams?"

Tracey shook her head. Then added, "They don't help." She didn't ask how he knew about her coming out here at night.

"Why won't you talk to me?" Cleaver asked again. "You used to ask me if there was any news."

"You never had much."

Cleaver chuckled at that. He was closer now. Tracey glanced across and saw that he was leaning on the rail. "True enough," he said.

"So? Is there any news?"

"Not good news. It sounds like they're wrapping up the investigation back home. No new leads, nothing to go on with, so they're tightening the purse strings and reassigning agents to more active jobs."

"How do you know this?"

"I'd rather not say. It didn't come from Franklin Johnson."

"What does all that mean, you know, for us?"

"Without finding those that were after you, it's not safe for you to return home."

"And you and Paul?"

Cleaver didn't answer.

"Ray?"

"They never found out who leaked the information about your apartment in the city. Paul and I are the natural scapegoats."

"They're going to charge you?"

Cleaver shook his head. "There's nothing they can charge us with."

"I don't understand." Tracey slid closer. She sensed Cleaver was troubled about something.

"Tracey, I think they mean to lose us over here."

"Huh?"

"I think we, all of us, are being kept here while they might need proof of our warm bodies, but when things have settled down enough they'll get permission for our permanent relocation and then we can all just disappear."

"You don't mean that in a good way, do you? A new life in New York as a shoe salesman or something." Tracey found it odd that she wasn't finding this news more disturbing.

"No. Not in a good way."

266

After a lengthy pause, he said carefully, "Tracey ..."

"What?"

"I'm telling *you* this because I trust you. I know you don't want to talk about Michael, but ..."

It was clear enough. "You're not telling him."

"No."

Tracey tried to fit this in with everything else going on inside her head. It was comfortable and comforting here in the dark beside Cleaver, despite the dire pronouncements. This was a man that had always treated her kindly and with respect, even though he thought she was a loony – it wasn't like she didn't understand why. And this was no longer her interrogator and jailer. Ray was a friend. The man inspired trust, not confusion. Tracey felt calmer now than she had in days.

After a period of silence, Ray continued, "Whether we realise it or not, there are things we know, or have seen, that someone doesn't want us to spread around."

"There's only one thing it can be," Tracey said.

Ray looked at her.

"I know you have never believed me, but *everything* I told you was true."

"Tracey—"

"Tilvy, are you still there?" Tracey called out, interrupting Ray's response.

Tap.

"Is it daytime, Tilvy?"

Tap, tap.

"Is it night?"

Tap.

"Do you think I should trust Ray Cleaver?"

Tap.

Ray glanced out into the dark, then turned back to Tracey. His eyes glinted at her, reflecting what small amount of light there was. His breath caught and he asked, "How are you doing that?"

"You said you trusted me."

"I do."

"Then believe me!"

14. Connection

Something was different this time, the memories that flickered up in Angel's mind weren't all horrors. When Asha first entered there was the now familiar line of dead faces, those that had sacrificed themselves to sustain Angel. Sacrifice, that was how Angel thought of those deaths.

But this time, after that line of faces, came a feeling of great joy. Angel was looking up at this house, its gardens obviously new. Angel thought it was a palace. Her four children were with her, as they hadn't been in a long time.

The scene changed. A series of confused images: a dead man on a beach being fed on by large carrion birds; a blurry vision of a beam falling and crushing a woman; fire and noise and people running and screaming.

The memories flickered again. Overwhelming happiness. The four children flying high above. Four children swimming in the ocean. Four babies floating on a lake. Newborn and being held in the arms of people that Asha didn't recognise. Something about these scenes disturbed Asha, but she pushed the thought aside, she was making progress.

More faces. Marking their foreheads as they lay dead. Sensual ecstasy that felt wrong, forbidden, but compelling and unquenchable.

A sudden darkness. A voice calling for her. A knife plunging toward her. Terror. Deeper shadows of monsters with huge teeth and claws that screamed with sounds like distorted words.

The monsters vanished. Physical pleasure that was new to her. A handsome man. An array of living human faces staring at her with hunger.

And darkness again. Confusion and fear. The sickly sweet and warm smell of stale wine on someone's breath. Someone panting in her ear, their fingers pressing painfully into her small breasts. Pain.

Contentment. A pretty blond woman holding her hand and looking down, her smiling face full of love. The scene paused, still like a photograph.

And then nothing.

In the confusion left by the buffeting of Angel's memories Asha thought she may have fallen out, that perhaps she had let go. But then she felt it. The memories were gone, swallowed up in the depths of Angel's mind, but the connection was made and growing stronger.

John was right. It was warm. There was heat beneath her breast. Asha was tempted to open her eyes to watch the golden beam that must be forming between Angel and herself, but she resisted, afraid it might break her concentration. She held the woman closer.

In her efforts to make this work Asha had tried to feel love for this old woman, but Angel hadn't made it easy. She had remained remote and aloof, cooperating only because she was more frightened of dying than she was of Asha. In the end it was the memories themselves that had fed the compassion that Asha needed. It was the pity she felt for the horrors that Angel had endured that made Asha want to help. It occurred to Asha that the trial by memories was as much a test, a preparation for Asha herself, as it was about being allowed through by Angel. Perhaps that was why it had to work this way.

Time was a paradox. In this trance-like state it barely existed. Asha knew nothing of what was going on outside herself and Angel. Years could be passing. The world could be ending. None of that mattered. There was only the connection. There was Angel and her hunger, and there was Asha and her need to fill that void. It felt like they had been connected like this forever, and it felt like they had only just started.

Concentration was getting more difficult now. Her mind was becoming cloudy. But she wouldn't give up yet, she couldn't be certain when she would make it through again.

Angel began to move in Asha's arms. At first the movements were slow and cautious, but they began to get stronger and more urgent. Asha relaxed her concentration. She was weak now, she couldn't hold on much longer.

The connection was fading and Asha became more aware of Angel's movements. The old woman was rubbing herself against Asha, one hand was stroking Asha's back and side, and now seeking for a way inside Asha's tunic. Asha's eyes snapped open and the connection winked out.

"Angel," Asha spoke loudly. Or tried, her voice came out soft and husky. "Angel!"

Angel's head snapped up. There was a look of surprise on her face, she hadn't realised what she was doing. There was a hesitation as Angel took in the situation, then she pushed herself away and got up from the bed.

"Sorry," Angel whispered. She kept her head turned away. "I'm sorry."

"It's okay," Asha tried to tell her, "I understand."

But Angel wasn't listening. She scuttled to the door and quickly left.

<It worked!> Peren proclaimed loudly inside Asha's head.

Asha winced. "Quietly."

<Are you okay?>

Asha nodded. Just tired. She didn't vocalise this time, it was easier.

There was a pause before Peren came back with, *<Mama seems worked up. Embarrassed.>*

Apparently the process affects the libido, Asha told her.

<Oh.>

Asha smiled at the embarrassment she felt coming from Peren. It's only one-sided, I'm afraid.

<You do feel exhausted, … diminished.>

I need to return to the trees. Rebuild my strength. Asha crept to the side of the bed and stood. She swayed for a few moments before steadying. She had given a lot.

<It all comes from within you.> Peren sounded surprised.

Yes, Asha answered flatly.

<I thought you must draw it from somewhere. Somewhere else.>

That would be a neat trick.

<I just mean ... I didn't realise what we were asking of you.>

Now you do.

There was silence for a time. Asha thought Peren might have gone away.

<I might know why it worked this time.>

Asha was working her way slowly down the broad staircase. She stepped aside as a human woman came up carrying neatly folded sheets. Why?

<I stayed out.>

Huh?

<Each time before, I was with you or Mama. I was seeing what you were seeing. I think my reactions might have made things worse, so this time I stayed out.>

Asha nodded, she supposed that could have been part of it.

Peren wanted to talk, she was obviously excited. Her presence would disappear for a moment, then come back to say what her mother was doing now, and how much better she seemed. Asha was too tired to pay much attention. She passed through the front door and looked out at the welcoming trees on the far side of the lawn.

<Mama's actually dancing now!>

Asha cringed at the intensity of Peren's enthusiasm. Peren, please. I need some time.

<Oh ... sorry.>

Peren's presence disappeared from her mind and Asha straightened up and walked out across the lawn.

Asha chose one of the larger trees just inside the line of the forest and rested her hands against the trunk. Even that felt good. She pressed her hands into the life of the trunk, and then quickly followed. The tree welcomed her like a friend. The relief was overpowering. She could feel the need of her own body drawing from the life of the tree. She couldn't stay here long. She would move soon and spread the load. It wasn't the tree's fault that she had let herself get so depleted.

- - -

"So where are we now?" Telia asked, pulling herself up through the gaps between the rocks.

Barma chuckled at the exaggerated exasperation he heard in her voice. "If you climb that ridge over there," he pointed with the arm that wasn't holding Ellie, "and look to the north-east you might be able to see the edge of the central forest – just."

Telia paused, thinking it through. "But we were …"

"I know. We were way out on the other side." Barma was enjoying himself. Telia was good company and he enjoyed showing off his knowledge of the Glade's secrets.

"Do we have to squeeze back through there to return?"

"You can't go back that way," Barma said.

Telia's face filled with relief.

It had been a tight fit even for his skinny frame. That was one of the reasons why he'd carried Ellie for the last distance. Telia wasn't fat, but she bulged in places Barma didn't, she'd had a hard time through the last part of it. Barma had remembered this tunnel as being bigger, but maybe it was just that he was smaller back when he and Andrei had explored these places.

"Some of them work both ways, but a few don't. Like that one. Andrei and I always thought they were probably the ones that once went to other Glades. We'd always hoped to find one that was still open, but we never did."

"You're doing well for someone that said it was all so long ago, old man," Telia teased him.

"It's coming back."

"I heard how much trouble you two were as kids, I'm getting a better appreciation for the grumbles."

"It was all Andrei's fault," Barma said, but grinned.

"Right. If you didn't look so happy about dragging me through all this now, I might have believed you. I think Andrei was set up."

Telia lifted Ellie from Barma's arm. Her affection for the child was obvious. Barma felt it himself, but it was a strange, one-sided arrangement. There was never much in the way of response, Ellie lay there and did little. Sometimes her arms would move weakly, and sometimes her head would turn as if to cast those white sightless orbs at a new target. But that was all.

"So where to next, my ancient leader?"

Barma looked around and tried to remember. They were standing on a rocky ridge about halfway up a gentle hill. At the top, to the north, was the higher ridge he'd pointed out to Telia. Down to the south was an area of rough scrubby bushland, the trees mostly small and twisted. To the west the scrub merged with a forest of heavily built gum trees; not as tall as the central forest, but still very substantial. He peered past the glare of the setting sun. Yes, that forest was familiar.

"That way." He pointed. "There's a small lake on the other side of those trees. I think there was a burrow or something under the water there."

Telia pulled a face. "Muddy burrows may have been your idea of fun back then, but they're not mine. Isn't there another way?"

Barma thought about it a bit longer and then shook his head. "We didn't come here much because it's not well connected. These were the only two ways we found. One in and one out. The one in the lake is a one-way tunnel too."

"So it's either walk back the long way, or swim through a wet tunnel. Is that it?"

Barma nodded, and gave Telia an embarrassed smile.

She sighed. "You do know how to show a girl a good time, old man. Come on, let's rest in those trees tonight. Maybe in the morning I can be more philosophical about adventures."

They made their way down the slope and into the forest. Telia chose a tree and they climbed into the branches, passing Ellie between them as necessary.

Telia nestled Ellie into the fork between three large branches, and took station on a branch next to her, one hand touching the child all the time. Barma moved onto a branch on the other side, and he too kept one hand near Ellie. It wasn't a conscious thought, just something that had become a habit. Later they would take turns at merging, never leaving the child alone.

Darkness descended. It was quieter here than it would be in the outside world. There were creatures here besides the aaranya, animal-like things they called pazuka, but they weren't as common as animals were outside. As if to contradict Barma's internal commentary about the nature of the Glade, there was a brief whooshing sound of wings as the dark shape of a night-bird flew past somewhere behind him.

"What are you laughing about?" Telia wanted to know.

Barma explained that he was determined to have a good

description of the Glade for Tracey and John when he met them again.

"I suppose we do take it for granted," Telia agreed. "I mean, look at all the places you've shown me in the last few days. Places I either never knew existed or I had forgotten about."

"Lots of kids explore."

"And lots got lost trying to follow you and Andrei."

"We never let them disappear for too long," Barma assured her.

"That's the main reason why the elders never stepped in to curb your excursions."

"I didn't even know they noticed."

"Of course they noticed. But sure, all kids explore. When I was growing up I probably did see some of the tunnels and destinations you've shown me, but we grow up and forget them. For you and Andrei, and eventually Tilvy, the adventures seemed to be something more."

Barma shrugged, feeling a little embarrassed. Had he just been accused of not growing up?

"Everyone thought you three were prime contenders to go wandering when you grew up," Telia said, "but you never did."

"Andrei has."

"That's a bit different. He wasn't showing much sign of leaving before this stuff started."

Barma wasn't so sure, but didn't argue the point.

"You miss your friends," Telia observed.

"I'm worried, that's all. Andrei has been gone so long, and Tilvy's out there somewhere, too close to Sando and whatever he's up to."

Telia reached across and squeezed his hand. "They'll be okay."

- - -

Asha stepped out from the trunk and stretched. The morning was bright, and birds and insects were busy all around her. She had moved several times through the night, and each time she felt better. This morning she felt almost good. Even her concern for John was lifting.

Casseta glided in from a nearby tree and alighted on Asha's arm.

"Good morning, darling girl," Asha greeted her.

The brevi climbed to Asha's shoulder and twittered in her ear, as if sharing her adventures.

"I know I told you to go, but I'm glad you didn't. It is good to see a friendly face."

More twittering.

Asha sat down on the branch and leaned back against the trunk. Birds started to gather near her. The brevi climbed across under her throat and disappeared beneath her tunic. There was a feeling of cold and then a sudden warmth as Cassey merged into her body.

"Welcome home," Asha whispered.

She was still talking to the birds a while later when a voice called up from the ground.

"So it's true. You really do recover quickly."

Asha looked down. Helix. Pale but radiant. Beautiful and compelling. And almost as frightening as Jaimee.

"Our mother looks younger. You've done well," Helix said. She looked around, as if assessing the forest and then looked back up. "If you're feeling up to it, why don't you come with me for the day? I think you might find it interesting."

Asha hesitated, she didn't trust this woman.

<It's okay,> Peren spoke into Asha's mind. <She just wants to get to know you better.>

Why? Asha asked, remembering just in time not to vocalise.

<She wants to know if you're good enough for our brother.>

I'm not interested in Jaimee!

<Jaimee's interested in you.>

What's he said?

<Nothing. He doesn't need to. My siblings aren't very good at keeping secrets.>

And you?

Peren didn't answer.

"It's all right," Helix called up to Asha. "I'm not going to hurt you. I thought you might like to get away from here for a while."

Asha climbed down slowly and stood in front of Helix. Although there wasn't that much difference in height, Asha felt small and insignificant in front of this beautiful woman.

"Walk with me," Helix said, and turned around.

Asha followed. She felt like a mouse scuttling, too nervous to be doing this but compelled nonetheless. Pull yourself together, she chided herself, Helix is just another narun. But it wasn't easy to

275

make herself believe it.

"What do you think of all this?" Helix cast her arm out, taking in the forest.

"It's lovely." Even Asha's words felt inadequate.

"You don't find it dull, confining?"

Of course it's confining, Asha thought, but didn't say.

"I never understood the aaranya," Helix continued as if Asha had given some anticipated response, "even when I got over our childhood phobia about them. You all seem so placid."

"Content," Asha suggested.

"Yes, that's it. With just this, you're all content. It's very strange."

Asha saw now that there were dhumraka around them. Keeping their distance, but also keeping pace.

Helix noticed her attention. "They're very loyal. A bit over the top sometimes, but useful."

"What are they?" Asha found the confidence to ask.

Helix glanced at Asha briefly. "A people with a long and proud history. We might share it with you some time."

"They feel like aaranya."

"No, not exactly."

Helix's rapid pace brought them out on the lawn. On the driveway were four vehicles, all large four-wheel drives, all a deep blue-grey, and all with dark tinted windows.

Both brothers were waiting near the cars, their smiles wide. Jaimee stood out in Asha's perception. Only he exuded the same self-confidence she felt from Helix. Not that Sando was shy and unassuming, far from it, but from Jaimee and Helix the certainty of their own worth radiated from them.

"A sight to warm the cockles of your heart?" Jaimee nudged Sando.

"Indeed. Two beautiful women strolling toward us. What more could we want."

"Maybe one for you, brother."

Asha noticed Helix stand straighter and preen in response to the flattery.

"Did you want to come with us?" Helix asked.

"Sando's got an errand in the city, and I've got some meetings lined up. We're just here to catch a glimpse of you both before you depart and leave us derelict," Jaimee rejoined.

Dhumraka approached from various directions and climbed into the lead and trailing two cars. Helix ushered Asha into the second of the cars and climbed in behind her.

"See you tomorrow," Sando called as the door closed.

The four vehicles moved smoothly off together, as if they were linked. There had been no typing of commands on the keyboard mounted on the back of the seat in front of them.

"Can they see us?" Asha asked, indicating the human driver.

Helix shook her head. "They are mine, they know what I want."

The vehicles made their way through the winding roads beyond the estate and Helix began questioning Asha about John.

"Tell me about this human of yours. The one we let live." There was something odd in Helix's tone. It was obviously a leading question, but leading where?

"What do you want to know?" Asha asked cautiously.

"Oh, I don't know. How did you meet him?"

Asha described how she came to know John. She tried to keep it brief, she didn't want to open up to this woman, but it was a subject she found difficult to remain objective about.

"What I really want to know is why?" Helix interrupted. "Why a human? Why him particularly?" She sounded genuinely puzzled.

"I don't think of him as human, not like you mean. Not as something separate and different. He's just a man." There was something equalising about sitting in the back of the car, Asha didn't feel as intimidated as she had earlier.

"But he's an animal." Helix emphasised this as only a narun could. Not that animals were worse than humans, but that humans were simply animals, no less, but no more.

Asha wasn't sure how to respond to that. She had never seen animals as lesser creatures. They were part of life, like the forest and the streams. Like the narun.

"Why him? Was it just that he could see you? Would any human have done?"

Asha shook her head vehemently. "No. I grew to love him, to love what he was, before he could see me. I didn't realise it at the time, but it's true. John becoming aware of me simply made it possible to take the extra step." Though there had been nothing simple about it,

Asha acknowledged silently.

Helix looked unhappy, dissatisfied. Silence ruled for a while.

"What do you think he might do?" Helix asked.

Asha turned back from watching the forest pass by. "Do?"

"You know, now you're not with him?"

"He'll return home to be with his daughter," Asha said. More quietly she finished, "To wait for her to die."

The expression on Helix's face suggested that she wasn't convinced, but didn't hint why.

- - -

"It's a swamp!" Barma looked across the tall reeds surrounded by dark water.

"It is," Telia agreed.

"It used to be a lake."

"Things change, even here in the Glade."

"But it's a swamp."

"You've said that."

Barma looked around hoping to find some sign that he was mistaken. Maybe the lake was further that way. ... No. This was it. What was left of it. He looked back at Telia. "Do you suppose the tunnel is still here somewhere?"

"Hey, I'm following you, remember?"

Barma turned back to the swamp. It was big, but it wasn't huge, not as big as he'd remembered the lake to be. The water was dark and smelly. There was nothing wrong with it, this was what happened in swamps, but that didn't make you thrilled with the idea of swimming in it.

"I'll look," he said at last. "You stay here with Ellie."

"If you weren't already spoken for, Barma, I could get a serious crush on you."

Barma glanced back over his shoulder to see if Telia was laughing. She wasn't.

He walked down the bank to the water level. From here the reeds were high enough that he couldn't see far ahead. He put a toe into the water, it wasn't cold. He put the rest of the foot in. When it touched the bottom there was a prickly, scraping sensation as his foot pushed aside the roots of living plants and remains of rotting vegetation, and then the mud squelched up between his toes; it was

278

colder than the water. Ah-huh. He pulled his other foot off the bank and sat it down near the first. See? that wasn't so bad. He took another careful step.

"It could take a while then," Telia observed from the bank.

Barma turned to look back and almost slipped over, grabbing at the reeds to steady himself.

"I was just saying." Telia held up one hand in surrender. "I'm not criticising, honest."

Barma returned her smile. He supposed it was pretty funny. "I've just got to get used to it, then I'll be able to speed up a bit."

"You taking notes to describe this to your friends?" Telia asked with a grin.

Barma poked his tongue out at her.

Her tone turned serious. "How about I climb up here." She pointed to a tree growing near the edge of the swamp. "I can point out the clear patches in the reeds."

"Good idea," Barma acknowledged.

Telia make quick work of scaling the tree, even with Ellie held carefully in one arm. Laying along one of the branches she surveyed the swamp near Barma. "Forward about six steps and to your left about two," she called down.

Barma turned back to the swamp, pushed the reeds to the side, and stepped forward.

"Maybe a dozen steps of that size," she commented.

"Ha ha."

They proceeded like that for a long time. Telia offered to take a turn, but Barma said he was used to it now. Each small clearing they found offered little but deeper mud. At times the water rose to chest height, and sometimes he had to work around thick patches of reeds, but otherwise the search continued smoothly.

"How did you find it the first time?" Telia called to Barma. He was fifty metres or more away, and slowly working his way back to her. "I mean, underwater like that, it wouldn't exactly have stood out."

"I don't remember," Barma admitted. "Andrei can be pretty persistent when he wants to be."

"You're no slouch either," Telia told him. "You sure you don't want me to take a turn?"

Barma shook his head.

"You're veering to your left."

Barma adjusted his path.

"That's better, just another few paces."

He found the clearing. It was bigger than most, but looked much the same. He took one step into it and the water was at his waist, the mud below rising around the calves of his legs. Another few steps and he was in the middle of the pool and the water was up to his chest, the mud to his knees. He couldn't see Telia from down at this level.

"You still there?" Telia called.

"Yeah. It's just another mud wallow. Where to next?"

"Find a higher spot, I've lost track of where you are."

The next step was firmer and he rose a little. Another step forward and he was suddenly under the water. He floundered at first, his arms waving trying to regain his balance, and then he broached the surface and tread water.

"Barma?"

"I'm okay," he called back. "I found deep water. I'm going under to see what's there."

"Don't leave a lady waiting too long."

"I won't."

The water was too murky to see any distance, it was probably bad enough before, but his movement had stirred up the mud. With his hands he found the muddy sides of this dip in the swamp, and followed the line down. The water cleared a little, but not enough to give much sense of anything in the distance. But there was distance, he could tell that much. His hopes grew.

It was definitely a tunnel now, not just a low place in the swamp, and he followed its slowly curving path. He was deciding that it was time to go back and get Telia when the tunnel came to a dead end. Was this the tunnel he wanted and it had closed over, or was this something else? He had no way of knowing.

He turned to go back and noticed a side tunnel. He swam to the start of it, but stopped himself from entering. If this was the tunnel he and Andrei had found years ago, it only worked one way. If he went too far he would leave Telia and Ellie stranded.

- - -

They were driven to a marina, and Asha, Helix and the dhumraka boarded a large boat. Hours later the engine went silent and the boat rocked gently on the empty ocean.

"Where are we going?" Asha asked.

"You were asking about the dhumraka, yes? It's time you met them."

At some point while Asha hadn't been watching, Helix had changed her extravagant, but elegant, white blouse and long skirt for a shape-hugging top and tights that left her midriff bare.

"Ready?" Helix asked, an eyebrow raised.

The strong sense of inferiority had returned, Asha couldn't help thinking that Helix was critical of Asha's appearance. She resisted the urge to try and change her tunic and shorts, there was no competing with Helix.

The dhumraka picked up weapons from a storage space at the end of the boat. Most were slender spears, the metal shaft was covered in places with material more suited for gripping by narun hands, and one end was shaped like a long double-edged knife. A few picked up more sophisticated weapons, they looked like long guns of some sort.

"Are we expecting trouble?" Asha asked, eyeing the array nervously.

"My loyal protectors like to be prepared," Helix answered carelessly.

Several dhumraka dived into the water and moments later came back to the surface, waiting.

Helix executed a perfect dive, timed exactly right so that she disappeared with barely a ripple into the smooth side of a wave. Asha felt like she should hang over the edge of the boat and drop herself into the water rather than try to match Helix. She looked around her. Some dhumraka had remained on board, they were waiting for Asha to move. There were men and women, strong and loyal apparently, but obviously selected for their beauty. Helix wasn't afraid of coming out second and must have believed that her companions' attributes only added to the effect she wanted.

Asha shook herself. She was procrastinating. She turned and dived into the water without giving herself any more time to think about it.

Helix was already swimming away, as elegant under water as she had been on the surface. Asha couldn't help but admire how smoothly and efficiently she moved, as at home in the water as any of the jalaja that Asha had met.

Another mental shake. She had to get over this reverence thing. Helix hadn't touched her. These feelings came from ... Asha didn't know where, and that only made it worse. It made it seem like the feelings were justified.

It was only when Asha forced herself to take her eyes from Helix that she realised they were swimming beside an underwater forest. Giant kelp. The large fronds wafted gently as they floated with the currents. The stipes (stalks), disappearing into the depths, looked impossibly narrow to hold such a mass of growth. Tilvy had told them about finding such plants above the Research Centre where Asha had been imprisoned, here was the evidence it had been no coincidence. The dhumraka were people of the forest, but also of the water.

They hadn't been swimming for long when many grey faces appeared among the leaves of the kelp. Helix turned, paused long enough for Asha to catch up, and then swam into the forest amid this sea of grey faces. So many! The aaranya were never this prolific.

There were fish here too, but they were nervous and quickly moved out of the way of the procession.

Dhumraka moved the kelp aside so that Helix could swim on with minimal interference. Asha swam beside, but slightly behind Helix. The few dhumraka that she caught looking at her gave her no idea what they were thinking.

They descended slowly, eventually coming to a clearing in the forest. The rocky surface below them was partly covered by a few low creeping plants. To one side, apparently anchored by a complex tangle of giant kelp, was the rippling silvery surface of a Way. Asha used the aaranya words, everything about this place made her think of the aaranya and their Glades.

Barely acknowledging the crowd that had assembled to greet her, Helix swam on and directly through the Way. Asha followed.

Beyond the Way the Glade felt much the same as the outside. The water was clearer, and the fish here more varied in their colouring and less nervous, but little else changed.

Asha noted that the dhumraka had been forced to leave their

human manufactured weapons outside. They each swam to one side and gathered new weapons from a cache on the inside. These were all simple spears, apparently wooden versions of the spears they had carried outside – but wood from inside the Glade.

Without explanation, Helix continued to lead them on, but instead of angling up, as Asha had expected, Helix made toward a deep green tangle of kelp. A broad dark tunnel became apparent, formed from the extra long leaves of this group of plants, and Helix swam into it.

The same group of dhumraka followed them through. A hundred metres or so later the tunnel ended abruptly and they came out into the open. Surrounding this area was another kelp forest, but the plants here were distinctly different to those they had just left. The green of the leaves was subtly luminous and the stems were more substantial. Nor did the plants grow straight up. Each plant arced in graceful curves that wound around each other in complex patterns.

Helix had stopped, she was watching Asha with a satisfied smile on her face. "The Glades of the aaranya no longer connect."

"No," Asha agreed, though it hadn't been a question.

"The Glades of the dhumraka do. We just travelled a hundred and fifty miles to one of my favourites. These Glades had a few small connections before, but since I've taken over the dhumraka it has all become much more satisfactory. I may do the same for the aaranya when I get time."

Asha didn't know how to respond to that.

"What do you think? Worth some small sacrifice to gain My Providence?"

Movement caught Asha's eye. The dhumraka around them had all bowed. Asha had to fight the urge to emulate them.

"Come," Helix demanded, and swam upward.

They swam up a long way. The twining growth of the kelp forest continued like the wall of a cylinder around them. Asha saw dozens of dhumraka lining the wall, each peering out from the spaces between the fronds to watch as Helix swam past.

"The attention does get tiresome sometimes," Helix said.

The dhumraka on the walls drew back among the fronds, but Asha could see that they hadn't gone far.

They broached the surface and Asha was surprised to see that the kelp continued to grow above the water level. The stalks grew thicker and turned brown, and the leaves were larger and more rigid. There were more dhumraka here, above the water, some had been reclining on the large leaves. They stood and bowed their heads to Helix.

The sky wasn't visible from here, but it wasn't dark. Many of the leaves had a mirror-like finish, they were hard to look at, and they reflected and scattered the sunlight in surprising patterns. Not bright, but still pleasant. It was all quite beautiful, Asha admitted reluctantly.

"This way," Helix said.

Near the edge of the open pool, Helix rose out of the water as if she was walking up a sandy beach. After a few clumsy missteps, Asha found the flat topped vine that Helix was using. It's surface changed from a delicate velvety touch under the water, to a hard wooden texture above.

Asha followed as Helix led the way up among the winding plants. Despite the closed in feel to the forest, the air was fresh and gentle breezes wafted past from one direction and then another. There were other creatures here, but they kept their distance.

At one point they stepped onto a floor formed from a mat of living leaves. A dozen men and women, all the uniform grey of the dhumraka, and all very old, were standing in the small arena, or perhaps a meeting area.

"The elders of this Glade," Helix cast her hand over the group.

The dhumraka bowed low. "Our queen," they murmured together.

Helix turned without acknowledging them. "This way."

The dhumraka elders straightened as Helix walked away. Asha expected to see disappointment or resentment on their faces, for the abrupt way they had been treated, but she saw only adoration. Was it the same in the Glades of the aaranya that Helix had subsumed?

Despite the beauty of this place, the unnatural deference and adoration that everyone paid to Helix was depressing. How could you fight something like that?

Helix walked nimbly along the paths formed by the intertwining branches. The dhumraka that had come with them from the estate began to fall behind, leaving Helix and Asha to ascend the last distance unaccompanied.

The sunlight grew brighter and abruptly they were in the open. A small number of the interwoven plants that Helix had been following continued their upward climb. Asha paused to look out across the top of the forest. She felt movement on her forearm.

"Cassey, no," Asha whispered.

The brevi paid no attention and continued to wriggle herself free from Asha's body. Cassey gave a brief, low twitter, leapt from Asha's arm, and glided down into the forest and disappeared.

Asha stopped herself from shouting for Cassey to come back and looked up quickly.

"Why am I not surprised?" Helix said. She was several steps higher, looking into the forest where Cassey had disappeared. "Jaimee will be intrigued. The brevi seem immune to our charms."

Asha didn't know what to do. Maybe Cassey could escape from here and make it home. As much as Asha would miss her, it would be for the best.

"Don't worry, dear," Helix assured her. "My people will keep an eye out for her. She's sure to come back to you, where else can she go?"

- - -

Telia, waist deep in the dark water of the swamp, kissed Ellie on the forehead. "I'm sorry, dear one, but we're about to go where it's wet and murky."

"It gets clearer further down," Barma assured her.

Telia nodded. "Ready when you are."

It was easier going now that Barma knew what to expect, and he soon found the side tunnel and led them through it. It wasn't a big tunnel, but there was enough room to swim without hitting the sides, and the water was clear. After a short distance the tunnel turned and then went on for a long way at a gentle incline. They reached the surface of the water and stepped out into a low muddy tunnel.

"Shouldn't we be back above ground by now?" Telia asked.

"I think we've definitely gone on to somewhere else," Barma agreed.

"Um ..." Telia was looking back at the water behind them, she sounded concerned.

"What?"

"You said this tunnel was one way. So if we turn around now, where would we end up?"

"I don't know. I don't remember if Andrei and I ever followed this one back all the way. I remember that some of them come out somewhere else, and some of them just dead-end, or shrink to nothing."

"So what you're saying is that there may be no way out, back that way."

"Possibly."

"So we'd better hope the way ahead is still open. Didn't you and Andrei ever worry about getting stuck somewhere? Or lost?"

Barma tried to shrug, but it didn't come out well while he was hunched over in this tunnel. "We didn't think about it."

"Oh. All right, I'll try that then. Here I am not thinking about it. Lead on."

They hadn't gone far when the tunnel ceiling began to get lower and they were forced to their hands and knees. Crawling while holding Ellie in one arm was difficult, so they took it in turns, swapping regularly.

Eventually they were forced to stop and rest. There was nothing for it but to lie back in the mud. Telia placed Ellie on her stomach to try and keep the child out of the worst of it.

"Have you noticed," Telia observed, "that all this is so wet it's sticking to us." She pulled some of her dark hair forward to look at it. "Even when I try to let it run off it stays put. Everything is so humid."

Barma ran his fingers through his mop of hair, they came back streaked with mud. "Maybe this is what it feels like to be human," he mused, "always dirty."

Telia pulled a face. "You've really outdone yourself this time, old man. Just the outing a girl really appreciates. This place is neither one thing nor the other. Not wet enough to merge nor dry enough to stay separate. Blah."

"It all feels ... odd. New."

"What do you mean?"

Barma thought about it. He ran his fingers over the ceiling of the tunnel just above his head. "I don't know. Just the way it's all so evenly wet and muddy. Like it hasn't had time to settle properly or something."

"You're not thinking it might close up again are you?"

"Probably best not to think about that either." Though now Telia had suggested it, Barma found the idea wasn't so easy to dismiss from his mind.

"Right," Telia agreed. "Let's move on. It's easier not to think if we keep moving."

So they crawled on … and on. Barma knew that he and Andrei had never been anywhere like this, it wasn't a place you were likely to forget.

"Erk," Telia complained. "I think the tunnel's getting lower. I keep rubbing my head in the mud."

"Me too. Break?"

"Yeah."

They had barely settled when the tunnel lurched.

"What the …?" Barma started in fright.

"Are these tunnels supposed to do that?" Telia asked.

"They never have before."

Another lurch and they were forced to lower their heads as the ceiling dropped.

"This is not good, Barma."

"What do we do?"

Barma heard the mud squelching as Telia moved around behind him.

"I was going to suggest going back," she said, "but it looks worse behind us. There's barely enough room to turn around anyway."

"So we push on?"

"Can you take Ellie?"

After a lot of squirming in the mud, Barma managed to work Ellie up past his body and sit her on the mud in front of him. He lifted her forward and crawled on his belly after her. He could hear Telia struggling to follow.

"Our Glade wouldn't do this to us, would it, Barma?"

"No." Barma tried to sound definite and confident, but he was no longer certain they were in their home Glade. The mud he was crawling through now had a faint smell of salt water; he and Andrei had never found an ocean in their home Glade.

They kept on pushing their way through the mud, neither daring to suggest they rest.

"How's Ellie?" Telia asked.

"Muddy," Barma answered. His tone was abrupt, he didn't mean it like that, he was tired and getting nervous. "I—"

The tunnel trembled.

"I think—" Telia started.

Barma turned his head. The tunnel convulsed and he was squeezed between the lowering ceiling and the rising floor. He was being pushed deeper and deeper into the mud. He thought he heard a shout, perhaps a scream from Telia, and then he passed out.

- - -

"Come on," Helix told Asha. "Not much further now."

A hundred feet or more above the level of the other forest plants, Asha could no longer think of them as kelp but they weren't exactly trees, the rising vine-like growth levelled out to form a wide platform. The branches split into a myriad smaller stems that wove themselves into a wooden floor. Around the edges of the platform the leaves grew into mats that formed an encircling curved bench, like a moulded green frame. In places, smaller leaved branches reached out into the space beyond the platform, seeking to grow further.

The main forest lay like an even green field below the platform. To the west, beyond the forest, Asha could see open ocean. In the other direction, in the distance, the land rose into green mountainous peaks, but they were too far to see what sort of vegetation grew on them.

"I like to come up here when I return from abroad," Helix announced. "My people still crave sight of me." She pointed down to the forest. Here and there were the small grey figures of dhumraka watching Helix. "But they're far enough away that I can gain some sense of distance. The perspective helps I think, don't you?"

Asha didn't answer.

"Far from the madding crowd's ignoble strife, their sober wishes never learn'd to stray," Helix quoted. When Asha looked blank, Helix explained, "It was written by a human a long time ago. His name was Thomas Gray. I learned the words when I was young, though I still don't know what they mean. Something human I guess," she dismissed the thought, "but I like the sound of them."

She continued, "Along the cool sequester'd vale of life, they kept the noiseless tenor of their way."

Helix paused again, and smiled. "Now that I think of them, I wonder if the words might apply to the aaranya. You've kept to yourselves for so long that your thoughts and actions have become fixed – sober and noiseless."

It didn't seem like Helix was expecting a response, so Asha turned away, walked to one side of the platform, and looked out. She was worried how Cassey would evade the populous dhumraka of this Glade.

"Do you read?" Helix asked.

"Not much."

"I don't get to it much any more either," Helix admitted. "We were encouraged when we were growing up. Sando was keen anyway, but it was Jaimee that kept pushing me. He recognised that humans were the main threat, so he made sure we all learned what we could of them."

Helix sat on the leafy bench not far from where Asha was standing. She held out a hand, indicating that Asha should sit near her.

Asha sat, but avoided meeting Helix's gaze.

"You've done wonders for our mother. Do you think you'll be able to do more?"

Asha risked a brief glimpse at Helix's pale eyes and then looked away again. "As I told Jaimee, I don't think I can heal her."

"But you can continue to feed her?"

"Probably. But the problem is still there, and Jaimee says it's been getting worse. What I can do may not be enough. It wasn't for Ellie."

"The preta you saved?"

Asha nodded. "John's daughter." *The girl you people have killed*, she added silently.

"Are you fertile?"

Helix's question took Asha by surprise. She faced the woman, those pale eyes were unwavering. It wasn't a frivolous question. "Yes," Asha answered, though her response was hesitant. Her hands went reflexively to her stomach.

"How can you be sure? Have you ever had a child?"

"No. But ... I ..."

289

"Did this healer you met discuss such matters with you?"

Asha nodded. Helix's gaze hadn't relented.

"Do you think you could help someone that was having trouble?"

"I don't know. It would depend."

"Would it require that same memory trick you do with our mother?"

Asha shook her head. "No. That's ... I don't know why that happens."

Helix turned away. "We've all tried."

<I haven't,> Peren intruded on Asha's mind.

Asha looked down at her knees, trying not to give away her surprise, both at the turn of the conversation and at Peren's keen attention. You've been listening?

<One of them was going to bring this up soon. I wondered who it would be. I should have guessed.>

"Aren't you going to say anything?" Helix asked.

Asha looked up. For once there was doubt in Helix's eyes, it didn't sit comfortably there. Revealing this failure couldn't have been easy for her.

"I don't have much experience," Asha prevaricated.

"So we should go find this jalaja you met? Maybe she could help."

"She left the zarana. I don't know if she still lives."

"So it's up to you then." There was metal in Helix's tone.

"How can you be—?" Asha began.

"Be certain the problem lies with us? We've each tried different partners. Jaimee and I have even tried together." Helix paused, her eyes hard, waiting for some hint of disapproval.

<They never told Sando,> Peren added quietly, *<not about any of the times they tried.>*

Asha tried to remain impassive. You're not helping, Asha noted to Peren. Anyway, I thought you said they weren't good at keeping secrets.

<Not from me.>

Unaware of Peren's input, Helix continued, "Jaimee thinks it's because of what we are. He thinks we may only be able to reproduce with an unrelated equal. He thinks *you* could bear his children."

Asha was stunned.

<I don't know why you're surprised,> Peren said smugly, *<I told*

290

you he liked you.>

"But that won't help me," Helix said, and turned, looking out to the ocean. "I was hoping this great healer they've spent so much time cultivating might offer something for me, but you don't inspire confidence."

"Is this why ...?"

<No.>

"No," Helix echoed her sister. "Our mother was always the priority. But we had hoped that you may offer more than that."

I didn't *offer* anything, Asha thought. Peren didn't respond.

"Do you think your problem may be because your mother was once human?" Asha remembered having similar questions about what might be possible with John in his saarvaya form.

"Our ancestry is more complex than you know," Helix replied, but didn't elaborate.

Peren?

<It's complicated,> was all Peren would say.

Helix was looking back at Asha now. "Would you at least try to help me?"

"What, now?"

"No. There's too much going on. But soon, I hope."

- - -

"... toes!" A voice imposed itself on Barma's consciousness.

He tried to move but couldn't. Mud! The memories came back, oozing like the mud that surrounded him.

"Barma!" Telia called loudly.

He tried to open his mouth, and succeeded enough for some gritty water to run between his lips before he could remind himself that he didn't need his mouth to talk. "I'm here."

"Prove it to me. Wiggle your toes."

He could feel hands on his feet, squeezing them. He moved his toes slowly through the mud. Telia's fingers squeezed gently, then rubbed over his feet.

"Thank you." The level of relief in Telia's voice surprised him.

"What's wrong?"

There was a catch in her voice as she answered, "I thought I was alone. You were so still for so long. ... I wanted so much not to be alone that I thought I might have imagined your voice. But toes,

291

muddy toes are real. In this place *they* are real." She squeezed his foot again.

Barma laughed, he couldn't help himself, though it was quickly curtailed by the mud.

"I know it sounds silly." Telia sounded embarrassed, but relieved. "And selfish too."

"Why selfish?"

"To want company while I die."

"We're not going to die here." Strangely, Barma found he believed it.

"Thanks." Another squeeze. "Do you still have Ellie?"

Barma had one hand still stretched forward and he found that he could move it slowly through the mud. Ellie was there. She wasn't moving, but that didn't mean much. "Yes."

"Any suggestions?"

Barma tried moving the hand that wasn't touching Ellie. It did move – slowly. He tried moving his head. It moved too, slowly and with great effort. He tried pushing himself away from the floor but made no progress. "No," he finally admitted.

"Let's try not thinking about it," Telia suggested.

"Huh?"

"Tell me about growing up with Andrei. Tell me about Tilvy. Talk to me. Remind me what it's like to live in our Glade."

It might have seemed a strange request, but Barma understood. Even though he had been conscious just a short time, the absolute helplessness of their situation made every moment draw out. Telia had been awake longer. Alone. It must have felt like she'd been trapped here forever.

"I can still remember a time when I wasn't friends with Andrei," Barma began. "I wasn't much of a flyer as a baby, but Andrei was. I used to watch him and the others play, envious that I couldn't keep up."

"You can remember back that far?"

"Yes." Barma paused to try and push some of the grit from his mouth.

"Are you okay?" Telia's concern was touched with a note of panic.

"Fine. I have trouble remembering not to move my mouth."

"Old habits. ... I can barely remember my youth, let alone when I could fly."

"And you were calling me old," Barma teased.

"But that's just it. I never have, not since I grew up. There's just snippets, the odd random image. Not the sort of detail you remember. I've always envied those that can remember their past in so much detail. Sorry, I interrupted."

"I stopped flying before the others, so when they finally did – Andrei really pushed it to the limit – I already knew more of how to get around on the ground than they did. I think that's when Andrei first started to take notice of me."

Telia squeezed Barma's feet. "I knew these would come into the story somewhere."

Barma chuckled. "Of course me showing Andrei things didn't last long. Soon I was following him, but now I could keep up. I was determined to keep up, and Andrei seemed to like having me along."

"He always liked to show off."

"I guess. Though Andrei always said, even back then, that fun was more fun with friends."

"Andrei the philosopher?" Telia sounded disbelieving.

"Sure. There's a lot about him that doesn't show to everyone. ... I miss that closeness. Not just now, but ever since Tilvy and I, you know, got serious. He drew back then."

"Giving you two space?"

"Maybe he was," Barma answered in surprise. "I hadn't thought about it like that. We drove him away."

Telia squeezed his feet again. "No. I wouldn't put it like that. I think Andrei was being considerate." Telia paused for a moment, then said, "You know, I think I'm starting to like him more now. I always thought he was just a cheeky little ... thing. Likeable in his way, but not someone I'd ever have taken seriously. And I wasn't the only one. I always wondered why elders like Kaia and Milla had so much time for him."

"We used to—" Barma started.

The tunnel trembled and they both stayed silent, waiting, and wondering if it was going to open up and set them free, or close completely.

"That was—" Telia started. There was another tremor. "Listen!"

Barma heard it too. The sound of water trickling.

The tunnel jerked with a savage spasm and the ceiling ripped away from them. Water gushed across their now exposed backs. Barma grasped Ellie's arm, and he felt Telia grip his ankles. They'd been pressed so tightly into the mud that it kept them from being washed away in the first flush of the sudden flood. Barma felt his body begin to lift away and called back to Telia to hang on, but there was no need. The rush of water slowed and eventually stopped.

"It's salty!" Telia said. "Seawater. You can taste the seaweed."

"I think maybe we found what we were looking for," Barma said. He peered through the muddy water to Ellie. She appeared to be unharmed by her experience, unaware that anything had changed. Being buried in mud was probably little different from what the rest of her life was like now.

"Here, let me," Telia said. She gently lifted Ellie from Barma's arm and began rinsing off the mud that had stuck to her.

Barma gave them a few moments and then asked, "Are we moving on?"

"You bet."

The tunnel opened out wider and the water became cleaner and much clearer. What should have been dark was still clear to their senses, so they were obviously still inside a Glade, but Barma assumed it could not be their home.

Large roots were now visible growing past the tunnel wall. A short distance further and the tunnel divided.

"Which way?" Barma asked.

"I thought you were leading."

Barma shook his head. "That was when I knew where we were."

"That way?" Telia pointed, apparently at random.

Barma shrugged and went that way. Then there was another divide, and another choice. And then there were a dozen choices. It was as if they'd entered a maze, or perhaps it was a wide cavern filled with closely spaced columns of tangled roots and mud.

"Stop." Telia said. "Let's just stop and think. I'm not sure seawater is a good sign. I assumed we would come out in another Glade, preferably one close to home. But this ... it doesn't feel right."

Barma touched a large root exposed on one of the columns. "Maybe we could merge and go up that way, take a peek. Try and see where we are before we say hello."

"Ellie can't merge," Telia reminded him, "but I suppose one of us could go."

Barma was about to volunteer when he saw something. He pointed.

"Casseta?" Telia spoke out in query.

The small ginger blur had disappeared behind a column, but quickly reappeared. Barma was astounded, he'd never seen a brevi swim – it was fast! The flaps of skin it used for gliding were like wings in the water. The brevi almost collided with Telia and quickly scrambled up her arm and twittered in her ear.

"John and Asha must be here," Barma said. "Was there a message?"

Telia took a moment to answer. She handed Ellie to Barma and scooped Cassey into her hand. "I don't think it was a message, or not for us. Just Asha's voice saying *Cassey, no.*"

"They must be here," Barma repeated.

"Cassey, can you lead us to them? Take us to Asha?" Telia asked the brevi.

The small ginger creature trembled in Telia's hand. Its twitter sounded nervous and agitated.

"Take us, Cassey," Telia insisted. "You have to take us. The child needs Asha."

The brevi twittered again, louder this time. To Barma it sounded like scolding.

"Do you think—?" Barma started, but Telia held up her free hand asking for silence.

"If Asha's here, Cassey, we need to find her. Lead us."

Casseta sat silent in Telia's hand for a moment and then launched herself off and started swimming. The brevi swam quickly, but she stopped at each turn between the columns and waited for Telia and Barma to catch up before rushing on again, as if impatient to get this over with.

"Do you think she understood what you wanted?" Barma asked.

"Milla always says they understand what we mean, even if they don't understand the words," Telia said. "I think Asha must be here. Maybe that's why the connection opened to this Glade."

"Or maybe it was Cassey," Barma suggested.

"Maybe."

295

Barma quickly lost track of their path as Cassey led them back and forth between the columns. Some places were a tight fit. The brevi waited impatiently for them as Telia and Barma handed Ellie between them and squeezed through, and then she was off again.

At last Cassey stopped. She was clinging to the side of a large root. Telia had Ellie, so Barma swam up to take a look at the space above the brevi.

"It's a tangle, but I think there's sunlight up through there. Wait while I see if I can get through."

Cassey gave a nervous sounding twitter.

Barma glanced at the brevi but couldn't work out what it meant. He swam up and squeezed through a pair of intertwined roots. He called back, "It's a fair way. I think we'll have to do it in stages."

Telia handed Ellie up, and Cassey swam through and waited with Barma while Telia pulled herself through. They continued working their way upward until at last Barma pushed his head through a gap and emerged into a dense clump of seaweed. It was vaguely familiar but he didn't remember why, not then. He saw no one after a quick look around so pulled himself out through the gap.

"We're there," he called back down.

Again Telia handed Ellie up to him, and again Cassey swam through.

Barma was about to take a better look around when Telia called to him.

"It's too tight, can you give me a hand?"

He lay Ellie to one side, nestling her securely among some roots, then reached down and grasped Telia's hands. After some squirming and grunts of discomfort, Telia popped through.

What happened next was too fast for Barma to react, but the memory of it would stay with him.

"Barma!" Telia shouted.

There was a loud panicked twitter from Cassey. She flew through the water, and clung to Telia's arm. Barma was still staring at Telia, he hadn't had time yet to turn and see why her face looked so shocked and afraid. There was a brown flicker at the edge of his vision and a spear tore through Cassey and into Telia's arm.

Golden prana gushed into the water. The combined shocked screams from Telia and Cassey filled Barma's head. He remembered noticing that the spear was gone, it had passed through the space between Telia's arm and her body. He remembered noticing that Telia had been cut deeply, both on the arm and along the side of her breast. But most of all he remembered Cassey. The hole in the side of the brevi was huge on such a tiny creature. Cassey's whole body was arched back and her head was thrust out screaming. The sound was so loud, and of such high pitch that it sliced into his mind and froze him in place.

- - -

"They followed your brevi through here somewhere," Helix told Asha. "She shouldn't be far away."

Asha hadn't wanted to find Cassey. She had hoped Cassey might be able to find her own way home, or at least hide away and stay safe. But Helix was insistent. Asha was sure now that Helix meant no good for the brevi. The siblings didn't like things that could defy their influence. Asha didn't like to think about what that meant for the brevi in the Glades already taken by Helix.

They had been led through the kelp forest by some of Helix's loyal band to where the brevi was last seen. The growth here was thick and they couldn't see far ahead.

"That way," Helix said suddenly.

They swam on quickly through the dense growth. Asha knew she had to get to Cassey before they others did.

Screams cut through the water. One in particular. So high and so loud. Like nothing Asha had heard before. Helix fumbled her stroke, as if distracted or disturbed by the shrill noise, but the sound sparked something in Asha. Her body reacted without thought.

Asha was away from Helix before the woman could reach out. She put everything she had into her movements, desperate to be in time. A dhumraka man placed himself in her way and Asha raked her fingers across his chest. He yelled and fell back, clutching at the cuts she had left behind. Another dhumraka thrust a spear across her path, but she ignored it; later she would find a shallow cut down one side of her leg.

And then she was there. Two people. And Cassey. Screaming Cassey. The cut was so big. How was the brevi still alive? The lessons from Ulvanya took over and Asha ran her fingers across the wound, closing off the major flows in a single quick stroke. It had never happened that fast for her before, but she had rarely been this desperate. Still the poor creature screamed.

"Cassey," Asha crooned softly and carefully lifted the brevi from the arm of the woman it had been clinging too. The wound was bad but the loss of substance was worse. However much Ulvanya may have warned her against such reckless expenditure, this was something Asha could do. She pressed her fingers into Cassey's wounded side and gave of her self.

"Please, Cassey, please. Be okay, my darling. Please." Asha continued to give of her own life to try and replace what the brevi had lost. She used the life emanating from her fingertips to sew the wound together. And as some of the proper structure began to form, she went back and reopened the quick closures she had first applied, this time redirecting them and rejoining flows that should never have been severed. Would it be enough? Had she been in time?

Asha heard the brevi twittering weakly and realised that the screaming had stopped, she didn't know when. "Hush, my darling girl, hush. I'm here." The worst of the wound was closed off now. If Cassey could survive the loss she had suffered then there was a chance the wound might heal. But it was only a chance. Asha wanted to spend more time on the main wound, but moved her attention to the flap of skin that the brevi used for gliding. It had been sliced right across. Slowly she began to rejoin the skin, still giving of herself in the hope that it might all be enough. Such a tiny creature, surely what Asha could give would be enough.

"Fascinating," Helix said. She was watching from beside Asha. She reached a hand out to the brevi.

Cassey screeched, rolled over and tumbled out of Asha's hand. Asha hadn't been holding her very tightly, she didn't dare. She bent down to try and catch the brevi, but Cassey righted herself and swam awkwardly to a gap in the roots.

"Leave her!" Asha yelled as a dhumraka woman tried to intercept.

The woman hesitated for a moment and Cassey slipped beneath the outstretched hand and down into the hole. A wisp of golden prana hung in the water where she had passed. Asha hoped it was only because she hadn't completely healed the flap of skin, but she knew Cassey might have torn open the main wound in her panic to get away.

Asha went to the gap and pushed her head and shoulders down through the hole. More wisps of gold gave evidence of the brevi's passing. "Cassey?" she called softly. There was no response. A firm hand on her shoulder pulled her back.

"I'll send someone down," Helix said.

Asha looked numbly at the hand touching her shoulder, and then followed the arm to the pale elegance of Helix. "Get your hand off me!" Asha shouted in shock, remembering what Helix could do.

Helix drew back in surprise. "I didn't. I wouldn't."

<She hasn't,> Peren's voice broke through Asha's panic. <It takes more than a touch, she has to mean to do it.>

"I'll send some others down there," Helix said. Her tone was abrupt now, reasserting her authority.

"No!" a man called.

Asha looked around. "Barma?"

<Who's that?> Peren asked. Asha ignored her.

"If you've done enough for Cassey you should leave her down there," Barma said. "Maybe you can help Telia."

It took a moment for Asha to recognise the woman standing next to Barma, he had his arm around her. Telia's head was bent over and she had one arm held over her breast and other arm. The thick flow of gold into the water spoke of a deep wound.

"It's a maze down there," Helix said loudly, trying to draw Asha's attention back. "Some of my people can try to find the brevi while you attend this woman."

Asha tried to clear her head. "I don't know ..." she started. She saw Barma shake his head in the negative. Had she done enough for Cassey? There was no way to tell now. But she didn't want Helix or any of the dhumraka near her.

Several dhumraka were already approaching the hole, the woman that tried to intercept Cassey was already pushing her way down.

"No!" Asha said. She glared at Helix. "Tell them no!"

"I don't take orders from you," Helix snapped back.

"But you want my help. You *need* my help. And now you've seen what I can do. Leave Cassey alone."

The dhumraka stopped. There was a long hesitation before they slowly pulled back.

"And you won't touch my friends," Asha pressed her advantage.

"You understand me? They're to stay free."

Helix glared at Asha. She wasn't happy about being coerced this way. Finally she nodded, the movement was barely visible.

Asha turned and went to Telia.

Telia lifted her head, her face was pale and screwed up in pain, but she refused to move her hand from over her wounds until she had Asha's attention. She nodded to the side. There, beyond the dhumraka that had been guarding them, still nestled among the roots, was Ellie.

15. Breakout

"Tilvy?" Tracey called quietly into the branches. It was early morning and the birds in the cage were making a lot of noise, she wasn't certain that Tilvy would hear. But the response came quickly.

Tap.

"This is Paul Aldercott."

There was a brief rhythmic rapping.

Aldercott looked at Tracey.

"I think that was Tilvy's way of saying hello," Tracey explained.

Tap.

He turned to the sound and peered into the shadows beyond the leaves. "Hello?" he said hesitantly.

The rapping was repeated.

"Um ... Are you real?"

Tap.

"Am I dreaming?"

Tap, tap.

"Give me five taps."

Tap, tap, tap, tap, tap.

Aldercott turned back to Tracey again. "This is your friend? The one you told us about?"

Tracey nodded. Tilvy issued another single, loud tap.

"And you've convinced Ray?"

"Yes."

After last night's revelation, Ray had told Tracey to bring Aldercott out here and show him. Ray was still inside, ready to distract Mike if he changed his usual routine and got up this early. Tracey was feeling bleary and vague after only a few hours sleep.

"So it's real … all of it?" Aldercott queried.

Another nod. Another loud tap.

Tracey was surprised to see a smile spread across Aldercott's face. It transformed him. He seemed younger; she realised that he probably wasn't that much older than she was. All of her ideas about Aldercott being snobbish and holier-than-thou suddenly seemed misplaced. Here was a young man that probably looked to Ray as a mentor and teacher as much as a partner. It wasn't a thought that had occurred to her before.

Paul was leaning over the rail and staring down at the walls on either side. Then he twisted around and studied what was above them.

"What are you doing?" Tracey asked.

"We've got to be able to get in there."

"What?"

"I want to meet her. Them. All of them. This is momentous, like first contact or something."

Tracey laughed at his enthusiasm, and didn't remind him that he was far from the first and the narun weren't aliens. This wasn't what she'd expected at all. Ray had been much harder to convince and looked very unhappy when he finally relented. She moved closer.

"They can get out of the mesh cage, but all the doors they've tried are locked," Tracey told him. It had taken a lot of time to extract that information last night. Tracey called softly to Tilvy, "Have you found a way out yet?"

Tap, tap.

Paul peered down again. "I wonder if we can cut through the screens and climb down from balcony to balcony."

"And what, be trapped down there with Tilvy and the others?"

"Ray is good with locks. He might be able to open one of those doors."

There was brief rhythmic rapping.

"What?" Paul asked.

Tracey smiled. "Tilvy's just reminding us that she's part of the conversation."

Tap.

"Sorry," Paul called into the branches. "Can you see me?"

Tap. A pause, and then a brief staccato rapping.

Paul glanced at Tracey.

"I think that was Tilvy laughing."

Tap.

"I guess it was pretty silly."

Tap, tap. Pause. Staccato rapping.

"No, not silly, just funny," Tracey translated.

Tap.

Paul's smile returned.

* * *

"I see that you and Cleaver have gotten all pally again," Mike said.

They were in the gym, it was where Mike was most inclined to speak openly about what was on his mind. Tracey was walking on one of the treadmills, it was better than sitting down watching Mike go through his workout – not that he minded being watched. She could still see him in the mirrors at the front of the room; Mike was running harder today than he usually did.

"I don't know why you don't like him," Tracey said.

"I don't know why *you* do."

Tracey didn't respond.

"You shouldn't trust him, he's government. You can't trust the government."

"It's supposed to be the government that's keeping us here."

"It doesn't feel like government."

Tracey stopped her treadmill. "See? Even you feel it."

"I've got no complaints. Whoever is supplying all this gets my vote."

"But what will they do with us when time runs out?"

"He's really got you worked up on it, hasn't he?" Mike asked. He slowed to a sedate jog on the machine. Their eyes met in the mirror. "Is he working up a plan to bust us all out?"

"It's not him," Tracey said without thinking.

"What? Monkey boy?"

"Stop saying that. Paul's all right."

"Oh, *Paul* is it? Aren't you just a cosy trio."

"It's not like that."

"Sure. Like *Paul* wouldn't like to get into your pants. Cleaver too, I wouldn't be surprised."

Tracey ignored that, it was a side of Mike she had seen before, one she didn't like. "They're just concerned that this isn't all it seems."

"They just don't like it when they're not the ones calling the shots."

"What if there was a way out?" Tracey asked, and stepped off her machine.

Mike stopped his machine and turned to face her.

"Would you come with me?" Tracey asked. She didn't like sounding so needy.

He stepped off the machine and walked toward her. "Just stroll out, like the American Wild West?" he asked. "Six-shooters blasting?"

Tracey shook her head. "Something secret."

"Do we lose the goons?"

"They're not goons. Paul and Ray would come with us."

"Suddenly it doesn't sound so good. Anyway, what do we do for money?"

"I don't know. Get a job I guess."

"And go hungry while we wait for our first pay. It may have escaped your notice, but we don't have *any* American money."

"Ray will think of something."

"You're losing me with all this *Ray* and *Paul* stuff." Mike stepped closer. "But I'd be happy to go with you. Somewhere private. Somewhere we can be together." He put his arms around her and pulled her close.

"You're sweaty," Tracey complained, but softly. She craved this, the physical comfort of another holding her close. And though she didn't like to admit it, she could feel her body responding to his warmth.

"I am," Mike agreed. He ran his hands down her back and pressed against her buttocks, pushing her against him. She could feel his erection swelling between them. "You could come back to my room," Mike whispered in her ear. "We could take a shower together. Really get a workout."

Tracey hesitated. She wanted to be held. And part of her wanted more, wanted what Mike wanted. But not now. She pushed him away so she could think more clearly. "Not now, Mike. I'm sorry."

He was reluctant to release her at first, but he finally stepped back. There was a hard glint in his eyes before he looked down at the bulge in his shorts and said, "I'd better be carrying something in front of me on the way back to my room, I don't want the boys getting envious." When he looked back up it was with the cute smile that Tracey liked very much. "Cold shower time," he said.

"Thanks for understanding."

He shrugged as if it was nothing. "Who wants an audience anyway, huh? We'd walk past trying to hide this and they'd just know we were going in there to bump uglies."

"It would be awkward," Tracey agreed.

Mike picked up his tracksuit and made a show of stretching it far out in front of him. Tracey laughed. He leaned forward and kissed her cheek. "We'll get there." There was something odd with the tone of his voice when he said this, but when Tracey looked at his face in question he was smiling.

After Mike had gone, Tracey sat down to think. She did want an end to the dancing around they had been doing. She knew a lot of it – most of it – was her own fault, her own indecision. Mike wanted her, he made that very apparent; this wasn't the first time he'd invited her to his room. And Tracey did want him. She wanted to regain what she thought they once had.

She walked back toward the common area and her room. She was still half toying with the idea of walking past, turning left and going to that second door and knocking on it. Sex might not be what she was really looking for now, but that didn't mean it couldn't be fun. It wasn't like she didn't feel the attraction, the need. Maybe it was something they had to get past before—

"Tracey."

She looked up. Ray and Paul were both sitting at the table in the common area. She felt a hot flush of embarrassment rising up her neck. She was sure they must be able to read what was going through her mind.

"Care to join me on the deck?" Ray asked.

Paul gave her a wave and a small smile. Tracey smiled tentatively in response before she turned to follow Ray. On the balcony it was warm and humid as usual. They leaned on the balcony rail and looked out into the foliage.

An involuntary gasp escaped from Tracey's mouth.

"What is it?" Ray asked.

"Nothing," Tracey answered hurriedly. But it wasn't nothing. She had come so close to going to Mike's room! She hadn't given a thought to the cameras that might be watching. Love may or may not be blind, but lust definitely did bad things to your memory and concentration.

"Sure?" Ray was watching her with concern.

"I doubt if Tilvy's here now," Tracey said quietly, as much to change the subject as anything else. "She's not expecting us."

"I wanted to talk to you. Your friend says they can get out of the cage, but they can't get past the doors down there," Cleaver said.

Tracey nodded.

"Paul's right, if we could climb down there we might be able to help."

"Do we tear up sheets to make a rope, like in the movies?" Tracey asked, mostly in jest.

Ray shook his head. "Sheets weren't what I had in mind. I don't know how much they've been watching us, but it's a good bet they're getting slack by now. We might be able to sneak a few things out here without being noticed."

Tracey looked down. It looked a very long way. She swallowed hard. "Okay. So let's say we make it down there without me breaking my neck and making lots of noise, what if you can't open the doors?"

"Then we all come back up here."

Tracey looked at Ray in surprise.

"You said your friends can jump from great heights without getting hurt, yes?"

She nodded.

"There are stairs next to the kitchen that lead to the roof. The door is locked and probably alarmed, but I'm sure I can get it open. Your friends can go up on the roof and jump down. We'll be doing it at night, so the streets should be quiet."

"But we'd still be stuck here."

"Maybe. When I set off the alarm to that door then the guards will come running. You and Paul can be waiting at one of the doors and sneak out when the guard bursts through."

"But then *you'd* be stuck here."

"If Paul gets out and can contact home then they won't dare do

306

anything to me. Obviously this is plan B. I'd rather we could all leave quietly."

"And Mike?" Tracey asked.

"Have you ever told him about your friends?"

"No. I've never known how to start."

Ray raised his eyebrows but didn't comment. "Do you think he'll want to come with us anyway?"

Tracey was slow answering, she was thinking about her earlier conversation with Mike. She could only answer, "Maybe."

"If he doesn't want to come, but knows we're leaving, is he likely to make trouble for us?"

Tracey shook her head. "He's not that selfish."

Ray looked doubtful.

"He's not!"

* * *

"I don't know why you all keep coming out here," Mike told Tracey. He stepped closer to her, pressing her against the balcony rail. "If you want to get hot and steamy just come back to my room, there's always lots of hot water."

Tracey pushed him back. "Mike, I want to talk."

He looked at her warily. "What about?"

"We want to get out of here."

"This again? Why stir the pot. You're not going to find anything this comfortable out on the streets."

"Keep your voice down."

"Why?" Mike said loudly. "You think the trees have ears?"

Tracey briefly considered trying to prove that they did, but she had decided with Tilvy last night that there was too much to explain. It had been different with Ray and Paul. They already knew all the background, believing in the narun was just the detail that made it all make sense. Anyway, if Mike decided he didn't want to come then it was probably better if he didn't know. He would have to get the crash course later, if he agreed.

When Tracey didn't answer him, Mike held up his hands in surrender. "All right," he whispered. "I'll play the game. Bring down the cone of silence."

"Will you come with us?" Tracey asked him.

"When?"

"Come on, Mike, it's not like you have to check your diary."

"I'm still not fussed about the *with us* part. Make it just you and me and I'll come. We can make love inside cardboard boxes in back alleys." He stepped closer.

"That's not going to happen," Tracey answered.

"Which part? The making love part, or the cardboard boxes?"

"The *just you and me* part. We're all going."

"So you haven't given up on making love?" Mike reached up and stroked the hair back from the side of her face.

Tracey leaned into his hand. "No. But I don't want to do it here." She wasn't going to forget the cameras again.

"All right then. I'm in. Where you go, I go."

Tracey smiled at him in relief. "Thank you."

"So do I get the date now? I need to mark it in my diary."

"Tonight," she said quietly, still smiling.

Tracey almost fell forward as Mike suddenly pulled back.

"Tonight!"

"Shhh," Tracey urged. She reached up to his face, but he brushed her hand away.

"You three have been cooking all this up and you're ready to go. Asking me was an afterthought. I suppose the other two wanted to leave me behind, is that it?"

"No," Tracey protested, though she knew it was at least partly true. "I didn't want to leave you, but I didn't know if you would want to come with us."

"So why not involve me in the planning?"

"It just seemed better to wait until we knew it was going to happen."

Mike thrust himself against the balcony rail and looked down. "So what's the deal? We going to jump out and climb down that mesh?"

Tracey came up next to him, put one arm around him and squeezed. Speaking quietly, and hoping that Mike would do the same, she explained, "No, we can't use the mesh."

"I suppose it is a bit flimsy."

"It's not that. You mustn't touch it. It burns."

"How do you know?"

"I just do." With her free hand, Tracey pointed down past the insect screens. "We're going to climb down through the screens and get out one of the doors at the bottom."

"And then what?"

Tracey shrugged. She didn't know, she hadn't asked Ray about that part, she assumed that he and Paul would know what to do. Just climbing down from here was as much of a challenge as she was willing to face right now.

- - -

Sando wished his brother was here tonight, but Jaimee had had to rush off to attend to some political crisis. Not that Sando needed Jaimee's help, he just wanted to show Jaimee that he wasn't the only one that could play mind games. Sando flicked around the video feeds.

The older human, Cleaver, was already on the move. He was in the gym now. He hung a bathrobe over the end of one of the weight-lifting machines and went to a cupboard.

"What do you want two sets of gloves for, old man?" Sando asked absently.

"My Sando?" queried Orinarya.

Sando ignored the small woman sitting next to him. Her adoration was nothing new or unusual, and her sharp, rat-like features didn't appeal to him any more.

On screen the human seemed to be adjusting the weights or something. Exactly what he was doing was obscured behind his hanging robe. After a few moments the man shrugged, as if changing his mind, and lifted his robe and walked out of the room, switching out the light as he went.

Sando stared at the dim room on the screen, but his mind was still going through what he had seen before the light went out.

"Ah. So that's your plan is it? Clever Cleaver."

Sliding a keyboard forward, Sando began typing out messages to get his team prepared. He made doubly sure they knew they had to stay out of sight until he told them to move. Trying to coordinate humans and dhumraka was always fiddly, but where was the challenge in doing it the easy way?

- - -

Tracey crept to the balcony door. She could see that Ray and Paul were already there, but there was no sign of Mike. She tiptoed back past her own room and turned left. She went past the first door,

Paul's room, and stopped at the second.

"Mike?" she gave a loud whisper. When there was still no response after a few seconds, she knocked gently.

She heard movement inside and a few moments later the door cracked open. Mike peered out, glanced at her, then looked down the corridor. When he saw there was no one else he opened the door wider. He was wearing only boxer shorts.

"Why aren't you dressed?" she whispered to him.

"I'm not coming."

"Shh." Tracey looked around nervously. "You said you were!"

"I changed my mind. You should too."

"I thought you wanted to come with me?" She couldn't stop the hurt entering her voice.

"I do want to be with you, I just don't think we should try to leave here. Stay." Mike reached out and grabbed her arm. "Come in and stay with me."

Tracey shook him loose. "No. I told you, I don't trust this place. I'm going."

He reached out again but Tracey stepped back. She tried to see his face. In the dim light she couldn't tell what he might be thinking, but then she never could, not really. She turned away before he could see the tears forming in her eyes.

"Tracey."

She risked a look back.

"You should stay."

Tracey turned away again and half ran to where the corridor opened into the common area. Once she was around the corner she stopped and took some deep breaths, trying to calm herself, trying to stop the tears from coming. She heard the click as Mike's door closed.

She wasn't able to move for a time. She didn't seriously consider going back, her mind was made up, but she found the rejection hard to come to terms with. She felt betrayed by her own desires and reactions. Mike's final words hadn't sounded like an invitation, there was no affection in them. They had sounded like a warning. Tracey shook free of her stasis and went to the balcony.

She slid the door closed behind her.

"Where's Mike?" Paul whispered in her ear.

Tracey jumped with fright and gave a small squeak.

Paul put his hand on her shoulder and squeezed gently. "I'm sorry."

Tracey pushed his hand away. "Mike's not coming."

Ray was looking at her, an eyebrow raised.

Tracey shrugged. She went to the rail and looked down. There was a cable tied to one of the rail posts, and it hung down through a cut in the insect screen where it joined the balcony.

"Where did you get that?" She pointed to the cable.

"One of the weight machines," Ray answered.

"It's not very long." In the dark she couldn't be sure, but it looked like it barely reached the next balcony

"It doesn't need to be." He turned to Paul. "Ready?"

Ray held Paul by one arm as he dropped over the edge and slid his feet through the cut in the screen. Paul grasped the cable with gloved hands. Cleaver held out a knife from the kitchen, Tracey couldn't help the shudder that ran through her at the sight of it. Paul held it between his teeth and quickly lowered himself down. Tracey watched, more than a little amazed, as he dropped smoothly down to the next balcony. He held the cable with one hand as he cut through the screens and then slipped quickly through.

"I can't do that!" Tracey told Ray. "I'll fall."

He shook his head. "You don't need to."

Cleaver pulled the cable back up and formed a loop at the end.

"Put this loop around you," he told her. "Sit in it. It won't be very comfortable, but it won't be for long. I'll lower you down." He reached across and handed her a thick jacket. "Paul left this for you to use as padding."

Tracey accepted the jacket gratefully, and folded it around between her and the cable.

As Ray assisted her over the rail she saw that he was wearing the same sort of gloves that Paul had used.

"More from the gym," he commented. "They didn't have any in your size, but you shouldn't need them."

"Just don't drop me." Tracey's voice came out in a nervous stutter, she was all too aware of the huge drop below her.

Ray smiled. "Ready?"

Tracey forced herself to nod.

"Lean back, let me take your weight."

After a long hesitation Tracey managed to do as she was asked. Even through her jeans and Paul's jacket, the thin cable cut into her hips and squeezed her painfully. The fine mesh of the insect screen brushed against her back, and her feet dropped through the hole.

"Now let go of the rail with one hand and hold the cable."

Tracey knew he was taking her through this like a child. In another situation she might be offended, but right now it was just what she needed.

"That's it. Now the other hand."

She stared at her other hand and willed the fingers to let go. It seemed they weren't going to obey, and then she was swinging free. She scraped against the balcony and her face rubbed against Ray's arm where it reached down to hold the cable.

"I've got you," Cleaver reassured her.

Tracey gasped softly each time she was lowered another few inches. The rough edges from the hole in the screen brushed up passed her. Some of her hair caught as it passed, and then flopped back over her face. She barely had time to realise she was swinging in the open when she felt hands grasp at her ankles.

Paul pulled her in through the screen and onto the lower balcony. His hands felt sure and strong and comforting as they held her legs, her thighs, her back. And then Tracey was standing. Paul held on to her, as if afraid she would fall over, and Tracey clung to him and rested. She was still shivering from the fear of her descent.

"Thank you," she said softly.

Paul's hold tightened for a moment, and then he stepped back. Tracey couldn't make out his expression.

"I—" he started. He cleared his throat. "We'd better get you out of that so Ray can come down."

It took a few moments to work the loop free. Tracey handed Paul his jacket, he tossed it to one side. He gave the cable a couple of quick jerks and they waited.

The cable twitched and jerked like something living. Feet appeared from above. Ray grunted quietly as he lowered himself a short distance at a time. Aldercott reached out and guided him onto the balcony.

"Not as young as I was," Ray panted when he was safely down. He pulled his gloves off and rubbed his hands on his legs.

"Not as light as you were either, boss," Paul remarked.

"Skinny bastard," Ray muttered.

Paul grinned. "The next bit's yours, Ray."

"I know. Give me a minute."

"What do you mean? How do we get down to the next one?" Tracey asked. She wasn't looking forward to repeating the experience.

"If Ray can do his thing we'll take the stairs from here," Aldercott answered.

As he worked, Ray explained that the door of the balcony above them wasn't connected to an alarm, so he was hoping none of these interior doors were. That just left the risk of cameras and patrolling guards.

"And those?" Tracey asked.

"Are in the lap of the gods."

- - -

Sando watched the three of them walking down the corridor, their images turning to dark silhouettes on the screen when they passed through shadows between the few lights left on. He was impressed with Ray's knack with locks, maybe he could get the old human to teach him before it became fodder.

The trio were walking quietly but it would have been more amusing if they were trying harder to be sneaky. Sando had an urge to turn on the speaker system and have the computer whisper something to them. Maybe, "I can see you." But he resisted the urge. He wanted to see how this played out.

- - -

Tilvy waited and watched from the small space between the building and the mesh. She had made out some movement when Tracey and the others had moved from the top floor to the next one down, but there had been nothing since, and she was starting to worry. Taiza and Beenae fidgeted near her, Pasith waited a few feet away.

There was movement on the balcony above them. Tilvy sensed three humans up there – Tracey and her two minders. Mike hadn't come, Tracey would be disappointed.

There was a tearing sound and a cut appeared where the insect screen folded back to meet the balcony.

"Tilvy?" Tracey's voice called down in a loud whisper.

Tilvy gave the two sticks she was carrying a single tap.

"Ray says you should come up here. We know this door is okay, the ones down on ground level may set off alarms."

Tilvy gave a single tap, and then rubbed the sticks together.

Tracey appeared to have guessed what it was Tilvy didn't understand. "Paul's getting something for you to climb up, hang on a sec'."

A short time later there were more sounds of movement, the whisper of voices and a tearing sound. To Tilvy it seemed very loud, but she knew the trees would swallow most of it. There was a soft rustling and the end of a length of cloth appeared. It quickly dropped lower, revealing knots tied at intervals.

"I can't tell what sort of material it is," Tracey whispered down to them. "Is it okay?"

When the material came within reach, Tilvy stretched up and touched it. Some sort of blend, not pleasant, but they would be able to grip it well enough. She gave a single tap.

"Ready when you are," Tracey said.

Tilvy put her sticks down and turned to Pasith. "Are you ready to meet some humans?"

His face bent into a grimace. "Do I have a choice?"

"Y' c'd stay," Taiza said.

Tilvy tugged at the cloth to make sure it was secure and started climbing. She pushed her way through the hole in the screen and saw Tracey looking over the rail with an expectant smile. Standing next to her, holding the cloth wrapped around the balcony rail was the younger man, Paul. The excited expression on his face made him look very young.

She got to the top of the cloth and had to reach out and grasp the young man's arm to pull herself over. He was startled by her touch but didn't pull away. Tracey, sensing Tilvy's presence, was reaching out to help as she climbed over the rail. The two of them hugged tightly.

"It's so good to feel you near again, Tilvy," Tracey whispered.

Tilvy wiped the tears from Tracey's cheek. "It is," she agreed, though Tracey wouldn't hear.

Pasith came up next, and moved quickly to one side of the

balcony. Beenae and Taiza followed.

"Is that it?" Aldercott asked, looking to Tracey.

Tilvy gave her friend a light tap on the arm.

"Yes," Tracey confirmed. She reached around behind her and pulled out a small pad and a pencil. The pencil had broken in half but was still usable. "Who's here?" Tracey asked Tilvy, then aside to Ray, "Can you shine your torch here?"

In the wavering light of the tiny torch, Tilvy scribbled four names.

"I don't know Pasith, do I?" Tracey asked.

Tilvy tapped her friend's arm twice.

"Hold out your hand, Ray," Tracey said. "Let Tilvy introduce herself."

The big man's hand almost swallowed Tilvy's. His head swung slowly from side to side as he stared down at his hand; it looked empty, but it wasn't. His mouth moved, but nothing came out.

"Come on, boss, my turn," Paul urged over his shoulder.

Ray stepped back and Paul put out his hand. Tilvy took it. The young man pressed it gently, glanced down and then looked up, trying to find her face.

"This is an honour, Tilvy. Thank you." His expression was one of awe.

Tilvy grinned. She'd never had that effect on anyone before.

"We'd better get a move on," Ray said. "Paul and I will take the lead, that way we won't fall over anyone."

Tilvy wasn't sure that was a good idea, but Ray had already turned away.

They made their way back into the corridor. Tilvy and Tracey held hands, partly so Tracey knew where her friend was, and partly in the relief of finally being close again. The carpet muffled their footsteps. It was very quiet.

- - -

Sando tapped on the edge of the keyboard and considered his options.

Until tonight he hadn't been certain the two male humans believed the narun existed, but the girl must have finally convinced them. Sando wasn't surprised that she had, in fact he was pleased. It was all much neater this way, and Sando liked things neat.

Having the narun prisoners climb up from the ground level was a

315

surprise. Sando had disabled the alarms on the ground floor doors, expecting them to try getting out that way. It wasn't a problem, just not what he had expected, and Sando didn't like unexpected.

So how far to let this go? If they got all the way out into the open, if they thought they had actually made it to freedom, their disappointment would be all the more crushing, and that would make for a fine conclusion to the game. But Sando hadn't forgotten the old woman at the Glade, and her smile as she snatched away the satisfaction he'd come for. Out in the open there could be more of the unexpected. If Jaimee were here it would be different, but Sando wasn't going to risk disappointment on his own.

He started typing commands.

They all froze as a speaker in the ceiling crackled into life.

"If you'd please stop where you are, your escort will be along shortly," came the smooth, pleasant voice.

Ray rushed the last few metres to the stair well. He opened the door and they could all hear the footsteps echoing.

"There's only one, I think," Ray whispered.

Tracey felt Tilvy tap on her arm; tap, tap, and then a rapid tapping that Tracey couldn't count. "No," Tracey voiced, "there's more. Ones you can't see." She felt a confirmation tap from Tilvy.

Ray pulled the door closed and made his way back quickly, murmuring his excuses when he bumped Tilvy and Pasith as he hurried past them. They hadn't gone far when the door at the other end of the corridor was pulled open.

"Plan B," Ray said, and tried the nearest door. It was locked. "Stand clear." He stepped back and kicked at the door near the handle. There was a deep thud and a metallic screeching, but the door held.

"Stop!" the big man approaching from the far end yelled.

Ray kicked out again. There was more metallic screeching and the door cracked open but didn't swing free.

The big man yelled again, and this time it was accompanied by a rapid series of muffled gunshots. Bullets hit high on the edge of the doorway in front of them and fragments of the door spattered out.

Ray stood back and raised his hands, Paul and Tracey followed suit. Tilvy moved her hand to rest on Tracey's shoulder.

"Don't move, or the next rounds don't miss," the man said, he was getting close now.

"Lower your gun, Cutler," a deep voice came from the other direction.

This was another large man, but in his hands was an antenna like device, a wire from it stretched to a backpack.

"Is that a weapon?" Paul asked Tracey softly.

"Yes," she whispered back.

Ray was still looking at the first man. Tracey saw Ray lower one hand, and raise it again. He smiled.

"Parsons?" Cutler called out.

"Put your gun away," the other guard called back.

"Does Cutler look jumpy to you, Paul?" Ray asked quietly.

"Yes, boss."

Ray started to lower one hand again, and then raised it. The smile remained. "Have you ever noticed, Paul, that anyone used to carrying a gun assumes that everyone is carrying?"

"You'd be talking about the Yanks again, wouldn't you, boss?"

Ray's smile widened, but he didn't look away from Cutler. "Is he someone whose reflexes might be faster than his brain, do you think?"

Paul was slower to respond this time. The two men had stopped about five metres away on either side, and Paul glanced back and forth between them. "Maybe, but I don't like where you're going with this."

Ray ignored that. "When I say drop, I want you all to drop flat to the floor on this side of the corridor – near the door if you can. *Everyone*. Is that understood?"

Tracey felt Tilvy tap once on her shoulder. "Yes," she confirmed, though she had no idea what he was thinking.

"This is *not* a good idea, boss," Paul said.

"That was an order, Mr Aldercott." Ray stepped away from the door he had been kicking, and moved one of his arms again. This time Tracey noticed the first man, Cutler, start to raise his gun, then to lower it again. The weapon wavered as it pointed to the floor, the man seemed to be gripping it very tightly.

Ray continued speaking quietly, "As soon as you get the chance, make your way into the room, the door should open now. Barricade

317

it behind you and then try to get out. We're only on the first floor."

"Ray?" Tracey queried.

"Don't argue, Tracey," Ray answered. "Better that some of us get out than none. We may not get another chance. That goes double for your friends, make sure they understand."

Tracey wasn't sure how to do that, she was only sure that she didn't like the sound of whatever Ray had planned.

"Maybe—" Tracey started, but was interrupted by a painful squeeze from Tilvy's hand on her shoulder. There was someone coming from the other way. An elegant, slender young man wearing a suit and a confident smile.

\- - -

Sando walked calmly toward the group. It was so good to see the disappointment and fear on all their faces. Almost all. Clever Cleaver looked like he still had something on his mind. Sando checked that the dhumraka were in their places, waiting behind the guards on both sides; the human couldn't hope to get past them.

He came up next to Parsons, nodded his head to his guests, then stepped back and pulled a small electronic pad from the guard's backpack. He tapped it to start playing his pre-recorded message.

"I got dressed up so you could all see me. The humans among you may not fully understand, and that would be sad. So here's a demonstration." Sando pulled the artificial skin from his left hand and waved his fingers at his guests. He smiled at the surprise on their faces. "I thought you'd like that.

"Since you are apparently bored with your current accommodation, I've come to escort you all to your new home. I suggest you cooperate quietly, though I'll be happy either way." Sando offered another wide smile.

"Down!" yelled Cleaver.

Sando froze in surprise as all the prisoners except Cleaver dropped to the floor. Cleaver turned his back on Sando and his hands dropped down as if he was reaching for something inside his jacket. Movement beyond Cleaver caught Sando's eye and he saw Cutler raising his gun. Not quite believing what he was seeing, Sando was slow to react. The gun was level before Sando managed to thrust out with his mind, wrenching savagely at the man's thoughts to try and make him stop.

But that was a mistake. Cutler's hand wavered as his finger came down on the trigger. It froze there and bullets fired wildly down the corridor. Cutler stumbled forward, his free hand reaching for his head. The gun was still firing.

Cleaver dropped. Parsons, whose body had partly protected Sando, jerked a couple of times and collapsed. A bullet grazed high on Sando's arm, the pain of it burned. He heard screams of pain from the dhumraka near him.

The bullets only lasted a few seconds before the magazine ran out, but that was enough. Cutler was still standing, as were the dhumraka behind him, but around Sando was devastation. Sando looked down, unbelieving, at the dead and wounded. When he looked back up he saw the prisoners entering the room off the corridor. He would deal with them in a moment. First there was Cutler.

Tilvy and Paul pulled Tracey into the room with them.

"Help me move this!" Paul called out.

They all worked together to slide a heavy cupboard in front of the door.

"Ray?" Tracey asked.

"This is what he wanted," Paul said. His voice thick, his words abrupt.

Screaming erupted from outside. Tilvy recognised it as human – barely.

"Come on!" Paul yelled at them.

They ran to the large windows overlooking the street. Aldercott grabbed at a chair and swung it at the window. It bounced off. He tried a couple more times and a crack appeared.

The screaming continued out in the corridor.

"Help me with this!" Paul grabbed the side of a desk.

Even with all the others on the other side they had trouble keeping up with Paul as he rushed the desk at the window. The window smashed and rained down in tiny pieces. Paul was almost carried over with the desk, but Taiza managed to grab him and pull him back.

The screaming had stopped. There was a light thump against the door.

"You others jump down," Paul ordered. "I'll lower Tracey and you can help her."

"But Paul?" Tracey started.

Paul didn't meet Tracey's eyes as he grabbed her by her shoulders and moved to the edge.

Tilvy hesitated. She didn't like the idea of being separated from Tracey again, but what Paul said made sense.

Pasith pulled at her arm. "Come on, before Sando puts his mind on us."

Tilvy and Pasith jumped out into the night, leaping beyond the desk and broken glass. They landed lightly at the side of the empty street. There was a loud curse and Tilvy looked back.

Taiza hadn't jump far enough, he had come down against the upturned desk and was clutching at his leg. Beenae was rushing back to him. Paul was lowering Tracey from the window. Tilvy tried to step forward to help, but Pasith pulled her back.

"Too late," he told her.

Sando was standing in the window, his suit and artificial skin gone. He was staring down at Taiza and Beenae. Taiza screamed, let go of his leg and clutched at his head. Beenae tried to hold him.

Pasith pulled at Tilvy. She didn't want to go, but Pasith wouldn't relent. She had to follow him or be dragged. They were almost across the street when Tilvy felt Pasith stumble. There was a car coming. It was almost on them. Tilvy threw herself against Pasith and together they rolled into the gutter.

The car was gone. Tilvy waited for Sando to take control of her. She wondered if this time she could find a way to resist it. But it didn't happen. Sando wasn't looking at her. His attention had returned to those close at hand. Paul was lifting Tracey back up.

"They're coming!" Pasith cried out. He pulled himself upright and dragged Tilvy to her feet.

There were dhumraka coming around the outside of the building, more leapt from the window near Sando.

Tilvy finally admitted to herself that there was nothing she could do here. To be captured again would help no one. They would have to escape now, if they could, and come back for her friends. She stopped struggling with Pasith. They turned and ran.

- - -

"Paul?" Tracey called up.

He didn't answer.

She was rising. She was being pulled roughly across the windowsill and the broken glass. She was falling again. But not far, she landed roughly on the carpeted floor. She struggled to her feet and looked at Paul.

"What—?" she started, but stopped when she saw the pain spreading over his face. She turned. There looked to be nothing there, but Tracey knew better. She stepped forward and swung her fist. She connected with something and it fell back. She stumbled.

Pain spiked through her temples. She struggled against it. The pain rose further, and then everything went black.

- - -

They ran. And always the dhumraka were behind them. So they kept on running. Up hill and down hill. Across streets. Tilvy had no idea where she was or what direction they were going. The wind was rising, swirling from unexpected directions around the buildings. They ran across a street that was still busy with traffic, narrowly missed by cars that couldn't see them. That bought them some time, but not much. Another turn and a glimpse of ocean was available far down the hill.

"Come on," Pasith urged her, and they made a renewed effort.

The tantalising glimpses of ocean came and disappeared as they ran. Pasith pulled her across the street and they were running across a low cut lawn. Past trees. Over concrete. A tiny beach. Gusts of wind blew stinging sand in their faces.

"At last," Pasith said in relief, and pulled Tilvy after him.

Tilvy knew this wasn't right, it wasn't safe, but she was too exhausted to argue. She allowed herself to be pulled across the sand and into the water.

Pasith swam so smoothly and easily through the water that he could have quickly left Tilvy behind, but he kept returning and pulling her forward, urging her on. They had gained a good lead on the dhumraka before they entered the water, but the grey narun couldn't be far behind.

An eternity later Pasith let Tilvy rest, she couldn't go on.

"Not long," he warned her.

It seemed like only moments and he was urging her to swim

again. There had been no sign of the dhumraka but it wasn't safe to remain.

It was daylight again, a small amount of light penetrated down to where Tilvy was resting near the ocean floor amid the low growth. Pasith had swum off a short distance, how he could keep going she didn't know. He came back in a rush. Tilvy forced herself to start moving before he had to say it.

They managed to stay ahead of their pursuers for the rest of the day. The sun had gone down again when they entered a mass of greenery so thick that at first Tilvy was bewildered by it. She finally recognised it as the kelp that she had seen so long ago in those pools at the top of the Research Centre. She clutched at Pasith and whispered in panic, "This is where they live!"

Pasith didn't respond. He pulled Tilvy up next to him and swam upward, winding his way through the thick kelp. Near the surface he pulled Tilvy into a thick mat of the velvety fronds and drew them both to a stop. The water was rocking up and down as strong winds swept over the surface. Pasith put his fingers to his lips to tell Tilvy not to speak, and they merged into the water amid the fronds, rising and falling with the waves in the darkness.

Tilvy felt the presence of dhumraka come and go around them for a time, searching. Pasith had hidden their presence within the abundant life of the kelp. If anyone came too close they might be found, and they would be vulnerable like this, but the dhumraka eventually passed on. The fiery life of a school of small fish passed through the water that Tilvy occupied, a strange hot tickling sensation. And then they were alone.

Pasith emerged from the water and Tilvy followed. He whispered in her ear. "Follow me. Slowly."

He slipped his way smoothly like an eel, barely disturbing the water or the plants. Tilvy tried to emulate his actions as best she could. She didn't know where he was going, his direction seemed random to her. The storm had passed, the surface had calmed and the sky was growing light above the water when he finally stopped.

"Some distance between us and where they were looking for us," he explained quietly. "This might be enough for now. We should rest here while we can."

Tilvy started to try and say something, but she didn't know what.

Her mind felt like it was drifting in a fog. So much had happened and now her friends were ...? She looked into Pasith's face.

He smiled gently and squeezed her arm. "Just rest," he said.

It was late afternoon when they emerged from the water. Dhumraka had passed close by a few times through the day.

"We've got to go back," Tilvy urged. "We've got to help the others."

Pasith shook his head, though his expression was sympathetic. "They'll be watching for us. We have to get away from here first."

"But—"

He took her hand. "Trust me. I'm not trying to run out. You and your friends rescued Neso and me when everyone else had given up on us. I haven't forgotten that."

Tilvy nodded reluctantly.

"Come on."

Tilvy again followed Pasith as he carefully threaded his way through the matted fronds. It was slow going, but the life of the kelp would help to obscure their presence from any distant watchers. Later that night they rested again, and then moved on at sunrise.

They came to a break in the forest. It wasn't far until it started again, but they paused briefly, trying to decide whether to risk moving into the open, or whether to try another way. Pasith led them down to the seabed, hoping that they could gain enough cover to cross the gap unnoticed.

The growth wasn't so dense near the rocky bottom. It didn't hide them as well. And that was enough. They heard a distant call coming from ahead of them somewhere, and then another, closer, from the left. Dhumraka entered the clearing not far from them, these were carrying spears.

There was no time to confer. Pasith pulled Tilvy around and they swam as fast as they could back into the forest.

Tilvy could hear more calls as the chase started again. So many voices calling out, it seemed hopeless. She kicked out harder, trying to keep up with Pasith as he wound his way back and forth.

Pasith turned suddenly to the left, Tilvy clawed at the water trying to follow him. She caught a brief glimpse of the dhumraka he was trying to avoid, and heard the man shout to his friends.

Tilvy was just too slow here. She could never outswim the dhumraka. On his own, Pasith might have a chance. She called out to him, urging him on. He turned back and grabbed her arm, pulling her with him.

They burst through a thick wall of kelp fronds. Pasith was reaching back to check on Tilvy. He looked up only just in time to stop himself being impaled on a spear. Tilvy cried out in despair. More than a dozen spears faced them in this small clearing. There was nowhere else to go.

She looked past the spear points into the faces behind them.

16. Choosing

"Would it help if he formed a tail?"

"No, my Lord Theseo," Polyphemo replied, "we tried that. He can't use it effectively. He's more agile as he is – and he can move quickly when he tries." The last given as a warning.

Senna was surprised when Theseo looked her way.

"Give him the blade," Theseo commanded.

Senna looked down at the sapphire sword.

"Now, girl."

Senna swam to Andrei. At least this session hadn't resulted in more bruising, not since Theseo arrived unannounced and decided to take a hand. It had all been practising movements and ways of holding the practice weapon, but it looked like they were moving beyond that now.

Andrei gave her an unhappy look as he accepted the hilt of the zakti. Senna tried to give him a reassuring smile, but it didn't come easily.

"Now bring me his staff, girl," Theseo demanded.

"He's definitely making it easier for me to consider sticking him with the sharp end?" Andrei whispered as he handed over the practice blade.

"Me first," Senna whispered back.

Theseo met Senna halfway. His eyes wandered over her, seeming to pause as they passed over her legs. Then his gaze moved back to her eyes. Senna was tempted to poke her tongue out, but lowered her eyes and passed over the weapon. Theseo brushed past her and took up position close to Andrei.

Senna returned to her place by Sarva. The water was crowded

with Marr warriors, the usual guard plus those that had come with Theseo. All were watching the demonstration with interest.

As Theseo proceeded to take Andrei through different movements, two things were immediately obvious: Andrei did much better with the zakti than he had with the practice blade, and Theseo was fast, powerful and agile, even in comparison to Polyphemo. Senna almost groaned aloud to see what Andrei would be up against.

Later, Polyphemo was called in. With Theseo on one side of Andrei, and Polyphemo on the other, Andrei was encouraged to keep twisting back and forth, trying to strike their weapons as they moved around him, and over him, and under him. Not once did the zakti ever touch one of their weapons. As fast as Andrei sometimes was, he just couldn't match the samudraka in the water. Soon he was exhausted. The only positive sign that the training was having any effect was that he didn't automatically try to align himself with the surface, nor with either of his opponents.

"You need to build your stamina," Theseo told him.

"Why?" Andrei asked. Senna cringed to hear the defeated tones.

"Don't you want to die with honour?" Theseo asked, his tone slightly incredulous.

"I don't want to die at all!" Andrei twisted around so that he was looking at Theseo directly.

Theseo didn't respond at first. He looked down at his blunt practice blade, turning it back and forth for a few moments. Then, in apparent disgust, he sent it knifing through the water to Polyphemo, who deftly caught it.

"Then kill me now," Theseo said, holding his arms out in sacrifice.

"I don't want to kill you."

"Why not? That's what I will do to you. Coward or not, I *will* kill you."

"I'm not a coward," answered Andrei, anger creeping into his voice. He moved forward slightly, and Senna saw the surrounding Marr guards all lean in, ready to intervene.

Theseo waved them back. "Who but a coward will not fight for his life?"

Andrei tensed for a moment, and then pulled back and shook his head. "What life? Why should I play your games?" Andrei glanced

326

around at the Marr, still tense with concern. "What good would it do anyone for me to kill you? Will I live? Will you let my friends go?"

"Fight me now, as we are – you with Zamayitar, myself unarmed – and I will command my guards not to interfere."

"And?"

"And, if you should win, I will command them to escort you out of here."

Senna felt the Marr guards near her move restlessly. She glanced around and saw they were not comfortable with the regent's offer.

Senna was surprised to see Andrei grin. "You make a tempting offer, Lord Theseo," he replied, "but no."

"You are too much of a coward even for this?"

Senna could see there was no anger in Andrei now, Theseo's goading was having no effect.

"I admit that I'm not in a hurry to fight with you or anyone. I'm allergic to pain – I break out in grimaces and they spoil the lines of my youthful face. But that's not the reason for rejecting your offer, Lord Theseo," Andrei emphasised the title with more than a touch of sarcasm. "I'm not the bravest person alive, but I'm not stupid either. Even if I had a chance of defeating you, which I doubt, none of us are leaving here with Zak."

"Your friend—?" Theseo started.

Andrei raised the zakti.

"Oh." Theseo paused, then said, "You have my word as regent."

Andrei looked across at Senna and smiled sadly. Looking back at Theseo, he answered, "If I thought such a promise meant anything then perhaps I would try."

"You doubt my word?"

Andrei shook his head. "No. But I doubt the power of your word after your death."

Theseo lowered his arms. "You are right. Even if the Marr would obey me, others would not. Zamayitar cannot be allowed to remain in your hands and there is only one way it can be released."

Senna was struck by how similar the two men appeared, her Andrei and this young regent. They looked nothing alike, but floating there facing each other, there was something of defeat and respect in their expressions that linked the two.

Theseo continued, "For the honour of the Marr, for my own

honour, and for the good of the samudraka, it must be me that does this when the time comes. I would rather not have to kill a helpless man."

"And I'd rather not be that man," said Andrei. "Being helpless or not has little to do with it."

"Perhaps," Theseo acknowledged, "but wouldn't you rather end it honourably?"

"Honourably?"

"To die in battle, having fought valiantly, brings honour to any warrior."

"I'm not a warrior. Anyway, what honour does a corpse feel?"

"But the memory you leave behind with your friends, your woman." Theseo pointed to Senna.

Andrei grinned across at her. "Senna thinks I'm an idiot anyway. I think I prefer it that way."

Senna laughed, though she felt more like crying.

"I do not understand," said Theseo.

"That's okay," said Andrei. "You probably had to be there."

Theseo shook his head and turned. Senna felt his gaze rest on her for a moment, before it moved on to Sarva. "A word, if you please."

Later, on the beach, night had fallen and a light, misty rain was blowing softly across the group as they listened to Sarva. Senna liked the feel of the rain, delicate and clean, almost a caress. She had one arm around Andrei, but his attention was on the sword, constantly touching it and turning it over in his hands.

"Theseo is running out of time and options," Sarva was saying.

"Why does he tell you this?" Garjae interrupted. "Why not tell us all?"

Sarva paused and thought about that, before answering, "Probably because he can justify speaking with me privately, because I appear to be our leader, or at least our spokesperson. To speak with us a group would mean having the guards overhear, and some of it I don't think he wants to admit in the open."

"So why tell us at all?"

"Because he believes us and he wants our help to defeat the papayamala. He's been doing everything he can to make sure we are willing to help, but it's costing him.

"He sent out people to search the region where his mother saw the papayamala. He's been hoping to get confirmation that doesn't come from aaranya – that, he thinks, might give him what he needs to take action as regent, but none have returned yet. He's been encouraging all the samudraka to wait for Holitto's return before deciding to choose a new king."

"That's not likely, is it?" Darnu put in.

"No. Theseo admits that, but tradition says they should wait and that's been enough to let Theseo convince them – so far."

"So what's the problem?" Senna asked, since all this was obviously leading to something.

"The longer he waits the more of Theseo's support is disappearing. A samudraka called Nelious, of the Raktana, is gaining confidence enough now to suggest that they don't need to wait, that they should choose a new king."

"And this Nelious thinks they're going to choose him?" Andrei asked, not lifting his eyes from the zakti.

"I'm not sure I understood it all," Sarva admitted. "But in a situation like this—"

"This has happened before?"

Sarva shrugged. "I doubt it, but I think they're working on the idea that the zakti is available to whoever can pick it up, and I suppose that might have happened before."

"It's nice to be taken seriously," Andrei muttered.

"It was you that rejected more training," Garjae reminded him.

"In a situation like this," Sarva repeated, "it seems that there can be multiple contenders, but each must have enough support or the selection could turn messy. So the assembly tries to agree in advance on who may contend."

"I'm confused," said Senna. "I thought the problem was having multiple contenders."

"If they have widespread support, then that's okay," said Sarva. "As far as I can understand, it's a matter of having people willing to accept the contender if he wins, even if he's not the one they want to win. That's what those assemblies we attended were about, and I assume more goes on in private. Theseo said that the final selection is usually a formality."

"If there are multiple contenders then we might not get Theseo as

329

king anyway," said Darnu.

"Theseo seems confident."

Garjae snorted.

Sarva ignored that and continued, "Theseo's problem is that he can't afford to lose any more support, and if he's not a contender then it might turn to war. The Marr have held the throne for so long that they won't give it up without a fight, whatever everyone else thinks."

"Crap," said Andrei, looking up from the zakti at last. "That's what this afternoon was about, wasn't it? Theseo was hoping I'd attack him, give him an *honourable* reason for killing me and taking Zak. He was trying to cheat and cut through all this."

"Theseo didn't tell me that, but I think so, yes," Sarva said.

"What happened to wanting our help?" Garjae asked, his tone sarcastic.

"That's easy," said Andrei. "In his eyes it would have been an honourable battle, and you'd all have been pleased as sunshine with my valiant but ultimately inadequate efforts. So pleased, you would have quickly forgiven him the necessity of relieving me of the dreadful burden of my cowardly life, and be falling over yourselves to help him in any way you could."

Senna squeezed Andrei against her side. Though the words were delivered in humour, she could hear the bitterness beneath them.

Sarva looked at Andrei quietly for a moment.

"What?" asked Andrei. "You going to tell me I'm wrong?"

Sarva shook his head. "Theseo did say to warn you that the next time we're called to the Hall of the King ... it will probably be to choose a new king. Theseo is going to add his voice to those saying there is no need to wait. He has no choice. He has to move while he has the support to be a contender."

"And I suppose he expects that the rest of us will still be happy to help, even after all this happens?" said Garjae.

Sarva nodded. "That's what he hopes."

"So it's all been an elaborate ruse." Garjae raised his voice. "Lord fucking Theseo getting all friendly, telling us stories so we'll stay happy even when he starts killing us off. John's already gone. Who's next after Andrei?"

Senna stopped listening then. She took the zakti from Andrei's

330

hand and lay it on the sand. Then she pulled him up and led him through the rain, heavier now than it had been, and into the ocean. She tried not to think about the fact that their remaining time together had suddenly been cut so short.

--- --- ---

"What secret?" John asked. He was whispering too, though he didn't know why. His body was insisting that he respond to this beautiful woman, so close and so naked. Though her body was currently hidden beneath the gold of the pool, he had seen it enough times that no imagination was needed to know what was there.

Lantea pushed herself back a little, though her hand remained resting high on his chest. John had to stop himself from reaching out to pull her closer.

"Yes," Lantea said ambiguously, perhaps answering some thought of her own. She spoke so quietly that John had to tilt his head forward to hear her properly. "My one little secret seems a poor payment for all the secrets that I know you carry. But what else do I have to bargain with?"

John made himself lean back. "What secret?" he asked again.

"There are so many to choose from, I hardly know where to start." Lantea smiled at him, but it didn't reach her eyes. "Like why the papayamala were so interested in taking your ... lover?" Lantea ran her hand slowly, tantalisingly, down John's chest. "Was she so very beautiful that they couldn't resist?" Her hand stopped and pulled away. "Or was there something else?"

When John didn't respond to that, Lantea continued, "Or perhaps I should ask what is so special about Sarva that he could escape from the one you call Helix? The one he claims is so powerful."

John remembered Senna asking the same question.

"No. There's one secret that's more interesting than any of those – to me."

He waited.

Lantea pressed closer and whispered, "What are you really?"

Trying to divert the conversation, John asked, "That's something I've never understood about the narun. How is it you are so certain I'm not aaranya?"

Lantea raised an eyebrow.

John thought back over what he'd just said and cursed himself for a fool.

"You taste different," Lantea said, apparently deciding to answer the question anyway.

"The narun have no sense of taste," John said, though he remembered what he thought of the samudraka accent when he'd first heard them.

"It is as good a word as any for the way that different people seem to our senses. You may look much the same, but you move differently, you hold yourself differently. You sound different when you speak." Lantea leaned in and ran her nose up the side of John's head, he felt her breasts brush over his shoulder. "You smell different." Lantea pulled back and finished, "You *are* different. Any *narun* can sense that. So what are you? You who know so much about humans. You who speak of the narun as something separate to yourself."

"We told you, saarvaya."

"A word that means nothing to us. You gave us a story that is full of things left unsaid. The men playing games with power may not have time for such details, but *I* think they could be important."

"You think we are lying to you?"

"About the papayamala, no. The samudraka won't move without confirming for themselves, my son sent out men as soon as Sarva first spoke of them, but I believe that part of your story. As for the rest ... at the least, there are some things you fear to tell us."

"You said you have a secret," John prompted.

"Oh no you don't," Lantea said, and rested her hand back on his chest. "I have only the one. I'm not giving it away without some reward in advance." Her hand moved lower.

John pulled away from her.

"I know you're tempted."

John didn't try to deny it. Whatever his mind might be telling him, his body was making its own preferences well known. "It's this pool."

"That's not a very flattering thing to tell a lady."

John shook his head in frustration. "You know what I mean."

"Does it matter?"

John tried a different tack. "I thought we had things to discuss."

"I thought you didn't want to tell me," Lantea countered.

332

John tried to think clearly, but was finding it difficult. "And will you share my secret with your son, the regent?"

"If you are a threat to the samudraka, I will have no choice."

"I'm not. I'm not much of a threat to anyone."

"In that case, speak. The samudraka do not jump at shadows."

John looked past her, no longer able to hold her intense gaze. Was there any harm in telling her what he was? It seemed likely that she might have guessed some part of it. Perhaps it would help if he was open about it, rather than keeping it a secret for her to worry over. It was possible it might distract her from the other questions about Asha and Sarva.

He could feel Lantea's attention still centred on him. He wasn't ready to look back at her yet, but she was hard to resist, in all senses.

His eyes involuntarily followed some slow movement out beyond Lantea. At first his mind was too busy to take in what he was seeing. Front-on, it was just another face of a creature coming to the pool of life. The eyes bulged out to the sides like so many of the creatures he'd seen, though these were more forward than most. The face was long, and the lips were thin and closed in a flat line, giving the creature a grim expression. The skin colour was a pale yellow-orange, the colour deepening to red at the sides.

Many things crowded in on John's senses at once. This wasn't some big creature up close, it was a huge creature still some distance a way – but not far enough. More red appeared on both sides as the long body coiled up behind it. That red was familiar. The grim lips began to part, revealing the glow of large white teeth. Those were familiar too.

John opened his mouth, but no words came out. Now that yellow-orange head was rapidly swelling. No! It was rushing at them as the huge body uncoiled. There was no time for words. John lunged forward and grabbed at Lantea. He had time to see the astonishment on her face before his arms went around her, and then he was dragging them both down into golden pool.

He felt Lantea struggle against him, and he drew his arms tighter, crushing her body against his. Something hard and rough crashed into his back, pushing them deeper into the pool. He felt the skin on his back and buttocks tear as the lower jaw of the serpent swept past. Moments later he heard that strange ringing, rasping call as the serpent screamed out its frustration.

The current of the serpent's passing pushed Lantea and John even deeper, swirling them around. John continued to hold Lantea, not wanting to be separated and fearful that the creature would be back. Their movement slowed as the currents quickly settled in the viscous mud, but still John clung to Lantea, as blind down here in the intense life of the pool as if he was staring into a spotlight.

"I knew you were tempted," Lantea spoke seductively into John's ear.

John opened his mouth and it filled with the mud of the pool. He tried to spit it out and to disentangle himself from Lantea, but now her strong arms held him tightly, and her powerful legs wrapped around him and squeezed him against her. What the panic with the serpent had quickly reduced, Lantea's insistent pressure was now restoring.

Speech. Milla had shown him a long time ago that the telepathic speech of the narun didn't require the use of the mouth, it was only a convenient focal point. John tried to think his words aloud.

"This is not what I want," he managed to say.

"Your body says different." Lantea squeezed more tightly with her legs in emphasis.

"There is another. ... Asha." Saying her name helped to steady John's resolve.

"What she doesn't know can't matter to her."

"It matters to me."

Lantea released her hold. "Rejection is an odd sensation. I don't think I like it."

John pulled away from her, but kept hold of her hand. "It is not rejection. It is a choice." He squeezed her fingers gently. "My people place a lot of importance on fidelity to a loved one."

"As do ours – in speech. But it rarely means that much, especially not here in the sarasi-jilvana of all places. Here, life is insistent."

"I know," John acknowledged ruefully.

"You are a strange—"

"Ow!" John exclaimed, forgetting himself and taking in a mouthful of mud. Something bit into his already injured back, an injury he had forgotten until now.

"The kravyada have found us, we must move." Lantea grasped John's hand strongly and began pulling at him.

John tried to help, but their movement remained slow through the mud. He hoped that Lantea knew what she was doing, John wasn't even certain which way was up. More nips at his back. John bit down on his lips to stop himself taking in more of the mud. There was a bite at his groin and he hurriedly swept the creature away. The pressure on his hand, still held firmly by Lantea, jerked, and John guessed she was being attacked too.

Their heads broached the surface. The serpent! John looked around quickly but didn't see it. Another bite distracted him and he flicked away the kravyada.

He saw Lantea try to rise from the mud, but without the rock ledge to grasp she couldn't break free. John glanced across, they were a long way from the ledge now.

"Here," he called to her. "Stand on me."

At first he thought she was going to embrace him again, but she simply smiled and touched his face before placing her hands on his shoulders and pushing herself upward. As her body moved past his, John reached down along one of her legs until he could get his hands under her foot, and he pushed up as hard as he could. He felt himself sinking deeper into the mud. Several kravyada were biting at his back and stomach, but still he kept pushing at Lantea's foot until the pressure disappeared. He took a moment to brush the creatures from him and swam for the surface.

"Give me you hand," Lantea called to him as he emerged.

John looked up. Lantea had transformed, her silver tail glowing gold above the pool. John reached out. He saw the serpent coming at them again. "The serpent!" he warned.

"I know!" Lantea grabbed John's hand and her tail thrust powerfully through the water.

The mud was reluctant to let go, John felt it clutching at him, sucking at him. And then he was free. Lantea's tail struck him several times, but she kept swimming. John, helpless to aid their progress, looked behind them. A wall of sharp teeth was closing in. Beyond the teeth a bright orange gullet disappeared into black. He could see the tongue, a short red, pointed thing, and even that seemed to be trying to stretch out, hungry for them both.

He knew the creature was huge, but being so close to those glowing white teeth was an emphasis he didn't need. This thing could quite literally swallow them whole.

He watched the jaws stretch in anticipation as the creature sped up to close the last small distance. John's arm was wrenched to the side. There was a flash of white. There was the rough surface of the serpents skin against his feet. And then a crash. His head and shoulders screamed out in pain and everything went black.

There was pain, a lot of it. For some reason John was surprised by this. His head hurt, his shoulders hurt, his back hurt, and there were lots of little hurts to add to the symphony. He groaned.

"Let that be a lesson to you," Lantea's voice came softly to him from close by. "No one rejects me without swift retribution."

John remembered why he was surprised. He hadn't expected to still be in pain after being chewed up by a serpent. He expected to be dead.

He opened his eyes. They were inside the cave. Lantea was smiling down at him, she was nursing his head against her breasts, but released him to float freely in the water, and drew back as he started to move.

"An honourable man would laugh when a lady makes a joke," she told him, still smiling.

John tried to smile.

"I am sorry about your head and shoulders. You don't turn as fast as a samudraka, you hit the side of the cave when we came in."

"Much better than the alternative," John managed. "Thank you for saving me."

Lantea seemed to consider this for a moment, and then smiled briefly before saying, "I think it's safe to return to the pool. We both need it." She indicated bite marks on her breasts and stomach, each bright gold with the prana still seeping from the wounds. More marks were visible further down. She had transformed again, now floating exposed in front of him. "The bites on my legs are less painful like this," she explained, "the stiff skin of a tail aggravates them. It's not a come on, not this time – although ...?"

John managed to smile more convincingly, but shook his head.

"No?" She shrugged. "Come on."

Movement was painful, but worth it. Settling back into the pool brought rapid relief to his injuries. John dunked his head beneath the surface for a while to try and relieve the headache.

"We may have to move again soon," Lantea said when John raised his head. "It was the tears in your back, which you forgot to tell me about, I might add—"

"I seem to remember being distracted," John interrupted.

"It's good to know I wasn't a total failure," Lantea acknowledged. "Those injuries drew the kravyada, and will again. So stay ready."

After a time, Lantea inspected John's back. "Your wounds are mostly closed now. We may as well move where we are less likely to be disturbed."

They settled into the pool again and Lantea turned to face John, staring at him with a familiar intensity. John wondered if it was all going to start over.

"You were about to tell me what you are," Lantea said.

"I was?"

Lantea nodded.

John supposed she was right, he had almost convinced himself. He went over the story in his head, working out what he could say without giving away Asha and Sarva's secret. It still meant leaving out any mention of his daughter, or the real reason why they had gone to the Samgha. Sarva's explanation was that they had been tricked into going there, and that still held up well enough, it was close enough to true. John thought it would work. So he started talking.

"You were human?" Lantea asked when he had finished.

"Yes."

"And there were others like you?"

"Not exactly. The Samgha said they weren't entirely human."

"But they were material creatures, like humans?"

John nodded.

"Why didn't you say so earlier?"

"Because we knew the samudraka don't like humans."

"We don't like aaranya either."

"We thought adding a human – ex-human anyway – might be a step too far."

Lantea stayed quiet for a time, looking across the pool.

"Are you glad we got interrupted now?" John was curious about what Lantea might think of him now that she knew the truth.

"The pool of life, sarasi-jilvana, makes no distinctions."

"And you?" John pressed.

Lantea looked at him. She was studying his face, perhaps looking for signs of what he had once been, John thought. Eventually she answered, "I am conflicted. ... It's not unlike how I feel about those children, the papayamala."

"That bad?"

Lantea shook her head. "I know I should be appalled, or disgusted or something. But they were beautiful and I can't help but remain curious about them." She paused and looked John in the eye. "I feel the same way about you."

- - -

Andrei felt reasonably at peace with himself, but he was worried about Senna. He could feel her clinging tightly to his hand. He wondered if she would let go when the time came.

The Hall of the King was a very different place this time around. Their group had been pushed up into their usual corner near the front, but the throng of samudraka were quiet and mostly still. Instead of the constant mix of colours, the floor of the hall was a patchwork, each samtaana keeping to themselves. There appeared to be a ranking to the groups, a hierarchy in which the most important samudraka communities were gathered together nearest the front. The dark jade of the Marr and the faded blood of the Raktana were next to each other immediately before the regent. There were no elders present at this assembly, their leaves had settled closer to the floor, and this made Theseo appear higher than usual upon his central leaf.

"It has been proposed that we should wait no longer for King Holitto, so long lost to the search for his nikasa." Theseo spoke loudly across the heads of the assembly. "We have before us convincing evidence that he will not return." Theseo waved vaguely toward Andrei. "As regent, I have been persuaded to support this view, though I would gladly give my beloved brother more time to take his rightful place before you."

Theseo paused there, as if waiting for someone to interrupt. The hall remained silent.

338

"People of Agadharastra, we mourn the passing of our king," Theseo called out in loud chanting tones. "Maharaja Holitto, Mahanidra Agadhajala."

"Maharaja Holitto, Mahanidra Agadhajala," chanted the assembled samudraka.

Andrei heard Darnu whispering a translation, "King Holitto, sleep-of-death in deep water."

"Mahasarpa greets you as an equal," intoned Theseo. The assembled repeated it, and Darnu continued to translate.

"Our father-kings welcome you at their side."

"Your life flows on through this kingdom."

"King Holitto, sleep-of-death in deep water."

Silence fell over the hall and Andrei could see that all those present had bowed their heads, so he hurriedly did the same. He felt Senna squeeze his hand. He looked across and saw the fear in her eyes. He pressed her hand against his side and whispered, "It will be all right." Senna turned her head, but continued to hold tightly to his hand.

"People of Agadharastra," Theseo called out loudly, and Andrei looked up to watch him. "My time as regent has passed with the passing of King Holitto. It is time for a new king to stand forward."

Theseo swam out over the group of Marr, and remained floating a body length above them.

The crowd stirred briefly and then silence settled again.

Theseo spoke out across the hall, "I, Theseo of the Marr, son of King Poseitto, brother to King Holitto, offer the power of my tail, the strength of my arm, and the length of my life in the service of Agadharastra."

From the group of red Raktana one man rose higher in the water. "I, Nelious of the Raktana, descendant of King Demetrious, offer the power of my tail, the strength of my arm, and the length of my life in the service of Agadharastra." The man looked greedily over the assembly, as if counting his winnings. This was the man that Sarva had pointed out to them previously. Older than Theseo, he also looked larger and stronger, but Andrei had seen Theseo in action and knew his youthful appearance was deceptive.

The two men floated above their groups, apparently waiting for other contenders to rise. Theseo looked bored, but Andrei thought such disinterest must be pretended. Nelious looked excited and his eyes continued to dart here and there as if expecting more.

A murmuring rose among the samudraka. Theseo's head turned quickly and a look of surprise showed briefly on his face before he could force his expression back to a sort of pained neutrality.

Uh-oh, thought Andrei, having Theseo surprised couldn't be a good thing. Andrei followed his gaze and found, near the back of the hall, another samudraka risen from his group. This was a young man, probably similar in age to Theseo. The man's skin was pale-yellow mottled with faded brown. He spoke loudly toward the front of the assembly, "I, Rindini of the Afflic, descendant of King Mardriti, offer the power of my tail, the strength of my arm, and the length of my life in the service of Agadharastra." His voice cracked with nervousness as he spoke, but the young man held himself proudly above his group.

Andrei looked to the front of the hall. Theseo was managing to maintain a blank face, but Nelious looked smug. This obviously wasn't part of Theseo's script. So much for formalities. Not that Andrei was sure what the formalities were supposed to be here. He leaned back to whisper to Sarva, "What happens now?"

Sarva shrugged and mouthed, "I don't know."

The hall was silent and the three samudraka remained floating where they were.

Andrei leaned in to whisper in Senna's ear, "Maybe the last one to get bored wins."

Senna released his hand and pulled him against her, laying her head on his shoulder. Andrei squeezed her tightly. He couldn't think of anything to say that might comfort her.

Rindini was the first to move. He held a hand out and a double-ended spear was tossed up from the group below him. Rindini fumbled his first grab, but got hold of it with the second. With the spear held across his chest he bowed deeply to Nelious, then to Theseo, and then he ascended over the crowd.

A spear rose rapidly beside Nelious and his hand closed around it without a glance. He turned to Theseo, gave a perfunctory bow and swam up to meet Rindini.

Theseo smoothly received a spear thrown up by his side and followed the Nelious toward the true centre of the Hall of the King.

All heads turned to follow the contenders.

The three formed a triangle beneath the bright yellow sphere of blossoms. Each of the men floated at an oblique angle about three body lengths away from the others. Their spears were held across their chests, at the ready, but Theseo and Nelious both looked relaxed.

A loud call, more like a grunt than a word, rose up from the assembly. The contenders began to circle slowly, each taking a different path but with a common centre, as if they were swimming around an invisible sphere.

It was Rindini that broke first, thrusting at Theseo. Theseo moved just enough, concentrating instead on blocking a blow aimed at him from Nelious, who had started his move immediately after Rindini. The warriors fell back into the sphere formation and continued circling slowly. Again and again the feints were repeated, and the contenders paths around the sphere changed after each attempt. Rindini, obviously so nervous at the start, began to settle and his spear thrusts gained speed and strength. Not all his blows were directed at Theseo, but Andrei began to suspect that his most determined attacks were.

- - -

Their time was cut short at the pool when the young Marr woman brought Lantea news that the Time of Choosing was at hand.

The path back to the tiirtha was long, and made much longer by the circuitous route that they followed. Lantea explained to John that the route was chosen to ensure that they were always within range of shelter if a serpent appeared. The deeps of the ocean were a rich source of life, but there were many serpents and they were always hungry. It was also made longer because John couldn't swim as fast as Lantea. She commented that she had made better time while carrying him and John could well believe it.

The first indication of reaching their destination was the presence of Marr guards, a dozen or more, arrayed irregularly before a large expanse of dark cliff face. The cliff face itself was only visible because of the small growths of plants, and occasional simple creature, living on its surface.

As they approached, John saw more guards emerge from grottoes in the cliff. Each guard was armed with what, at first, John thought to be the usual double-ended spear. As they got closer he could see that these were different, thicker and heavier in appearance, and black and lifeless. He remembered that material weapons could not be carried through the tiirtha, so these must be stored somewhere out here when not in use. He shuddered to think what it must be like to fight with such weapons down here, to be unable to see the blade slashing toward you in the darkness.

"Has it begun?" Lantea asked one of the guards.

"Soon, my Lady," was the response. The guard bowed his head to Lantea but ignored John.

"We must hurry," Lantea said. She swam to a small, dark expanse of cliff face. It was distinct from the surrounding area because there were no plants or creatures over this small oval. The surface was faintly visible, ebony polished to a deep sheen.

She swam through ahead of him, and John saw a brief and faint flicker flow across the tiirtha, like a distant search light against the clouds. The tiirtha was not much larger than a double doorway from back in his human life. John hurried after her. The sensation was familiar. A gentle pressure, like passing through the surface of a pool of water, passed down his body. Inside the tiirtha there was no sensation at all. And then, as the pressure passed over his feet, he felt it start again at his finger tips and he emerged into the zarana.

"The way is small," commented John.

"It keeps the larger serpents out," she answered, "and the smaller ones we can deal with. Hurry now."

John had enough time to notice a large cache of spears inside, and many guards. He didn't know if this was unusual, he'd been mostly out of it when they left.

They passed through the first great blue wall, out of sight of the guards, and Lantea stopped. "This is too slow. I must carry you."

Before John could comment Lantea scooped him into her arms as she had before, though John was larger now and felt rather ridiculous. Lantea started out strongly, her grip almost painful as she held John against her.

They passed beneath more of the great walls, there were fewer here than John remembered coming in from the other zarana, and emerged into the open. The mountain loomed before them. Lantea swam down and kept close to the ocean floor, apparently familiar with the paths through the abundant plant life.

In less time than seemed credible, Lantea carried John into a tunnel at the base of the mountain and began to wind her way upward. Whether it was the paths Lantea chose, or some other reason, John didn't know, but they met no others as Lantea forged on.

At last she slowed and stopped. She placed fingers to her lips, indicating he should be quiet, and began pushing through an apparently dense growth of vines. She found her place, reached back and pulled John after her. On the other side was a narrow, overgrown pathway, and John followed as Lantea moved ahead.

Not much further on she stopped again, pushed some vines to the side and pulled John into a large room, much higher than it was wide or deep. "The Hall of the King," she whispered, pointing at the wall of vines in front of them.

The vines of this wall were loosely spaced and John followed Lantea's example, squeezing between them until he was confronted with the back of silver and gold blossoms. By moving his head he could see out beyond them to the crowded hall.

John searched until he found his friends standing high to one side, he could only just see them from his position behind the throne. They had their attention directed high into the hall. All the samudraka were looking the same way, and John followed their gaze. He saw three men swimming with little apparent urgency or effort, their patterns forming a sphere above the crowd.

"My son, I warned you the Raktana would play tricks," Lantea whispered angrily.

John peered through the vines to try and read her expression. He saw her eyes widen and he looked back out. The elegant sphere pattern had gone, there was now a whirl of figures moving too fast for John to make out clearly. And then, just as quickly, the figures returned to their elegant pattern.

"What is it?" John whispered. "What's happening?"

"The Choosing of the King," Lantea answered.

"They fight for it?"

"The survivor is king."

John stared at the three figures in disbelief. They had talked about the king being chosen from the contenders, but John thought

343

there must be some sort of vote or something.

"I thought there was only one other contender," John whispered. "There's three up there."

"The Raktana must have done a deal with the Afflic – the yellow one."

"I don't understand."

"Nelious knew he couldn't defeat my son on his own, so they have convinced the Afflic to sacrifice one of their own to the Choosing. He is not expected to live, none of the samtaana would follow him, he is only there to help kill my son." Lantea's whisper grew loud with her anger.

There was another flurry of movement. This time John was better able to keep track of the figures, and it seemed to him that the yellow samudraka had attacked the red one. "But just then—" John started.

"It would not be decorous to be open about it. The Afflic must attack both, but if you watch carefully there is a pattern to it. Even the Afflic's attacks on Nelious are intended to draw my son into exposing himself."

"If it's so obvious, why doesn't someone stop it?"

"Everyone knows what is happening, but as long as etiquette is followed there will be no complaint."

"Couldn't your son have evened the odds? Brought his own sacrifice?"

"Even if he had known, my son would probably have refused. He is strong and proud."

John could hear the pride in her voice, and thought of telling Lantea where her son had got it from, but Lantea continued speaking.

"Even our allies may have supported this. My son is very young and untried. This is his test. It may turn out to be a good thing. If my son can win here there can be no question whether he has the strength to be king. He is as good as any of the Marr that came before him – better!"

The circling warriors burst into another whirl of movement. Theseo, trapped between opponents, managed to spin his spear to intercept an attack from the Afflic and then fold back on himself so fast that John didn't know how he managed it, and slip past a thrust

344

from the Raktana. In a moment the three were circling again as if nothing had happened.

John thought it looked like the Afflic had an injury on his back and another near the end of his tail. Both Nelious and Theseo appeared to be untouched.

"How long does this go on?"

"As long as it takes. Poseitto's great-grandfather fought for three days to take the throne back from the Raktana. But this won't take that long, Nelious doesn't have the patience. My son is a match for this pair."

John wondered at her confidence.

The next action took place between Theseo and Nelious, with the Afflic on the other side of the empty sphere. Nelious spun his blade around and forced Theseo to move back fast to avoid it. From his place on the other side, the Afflic threw his spear hard at Theseo. Cries of outrage rose from the assembly below the fight. With a subtle twitch from one end of his spear, Theseo guided the blade of the incoming spear away from his body, but the shaft came on, tumbling over and tangling itself between Theseo's spear and his body.

Taking advantage of the distraction, Nelious thrust his spear at Theseo's chest. Theseo tried to twist to the side, but the blade caught him, cutting a deep line along one breast and prana spilled into the water. Nelious kept coming with his spear, spinning it over to bring the other end down while Theseo was still trying to recover.

This is the end, thought John. Theseo seemed a tangle of arms and spear shafts, partly lost amid a foggy gush of golden prana spilling from his chest. The Afflic had moved closer but couldn't engage now that he had effectively disarmed himself.

Theseo slid away as Nelious's spear sliced down. Moving closer, Nelious pulled his spear around in a slash across Theseo's tail. But Theseo wasn't there. Rising forward and up from the gold-stained water, Theseo now had a spear in each hand. With one he reached down and dragged a blade across Nelious's back, with the other hand he thrust out and let the spear fly.

The Afflic was too close and too stunned by Theseo's sudden recovery to move. The spear passed right through his chest and protruded from his back. An expression of surprise remained on his face as prana gushed out front and back. Soon the pale-yellow samudraka body was lost inside a globe of golden, life-stained water.

Theseo ignored the flight of the spear and followed Nelious. Theseo drew a second slice across the red back and then pulled up and waited for his opponent to turn.

"Always so damn noble," John heard Lantea complain.

The Raktana was slow to come fully face on, depending on Theseo's character while he took time to recover himself. The two were now upside down, from John's perspective. It all looked unnatural, surreal, to him. John could see that the cut on Theseo's chest was still bleeding into the water, he couldn't afford to wait too long.

Apparently Theseo thought the same thing. As soon as Nelious brought his spear up ready, Theseo snarled words that John couldn't hear and moved in fast. The tips of Theseo's spear moved in a blur. Nelious managed to block some blows, but his arms were moving stiffly, a result of the wounds on his back. A score of shallow cuts appeared on his chest. Theseo's spear swiped lower and John saw the tip of a red tail float away.

"Stop playing with him," Lantea murmured.

As if he'd heard his mother's words, Theseo pulled back and aligned one blade of his spear with Nelious's chest. But he hesitated then, as if waiting for Nelious to defend himself. Nelious tried to raise his spear with one arm, but it was obvious he was already finished. Theseo thrust the blade deep into Nelious's chest and twisted the blade. There was a gush of gold, Nelious issued one loud shout of pain, and then he went silent and still.

Theseo swam up and touched the ball of bright yellow blossoms that had shone like a sun over the fight, and then turned to look down over the upturned faces. He spread his arms, the spear held exultantly in one hand.

From below him the samudraka raised a shout in one great voice, "King Theseo! King of Agadharastra! King Theseo! King of Agadharastra!"

Even over the din of the samudraka, John heard Lantea say, "My son."

"My Lady," a call came from behind them.

John turned, it was the same young Marr woman that had come to them at the pool.

"What is it, Thalia?" Lantea asked.

"You must come."

"My son has just—"

"Please, my Lady. It is urgent," Thalia insisted.

Lantea looked back out to her son, then pulled herself out from the vines. To John she commanded, "You stay here."

John nodded.

"I mean it. Whatever you see or hear out there, you must not interfere. Do you understand?"

John wasn't sure what she thought he might do, but nodded again.

Lantea looked at him doubtfully.

"Please, my Lady," Thalia repeated.

Lantea turned and followed Thalia out between the vines at the back of the room. John turned and pushed into the vines at the front, watching as Theseo swam closer, coming to claim his throne.

- - -

Senna watched in dread as the new king approached his throne. There couldn't be much time left. She could feel that Andrei had gone tense at her side, and an occasional shake or shudder ran through his body. The calm he had maintained earlier was slipping.

The crowd of samudraka continued to shout while Theseo took his place over the vine throne. He floated erect, the tips of his tail rested lightly on the long vine bench. The cut across his chest continued to bleed gold into the water before him, but it looked to be slowing.

Theseo raised his arms, his spear still held in one fist, and the calls of the samudraka gradually quietened to an expectant hush.

"I, Theseo of the Marr," Theseo called out loudly, the pride and excitement clear in his voice, "by the power of my tail, the strength of my arm and the length of my life, proclaim myself King of Agadharastra. Are there any here who would deny me?"

The room remained silent. Theseo drew the moment out, staring over the assembly, his eyes resting for long moments on the group of Raktana near the front. He lifted his gaze to the cloudy masses of the defeated contenders, and then again to the bright yellow ball at the top of the hall. As if calling out to the sun itself, he proclaimed, "I am King Theseo, King of the Agadharastra. My life is your life."

Again the crowd erupted, repeating Theseo's name and title over and over.

Senna could hardly bear it. She wanted the cries to go on forever so that Andrei could remain at her side, but the pressure of waiting these last few moments was tearing her apart. She wanted to scream.

All too quickly the calls of the samudraka began to fade, but even before they had stopped, Senna heard the cry she had been fearing.

"Zamayitar!"

Senna glared out, trying to find the one that would hurry these last moments.

"Take up Zamayitar!" the call came again, this time from someone else.

Quickly the cry was taken up by more until it became a chant. Theseo looked over and beckoned to Andrei.

Senna felt Andrei begin to move and she clung all the more tightly to him. "No!"

Andrei turned to hold her, lifted her head and kissed her gently. He broke the kiss. "We talked about this," he reminded her.

And they had. They had talked and Senna had screamed at him. They had made love and then talked again. There were only two possible outcomes. They could all fight, and all die, or Andrei could do this and give the others a chance to live. "Would *you* choose differently if our positions were reversed?" he had asked. Senna had shaken her head. Andrei had continued, "I get the easy bit. It will be over quickly for me, Theseo will see to that. You're the one who has to go on without your idiot." Senna had shrieked at him then, just screaming meaningless sounds as Andrei held her tightly.

They had talked, but that didn't make this easier. It didn't make it right.

Andrei began to pull himself free from her. Senna knew she should let go but couldn't make herself do it. Darnu and Sarva came up on either side and held her while Andrei broke free.

"Take care of her," Andrei said.

"Of course," Sarva responded.

Andrei kissed her forehead and then impossibly, unbelievably, turned his back. Senna could see him straighten himself. "Now," she heard him say, "let's see if I can get through this without stabbing myself in the foot."

- - -

John could barely make out what was happening with his friends, the vine throne was getting in the way. He knew something was happening there because most of the samudraka were looking that way. Eventually he saw Andrei swim out in front of the throne. John remembered how he'd admired his friend's skill in the water, but after watching the effortless ease of the samudraka, and their sheer power, Andrei looked vulnerable and slow.

Andrei stopped when he was before the king, still some metres out, hovering above the leaf where Theseo once held court as regent. "You rang, my lord?" Andrei said with a grin, and bowed his head.

"King," corrected Theseo. John couldn't see the new king on his throne, only hear him.

"Congratulations, King Theseo," said Andrei amiably.

The samudraka had gone very quiet, they were all straining to hear what they could of the conversation passing between the king and Andrei.

"Are you sure you want to do this now?" Andrei asked. "You must be tired after your valiant efforts. Perhaps you'd like time to heal that nasty cut? I'd hate to have you at a disadvantage."

Theseo laughed, and some of the samudraka near the front joined him.

"I regret calling you a coward, Andrei of the aaranya," Theseo said loudly enough for most to hear.

"Think nothing of it," Andrei said cheerfully. "It was close enough."

"I think not," Theseo disagreed. "It may not be the courage of a warrior, but it is courage of its own kind."

"It would be unseemly for me to disagree with the king," said Andrei.

"It would."

Andrei glanced behind him and looked up at the yellow ball of flowers and the golden shrouds that enveloped the defeated contenders. "Is that where we do this?" Andrei asked, looking back at the throne.

"No. Where you are is good enough."

"You sure? I don't mind moving. Do you think those at the back can see well enough? I hate to disappoint an audience."

Theseo drifted forward off his throne. "They will see all they need to see."

John watched Theseo's strong back, his tail and hands barely moving as he guided himself slowly forward. Tufts of gold-tinted water wafted over one shoulder from the wound on his chest. It was starting to dawn on John what he must be witnessing, but his mind just wouldn't accept it. John peered to the side, he could see the rest of his friends better now, they had pushed forward. Or perhaps they had been pulled forward; John could see Darnu and Sarva holding Senna back, her face a mask of horror and devastation.

He couldn't make sense of what he was seeing. His friends weren't being held back at spear point. They were waiting there, watching, apart from Senna, apparently willingly. And Andrei? Andrei sounded cheerful and optimistic. It couldn't be what it looked like.

"Is there a protocol for this?" Andrei asked Theseo. "Do I draw Zak now? Or maybe I should wait for the last moment, give everyone a good show."

Theseo stopped. He seemed puzzled, perhaps confused, by Andrei's chatter. He answered, "Draw the zakti. Let everyone see that it is Zamayitar."

Andrei did as he was asked, raising the sword high over his head. The blade shone a brilliant ice blue.

After a moment, Theseo pointed one blade of the spear forward, and asked, "Are you ready, Andrei?"

"No," said Andrei, lowering the sword across the front of his body.

"No?"

"No. But if you're waiting for me to be ready, you could be waiting a long time. So how about we start when *you're* ready."

"As you wish," said Theseo, and lifted his spear higher.

17. Violation

The wind wailed through the trees, and the upper reaches tossed and twisted in the darkness. Asha clung tightly to the tip of the tallest of the trees and let the wind tear at her. She was here by choice. The news from Barma and Telia had seethed inside her all through the long return journey. To merge now was to risk having her anger take possession of her, as it had once before. Up here the angry force of the storm gave voice to the rage and frustration that she could not express.

<*Asha?*> came the tentative query from Peren.

The normal telepathy of the narun entered the mind as if it were sound, competing with external sounds. Peren's voice entered directly, a memory of hearing the words. On top of the other insults, this intrusion was more than Asha could stand. "Get out of my head!" she screamed into the wind. Peren's presence quickly faded.

Asha screamed again, a wordless outpouring of emotion. The wind screamed back. Asha screamed louder and harder, until the very effort of it filled her mind. The wind met her scream and raised it with a howl. Asha's fingers slipped on the bark. It would be so easy to let go and let the wind take her. Kill her or set her free. The wind's choice.

<*Please come down,*> Peren said softly. She sounded frightened.

Asha's screaming dwindled and stopped. Her mind felt clearer now. She tightened her grip on the trunk of the tree. She felt embarrassed for having tried to compete with the wind. "I thought I told you to go away."

<*I was scared for you. What if the tree breaks?*>

Asha laughed at that.

<Why do you laugh?>

"Do you think I care if the wind takes me?"

<Asha?>

"You knew, didn't you?"

Peren didn't respond.

"You knew that Sando had closed my Glade. My home. You let me go on believing that my bargain would keep them safe. Did you all have a good laugh at that?"

<No, Asha. I never thought it was funny.>

"Sando won't let it open again, will he?" When Peren was slow to respond, Asha pressed again, "Will he?"

<But now there's a connection to another Glade— >

"If the connection is still there, and if it can be found again, it goes to the dhumraka. Do you think that's what I want for my people? To be your sister's plaything? And if my home doesn't open again it will fade and die, and the elders with it."

Asha could still feel Peren there in her mind, silent and uncomfortable. Asha was getting good at sensing Peren's coming and going. That was something that had surprised the shy girl, even her own siblings didn't always notice.

"And what of the promise from Helix? Does it really mean anything? Will the dhumraka keep them safe? Or has she already gone back there and taken Barma and Telia? Has she let Ellie die so I won't waste time trying to keep her alive?"

<No! Helix won't do that.>

Though Asha felt the honesty of Peren's words, she couldn't stop her accusation. "Why should I believe you? After all this, why?"

<I'm telling you the truth.>

"Really? How am I to tell?" Asha could feel the words cutting, and took pleasure in it.

<I ... I wouldn't lie to you. Not now.>

"What's to stop Helix going back anyway? It's not like your siblings pay any attention to you."

Peren's presence was still there, trembling. The girl was crying. Asha almost felt sorry for her, but there was something else she needed to know.

"Peren?"

<Yes.> The response was hesitant.

"Did my bargain with Jaimee achieve anything at all? Is John safe?"

There was no response, though the shaking of Peren's presence settled and went still.

Asha's whole body went tense. She became aware of the storm again, and how easy it would be to let go and let it take her. Is that what she would do with the answer she thought was coming? "Is John safe?" she asked again.

< ... *Yes.*>

"Yes?" Despite all her hopes, it wasn't the answer that Asha had expected. Could she believe it?

<*Sort of.*>

"Sort of? What does that mean? What have your brothers done to him?"

<*It's not them.*>

Asha couldn't work out what to make of that.

<*Please don't make me explain. Don't make me choose.*>

"Choose what?"

<*Between my family and your friendship.*>

Friendship? Is that what this was? "Friends don't lie to each other."

<*I'm not lying. He is alive.*>

"How do you—?" Asha started.

<*I've got to go,*> Peren said abruptly, and her presence vanished.

Asha climbed down a short way, holding tightly to the trunk against the pull of the wind, and then merged into the tree. Suddenly she didn't want to risk being blown away.

- - -

Tracey woke to someone shaking her shoulder gently. Her head hurt.

"Tracey?"

She opened her eyes. Paul was kneeling next to her bed, peering down at her with concerned eyes. "Is Ray—?"

"I don't know. There's been no one to ask."

Tracey sat up slowly. She was on a low bed in a small room. It had a cheap, mass-produced look to it, very different to her previous room. "Where are we?"

"I don't know that either. A long way from anywhere. A bad storm

353

went through here last night, that's about all I know." Paul thrust a small notepad in front of her. "Read this."

Tracey recognised it as the pad she had been using last night. The writing on it was scratchy and unpractised, she knew it wasn't from Tilvy.

It read: "Beenae, Taiza in cage with tree. Beenae's okay, Taiza's not. Leg hurt not bad, but think Sando damaged mind. Not talking. No sign Tilvy or Pasith. Don't know Pasith."

Tracey stared at the cramped writing for a few minutes trying to take it in. She looked up. "Who?"

"Oh." Paul took the pad and flipped back a few pages. "We started there."

Tracey skimmed over the page. "Asha?" She stood up hurriedly.

Paul reached out and steadied her as she wavered. "Are you okay?"

She nodded. "Where is she? Is John with her?"

"We're in a cage of some sort, she's on the outside of it. Or she was."

"Show me."

Paul led the way out of the room into a short narrow corridor that opened into a wider area, a small combined kitchen, dining and lounge room. Mike was sitting in one of the scruffy lounge chairs watching the small television with the sound low. He looked up when he heard them arrive. He opened his mouth.

"Don't start," Paul told him.

Tracey hesitated for a moment, meeting Mike's hostile gaze with puzzlement, then she followed Paul outside to a rough-hewn porch. "What was that about?"

"Asquith's been griping at me all morning about getting him into this. I didn't want him starting in on you."

"But he's right, isn't he? We did get him into this."

"No. Ray was right. Something like this was coming anyway. Or worse."

There were two steps down from the porch, and Tracey turned back to see where they had been. It was a small cabin, a flimsy looking thing like they have in caravan parks. Surrounding this was an area of lawn enclosed inside a tall mesh fence. It was a normal chain-link fence, rather than the special mesh used to contain the narun, but it was high. The top curved inward, and drawn between the posts was tightly coiled razor wire.

The real surprise came when Tracey looked beyond her own cage. There were two rows of these caged-in cabins facing each other in a long line, at least ten on each side. In a few of the distant cages she could see people wandering aimlessly about their enclosures. Tracey had once visited a dog boarding kennel with a friend, the scene here reminded her of that place.

"This way," Paul said.

A tall pine forest surrounded the line of cabins on all sides. Between the cages and the forest was a space of uneven grass, not as well kept as the lawn inside and between the cages. Their cabin was at one end of the line. A path from between the line of cabins led past them and up through the trees, beyond which Tracey caught glimpses of what looked like a hedge and perhaps the top of a large house.

At the back of their cabin, in the space between it and the fence, was an area of gravel. Beyond the back fence, past a handful of isolated trees, Tracey saw another cage out on its own. There was a tree in the centre, much shorter than the surrounding forest. Now she knew where Beenae and Taiza were.

The mesh in front of her rattled as if it had been tapped.

"Asha?"

The mesh rattled again.

Tracey put her fingers through the mesh and felt them grasped by invisible but warm fingers.

"Is John here somewhere?" Tracey asked.

There was no response for a time.

"One tap for yes, two for no," Tracey prompted, remembering that Asha had rarely participated in this way, John had usually been there to translate.

Tracey felt two gentle taps on her fingers.

"Here, this might help," Paul curled the pad around to squeeze it through the mesh.

- - -

<You're not supposed to be here,> Peren said.

"I can see why. How much more haven't you told me?" Asha responded angrily.

<They only got here last night.>

"Sando's had them longer than that, and don't try to tell me you didn't know!"

<You weren't supposed to know.>

"A *friend* would have told me anyway." Asha scribbled "Wait" on the notepad and held it up for Tracey. She couldn't concentrate on both conversations at the same time.

<I ... it's hard.>

Asha laughed without humour.

<I didn't know I was going to like you, not an aaranya. And when we started to get along I was too scared to tell you any of this. I was afraid of what you might do, that you might refuse to help Mama. I've never had a friend before, I— >

"Is it any wonder? You don't make friends by destroying everything they love!"

<I can't betray my family. They're all I have. All I've ever had. I can't.>

Asha could feel that Peren was crying again. Asha waved the pad at Tracey and Paul, hoping they'd understand that she meant she was coming back, and then she walked across to the cage holding Beenae and Taiza. She couldn't touch the mesh of this cage.

"You can see out my eyes, can't you? Look at that man." Asha stared at Taiza. "See what Sando has done to him? Taiza is a friend. He helped to save my life."

<He ... he seems all right.>

"He's not. Taiza is a gentle man, full of life and energy. He creates things. Beautiful things. He can't sit still unless he's creating. *But now look at him!*" Asha felt Peren cringe in response to her anger, but Asha had no sympathy, not while looking at the strangely quiet and passive Taiza.

"Asha?" Beenae asked. "Who are you talking to?"

Asha held up a hand, she would try to explain later. "You've got to let me help him," she pressed. "Let me in there. At least I can ease the pain in his leg."

<I can't.>

"Get Reyndani to let me in. If you want to be my friend you *have* to do this."

<You won't let them out?>

356

"Where would we go? The tree only knocked over the fence between the front and the back, there's still no way out of the estate."

- - -

"Sando, my brother, things haven't turned out so well for you lately, have they?" Jaimee said.

Sando shook his head, just slightly, but remained staring out the window at the trees in front. Asha was back out there somewhere now, while they had men repair the fence, but there would be no keeping her from insisting that she should go back to her friends whenever she wanted.

Jaimee continued talking, enumerating Sando's follies. "The Glade you supposedly closed is popping up connections in unexpected places. You've lost two of your guests. You almost killed one of the humans we had promised for Mother. You did lose three dhumraka and two humans that we had nicely settled into our arrangements. And to top it off, we now have Asha upset over the things we forgot to mention and the promises she thought we'd made."

<It's not Sando's fault,> Peren said into their minds.

"No one's saying it is," Helix said. "Jaimee's just saying things haven't gone well lately."

"Exactly, sister," Jaimee agreed.

Sando turned from the window. "We might continue that list, brother, by also noticing that Asha's human and his friends are still alive and well. That wasn't part of your plan, was it? It certainly wasn't part of mine."

Jaimee waved that away. "They're with the samudraka, they're as good as dead."

"And yet, strangely, they're still alive after all this time. Even the human, ex-human, that should have died long ago. That's still right, isn't it, Peren?"

<Yes,> Peren answered softly.

"The samudraka have remained isolated in the depths for so long they wouldn't know what the sun looked like," Jaimee responded. "We'll deal with them when the time comes."

"Asha still doesn't know about you, does she, sister?" Helix asked.

When Peren was slow to respond, Jaimee prompted, "Peren?"

357

There was silence for another few moments, and then Peren said, *<Sorry, I was just checking on Mama. Hope I didn't miss anything. I think, if we want Asha to keep helping Mama, and you Helix, then we're going to have to keep her friends safe.>*

"And what about me?" Jaimee asked.

<I think your only chance with Asha would be to let her friends go.>

"So we take them away and dispose of them somewhere else," said Sando.

<I don't think she'll fall for that. She'll want her Glade to be allowed to open, and she'll want proof that her home and her friends are safe.>

"So we keep things as they are," said Helix. "She's agreed to keep helping Mother, as long as her friends remain untouched. She hasn't asked for more."

"Yet," said Sando. "She also agreed to try and help you, sister."

Helix smiled at him. "I had to make the most of an awkward situation."

"I was hoping for rather more," Jaimee said sadly.

Helix walked to him and stroked his face. "I know, my brother, but it was never very likely, was it? Keep things as they are for now, maybe she'll come around. Eventually she will see what she's missing."

"And you're happy to keep carting her back and forth to feed the preta?" Sando asked.

Helix shrugged. "Keeping them with the dhumraka was her idea. I agreed because it was the easiest way to make her cooperate after learning that her own Glade was closed. But it's no great trouble, and I doubt it will be a problem for long. The little thing doesn't have much time left, not even in the Glade."

<And what about Mama?> Peren asked. *<Asha can't heal her, not properly. Mama is still going to die. We have to start looking for this other person she told you about, Jaimee. The one that can see the connections of life.>*

Jaimee glanced uncomfortably between Sando and Helix.

<Jaimee?>

"Sister. Peren. I think we may have to face up to reality. Whatever time Asha can get for our mother is probably all the time she has left."

<No!>

"What choice do we have? Asha has no idea if such a person exists. Where would we start looking?

<We can't just give up. Asha wouldn't. She hasn't. If we weren't keeping her here she would be out searching for a person to save Ellie.>

"You seem certain of that."

<You can tell. It's in everything she does and says. She spends a lot of time thinking about that child.>

"The preta is doomed too," Helix said.

"It always was," added Jaimee and Sando together.

- - -

Barma gave up trying to count how many days they had been here, and watched Ellie lying quietly in Telia's arms. The child was looking a little stronger again now. Helix had not long taken Asha away again, but for all that Asha had given of herself, the improvement in Ellie was only very slight. The end could not be far off. Would Asha ever stop trying to prolong it? What would she do when the end came?

"You must be pleased," Telia broke into Barma's thoughts.

"What?"

"The news that Tilvy escaped."

"I'd be happier to know she was safe."

Telia shrugged one shoulder.

"This is hard on Asha," Barma said.

"She's not looking well," Telia agreed.

Forinay, one of the dhumraka women guarding them, had been standing close. She edged closer. She was older than Barma but still quite young, and thin almost to the point of emaciation. She made up excuses to be close to Ellie, often staring at the child in wonder. Forinay generally spoke to Telia, not avoiding Barma particularly, but often acting as if he wasn't there. The other guards disapproved of her but didn't reprimand her in any way, they appeared to ignore her most of the time.

"They say that what the healer does for this child she also does for our queen's mother," Forinay told them.

"What do you mean?" Barma asked. This wasn't something that

359

Asha had spoken of.

Forinay didn't acknowledge him but spoke as if Telia had asked the question. "Their mother is not well, so the healer feeds her too, like she does this child. ... I think it must be very hard. If feeding the child takes so much of her, feeding an adult must be worse."

"What is wrong with their mother?" Telia asked.

Forinay shrugged. "I do not know. I have never seen her. May I touch the child?"

Telia nodded.

"She is very pretty," Forinay said softly. She gently stroked the bald, pale grey head of the preta.

Even with the affection that he felt for Ellie, this wasn't a description Barma would have used, but he kept silent.

"I had a child once," Forinay continued. "He died. Now I shame my people by not having another."

"Shame?" Telia asked.

"It is expected of us," came the vague answer. "I would leave ... if I could." Forinay glanced around quickly to make sure none of the other dhumraka were within hearing. "You know that they did look for the connection you came through, even though the healer forbade it."

Telia nodded. "I thought they would."

"They didn't find it. Nor that little creature that was with you." Forinay stopped stroking Ellie, and ran her fingers lightly over the still healing scar on Telia's arm. "It must be a wonderful thing to be a healer. If I was a healer I might have saved my son."

"Why can't you leave?" Barma asked.

This time Forinay did look at him, a mixture of fear and surprise on her face. She shook her head and turned back to Telia. "Unlike the others I probably could. I think the Glade has rejected me." Another nervous glance around and then she added hurriedly, "I still love our queen, of course I do." Then more quietly, "It's just that she ... she doesn't seem as close to me as she once did. ... I probably could leave, but where would I go? Who would take in a reject like me?"

Telia reached out her free hand and placed it gently on Forinay's shoulder. "You could come with us when we go. Our Glade would welcome you."

Forinay stared at Telia in shock and hope.

"Ours are a gentle people, Forinay. I think you would fit in very well," Telia assured her. "Wouldn't she, Barma?"

Barma looked at Telia in surprise. Take in a dhumraka? Telia nodded at him. "Yes, of course," Barma said, though he wasn't sure how convincing he sounded.

Hope seemed to grow on Forinay's thin face, and it clung there for long moments before starting to fade again. She told Telia, "You won't be leaving here. Not ever."

\- - -

Asha was exhausted from her time with Angel. It was always draining, but so soon after the long journey to feed Ellie, Asha was feeling it worse than ever. But she argued with Peren anyway. Angel was still feeding as she always used to, despite what Asha now did for her. "There's no need, I can feed your mother!"

<It takes too much out of you.>

"She doesn't get enough from the humans to make any difference, not any more. Why keep killing them?"

<Jaimee insists that we spare you as much as we can. I think he's right. Between Mama and Ellie you aren't getting enough time to rest properly.>

"What if I insist?"

<Then Jaimee will tell you it's a choice between the humans and Ellie.>

"How do you know?"

<They've discussed it. His mind is made up.>

Asha gave a half-amused snort. "I suppose I should be happy that he's given up trying to impress me."

<Not exactly given up,> Peren corrected her. *<He's just resigned himself to waiting.>*

Asha paused at the bottom of the stairs until she remembered what she wanted to do. "Can you remind me how to find Tracey's friend?"

<You should rest first.>

Asha ignored that and started walking in the direction she thought was right.

Inside a secure room below ground, Asha found Raymond Cleaver still lying on the bed as she had found him each time before.

But he was awake now and reading a magazine. He looked up as the door opened and closed.

"Are you the friendly one, or one of the others?" he asked. His voice was husky from lack of use, but he was much improved from what he had been.

Asha reached out and squeezed his large hand gently.

"You're her." He sounded relieved. Asha wondered what other visits he had received.

She took the magazine from his hand and lay it on the bed, and then gently pressed his arms down at his sides. When she opened up his shirt she found that the dressings had not long been changed. On the front here they were only small. She ran her fingers over his skin, avoiding the strange material of the dressings. There wasn't much she could do, but she checked anyway and eased away some of his pain. Then she started lifting at his shoulder and Ray obliged by rolling onto his side with a pained grunt. One of the exit wounds had been very serious and slow to heal, but it appeared to be coming together better now. Again she did what she could to ease the pain and to aid the healing. It wasn't much, but this was what she did. She couldn't ignore it.

Asha pressed lightly on his shoulder and he lay back again. After straightening and buttoning his shirt, she placed the magazine back where he could reach it without stretching. There was nothing more she could do, so she patted his hand and turned to go.

"Who are you?" he asked.

She scanned the benches and found a pen. It was plastic and very awkward to hold, and she wasn't good at writing at the best of times. Using both hands she managed to scrawl her name on the corner of his magazine.

"Asha," he read. He thought for a moment and added, "If you are who I think you are, then you're one of Tracey's friends. Is she here? Is she well?"

Asha tapped his hand once in reply to each question.

"Take care of her, won't you?"

She patted his hand.

Ray stared at it. "Was that a *no*?"

Asha cursed herself for not paying more attention. She brushed at his hand, trying to suggest she was wiping away her last response, and then picked up the pen again. She managed to scrawl "I will" on the corner of the magazine. It wasn't a promise she was sure she could keep, but she wasn't up to writing out a longer explanation.

"Thank you," Ray called as she was leaving.

Asha was walking across the lawn, looking forward to regaining her strength from the trees, when Peren spoke again.

<Why do you do it?>

"What?"

<Help humans. They're the enemy. They destroy your forests.>

"They don't know any better."

<Sando says it wouldn't make any difference if they did.>

"He could be right."

<So why?>

"Whatever their faults, they are part of the life of this world. They are living creatures, as we are. They suffer pain and loss, as we do. I can't ignore that."

<You could. They wouldn't know any different.>

"But I would. ... It's possible I do it as much for me as I do for them."

<I don't understand.>

"Nor do I."

- - -

The days passed quietly. The few humans they saw outside the cages didn't answer any questions. They occasionally gave commands as they delivered food and exchanged clean bedding and clothing for used, but that was all. There were no prisoners in the cabins close to them, and when they tried to call to those further off they were ignored.

A few days ago there had been some new arrivals to these kennel-like cabins. They all looked thin, dirty and unkempt when they were brought in, and they seemed resigned rather than upset by their imprisonment. These, too, were housed in distant cabins. From what Tracey had seen, these new people were already looking healthier than when they had first arrived.

Tracey had taken to going to bed early, as much to get away from Mike as anything else. Paul's presence usually prevented Mike from spouting off, but he couldn't stop the burning of Mike's unhappy gaze whenever it fell on her, and that was happening more and more often. Tracey got the impression that Mike was nurturing his discontent, brewing it into something stronger. So she avoided him. But despite the early nights, her sleep was broken and unsatisfying. She spent hours lying awake and thinking, usually in circles, but sometimes just going over events and trying to make sense of them.

Earlier, Tracey had seen Mike rubbing at his temples as if he had a headache. She had made the mistake of asking Mike if he was okay.

"Of course I'm not fucking okay!" he snapped back. "Your voodoo friends are still sticking pins in my head."

"There's some pills in—"

"You think I haven't tried them? They don't fucking work."

"Mike—"

"I've been getting these ever since you decided to check out of the hotel. You think—"

"Shut up, Mike," Paul told him.

Paul had taken it on himself to act as Tracey's protector. He made sure he was around most of the time to intervene when Mike started griping again, and he was reluctant to leave Tracey alone with Mike, even for short periods.

It wasn't the first time Mike had tried to tell them how he had been dragged from his room. Tracey and Paul had been unconscious and had seen nothing of it. Mike had argued or resisted, and felt the brunt of Sando's anger and frustration.

She felt sorry for him, but he didn't make it easy. Mike was no longer hiding behind the facade he used to get what he wanted. It had been wiped away. Tracey felt she was seeing the real Mike for the first time, and it wasn't attractive. Worse. The way he looked at her now was a little frightening, and she wondered how she could ever have found him so appealing.

Tracey rolled over and thumped the pillow. She squeezed her eyes closed, determined that she should go back to sleep, but in a few moments her head was starting to go back over old ground again. Sleep wasn't going to happen, however late or early it must be.

She got out of bed as quietly as she could, put the bathrobe on over her nightie, and crept out into the small hallway. The floor creaked beneath her feet. There were a few lights, like dim street-lights, running down between the line of cabins. These cast enough of a glow through the front windows that she could make her way without bumping into anything.

The shadow of the empty table made her think of Ray and the middle of the night meetings they used to have in the safe house back home. It seemed such a long time ago. The tension in this small cabin had reduced after Asha had given them the news that Ray was alive. It now seemed less likely that Paul would try to kill Mike for his next insensitive remark.

The door to the outside opened with a squeak and the closing click sounded very loud in the night air. It was colder than she'd expected. The boards were rough against her bare feet, she probably should have put on shoes. She crossed the porch and stepped down onto the damp grass.

The sounds of the night came to her. Insects and frogs, she supposed. Who knew what else? Still, it wasn't as foreign to her as the jungle inside their last prison.

At the side fence she grasped the cold mesh and peered along the path and into the trees. She thought she could make out a bit of light coming from the house through there. That was where Ray was, apparently. They were helping him to recover. That had to be a good sign, didn't it? Why make him better just to kill him? That wouldn't make sense, but Tracey had the uncomfortable feeling that she was missing too many pieces of the puzzle.

They had watched a tall Asian man walk prisoners down that path toward the house. Each of the prisoners looked lethargic and compliant. Paul suggested they had been drugged. None of them had ever been walked back again. Paul was disturbed by that. Tracey preferred to think the people were being released or something. Why keep people like this if they only wanted to kill them? When they had tried to ask Asha about it the answers were brief and vague. And Paul was worried about that too.

Tracey turned around to look down the line of cabins, and fell back against the mesh in fright. There was a shadowy figure just a few feet from her.

"I wondered if I'd ever get to talk to you alone."

The words were spoken quietly, but Tracey felt their menacing undertone and pressed herself harder against the mesh.

"That's not the welcome I expected from the woman who

promised we would make love in cardboard boxes."

"You scared me." Tracey managed to keep her voice calm, but only just.

"I'm sorry," Mike said, and stepped closer.

"No." She tried to slide to the side, but Mike's hand came out and caught the mesh, blocking her with his arm.

"You want me, admit it."

"No," she repeated.

Mike reached out with his other hand and squeezed her breast through the bathrobe.

Tracey pushed it away. "No!"

She wished she could say more, but nothing else would come. She tried to slide the other way but Mike blocked her again. He pushed his body against her, pressing her painfully against the mesh.

"I know better. I know women, and I know when they want me." He leaned in and nipped her earlobe.

Tracey was trying to push him away, but he was too strong. "I don't want to. Not any more."

"You'll come around," Mike whispered beside her face. He rubbed his swollen groin against her. "Feel that?"

"Let me go!" Tracey spoke louder now, wondering if she should scream. But she didn't want to cause a fight between Mike and Paul, things were bad enough already.

She managed to pull one of her arms free and slapped Mike across the face. He barely flinched. He forced one hand between them and into her bathrobe, searching for her breast. At the same time he pushed his mouth against hers, mashing her lips against her teeth. Tracey reached up and pushed his face away, raking her fingers down his cheek.

Mike stepped back and hit her hard across the face. The open-handed slap rang loud and her head reeled back, slamming into the mesh.

"A bit of struggling is fun, but no nails," he told her in reasonable tones.

He pulled open her bathrobe. "Nice nightie, though I have seen it before." With both hands he rubbed at her breasts through the thin material.

Tracey's head started to work again, and she realised she was in serious trouble. She was no longer pressed against the mesh. There was room to move while Mike was distracted, but there was no point in trying to run. She could scream, or she could try one more time to deal with it herself.

She leaned in toward him and Mike started to push her bathrobe from her shoulders. His feet were apart, standing firm and ready to grab her if she tried to get away. She slid one leg back slightly and then slammed it forward, driving her knee up between his legs.

Mike gave a quiet shocked groan, a long wheezy exhale, and started to fold up.

Tracey tried to move away, but was pulled up short. Mike had a death grip on her bathrobe. As he collapsed in slow motion he was dragging her down with him. They were both on their knees now, Tracey was twisted awkwardly, pushing away as Mike was dragging at her. One of her arms was bent back painfully, caught in the robe. She finally managed to slip it free and let the bathrobe drag away.

She pushed to her feet and tried to spring away from him. A hand grabbed at her foot and she tripped, falling hard, face first into the ground. Fog and bright stars filled her vision. She shook them clear. As she rose up on her elbows she felt his hands grasping at her buttocks, scrabbling at the shiny material of her nightie. She pushed forward and felt the nightie tear.

Pushing up with her hands, and drawing a leg up under her, she felt his hands slipping from her nightie. She was sure she was free now, and tried to lunge away. His fingers closed around her wrist and pulled her hand back. She crashed painfully to the ground. He was on top of her now, pushing her face into the grass so she couldn't scream. She flailed ineffectually at him, reaching back with her hands and kicking out with her legs. She could hear his hoarse breath rasping above her.

He forced her head to turn to one side. When she opened her mouth to scream he pushed a wad of her bathrobe into it, and kept pushing until Tracey thought she was going to choke. He wriggled about on top of her for a moment, she didn't know what he was doing until he caught one hand and then the other inside some sort of rope. It took her long moments to realise that it was the belt from her bathrobe.

He slid back and pinned her legs. Moments later her ankles were locked together with the leather belt from his jeans. The bones of her shins crushed painfully together as he pulled it tighter.

The nightie was torn off her shoulders, down her back and then pulled out from under her. He flipped her over roughly and pulled the bathrobe from her mouth. She didn't know what he had in mind, but quickly pressed her teeth together so he couldn't jam it back in. He punched her in the stomach and her mouth opened in a gasp. The nightie replaced the bathrobe as a gag, the fragile material barely enough to satisfy Mike's insistent pressing. One of her nostrils was partly clogged with blood, making it difficult to breathe.

Tracey squirmed, trying to pull herself away from him. He reached out and slapped her across the side of the face. "Quiet!" he told her.

The noise was loud in her ear. Surely Paul would hear that? But his room was on the other side of the cabin. She could only hope he might wake in the middle of the night, as Ray always had.

Mike spread the now free bathrobe on the grass next to her, and rolled her onto it. Her hands were underneath her, pushing her belly into the sky.

"You can't say I'm not considerate," he said. His voice was still coming out strangely. "Now sit quiet for a bit while I get my breath back."

Tracey tried to think. She should have screamed when she had the chance, but she had never dreamed it could come to this. There had been so many times that Mike could have pressed her, but he never had. How could she believe this was even possible?

The night was cold and her body was wet from the grass. Her skin was covered in goosebumps and she was shivering. If it wasn't for the gag her teeth would be chattering.

"I'll warm you up in a minute," Mike commented. He sat next to her, his knees pulled up, one hand covering his groin. "It's your fault there's a delay. ... Fuck that smarts! That's three I owe you."

Tracey tried to call out through the gag.

"Quiet!" Mike thumped her side with his fist.

He continued talking, all the more terrifying for his mild conversational tone. "I owe you for getting me into this weird shit in the first place, and never telling me what was going on, for treating me like an idiot. I owe you and the others for getting me dragged out of the Hilton and into this sty. And now I owe you for a pair of swollen balls, and you can bet I mean to get paid for that. God! It feels like they got sent up into my gut."

There was a long pause while he took deep breaths. "You realise this means I'm going to have to kill Aldercott too. He's not going to like me breaking in his precious virgin."

Tracey tried again to speak through her gag. She wanted to tell him that wasn't necessary. He could do what he wanted. She wouldn't tell. But Mike wasn't listening.

"You want to hear something really funny? You were right. I was being paid again. When that Johnson turned up to interview us, he told me that he could make it worth my while to get close to you. Isn't that a killer?

"I mean, it's not as though you're ugly. I told you on the plane that I'd have been happy to get you off." He ran his hand briefly over her belly and down her thigh. "But both times I was told not to upset you. They told me to take it slow. So I did. *Fucking frustrating!* I've never had to go through so much for any piece of arse I've wanted before, and I've had better than yours." He ran his hand under her and squeezed hard. "Though it's not bad. I'm not complaining."

Despite the cold and the pain, Tracey couldn't stop herself from listening to Mike's recital with a peculiarly remote dread, as if she were watching an accident happening to someone else.

"Johnson wanted me to keep an eye on what you and the others were doing," Mike continued. "He warned me to be careful. He knew that Cleaver and his monkey were protective of you. It wouldn't do to get into a fight, two against one wouldn't have been fair."

He paused again and stroked the side of her face. Tracey turned away from his hand.

"He made several very generous offers." Mike was running his hand over her breasts now. "Money, of course, and safe passage out when the time came. So you can see why I'm so upset." He squeezed one nipple until Tracey tried to call through the gag in pain. "Your messing around killed all that. No money, no safe passage."

He pressed down on her shoulder, to stop her turning away, and then forced her head around to make her look at him. "But there was another little side benefit. They had to help me spy on my

369

compatriots, so they gave me some extra channels on the television. You might have played the reluctant virgin when we were together ..." Mike leaned forward so their faces were close. "But I've seen *all* your most personal and intimate moments."

Tracey shuddered.

Mike smiled. "You know, I think I'm starting to feel better." He leaned over and bit her breast, and ran one hand down between her legs and squeezed.

Tracey tried to scream through her gag. She twisted and thrashed out with her legs. Mike pressed her back down and pushed the gag more firmly into her mouth.

"Hold your horses, girl." He pulled back, removed his shirt, kicked off his shoes, and started to undo his jeans.

While Mike was distracted, Tracey pushed out with her numb hands and feet and rolled toward the fence. She reached the mesh but could feel Mike's hands grabbing at her, pulling at her. She kicked and kicked at the mesh, trying to make it rattle as loudly as she could. Someone *must* hear. She could barely feel her feet now, but she could feel enough to know they were hurting as they mashed into the wire.

And then she was being dragged again, face down, by one arm. It seemed certain that her arm must pull from the socket or break at the wrist. She was dropped and then flipped over onto her back. Mike pushed his jeans down and let them drop to his ankles. She kicked out at his groin, but he was ready this time. He caught her feet and pushed them to the side.

He picked one foot free of his jeans and kicked her in the upper thigh. The pain knifed through her as he connected with a nerve. He climbed onto her. Her ankles screamed in pain, the leather belt cutting into skin as her knees were forced apart.

"Come on, girl. This can be fun. You've always wanted it, now here it—"

His voice was cut off, and his weight was gone. There was the sound of a scuffle, a pained grunt and a thud. Tracey turned her head in time to see Mike falling to the ground, his jeans still tangled around one ankle.

Out of nowhere a half-naked man appeared on the other side of her. Tracey jerked away in fright.

"It's all right," Paul said. "It's me."

He carefully pulled the gag from her mouth, and turned her gently onto her side so he could get at the belt around her wrists. She closed her eyes, thankful that the nightmare was over.

"I'm sorry I didn't get here sooner," he told her.

Her wrists tugged back and forth, Paul was obviously having trouble with the belt. He apologised under his breath for taking so long.

Tracey sensed movement and opened her eyes. Mike was coming at them, doing up his jeans as he came. "Paul!" she screamed.

Mike's foot sped over her shoulder and there was a hard snap as it connected with something. Mike stepped over her. Tracey twisted up to try and slow him down. She heard him stumble. She twisted again to try and see where he was. His bare foot crashed down onto her shoulder and forced her to the ground. "Lie still!" he yelled at her.

She heard fists strike flesh. She turned her head but couldn't see them. As she rolled onto her side she realised that sensation was returning to her wrists. The pain was welcome, it meant that the belt had been loosened. She pulled at it as she tried to sit up.

Paul was winning. Mike was being forced back closer to the porch under the onslaught of blows. Mike suddenly rushed in as if to embrace his opponent. The two men came together and wrestled, and then slowly toppled over. Paul was underneath. There was a thud and the loud sound of expelled breath. Mike began to pound at Paul's face.

Tracey's hands were free now, and she struggled with the belt around her ankles. Her fingers were wet and numb, she couldn't get a grip on the leather.

The two men were rolling over on the ground, back and forth, grunting and gasping, each trying to land a telling hit.

The belt came free. The rush of blood to her feet was excruciating. She tried to stand but her legs wouldn't support her and she crashed back to the ground.

When she looked back up she saw Paul was under Mike again. They were at the steps to the porch, and Mike was smashing Paul's head against the step.

She forced herself to stand, calling out in pain as she forced herself to walk. She started to fall and pushed out with everything she had. She landed against Mike, dragging him off Paul as she crashed down.

She grappled with him as they rolled, trying to stop his fists. She could hear his breath rasping near her, could feel him trying to get a grip on her slippery wet skin. And then he was above her. A fist smashed down below one eye. She cried out. Another strike and her world went dark for a moment.

Mike's weight slowly lifted off her. She opened her eyes. Her vision was blurry at first, she could barely make out his shadowy figure above her. She stirred groggily, trying to clear her head. Pain exploded in her ribs. Her vision cleared enough to see Mike waver and then steady himself, ready to kick her again.

"No," Tracey said weakly.

"Oh yes," Mike contradicted.

Tracey pulled herself away from him.

Mike stepped closer.

And then he stopped. He straightened up. He turned. He looked toward the mesh fence at the side and started walking. When he got there he lay his head against the mesh for a moment, as if waiting for someone to pat him. Then he stepped back from the mesh, looked up, and stepped forward again. He started climbing, driving his bare fingers and toes into the gaps in the mesh.

Tracey pulled herself over to where Paul lay with his head still resting on the step. There was a lot of blood. He was so still that she thought he might be dead, but when she touched him he groaned and his head moved slightly. She didn't know what she should be doing for him.

There was a scream of pain. She looked up to see that Mike had reached the top of the fence. He had reached out through the razor wire, trying to grasp the post where it leaned in. She could see the blood running down his arm from his lacerated hand and wrist. Still screaming, Mike reached out with his other hand and dangled from the top of the fence. Dark streaks of blood ran down his chest.

She didn't move, couldn't move, as she watched him pull his chin up and then throw a leg over the wire. Mike pulled his stomach and groin over the vicious barbs and his screaming turned into something inhuman. And then, abruptly, he was silent. The only movement was from the fence still wobbling under his weight. His grisly corpse hung there like a slaughtered beast waiting for the butcher. The only sound was the dripping of his body's fluids draining onto the ground below.

- - -

"I thought you'd be pleased." Sando looked at Asha in surprise.

She couldn't answer him.

"It's amazing what my brother can get someone to do, isn't it?" Jaimee commented cheerfully. "Usually there are limits, but once he's touched you and locked your mind on a task, that's it."

"An awful ruckus though," Sando said. "I'm pleased you shut him up, despite the waste."

"A life without merit. To offer something like that to our mother would have been an insult. It is better gone."

Asha couldn't pull her eyes from the body dangling on the fence. Peren had called her, told her to hurry. Beenae had tried to raise the alarm, a dhumraka had heard him and ran to fetch the brothers. By the time Asha got here this man was already pulling himself over the savage wires at the top of the fence. "Why?" she managed at last.

"He was trying to rape your friend," Jaimee told her.

"I thought you'd approve of his punishment," Sando added.

Asha could see Tracey kneeling at the steps to the cabin porch. She was naked, shivering with the cold and shock. Tracey had one hand on the shoulder of the man in front of her, Paul, but her eyes were still locked on the body hanging on the fence. Paul was moving weakly.

"Let me in there," Asha demanded.

"Sure," Jaimee agreed. "Reyndani is on his way with the keys and someone to help get rid of this," he waved his hand at the body. "It will be a while before we can get the doctor here to see to your friends."

Asha pushed Reyndani back after he had unlocked the gate, stopping him from entering while she went in. She picked up the bathrobe off the grass, it was damp but better than nothing. Tracey gave a frightened jerk as Asha lay the robe over her shoulders, but then the young woman seemed to sense who it was and turned and embraced Asha, crying and shaking against Asha's shoulder. They knelt there together. Asha held Tracey tightly in return and whispered words of comfort that the girl couldn't hear.

While Tracey sobbed, Asha let her senses reach out. The girl wasn't badly hurt, though there would be pain in many places when the shock gave way and let her feel it. Asha put a hand out and touched the man beside them. This one was worse, but not critical. Asha needed to do what she could for him, but she was reluctant to pull away from Tracey just yet.

"We'll take them up to the house," Jaimee spoke from behind her.

Two humans carried Paul on a stretcher between them. Tracey leaned against Asha, limping on badly bruised feet, and constantly tugging at the bathrobe as she walked. As they walked out the gate and down the path, Asha found that both she and Tracey kept glancing at the bloody body on the fence. Asha squeezed Tracey firmly and led them on.

At the house Asha spent a few moments with Paul and then turned her attention back to Tracey. Asha helped her through a long hot shower, doing what she could to reduce the pain that Tracey felt from her feet and face and wrists. Tracey rejected another robe like the one she had been wearing, Asha managed to insist that the brothers arrange something else.

Some humans had cleaned up Paul. Tracey was content for Asha to leave her side provided she could stay close to Paul, so Asha let her sit there while Asha spent more time trying to do what she could to reduce his pain and aid his healing.

The human doctor arrived and Asha stepped back. Tracey stayed at Paul's side, holding his hand. The doctor frowned at her, then shrugged and worked around her.

"How could you let this happen?" Asha asked Jaimee.

"There was supposed to be someone watching the monitors," Jaimee said.

"A human," Sando added.

"He said he felt ill and had to lie down. He regretted his lack of attention."

"But he won't be making any more mistakes," Sando finished.

Asha shuddered at their casual disregard for human life.

<They're coming for us!> Peren called loudly in their minds.

Asha saw the shock register in Jaimee and Sando's faces. Something must have shown on her face too, because Jaimee looked at her strangely.

Who's coming? Asha asked silently, but there was no response.

The brothers turned in unison, their faces grim. They left the room quickly without saying anything.

18. Legion

Though his lessons had told him to watch the man, not the weapon, Andrei could not stop himself from watching the blade of Theseo's spear as it pulled back.

Should he try to defend himself, or just let that blade do its work? It was a question he hadn't managed to resolve despite the sleepless nights he'd spent pondering it. Now, in this final moment, it seemed better to just stand and meet his fate. To struggle and make his inadequacy so obvious to all, especially to Senna, was demeaning. Just accept it, he thought. It's coming anyway. Let it come. He let the zakti drop lower.

He saw the spear blade stop, hesitate, then start to move. Zak began to rise to intercept the spear. Either his body or his sword didn't agree with his decision. He would try to live.

"King Theseo!" cried a woman's voice from the back of the hall.

The spear blade stopped quickly, and Andrei watched it quivering in the water. Zak stopped too. The rise would have been too slow anyway, that much was obvious.

"Why do you interrupt, Lantea, Mother of the King?" Theseo called out.

Mother? That brought Andrei's attention back from the sharp edge of the spear blade. The man has a mother?

Theseo had pulled back slightly, so Andrei turned to look across the sea of samudraka faces to the back of the hall. A beautiful woman floated there, and behind her trailed a score of Marr warriors. With them were Tilvy and a jalaja, a stranger. Or was he? Andrei thought he looked familiar. Some of the Marr had been wounded. Tilvy looked exhausted and frightened.

"My son, King of Agadharastra, we have news of the papayamala. News that may bear upon the fate of that young man." Lantea pointed to Andrei.

"Zamayitar!" called one of the samudraka near the front of the hall.

Andrei glared down at the group of lime-green samudraka, the voice had come from there somewhere. Do you want the bloody thing? he felt like yelling. But he bit his tongue and looked back to the new-comers.

No one else took up the call.

"Come forward," Theseo called over Andrei's shoulder. Quietly, Theseo continued, "Andrei, put the zakti away. I must hear this first."

Andrei was more than happy to slide the sword back into its sheath.

"Wait there," Theseo instructed him, and pointed to one side of the throne.

Andrei went to the indicated position while Theseo ascended to his place above the throne.

"Are you mad?" Andrei heard whispered from somewhere behind him.

It took him a moment to recognise the voice. "John?"

"I'm here, behind the vines."

"Are you all right?"

"Yes. Are you?"

"For now. Where have you been?"

"Lantea took me somewhere to get better."

"Typical. You wander off with the beautiful woman while we do all the work," Andrei answered.

"That's my mother you're talking about," interjected Theseo in a quiet voice.

Andrei couldn't see the king very well, the vines of the throne got in the way. "Sorry, King."

"Sure you are," said John, sotto voce.

"Quiet now," said Theseo.

Lantea and the new arrivals assembled before the king, their heads bowed.

"Speak," Theseo commanded loudly.

One of the Marr, his left arm held against his body to hold his wounds still and closed, raised his head. "King Theseo, we did not see the papayamala for ourselves, but we found these two, who speak the same story that you have heard. Also, we were attacked by grey ones, the dhumraka of whom these people speak. The dhumraka are not like samudraka, but they are strong in the water. We captured one and he spoke of his pale queen, Helix. More attacked and – it shames me to tell it, my king – we were forced to retreat. We brought this aaranya and this jalaja back with us rather than leaving them to be killed by the dhumraka."

Andrei had been watching Tilvy, waiting to see if she would notice him, but mostly she kept her eyes down, every now and then stealing glances up at the king, but not noticing Andrei to the side.

"Lantea, Mother of the King," Theseo said. "You said this had relevance to this aaranya?"

"Yes, my son and king—" Lantea began.

Tilvy looked up and her eyes met Andrei's. "Andrei!" she screamed. She pushed hurriedly past the guards and swam into Andrei's arms. He squeezed her tightly. "I didn't know what had happened to you." She hugged him hard and then pulled her head back. "The others?"

Andrei pointed, and Tilvy waved at them.

"Ahem." King Theseo was peering down at them from the edge of the throne.

"Sorry, King Theseo," Andrei said as contritely as he could manage. "She's not accustomed to royal company."

"I'm sorry," Tilvy added meekly.

Theseo turned back to the hall. "You were saying, Mother?"

Lantea said simply, "The jalaja, Pasith, can explain."

"Speak, jalaja," Theseo commanded.

Pasith recounted the tale of his capture and imprisonment briefly. "A samudraka was captured too, while I was imprisoned, though she did not live long. She called herself, Hartdarika Barethusa—"

"Are you sure?" Theseo interrupted.

Pasith nodded his head.

"Say it again," Theseo demanded. "Loudly."

"A samudraka was captured too. She called herself Hartdarika Barethusa. She did not live long enough to escape with the rest of us."

The samudraka of the assembly all began talking. Theseo gave them a few moments and then called for quiet. "Continue, jalaja."

"Neso and I were certain we would die there, but that man," Pasith pointed to Andrei, "led his friends to rescue not just his own kind, but us as well. Had Barethusa been alive, I am certain they would have done what they could for her too."

Theseo pointed across to Senna and the others. "Were those among your rescuers?"

Pasith looked across and then back to the king. "I remember all except one of them, yes, my Lord King. There were also two humans helping them."

This raised a murmur from among the samudraka near the front of the hall.

"A woman called Tracey," Pasith continued. "The papayamala have her now. And there was a man that I never met, they call him John."

Andrei tried to think quickly. Even though they had avoided naming John, Andrei was pretty sure he'd given it away more than once over their time here. Would the king make the connection?

"Thank you, jalaja Pasith," Theseo spoke loudly. "Hartdarika Barethusa was known to us. You have given us much to think about."

Theseo bade his mother to take the guard away, Pasith was sent to be with Senna and the others. It seemed that Theseo was happy to ignore Tilvy still clinging to Andrei's side.

"Zamayitar!" a voice cried out from the middle of the assembly, before Lantea and the others had even reached the back of the hall.

Oh bugger, thought Andrei. He'd hoped they might have managed to forget for a while longer.

"Zamayitar is already in my power," Theseo spoke out loudly. "I can reach out and take it up at any time I choose. Are there any here that doubt it?"

"Zamayitar and nikasa!" a voice called from among the Raktana near the front.

Theseo glared at the Raktana for long moments before looking up. "I have Zamayitar within my reach. Within one year I will stand before you with Zamayitar in one hand and my nikasa in the other.

These are the commandments of our father-kings. I have been chosen. I am King Theseo. King of Agadharastra by the power of my tail and the strength of my arm."

Then, looking back down at the Raktana but still speaking loudly for all to hear, Theseo continued, "Hesperous of the Raktana, I give you leave to contest this now, if that is your desire."

There was silence in the hall.

"No? Then I will hear no more of it. I am King Theseo!"

Led by the group of Marr, the hall erupted into the chant. "King Theseo. King of Agadharastra."

The chant continued as the king departed. After the chanting had died away the hall began to empty.

Andrei enjoyed a tearful reunion with Senna. A reprieve of limited duration was better than no reprieve at all. Their group was not permitted to return to the island, Polyphemo explained that the king must keep Zamayitar close at hand, so they were instead led to a small cave further down in the mountain. It was a true cave with solid walls. The one small entrance was closed over with thick leafy growths.

This felt more like a prison, Andrei thought, but being a prisoner was a step up on being a corpse. Senna seemed to agree, she wouldn't let Andrei's hand go, and she was smiling brightly at him every time he looked at her, which was often. Some privacy might have been nice, but for now they celebrated with hugs and kisses.

John had returned to them looking fit and happy, albeit confused by recent events. Polyphemo said that the king wished to speak with them, but he would be busy for some time, so the group used their time to catch up on each other's stories as best they could. It took a long time, and despite the shocks that came in the telling, there remained a festive air to the group.

Except for John. His earlier happiness at their reunion faded quickly with the news that the Glade had been closed, and he had pulled back from the others to lean against the cave wall. The news had been a shock to them all, but Darnu assured them that in time it should open again.

"What is it, John?" Andrei asked.

John's eyes were closed and he didn't open them when he answered, "That's it."

"What?"

"If Ellie is locked away in the Glade then there's nothing we can do for her, even if we can find what we need."

"Oh." Andrei hadn't thought about it like that.

"You can't *know* that, John," Senna insisted from Andrei's side. "Not yet. Glades are strange things."

"You mean, there will be time to be unhappy later?" John asked. He opened his eyes and looked at Senna sadly.

"That's not what I meant," Senna replied, "but it will do. It applies to all of us."

- - -

The group had a day of relative quiet, locked away in their cave, before Theseo came for them. He looked to Sarva first.

"You still intend to cooperate?" Theseo asked.

"Of course," Sarva replied.

Theseo nodded and turned to Andrei. "You have no choice. You *must* stay next to me at all times. The samudraka must see that Zamayitar remains within my reach."

Senna huddled closer to Andrei.

Theseo looked at her curiously for a few moments. John thought Senna looked on the verge of offering some retort, but must have thought better of it.

Theseo turned to Pasith. "You may depart if you wish, I can have you escorted to a tiirtha close to your home."

"I will remain with my companions, Your Highness."

Tilvy whispered something to Pasith, but he shook his head.

Theseo's eyes fell on John. The intense scrutiny left John in little doubt that Theseo understood what John was.

"I do not know how long we may be away," Theseo said, "and I cannot guarantee that we will always have access to sarasi-jilvana to sustain you. Would you like to remain here?"

John shook his head. "Thank you for the time you have given to me, I would use it to help my friends if I can."

Theseo nodded his head in approval.

"That's the way," Andrei whispered in John's ear, "talk like a warrior, he appreciates that."

The amused look that Theseo flicked at Andrei suggested that he guessed what was said.

"We go," Theseo announced, turning away.

"What? Now?" Andrei asked in surprise.

Theseo turned back and raised an eyebrow. "We must act while passions are hot. Right now the samudraka still remember Pasith's description of what happened to Hartdarika Barethusa. They remember how my warriors appeared after their battle with the dhumraka. They are ready for revenge. If we linger then people will start to think and to talk. Some will start to question. A short delay will lead to a long delay. We must act now."

"But can you be ready so quickly?" Darnu asked.

"I started making preparations as soon as I heard Sarva's tale for the first time, and the samtaana of this ocean were already preparing for battle – the time of choosing is a volatile period for our people. We are as ready now as we can be."

They followed Theseo out to find Marr guards waiting. As Theseo had said, Andrei was to swim next to him, but the rest were moved well back. Even Senna was obliged to release her hold on Andrei for the moment.

After a winding journey up through the mountain, they swam through a large passage lined with bright yellow flowers and out into the open water. But it wasn't open. It was crowded and noisy. The dark jade of the Marr dominated, but there were areas populated from other samtaana, and in some places the colours mixed to give an almost psychedelic aspect to the scene.

"So many?" Tilvy whispered in awe.

Theseo and Andrei swam out into the crowd and a cheer started that grew as it spread out.

Sarva called over the noise, "Andrei's in his element."

John grinned. Sarva was right, Andrei was waving to the crowd and smiling. Incredibly, some of the cheers seemed to be directed specifically at him. A few pretty girls along the path, showing less reserve – as Lantea had phrased it – than the older women, reached out to him. Andrei paused a few times to take their hands and kiss their fingertips.

"I'll kill him," Senna said.

"Give him a break," Sarva called back to her. "It's only a few days ago that they all wanted to see him dead."

"That hasn't changed," Garjae reminded them.

John realised Garjae was right. This was just the power of the crowd, and the fact that Andrei was in the company of the king.

Another sound started, mostly lost in the cheers of the crowd at first, then gaining cadence and strength until the water was shaking with the power of it. A rhythmic cracking sound, like the breaking of rocks. John glanced back to make sure the mountain was still standing. Behind him, John saw that Pasith, too, was looking around nervously.

Sarva touched John's shoulder and pointed. The samudraka were pairing up, holding each other by their arms and snapping their tails together, issuing a sound like a rifle shot. Many pairs spun around each other, making a dance of their celebration.

Theseo led them up through the ranks of samudraka, and the rhythm of the tail snaps was now interspersed with a chant: "King", snap, "King", snap. Repeated over and over.

It felt like the crowd was generating its own power, and multiplying it as they sent it on to the king and his companions. John felt strangely strong and confident. For the first time in his life he could understand why people sought positions of fame and popularity. The sheer exhilaration he felt from the mere side-wash of this outpouring was almost overwhelming.

They reached the top of the crowd and Theseo and Andrei kept rising, but the guard kept John and the others lower.

Theseo and Andrei stopped high above the crowd. Theseo leaned in to speak with Andrei. Andrei drew the zakti. It was shining even as he drew it from his sheath, and as he raised it above his head its intensity became hard to look at. Theseo reached out and joined his hand with Andrei's holding the sword. The rhythmic chanting increased and the sword shone even more brightly. John had to look away.

"Agadharastra!" The word echoed out through the water. A single voice, impossibly loud.

It was Theseo. How he made such a call John didn't know. The noise of the crowd stopped abruptly.

"We go to battle as our ancestors once did," Theseo continued, his voice carrying as if amplified. "For the Agadharastra. For the samudraka. For *all narun*!"

Cheering broke out again, mixed with loud snapping of tails.

"Victory will be ours!" Theseo called over the tumult.

Theseo and Andre started swimming, the blade of the zakti held in front of them still blazing. John and the others were urged forward by the guard to join them. John was still astounded by the size of the crowd. From this new viewpoint above them, he could see that there must be many thousands. In a few places there were even young children carefully kept together in groups, the parents or guardians keeping a protective stance around them so they wouldn't be swamped by the crowd. Warriors started to pull themselves clear of the crowd and follow after their king.

Sarva nudged John's side and pointed ahead of them, grinning. "I don't think Garjae's happy being relegated to follower," he said.

They swam for a few hours, travelling slowly by samudraka standards. Theseo halted beyond the last of the blue rock walls that surrounded the mountain.

"I've got some organising to do," Theseo explained. He eyed the random arrival of warriors still coming through the gaps in the wall with dissatisfaction, and then looked back. "We'll be swimming harder from here. Pair-up." He flicked his fingers between the guards and the aaranya.

Theseo took Andrei's arm and showed him how to hold himself out, clear of Theseo's tail, but still able to hitch a ride on Theseo's strength. When Andrei was getting it right, Theseo turned back to the guards. "Practise," he told them, and then towed Andrei with him on his way to survey his army. A dozen or more of Theseo's personal guard went with them.

Polyphemo was shaking his head as he watched his king swim away.

"You don't approve?" Sarva asked him.

"I don't ... I think it is difficult," Polyphemo managed finally.

"What do you mean?" asked Garjae.

Sarva glanced at Polyphemo and answered for him. "He means it is not good for the king to be seen with an aaranya as a constant companion, nor is it good for the king to be seen without his sword. A choice between the distasteful and the embarrassing."

"I just meant—" Polyphemo started.

"It's okay," Sarva assured him. "You're right. It is a difficult situation, and King Theseo hasn't taken the easy way out. Not

384

everyone would have the courage for this path."

"We should practise," Polyphemo changed the subject. He held out his arm to Sarva.

Other guards came to pair with each of the others. Garjae got one that looked almost as unhappy as he was. A large but shy young man approached Senna, and held his arm out tentatively.

None of the guards approached John. He wondered what he was expected to do. A hand touched his shoulder. He turned to see Lantea's face hanging upside down in front of him.

"You're not too proud to accept the aid of a woman, are you?" she asked with a smile. "You weren't before."

John tried to turn his head to see her better. "No. I'm just surprised to see you here."

Lantea twisted around in the water until they were face on. "Better?"

John nodded.

"Some samtaana have women warriors, but even the Marr like to have some women with them. As nurses and minders – and for other reasons."

"Does everyone know about me?" John asked. "Is that why none of the others offered to help?"

"No. My son knows. Perhaps some others guess, it is hard to tell. Mostly it is just that you are still too strange for the conservative Marr." Lantea held her arm out. "Shall we practise? This way will be tiring on our arms, but it is a little more dignified than the altern-ative."

- - -

Garjae rubbed at his shoulder. He wasn't sure what bothered him the most. His arm and shoulder were aching from trying to hold himself clear of the tail of his samudraka guide all day, his dignity was offended by having been hauled about like a helpless child, and his confidence was bruised because he knew that the aid was necessary, he could never have kept up the pace without it.

If that wasn't enough, John was over there, hovered over protect-ively by Tilvy and Pasith – the two of them speaking quietly while John slept beneath them. The beautiful samudraka woman had not long left. What was it about that strange once-human man that attracted such dedication from those around him? Garjae was at a

385

loss. He gave his shoulder a savage squeeze. If being hopeless and helpless was what it took then maybe Garjae was better off as he was.

A hand touched his shoulder.

"Let me," said Darnu sitting down just behind him.

Darnu pushed Garjae's hand out of the way and began to massage the shoulder.

"Thanks," Garjae acknowledged his friend's comforting presence.

"If Asha were here she'd soon see to our painful limbs."

"If Asha was here she'd be over there doting on him," Garjae answered bitterly.

Darnu didn't respond to that, just moved his massaging fingers further down Garjae's arm. "This is the one you hurt before."

Garjae nodded. "Where are we, do you know?" he asked to change the subject.

"The home of the Eadie, I was told."

"Doesn't tell me a lot."

"No," Darnu acknowledged.

Theseo had led them through connections between three different zarana so far, each one subtly different to the last, but each one just another watery world of samudraka as far as Garjae was concerned. In each zarana there had been yet another enthusiastic greeting for the new king, and more warriors had joined their army.

Sarva swam in from wherever he had been. "Long day," he commented as he settled against the rocks near them.

"How many more?" Darnu asked him.

"I don't know. Theseo is now dispersing parts of his army to join up with others coming in from further away."

"Sounds like it could take months," Garjae said.

Sarva shook his head. "The zarana are amazingly interconnected. Polyphemo said that you can get from one end of the ocean to the other in a matter of days if you know the way and can rely on a friendly reception at each zarana."

"What do you mean?" Darnu asked.

"The connections seem to be related to the affiliations between the different samtaana. The ones that like each other connect their zarana, if the relationship falls off then the connection may close or become more difficult to access. It is sometimes faster to go forward

386

by following a connection to a zarana behind you that has a more direct link to where you want to go."

"Sounds like a messy arrangement," said Garjae. He just wanted to get away from all this and back to the air and real forests.

Sarva shrugged. "I guess it has its uses."

"Where's Andrei?" Darnu asked.

"He's been given time off for good behaviour. He and Senna are trying to make the most of it."

"Is there still no way out of it for him?" Darnu's hands had stopped massaging Garjae's arm, but they remained resting on his shoulder.

Garjae looked around at his friend and saw the concern written over his face. "Maybe in the heat of battle we can sneak him off."

Sarva chuckled at that. "I like your thinking, Garjae, but there is one problem."

"What?"

"The samudraka would come for their Zamayitar. We'd start another war."

"So we leave it behind."

"It's no good to Theseo while it belongs to someone else."

"Maybe Theseo will get killed and solve it for us," Garjae said.

"That would be worse. Theseo has been a streak of luck for us. No other samudraka that I've ever heard of would have gone so far out of his way to keep us alive. Even after Tilvy and Pasith turned up he could have finished what he started. Andrei would already be dead, the rest of us too probably, and they'd still be trying to attack the papayamala."

"I still don't trust him."

"I think you should. I don't know whether it's his mixed heritage or what it is, but he's the best chance we've ever had of improving relations between the aaranya and the samudraka. Andrei can't be allowed to stand in the way of that."

Garjae glanced sharply at Sarva, and he felt Darnu's fingers dig into his shoulder.

Sarva saw their expressions and hurried on, "That came out badly. I'll do everything I can to get Andrei out of this, *everything*, but you must see that this is an opportunity we haven't had in thousands of years. It would be one thing if we could save Andrei, just whisk him away like you suggested, but that can't happen. It would be worse, much worse, for aaranya everywhere."

"He's part of our stand," said Darnu.

"You've been away a long time," added Garjae, "perhaps you've forgotten what it's like to belong."

"I haven't forgotten, Garjae," Sarva answered. "I have never forgotten."

More exhausting days of travel through zarana. When they weren't actually travelling Theseo had the guards give weapons training to John and the others. Theseo dedicated himself to training Andrei.

"Aaranya pacifism won't protect you in the middle of a battle," Theseo told them. "At least learn how to defend yourselves."

Sarva had taken to it fairly well, John guessed that he had seen other battles. Pasith did reasonably well, if only because of his greater natural agility in the water. The rest of them? If they were attacked while still underwater their survival would depend on luck more than anything else.

In this zarana lived the Mieten. These samudraka had skin of an even, deep tan colour, their tails a darker shiny brown. Their home consisted of a series of long straight ridges that formed layers of immense cliffs. John and his companions were currently situated on the edge of one of those cliffs, looking out through the huge expanse of open water before them. Though the water was very clear, the ocean floor was so far below the cliffs that it was almost lost in the haze.

Sometimes John caught sight of creatures swimming out in the distance, some of them very large, but none came close enough for him to get anything more than an impression of size.

John and Sarva were sitting some way off to the side of the others. Andrei and Senna had swum away below to try and find some privacy.

"I still can't quite get my head around all these different worlds sharing space with my own," John mused.

"These are your worlds too now," Sarva said.

"I guess," John agreed, "but it still doesn't feel like it."

"When we get out of this you'll find that Glades feel less foreign to

388

you. More like a home."

John didn't respond to that. It wasn't likely to be an issue.

"There is more to all of this than just you and me and our friends," Sarva said.

John turned to look at him. Sarva was watching him with a strange, questioning expression. "I understand that," John answered cautiously, wondering where this was leading.

"I'm not sure the others do."

Further along the edge of the cliff, John saw that the others were resting rather than conversing. Tilvy saw him looking and smiled. John smiled back. "It's not easy to look beyond the needs of those you love," he said quietly to Sarva.

"Especially when they have spent their lives in isolation. Until you brought them out here," Sarva pointed back over his shoulder to their friends, "they had little to do with anyone not of their own stand. They still see everyone else as somehow separate and different."

"Most of those we've met really are different."

Sarva shook his head. "Not in essentials. The samudraka, the jalaja, and even the yaayaavara are just people like us. Their lives are like ours in every important respect. They love just as we love. They hurt the way we hurt. Their basic needs are all the same. These are all people we would care about if only we got to know them."

John nodded slowly.

"I've seen a lot of the world, John. It has given me a different perspective."

"I guess it would," John agreed, he still wasn't sure what this was about.

"Out there, on every piece of land, the narun are under pressure from humans."

John flicked his eyes up to Sarva's in surprise.

"They don't all feel it yet. We are few enough that it has been easier to move out of the way than to try and do anything about the problem. But the problem is there, and it's getting steadily more serious."

"I know it did surprise me to find so little animosity towards humans among the aaranya."

"That's isolation again, John. You have been to some very select, out of the way, places. Life has been much harder for others. It is also what the aaranya have become. There is very little animosity even where the aaranya and jalaja have been pushed out by humans. You've seen some of that for yourself with Senna and her people. We'd rather die than kick up a fuss. What you and Asha have brought out in this small group is very much out of the ordinary, believe me. The samudraka see us, the aaranya generally, as too passive, and they might be right."

"But even if that is right," John said, "I don't see what can be done. Where are you going with this?"

Sarva met John's gaze for a time and then looked away. "I don't know."

They sat quietly for a time. A comfortable silence.

John's thoughts turned to Asha, perhaps because Sarva's presence beside him reminded him so much of her. The same compassion existed at the centre of both. Sarva's had grown worldly and all encompassing. Asha's was more personal and intimate.

"In amongst all this, do you think we will be able to find Asha?" John asked. "To save her?"

"My dear sister?" Sarva answered loudly, as if he had been pulled away from other thoughts. "Asha will be where they are. If—"

"You two look very serious."

John looked up and smiled as Lantea swam in and settled on the other side of Sarva. "We were talking about the problems with humans," he said.

"You could be here a long time."

John grinned back at her.

"I know this place," Lantea said. "These people and mine have always been good friends. My son will do well here."

"He has done well everywhere, hasn't he?" Sarva said.

"He is a new king on a popular quest, so of course he is welcomed. But here he is truly welcomed for what he is."

"And how do the Mieten feel about Andrei?"

"That he still has the Zamayitar?"

Sarva nodded.

Lantea shrugged. "No one is happy about it, but for now the story of Andrei's heroics against our common enemy is enough to keep them content." She fell silent for a time and studied Sarva's face.

Sarva met her scrutiny with his own. "I think I know something about you," Lantea said eventually.

Sarva raised an eyebrow.

"Your friend – Karya?"

He nodded.

"Her friend among the samudraka was a relative of mine. I heard something of how it came about. Karya was a special girl – woman. Very brave."

Sarva looked away. "Yes. She was."

"I heard something of you too. Not much, but some. Most of it suggested you were unusual."

Sarva shrugged.

"What is your power?"

John stared at Lantea in surprise. Lantea ignored him, continuing to study Sarva. Sarva continued to gaze out into the ocean depths, as if he hadn't heard.

"I know what you are. I finally have all the pieces put together. Asha is your sister – your twin." Lantea looked across at John. He tried to keep his expression impassive, but it wasn't something he was good at.

"Will you tell your son?" Sarva asked.

Lantea didn't answer for a long time. Eventually, she rose and turned to go. "One war at a time is enough, don't you think?"

"Lantea!" Sarva called before she had gone far. She stopped and looked back at him. "Tell your son that the papayamala may be expecting him. They may anticipate his moves. He should be prepared for that."

"An army of this size doesn't do much by surprise," Lantea answered, turning away.

- - -

Andrei stared out into andhakara-nitya, the eternal dark ocean. Except, just maybe, it wasn't quite so dark here. The tiirtha from this latest zarana had brought them out near the top of a ridge. Andrei thought he could feel, if not actually see, a slight hint that sunlight was trying hard to make it to this depth.

Senna touched his arm. "It's getting crowded," she said, and pulled him away. John and the others came with them, as did Lantea.

Theseo stayed holding his position not far in front of the dull flat surface of the tiirtha, directing warriors one way or another as they continued to emerge. He was showing them where to collect their spears. Part of Theseo's preparations had been to cache physical weapons outside selected zarana – such things had to be carried through the outside ocean itself, and that had taken much longer than their journey through the zarana. Andrei's zakti was one of the very few weapons that could be carried through the tiirtha, that could exist as a weapon both inside and out. A handful of samudraka from other samtaana had similar weapons, though none held the same importance to the samudraka as the king's Zamayitar.

Well away from the assembling army their small group came to a stop. The more colourful praanin creatures slipped away from them, but there were still a few material creatures near them, gaping at the light snow of material dropping from above.

Senna held tightly to Andrei's arm as she pointed at different creatures.

Andrei pointed to one small fish with huge, vicious looking teeth that were too large for its mouth. "Now that's ugly." He called across to Garjae, "Here's something to make you feel better about yourself."

The fish was already swimming away by the time Garjae and Darnu turned around. But Garjae smiled anyway, and answered, "You're right, Andrei, I do feel better."

Andrei stared at Garjae for a few moments, then pulled Senna close and whispered in her ear, "Okay, now I'm spooked. Out of everything we've seen since we left home, Garjae smiling and being friendly to me has got to be the scariest."

Senna flicked Garjae a glance and then huddled close. "Even worse than the nirarkta?"

"Much!" Andrei answered fervently.

They both erupted into giggles. Andrei, looking over Senna's shoulder, saw Garjae's smile fade and his expression turn sour again. Andrei felt a pang of guilt. "I think I've upset him. I should apologise."

"He'll get over it," Senna whispered back. She pulled on his arm and pointed, "Look."

Pasith was swimming up close to a large jellyfish. He reached out and touched it lightly on one side and pulled back quickly. Light flared out from the creature, and then flashed up in pulsing lines that looked like small lightning strikes. Andrei heard Tilvy call out in surprise. Pasith swam in and touched it again, and again the creature lit up.

The army was still swelling out from the tiirtha, so they and the fish moved out further. Andrei and Senna caught up with John. He appeared to be entranced by something like a cross between a tiny whale and a gaunt eel. Just a couple of feet long, its head and mouth were huge compared to its whip-like tail. Most of the body was a pale, almost transparent yellow to Andrei's senses, but the end of its tail was glowing pink.

John saw them coming and smiled. "I haven't seen much of you lately."

Andrei waved a hand dismissively. "Well, you know. It's busy and important work that I'm doing for the king. It doesn't leave much time for the little people."

"That must be why I noticed this poor thing," John said. When Andrei looked puzzled, John continued, "With its swollen head."

"Don't forget who's carrying the sword around here," Andrei warned him. They grinned at each other.

"It looks like it could turn around and swallow itself," Senna said.

"It looks like it already did," said Andrei.

They watched it for a few minutes more. Its pink tail flashed red a few times and it moved on. They didn't try to follow it.

"What happens now?" John asked.

"Hey, don't ask me. I just carry the damn sword."

"What happened to busy and important?"

Andrei shrugged and looked away. It was Senna that answered, "It was always just worried and scared." Andrei didn't try to contradict her. "And now we're back in the outside world, it feels like the war is almost on us and that means ..." She trailed off, unable to finish. Andrei squeezed her hand.

"I'm sorry," John murmured.

Andrei felt a little selfish at having let his mood swing at the thought of what was coming, John's life expectancy wasn't much different to his own. Win or lose, neither John nor Andrei could hope for much on the other side of the coming war.

"You were just trying to make me laugh, right? That's your job after all."

"Sure," John answered, a weak smile returning to his face.

"Looks like they're all out," Tilvy announced as she and most of the others swam up to them.

No more samudraka were emerging, and Theseo was off to one side, speaking with a rainbow of leaders from different samtaana. Arrayed for a considerable distance on either side of them were ranks of warriors waiting patiently, their spears mere shadows in their hands. Andrei shook his head. So many of them, and this was just part of the army. If the samudraka wanted to wipe out the aaranya there would be no stopping them. He felt some reservation about what they were doing. At least the papayamala weren't wiping out the aaranya, not all of them anyway. Might it be better to live in the bondage of the strange siblings than the possibility of all dying at the hands of the samudraka?

"Where's Sarva?" Senna asked.

Andrei glanced around their small group. "And the king's mum?"

"They swam off earlier," Pasith said, and pointed into the depths below the ridge. "Down that way somewhere."

"Theseo won't like it if we lose his mum. Maybe we should go get them."

"Looks like you're wanted," Darnu said, nodding in the direction of the king.

Andrei turned. A samudraka, one of Theseo's guards, was approaching them.

"You are to come," the guard announced.

His manner suggested that he meant all of them, so they followed him back.

Theseo called Andrei to his side, but waved the others back behind him. "You'll want to see this," Theseo said.

A booming sound ran through the water, and then another. Andrei glanced down and saw that a group of Marr warriors were assembled at some structure they had built against the ridge below them. They were hitting it with their tails, and the sound was somehow being amplified. The booming continued in a deep, strangely syncopated rhythm.

"What's this for?" he asked the king.

Theseo held up one hand. "Just wait. It won't take long. We've been keeping them close so they would be ready when we needed them."

All the samudraka were looking out into the distance, so Andrei turned to watch as well.

Minutes passed. The sound was starting to give Andrei a headache. He fidgeted and looked back at his friends. Senna smiled at him, mouthing a question. Andrei shrugged.

Theseo touched his arm. "There."

A long smudge in the darkness of the water. And then another one. And another. As the smudges drew closer they resolved into snake-like shapes in a variety of dull green and yellow shades. Andrei wondered why they would want to call snakes. The shapes kept growing and he realised these were large creatures.

"Serpents?" he asked.

Theseo nodded. "Young males. Smaller than the one your friend will have told you about. The females are vicious even as babies, and can't be trained, but the males remain amenable to command until they reach maturity, if you start them young enough."

"These are small?" The creatures looked pretty big to Andrei, certainly big enough that chewing on the occasional aaranya like himself wasn't going to be a problem.

Theseo laughed. "Ask your friend about the one he met. These are tiny in comparison."

The serpents stopped fifty metres or so in front of the line of samudraka. There were dozens of them surging restlessly back and forth, snapping at each other irritably.

"Come," Theseo pulled at Andrei's arm, "come and meet Zizu."

"Baby?" Andrei translated in disbelief.

"He was when I started training him, the name stuck."

They approached the line of writhing serpents, Theseo confidently and Andrei nervously. Theseo began calling. The repeated "Zizu" call came out as a continuous buzzing sound.

One of the largest of the serpents snapped savagely to clear a space around it and then extended its head forward. Theseo swam directly to the protruding muzzle of the creature and stroked it. It had only to open its mouth, Andrei thought, and the king would be gone. It would barely have to chew.

"Come forward," Theseo urged. "Let Zizu get used to you."

Andrei swam slowly closer. The serpent moved its head toward him and Andrei pulled back.

"It's all right," Theseo assured him. "Zizu is just curious."

Andrei told himself that he was dead anyway, so there was no need to panic, and forced himself to approach it. The serpent seemed to sniff at Andrei's body as Andrei tentatively stroked the side of its head.

"He's cute," Andrei said, trying to sound confident.

"He's almost grown up. I'll have to release him soon and start with another. This will be his last battle. I'll be sorry to let him go."

"Why do you have to let him go?"

"He will soon be old enough to want a mate. He'll get unpredictable and dangerous to be around." Theseo laughed when he saw Andrei start to pull back. "Don't worry. He's fine for now."

Around them, other samudraka had come out to make contact with their serpents. The water was quiet now, each serpent had found its master and lay still while it was stroked. Theseo led Andrei along the long line of Zizu's body, apparently checking for injury. The skin of the creature was covered in large shiny scales. Zizu was mostly yellow, brighter than most of the other serpents, and his scales were edged with a dark green.

"They change colour as they mature," Theseo explained. "Soon Zizu's scales will begin to turn orange, and that's when I will know it is time to set him free."

"What do they eat?" Andrei asked.

"Whatever they want." Theseo chuckled. "Sorry, it's the punchline of a joke among the warriors. They spend most of their time in water deeper than this and feed on other praanin creatures."

"Including narun?"

"The older ones, yes. And the females of almost any age."

The booming rhythm had stopped a while ago, but it started again now. At first Andrei thought it was the same, but as the sound repeated he realised it was a subtly different beat.

"What now?"

"Some zarana open at this level, or even shallower," said Theseo, "where serpents are not so prolific. So they find it convenient to use material creatures, squid. They're good, but no match for a serpent like Zizu." He gave his serpent a hard slap on the tail.

Andrei turned in surprise as Zizu nudged him in the back. The serpent had folded back on itself to follow their progress. Andrei patted its muzzle nervously. "Nice Zizu, good Zizu. You won't like chewing on me, Zizu, I'm videzaka."

Theseo laughed. "Serpents are not prejudiced."

"Maybe we could work on that," Andrei suggested. Another thought occurred to him. "Squid," he said. "You mean those small, funny little things with lots of arms trailing out the back?"

Theseo laughed again.

"And that was funny because ...?" Andrei prompted.

"You got it all right except the part about being *small*," Theseo told him.

"Oh. And they know about us? They can sense the narun?"

"They wouldn't be much use if they couldn't. There you go." Theseo pointed.

A hundred metres above them were large pale shapes, each coming into position in a series of surges. It was only as samudraka swam up next to them that Andrei realised just how large the smooth bodied creatures were. They were small compared to the serpents, but even so the smallest of them had to be a dozen metres or more from their rounded bulbous mantle to the end of the longest tentacles. Andrei was suddenly feeling better about swimming next to a serpent and it took him a moment to realise why. And then he understood. The main body of the squid reminded him of the nirarkta. He shuddered at the thought.

Andrei let his eyes wander over the assembled host of warriors, back to the squid, and finally down to the serpents. "Any more surprises?" Andrei asked while absently stroking Zizu's muzzle.

"Not yet," Theseo answered. "Now it's time to find our enemy. Let's see if we can make them as nervous as you are."

19. Preparations

"How long have we got now?" Jaimee asked.

<I don't know. Just a few days I think,> Peren answered.

"How can they come so quickly?" Sando asked.

"Their zarana are connected," Helix reminded him.

"But I didn't think they cooperated this much."

<They're coming for us. They united because they all hate us,> Peren said. She sounded more upset by the hate than the samudraka coming to kill them.

"Do you know how many?"

<Not really. But a lot. Thousands.>

"How many aaranya have we got?" Jaimee asked Helix.

Helix was silent for a few moments, concentrating, before she answered, "About two thousand so far, I've got more still converging on airports. Some are probably too far away to get anywhere useful in time. You may need to get me some more planes. Arming them effectively is the problem, they have no weapons of their own."

"I'll talk to Stephenson, see what he can arrange. Sando, what have you got?"

"There's a good stock of field generators, so we could give human contingents some idea what direction to shoot. The ray-guns are harder and more expensive to produce. If I really push we might have a few hundred by the end of the week, if we're lucky. We never expected a full-scale war among the narun. We were concentrating on making them more effective against humans before we scaled up production. But that's not the real problem."

"What is?" Jaimee asked impatiently.

"Most of it's been made for land use. We never contemplated

underwater battles. There are only a few dozen that you can use in the water, and they're not very effective. The samudraka weren't supposed to be a problem for us, not yet."

"Fuck!"

"You should have let me kill the others while we had the chance," Sando said.

"And you shouldn't have let those two escape!" Jaimee snapped back. "Peren says that's what brought them here."

<That's what it looked like,> Peren agreed quietly, *<but I can't be sure.>*

"We will have a good number of aaranya to throw at them," Helix put in before the brothers could argue further. "The dryads will be almost useless underwater, but we can use them to distract the samudraka while the dhumraka make more effective attacks."

"The aaranya aren't going to be much better on land," Jaimee said. "They're not fighters."

"We'll need to bring some of them past you," Helix said to Peren. "You'll have to be our eyes in the battle, I don't fancy being there myself."

<I know,> Peren agreed in a quiet voice.

"It will be better if Asha doesn't see it happen," Jaimee said, ignoring the hesitation he heard in Peren's tone.

"Do it after one of her sessions with Mother," Helix suggested. "She always merges for a long time after that. She won't see anything."

Jaimee nodded.

"What else have we got?" Sando asked.

"I've got a few ideas," Jaimee said enigmatically. "I'll need your help, Sando, my brother."

Sando nodded, starting to sense what Jaimee had in mind.

"We probably need to experiment a bit," Jaimee continued. "Can we borrow some of your aaranya, sister?"

"Don't waste too many, we might need them."

Jaimee shrugged. "What I'm still trying to work out is how to get the human military involved. It's all National Parks and populated areas around here, they won't accept it as a training exercise."

"We won't need them. The samudraka must never reach land," Helix argued.

"And what if some get through? Most of your dhumraka will be out at sea."

"The samudraka don't know where we are," Sando argued.

"Are you ready to bet your life on that?" Jaimee responded.

<And Mama's,> Peren added.

"All right then," Sando said, "so we pull out some terrorists."

Jaimee grinned. "Great idea. We won't even need Helix to help. The right threat and the humans will happily torch half the west coast looking for them."

- - -

There was still a dark stain beneath the fence. The rain last night hadn't been enough to shift it. Tracey stared at it and shivered. There was also a dark stain in her mind, confusing her thoughts. Guilt, sadness, relief, shame, fear and horror all still whirled through her mind, each visiting for a moment before being pushed away by the next impulse clamouring for acceptance.

"Tracey?"

She turned. In the days since they had been returned to this cabin the worst of their physical injuries had healed. The bruises on Paul's face had faded to an ugly yellow, and most of the scratches were nothing more than fading white lines. It would take longer for the hair to grow back properly on the back of his head where a patch had been shaved to receive stitches.

"You shouldn't keep doing this to yourself. It wasn't your fault," Paul said quietly.

"Whose was it?"

"You said this was Sando's work."

"That's what Asha told me," Tracey admitted.

"And you know she's right. You've met him before. You told me about it."

Tracey nodded. "But if I hadn't led Mike on—"

"You didn't!" Paul's tone was vehement. One hand came out toward her, but pulled back again.

He doesn't even want to touch me now, Tracey thought bitterly. The first days back here had been okay. Tracey had kept herself busy doing as much as she could for Paul so that he could rest. He had seemed natural with her then, appreciative of her help. She had filled the rest of her time scrubbing everything in the cabin, again and again, and talking with Asha. Asha visited regularly, let in via the gate by the tall Asian man that she seemed to know. But since Paul had regained his strength, his reactions to Tracey had changed. Their time together became strained and awkward, full of things left unsaid.

"Mike brought this on himself," Paul was saying.

"But I—"

"You thought Mike was sincere. There is no shame in that." Paul stepped closer.

"I feel like such an idiot."

"He was a good actor. He had us all fooled."

"No he didn't!" Tracey snapped. Paul took a step back. "You two both knew. You tried to tell me but I didn't listen."

"We didn't like him, we didn't trust him, but we didn't know what he was doing."

"I should have had better sense."

"It's not your fault, Tracey."

"I feel guilty because I'm relieved he's gone." Tracey's tone changed as a new mood caught hold.

"I am too."

"Whatever he did to me, or was going to do ... no one deserves to die like that."

Paul didn't respond. Tracey looked up and recognised the carefully neutral expression on his face. It had been there the first time she met him.

"You didn't see it. Didn't hear it." Tracey shuddered. She felt tears on her face and wiped them away. Then she laughed bitterly. "At least I have more variety in my nightmares now."

"I know. I hear them."

"I'm sorry if I keep you awake." She hadn't meant the words to come out so harshly. She turned away from him.

"I just wish I could make them go away," Paul said.

Tracey shook her head.

"I wish I could do something. Get you out of all this. Somewhere safe."

Tracey almost laughed. Safe? How did you hide from an enemy you couldn't even see. How did you resist someone that could force you to disembowel yourself on a razor-wire fence?

"I think we should try to escape," Paul said in a whisper.

Tracey turned back in surprise.

"When Asha was here yesterday, she said that they might be sending Ray out soon, that he has recovered enough to get around now."

Tracey nodded. They hadn't been allowed to visit him, but Asha had passed messages back and forth.

"With Asha's help we can all escape."

"It's complicated for Asha," Tracey reminded him.

"I admit I don't get all of it," Paul acknowledged, "but we will need her. And there's this war she spoke of, people coming for the others. It seems to me it would be a good time to be somewhere else, and it also means they will be distracted, so our chances will be better."

"I don't even know where we are."

"I got enough from Asha that I think I know. It's a long way from anywhere, so we'll have to steal one of their cars – we probably need that to break through their fences anyway."

"It sounds like you have it all worked out."

Paul shook his head, but said, "I've been thinking about it since I found out that Asha has the run of the place. We need her help to get us out of this cage."

Remembering their last disastrous attempt to escape, Tracey was sceptical. "Where would we go?"

"Ray knows people over here. If we can get free then he can get us help."

Tracey shook her head, it seemed hopeless.

"We can do it. We have to do it. I have to get you out of here." Paul stepped closer. Again his hand reached forward and drew back.

"I'm not contagious you know." Tracey's words came out flat and depressed.

A look of shock filled his face. "It's not ... I'm not ... I thought you might not want to be touched after ..."

"Hold me," Tracey whispered. Paul hesitated. "Please," she pleaded.

Tracey leaned her head against his shoulder, she could feel her tears starting to run. Paul's hands rested only lightly on her back, as if he was afraid she might break. Her emotions welled up and breathing got harder. She pulled herself against him, wishing she could bury herself in the strength she felt there. Paul's arms tightened and the feelings she had been holding tightly inside finally burst loose. She howled and sobbed into his shirt.

Forinay had somehow managed to persuade the other two guards that there was no reason why Barma and Telia shouldn't be allowed to move around within the Glade. Barma guessed the guards were as bored as he was, that any diversion was welcome.

"Where is everyone?" Telia asked the nervous young dhumraka woman.

Forinay glanced back to make sure the other two guards weren't paying attention. "Preparing for war," she whispered. "The samudraka are coming."

Barma glanced at the woman in surprise. There had been a lot of activity over several days, people rushing back and forth, meeting briefly and exchanging hurried whispers. A feeling of tension had grown around them but they hadn't known why. And then, slowly, it had all changed. The Glade grew quiet and they rarely saw anyone but their guards. It was almost peaceful now, but an indefinable tension remained as if carried by the water.

"Why?" Barma asked.

Forinay ignored him.

"Why are the dhumraka making war on the samudraka?" Telia asked.

Forinay shook her head. "We didn't start this. Not even our queen wants this, not now. But the samudraka are coming."

"The samudraka wouldn't attack for no reason," Barma said with more confidence than he really felt.

Swimming closer to Telia, Forinay whispered so that Barma could barely hear, "Someone told them about our queen and our lords. They are jealous and coming to take our queen." She glanced around nervously again. "They say it was aaranya that told them." A pause and then she repeated the mantra, "The samudraka are coming."

Barma hitched the tiny form of Ellie into a more comfortable position in the crook of his arm. He knew little of the samudraka, other than tales from the Aeonian War. Now they were an enigmatic people who were said to have no love of the aaranya. But they couldn't be that different, could they? Surely, if the samudraka found Barma and Telia here as prisoners, they would help?

"Where are you taking us?" Telia asked Forinay.

The nervous woman shook her head. "You will see."

Forinay led them deeper into the Glade and the kelp got thicker and darker.

One of the other guards swam closer. "We should not be here," he told Forinay.

"Where are they going to go?" she asked innocently.

The guard didn't look convinced, but didn't stop Forinay from venturing further into the kelp. The other guards swam closer now, they had to if they wanted keep sight of their charges.

"Why back here?" Telia asked.

Forinay whispered, "I've seen her."

"Who?"

"Your little ginger creature."

Barma felt a surge of relief to hear that Cassey was still alive.

"Was she okay?"

"I only saw her for a moment," Forinay whispered, "but I think so."

They came to a stop not far from the hole where they had been captured. The other two guards looked around nervously.

"I thought she might come to you," Forinay whispered urgently. "Then she could lead us back to your Glade."

"Move on!" one of the guards insisted. "We can't stay here."

When Forinay hesitated he thrust his spear forward, indicating the direction they should take. Reluctantly, Forinay started to swim away.

Telia spoke quietly to Forinay. "If Cassey is still here then that must mean the connection is closed. I don't think we can leave that way."

- - -

Beenae was smiling widely at her. Asha smiled back. She didn't point out to him how far Taiza still had to go.

She looked past Beenae to watch Taiza. He was kneeling at the base of the tree, fiddling with some small twigs. It looked like he was trying to build something. She could hear a faint murmuring, and her smile deepened. That constant chattering to himself as he worked was familiar. So what if he didn't recognise Asha when she had arrived at the fence, they had never been that close, maybe this really was the start of a recovery. They had to hope.

"Has he said anything to you?" Asha asked.

Beenae shook his head. "Not really. But sometimes he looks at me like he's trying to remember."

Asha smiled gently at Beenae. She wished she was inside, she wanted to give him a big hug just for being so constantly optimistic and enthusiastic. She found herself coming here often, just to get a dose of Beenae.

Before the news of the samudraka, Asha had been allowed in the cage with Beenae and Taiza a few times, but Jaimee was being difficult now. Asha was afraid to push things in case he decided to restrict her movements.

"He's here," Beenae said, pointing across to the path from the house.

"I'll be back soon." Asha managed to stop her hand before it touched the burning mesh.

"Maybe Taiza will be talking by then."

"Maybe."

Asha jogged lightly across to meet Reyndani at the path. Reyndani stopped pushing his trolley and gave a small bow when he sensed her approaching. It was a bit disconcerting the way he could recognise her without actually seeing her, and he retained that strange formality he'd been brought up with in the Samgha. He was much the same man as he'd always been, with the stark exception that his priorities had changed. He never spoke of his wife and son, nor his parents, back in Myanmar. Asha had tried to question him about them, but the most she ever saw was a slight tightening around his eyes and then he would change the subject.

Reyndani unlocked the gate and Asha picked up the small basket of clean sheets and clothes from his trolley while Reyndani picked up an identical basket of used items that Tracey or Paul had left inside the gate.

Tracey opened the door to the cabin as Asha came up the path. The smile on Tracey's face looked warm and natural. Though the young woman wouldn't see it, Asha smiled in return. She was pleased to see that Tracey was looking so much better.

"I'll take them," Tracey said, and took the basket through to a room at the back.

Paul was sitting at the table in the small living area. "Ah, just the woman we wanted to see," he welcomed her. "Well ... you know what I mean." He slid a large pad across in front of an empty chair. "Any news from Ray?"

Asha settled herself in the chair and picked up the pencil. "He is well," she scratched.

Tracey returned and sat next to Paul. "We have something we wanted to ask you."

Asha waited.

"We want to get out," Paul said.

Asha was trying to understand exactly what he meant when Tracey chimed in, "We want to escape. To take you and Beenae, and Taiza and Ray with us."

"But we will need your help," Paul added.

Asha felt a sudden panic. Was Peren listening? She didn't think so. But this wasn't safe, Peren could come into Asha's mind at any time. How could she explain that?

"Asha?" Tracey queried when Asha didn't respond.

"Not safe," Asha wrote. "I am watched."

"Not all the time, surely?" Paul said.

Asha tried to think it through and then scribbled, "Watching my mind. Any time. I give you away."

"Are you being watched now?"

"No."

"Would you know?"

"Yes," Asha wrote. The word on the paper looked more certain than she felt. She was worried that even thinking about Peren might bring the girl into her mind.

"Asha, you are the best chance we have," said Paul. "I'll explain what I have in mind and then you can tell me if you think we can make it work."

Asha listened as Paul outlined his plan. He made it all sound easy. She could leave here! ... No. She couldn't. With Peren in Asha's mind there was never going to be an escape for her, and Asha would be a liability to any attempt. And there was more—

406

"What do you think?" Tracey interrupted Asha's thoughts.

"Need to th—" Asha started to write.

<You're a twin!> Peren's voice exploded in Asha's mind.

Asha swept the page of the pad over and started tapping the table urgently with the pencil. Tracey and Paul looked at the pencil with puzzled expressions that slowly transformed to frightened understanding.

<You're a twin,> Peren repeated.

Asha got up from the table and rushed out the door of the cabin. So? she answered, trying hard not to think about what Paul had just told her. Thankfully, Peren had other things on her mind.

<You never said.>

I thought it must be obvious.

<We talked about it once, back when Sando first found you, but Jaimee said that even if there had been a twin, it must have died or you would be together.>

"We're not." Asha spoke out loud with deep finality.

<You never speak of him.>

"So you can't really read my mind then, or you would have found him. He's always there."

<I had seen him, but he is so much younger – softer – in your mind. I didn't realise. I thought he must just be a brother.>

Asha paused at the gate. She would have to wait for Reyndani to come back from the other cabins and let her out. She looked back and saw Tracey looking out the door. Asha stopped herself from waving. The significance of Peren's conversation finally caught up with her.

"How do you know about my brother?"

<Sarva is with the samudraka. So is your John.>

Asha was too stunned to respond.

<They're coming to kill us, and your brother and your lover are helping them.>

Have you told Jaimee about Sarva? Asha asked silently.

<About Sarva being your twin? Not yet.>

But you're going to?

<I'm not sure. I'm scared Jaimee will do something silly trying to get hold of him. What can your brother do?>

Do?

<You know? Like you. Like my brothers and Helix.>

I don't know. Neither of us had any talent when last I saw him.

Reyndani arrived back at the gate and let Asha out. She patted his arm absently before she parted.

Peren questioned Asha for a while about Sarva and why he had left. Asha had little in the way of answers, she had never understood it.

<And you've been apart all this time?>

Asha nodded sadly.

<How can you stand it? I think I would die if my siblings left me.>

There were times when I wished I would.

<What am I going to do?>

"I thought you said the samudraka were coming because they don't accept twins," Asha said. "If they know about Sarva, why haven't they killed him?"

<Only one of them knows what he is, I don't know what she's going to do about it. You know they will kill you too, if they find you here?>

Asha had already assumed that, but she had also worked out it was probably for the best. It was probably her only way out, the only way for aaranya everywhere.

<You really feel like that?> Peren sounded devastated.

Of course Peren was upset, Asha had as good as said that she wanted Peren dead. Asha cursed herself for expressing the thought so clearly, or maybe Peren was getting better at reading her, just as she was getting better at feeling Peren's presence. "How do you expect me to feel?" Asha asked out loud, suddenly angry. "I'm a prisoner here. My friends are under constant threat. My people are enslaved. Tell me, *friend*, just how do you expect me to feel?"

Peren didn't answer for a long time, Asha could feel her presence trembling. *<I thought ... in time ...>*

"What? That eventually I'd stop caring about my people, about my friends?"

<No. I thought ... I thought we might work things out.>

"Are you really that naïve? Have you looked at Jaimee lately? At Helix? Would they ever release my people unless someone forces them to?"

408

<I thought ...> Peren started. <I've never had a friend before. I didn't realise it would be so hard.>

Asha was almost feeling sorry for Peren and the impossible position she was in. Almost, but not quite. "It's not just me the samudraka will kill. They will probably kill everyone they find here."

There was a sense of movement, a tentative nod from Peren's presence.

An idea flickered into Asha's mind. She started to push it away, but changed her mind and pushed ahead. Would you help me to get them out? she asked silently. One of the children of the estate was walking nearby and she didn't want this conversation overheard.

<What do you mean?>

I mean I want my friends away from here. Away from the war your siblings have brought on themselves.

<The samudraka will never reach us.> Peren's words were more confident than her voice.

Underestimating the samudraka would be a mistake.

<What would I have to do?>

Nothing.

<I don't understand.>

The child was gone now, so Asha spoke out loud, "All I need is for you to do nothing. Whatever you see me do, don't tell your siblings. Don't interfere."

<Will you stay?>

"Do I have a choice?" Asha regretted her words the moment they came out, she could feel Peren cringe at them. "I will stay," Asha said more gently. "If my brother and John are coming here then perhaps I can see them before the end."

20. Battle

They left Stephenson speaking with the general. There had been no evacuation of civilians and the general was concerned that some might venture into the area and be at risk. Stephenson was assuring him that it wouldn't be an issue. The army was there only as a precaution.

The army contingents shouldn't be necessary tonight, they shouldn't be necessary at all, but the precaution did seem sensible. After all, Sando reflected, it wasn't that far from this beach to their estate if you went directly through the forest rather than following the roundabout route of the road. If the samudraka found some unexpected reason to turn this way, then the siblings might be thankful for this extra defence.

The siblings stopped at the top of the ridge and looked out over the beach and the ocean.

"Why here?" he asked his brother. They had no reason to come closer to the battle. Distance didn't matter to what Helix could do, and they wouldn't see anything from here.

Jaimee gave his trademark shrug. "It seemed fitting. Our home of so long ago. We met our first samudraka not far up that way, you remember?"

<I do,> Peren put in.

"You would," Jaimee answered wryly.

"Everything ready, Helix?" Sando asked.

Helix nodded slowly. "Keeping them still is harder than I expected. They want to attack now."

"Don't let them go," Jaimee cautioned. "Timing is important."

"I know. I understand the plan."

Sando watched the ocean. The wave crests were tipped with gold by the low sun. When sunset came the colour would turn red.

"Let's go down to the beach and get comfortable," Jaimee suggested.

Sando agreed readily enough. He didn't like standing here with human soldiers behind him, soldiers armed with detectors that would let them see the narun. They also had ray-guns, though normal bullets would be good enough once they knew where to point them.

They climbed down the ridge and settled on the sand above the high tide line.

"Would you like me to massage your shoulders, dear sister?" Jaimee asked.

"Shut up and let me concentrate," Helix snapped back.

Jaimee grinned at Sando. "Tetchy, isn't she? And here I was thinking she could manage a few warriors without a crease in her beautiful brow."

"It's more than a few," Helix reminded him. "I don't normally need to be so specific. They're ready to tear apart any samudraka they can see—"

"They wish," Jaimee interrupted.

"Yes, they do. I got them worked up to this, but now I have to keep them in check. If you think it's easy, you try it."

"I'm happy to leave it in your capable hands, dear sister."

- - -

The speed of the serpent was incredible. Zizu rushed through the water past the assembled ranks of samudraka warriors. In front of Andrei, Theseo's position on the serpent looked precarious. His tail was folded as if kneeling, and the broad flukes lay across Zizu's back as if Theseo could grip the scales with them. However fast the serpent swam, however quickly it turned and writhed through the water, Theseo sat there like he was glued in position. It was all Andrei could do to hold on, his knees gripping tightly and his hands clutching at the edges of the scales.

Along the line were other serpents and huge squid that rippled restlessly. The samudraka saluted their king as he passed. In other circumstances Andrei might have thought this was fun, but not now. Battle was almost on them.

There was nothing subtle about Theseo's strategy. His huge force had been split into three, but they would all attack the same point together. His intention was simply to overwhelm the dhumraka. He would start here, not far from where his mother had first encountered the papayamala as infants, and cut a swathe along the coast, working south past the large human city until they found the papayamala and destroyed them.

Scouts had returned late in the afternoon. They reported a large army assembling ahead of them, near the surface, at the edge of the shelf where the ocean floor fell away into the depths, but they hadn't risked going close enough to determine any details.

Despite initial surprise at the size of the force confronting them so soon, Theseo was not concerned. He wasn't worried about being outflanked, or even outnumbered. No other narun could hope to compete with the samudraka in their own environment. "An army ten times our own size wouldn't worry me," he had boasted. Andrei wished he shared the king's confidence.

John and the others had been kept back with the majority of the samudraka women – those that weren't warriors. A small reserve of warriors remained with them. Theseo was hoping that he could find the papayamala without going on land, but he held the aaranya back in safety in case their help was needed later.

Theseo brought the serpent to a halt at the head of the assembled Marr warriors. Zizu twitched back and forth, still worked up from his fast dash across the front of the armies. Theseo leaned forward and called to the serpent, slapping firmly at the scales behind its head. A shiver ran down the body of the serpent and it finally settled.

Andrei looked up. A dim residue of sunlight continued to filter down to them.

"Remember what we practised," Theseo said, speaking quietly over his shoulder. "When the battle starts keep well back so I don't accidentally get you with this." He held up his thick, double-ended spear. "Zizu isn't likely to let anyone get near you, but keep watch. If anyone does get close, tell me."

"And if I fall off?" Andrei asked.

"Don't." Theseo twisted himself a bit further so Andrei could see his grin. "We can't afford to lose Zamayitar."

Andrei grinned back at him.

When Theseo turned back to the front, Andrei shook his head in disbelief at the strangeness of their situation. The more time he and Theseo had spent together the more they had grown to like each other. Senna thought Andrei was mad, but friendship and love are resistant to reason. Sure this man intended to kill Andrei, but he had no choice, and Andrei understood that. In fact Andrei felt sorry for Theseo. The slaughter that Theseo had so obviously found distasteful from the start was turning into something much more difficult, the killing of a friend.

As incomprehensible as it was to others, it was this tragedy that both found funny. The humour of it wasn't apparent to anyone else so their words were usually misinterpreted by anyone listening to their banter, and that only made the joke that much funnier. Andrei had tried to explain it to Senna.

"He could have avoided all this by doing what any of the others would have done as soon as we met. The longer he leaves it the harder it gets, and yet he keeps finding reasons to avoid doing it."

"But it's *not* funny," she had argued.

"Not when we're apart, no," Andrei admitted, "but when we're together the ridiculousness of it is too much not to laugh at."

Senna had shaken her head.

A deep wordless shout, part grunt and part cheer, issued from thousands of samudraka. Shaken out of his thoughts, Andrei looked up and saw that the dim sunlight was gone. The time for battle had come.

At some signal Andrei didn't see, Zizu started to rise and the army rose up behind them. The deep shouts of the warriors kept up a slow, steady rhythm.

"You're the king, shouldn't you tell someone else to go first?" Andrei called to Theseo.

"I am the king. I lead," Theseo answered.

"Well, be careful. Don't forget I'm back here."

All Andrei heard of his response was the laugh.

They rose from the depths, moving quickly, as if keen for the battle to start. Andrei knew they were, but he still didn't understand it, and he certainly didn't share the feeling.

Andrei could feel the presence of the opposing army before he

413

could see them. It stretched out before them like a single huge creature. Something about that presence troubled him. Theseo must have felt it too, because he called out a command that Andrei heard echoed down the line of warriors. Their progress slowed.

The enemy appeared. A swarm of dots that slowly resolved into men and women carrying spears. Another call from Theseo and the samudraka stopped.

Theseo twisted and looked at Andrei. "You see?"

"It's not possible," was all Andrei could say.

These weren't dhumraka. There wasn't a dhumraka to be seen. They were aaranya. Aaranya from many different places. Thousands of them forming a wall across the ocean. More of his own people than Andrei had ever seen in one place before. More than he even realised might exist.

"They aren't warriors. They can't be."

"No, they're not," agreed Theseo. "But they're here and they're armed. I'm sorry, Andrei."

Theseo called out savagely and two of the Marr on serpents departed hurriedly along the lines of the samudraka.

"We must find the dhumraka before we attack."

The samudraka had fallen silent as they waited impatiently for word from their king. In this quiet, Andrei heard a mechanical thrumming sound. They were still some hundreds of feet below the surface, when he looked up he caught sight of lights and shadows that could only be large ships.

"Humans," Andrei said.

Theseo shrugged. "They're up there, we're down here."

Andrei couldn't argue with that logic, but he didn't think it could be normal, nor a coincidence, that so many human ships would be present in this one place.

"Maybe we should go back. Think about this. Maybe talk to John," Andrei suggested.

"The samudraka will not retreat," Theseo said flatly.

"I'm not suggesting we surrender," Andrei argued.

Theseo held up a hand to stop Andrei saying more. One of the riders was returning. The rider stopped his serpent a short distance away and swam to the king.

"King Theseo, there are no dhumraka visible. Just these," the

414

man flung a hand out at the motionless aaranya before them.

"Leaders?" Theseo demanded.

"None that can be seen."

Theseo shook his head. "This makes no sense. They know these aaranya cannot stand before us. Why are they here?"

Zizu trembled beneath them, and then Andrei felt it himself. A faint, disturbing buzzing that seemed to reach right through him.

"Theseo!"

"What?"

"The humans. They know we're here!"

"So?"

Andrei didn't know how to answer that, but it had to mean something.

Shrill cries made them look forward. The aaranya were attacking. As they started to move the loud shrieks coalesced into an incoherent howl of noise.

"Draw Zamayitar!" Theseo called back to Andrei. "Hold it high."

The messenger was already on his way back to his own serpent. Behind them, the loud rhythmic chant of the samudraka started.

Andrei held the zakti high, and Theseo reached back and put his hand around Andrei's. The sword flared brightly, and Theseo waved it back and forth.

"Agadharastra!" Theseo yelled.

His voice, impossibly loud, rang through Andrei's head. Theseo released Andrei's hand and leaned forward, urging Zizu on.

Andrei was astonished to see that there were samudraka keeping up with the serpents. The calls of the samudraka had quickened until now it was just a continuous roar, deeper and louder than that of the aaranya.

- - -

"Why teach us to fight and then leave us behind?" Garjae asked.

Darnu put a hand on Garjae's arm. "Did you really want to fight? To kill other narun?"

Garjae slumped slightly. "No. But what if Asha is up there? Who will tell the samudraka when to stop?"

"She won't be there," Sarva said. "Neither will the siblings, the papayamala."

"How can you know?" Garjae demanded.

"It's not their style. If they were certain of winning, of it being a walkover, they might be there, but against the samudraka?" Sarva shook his head. "It's not likely."

Garjae looked around. There were a few hundred samudraka still here, mostly women of varying ages. The few dozen warriors looked as frustrated at having been left behind as Garjae felt.

John, Tilvy and Pasith were with Senna. It looked like they were trying to distract her with conversation. The worried expression still fixed on Senna's face suggested it wasn't working. Not far from them was Lantea. She was accompanied by two samudraka warriors, men matching her pale cream skin and silver tail. He wondered what that was about, the rest of the reserve warriors had kept to themselves, floating above, as if trying to shorten the distance between themselves and the battle.

They were waiting on a ridge that reached up from the ocean floor, just one of the many roots stretching out from the continental shelf. For the want of something to do, Garjae swam out and peered into the depths below the ridge. Darnu went with him.

"I've been thinking about home," Darnu said quietly. He had called Nuttachen out, the pale brevi flicked back and forth between the two men.

"Hmm, what?"

"There will be a lot to do, preparing the forest for the Way."

"I guess. Tilvy said Ceeda was going back, there may be others," Garjae answered absently. Despite his impatience to leave the samudraka, returning home hadn't been high in this thoughts.

"Have you thought what it will be like?" Darnu asked.

Garjae shrugged.

Darnu said, "It will be busy, but peaceful too. Our own people for company again, and when the Glade opens, our own elders. I miss Milla and Kaia. I miss home. ... And if we get sick of company we can seek out our own space like we used to. Just you and me, like it was before all this started."

"Before it started," Garjae mused. When did it start? He remembered seeing Asha as a young girl. He had loved her then. Not in the same way, but there was something even then. He had seen she was special. He had seen something of what she would become. He had been happy to wait, he just hadn't expected to wait so long. And now?

"I think about home a lot," Darnu said quietly, "and the way it was before."

Floating in the dark water, they maintained a companionable silence as they watched and waited.

- - -

The two armies came together in a confusion of swirling currents. Spears lashed out. Teeth and tails and tentacles smashed at bodies. Shouts turned into screams.

It was a massacre. It should have been a rout, but the aaranya kept attacking. Even the mortally wounded kept coming. Andrei watched in dismay as his people were slaughtered. Many fell to the teeth and tails of the serpents, some to the ripping claws hidden in the tentacles of the squid, but most fell to the spears of the samudraka warriors. The water was soon filled with golden clouds, the life of his people spreading quickly through the water.

Theseo was concentrating on a group of aaranya in front of him. Zizu's huge mouth stretched forward and took one of the men. The lifeless body, still spurting prana, was quickly cast aside and the serpent reached for another. Theseo reached out to one side of the serpent's massive head and his spear slashed out across a man's throat.

A scream of rage made Andrei look up. Out of a cloud of gold came an aaranya woman, her face distorted with pain and savage intent. One of her arms was almost severed from her body, but the other still held a spear. She ignored Andrei, seemed not to notice him, as she lunged at Theseo's exposed back.

Zak was still in Andrei's hand, forgotten in the horror of battle. The zakti rose without conscious thought and sliced across the woman's spear. The tips of her fingers vanished with the end of the spear. She turned in surprise. She lashed out with what was left of her spear, perhaps she didn't realise the point had gone. The end of the spear and the woman's ruined hand smashed across Andrei's face. And then she was silent. Only as her body drifted away, spilling prana into the water, did Andrei see the zakti slide clear of her body. He had killed her. He almost dropped the sword in shock.

Thunder boomed through the water. And then again, closer. They were rolling over, serpent and riders together, pushed by the force of an immense pressure wave. Andrei clung desperately to the scales, trying not to be torn loose. Their movement slowed and Andrei quickly slid the zakti into its sheath so he could hold on with both hands. More thunder and they were pushed backwards by another expanding wall of pressure. A screech of fear or frustration came from Zizu as the serpent's body thrashed at the water.

Andrei thought that the ocean had turned against them, refusing to countenance the horrific slaughter of the aaranya. Theseo was calling to Zizu, trying to calm him. Everywhere Andrei looked there were walls of white bubbles laced with the gold of spilled life rising through the water.

More distant rumbles came to him and he recognised them as explosions. The humans! He looked up. A small, dark, lifeless shadow was falling toward them. He shouted a warning to Theseo, but the shadow came too quickly. It missed them. Andrei felt the strong wash of its wake as it passed close to his side.

Moments later the world flashed bright, like a lightning strike, and then the concussion hit.

- - -

Helix cried out in pain and Jaimee raced to her side.

"Helix. Sister. What is it?"

<They're dying,> Helix whispered into their minds, too shocked to speak out loud.

Jaimee looked up at Sando, his face puzzled.

"Who are dying?" Sando asked.

<The aaranya. I've never lost so many at once. Hundreds of them gone already.>

"We expected that," Jaimee said, still puzzled.

<I didn't expect the pain.>

"But ...?"

Helix didn't answer, so Peren, ever present in their minds, answered in her stead. *<Helix is connected to their stands, to their home Glades. The Glades feel the loss, so Helix feels it too.>*

<I didn't know. Didn't guess,> Jaimee answered. *<I would have found another way.>*

Helix winced. *<It's okay,>* she said at last, and squeezed Jaimee's hand on her arm. *<It will be worth it.>*

Sando stood up and looked to the west. There was nothing but the

418

ocean stretching into the darkness. He heard and felt Helix cringe as more of the aaranya died. Moments later he heard a faint rumbling. It felt too soft and gentle to be the aftermath of a massacre.

- - -

The water that Andrei occupied was twisting and coiling, threatening to tear him apart from within. Beneath him, Zizu shrieked and then fell silent. Theseo yelled in pain. Or was it Andrei himself? He couldn't tell. They were rising. The water around them was hot.

The body of the serpent rolled over in the roiling currents. Theseo was falling free. Andrei pushed himself away from Zizu's corpse. The rising bubbles pushed at him and tore at him. He fought through them and reached out for his friend. He caught the tip of Theseo's tail and held on tightly. They were still rising.

Andrei pulled himself up Theseo's body. Now they were being pushed to the side into cooler water and Andrei tried to use the currents to get further from the turmoil.

Free of the white water, he could hear other explosions off to one side. A different sound intruded. Engines and propellers churning the water. Above them was the dark shadow of a ship. Holding Theseo over his shoulder with one hand, he swam deeper as fast as he could. He wished he had a tail.

Theseo groaned and moved weakly in Andrei's grasp.

"Hold still, partner," Andrei called to him.

Three figures came out of the gloom below. Andrei slowed. Aaranya. Three men.

"Guys?" Andrei called to them. "Look, I'm one of you!"

They kept coming.

"Please, don't make me do this," he pleaded.

They kept coming.

Andrei let Theseo slip from his shoulder and drew the zakti. It glowed brightly in his hand as he swam to meet them. "Just go!" he yelled at them and waved the blade.

At the last moment he realised they were going to swim past him. They wanted Theseo. "No!" he cried, and lashed out with the sword. It sliced right through the man's neck and gold exploded into the water.

Andrei spun around in time to see a spear thrusting at Theseo. Andrei pushed himself hard and stretched full length, the tip of his sword reached just far enough to cut into the man's arm. The spear kept going and cut a shallow groove over Theseo's shoulder. Theseo flinched at that, shaking his head.

The aaranya men were confused about where the attack had come from, looking everywhere but down at Andrei. Andrei was torn, he didn't want to kill these men, but what choice did he have?

"Here!" he yelled.

They both turned. Andrei swam in, heedless of the hatred glaring back at him. A spear thrust came at him. He tried to cut away the tip. He missed, but the aim had been poor and the spear passed by his side. Andrei pushed away the shaft with his free hand. As Theseo had shown him, Andrei kept the zakti slicing in, using the man's own momentum against him. There was shocked expression on the man's face as the blade cut smoothly into his chest. A single frustrated shriek was cut short.

Andrei yelled in surprise and pain as a spear cut the side of his chest. He was slow to turn and already the third man was drawing his spear back to strike again. Andrei twisted, sliding Zak through the water. The spear came at him but slid past. He brought the zakti across and felt it catch for a moment, and then his attacker's arm fell free.

There was a moment of hesitation from both of them, and then the aaranya screamed and clawed at Andrei with his remaining hand. Andrei was too surprised to move or react. The man's fingers reached for Andrei's eyes. And stopped. The man was suddenly still and silent, as if he had been switched off.

Andrei drew back slowly. There was a spear buried in the man's chest.

"I hope you don't mind," Theseo said from behind.

Andrei turned. "Are you all right?"

"I will be. Zizu?"

Andrei shook his head.

Theseo turned away, studying what remained of the battle. The explosions had stopped now. "What happened?" he asked quietly.

It wasn't clear whether the question was directed at him, but Andrei answered anyway. "Humans. Bombs from the ships." When it looked like Theseo might try to swim into the golden clouds that marked the battlefield, Andrei touched his arm. "We should go. The samudraka will have descended. All you will find there are mindless aaranya and ..." he trailed off.

Still Theseo hesitated.

Several faces, all aaranya, emerged out of the murky clouds. Their attention turned and centred on Theseo and Andrei.

Theseo nodded at them.

- - -

Their first indication that something was wrong was a distant rumbling like a savage thunderstorm at the height of its fury.

John thought he knew what it must be. Nothing the samudraka did, nor any narun, could be responsible for such a sound. Had Theseo listened to any of the warnings that John and Sarva had tried to give him? When Senna looked at John with panic in her eyes, he shrugged his shoulders, he wouldn't confirm what she must have already guessed.

It seemed like an eternity before the first warriors began to return. It was obvious that there had been no victory. The warriors were returning in small groups. Every group was carrying some of their number. Too many. Few of the wounded were cut, but many were incapacitated, unconscious or groaning and unable to coordinate their movements properly.

The women that had been waiting swam up to meet them and took the wounded from their comrades. The women carried their burdens down into the depths below the ridge, quickly disappearing into the darkness below.

Senna was tense beside him, peering into the water above, straining for some sign that Andrei was approaching. John wanted to tell her that it would be all right, but couldn't find the conviction to utter the words.

"Where are they taking them?" Tilvy asked. She was pointing to more women disappearing below.

"To sarasi-jilvana."

Lantea's voice came from behind John. He turned in surprise. She was there, still accompanied by the two warriors of her samtaana.

"There are some small pools of life down there," she continued. "It is why we chose this place rather than closer to the battle."

As more warriors returned, the reserves departed, going up to offer their help to others. Lantea and her companions remained close to John and Senna. They all waited impatiently.

The flow of returning warriors continued. They settled in widely spaced groups. John couldn't keep track, he couldn't tell how bad it must have been. Thousands had gone. Had thousands returned? He couldn't guess.

Polyphemo returned with a small group of Marr warriors. He had a look of shock about him when he came over and spoke quietly with Lantea. When Senna tried to question him, he shook his head. "I haven't seen them," he said flatly, and swam away.

The flow of warriors slowed to a trickle and then stopped. John could feel his hopes fading away, and the more he clutched at them the faster they receded.

"Andrei!" Senna yelled suddenly, and began swimming as fast as she could.

In moments Lantea was beside her, grasping her by one arm and pulling her faster. The two women rushed forward. John couldn't sense what Senna was reacting to, but he didn't doubt her.

Theseo and Andrei were the last to return. Neither were badly hurt. Both were sombre. Theseo left Andrei with Senna and swam off to speak with his warriors. Lantea and her companions went with him. John and the others listened in horrified silence as Andrei told of the battle.

When he had finished, Andrei looked drained. Senna took him by the arm and led him away before the others could say anything.

"What does it mean?" Pasith asked, the first to recover his voice.

"Are the samudraka defeated?" Tilvy echoed his concern.

"No," Sarva answered flatly. "But the papayamala aren't going to fight the way Theseo wants them to."

- - -

<I think it's over,> Peren said. <The last aaranya I had connection to is gone.>

"Helix?" Jaimee asked gently.

<Some are still dying. But yes, I think it's almost over.>

"How many?" Jaimee asked. "How many did we kill? How many did you lose?"

Helix opened her eyes and glared at Jaimee. "After a century you still don't understand. You never listen!"

Jaimee grinned at her. "Feeling better, sister?"

Helix turned away, but Sando could feel the turn of her mood and the smile that had come to her face. Jaimee could be hard to resist when he turned on his charm.

"So? How many, sis'?" Jaimee pressed.

"I don't know. More than half, less than two-thirds of the aaranya are gone from me. That's the best I can do."

"And the samudraka?"

Helix shook her head wearily. "I don't know. I can't know. Ask Peren, she was the one that had their eyes."

Peren's voice was hesitant, the horror of it all was obvious in the way her presence trembled in Sando's mind. *<It was all so confused. There was so much death. I couldn't watch it all. ... I just couldn't.>*

"Peren." Jaimee's tone was impatient. "What's the point of being able to see what they see, if you don't watch?"

<I'm sorry.>

"Can you guess?"

< ... Not really.>

"Try."

< ... I don't think the samudraka died as easily as the aaranya. I don't think as many of them will have died.>

"So maybe half?" Jaimee pressed.

<Maybe.>

"Will that be enough?" Sando asked.

Jaimee shrugged. "We'll have to wait and see. You can at least keep watch for that, can't you, Peren?"

"Jaimee?" Helix interrupted.

The brothers looked to where Helix was pointing. A young human man was walking along the beach.

"No uniform," Jaimee observed.

"A camper on a night stroll, maybe," suggested Sando.

"I would feel so much better with a pick-me-up," Helix said.

<No!> Peren objected. *<You weren't going to do this so close to home.>*

"You've got a point," Jaimee said, purposely misinterpreting Peren. "If mysterious deaths happen everywhere but here, then we might draw attention." He stood up and put his hand out to assist Helix to her feet. "Shall we?"

"We shall," Helix agreed.

Jaimee stepped lightly across the beach and knocked the man out with a quick slap to the head. Sando turned off the man's small flashlight.

Jaimee took one shoulder, Helix the other. Pressing up from beneath the man's neck with their hands, they pushed until the prana of his body was exposed like a translucent second skin. The man's body gave a jerk and he woke screaming. Sando was ready for it and quickly slapped harder at the man's head. The scream cut off and the man lay quiet. Jaimee and Helix leaned in and bit into the prana, drinking hungrily at the golden life that flowed from the wounds.

While his siblings fed on the man's life, Sando stood and watched the ridge above them. No one came. The man's last cry had gone unheard.

Sando looked back down, deciding where to join in the feast. He could feel Peren's disapproval. He always seemed to feel it more than Jaimee or Helix. The draw of life was too much, he pushed his sister's disapproval aside. He knelt by the man's thigh and pushed the prana up. He bit down and the hot fluid prana burst into his mouth and down his throat. The heat flowed quickly to his stomach and spread into his body like liquid fire.

Three days passed in which they saw little of Theseo, he spent the time among his warriors, assessing the damage, and – John supposed – trying to work out what they should do next. When he did come to them it was to press them for details of how the humans had known where they were. He pushed John for information about the bombs and ships that the humans used, but John couldn't tell him much, he knew almost nothing of such things.

Sarva spent time talking to Lantea. Later he spoke softly to John out of hearing of the others. "They lost close to half their warriors. More than half of the serpents and squid. Some samtaana fighting in tight groups were almost wiped out."

"Will they keep trying?"

Sarva nodded. "Yes. But ..."

"But what?"

"Some are saying this happened because of us. Because of Andrei.

424

Many are reluctant to continue following a king that does not wield Zamayitar."

"But they were okay with it before."

"They thought they were invincible then. They know better now. They lost half their army and they still haven't met the dhumraka."

It looked like Sarva was going to say more, but Theseo arrived with a small retinue of Marr warriors. He looked tired. He hadn't rested much since the battle.

The group assembled at the top of the ridge. Most of the samudraka were content to float in the water, but John and the others settled on the exposed rock. Lantea floated off to one side with the warriors that had become her constant companions.

"Are you recovered?" Theseo asked Andrei.

Andrei shrugged. "The bits that heal."

"You are a warrior now."

"I was happier as a coward."

Theseo gave him a doubtful look.

"What are your plans?" Garjae interrupted them.

"Plans?" Theseo looked at Garjae in surprise. "We keep going."

"How?"

"We still have enough warriors to defeat the dhumraka and their allies—"

"The aaranya were *not* allies," Andrei corrected him.

"No," Theseo agreed. "They were decoys to draw us in. We won't make that mistake again."

"How many more of our people must die?" Darnu asked.

Theseo looked at him sadly. "I do not know. Would you rather we withdrew and left them enslaved?"

"Would you, if we asked you to?" Tilvy asked.

"No. The samudraka will not permit the papayamala to remain. Whoever stands in our way will be removed."

"But you still don't know where they are," Garjae reminded him.

"So we track them back." Theseo looked at Tilvy. "You will help?"

"I ... I'm not sure I could—" Tilvy started.

"I know the way," Pasith interrupted her. "I'll show you."

"What about the ships? The humans?" Garjae asked.

Theseo eyed John carefully.

A dozen or more samudraka arrived, interrupting whatever

425

Theseo had been about to say. These were men from many different samtaana. John thought they looked like leaders he had seen Theseo consult with before. To the front was the faded red of the new Raktana leader, Hesperous.

"I was hoping to rest," Theseo told him.

"You may rest when this is resolved," retorted Hesperous.

"It is resolved."

"Are you too frightened to do this when my son is at full strength?" Lantea demanded across the group.

Hesperous didn't acknowledge her. "You must take up Zamayitar now, or face another choosing."

Theseo raised himself level with Hesperous. "And you think *you* can defeat me?"

"If not I, then one of us will." Hesperous indicated the others behind him.

Sarva swam in close behind Andrei and Senna.

"This is not the time," Theseo argued, but his words lacked strength. "This man saved my life."

"That you will admit—"

"Don't I get a say?" Andrei asked. He broke Senna's grip on his arm and rose up from the rock.

"You may, of course, defend yourself." Hesperous sneered at him.

Andrei looked at Theseo. "We knew this was coming." He drew the zakti from its sheath. It glowed so brightly in his hand that even Hesperous and his cohort looked surprised.

"Andrei, no!" Senna cried.

One of Lantea's warriors came from behind and restrained Senna. Marr warriors descended to block John and the others from trying to interfere. Polyphemo was blocking John. He peered past the huge man trying to work out how he could help Andrei, but there was nothing he could do. The other of Lantea's companions was close to Sarva but not yet touching him. Senna was struggling in the pale arms of her captor.

"Sen'," Andrei called to her. "We talked about this."

Senna was only able to respond in agonised denial. "No!"

Theseo was looking at Andrei, a great sadness on his face. His head was shaking.

Andrei held the zakti up. "Come on, my friend. If you want Zak

426

you're going to have to do what kings do."

No one was holding Sarva. No one was blocking him as he started to move. Theseo's expression turned puzzled as he watched Sarva rise up behind Andrei.

Sensing that something was happening behind him, Andrei turned. Sarva reached out and put his hand over Andrei's. For a moment they floated there, sharing the sword, holding it out like a beacon.

"What—?" Andrei started.

"I am sorry, Andrei," Sarva said.

And then the zakti was turning inwards, folding down. It thrust into Andrei's side and gold gushed from the wound. John saw the look of surprise and pain on Andrei's face before the struggle became obscured by the prana in the water. It looked like they were embracing.

Andrei cried out. The sound was cut short and he fell silent.

Senna screamed. The Marr guards struggled to restrain Garjae and Darnu. John, Tilvy and Pasith were rooted to the spot in shock. Theseo started to move in, but Lantea was suddenly there and placed her hand on his chest.

The zakti dropped free and fell slowly through the water. Its bright glow glimmered, dulled, flickered a few times, and then went out. The sword was now just a dull dark blue, barely visible against the rock on which it rested.

Senna was still screaming, reaching out desperately to Andrei. Everyone else had fallen silent, they were staring at the sword. The impossible meaning of that dull blade took time to sink in.

When John looked up, Lantea had taken Andrei's body from Sarva and was carrying it away. A stream of gold marked her passage. Her guards followed behind, one holding tightly to Senna as she continued to struggle in his arms.

"Let her grieve away from here," Sarva called after them. He was holding his side tightly, prana seeping through his fingers. The sword had cut him deeply during the struggle.

"Why?" Theseo managed.

"Because it had to be," said Sarva. "And because it is better that my people hate me than to create further enmity with the samudraka."

"I don't ..." Theseo shook his head.

"Pick up your sword," Sarva told him.

Hesperous made a sudden move toward the zakti. He stopped just as suddenly when the blade of Theseo's spear appeared at his throat. John hadn't even seen Theseo move.

Theseo scooped up the zakti. He flinched as if the sword had burned him and stared at the blade, not quite believing it was there in his hand. He glanced at Sarva, frowned and shook his head, then looked around at the others. No one spoke.

After a few cautious swings, Theseo held the blade before him, unable to take his eyes from it. The blade glowed weakly.

"Zamayitar," Polyphemo called out. A moment later other warriors repeated the call.

The blade flickered.

Theseo rose above the group, holding the sword high. "Zamayitar!" he cried exultantly, and the zakti flared. "Zamayitar!"

The voice of the king spread like a shock wave across the samudraka, and the call came back magnified by jubilant warriors, "Zamayitar!" The blade flashed brighter. "Zamayitar!"

John couldn't make it fit. The happy cheering that erupted around him was echoed from further away as more joined the triumphant chorus. That sound was wrong, but it kept washing over him. It ate into the back of his head and prickled down his spine. His body shook from the offence of it. His friend was dead! But still the people celebrated.

Touching

21. Revelation

Asha sat on a branch and looked out at the front gates of the estate. Paul had said that if they stole a car they should be able to crash through the gates and escape. She could send them on their way and they would be one less thing pressing constantly on her mind. She would still worry about them, but perhaps the samudraka would solve that problem forever.

These thoughts were all about distraction. Asha didn't dare try to merge yet. The anger and frustration was still boiling away inside her. Peren had told her about the battle. About the huge losses on both sides. About the thousands of aaranya that had been brought in and sacrificed as mere decoys in the siblings' fight against the samudraka. Asha had raged against Peren. She had screamed that she would do no more for Angel, that she would tell Jaimee the secrets Peren was keeping from him. That she would do what she could to destroy the siblings.

But the threats were idle, they both knew it. The battle was done, it couldn't be undone. Asha remained hostage to the situation and her own nature. And, ultimately, she couldn't find it in herself to hate Peren. The girl had seen the battle through the eyes of the aaranya. It had been as if she was there herself, not just once, but again and again with each of the aaranya she had touched. Asha shuddered at the thought. Peren was devastated by the experience. She hadn't understood what Jaimee's plans really meant, not until she experienced it. She had been a wreck afterwards, and Asha screaming at her hadn't helped. Peren was torn between the desire for her family to survive and the knowledge of what this cost. And the costs kept climbing. Peren was as much a hostage to the situation as Asha.

Asha wanted the samudraka to win. It would mean her own death, and Peren's, probably John and Sarva too, but it would mean the release of aaranya everywhere. After what had just happened that was a thought to cling to. This should have put her at odds with Peren, but the girl was more willing than ever to help Asha get her friends out of here.

Escape. Asha looked again at the front gates. If she was helping friends to escape then she should do all she could for Barma and Telia as well. If she could contrive a way to get them brought back here then they could leave with the others. It would have to be soon.

Ellie? Inside the Glade of the dhumraka Ellie might have weeks left, and only if Asha was allowed to visit often. Asha should have been back there before now but Jaimee and the others were busy. If Asha asked them to bring Ellie here then it would be a matter of days before Ellie faded and died. Could Asha do that to her?

Asha remembered the bright precocious child that Ellie had been when she was human. Asha smiled sadly. It had been too long. She had spent so long struggling to keep Ellie the preta alive that she rarely took the time to remember the human child that Ellie had once been. It was that child that she had been trying to save, not the listless preta. But the child was gone, and there was nothing Asha could do to get her back.

There were tears on her face but a sense of relief in her heart as Asha made her decision. Ellie would be here with Asha. Even if there was no other consolation, at least Asha could be with Ellie when she died.

Rising up from the depths, a pair of thoughts connected in Asha's mind. Peren! she called out as loudly as she could in her mind. She hadn't tried to call Peren before, but she was confident it would work.

<Asha?> Peren's tone showed her surprise, and her fear that Asha might continue raging at her. <Is everything all right?>

You said John was with the samudraka.

<Yes.>

He's been with them all this time – in the ocean?

<Yes.>

So he can't be in his human body, can he?

Peren was slow to answer this time.

Where is his human body? Asha insisted.

<It's dead.> Peren's response was so soft that Asha barely heard it.

"And this was something else you didn't think to tell me?" Asha said out loud. A dhumraka guard on the other side of the gates looked up.

<You were so happy that he was still alive, I didn't want to spoil that. ... I thought it wouldn't matter.>

But how is he still alive? He should have faded by now.

Peren explained what John had been through.

How do you know all this?

<I touched her, the woman John was with, a long time ago. She was my first. The first time I realised what I could do. She's how I know what the samudraka are doing. Sometimes I think she hears me. That she knows when I'm with her – like you do. I like her, she's very bold.>

So you live your life vicariously through the eyes of others? Asha asked.

A faint acknowledgement.

Why don't you come out from your trees and live your own life?

<I can't.>

Why not? It wasn't the first time Asha had asked.

<You don't seem jealous,> Peren said, changing the subject as she always did. She hurried on, *<I mean, John didn't do anything wrong, not really, I just wondered that you didn't react more when I told you.>*

There had been a twinge, maybe more than that, Asha acknowledged to herself. I want him to live, Asha expressed more clearly in her mind. But now he's going to die. Ben, at the Samgha, said it was certain. All saarvaya die when their saardha is lost. Ben lied about many things, but not that. Sando will get his wish. John will die.

The words kept repeating over and over in Asha's mind. She had been so happy to learn that John was alive that she hadn't let this unacceptable conjunction of thoughts enter her mind. But now it was there and it wouldn't let go.

<Mama has lived a long time.> Peren ventured.

Asha shook her head. Your mother's situation is special. You four may have something to do with it. No. With or without my help, with or without the help of the samudraka, John will die.

<*I don't— *> Peren started.

"Leave me," Asha said.

Peren hesitated, seemed about to speak, then her presence faded.

Asha turned back to the tree trunk and climbed higher. Maybe John would get here in time. Maybe they could be together, a makeshift family for a short time, as they waited for the end of all their hopes.

- - -

Forinay made almost no pretence of being their guard any more. She sat with them and slept next to them, always edging close to Ellie. The spear Forinay was obliged to keep with her usually lay forgotten to one side. Barma found himself eyeing the spear and wondering if he could use it. Telia caught his eye and shook her head. She was probably right.

The other guards paid little attention to them. Previously the guards had been changed once or twice a day, but since the Glade had gone quiet the same guards had been with them constantly. Barma thought they looked distracted, he imagined they were wishing they were somewhere else. If Andrei was here he would probably be suggesting a deal: the guards could go wherever they wanted if they let their prisoners go. Barma grinned at the thought and wondered what his friend was up to now.

"A happy thought, Barma?" Telia asked.

"Andrei," he said in explanation.

Telia smiled.

"Who is Andrei?" Forinay asked.

Barma blinked in surprise. It was the first time Forinay had asked him anything directly. "A friend," he answered, but that didn't seem enough. "We've been friends since childhood."

Forinay sat up straighter, obviously interested, and Barma found himself recounting some of the same stories he'd already told Telia. Forinay was spellbound, childlike herself in her fascination with the tales. Barma thought it sad that such simple stories should mean so much to her.

"He caused a great panic once," Barma told her. "He fell asleep during a game of hide-and-seek. We were still very young and someone thought he had gone outside unsupervised."

"It wouldn't have been the first time," Telia put in.

Barma grinned. "But not during a game. If he cheated it was only so someone would actually find him. He was very good at finding places no one thought to look. He woke up with people rushing about organising a search party. He tapped someone on the shoulder to ask what was happening."

"It was Darnu," Telia said, smiling. "Where were you through all this?"

"I was *It*. I had found everyone else. I knew Andrei must be still around somewhere, but no one would listen to me. One of the older kids brought the adults into it."

Forinay's face had taken on a dreamy expression.

"Are you okay?" Barma asked her, wondering if he'd finally managed to bore her.

She looked at him, her eyes bright. "We could play hide-and-seek."

"Huh?"

Forinay rose and looked at them. When they were slow to respond she said, "Come on."

Telia and Barma glanced at each other. Barma shrugged.

They followed Forinay on a circuitous route through the kelp and eventually up out of the water, where the stems and leaves of the plants grew thicker and more tree-like. They hadn't been permitted up here before, but the disinterested guards followed without complaint.

After a lot of climbing they came to an area floored with woven leaves.

"The elders are usually here, but they're guarding the Way from intruders while everyone else is gone," Forinay told them. She kept climbing.

Eventually they reached a place where intertwined stems formed a path rising above the surrounding forest.

"We shouldn't be here," one of the guards called from behind them.

"Why not?" Forinay asked. Barma thought her bright tones, so different from her usual nervous and meek behaviour, would betray her excitement to the others, but they didn't seem to notice.

"This is the queen's place."

"She won't mind, she's not here."

The other guards, one man and one woman, looked doubtful and nervous.

Forinay started walking up the path formed by the stems. Telia and Barma followed. The guards came a short distance and then stopped. Forinay saw that and smiled in satisfaction.

High above the level of the main forest was a platform. The sun was low in the west, sinking into the ocean beyond the forest, it would be night soon.

"What do you think?" Forinay asked Telia.

"It's very pretty."

"No." Forinay stopped and peered back down the stems they had walked up. Apparently satisfied, she turned back. "We jump," she said, "and then we hide." She turned to Barma. "I know places. I wasn't popular like your friend Andrei, but I did explore on my own. I know places they won't look."

Telia looked down at Ellie lying in the crook of her arm. Barma guessed she was wondering what would be best for the child. Telia looked back up. "And what do we do when your people return, when your queen returns?"

"I thought we might escape before then," Forinay answered. "Sneak up on the Way and swim out."

"But you said the elders were there," Telia reminded her.

Forinay's face fell and her shoulders slumped.

Telia reached out her spare hand and squeezed Forinay's shoulder. "It's a good idea. Asha hasn't come, maybe she can't come. This is a chance for Barma, Ellie and me, perhaps the only chance we have. But what about you, Forinay?"

"What do you mean?" Forinay looked puzzled.

"If you come with us you will be in trouble. Lots of trouble."

"Don't you want me to come?"

Telia shook her gently. "Of course we do, but it's dangerous. If you come with us now there can be no turning back."

"I don't want to come back. I don't want to be here any more."

"And your queen?"

Forinay shook her head, there were tears in her eyes. "I don't feel her. She's left me."

436

Telia pulled Forinay close and hugged her. "I'm sorry."

"I'm not." Forinay stroked Ellie's face gently. "I would rather be with you."

Forinay pulled herself free of Telia's embrace and went to look back down at the guards. "They're not paying any attention to us," she said. "They're watching the sunset."

"So we jump that way?" Telia asked, pointing east to the distant mountains.

"If we stay quiet it might be a long time before they work out we're gone."

They climbed onto the edge of the platform and glanced nervously at each other.

"Ready?" Telia prompted.

Barma and Forinay nodded.

They jumped.

- - -

"Now is not the time to be going," Sando told his brother.

"The samudraka are quiet," Jaimee answered.

"Until Peren's contact returns to the king we can't be sure of that."

"Helix will know if they start attacking her people."

Sando had to concede that, so he tried a different tack. "How much more are you going to do to try and win this woman's approval?"

"We need her!"

"Do we? Mama's going to die anyway, you said that yourself." It was obvious Peren wasn't paying attention to them or that would have drawn an argument.

"You know that's not the only reason we want her," Jaimee snapped back.

"Right, so you and Helix can procreate. Where exactly does that leave me?"

"And Peren."

Sando ignored that. "Well?"

"If Asha can help Helix she might be able to help you too."

"But you've got dibs on the direct approach?"

"She doesn't like you."

"She doesn't like you either, brother," Sando reminded him.

Jaimee shrugged. "She'll come around. We've lived over a hundred years, Sando, a little patience is the least we should have learned."

Sando turned away.

"Look," Jaimee said, trying to sound reasonable. "We bring her friends back from the Glade and the preta will die quickly. It's at her request so she can't complain about it, and one more problem is out of the way. Where's the downside?"

"I still think you should take Helix, let her take control of them."

"And upset Asha again?" Jaimee shook his head. "I can manage. Helix needs to spend time with her dhumraka, and I need you and Stephenson to get things ready in the city."

"What for? We already know how to defeat the samudraka."

"It won't work so well a second time. What little they know will take them to the city, we need to be ready for them when they get there."

"Who cares about the city?" Sando argued. "Let the damn humans worry about it."

"That's the difference between us, brother. I plan ahead. Contingency plans to cover us whatever happens."

"I'm not convinced about this plan. We can't control the samudraka through their king, like Helix does the aaranya. He's not an elder."

"There are other ways."

"More of your games."

"Ah, brother, you're just jealous because I'm so much better at them than you."

The helicopter was now hovering low over a bare patch of ocean, and Stephenson opened the door. Wind gusted in around them.

"Don't forget to come back and get me," Jaimee reminded Sando, "it's a long swim back."

"As if."

Jaimee gave his brother a grin and waved. "Don't worry about it, brother. It's all under control."

Sando grimaced and nodded.

Jaimee leapt out and dropped to the water.

- - -

Ray was pale and much thinner than he had been, but otherwise he looked remarkably well for a man that had received three bullet wounds in the chest not so long ago. He sat across the table from Tracey and Paul, sipping at his coffee and eyeing the two of them with a faint smile twitching at his face.

"What?" Paul asked him.

"It's nice to see you have finally relaxed," Ray said.

Tracey glanced at Paul, he was looking down at his coffee now. He looked embarrassed. She looked back at Ray.

Ray grinned at her. "You used to make him nervous."

"Nervous?" Tracey didn't quite believe it.

"Self-conscious anyway."

"We're not supposed to let our personal feelings interfere with the job," Paul muttered, still looking down.

"I told him he was overdoing it," Ray said.

Paul looked up. "Boss, we're supposed to be talking about getting out of here."

"Right." Ray put his cup down. "Asha filled me in on some of it."

"And you agree?"

Ray nodded. "Asha says there's something we should look at before we go."

"Which is what you want to do tonight?" Paul asked.

"While the problem children are away," Ray agreed.

"I think we should take this chance and just keep going."

"She has two more friends she wants us to take, and they're not here yet."

"I wish Asha would come with us," Tracey put in. "John won't like us leaving her behind."

Ray looked uncomfortable for a moment, and Tracey wondered if Asha had said more to him than she had to herself and Paul.

"I'm not sure I like this friend in her head thing," Paul said.

"There's a lot about this I don't like." Ray shrugged. "I didn't like the idea of invisible people either, but if there are more like Asha I could get used to it."

"There are," Tracey said.

He smiled at her in understanding. "The point is that we have to work with what we've got. If Asha says this voice in her head is going to help us then I'm willing to accept that. She can get us past the surveillance cameras they have outside, and through the doors we have to open. If it all works tonight then I'll have better confidence we can do it again when the time comes."

After dark they all dressed in dark clothing and waited by the door to the cabin. At the sound of metallic clinking noises from the gate, Ray opened the door and they looked out. There was silence for a while and then the gate swung open. The three of them jogged to the gate and quickly through it.

The gate closed behind them, the keys swinging in the lock. Ray was moving again, one hand held forward, being led somewhere by Asha. Tracey and Paul followed behind.

They stopped beneath the shelter of the trees. A hand touched Tracey's arm. She turned and someone hugged her. It took her a moment, but when she recognised it was Beenae she hugged him tightly in return. Tonight was a full dress rehearsal. Asha was also making sure the aaranya would be able to escape with them.

Through the trees, past a thick hedge, and then to one side of the house. There was little light here, but enough to see the paved area and clothesline, rubbish bins and other paraphernalia of human existence. The servants entrance, Tracey assumed.

A light came on and there was a moment of panic as they pulled back behind a small garden shed. Tracey heard, but couldn't see, the sound of someone moving around at the rubbish bins. The light went out and after a few moments they were led forward again.

- - -

Asha wasn't sure if this was a good idea, but she wanted them to see where the garage was before they went on, at least then they'd know how to find it later if Asha was prevented from helping them for some reason. There wasn't much chance of discovery here, there wasn't any reason for the human servants to come this way. She opened the door at the end and led them into the large open area. Two spots were empty, Helix had taken two of the vans with her, but the other cars were all still there.

"Wow," Paul said in appreciation, staring at Jaimee's Ferrari. The deep blue was almost black in the dim lights of the garage. He walked over to take a closer look at it.

"The Suburban will be more practical for our needs." Ray pointed to one of the large station-wagons.

Paul pulled himself reluctantly away from the sports car.

Asha left the humans to look over the car and turned her attention to Beenae and Taiza. "How's he doing?" she asked Beenae.

"Better," he answered. "Almost as soon as we came inside he started to get more alert. Look."

Taiza was studying some panel on the wall. It had a few small red and green lights on it. Asha had no idea what it was for, but when Taiza reached up to it she rushed to stop him.

"Might be better to leave that alone," she told him softly.

Taiza turned and looked at her. He raised an eyebrow, as if in question.

"We don't want to draw attention," Asha explained.

Taiza nodded slowly.

Asha was surprised, it was a real response. Beenae was beaming. She smiled back at him and squeezed Taiza's hand.

<*Jimmy's gone back inside the monitoring room now,*> Peren spoke into Asha's mind. <*The others are busy or gone to their rooms, you should be able to sneak past now.*>

Asha went to Ray and grasped his hand. It was time to show him what she had brought them to see. He smiled at the top of her head. "I'm not that tall," she said, not that he would hear her. She tugged on his hand, indicating they should continue.

As they neared the monitoring room and the stairs to the basement, Asha paused and put a finger to Ray's lips, then she pointed the fingers of his hand at the door.

"Someone in there?" he mouthed.

Asha tapped his hand once.

They walked quietly to the stairs and made their way down. Ray risked turning on the lights so they could make their way through the storage area without banging into things.

"There's a lot of food here," Paul remarked.

"A lot of people," Ray answered.

"Many of them are children," Tracey said. "I keep thinking we should be doing something about them. If there might be a battle here they won't be safe."

Asha had had the same thought, but she could think of no way to try and save them. They were all connected to Peren and to Helix, they had no escape, just as Asha had none.

Through the heavy door into the machine room.

441

"Generators," Paul said. "They're well prepared for a siege."

"Asha, look," Beenae called to her.

Taiza had stopped following them so he could study one of the engines more closely.

"Don't let him start anything," Asha warned.

Beenae grinned at her.

At the brick wall Asha placed her hand in the hole and the door opened. Peren gave her the combination and she opened the inner door.

- - -

Tracey opened her mouth in amazement at the mass of high-tech equipment that confronted them. Paul whistled softly. Someone closed the doors behind them and Tracey turned in alarm.

"It's okay," Ray reassured her. "I wanted to be sure no one could hear us if they came down this way."

Ray was pulled along to a desk. He sat down and tapped a key. The screen woke up and a bright blue logo appeared. Tracey made out the words "Federal Bureau of Investigation" written in the bottom half of the circle.

"Is that what I think it is?" Paul asked.

Ray tapped a few keys and brought up a screen that asked for his password.

"Careful, boss," Paul warned, "you may draw attention."

"I doubt it," Ray answered. He clicked the "Enter" button.

"Straight in!" Paul exclaimed.

Ray was shaking his head.

"What is it?" Tracey asked him.

"I thought they must have a few contacts." He stopped and shook his head some more. "But they have access to everything. The people I was going to contact when we got out, anything they do can be tracked from here. We might have to change our plans."

"Want to know the President's bank balance, Tracey?" Paul asked. He had sat at another desk and brought up a different screen.

Tracey looked over his shoulder as he flicked through different displays.

"This is amazing. They're linking stuff from all over. Corporate records, bank records, purchase and credit history. ... There's a log here of people they've been following. Senators. ... I don't know

442

these names but from the details they look like cardinals and bishops. ... Shit! We're here, Ray. And you, Tracey. And John Caldor." Paul clicked to go further into John's details. "There's nothing new from Caldor in months."

"There's the emails I was telling you about," Tracey pointed. The details had been mysteriously wiped from her computer, she had no proof to show Ray and Paul what had gone on between her and John.

Paul flicked through them briefly and then returned to the outer screens. "Aside from us, most of the rest of it's American. ... Some from the UK, and a bit of Europe but not much. ... Hell, they've even got the White House on here. ... Yep, straight in, like all the others. How the hell are they doing this?"

"I'd say they've been at it a long time," Ray answered from where he had sat at another desk. "They've got defence systems online here."

Paul turned in shock. "Can they launch missiles?"

Ray shook his head. "I don't think so. Not directly. ... At least, not from what I can see here." He looked up past his shoulder and patted a hand that Tracey couldn't see. "I think Asha is trying to tell me that they may have other ways of controlling the people needed to do it."

"Aren't those systems supposed to be isolated?"

Ray shrugged. Tracey thought he looked tired. He really should be resting rather than getting worked up over all this. As far as Tracey could see there was nothing they could do about any of it.

A loud beeping started from across the room.

- - -

Asha turned in fright. Taiza had the side off one of the boxes of equipment and was fiddling with wires.

"What's he doing?" she called.

Beenae looked up and grinned. "Being himself."

"Now is not the time!"

Beenae's smile dropped. "When is?"

Asha didn't have an answer for that. "Get him to put it back together. We don't want anyone to know we've been here."

While Beenae turned and spoke softly to Taiza, Asha tried to reassure Ray. Are you there? she called to Peren in her mind.

<I am now,> Peren responded. *<The samudraka are on the move again.>*

Asha frowned. Where are they going?

<I don't know. I just know that most of the army has moved on.>

And John?

<I didn't see him, but they said he was okay.>

Relieved at this news, Asha returned to thoughts of her friends' escape. What happens if Helix is here when they want to escape? she asked. Where will her personal guard be?

<They normally wait inside, up the other end of the house. They have a room on the second floor. If there are any outside when you're doing it, I'll let you know.>

Asha nodded. Can you tell if we've disturbed anyone?

There was no response for a time, then Peren answered, *<Not as far as I can tell.>*

Even so, Asha thought, they should probably get out of here. Ray needed to rest, and they'd already pushed their luck a long way. It felt wrong to be locking her friends away again, but she had no choice. They couldn't leave yet. Ray reached out and found her arm. He worked his way down to her hand and patted it.

"Thanks, Asha," he said, "we really did need to see this."

- - -

Garjae tapped on Darnu's arm and pointed. "She's back."

They watched as Lantea and her guards swam in and spoke to a group of the remaining warriors. The king, John, Sarva and most of the army had left before nightfall, it was now late evening.

"I wonder where Senna is," Darnu said quietly.

"Let's ask," Tilvy said. She started swimming without waiting for the others to respond.

Lantea saw them coming and met them part way. Garjae noted that they were meeting close to where Andrei had been killed. He had never considered himself sentimental but the proximity made him uncomfortable.

"She didn't want to return," Lantea answered the question before Tilvy had a chance to ask. "We took her to the beach. She said she'd make her own way home."

"How?" Garjae demanded.

"One of us should be with her," Tilvy said.

Lantea shook her head slowly. "She said you should stay and look after John."

"Why should we believe you?" Garjae asked.

He felt Darnu's hand rest on his arm, trying to restrain his anger. Darnu wasn't the only one to notice, Lantea's guards moved closer. She waved them back.

"I have no reason to lie about this," Lantea answered calmly. She looked to Tilvy. "How is John? How did he take it?"

"How do you think?" Garjae snapped at her.

"He tried to kill Polyphemo," Pasith said quietly. "He got closer to succeeding than you might expect."

Lantea's eyes widened.

"I think he took him by surprise."

"Is he all right?"

"Polyphemo wasn't seriously hurt," Garjae's sarcasm interrupted Pasith's response.

"I meant John," Lantea answered and looked back at Pasith.

Pasith nodded. "A bit dazed for a while, but nothing permanent."

"He was well enough to go with the king. They want to—" Tilvy started.

Lantea held up her hand. "Stop," she said. She looked around uncomfortably for a moment. "I must go." She turned with her guards and departed. It looked to Garjae like she was avoiding other groups of warriors as well. A strange woman.

"I still think one of us should go to Senna," Tilvy said.

"How would you find her," Pasith asked. "It's a big beach. And what about John?"

"John's doing okay," Garjae said. "He and Sarva are still great friends." It was quite bizarre to watch. He noticed the others looked away at this reminder. They had all noticed.

Sarva had been away for a time, taken by one of the Marr women to a pool of life to help heal his injury, and when he returned, Garjae and the others had refused to talk to him. It seemed an inadequate response to his betrayal, but it was all any of them could do. Except John. John had approached Sarva like an old friend, as if nothing had changed.

"I don't think he's accepted it yet," Darnu said.

"If that's true, I don't think I would like to be Sarva when he does," Pasith said, "not after what he almost did to Polyphemo."

"I think it's because Sarva feels a lot like Asha," Tilvy said. "I don't think he can separate them in his mind."

"Sarva is nothing like his sister!" said Garjae. "And John was once human, maybe that's a normal response from one of them."

Darnu frowned as he looked at Garjae. "He has been our friend."

"So was Sarva!"

There was silence for a while.

"I hate thinking of Senna out there all alone," Tilvy whispered.

"Just hope that she is," Garjae told her. "Who knows what she might find – or what might find her?"

Garjae heard Pasith whisper to Tilvy, "Andrei was right about him." He opened his mouth to retort and then decided against it.

"We might be able to find her," Darnu said unexpectedly.

Everyone turned to look at him. He looked around, and satisfied that no one was paying attention to them, he led their group away from the samudraka. But he didn't go far.

He stopped and said, "We can't all go. I doubt if the samudraka will be happy with that, and some of us should stay to keep an eye on John." He paused to wait for responses. When there were none, he continued, "I think Tilvy and Pasith should try to find Senna. Garjae and I will stay here." He looked at Garjae with concern. "No offence, but Senna and you never got on, she's unlikely to be pleased to see you."

Garjae shrugged. It was true enough, though it wasn't as if things were much better between himself and John.

"The king expects us to lead him into the city," Pasith reminded her.

"I'll go alone," Tilvy said. "I'd be no help in the city, I don't remember it. It might be better this way anyway, Senna knows me."

Darnu frowned, obviously not happy with the idea.

"One, two or three, it's not likely to make much difference if we run into the wrong people," Tilvy said.

"How will you find her?" Pasith wanted to know.

Darnu murmured to his arm and the small cream form of Nuttachen emerged. Darnu looked up. "He's found Senna before, he can do it again."

"What do I do when I find her?" Tilvy asked.

"Garjae's right, it's dangerous out there. I think you should try to persuade her to come back here. We should stick together."

"And if she won't?"

"I wouldn't blame her," Garjae said before he could stop himself. "I wouldn't be staying near Andrei's killer either, if I had a choice." He was gratified to note that none of the others seemed inclined to disagree.

Darnu continued, "If she won't come then stay with her and send Nuttachen back to tell us where you're going."

- - -

Senna wandered among the human soldiers, her body still cloaked against the detector field. They had felt it as soon as they climbed the ridge above the beach. Now she was cloaked, none of the men watching their screens noticed Senna's presence added to their own, she appeared merely human.

Lantea had gone, returned to her people. Senna wasn't sure what to do with herself. She couldn't sleep, and with these humans and their detectors around she didn't dare relax her vigilance. She needed distraction from her restlessness, and studying these men, soldiers in camouflage uniforms, was as good a way as any.

What did their presence here mean? The battle had been out at sea. Were these just a precaution, or were they guarding something that the samudraka should know about? And if the samudraka should know, should Senna try to tell them?

She had answers to none of these questions, so she kept wandering among the soldiers, watching and listening, and trying to understand.

Night fell and Senna rested against the tree she kept returning to, comforted by its presence. Her mind was still a maze of thoughts too overwhelming to push through. Many soldiers crawled into small tents to sleep, but several remained watching their screens and listening to the sounds of the forest.

The constant buzzing of the detector field abruptly stopped and Senna became alert. There were people coming. Some soldiers stirred themselves to go and meet the new arrivals.

Some instinct made Senna hide herself behind the tree. There were two human men among the arrivals, one a soldier himself, the other a huge man in a suit. But there were also half-a-dozen dhumraka and a tall pale woman, almost glowing in the darkness. She was beautiful. She could only be Helix, the one that Sarva had spoken of.

Helix and her dhumraka companions broke away from the men and walked through the low scrub to the ridge above the beach. While their attention was turned away, Senna carefully worked her way past the trees to get closer to the humans that had arrived.

"The men can take a break for a few hours," the new, senior ranking officer was saying. "We'll let you know when they need to start monitoring the detectors again."

"Yes, sir," came the response, and with a brief wave sent a few men off to pass the word. Senna stepped behind one of the trees to stay out of the way of one that passed close to her.

"All quiet?" the officer asked.

"Yes, sir. The occasional false alarm, but they don't last long."

"What sort of false alarm?" the big man asked.

The soldier addressed his response to the officer. "Several hours ago there were a couple of blips near the ridge, more like normal soldiers than those you showed us in training, but they vanished quickly. We sent men forward with one of the portable detectors, but they found nothing. There's been nothing since."

"Very well," the officer acknowledged. "Do you have a seat for us? Walt here brought a very nice drop of whiskey with him. I thought we might sit and share it out."

The humans walked off and Senna turned her attention to the beach. Helix and her companions appeared to be just standing at the top of the ridge. Not sure if she should, but determined to find out anything she could, Senna crept closer. Using her cloak and every trick she had learned from Litak to hide her presence, she worked her way slowly through the low growth. Finally she stopped, she dared not get any closer. She could hear the murmuring of their voices but couldn't make out what they were saying.

22. Attack

Sarva was looking at him strangely.

"What?" John asked.

"I do not understand you."

"What's to understand?"

"The others refuse to look at me. They turn away when I come too close – and that is better than seeing the look in their eyes. Tilvy almost falls to pieces. If they were human I believe they would spit on me. If it wasn't for Darnu's restraining influence it would be much worse from Garjae."

"It is ... difficult," John defended his friends.

"I know. I understand them. It's you that I don't understand. Why are you even talking to me?"

John didn't try to answer that. He couldn't. He couldn't look at Sarva and think of the death of his best friend at the same time. Somehow the two just didn't go together. That event, only a few days past, was hazy in his memory, as if his mind was rejecting it. He would still look around expecting to see Andrei making some joke at John's expense. The disappointment when he saw that his friend wasn't there, and remembered he would never be there again, was crushing. But never did his mind connect Sarva to that fact.

"Our bond is still there," Sarva continued. "I can see it, barely changed from what it was. It should have shrivelled and broken away."

"Is that what you want?" John asked him.

"What I want doesn't come into it. It never has."

John felt he should say something, but nothing he could think of felt right. He looked up at the shadow of the great ship. "Is this going to work?"

"Maybe. Depends on whether they're expecting it."

"Why wouldn't they be? They've been a step ahead all the way."

"Looks like it's time," said Sarva, indicating the samudraka approaching.

The Marr warrior saw he had their attention and indicated they should follow him.

The ship was drifting silently but occasional movement on deck had showed that it wasn't derelict. The rest of the fleet wasn't far away. John had no idea why this one had stopped, but it was a good opportunity for their first attempt at boarding. A few dozen warriors from many different samtaana were spread out beneath the hull, waiting for their chance to board and learn about human ships. If all went well these would become the leaders of groups assigned to board other ships in the fleet.

Theseo was waiting for them just below the waterline. He gestured for John to come closer.

Previously, Theseo had preferred to deal with Sarva or Andrei, but since Andrei's death Theseo's reaction to Sarva was unpredictable. Sometimes he looked at Sarva with gratitude, sometimes with sadness, and sometimes with hatred. The one constant was a lack of trust. He rarely spoke to Sarva at all now.

"Are you ready?" Theseo asked John.

"How?"

Theseo pointed. There were bony looking protuberances on the grey metal hull, they formed a sort of staircase sloping up and out of the water.

"You did this?"

"The metals of human creation are not unknown to my people," Theseo explained. "Everything falls to us eventually. In the depths there are creatures that feed on it. Up here their time is limited. In sunlight the creatures will dry out and die, and some of these steps may fall off, but we attached many, some will remain welded to the surface."

"Is it safe?"

"Why not? The worst that can happen is falling back into the water. Come on."

One of John's unasked questions was answered. Theseo's tail

split, but didn't form human looking legs, the result was more like two independent tails until the flukes contracted into thickly shod feet. The legs moved oddly, seeming to bend where they wanted. John tried not to stare as Theseo began climbing up the hull.

Polyphemo pushed John forward, indicating that he should go next. The water dropped away as he rose above the waves, leaving him instantly dry. This was no small pleasure boat, it was an immense warship. They were climbing near the stern, where the deck was closer to the waterline, but it still felt like a long climb.

"How are you going to do this when the ships are moving?" John called up to the king.

"It is more difficult, but it can be done. Others are already placing the steps on other ships."

Theseo climbed over the rail and turned to help John. Polyphemo wasn't far behind, and after that Sarva. The warriors that followed formed a chain passing up spears. These would be visible to humans, so as each warrior climbed up they grabbed their spear and crouched near the edge, taking advantage of the shadows cast by the sparse lighting around the deck.

John looked around. They needed the human lights here, there was no life for their vedana to sense. From the water the ship had seemed huge and daunting, but from this low part at the back of the ship John couldn't see far forward, so it felt a bit more manageable. This deck was mostly clear, John thought it must be a helicopter landing pad or something.

Theseo was under the impression that John might be able to help, it was why he had insisted John come along, but John was thinking now that this place was as foreign to him as it was to the samudraka. The deck, rolling gently under his feet, felt very strange against his skin but it wasn't too slippery.

"Where to?" Theseo asked him. "The pointy end?"

John smiled, maybe not *quite* as foreign. He pointed to the part of the superstructure visible over the next deck. "I think somewhere under that will be what they call the bridge, that's where they control the ship from."

"The leaders will be there?"

John shrugged. "At this time of night I imagine some are probably sleeping."

"Where?" Theseo queried.

"In there somewhere, at a guess," John said, pointing to the wall in front of them, "or maybe the captain has a cabin up near the bridge. I don't really know."

"Captain? What about their king?"

"Americans don't have a king," John said. Theseo gave him an incredulous look. "Their equivalent is the President, but you won't find him here."

"Where? On one of the other ships?"

"No," John said patiently. He had tried to explain this before, but Theseo was having a hard time accepting it. "Human leaders ... they lead from behind. Far behind. It's safer that way." Before the conversation could continue into renewed explanations of what humans had become and what they could do, John continued, "But the captain is sort of like the king of this boat."

Theseo nodded at that. "Let's find him."

Torchlight flickered over them. John ducked down, and then stood back up feeling foolish, the human wouldn't see him. The human came down the ladder from the higher deck and concentrated his light on an area that had caught his eye. In the yellow circle cast by the torch was a spear held by a crouching samudraka.

The human drew closer, a puzzled expression on his face. Polyphemo came up behind him, a reminder to John just how large this samudraka was. The young human man started to lean down, his reaching hand almost touched the samudraka warrior holding the spear. Polyphemo clapped him hard on each side of the head. The crouching warrior grabbed at the torch as it started to fall, but it slipped from his hand and clattered to the deck. Another picked it up and threw it over the side. The warrior had better luck catching the collapsing human. With help from Polyphemo, he lifted the unconscious human and tossed him over the side. Moments later the sound of the splash came back.

"He'll drown!" John said.

Theseo ignored that. "Which way?"

"How many are you going to kill?"

"Which way?" Theseo repeated.

It was only now dawning on John that he was helping the samudraka to fight what had once been his own people. Those on

452

this human ship might be the human equivalent of the samudraka warriors, but they didn't know what they were fighting. They couldn't even see their enemy. It wasn't fair.

Theseo gave up waiting for John to respond and started walking. Polyphemo grasped John by one arm and pushed him ahead, forcing him to walk or fall over. Theseo led them up the ladder that the human had just come down.

"Is this any more unfair than all the samudraka that were killed by the bombs these humans dropped?" Sarva asked when they reached the top. At times his ability to sense what John was thinking was disturbing, especially so when John wasn't sure of his own thoughts.

"They didn't know."

"And that makes it better? What did they think they were doing if not killing?"

John couldn't find an answer for that. Aaranya and samudraka had died by the hundreds at the blind thrusts of these humans. Thousands.

The higher deck contained sets of large cylinders mounted above the deck and embedded in the deck itself there was an array of small square panels that John thought might cover rocket launchers. Perhaps the very things that had killed so many of the narun.

The samudraka spread out across the area, carrying their spears openly. Many things seemed wrong to John. That they weren't trying to be stealthy felt wrong, though they had no reason to hide. That their various gaits were peculiar, some so smooth they seemed to be gliding, others rocking back and forth, their legs bending in strange ways, was all wrong. That John was here among them, helping these people to kill his own kind was absolutely wrong. But what choice did he have? Whatever he did, people were going to die.

Another human guard. A look of puzzled surprise on his face at the sticks floating in the air before him. A flash of a spear. A brief gurgling gasp. The human was caught before he hit the deck and quickly carried to the side. Another splash. Theseo led them on.

"In there?" Theseo asked John eventually.

John had no idea really, but he nodded.

Theseo stopped at the door and turned to John. John opened it for him. Theseo swung it back and forth a few times and fiddled with the latches, puzzling over them. Then he called the others forward and John opened and closed the door repeatedly so that each could see how it was done. In other circumstances it might have been funny.

"What the fuck are you playing at?" a hard voiced called out from the passageway.

One of the samudraka went in without his spear, a few moments later there was a thump as the human hit the floor.

Theseo moved on into the passage and John followed. The human was lying very still but John thought he was probably alive. For how long? John moved on. He would try not to think about what he couldn't change.

The interior was a maze of tight passages and steep stairwells, and John soon lost track of where he was. Pipes and cables and dials and labels that meant little to him. It really was a different world, more alien to him than the zarana of the narun.

When asked, John demonstrated a few more doors that were slightly different to the first, and then followed on behind Theseo.

He looked up a stairway to see a samudraka coming down. John was sure they hadn't been that way before. The Marr warrior held up a hand with four fingers, and grinned at his king. Theseo nodded and moved on.

They found a door into a large room, maybe a dining area – mess hall, John thought it would be called, though it was anything but a mess. There were no humans here now. He turned back to look over his companions and frowned, many of the warriors were missing.

"They're exploring for themselves now," Sarva said. He looked amused.

"They do realise there's things here that go bang?" John asked.

"Probably best you keep that to yourself," Sarva said, grinning, "or they'll ask you to show them how."

John wasn't sure whether to be happy that Sarva's sense of humour was returning after such a long absence. Past experience suggested it didn't bode well for their situation.

Theseo, apparently convinced that John wasn't much use, had ceased asking for suggestions about where to go next. He spoke to a few of the remaining warriors and sent them out, and led the rest on down another passage.

More confusing passages, more doors and hatches, more stairs and pipes and cables. John was thoroughly confused. They met samudraka coming from various directions, each would murmur a report to Theseo and then go away again.

Sarva reached out and grasped Theseo's arm. When Theseo glanced at him, Sarva put his fingers to his lips and pointed to a door ahead. Theseo frowned as he concentrated, then a smile broke over his face. He drew the zakti from a loop formed in the skin at his side and the blade brightened. He pointed to Sarva and mimed opening the door. Sarva nodded.

Theseo held his hand up, indicating that the others should wait, and gestured Sarva ahead. Sarva moved casually to the door, turned the handle and pushed it in a single smooth movement, keeping to one side as Theseo stepped inside.

There was one sharp cry of surprise and then silence. A moment later Theseo emerged from the doorway. He was splashed with gold, and liquid prana still dripped from the zakti to the floor, quickly evaporating in a faint mist.

"The first of the dhumraka have fallen," he said with satisfaction. There was a cheer from the warriors behind John, but Theseo raised his hand to silence them. "There could be more. Be wary."

John glanced briefly into the room as Theseo led them past. As best he could tell, there had been two dhumraka in there, a man and a woman, though it was difficult to be certain. Their grey bodies were now in pieces and quickly evaporating, the room was already filled with a haze of lost life.

"What were they doing here?" John asked Sarva.

"Probably keeping watch for us."

"But not doing a very good job of it," remarked another warrior.

"Not a mistake they're going to learn from," added another.

"So they were expecting us?" John asked.

"Looks like it," Sarva answered.

"Our enemy would be ignorant in the extreme not to have considered this possibility," Theseo said. He paused and looked at Sarva. "And I should have been paying more attention. I thank you."

Sarva shrugged.

They moved on. Theseo appeared to be leading them generally upward again now.

Voices ahead, and brighter lighting. John followed Theseo into what had to be the bridge. A large area full of screens and cabinets topped with levers and dials. Cables dangled from the ceiling and electronic sounds issued from speakers. Dark windows that went around three sides of the area reflected back the lights of the interior. And humans. Six of them.

More warriors entered the room. One of the human men saw a spear moving.

"What the—?" he started, but never got a chance to finish. The spear slashed across his throat and he fell to the floor gurgling and grasping at his neck.

Warriors rushed past John and Sarva. John saw Theseo's blade flash brightly and a woman fell. Shots rang out as a human man started to shoot blindly at attackers he couldn't see. A yell of pain came from a samudraka hit by a ricocheting bullet. The sound of an alarm filled the space, drowning out any further cries from the humans. In moments the humans were all dead.

Theseo directed his warriors to the entry ways with signals from his hands.

The first humans that tried to enter the bridge died quickly. The ones that followed saw their fallen companions and hesitated. They fired shots randomly into the bridge, but none of the samudraka were hit. The alarm continued to whoop.

Polyphemo found loose objects on the bridge and threw them out at the humans. Hiding further back, John didn't know what he was doing, but other warriors followed his example. The objects drew more gunfire. A human rushed to one of the doorways and died with a spear in his throat. More ineffective gunfire followed quickly after he fell.

Abruptly the gunfire ceased and moments later samudraka warriors appeared in the doorways, grinning with excitement. Blood spattered their arms and shoulders. Theseo nodded his approval and then turned to John.

"How does this work?" He held up a vicious looking black rifle.

John didn't know much about guns, but he'd seen enough television that it didn't take long to work out. When he looked up he saw that he had an audience of enthusiastic warriors. John pointed the rifle to one of the windows and pulled the trigger. The gun

456

rattled and shook in his hands like something alive, he almost dropped it. The window blew out.

The gun was taken from his hand and a pistol put in its place. He demonstrated that as well. There was a brief period of pandemonium as warriors experimented with weapons salvaged from bodies. Ricochets threatened to kill everyone, but miraculously, it seemed to John, hit no one.

Theseo called for quiet. He gave John a nod, satisfied that he hadn't been a total waste of space. "Will these things work under water?"

John shrugged, he had no idea. "Probably not very well," he hedged his bets.

The king directed his warriors to scavenge more weapons, they would experiment. John hoped he wouldn't be too close when they did. Theseo found a door to the outside and led the way down the stairs to the deck. They were much higher above the water here.

At the rail, Theseo pointed to those that were to come with him, the others scattered. Some returned to the depths of the ship, others went along the deck to take care of any humans that emerged. He looked at Polyphemo. "Go back and get the others, we won't be retreating again." He spared a glance for Sarva and John. "Take these two with you."

Polyphemo didn't look happy at the command, but didn't argue.

Without hesitation, Theseo leapt from the rail. John saw his legs transform back into a tail as he descended. His warriors followed quickly.

"Come on," Polyphemo said brusquely to John, pushing him at the rail.

"It's no problem," Sarva assured John. "You've jumped further than this, remember?"

John nodded, but wasn't reassured. Polyphemo was already gone.

"You want me to lead the way again?" Sarva asked.

John shook his head, gritted his teeth and climbed over the rail. He looked down and wished he hadn't. Movement at his side, Sarva was on his way down. John jumped.

- - -

It had been quiet for a long time, just the sound of the waves gently washing the beach below, and the occasional whispering murmur of Helix speaking with her dhumraka. Senna found herself almost drifting off to sleep.

Helix cried out in frustration.

Senna gave a small yelp of surprise. She peered fearfully at the others, but it didn't look like they had heard.

"Where is he?" Helix called out angrily.

Senna couldn't tell who she was talking to, it didn't seem to be any of the dhumraka.

"What fucking use are they to anyone?" A pause. "All for the aaranya bitch. Christ! You'd think he was an adolescent. Did you tell him we are losing ships?" Another pause. "Tell him to leave them, they don't matter!"

Senna had heard humans talking on the phone, this was something like that.

"There! Did you feel that? That's another one. ... Two!" A brief pause, and then, "I've had the human crews on alert since the first one, but it hasn't helped. They've shot more of themselves than they have anything else. They even killed some of my people! ... Yes, I know you felt it too." A break. "Of course the aaranya are going in, what the fuck does he think I'm doing? But they're useless, they'll never get through. We're going to lose all the ships."

Anything that made Helix this upset had to be good. Helix's voice was growing softer now. Senna risked getting a little closer.

"What?" Helix yelled suddenly. "Fall back? Tell him to make up his fucking mind. ... It's too late for the aaranya, they're committed, the samudraka are already on them. I can feel them dying."

Senna cringed to think that more of her people were being slaughtered out there. Innocents caught in a power struggle.

"Tell Jaimee to get out of there. If we're going to fall back it's going to happen fast. If he's not careful he'll get caught in the middle of it."

Helix turned suddenly and started walking back to the forest. Her companions hurried after her, not saying a word. One of them came so close to Senna that she felt sure she would be discovered, but the man was concentrating on his furious queen.

"If my brother gets out of there alive I'm going to kill him myself," Helix ranted as she walked.

Helix joined up with the humans she had come with and they all walked away. Senna lay back and tried to let herself relax. Maybe it would work. Maybe the samudraka really could defeat the dhumraka and their queen. Something had to make the sacrifices mean something.

She heard the vehicles start and drive off. Still nervous, she sent her senses out as far as she could. She couldn't feel any narun left behind. She stood up and looked out over the ridge at the ocean. There was a battle going on out there and more of her people were being killed. Her people. It was a strange thought. One that encompassed a lot more than it had when she was growing up in the city. The world was a much bigger place now than it had been.

Her body tingled with the effects of the detector field as the soldiers turned their equipment back on. She jumped over the ridge, lost her footing, and slipped and slid down the steep slope to the beach. Landing roughly at the bottom she shook herself angrily. Now she'd have to work her way back slowly behind the human lines where her cloaked presence wouldn't be noticed.

There was time yet, and it was pleasant down here on the beach where the detector field didn't reach. Senna strolled down to the waterline and splashed through the ebbing waves.

Further along the beach was a small presence, something caught in fronds of kelp washed up on the sand. As she got closer she thought she recognised it and hurried.

She pushed the fronds apart and there, looking sodden and bedraggled, was a brevi. Senna picked up the creature, and patted the ginger fur. She whispered gently, "Oh Cassey, what happened to you?"

The water fell away from the creature and it twittered weakly. Senna stroked at the line of white running across one side, at right angles to the natural lines of darker ginger and white that ran the length of the body. The scar ran right across the fold of skin stretched between the legs on that side. There was a badly healed tear at the edge of the skin. "What did this?" Senna whispered.

Remembering that brevi could pass on messages, Senna lifted Cassey to her ear. Faintly she heard Cassey echo Asha's voice, "Cassey, no."

She looked at the brevi in wonder. "What does that mean?"

Before she could react, Cassey had jumped from her hand, part fell, part glided to the sand and began making its way to the ridge.

"Cassey, wait!" Senna called.

She ran after the brevi. Cassey was obviously weak, Senna had no trouble scooping it back up.

"Don't go," she whispered. "Rest with me for a while. We can't leave, not yet. A couple of days and then we can go. All right?"

Cassey twittered again. Senna held her firmly. The brevi relented and merged into Senna's body.

Senna could feel the warmth of the brevi moving about her body restlessly for a time before it settled somewhere under her right breast. Senna walked slowly along the beach, looking for the spot where she could sneak back over the ridge and into the forest. She continued speaking to Cassey, hoping the sound of her voice would be reassuring to the obviously distressed creature. "Where is it you want to go? Wherever it is, we'll go together. Okay? We just need a few days."

- - -

Asha lay back on the pillow exhausted. Angel lay next to her, still weak. The dramatic early successes were a thing of the past. Now, however much Asha gave of herself, it wasn't enough. The woman was fading. She would outlast Ellie, but not by much. Whatever had gone wrong was getting worse. Angel, like Ellie, was beyond the possibility of cure. Asha tried not to express the thought too clearly, Peren was still there in her mind.

Angel rolled onto her side. She placed her head on Asha's arm and her hand on Asha's belly. Asha glanced at the woman in surprise, and then relaxed again. Whatever this was, it wasn't an excess of libido. The woman appeared to be trying to offer comfort, her hand gently stroked Asha's stomach. Strange, but Asha decided not to risk embarrassing Angel by stopping her.

She should be moved to a Glade, Asha said to Peren. It may give her more time.

<Mama doesn't want to live in the ocean,> Peren said.

So take her to the forest. You must have aaranya near here.

<The others won't. Anyway, the close ones were closed long ago.>

Your siblings?

A response that felt something like a reluctant nod.

You know we have to find something – soon.

<My brothers have given up. And Helix.>

Asha could feel Peren's distress and wished she could find some way to comfort her. But there was nothing she could say. Lying wasn't possible even if it had been in her nature.

Could you persuade your mother to go to a dhumraka Glade, even if it was just for a while?

<We can't.>

Asha sensed there was something more, something Peren wasn't saying. What is it?

<The samudraka have already taken some of the Glades. No one's trying to stop them.>

Ellie? Asha asked, suddenly tense.

<Jaimee went to get them, but they had tried to escape. He's having trouble finding them and the samudraka are getting closer all the time!> Peren said in a rush. *<Now I'm worried they're all going to get caught.>*

I don't understand.

<Jaimee wants the samudraka to go to the city. He's having the dhumraka lead them that way, but now they're getting close to where he is, and I'm scared.>

Asha was confused. She didn't know what Jaimee must be planning or why he was putting himself in danger for her request. But even more, she was worried now that she might have stopped her friends from escaping on their own. Or might they be in even more danger from the samudraka?

<Two of the Glades have been closed already, their elders killed. Helix is furious. It hurt her a lot to lose them.>

It wasn't something that Asha could feign sympathy for.

Angel's hand reached up and touched Asha's face. "You shouldn't be wasting your efforts on me," the woman told her. "You have something much more precious to protect."

Asha looked at her in surprise.

Angel's blue-grey eyes looked back at Asha calmly. "You should try to relax," she said, and then she turned her attention back to Asha's stomach, gently stroking it. "The baby feels it when you are tense," she added quietly.

"What?" Asha's voice was barely a whisper.

"My son is not doing his duty. He should spend more time with you before the child fades. It is already very small. You should tell him."

"What baby?"

<What baby?> Peren's voice echoed.

"Can you hear its voice yet?" Angel asked, oblivious to the question.

"No," Asha whispered.

"I could hear my daughter from very early. She kept me safe when all was dark."

Could it be true? Asha wondered.

<I told you I heard echoes,> Peren said.

Asha reached inward with her senses. She rarely turned them on herself.

<Is it true?> Peren wanted to know.

Asha ignored her. There was something there. Tiny and weak. Barely discernible. A life that was separate from herself. Asha remembered those last desperate weeks with John. She hadn't been seeking a baby. Not consciously. She had just wanted to be near him, wrapped in him, part of him. She had wanted him to be part of her. And now he was.

Angel was wrong about who the father was, but she was right about something. Narun babies weren't like human babies. The father *had* to be there. The union had to continue for the entire gestation, both of them adding to the substance of the baby. If they didn't the baby would fade back into the mother's body. That the fragile start had lasted this long was a miracle in itself. But to what purpose? They had started a child together, but now it could never be finished.

Asha ignored Angel, ignored Peren's pleading in her mind, and rushed from the room. Brushing past humans on the stairs, Asha ran outside and into the trees. This one last tragedy was more than she could stand.

- - -

Barma slipped through the tightly woven vines and into an open space. It was good to be out of the water, but they were still inside the Glade somewhere. Forinay said she knew where she was leading them.

462

"It's an old connection," she claimed, "hardly used any more because this end is so far out of the way."

From this clear space on the side of the hill, Barma could see down to the water. They wouldn't be dry for much longer.

Forinay tugged at his arm and Barma knelt down to follow her back into the complex tangle of vines. By taking this overland route to the inlet and remaining hidden in the tightly packed vines that covered it, they hoped to remain out of sight of anyone looking for them. So far it seemed to be working.

He turned back and took Ellie from Telia while she crawled in after them.

It was awkward going. Some of the vines had long sharp barbs, and they had to wind back and forth to try and avoid them. Barma and Telia kept passing Ellie between them as they worked their way down the slope.

Telia caught his eye during one of the hand-overs. "I might have said this before, Barma, but it's worth repeating. You sure know how to show a girl a good time, old man."

Barma laughed.

The vines ended several feet above the waterline. They stayed within the cover of its growth while they surveyed the scene. The water of this narrow inlet was calm, the small waves barely made a sound as they lapped at the muddy bank.

"Are we sure this is a good idea?" Barma asked.

Telia shrugged. "No, but we can't stay here. The dhumraka will return eventually."

"Or the samudraka," Barma noted.

"The samudraka are coming," Forinay intoned. Barma wished she'd find a new refrain.

It was Forinay that descended first, carefully carrying her spear to one side. Telia followed.

Barma hitched Ellie into a more comfortable position in his arm. "Time to get wet again, Ellie. I hope you don't mind too much." Of course there was no response, not so much as a twitch. He checked her to make sure she was still alive – it had become a reflex – and then he followed after Telia.

The water was warm and clear. There was no kelp growing here. The slope they descended turned rocky not far beneath the surface, and small shrub-like plants, apricot in colour, grew up from between the rocks. Forinay led them down through the shrubs, taking what little cover these offered.

"Where are we headed?" Telia asked.

Forinay pointed the spear. On the far side, near the bottom of this submerged valley, was the entrance to a cave.

They reached the bottom, mostly levelled off with sediment. Creatures like soft-shelled lobsters moved about in the mud. There was not much growth here, so they hurried across to the other side and ascended towards the cave.

At its entrance Forinay stopped and turned to speak with them. Her eyes went wide with panic. "Someone's coming!"

Barma turned but saw no one. Forinay was tugging at his arm and he quickly followed her into the cave. It arced gently upward and then levelled out.

They approached another bend in the cave and Forinay stopped. Moments later the reason appeared. Three figures. Pale-blue men with tails. Samudraka. Barma had never seen one before but knew this must be what they were.

"The samudraka are coming," Forinay whispered.

Both sides stopped and watched the other. Nothing was said. Thoughts raced through Barma's mind: they should turn back, they should try to surrender, they should plead for mercy.

Forinay started to move forward, but Telia caught her arm. "Let me try," she said quietly.

Telia swam slowly toward the samudraka. "I am aaranya," she said, "as is my friend." She waved vaguely back to Barma. "We are not part of this. We were prisoners. We only want to leave this place. This woman is helping us."

One of the men said something, Barma couldn't make out what it was.

"No. Please!" Telia called out.

One of the warriors gave a flick of his tail, as he came forward his spear flashed out across her neck. Telia didn't even have time to raise her arm in defence. Her body twitched once. Her head and shoulders were quickly lost in a cloud of gold.

Forinay screamed in rage and rushed at them with her spear raised. Barma was torn. He wanted to join Forinay in seeking retribution, but he had no weapon and he had to protect Ellie. He should try to escape. Before he had a chance to turn, a hand touched his arm.

"Sando?" he said in surprise to the pale face smiling at him.

"Wrong brother," Jaimee answered cheerfully.

Barma turned back at Forinay's scream. He saw another flash of movement and she fell silent. Her spear dropped from her fingers. Gold poured into the water from the holes in her chest as she sank slowly to the bottom of the tunnel.

The samudraka swam past the bodies of the two women. Barma didn't know what he should be doing, or what he should be hoping for.

"I could have told your friend that the samudraka weren't kindly disposed to the aaranya at the moment," Jaimee said mildly. "Borrowed spears," he called to the samudraka, "and us unarmed. That's hardly fair."

The men slowed. Jaimee waved one hand and then the other, and cries of pain and surprise erupted from two of the men. The third threw his spear. Jaimee twisted in the water and the spear brushed past, grazing his shoulder. He ignored that and waved his hands again and again. Gold erupted from the man's chest and neck. Another flick of Jaimee's hands and the samudraka stopped moving, his limbs floating slack.

One of the remaining warriors turned to try and swim away. Again Jaimee's hands flickered. The man arched in pain as stripes of gold appeared across his back. He half turned and then went still.

The last warrior was clutching at his neck, as if he could hope to keep his life from flowing from the wound. Despite the gold pulsing from between his fingers, the warrior swam at Jaimee. Jaimee grinned at him, and waited.

The warrior closed the distance and thrust out with his spear. Jaimee flicked his hand and the warrior's arm floated free. The man tried to scream but only golden prana erupted from his mouth. Another movement from Jaimee's hand and the samudraka was dead.

"Come on," Jaimee said, turning around. "Best get out of here before their friends arrive."

23. Tactics

<Asha?>

Asha tried to ignore her.

<They'll be here soon.>

Asha had picked a spot near the tip of a tree where she could glimpse the ocean in the distance. Her home lay far behind that horizon. Kaia, her grandmother, would have been pleased to have yet another generation to refer to her as simply grandmother. "Drop the greats from in front of grandmother," Kaia used to tell Asha, "and I get all the joy of loving another child without feeling any older."

<Ellie is very weak,> Peren persisted. *<She will need you.>*

What would it have been like to raise this child with John? For it to have had an older sister in Ellie? Such were the impossible dreams that had grown in Asha's mind since learning of her child. A voice? Angel had said she might hear the child's voice. Peren said she heard echoes. That wasn't something Asha had heard of before in the narun. It might have been good to hear her child's voice, or it might have made losing it that much harder.

<Asha, I will have to tell Jaimee.>

Asha sat up. Why?

<Mama will tell him anyway. You heard what she said. She thinks it's his.>

As if.

<If I don't tell him, he will know I've been keeping secrets.>

Asha nodded reluctantly. What will he do?

There was a hesitation before Peren answered, Asha knew she wouldn't like what was coming.

<He may offer to stand in as ... surrogate.>

The revulsion Asha felt came from two levels. The first was simple. The aaranya just didn't do that. A child had just one father. Great care was taken to make sure no one ever thought that more could be involved. The second was more visceral, the thought of letting Jaimee get that close to her. *If he tries, I will slice him open,* she told Peren.

<He won't push. He's not like that.>

Still defending the indefensible.

<I'm sorry about Telia, but Jaimee had nothing to do with that.>

This time.

<I saw it through his eyes, he got there too late to save her.>

They were only there because he held them there.

<And because Ellie had to be in a Glade.>

So it's my fault.

<No! I just meant— >

I know. I'm sorry. But it does feel like that sometimes. That if I hadn't started visiting Ellie, and then John, that none of this would have happened.

<You didn't start this.>

So now I'm vain as well?

There was the unusual but pleasant sensation of Peren laughing in Asha's mind.

Asha resisted for a moment, but a smile pushed at the corners of her mouth and she laughed with her friend.

<They're about to land,> Peren said. *<I'll get Reyndani to come and tell you officially so you have an excuse to be there.>*

Your siblings still don't suspect us?

<Jaimee does, or has. So far I've managed to divert him.>

What will he do if he finds out?

<I don't know,> Peren answered, and then her presence left Asha's mind.

Asha climbed down and started walking to the house. Reyndani met her and led her into the house and up the stairs to the roof. As they walked he told her about Telia's death. Peren had arranged this with Jaimee on the excuse that it would save him suffering the initial brunt of Asha's anger, but really so that Asha wouldn't have to pretend to be surprised in front of Jaimee. Asha wondered how she really would have reacted if she had first heard the news this way. Reyndani, who couldn't hear her, would have made a very unsatisfactory wall to vent her anger on.

Reyndani kept her inside the door at the top of the stairs while they waited for the helicopter to land on the area marked out for it. The large, insect-like beast landed and the door slid back. As the blades slowed, Barma made his way unsteadily out with Ellie in his arms.

Asha pushed past Reyndani and ran to meet them. Barma looked pale and drawn, and he didn't lift his eyes to meet Asha's.

"I know about Telia," Asha said softly, "I'm sorry."

"She—" he started, then leaned against Asha and cried.

They held Ellie between them while Barma clung tightly to Asha with one arm, seeking strength she felt inadequate to supply. She waited. No tears came. It wasn't because she didn't care, she truly did share Barma's grief, but there wasn't room for her to express this new loss. Not yet anyway.

Eventually Barma straightened. "Sorry," he murmured.

Asha stroked his face and then look down at Ellie. She was fading fast now, outside the Glade. Asha picked the tiny child carefully from Barma's arms. She would have to feed her soon, and keep feeding her often. Maybe if she kept it down to many short feeds she could manage to sustain both herself and Ellie for a few days.

There was someone in front of her. Asha looked up. It was Jaimee, Sando was standing not far behind him.

"You'll want to feed the preta," Jaimee said.

Asha nodded.

"You'll have to do it in the cage."

"Why?"

"Because I say." Such a hard response from Jaimee was unusual.

"There's only one tree, it's not enough."

"I'll get someone to let you out when you're done, but the preta stays locked up with your other friends."

"That doesn't make any sense," Asha argued. "I need to be with her."

"So stay in the cage. In fact, that's probably best. If you kill the tree we'll plant another one."

There was something wrong. What is it, Peren? What's

happening? Asha asked in her mind, but her friend wasn't listening.

When Theseo learned that Tilvy had gone to find Senna, he merely shrugged. John was worried about them both, but there was nothing he could do. The samudraka attack was moving to land, to specifically human territory, and Theseo wanted John near.

The second sea battle had been a greater success than Theseo had hoped. Some warriors were lost on ships better prepared than the others, but the few dhumraka guards on each had been unable to prevent the samudraka from boarding and the humans stood no chance. The ships had been disabled long enough for the main force of the samudraka to wipe out the remnants of aaranya without interference.

Only a few small groups of dhumraka warriors were found in the water, and these fell back quickly. Theseo moved his army on, pushing the dhumraka in front of them. As they passed the entrances to Glades he sent small forces to investigate. They met little resistance.

"This isn't right," Sarva said quietly to John. "There can't be so few dhumraka. They're drawing us into something, like they did before."

"So tell him," John replied.

"He won't listen to me, not any more. *You* have to say something."

John nodded reluctantly.

Theseo called the army to a halt while they were outside the entrance to the bay. Pasith was called to tell what he knew and John swam forward with him.

"What is it?" Theseo asked John.

"This doesn't ... it isn't," John started hesitantly. Advising kings on battle strategy wasn't something he felt qualified to do. "Sarva ... we were thinking that it feels like a trap. There must be more dhumraka than we've seen. It feels like they're leading us here."

Theseo nodded. "It does. It's also where we wanted to go, and that makes it convenient."

John opened his mouth to say more, but Theseo had already turned back to Pasith.

Night had fallen before they swam in under the Golden Gate Bridge. John had never seen it before, and had never imagined

469

seeing it from this perspective. The long line of the roadway stretched above him, marked out in lights softened by a light mist that was rolling in from the ocean. John thought it was spectacular, a reminder of his old life. The samudraka ignored it.

Some distance in, Theseo called a halt and they waited. Eventually Theseo nodded to a few of the Marr and small groups went to scout ahead. He nodded to Sarva, Pasith and John, "You three stay close."

Theseo was attended by a dozen Marr warriors, including the Polyphemo, whose unhappy job it was to keep an eye on John and the others. John glanced back to locate Darnu and Garjae, they were following not far behind.

The scouts reported back that all was clear and they closed the last distance to the small beach. The samudraka rose out of the water and strode up the sand. Again John was struck by the way each moved so differently. The thought occurred to him that perhaps he should be surprised they walked at all, considering how little practice they must get. The beach wasn't very wide. Further along the samudraka were pulling themselves out of the water over concrete edging.

Despite the scouts having checked the area it was a tense time. Everyone was waiting for some unseen danger to materialise. But there was no sign of the dhumraka and no sensation of a detector field in use. Nothing to suggest anyone was watching for them.

"But there should be," Sarva commented. "Something's not right."

Progress was slow at first. Samudraka kept stopping to prod their spears at unfamiliar objects: the concrete and tarmac covering the ground, and the metal, tyres and windows of a parked car. Some stared up at the lights. The king's small group passed over an area of close-cropped grass and reached a road. A loud noise approached and Theseo drew his zakti.

John reached forward and touched Theseo's arm. "It's a truck," he said.

The large truck appeared and roared past them. Many of the samudraka flinched back.

"A ship that sails on land," Theseo observed. "Were there people in the back?"

"No, probably food or something. The ones that carry people in the back have windows along the side, they call them buses."

Theseo stepped forward onto the road, and John put his hand on the king's arm again. "It might be a good idea to remind your men that the humans driving those things can't see them. A spear won't stop them, it's up to your men to stay out of their way. The trucks and cars will stay on the road, your men should be safe enough on the footpaths." John pointed out the areas as he spoke. He remembered, what seemed a very long time ago, offering similar advice the Darnu and Andrei and the others.

Theseo nodded thoughtfully and then waved to two of his warriors. They departed to each side to pass on the warning.

They worked their way slowly up a steep hill. The warriors had all spread out, some taking different streets, and some investigating areas around the low two and three storey buildings that they passed. It was very quiet on the streets, few vehicles and no people. John wondered what day of the week it was, but he couldn't even guess. He had expected a city like San Francisco to be busier, even at this time of night, on any night. It added to the feeling that they were expected.

Eventually they came to larger buildings. Some of the samudraka looked around nervously, as if expecting the buildings themselves to move.

Pasith, on the other side of Theseo, murmured something to the king and pointed. Theseo nodded and started down the way Pasith had indicated.

More turns, more walking, and still few signs of human activity. There were more cars somewhere, John could hear the distant hum, but they weren't here.

"There should be more people," John said softly.

"Obviously," Theseo answered him, but kept walking as if he wasn't concerned.

Pasith pointed to a building maybe ten storeys high. From the outside it looked much like any of the others, perhaps broader than most. John found it hard to believe that it enclosed the small rainforest described by Pasith and Tilvy.

"How do we get in?" Theseo asked John.

Some flippant responses passed through John's mind, he wasn't sure where they came from. See if someone left the bathroom

471

window open, came top of the list. Try the basement came later, but with greater strength for some reason. He started to walk to the driveway that disappeared under the building. He couldn't have said why, it just seemed like the best way to go. The others followed.

John noticed that more samudraka were converging on the building from the different streets that they had followed. Darnu and Garjae had dropped back and were walking with another group of Marr warriors. He lost sight of them as he passed beneath the building. Only Theseo and his small band followed John down the dimly lit driveway.

John started to have reservations about what they were doing. He shouldn't be leading the king into such a vulnerable position. Then he thought of Asha, that she could be here somewhere, and walked a little faster. Somewhere further down in his mind a voice was telling him this was stupid, she wouldn't be here. She wasn't here. He would know. The thought that Asha could be here pushed itself forward again. He couldn't let the possibility go.

"Wait," Pasith said.

"The papayamala are near," Theseo said, "I can feel them."

John and Theseo were walking side by side now, with the same intense concentration, and with the same conviction that what they were seeking was near.

Sarva jogged up next to John. "Slow down."

John shrugged off Sarva's hand. "She's near, can't you tell?"

Pasith had fallen behind. The other warriors were similarly lagging, nervous in this unfamiliar environment.

"No, I can't," Sarva said.

There was a huge door made for trucks to come and go from some enclosed area. To one side of that was a smaller, human-sized door. John made for that.

"At least wait for the others," Sarva insisted. He tried to stand in Theseo's way, but the king brushed him to the side.

"They're here," Theseo said.

John pushed the door open. Yes, Theseo was right, someone was close, John could sense them. Could it be Asha? He stepped through.

It was a docking area for the loading and unloading of trucks, but there were no trucks here now, just a large open expanse of

472

concrete. It was brightly lit, almost dazzling.

There was a scuffle. John turned and saw that Sarva was trying to block the king from entering. Theseo pushed him hard and Sarva fell through and onto the floor. Theseo stepped in after him.

The door slammed closed with a loud clang and a screech of metal as a locking bar slid into place. Almost immediately, banging could be heard on the other side. But it went unheeded, all of John's attention was taken with the trio that confronted him. Sando twice, one had to be his twin brother, and the hulking figure of Waldron Stephenson carrying a ray-gun.

One of the brothers was grinning at John, the other was staring at Sarva still lying on the floor. Theseo had already drawn the zakti, it shone brightly as he raised it. Then the sword dropped and rang like a large crystal bell as it hit the concrete. Theseo fell beside it, groaning. Moments later John's world started spinning and tearing at him, and he collapsed to the floor with the others.

- - -

Sando was tempted to kill John here and now, before Jaimee and his concerns about Asha got in the way yet again.

<No, Zandy,> Peren whispered in his mind.

What do you care? Sando asked. All he felt in response was her disapproval.

Jaimee spoke to Stephenson. "We got what we came for, you can bring out the troops."

Stephenson, still holding the ray-gun over the prisoners, to knock them down again if they looked like getting up, used his free hand to pull out a radio and pass on the instructions. Several dhumraka came out from a small room, specially painted to obscure their presence to vedana, and began to pick up the three prisoners.

"You made that look easy," Jaimee said.

"It was," Sando admitted. "What they both wanted was already pushing them, I just eased aside their doubts. It doesn't get any easier than that."

Jaimee waved the sword that the samudraka had dropped. "This is a strange thing. It's pretty enough, but unwieldy. What do you think?"

Sando took the blade and gave it a few swings. There was something wrong with it. It felt like it was turning in his hand, as if

473

the balance was constantly changing. "Glad it's not mine." He handed the blade back to Jaimee.

Jaimee gave a strange smile and inclined his head. "The unexpected spare is an interesting addition, don't you think?"

Sando took a closer look at the prisoners on the floor of the lift. The human, ex-human or whatever he was. The samudraka, young and strong, bare torso of dark green, legs thickly clad in shiny black, and a strong presence that went beyond just the life of his body. Then there was the aaranya. Ruffled light brown hair, slender but still strong. Groaning and obviously disoriented by the effects of the ray, like the other two. Nothing remarkable.

The man's eyes opened and glanced at Sando briefly. It was enough. That pale green flicker was very remarkable. Sando took in more of the feeling of the man's presence and it became so obvious he didn't know how he had missed it before. He turned back to Jaimee and grinned.

The sound of vehicles drew closer. Trucks. Garjae and Darnu joined the samudraka in getting off the street and looking around to see what was coming. Large dull green trucks came from both directions on this street, and by the sound of it from other streets as well.

"I don't like this," Garjae said quietly to Darnu.

"I can only sense humans," Darnu answered.

The trucks stopped in apparent synchronisation. Pasith and several Marr warriors came running out from beneath the building.

"They have the king!" Polyphemo shouted.

The samudraka turned their attention from the trucks and rushed to the building. Garjae kept watching the trucks, waiting for the branch to crack.

A sudden strong buzzing sensation ran through his body. A Karlin Field.

"Detectors," Darnu stated the obvious. "They know we're here."

Humans poured out from the back of the trucks. Some were carrying screens in front of them, others were carrying devices that Garjae knew too well.

"And ray-guns," he said.

They ran together to the corner of the building. There were trucks down this street too, unloading a similar cargo. Samudraka were still converging on the building, disappearing into the tunnel that had swallowed their king.

Darnu ran and grabbed hold of Polyphemo. "You can't go back in there, you'll be trapped."

Polyphemo might have ignored him but then the screams started. There were samudraka still arriving from the various streets they had wandered down, these were the first to be picked off. Polyphemo grabbed at a number of samudraka and barked instructions at them.

"They're herding us together," Pasith spoke so quietly that Garjae almost missed it.

"Dhumraka," Darnu said, and pointed.

From one of the trucks there were dhumraka emerging, throwing back cloaks that had obscured their presence. Some of the dhumraka were carrying knives. They followed behind the humans, finishing off the samudraka that had fallen.

"Down here," Pasith called. He'd gone to the corner and was looking down the other street.

On this street a few samudraka had recovered enough to defend themselves from the dhumraka. A couple had picked up their spears. There were gunshots and one of them dropped.

"You two know how to do that cloak thing?" Pasith asked.

Darnu nodded.

"You might—"

"We'll go," Darnu interrupted him. "You get Polyphemo to lead everyone down this way. Tell him the king will have to wait until we deal with this."

"Or they will all be slaughtered," Garjae added, "not just the king." He concentrated and the hooded cloak formed around his body.

Darnu started to run and Garjae followed closely. They passed samudraka coming the other way, many of them glancing over their shoulder, reluctant in their retreat.

There was a long moment of pain and disorientation and then it passed as Darnu pulled Garjae behind the column of a building. They paused a moment and Darnu leaned out to take another look. "Now."

Garjae followed at a run, trying to keep the cloak around him.

Ahead he could see the humans directing their weapons down the narrow space between buildings. The dhumraka had fallen behind, still struggling with samudraka that turned out to be hard to kill.

The human soldiers returned their attention to the street. Darnu and Garjae rushed to another column and crouched behind it. The screams of samudraka caught in the ray got closer as the soldiers made their way forward.

Those far enough away stumbled, groaned and kept going. Those closer to the guns fell to the street. A few recovered fast enough to get up and run again. Some of these were lucky enough to get out of range. Most were not.

The thick columns of the building gave some protection, and Garjae wondered why the samudraka weren't trying to hide. He took a chance and peaked down the street. The soldiers where being thorough, checking with their detector before moving on. Darnu pulled him back.

They crouched down beneath their cloaks and hoped it would be enough to hide them. Garjae felt the detector field, faint at first, the column partly blocked that too, but it was getting stronger.

The soldiers were close now. Garjae could hear their footsteps, and even some of their conversation.

"Know what this shit is?"

"I don't want to, and neither do you."

"Ghost shit, that's what it is."

"Your ghost shit took out Dane and Crocker back there, or didn't you notice?"

"I didn't say it wasn't dangerous ghost shit."

The soldiers were level with them now.

"Just remember, we only shoot—"

"Yeah, I know. Shoot the ghost shit in front of us, not the ghost shit behind us. But it's all shit, man."

Darnu squeezed Garjae's arm. "Ready?"

Garjae nodded.

Cloaks held tightly around them, they ran lightly out to the line of soldiers. Each took position behind a man with a ray-gun, bypassing the man between them carrying the bright screen. With timing born of a lifetime together, they threw back their cloaks and attacked.

The soldier's helmet meant the first blow was awkward, the man stumbled and groaned. Garjae pushed the helmet forward and struck again, and the soldier fell to the ground. The soldier between them was ignoring his screen now, turning first to one companion and then the other, asking what had happened. Garjae picked up the ray-gun from where it had fallen, it was still attached to the soldier's backpack by a cable. Careful to keep Darnu out of the line of the ray, he pulled the trigger. Man and screen collapsed to the street with a rattle and crunch.

Something buzzed passed Garjae's ear, followed immediately by the sound of the gunshot. Darnu took the shooter out and together they turned their weapons on the nearest soldiers. The line fell quickly and they directed the rays back to the soldiers and dhumraka rushing toward them.

Human soldiers were not as badly affected as narun unless they were close. They went down but few died. Those that could, tried to crawl away. Some pulled guns and started firing blindly around them. Garjae concentrated the ray on those and they went still. Most of the dhumraka lay unmoving on the street.

The soldier at Garjae's knees struggled to get up. Garjae turned the ray on him. The man screamed briefly and went still.

A truck came roaring up the street. Darnu and Garjae concentrated their fire on the cabin. The truck kept coming, running over bodies, soldiers and dhumraka alike. At the last moment it veered off to the side and smashed into a column of the building. There was a deep thud, the tearing of metal, the rattle of broken glass and plastic, and a hiss of steam.

Cries and moans from human soldiers filled the void left by the now quiet truck.

The samudraka arrived, and Pasith with them. The samudraka began salvaging guns from the human soldiers, what they lacked in accuracy they made up for with enthusiasm. Darnu and Garjae showed a few how to operate the ray-guns and the warriors quickly went to the other weapons lying on the street.

There were hundreds of samudraka, Garjae hadn't realised how many had come on this futile mission. They flooded past, pushed on faster by the soldiers coming the other way.

"We can't go back the way we came," Pasith said loudly.

Polyphemo nodded.

"Follow me?"

Polyphemo nodded again, he seemed lost and indecisive with Theseo gone.

"The king?" Darnu asked.

Polyphemo pointed. A helicopter was rising from the building. It hovered over them for a moment and then vanished over the city.

"So we get out of here," Garjae said.

"If we can." Pasith pointed down the street, the way Garjae had thought was open to them. More trucks were pulling up.

- - -

It took a long time for the world to stop spinning and the pain to subside. He thought the noise was part of the effect until he opened his eyes and took in his surroundings. A helicopter. He was in the back of a helicopter. Not far in front of him was a mesh screen, beyond that were Sando and his brother, as well as Stephenson and a few dhumraka.

"Are you okay?" Sarva asked.

John turned. Both Sarva and Theseo looked like they had recovered already. Theseo was glaring through the mesh, Sarva was watching John with concern.

"Okay?" Sarva repeated.

John nodded in belated response.

"It's a pretty toy," one of the brothers was saying. "I hope it works better under water than it does up here."

"It was made for slicing the heads from papayamala," Theseo answered in a low voice.

"It doesn't work very well, does it?"

"Which one's which?" John whispered to Sarva.

"I'm the one you've met before," answered the pale face on the left. He nodded to the one holding the zakti, "This is my brother, Jaimee."

Jaimee turned his bright confident smile on John. "Ah, the now ex-human. You're looking surprisingly well for a man that's supposed to be long dead."

"Some days are better than others," John answered.

The brothers both laughed.

"I must say," Jaimee continued, "that I don't know what she sees in you. At least as a human you had some novelty value, but this?"

He shook his head.

"Is Asha safe?"

"Perfectly."

"It would be simpler to just kill him now and drop him out the door," Sando said.

Jaimee shrugged. "Maybe. Maybe not. I like to keep my options open, and who knows, perhaps I will win a few brownie points with my favourite girl. ... At least one of our sisters agrees with me."

"Where are you taking us?" Theseo asked.

Jaimee turned his attention back to the king and lifted the zakti. "As I was saying, this really doesn't work very well. I think you might need a new one."

"Pass it through to me, I'll show you how well it works," Theseo snapped back.

"What, like this?" Jaimee flicked his hand.

Theseo grunted in surprise and raised a hand to the cut on his cheek.

"So, Sarva," Jaimee said. "Your head is still attached I see. Does that mean you never told him?"

"Told me what?" Theseo demanded.

Jaimee grinned at the king. "You can't guess?"

"Stop playing games with me, videzaka."

Jaimee's fingers flicked again and a matching cut appeared on the other side of Theseo's face. "I happen to like games."

Sando, joined in the spirit of his brother's taunting. "How about we play *I spy a papayamala?*"

"That does sound like fun, brother. John, I never thought to ask, did you have a twin brother or sister back when you were human?"

John never got a chance to answer. Theseo was glaring at Sarva.

"Not such a good game after all, Sando, I think our samudraka has guessed it already. They didn't choose him just for his looks."

"Is this true?" Theseo asked Sarva.

Sarva nodded.

"That's right," said Jaimee. "We've already got the other half." Jaimee looked at Sarva curiously. "She never speaks of you. Why is that?"

"This Asha you speak of is your twin sister?" Theseo asked Sarva, ignoring the brothers.

479

Sarva nodded again.

John watched as the muscles of Theseo's face and shoulders twitched. He wondered what they would do if the king lost his temper in this confined space, but after a moment Theseo turned away and looked out the window.

Jaimee laughed. "You've come all this way to destroy the evil papayamala, and yet you've had one right beside you every step. That's got to sting."

- - -

It was now somewhere in the early hours of the morning, dawn couldn't be far away. Asha emerged from the tree and went to where Barma was lying on the ground near the others, cradling Ellie carefully against him. He woke briefly as Asha eased Ellie from his grip. He smiled sadly at the child and released her.

The others had all agreed not to use the tree, they understood it would only be for a few days. Once Ellie was gone Asha's need would not be so strong.

Asha took Ellie across the small caged area and looked out to the cage and cabin that held Tracey and the others. There had been no opportunity to explain what was happening, they must be wondering why they hadn't heard from her. Perhaps she should have let them go when they had the chance. Now she was locked up too, with no way to get the keys and let them out.

<I'll do it,> Peren said. <If it comes to that, I will do it.>

Where have you been? Asha asked in surprise, she hadn't felt Peren arrive.

<It's been busy.>

What's wrong? Why has Jaimee locked me up? He must know I'm not going to run off.

<He's been acting very weird since I told him you're pregnant.>

It felt strange to hear herself described like that. Asha hadn't told any of her friends here about the baby, there wasn't any point. In what way strange? she asked.

<At first I thought it was just jealousy. He thinks of you as his own. But now I think he's worried. You've proved you can get pregnant, so if he tries with you and fails— >

He'll never get the chance.

<He doesn't believe that, and if he fails then he knows the fault

must be his.>

Asha shook her head. So he doesn't want to be seen as a failure?

<Jaimee doesn't fail.>

Everyone fails sometimes.

<Jaimee isn't everyone.>

Asha didn't argue further.

<There's something else.>

What?

<They have Sarva and John. And the king of the samudraka. They're bringing them here now.>

Asha didn't know how to react. She desperately wanted to see John, and her brother, but not like this. Does this mean the samudraka have lost?

<I don't know. Lantea isn't with the army, I don't know what they're going to do. ... I hope John is careful. Both my brothers would prefer he was dead. Jaimee's holding out mainly because he hopes it might make you like him better.>

Your brother is delusional.

<Be glad, it's the only thing keeping John alive.>

- - -

"What do you want to do with them?" Sando asked quietly, out of hearing of their prisoners.

Jaimee was staring out the window and didn't answer at first.

The sky was turning grey with the approach of dawn and the noise of the helicopter was dwindling as the engine wound down. It was good to be home. Sando was weary and he could feel that his brother was the same, they had been going for days with little time to rest.

"Should we lock them up with the others?" he asked.

Jaimee glanced at the three prisoners and shook his head. "Lock them up, yes, but not with the others. I want to find out more about *him* first."

Sando understood that Jaimee was referring to Sarva. "But not together."

"No. Sarva and the human, okay, but the samudraka better remain isolated."

"He might solve our problems for us."

"I prefer to solve my own."

481

"What's wrong, brother? You don't seem your normal self."

"You don't feel it?

Sando shook his head.

"Are you there, Peren?" Jaimee asked. There was no response. "Our sister has been getting a little strange lately, don't you think?"

"More than usual?"

"Not that. Haven't you noticed anything different?"

Sando considered it for a moment. "She was very upset after the battle with the samudraka. She saw a lot that she didn't like."

"I think it's more than that."

"She's also upset about Mother. She doesn't think we should be giving up."

"Give me a direction and I'll start looking," Jaimee said in exasperation. "We've been at it for years."

"And the healer hasn't given us the time we were hoping for."

"No. I had hoped for better. I was sure she could give us time," Jaimee acknowledged.

"You don't think she's holding out on us, do you?"

"Asha? I doubt if she could hold back to save herself. Peren would soon let us know if there was anything going on in that way."

"So our darling little sister, what worries you?"

Jaimee shrugged. "Maybe I'm just tired. Let's get these put away and get some rest."

They followed Stephenson and the dhumraka out of the helicopter and prepared to take the prisoners down to the cells.

24. Tonight

"We don't need these any longer," Hesperous cast a disparaging hand at Garjae, Darnu and Pasith.

Polyphemo glared at him but didn't respond.

"You are not king yet," another samudraka reminded Hesperous, this one a pale blue.

"King Theseo may yet return," said another.

Hesperous looked at him with open disbelief before composing his expression. "We will, of course, wait the required time."

"Zamayitar must be recovered," the pale blue samudraka said.

"That has apparently been whisked away with our noble king in a human flying machine. Just how do you propose we locate it?"

Garjae turned away from the conversation. They weren't needed, nor wanted. The others followed.

"I'm starting to think we should make ourselves scarce," Pasith said quietly when they were away from the samudraka. "I don't care for our chances without King Theseo's protection."

"Protection?" Garjae gave a snort of disgust.

"Pasith's right," Darnu said. "It was Theseo's presence that protected us from the others."

"And his mother," Pasith noted. "I wonder where she is."

Garjae looked at the loose groups of samudraka warriors dispersed around them. More were still coming in from their widespread fights with the dhumraka. They had fought their way out of the city, against dhumraka and humans. Only by constantly moving and never giving the enemy time to get their equipment set up, did they avoid getting trapped and wiped out.

It had been Pasith's instincts that had guided them to the closest shore. Once in the water they were pursued only by the dhumraka, but there were hundreds of them, and more kept arriving. Many samudraka were lost but it might have been worse. Theseo had left the largest part of his army in the bay, and once they joined the fight the dhumraka proved inadequate to the power of the samudraka. Had Theseo still been with them, the samudraka may have pressed the dhumraka then, but the army was in disarray and had fallen back to regroup.

"Do we just swim away?" Garjae asked. "What if we run into samudraka that object, or that think we're aaranya left over from those they were killing before?"

"I'd like to find Tilvy and Senna," Pasith said.

Darnu nodded.

"And then we try to find Asha," Garjae added.

- - -

To be swimming back to the samudraka without seeing Senna seemed wrong, but what choice did she have? The message that Nuttachen had brought back had been clear.

"Nuttachen, slow down!" Tilvy called ahead to the tiny creature. It moved so fast in the water, it was all she could do to keep up.

She missed Pasith. His strength and confidence in the water might not match the samudraka, but his presence would still have offered a sense of security and comfort that she needed now. What would she do if she met a strange samudraka, one that didn't know her?

Tilvy swam over a familiar ridge, at least she knew she was still going the right way. It looked deserted and she was very tired. "Nuttachen, come back. I want to rest."

She settled on an area of exposed rock. Nuttachen nuzzled at her chin. "Yes, you deserve a rest too," Tilvy agreed, and let the brevi merge into her body.

Tilvy closed her eyes and tried to relax. She wouldn't stay long, she just needed a break.

"You shouldn't be out here alone."

Tilvy opened her eyes and looked around in alarm. It was Lantea with her two warrior guards.

Lantea continued, "It isn't safe for your kind to be out here."

"I have to get back. I have a message for the king."

"The king is lost. Taken by the papayamala."

Tilvy saw now that Lantea looked reduced, her usual confidence was missing. "The others?"

Lantea gave a brief, flat summary.

"What does this mean? Will the samudraka give up now?"

"No. But leaderless and with no obvious target, it is doubtful they will achieve much." She finished in tones of finality, "And there is no one to tell them when to stop. They will keep killing dhumraka until one side or the other ceases to exist."

"I know where the papayamala are," Tilvy said. "That's why I came back."

Lantea stared at Tilvy for a time, conflicting emotions swept over her face. Then she looked away. "You shouldn't have told me that," she murmured, mostly to herself it seemed. "I could just go ... but she needs an escort."

"Even with Theseo missing, they still need to know," Tilvy insisted.

"They do," Lantea agreed and turned back. "All right, come on. I'll take you."

- - -

A spear lashed out. Pasith managed to pull himself out of its path.

"We're friends!" Darnu was still trying to convince the samudraka that were attacking them. "Friends of the king!"

These were the faded blood-red of the Raktana, Garjae wasn't sure that claiming to be friends of the king was a good idea.

"Stop!"

The attackers paused and everyone turned. Polyphemo came in rapidly with half-a-dozen Marr warriors.

"Are you so simple as to forget these are allies?" he accused the Raktana.

"So they are not enemies but deserters," one of them responded. "It is the same penalty."

"I asked them to come this way," Polyphemo said.

Garjae wasn't the only one to meet this revelation with surprise.

"Then we will leave you to your friends, with pleasure," the Raktana answered, and indicated to his companions that they should leave.

When they were all out of hearing, Polyphemo turned to Darnu.

"What were you doing out here?"

"We got the impression we were no longer required," Darnu answered.

"Not all the samudraka are as short-sighted as the Raktana. Others saw you break us free of the human city. If we must go on land again your help will be needed."

Garjae was impressed, it can't have been easy for Polyphemo to make such an admission.

"Someone's coming." Pasith pointed.

"What's she doing back?" Garjae asked, not expecting a response.

The pale figures of Lantea, two of her guards and Tilvy appeared.

"My Lady," Polyphemo said, and bowed when Lantea got close.

"We have news," Lantea announced, and turned to Tilvy.

Tilvy smiled nervously and murmured to her arm until Nuttachen emerged. The samudraka watched with wary interest. They had seen the creature with Darnu before but didn't know what to make of it. They had similar creatures in their own zarana, but they were rarely seen with any but the elders.

"It's best you hear what I heard," Tilvy explained. "Nuttachen was supposed to be leading me to Senna, but he left me behind, ignoring me when I called. I didn't know what to do. You said to trust him, so I waited to see if he would come back. He finally did. This is what he told me." She murmured to the brevi and it swam to Darnu.

Garjae leaned in so he could hear the message repeat. It was Senna's voice that emerged from the brevi, "I've seen Helix a few times, they must be close. Humans watch above the beach with detectors. Stay away until the samudraka come."

"What does it mean by *above the beach*?" Polyphemo asked.

"The land drops away, leaving a ridge running along behind the beach where I left Senna," Lantea explained. "I didn't go up there, so I didn't sense these humans she speaks of."

"If the papayamala are close," Darnu started.

"Then Asha can't be far away," Garjae continued.

"And perhaps the king," Polyphemo finished.

- - -

"How did they find us?" Jaimee demanded, still tired and irritable after waking.

<I don't know,> Peren answered in quiet guilty tones. *<One of*

486

the aaranya found out, I don't know how.>

"Weren't you watching?"

<No, not when the news was first told.>

"Fucking hell, Peren. We have just one contact with the samudraka, why weren't you watching her?"

<When she left the main force of samudraka there didn't seem to be any point.>

"Of course there was a point. *This* was the point!"

<I was checking back, she was staying away from the army. ... I'm not like Helix, I can't be with everyone at once.>

"But this one was important. Who the hell *were* you w—?"

Sando interrupted his brother. "When, Peren? Do you know when we might see them?" He felt his sister hesitate, not because she was checking, but because the answer wasn't a good one.

<Tonight,> she said at last.

"How can they be here that fast?"

<Helix says they fell back this way when they left the bay, they were trying to get clear of the dhumraka she sent against them and this way was open.>

"Is Helix coming back?" Jaimee wanted to know.

<Yes, she'll be here soon. She wants you to arrange buses so she can get others here.>

"At least one of my sisters is thinking," Jaimee said. "We have to keep the dhumraka back behind the human front lines, and keep them clear of the samudraka. With buses we can do that. Sando, get Stephenson on it while I think."

- - -

"Tonight?" Asha said out loud in alarm, the others all turned to stare at her.

<I was supposed to be watching Lantea, but I wasn't.>

Asha could feel the trembling in Peren's presence. She was obviously afraid, she had reason to be, but there was more to it, a profound sense of shame and failure.

<I let everyone down. You, Mama, my brothers, everyone.>

"You couldn't know this was going to happen," Asha said softly.

<Jaimee's right, I should have been watching.>

Feeling the attention of her friends on her, Asha reverted to speaking silently with Peren. I need you to concentrate. We need to find a way to get my friends out before the samudraka get here.

<The house is a mess. Jaimee's got people running around doing all sorts of things. I think he's going to bus some of them out.>

I didn't expect him to be that considerate.

<It's not that. If the samudraka make it this far he plans to fly us out. He wants to make sure our servants survive for when we set up somewhere else.>

Oh. And the rest of us? My friends?

<I don't know.>

Can you get the keys for us?

<Jaimee's calling,> Peren said in a hurry, and her presence vanished from Asha's mind.

- - -

Tracey, Paul and Ray stood by the fence and watched a group of burly men lead the small troop of prisoners past. One of the prisoners, an older woman, glanced across at them, and then looked away. No one else acknowledged them.

"I've never seen them take more than one at a time," Paul said.

"Do you suppose they'll come back for us?" Tracey asked.

Ray was looking down through the fences to the cabins at the end where some prisoners still remained. "Notice anything about the ones they took?"

"The old?" Paul tried, and then glanced back at the departing prisoners and answered himself, "No."

"No. My guess is they took the most amenable. The ones least likely to cause trouble."

"Why?" Tracey asked.

"If you had to set up somewhere new in a hurry, who would you take?"

"So you think ...?"

"I think the war might be getting close enough to make them nervous." Ray turned his attention to the lock on the outside of the gate.

"You can't pick a lock you can't touch, boss," Paul told him.

Ray walked past them, following the line of the fence. Tracey's eyes were drawn to that same area of grass, still finding traces of darkness staining the ground, whether they were real or only in her mind she didn't know. Paul pulled her past but didn't say anything.

When they got past the cabin they looked out at the cage that held the aaranya.

"Do you suppose Asha is in there?" Paul asked.

"Either that, or evacuated already. Those are the only reasons I can imagine would keep her away." Ray turned back and looked along the line of the fence.

"The only other way is over," Paul mused.

Ray nodded.

Tracey looked up at Paul's face in disbelief. "No."

Paul squeezed her hand. "It won't be like that."

"I couldn't."

"If they're busy and short staffed up there, the cameras might not be monitored," Ray said. "A couple of mattresses over the wire."

"A few sheets tied together for rope," added Paul.

Ray nodded. "Over and then out as you had planned before."

Tracey stared up at the razor wire. All her eyes could see there was Mike's body, twitching and bleeding and dying.

"When?" Paul's voice seemed to come to her from a distance.

"Tonight," Ray answered, "I don't think we can afford to wait for Asha any longer."

- - -

Asha spared a glance to the cabin that held her three human friends. "Are you going to take them to safety?" she asked Jaimee as she followed him to the house.

"It won't come to that," he said dismissively.

"But you want me to feed your mother now, in case we have to move."

"Just a precaution."

"You could take them to safety as a precaution too."

Jaimee glanced across and shrugged. "If it comes to that, there'll be room for them when we leave."

"And the aaranya?"

"Could be a squeeze," he grinned at her and sidled closer.

"They can have my space." Asha stepped away from him.

He laughed. "It won't come to that."

Jaimee escorted Asha all the way up to his mother's room.

"Are you going to lock me up again afterwards?" Asha asked him before he opened the door.

489

"It's for your own safety," he said. "Everyone's jumpy with the samudraka coming this way. We don't want someone mistaking you for the enemy."

"It would help if I could have a fresh tree for a time."

Jaimee eyed her carefully. As always, Asha felt vulnerable to his penetrating gaze. His eyes lingered on her stomach before they returned to her face. So far he hadn't mentioned anything about her being pregnant. "Okay," he said at last, "but not for long. Out front and close to the house. I'll come out to get you before dark."

"Thank you."

Jaimee opened the door for her.

Angel's eyes flickered open at the sound of the door. She sat up a bit straighter and smiled. It made her look younger. Asha wondered what Angel had been like as a human. Meek and unassuming, Asha guessed, but with a subtle strength. More like Peren than her other children.

Asha walked around the bed and sat next to her. "Are you ready?" she asked.

"My son told me it wasn't his." Angel reached over and laid her hand on Asha's stomach. "The human's?"

Asha nodded.

"Was he a good man?"

"Is."

"My son ... he could help you. He would help you, if you'll let him."

"No," Asha said firmly.

"Wouldn't it be better to keep even this small part?"

"Not like that."

"It's alive. I can feel it even now. I thought you were a healer. How can you let this life go without fighting for it?"

Asha opened her mouth but couldn't find the words.

"My children saved me. Children are our reason for being. They are precious, worth every sacrifice you must make. Why won't you do this? Whatever you think of my son, won't you do this for your child?"

"Did Jaimee put you up to this?"

Angel looked surprised at the question. "No. He doesn't even know I'm asking, but I'm sure he would help if we asked him. He likes you very much."

Asha pulled Angel to her. "Let's do this."

Angel put her hand between them. "Are you sure we should? The baby."

No, Asha wasn't sure, but she said, "It's been okay so far."

When they were done Asha lay back exhausted. Angel, fed before she had really needed it, was brighter and talkative, though her mood was sombre.

"I don't want to leave here," she said. "It's been my only real home. Everywhere I've ever lived someone has driven me out. My father. The aaranya. The dhumraka."

"The dhumraka?" Asha asked, curious despite being so tired.

"When the children were young," Angel answered vaguely. "And now the samudraka are driving us from here. ... If I must die, I think I would rather die here, where I've been happy for so long."

"That much I understand," Asha answered with feeling.

\- - -

Theseo had come from his cell willingly enough, but from his stance, and the darting of his eyes, it was obvious he was nervous and ready to take advantage of any lapse on their part.

"So what do you think of our intrepid king of the samudraka, sister?" Jaimee asked Helix.

"The ponytail is a nice touch," Helix commented as she circled widely around Theseo. "Good body, but he could do with some fashion tips, I can't stand the trousers."

Helix approached closer. Theseo raised a hand to strike. Sando had been watching for this, and had already felt out the right pressure points. He pressed. Theseo's arm wavered. Sando pressed harder. Helix didn't move or flinch, she merely watched the struggle with amusement. Theseo's arm was trembling, there was a puzzled frown on his face and a twitch that spoke of pain somewhere behind his eyes.

"Not too much, brother," Jaimee warned quietly. "We may need him functional."

Sando held the pressure steady. While there were no distractions he could keep this up indefinitely. As long as Theseo failed to recognise the source of the struggle he was effectively fighting himself. He couldn't win. Sando reflected, as he waited for the king to weaken, that it was convenient to be back with his siblings. Helix and Jaimee naturally drew everyone's attention. Theseo, like so many before him, concentrated on Helix, not Sando. And Helix played her part well. She smiled knowingly, alternately flirting and looking concerned at Theseo's distress.

Still the king's hand trembled in the air. Sando was surprised, there weren't many who could last this long. Sando had been actively resisted a few times, but only by those that recognised their true adversary. One example sat in a cell downstairs. John had surprised him back then, Sando hadn't expected the resistance, that was the only reason he could accept.

At last the king's hand began to drop. Slowly. Theseo was still fighting it, but inch by inch the hand lowered to his side.

"There," said Helix, "you're just a big softy at heart, aren't you?"

Sando kept the pressure applied, Theseo was still struggling.

Helix reached out and stroked Theseo's bare chest, then ran her fingers through his neat beard.

"Enough play, sister," Jaimee said. "Take him."

She reached up and placed her fingers to Theseo's temple. "Ooh. That's nice. Are there more like you back home?"

Sando slowly released his pressure.

"This one special?" Jaimee asked.

"Every new connection gives me something, but this one, he's quite a buzz." Helix leaned in and kissed Theseo on the lips. "Sealed with a loving kiss."

Sando still hadn't relaxed. He knew that it sometimes took time for Helix's connection to come to full effect. There was confusion on Theseo's face now, but the anger that had been so evident was starting to fade.

Helix took a step back. "Have you no words of welcome for your new queen?"

Theseo's face twitched for a few moments and then relaxed. He moved smoothly to one knee and spoke in formal tones. "I, Theseo of the Marr, King of Agadharastra, offer the power of my tail, the strength of my arm, and the length of my life in the service of my queen." He bowed his head.

"The power of your tail," Helix mocked the king, "how intriguing." She stepped forward and said in tones matching the king's formal speech, "I, Helix, Queen of the Dhumraka, angel of Angel's, accept your service. Stand, good sir, and be prepared to do battle in my defence."

Theseo stood but kept his head bowed. "It will be an honour, my queen."

"Is it safe to return his sword?" Jaimee asked.

"He's mine," Helix answered smugly.

Jaimee crossed to where he had left the sword and carried it back to Theseo. It flared brightly when Theseo took it. The siblings tensed as Theseo moved rapidly with the blade. After a brief flourish the king knelt on one knee, the sword held upright before him.

"With Zamayitar in my hand no one shall harm you, my queen."

"Oh. Good," Helix answered, taken aback.

"Time to bring up Sarva," Sando suggested, "see if we can find out what it is he does."

"Do you know?" Helix asked Theseo.

"No, my queen. He has demonstrated no extraordinary powers in my presence."

"I must admit that I'd like to meet him," Helix said to her brothers. "If he's handsome enough maybe I'll become as bad as Jaimee is for his healer. We can double-date."

"Speaking of which," Jaimee said, "Asha's probably out front by now. I think we should hold off with her brother until I've got her locked away again. I'd rather not risk them mixing until we know more. It's not like we don't have other things to do."

"You're much too soft on her," Helix said.

Jaimee shrugged.

"Anyway, perhaps you'd like to explain what you want me to do with this now I've got it?" Helix waved her hand at Theseo, who was still kneeling, waiting for his queen.

- - -

Garjae slid one hand up to the top of the ridge. The familiar tingle of the Karlin Field touched his fingers and he drew them back down again. "Here too," he called to the others. He stepped off Darnu's upraised hands and slid back down the slope.

The sand was warm in the afternoon sun. Ominous, dark and billowing clouds obscured the western horizon. They were advancing quickly, soon they would cover the sun. Perhaps a storm,

Garjae thought, though he wasn't sure if that would be a good thing or a bad thing for what was planned for the coming night. He turned back to the others.

"I can hear a lot of activity up there," he said, "it sounds like they're still setting up."

"They must know we are coming," Polyphemo noted in disappointment.

"Did you expect anything else?"

"It's a wide front," Darnu said. "They must be spread thin."

"Or there are lots of them," Garjae said.

"We could keep looking," Pasith suggested. "Their cordon must run out eventually."

"And go where?" Hesperous asked, his tone showing his distaste for the continued involvement of Pasith and the aaranya. "The ridge gets smaller, see? Less cover for us. And the point is to find our king and the papayamala."

When Pasith still looked puzzled, Polyphemo explained, "We must assume that the humans are guarding the way to our destination. To go around them is to miss what we came for."

"So it's through them or leave unsatisfied," finished Hesperous.

"I'm not sure—" Darnu started.

"Let's go back," Hesperous interrupted. "We attack through the centre. Like you say, they must be spread thin, we will force our way through them."

"Where do you think Senna is?" Tilvy asked quietly as they followed the samudraka back down along the beach.

"If she's smart she's a long way from here by now," Garjae said.

Darnu nodded. "That's one of the reasons why I don't want to send Nuttachen. It's dangerous up there for anything that shows up on their detector. If Senna *is* there then we might draw attention to her, and if she's not then it's risking Nuttachen for nothing."

Polyphemo had dropped back from the samudraka to walk with them. He asked, "Do you think you might be able to sneak up and disable their detectors for a time? We wouldn't need long. Once we get among them their guns will be less effective weapons."

"You want us to lead the attack?" Garjae asked.

"You did before, in the city," Polyphemo reminded him.

Garjae grunted. That was different.

494

They had tried to teach some of the samudraka the trick of using a cloak to hide from the detector field, but the samudraka didn't use clothing as such, unless you accepted the way they converted their tails into covered legs. Few of the ones they tried to teach could even manage simple clothing common to the aaranya and jalaja, and none of them came close to the fine detached material needed for a cloak to be effective.

"Asha must be back there somewhere too," Tilvy said, "and John now."

The sun was already partly obscured by clouds, it would set in little more than an hour. Sometime after that the samudraka would attack, with or without help from Garjae and the others. Tilvy was right, Garjae acknowledged to himself, Asha must be up there somewhere and that was why they had come all this way.

- - -

Asha had drawn more strongly on the tree than she should, but it might be her last chance and she needed as much strength as she could get. What made it worse was having drawn at it so quickly, pulling at the life of the tree as if she had been truly starving. Standing out beside it the effect was obvious to her senses. Given time without other stresses it should recover. She stroked the bark with her hand, silently apologising for what she had done.

For herself, the force feeding had worked. Life surged through her body. Her depression had been pushed aside by the sheer energy she had consumed. She felt good, even confident. Not to put too fine a point on it, she felt amorous, aroused. The knowledge that John was close by only exaggerated the feeling. She was pleased Jaimee wasn't nearby, it was exactly the sort of thing he was likely to pick up on.

She placed her hands over her stomach, sensing for the life within. Even her child felt a little stronger. It might not be enough, no amount might be enough, but she had done what she could to prepare herself for the night to come. There may be no more nights to worry about.

The light faded abruptly. The trees obscured the western sky but they had already warned her what was coming, and Asha could feel the change in the air. A tingly feeling that was oddly suited to her excited body. A storm. But not for a while yet, not until after dark.

Jaimee said he would come for her before dark, he hadn't said how long before. She had about an hour before sunset, she hoped it would be enough.

Peren?

There was a brief delay before Asha felt Peren's presence enter her mind. <*You feel different,*> she observed.

Asha ignored that. Where is everyone?

<*Helix has gone out, I think she'll be gone for a while. Jaimee, Sando and Stephenson are all down in the computer room.*>

John and my brother?

<*Still locked up. They haven't been let out since they got here.*>

Why not?

<*I think Jaimee is nervous of your brother. No one knows what he does.*>

If he does anything. Asha forced herself to concentrate. And Reyndani?

<*Reyndani has not long returned after delivering meals to the cabins. The few staff left are getting ready to eat in the kitchen.*>

Dhumraka?

<*There's a few around, but they're all outside the fence line, they won't see you.*>

Keep an eye on your brothers.

<*Yes, ma'am.*>

Asha felt a nervous chuckle come from Peren as her presence faded. Asha guessed she had been a bit abrupt, she had too much energy for subtlety. She ran across the lawn to the front door. It felt good to be moving. She pushed her way through the door and ran to the first intersection of passageways. The temptation was strong to try and see John. She pushed the thought away. He would understand.

She ran lightly the other way and then stopped. This would take her past the kitchen. There were still some staff that might sense her presence. Reyndani would certainly recognise her. She backtracked to the large room that opened into the courtyard. She opened one of the glass doors, slipped through and carefully closed it.

"Oh! You startled me," Angel said.

Asha turned and tried to push the shock and guilt from her face. "I thought you would be resting."

"I came out to enjoy my garden, and my daughter's trees," Angel explained. "Jaimee insists that we might have to leave tonight. I really will miss this place. I'm afraid ... I was going to say I'm afraid I won't know what to do with myself, but, Asha, I'm just afraid." Angel stepped close to Asha and hugged her tightly. "I'm scared," she whispered. "I haven't been this frightened in a long time."

Asha returned the old woman's embrace, and murmured, "There's no need. Jaimee's just being careful, they're all very protective of you."

Angel nodded against Asha's shoulder. "They've been very good to me. Everything a mother could possibly hope for, and more. More than I deserve."

"I'm sure that's not true," Asha murmured, absently. This side of the house lay in deep shadow. It wouldn't be long until dark.

"I've never really thanked you," Angel said. "I know it's not working. My children keep telling me otherwise, but I'm not so far gone that I can't tell for myself. You have tried very hard to help me, and you've kept trying."

"There's really no n—"

"There is," Angel interrupted. "I have treated you abominably at times."

"You were afraid."

Angel nodded. "But still you tried. Very few people, other than my children, have ever shown me true kindness. Thank you."

Asha kissed the woman's cheek. "It's what I do. Now come on, you'd better go up and rest or you won't feel up to coming out and enjoying your home again tomorrow."

Angel smiled and let Asha urge her in through the door.

Asha resisted the impulse to slam the door behind the old woman. As soon as Angel turned away, Asha ran as fast as she could for the entrance on the far side. She forced herself to stop and feel her way inside. No one. She went through and ran quickly down the corridor.

She could hear talking in the kitchen, but there was no one in the corridor itself. She slipped into the surveillance room. The placed confused her. So many screens and pieces of electronic equipment, it all seemed a jumbled mess. Peren had said there were spare keys here.

It took a conscious effort to calm herself down and concentrate. She found the drawers that Peren had described and quickly rummaged through them. No keys in the first draw. In the second drawer were several bunches of keys, but these were the primary set. Asha moved down to the third. More keys. Too many. Which ones were the right ones?

<Those ones,> Peren said.

In her panic Asha hadn't felt Peren's presence arrive. Thanks.

<Hurry, I think Jaimee's getting restless.> Peren's presence vanished again.

Asha grabbed the keys that Peren had indicated and rushed out. The door closed with a slam that echoed down the passageway. Asha bolted before anyone could come to investigate.

Outside again. Asha ran down the path between the trees, the bundle of keys jangling in her hands. She got to the gate outside Tracey's cabin and started fumbling through the keys. Which one? Peren hadn't come back, so Asha tried a key. It didn't fit. The metal was awkward to hold and the whole bunch slipped through her fingers and dropped to the ground. She picked it up again and tried another key – it could have been the same one for all she could tell. It didn't fit.

"Asha?"

Asha dropped the keys again in fright. It was Tracey with Ray and Paul not far behind. Asha tapped the mesh once and bent for the keys again.

The next key fit in the lock but wouldn't turn.

"Show me," Ray said.

Asha held up the set.

Ray squeezed his fingers through the mesh and grasped a key. "That one."

It worked, Asha unlocked the gate. When Ray tried to come out she put her hand against his chest and rapped the keys against him twice.

"No?"

Asha pulled at his hand and led them all back inside the cabin. The pad and pencil were still on the table. She dropped the keys on the table and scribbled out the message she had been preparing in her mind. When she was done she stepped back. She wanted to run,

498

but first she had to make sure they understood.

Ray read it over then looked where he thought Asha must be standing. "Okay, that's clear enough. We'll see you later."

Asha turned and ran, the cabin door slamming behind her. She paused at the gate and closed it carefully so that from a distance it would still look to be locked, then she ran back to the house.

<Jaimee's coming out!> Peren warned her.

The others?

<Still down there.>

Where is he?

<He's already in the passage, he's in a hurry.>

I can't get out front before him. Let me know when he goes out the front door. Asha reached the house but waited outside the glass door.

<Now.>

Asha eased herself in and ran as quietly as she could to the front. Where is he? she asked, but she didn't need an answer, she could hear him calling for her.

She tried to calm herself and then pushed out through the door. "Jaimee?"

He turned in surprise.

"I was waiting in there." Asha pointed to the room at the side.

He frowned for a moment and then relaxed.

<I assured him that's where you had been,> Peren whispered, then disappeared again.

"There's a storm coming," Jaimee noted.

Asha nodded.

"It could complicate things."

She shrugged. She could only hope that they complicated things in her favour.

"Come on, let's get you safely away. Everyone's going to be even more jumpy with a storm about."

Asha followed him meekly back into the house. Jaimee collected the main set of keys from the surveillance room and led her back to her cage. He unlocked the cage and turned. He seemed to see her properly for the first time.

"You look good. Very good." He stepped closer.

Asha considered trying to take advantage of the situation. She could pretend to be attracted. From the way Jaimee was looking at her, she knew that her body was giving out all the right signals. Jaimee was vulnerable to her as perhaps no one else. Once she was close to him, perhaps holding him, she could cut – Ulvanya had shown her how. Jaimee wasn't expecting anything. Perhaps she could end it all right here. The abhorrence she felt at the thought of causing injury, worse, she knew she must not stop at just injury, fought with what she knew about Jaimee.

The moment passed. Jaimee shook himself free of his daze and stepped back. He warned the others away from the gate and motioned Asha inside.

Jaimee locked up behind her. He gazed at her for a long time before turning away. He started to walk, then stopped and looked toward Tracey's cabin. Asha froze. What would she do if he went over there? Jaimee shrugged and walked back to the house.

Asha took Ellie from Barma. The others pressed questions, even Taiza seemed alert now, but she shook her head. She needed time to think.

Her people were dying. Aaranya, narun of all kinds, were dying or being made slaves. All at the whim of these few who thought they had the right. The thought of all that suffering sickened her ... but it was also nebulous, outside herself. More personal concerns pressed at her. Her friends. Her brother. John.

John was close by. Asha could feel him. She couldn't be certain the feeling wasn't imagination fed by the knowledge that Peren had given her, but it didn't matter. It only mattered that he was close. Within reach. But Jaimee had said nothing. He controlled access. The only reason why he didn't control whether John lived or died was that John was going to die anyway, it was too late to change that. All Asha could hope to change was how he died, and perhaps where.

She stroked Ellie's tiny bald grey head. The child was fading fast, Asha would have to feed her again soon. But not too much. Enough that Ellie might survive until John was with them, she wouldn't survive much beyond that whatever Asha did now. Asha would conserve the rest, perhaps even top up again from the tree here. Her plans were drastic, they called for drastic measures. She was thankful that Peren was too distracted to be watching Asha's thoughts.

Some time through the day, Asha couldn't have said exactly when, her mind had fastened on a single definite conclusion. Whatever else happened, whether the samudraka won their way through or not, whatever the cost, Asha was determined that it would end tonight.

25. Storm

The stream was tiny, not even deep enough to let them submerge. But Pasith suggested that its life may add to the protection of their cloaks and further obscure their presence from the detector field – Garjae could feel it passing through him as a constant annoying buzz in his head.

Garjae looked back to Darnu wriggling up the stream behind him. "Is it working?" Garjae whispered. He was worried that the water was spoiling the effectiveness of their cloaks.

Darnu nodded.

Behind Darnu was Tilvy, and Pasith drew up the rear.

There had been some argument about Tilvy coming with them, but Tilvy was insistent. She wasn't going to be left behind. Garjae could understand that. He mightn't like the idea of putting her in danger – and most of the samudraka men had similar ideals of gallantry – but to be left as the solitary remnant of their dwindling group was not something Garjae would want either.

Garjae crawled forward again. There could be dhumraka close by, the dhumraka knew the secret of the cloaks now too and could be hiding among the humans.

He could hear the storm rumbling behind them, it wasn't far away. Gusts of wind that smelt of sea and rain swirled down into the gully that held the stream. It was hoped that the rain may help their attack, obscuring their presence even further.

It was full dark now, even if the moon had been up it would have been hidden by the thick clouds. John had told them that humans had night-vision glasses, but such things wouldn't let them see the narun, so the advantage would lie with the samudraka if they could get close enough to make use of their spears.

Darnu touched Garjae's foot and they stopped and listened. Human voices, still distant. Garjae crawled on.

They stopped when they reached the low trees where the humans had established their line. The land had risen here and gave a good view over the rough ground and low growth that lay between the trees and the ridge above the beach. An ideal place on which to mount their detectors and watch for attack.

The stream gully was shallow here so they were careful to stay quiet and low to the ground. Darnu slid up one side and peered out from beneath the hood of his cloak. After a few moments he slid back down and whispered to them.

"There are a couple of dhumraka up there, cloaked and spaced out behind the humans. They don't seem to be armed."

"Can't be seen carrying spears around by the humans," Garjae whispered.

Darnu nodded his agreement.

"What do we do?" Tilvy asked.

"You two concentrate on the equipment," Darnu said to Tilvy and Pasith. "Try to destroy it if you can. Pull the cables or smash the boxes or something. Garjae and I will try to keep the dhumraka off you." He glanced at Garjae.

"Fine with me," Garjae said.

"The important thing is to keep moving," Darnu continued. "We want to get as many of those things as we can, and we don't want to give the humans a chance to work out where we are."

They prepared to rush out, but turned their heads as a noise came to them out of the west. Rain. In the darkness of the night it was a dark grey sheet sweeping in from the ocean.

"I vote we wait for it to get here," Pasith said.

Darnu nodded.

Lightning flashed overhead and the immediate concussion of thunder shook the ground beneath them.

- - -

The constant repetition of draining herself to feed others and then trying to rebuild herself from the life of the trees had honed Asha's natural talent. What she had done only once before, lost in the grip of rage and despair, she had now done deliberately. She was sorry, of course she was. She hated what she had done, but this was the path she had chosen. Sacrifice. Angel's word. And that thought led to doubt. What right did Asha have to do this? The tree's life had been sacrificed to her need. Where would it stop?

Only thin tendrils of life were left now, the tree could hardly hold Asha's substance within itself. I'm sorry, she whispered silently, guiltily.

She felt a hand try to merge with the tree. Barma. Such life as there was left now was mostly hers. His presence touched her.

"They're here," he said, and withdrew.

She emerged, stumbling slightly from the unexpectedly easy exit. She glanced back and looked up into the branches. There was so little life left that the tree was barely visible in the dark, just a faint and fading ghost. She felt another stab of regret at the life she had taken. It wouldn't be the only life lost tonight. Make it mean something, she told herself, and turned back to the others.

Tracey, Paul and Ray were standing outside the gate. For some reason the others were still inside. It took Asha a few moments to realise that they were all standing perfectly still, as if frozen in place, and another few moments to understand that they were all staring at her. Even the humans.

- - -

"Do you see what I see?" Paul whispered quietly.

Tracey nodded, though in the dark the response was pointless.

Gusts of wind blew one way and then another around them. A couple of heavy spots of rain fell, but the expected downpour didn't follow. No one moved.

"Who is it?" Ray asked.

"Asha." Tracey was surprised at the confidence of her own response.

Standing not far inside the gate was a faintly glowing figure. Most of the shape was barely visible, like trying to follow fireflies in the dark. A curve of a hip would flicker into sight, then the line of a leg or an arm. But the upper torso and head showed distinctly in the blackness of the night and approaching storm. The subtle curves of small breasts showed over a brighter glow from within. The delicate lines of a feminine face were visible, a brightness where there should be eyes, and even wispy lines that might have been hair.

504

The figure walked toward them. Tracey almost stepped away, fearful of the power she sensed emanating from this being, but then she remembered the comfort that Asha had given when Tracey most needed it. There could be no harm from this woman. Tracey held out her arms.

Asha stepped into the embrace. Tracey felt as if she were holding fire. Heat suffused her body. The feeling was distinctly sensual, sexual, urgent. In embarrassment, Tracey broke contact.

"We should get moving," Ray said.

Tracey was thankful for the intrusion.

"But before we go, Asha, I need to visit their computer room again. Can we do that?"

\- \- \-

Tracey's acceptance of Asha had broken the stasis that had fallen over their group, but still none of the aaranya had found words for what they were witnessing. Barma remembered Ceeda describing how Asha had appeared to glow after drawing heavily on the trees in the prison, Barma had thought that must have been exaggeration. It wasn't. Life was radiating from her. Always a pretty woman, now Asha was spectacularly beautiful. It was difficult to look at her and remember what they should be doing.

Asha came to Barma and reached out. He released Ellie into her arms. "I'm sorry we were staring," he said quietly. "You look ..."

"Freaky?" Asha asked, a slight smile at one corner of her mouth.

"I was going to say good."

"Understatement, lad," Taiza said.

They both turned to him in surprise. Taiza's recovery had come a long way, but words were still unusual. He said nothing more.

Asha went back to the humans and took Ray's hand.

Barma took this opportunity to go to Tracey. When he took her hand she turned to him with a look of surprise.

"Barma?"

He patted her hand once.

"How did you—?" she started and then broke off. "I guess explanations will have to wait."

Asha was already leading Ray away and Barma pulled on Tracey's hand to follow. Beenae took Paul's hand, Taiza came behind.

"I'm glad to be led," Paul said quietly. "I can't see anything except

Asha."

"I fell over three times just getting here from the cabin," Tracey whispered to Barma.

Barma rubbed her arm in reassurance. He could see clearly enough here, the life of the grass and the trees they were approaching were clear to his senses.

"How come she doesn't cast any light around her?" Paul asked.

"I don't think it's really light," Tracey said, "it's just the way we see her."

Barma tapped her hand once.

The wind was getting stronger now, and as they passed beneath the trees the branches creaked and groaned. There were more heavy spots of rain, a few of which made it through the leaves writhing overhead. There was the hint of a flash of light somewhere high and far ahead of them, a few seconds later came the rumbling of thunder. The storm would break soon.

- - -

"What are you doing, Peren?" Jaimee asked impatiently.

There was a delay before she spoke. *<I was checking with Lantea, she's still a long way from the beach. I don't think she's going to take part.>*

"So you still don't know what they're up to? When and how they're going to attack?" The frustration made his voice loud and abrupt.

<No,> Peren answered meekly.

"And the king?"

<Still sitting with the dhumraka.>

"Don't worry, brother," Helix said, "he's mine. He's not going anywhere I don't want him to."

Sando was looking out the window. They were in a large room on the top floor. Normally it had a good view through the tops of the trees to the hills below them, but tonight the view was only darkness, broken with the occasional, still distant, flash of lightning.

"The storm could make it difficult to take the helicopter out of here," Sando remarked.

"It won't be a problem," Helix said confidently, "not even if they get past the humans. The samudraka may be supreme in the ocean, but they won't find the dhumraka such easy pickings in the forest."

506

"And even if some do get through, they're unlikely to get this far much before dawn." Jaimee added. "The storm will be gone by then."

There was silence for a while, each lost in their own thoughts. Sando glanced into the corner of the room where Stephenson sat quietly at a table, waiting to answer the radio if anyone called, or to respond to the demands of the siblings if they should want anything. Over the table was spread a large map with various labels sitting on it, designations agreed with the army so they could coordinate actions from here.

Stephenson noticed Sando's attention and nodded. Stephenson looked supremely confident, Sando thought, and why shouldn't he? He had been with Jaimee one way or another for most of his very successful life. He had no reason to doubt anything that Jaimee said, and Jaimee said they would defeat the samudraka tonight. Sando wished he shared his brother's confidence. Since reaching their maturity they had never faced such a hazard. If enough samudraka made it through, they could overwhelm the siblings despite the power that each of them possessed.

"I'm bored," Jaimee announced. "Why don't we bring up our two guests? We can introduce Asha's brother to Helix and see how they get on."

<No!> Peren said urgently.

"What? Why not?"

<I think it's starting. Just wait a minute while I check.>

Out the window a bright flash of lightning filled the sky. The thunder, when it came, vibrated the windows.

- - -

It didn't take long. The rain fell in huge heavy drops and visibility dropped to a few metres. Garjae waited a few moments then rose to his feet. The others were right behind him. He had only gone a few steps when gunshots rang out. Garjae ducked down, waiting for death. Darnu crouched on his left, Tilvy and Pasith on his right.

Darnu called over the noise of the rain. "I don't think they're shooting at us."

"The samudraka must have attacked early," Pasith called back, "using the rain for cover."

There was no safety here, no reason to wait, so they ran on. The noise and flashes of gunfire made it easy to find the first group of soldiers. There was light glowing from a large screen amid a cluster of men, most of them were shooting blindly out into the rain. Even from where he stood, Garjae could see the mass of glowing spots moving down from the top of the bright display.

Without much thought for what he was doing, Garjae pushed soldiers aside as he came in from behind. He was aware of Darnu behind him, knocking out soldiers to protect Garjae as he went for the screen. The soldier behind the screen turned to see what the disturbance was, one hand reaching for the rifle at his side. Garjae swung a hand at the soldier's face, felt the slight give as the substance of his hand met the prana of the man's body, and the soldier fell back unconscious.

Garjae tried to pick up the screen, intending to smash it on the ground, but his fingers couldn't find purchase on the strange material. He had better luck with the gun the soldier had dropped. He fired it at the screen. Pieces of glass and metal and plastic flew out in all directions, Garjae felt the sting as a few of them hit him. The screen went dark.

He heard a grunt from Darnu and turned to see him in a struggle with a dhumraka. Garjae swung the gun he still had in his hand. The barrel buried itself in her neck. It was a woman. She turned, calling out in pain and clutching at the wound. Garjae was still staring at her in surprise when a soldier, stumbling past them, blundered into her and they both fell down.

Darnu pulled at his arm. "Come on. Keep moving."

"Where are the others?" Garjae shouted over the noise.

Darnu waved vaguely ahead of them. So much for plans, thought Garjae.

They passed a confused group of soldiers. Two of them were trying to get their screen working – Tilvy and Pasith had obviously been here. Garjae realised he still had the rifle in his hand, so he fired it. The screen blew into pieces. Soldiers swore and turned around, looking for the source of the attack.

Darnu tore the rifle from Garjae's hand and threw it to one side before pushing Garjae the other way and pressing him to the ground. Gunfire erupted over them. Soldiers screamed as they were hit by others firing at the unseen enemy. Keeping low to the ground,

Darnu and Garjae made their way out of the confusion, eventually pulling themselves up behind one of the larger trees.

Garjae wondered whether there was any point trying to get to any more detectors. It looked like every soldier was already firing their weapons in one direction or another, even when they no longer had access to a screen.

"We should find Tilvy," Darnu called over the noise of gunfire, wind and rain. "We should be together when the samudraka reach here."

Garjae nodded. In all this confusion the samudraka were as much a danger to them as the humans.

- - -

The doors to the computer room closed with a light click.

"What are we doing here, Ray?" Tracey asked.

Asha thought it was a good question. She had her own plans, but she couldn't start them until she got her friends on their way out, and she hadn't allowed for this side trip. The energy she had taken in was pressing at her and making her impatient.

"We need to try and get the links closed," Ray answered. "If these people win through tonight, they'll be able to use all this to pick us up within a few days."

"Only if we use your contacts, boss," Paul countered.

Ray shook his head. "If we want to go home then it's going to show up on here somewhere. But that's not the only reason. Even if they lose tonight, these links will still exist. Someone else might stumble on them. They have to be closed."

Paul sat at one of the keyboards, pressed a couple of keys, and looked back to Ray. "Okay, boss. What do we do?"

Ray slumped. "You're the young one that's supposed to know all this stuff, I was assuming you could tell me."

"I know how to get in and find things, usually that's the hard part. It's not an issue here, everything's open. We're already in and no one seems to have noticed."

The room lights flickered and went out. There was a series of clicks and beeping sounds came from boxes all around the room. The computer screens stayed on. Asha's first response was to look to Taiza, but he was standing quietly next to Beenae.

Paul continued speaking slowly, looking around the room, like the others he was wondering what had happened. "... I have no idea how to close a link that's wide open like these."

One dull rumble shook the room, and then another, and a third. The room lights flickered on and the rumble settled back to a low hum.

"Generators kicked in," Paul said. "They must have lost power."

"Storm," Taiza said. Asha glanced at him again. He had moved to one of the computer terminals and was pressing keys. She frowned at Beenae, he shrugged.

Ray fiddled with the keyboard in front of him, and the screen changed a few times. Tracey was watching over Paul's shoulder looking as bewildered by it all as Asha felt.

"Noise," Taiza said.

Beenae reached out to move his hands from the keyboard.

Taiza pushed him away. "Noise," he repeated. "Make noise. Delete. Change. Create."

It slowly dawned on Asha that Taiza's mind may be working better than they realised. The problem was getting it out. His speech had always been strange, perhaps this was just a variation.

She hitched Ellie into a more comfortable position and bent next to Ray. Slowly, with her one free hand, she typed out Taiza's words.

Ray repeated them out loud.

"It might work," Paul agreed.

"But these are important systems," Tracey said. "What if you delete people's bank accounts, or, or ... set off missiles or something."

"I don't think that's likely," said Ray.

"And they'll have backups of most of it," said Paul. "The point is to make them notice that something changed without proper authorisation. It will all appear in audit logs and security alerts, they'll be able to track it."

"And the bigger the changes the faster it gets noticed," said Ray. "I just got us kicked off the FBI."

"You've started?" Paul asked in surprise.

"Why not, do you have any better ideas?"

Paul turned back to his keyboard. "Whose bank account would you like me to delete?" he asked Tracey.

"I think Taiza just deleted a whole computer," Beenae said

proudly from his place behind Taiza. "Would it be all right if I tried?" he asked Asha.

She shrugged helplessly, she understood little of what had been said. She looked at Barma. "Did you want to get in on it too?"

Barma shook his head but smiled. "Sounds like Andrei's sort of fun, but I think I'll skip it."

Tracey too was standing back out of the way.

<Asha, your friends had better hurry. The samudraka have broken through the first line of humans. I don't know what's going to happen next, but you're running out of time.> Peren's presence vanished as quickly as it had arrived.

- - -

"He wants to pull back," Stephenson reported after a brief conversation on the radio.

"What? No!" Jaimee snapped back.

"It's pouring rain there. His men are in confusion, many are already dead from their own gunfire."

As if to emphasise what Stephenson had said, the rain swept in against the house, pounding the windows in bursts of loud static.

"I don't care how many of his men are dead," Jaimee shouted back. "That's what they're there for. I want him to take as many of the samudraka out as he can, whatever it costs."

Stephenson picked the radio back up. "Negative, Point Prime, you are not cleared to withdraw. I repeat, *not* cleared to withdraw."

"Peren?" Jaimee called.

<What?>

"What can you see?" he asked in exasperation.

<Not much. Two of the dhumraka I had contact with are dead, the others can't see much in the rain. They're mostly hiding from humans that are firing in every direction.>

"Have the samudraka really reached them? Can you tell that much?"

There was a pause. *<Yes. They're everywhere.>* Sando felt Peren flinch. *<Another dhumraka just died,>* she reported flatly.

"Helix?" Jaimee asked.

"What? I'm not sending more of my people into that!"

"Can you add to what Peren said?" Jaimee asked as if it should have been obvious.

Helix shook her head.

The lights flickered and when out.

"Fuck!" said Sando.

"Is this—?" Helix started.

The lights came back on again.

Jaimee seemed not to notice that anything had happened. He walked to the table and looked over the map. Stephenson stood, anticipating orders.

"Sando, did you manage to get what I wanted?"

"Sure, there's some with Point Angel." Sando kept it short, aided by the military designation for the last line of human soldiers between the estate and the coast. With Jaimee in this mood it didn't do to go into long explanations. More thunder rattled the windows and still the rain kept up its roar.

"Peren, I want you out checking with everyone."

<Okay.>

"Check with Lantea too, and this time make sure. I don't want any more surprises."

<Yes, Jaimee.>

Jaimee waited a few moments, waiting to be sure that Peren was gone. "Helix, drop your people back behind the next line of humans. Drop far enough back that they won't be seen, but keep them between us and the samudraka just in case."

"Keep the humans out of it," Helix argued, "and let my people fight, Jaimee, they're a match for the samudraka on land."

"Just do it, sister."

Helix looked at Sando. He lifted his shoulders. He didn't know what this was about either, but they had always deferred to Jaimee's judgement when it came to tactics, and Sando wasn't about to change that now.

"But leave the king behind," Jaimee added. "It's time we gave the samudraka back their leader. You'd better rough him up a bit first, it will be more convincing. Walt?"

Stephenson nodded.

"Consolidate Point Angel back to here," Jaimee pointed to the map. "We'll leave the dhumraka to watch for any stragglers, they're better equipped for it. I want all the rest of the forces to converge here." Jaimee's finger slid over to one side.

Stephenson frowned.

Helix, watching over Jaimee's shoulder, looked puzzled. "But ...?"

Jaimee turned to her and grinned. "I'm not mad, my beautiful sister. All will become clear."

- - -

They found Tilvy huddled over Pasith. He was okay, just having some trouble getting himself together after being knocked over by a soldier that had run into him.

The wind and the torrential rain continued, making it hard to see any distance. It obscured and distorted the sounds coming from all around them. Rapid gunfire. Screams, both human and narun. Shouting voices, and the clash and rattle of people fighting.

"Time to get out of everyone's way," Darnu said.

Garjae and Tilvy helped Pasith to stand, and they made their way through the rain. They passed two human soldiers wrestling in the mud, apparently each was unaware that the other was a friend.

They passed many bodies. Mostly human, some dhumraka, and a few samudraka. One of the samudraka was still alive. A woman, her yellow-brown skin dashed with black. With one hand she clutched at a wound in her stomach, the golden prana leaking quickly through her fingers, with the other hand she threatened them with her spear. When she recognised them she lowered the point.

"I weaved left when I should have ducked right," she told them.

Pasith was managing okay now, so Garjae and Darnu knelt down to see if they could help the woman to shelter. Garjae went to put the spear to one side, but the woman clutched at his arm. "You might want to hold onto that."

Mostly carrying the warrior, they found a tree with a hollow where the ground fell away to one side. It was wet and miserable, everywhere was wet, but here most of the water gushing down the hill was diverted away from their hollow by the trunk of the tree.

A group of four samudraka came upon them and probably would have attacked except the wounded woman called out and told them to stop. "These are the king's," she said. The pale blue warriors disappeared back into the rain.

After a time the rain diminished and the sounds of battle grew less. Gunshots still rang out, but were quickly silenced. The screams now were all human, and those didn't last long.

Footsteps, too heavy to be narun. Garjae picked up the woman's spear. He glanced at her to see if she disapproved. She had gone still. Her hand had fallen away from her wound and lay limp at her side. She had died without a sound.

The footsteps stopped beside their tree. They could see the soldier, but in the darkness the young human was virtually blind, he looked pale and frightened. Garjae could hear the soldier's heavy breathing and the occasional rattle of the equipment he was carrying.

The soldier's head snapped around when he heard something to the side. He took a step back, lost his footing on the slope and fell. He landed heavily, splashing mud over Garjae and the others, and began sliding down the slope. He lost grip on his rifle and flailed around with his arms trying to stop himself. He came to a stop, swore softly and started to get up. A large figure came out of the rain and swung a spear under the man, slicing it up through his throat. The soldier gurgled and twitched for a moment and then lay still.

"Polyphemo?" Darnu called out.

The figure looked up at them and Garjae saw that Darnu was right. Another four of the jade green Marr warriors emerged through the rain.

"I thought you might have kept going," Polyphemo said when he came up to them.

"I doubt if there's anything better further on," Darnu replied.

Polyphemo nodded at that and then studied the dead samudraka woman for a moment before looking around. "You'd better stay with us. The humans continue to attack from the sides but they have lost the advantage."

They followed Polyphemo down the slope. The rain slowed to a windswept drizzle and Garjae could sense more figures in the dark around them. He didn't know how many samudraka must litter the ground behind them, but there were a lot still moving, undaunted by the battle they had just been through.

"You started early," Garjae said.

"Hesperous insisted," answered Polyphemo.

- - -

Tracey stood beside the car, the door was open waiting for her to get in.

514

"Come with us," Tracey said again to the glowing figure before her.

Two taps on her hand.

"It feels wrong to be leaving you behind."

Her hand was squeezed warmly.

"Come on, Tracey," Paul called.

Tracey couldn't hold back the tears so she let them flow. She didn't ask whether she would meet Asha again, the answer seemed self-evident. They hugged. That same warmth filled Tracey's senses but her sadness kept other feelings at bay. "Thank you ... for everything," Tracey whispered. Asha gave her a squeeze and then pulled out of her arms.

Feeling bewildered and guilty, as if she was doing something very wrong, Tracey climbed into the car. The door was closed behind her. An arm went around her and squeezed. It was Barma. Paul was in the front passenger seat, Ray was driving. Tracey and the aaranya were in the back.

Through the windscreen Tracey watched the indistinct glow of Asha make its way back to the door into the house. Ray pressed a button on the dashboard and the garage door behind them began to open. He started the car.

"I was hoping I wouldn't need lights," Ray muttered.

"Parkers only?" Paul suggested.

Dim light filled the garage space. Tracey couldn't see Asha any longer, but didn't know if that was because she was gone or because of the light.

"Wait a minute," Paul said. He opened the door and got out. The car shook a few times and Tracey heard the tinkling sound of breaking glass. Paul got back in.

"We don't need tail lights," Paul explained.

The rain was still falling heavily as the car crept back, the sound on the car roof drowned out the engine. The car stopped and then crept forward slowly.

"Damned if I can see where we're going," Ray said. He had his head pressed against the side window to try and follow the edge of the road in the weak glow of the parking lights.

"Damned either way, boss," Paul remarked. "If they see us they may call ahead."

"And the longer we take, the more time someone has to look," Ray finished.

Tracey squeezed Barma's hand. She had imagined this escape since Paul had first described it. In her mind it was always a headlong rush, but here they were creeping along at barely a walking pace.

They had been driving for what seemed an eternity when the car jerked to a halt.

"What's wrong?" Tracey asked nervously from the back.

"Tree," Ray answered. "I lost the road. Did you take out the reversing light too?" he asked Paul.

"Dunno. You want me to check?"

"Don't bother. I think we're far enough."

The car moved back a short way and then slowly forward again, as if feeling its way through the dark and rain. Another eternity. Tracey was shivering, she couldn't tell if it was cold or fear.

"Doesn't look like they're expecting us," Paul announced.

The rain had slowed. A light was visible in the darkness ahead of them, coming from the cabin for the guard at the gate.

"No point sneaking any longer." Ray turned to Tracey. "Better put your seat belts on back there, we'll be going faster from here on out."

Tracey helped Taiza and Beenae to share a seat belt, Barma took the centre one, and then she fastened her own.

"All set?" Ray asked.

"Guess so," Tracey answered.

"This is it," Paul said loudly. "Time to get the hell out of here."

Tracey blinked in the sudden brightness as the headlights came on. The engine made itself heard over the rain and the car leapt forward.

There was a loud bang as they hit the first gate. Nerve shattering metallic screeches filled the car and then another bang as they went through the second. The screeching continued for another few seconds before the tangle of gates caught on something at the side of the road and dragged off over the roof.

Tracey was pressed back into her seat as the car accelerated again. She was thrown to the side as they took the first bend.

"Bugger!" Ray called out.

When the door opened, John and Sarva both stood up. When it was Asha that walked in, John's mouth dropped. She was even more beautiful than in his dreams. He took one pace toward her and stopped, noticing the tiny figure held in one arm. Ellie. He looked up into Asha's face. Those eyes.

Unable to move, he said, "Now you're breaking down doors for me?"

"As many as it takes," she answered and smiled. She stepped closer.

John closed the gap and wrapped his arms around her, the tiny figure of Ellie held tenderly between them.

"Would you like me to hold her?" Sarva asked quietly from the side.

John felt Asha's arm loosen and then release him. Reluctantly, John let her go.

Asha turned to Sarva and stared at him silently for a long moment. Without saying a word she handed Ellie to him. She made certain that he had the child securely, then whirled back to John and threw herself against him. John was forced to take a step back. She squeezed him hard and John tried to match her. He lifted her from her feet and twirled. John set her back down and they leaned back so they could see each other's faces. Their hands explored the contours of neck, cheek and eye. A fierce kiss and then another look. Neither quite believed this moment had come.

Once again holding tightly cheek to cheek, John ran his hands up and down Asha's back, feeling her familiar lines. He felt the heat of her body penetrating his, and his body began to respond.

"It's what I want too," she whispered in his ear. "So much you wouldn't believe."

"But ..." he answered.

"But ..." she confirmed.

"Would you like me to step outside?" Sarva asked.

John and Asha tore their bodies apart but their hands refused to let go. They laughed. Being together again was too good to be embarrassed about anything.

"I'm guessing you're not normally this ... intense," Sarva observed. "Someone would have said something."

"I've been preparing for tonight," Asha answered without taking her eyes from John.

"Some preparation. I've got the hots for you, and you're my sister."

That broke Asha's trance, she let go of John to look at her brother. "Where the hell have you been?"

"It's a long story."

"It had better be a good one."

Sarva glanced at John.

"Can I have my daughter?" John asked.

It was still difficult for him to believe that this tiny creature was what was left of his daughter. There was no reaction from the preta as he lifted it high to try and study it. The last time he had touched his daughter her hunger had torn at his prana. In this new body he could feel the draw of her need, but it no longer burned. "Ellie?" he whispered. Still no response. The last time he had held his daughter it was just her human shell. He had cried over it before it was placed in a box to be buried beside her mother. This tiny, grey, shrunken and insensate being was all that was left, and he didn't need Asha to tell him that soon this, too, would be gone. "I won't be far behind," he whispered to his daughter.

It was much quieter now with the susurrus of gentle rain and the musical trickling of water running along small gullies on the hillside. The wind had died down to a soft breeze, with just the occasional stronger gust that shook drops from the leaves in a sudden heavy patter. The samudraka made more noise moving through the forest than the aaranya, but not enough to disturb the deceptive tranquillity of the forest.

When they reached the crest of the hill other sounds came to them from across the valley. Humans on the move. Garjae felt the buzzing of a detector, but too weak to be much concern.

"I can't feel any dhumraka," Pasith said.

"Too far to be sure," Darnu answered.

"What do you suppose they're up to?" Tilvy asked.

"Nothing good," grumbled Garjae.

Polyphemo glanced at him and then away.

Garjae knew that the others thought he was a sour pessimist, but

518

it wasn't pessimism if it was right.

They started slowly down the slope into the valley accompanied by the indistinct forms of samudraka to the side and behind them. Darnu grabbed Polyphemo's arm and pointed. There was someone coming. Spears were brought to the ready. Everyone tensed.

"But ...?" Darnu trailed off.

Polyphemo knelt, his spear held upright beside him. "My king," he said.

Theseo appeared through the trees and the other samudraka warriors knelt.

"I am gratified to find you this far advanced," Theseo announced. "Stand, please," he said to the samudraka, ignoring the fact that none of the aaranya had knelt. "This is not the place for formality."

"You were captured," Garjae said. He received several glares from the samudraka for the accusation in his voice.

"I escaped," Theseo said. "Not without difficulty, as you see." He indicated the cuts and bruises on his torso, and there were two evenly matched cuts on his face, one on either cheek, but these looked older and almost healed.

"And the papayamala?" Darnu asked. "Helix?"

"I didn't meet ... her."

"John and Sarva?" Tilvy asked.

"Are still in their hands."

Theseo spoke with Polyphemo about the disposition of the samudraka, and soon several other samudraka arrived, leaders of other samtaana.

"I don't trust this," Garjae said softly.

"He seems okay," Pasith said. "Nothing like what was said about the aaranya under her control."

Voices grew louder among the samudraka speaking with Theseo. There was a bright flash and Theseo held the zakti over them, it glowed strongly. "By the power of my tail and the strength of my arm, I am King of the Agadharastra. I carry Zamayitar. Are there any here that would challenge my right to command the samudraka?"

The others of the group fell silent, but from around them a cheer rose from the warriors and the zakti flared brighter.

Satisfied that he had asserted himself, Theseo said loudly, "The humans were deployed to divert you from the true path. They didn't expect you to get this far. But, my brave warriors, you have them worried now. You can feel them moving across the valley. They are redeploying to protect the ones we seek. Now is the time for us to show our true strength."

The warriors cheered again, and again the zakti flared.

Theseo lowered the blade. More quietly, he spoke to the leaders around him, "Our forces are too spread out. The humans are consolidating theirs, we must meet strength with strength."

"And the dhumraka?" Darnu asked.

Theseo flashed angry eyes over the aaranya and turned back to the samudraka. "They do not want to match our strength, most have withdrawn behind the humans. I have come through them, I have seen this. When we have wiped away the humans the dhumraka will break before us." Theseo paused to watch the reactions of the other leaders. "Delay serves the enemy. Gather your warriors, we must move on."

The samudraka leaders dispersed, Theseo turned and started back down the slope. Garjae and the others got shunted off to one side by the warriors that drew together to follow their king.

"Am I the only one that thinks he's acting strange?" Tilvy asked.

"He's a king, he's allowed to be rude," Pasith said.

Tilvy looked doubtful.

Garjae didn't like it either, but if Theseo was right about the direction they should be headed then they had little choice but to follow. They had to be there when the samudraka reached Asha to have any chance of saving her.

He noticed Darnu looking off to one side. "What is it?"

"Maybe nothing," Darnu said.

- - -

"Do you see it now, sister?" Jaimee asked.

Helix smiled in return. "We use Theseo and the human forces to draw the samudraka together in a clump."

"The humans will put up a fight, which will draw the samudraka in tighter."

"And then," Sando added his contribution, "we launch the missiles."

"If there are any survivors the dhumraka can clean them up,"

Jaimee finished.

"Point Angel won't be happy about firing on their own men," Sando pointed out.

"Probably not," Jaimee agreed. "They may need persuading. Do you feel like a run down to the front gates to meet a few burly marines from our Point Angel contingent, dear sister?"

<The soldiers are at the front gates?> Peren asked in obvious surprise.

"Didn't I tell you that?" Jaimee asked innocently. "Must have been while you were busy."

"Skin or no skin?" Helix asked.

"Your choice, though a bit of skin always perks up the soldiers."

The radio buzzed and Stephenson picked up. "Go ahead, Point Angel."

"Speak of the devil," Jaimee said cheerfully.

- - -

Asha looked over her brother and tried to adjust to the idea that the mature man before her was what had become of her twin, the youth that had deserted her so many years before.

"I'm guessing this is not the right time to tell it," Sarva was saying.

"No," Asha answered absently. Then more definitely, "No. You should go. I would have sent you with the others—"

"Others?" John interrupted.

"Tracey, Barma," Asha waved her hand vaguely, it was too much to explain in a hurry. "But I wasn't sure I would be able to get to you, and I'm still not sure Jaimee will let you go. The others aren't that important to him, but he will probably hunt for you, Sarva, so it seemed better that you leave separately."

"And you, my long-suffering sister?" Sarva asked.

Asha found Sarva's tone and phrasing irritating. She had spent too long listening to Jaimee and Sando refer to Helix in a similar manner.

"You're not planning on leaving, are you?" Sarva continued.

"No." She looked to John. "I had thought to try and send you away with Sarva, but I don't think I can do it. I know it's selfish but … will you stay with me?"

John stroked the side of her face. "I didn't come all this way just to leave you again."

"What's your plan, Asha?" Sarva asked. "You've obviously prepared yourself for something."

Asha shook her head. "Nothing specific, but Jaimee and Helix have to be stopped. If the samudraka don't make it then I will try to do something. All this," she waved her hand over her body, "is just in the hope that I will have the strength to do what is necessary when the time comes."

"Sando?" John asked.

"If I can. But Jaimee and Helix are critical, it's their ambition that —" Asha stopped to watch Sarva.

He had stepped closer and was studying her.

"What?"

"And the fourth?" Sarva asked. "You haven't mentioned the fourth sibling, yet I think you know her very well."

"Peren," Asha answered. "She's not like her siblings. She helped me get the others out, she helped me get here." Sarva's hand was reaching up to Asha's forehead. She frowned at it.

"No, Sarva," John said. "Wait."

Sarva's hand withdrew.

"You like this woman?" John asked. "You trust her?"

"Yes ... sort of. It's complicated."

"So whatever connection you feel with her, you want to keep it?"

Asha blinked a few times and glanced back and forth between Sarva and John. "Yes."

"Do you think that's a good idea?" Sarva asked.

"Yes! It's too much to explain now. We have to get you out of here."

"I ran out on you once, Asha, I don't plan on doing it again."

"That was a long time ago. It's forgotten."

Sarva raised an eyebrow, giving the statement as much acceptance as it was worth. "You may need some help," he said.

"Either the samudraka will kill whoever they find here, or the siblings will win and kill or enslave whoever is left."

Sarva nodded.

"Is that what you want?" Asha asked, her voice loud in frustration.

"As I told John, what I want doesn't come into it. It never has,"

Sarva responded mildly.

Asha was still trying to understand what that meant when Peren's presence exploded in her mind, *<Jaimee knows everything!>*

"Indeed he does," came Jaimee's voice from the doorway.

26. Touched

When they reached the crest of the next ridge most of the humans had already retreated. One small emplacement held position, their detector radiating strongly. Theseo attacked recklessly, running directly up the slope, ignoring the gunfire blasting down at him as if he were invincible. And it seemed he must be. Warriors on either side of him dropped, but Theseo ran on untouched. He fell among the humans, swinging Zamayitar. The blade flashed brightly again and again. Moments later Theseo stood amid the carnage, looking around for more.

Garjae watched from a safe distance, though safety was relative when guns were being fired in all directions. He could hardly believe it when the warriors arriving after Theseo cheered their king loudly.

"Did they count the bodies he left behind him?" Garjae asked out loud.

"The warrior's creed," said Darnu.

"It looked like more than that to me," Tilvy said. "More like a suicide run."

"Or inspiring his warriors," Pasith offered.

"That much worked, anyway," Garjae said. "Come on, or they'll leave us behind."

The rain got heavier and thunder rumbled, the next front of the storm was coming through. Even beneath the trees they could feel the wind picking up strength.

The samudraka were moving quickly now. Garjae and the others were forced to run wide around the increasing swell of warriors that swept up behind their king. At the next crest the scene would have been repeated except that a group of warriors overtook their king and slaughtered the soldiers before he could get there.

They were down in the next valley when Pasith called out, "Where is Tilvy?"

Garjae and Darnu stopped and looked back. Visibility had dropped again in the heavy rain.

"She saw something and ran out to the side," Pasith pointed, "but there were warriors coming up behind me and I was forced to get out of the way. When I got a chance I ran out wide again but she wasn't there. I thought she'd be back quickly."

"Tilvy!" Darnu called out.

Samudraka warriors were still passing them, some still coming in from the sides. A few glanced at their small group but most ignored them.

They spread out calling for her. It seemed a silly thing to do in the middle of a war zone, but there wasn't much choice.

Garjae turned at the sound of gunfire. He saw flashes from the muzzles of the guns. They quickly fell silent, leaving just the sound of the rain and rapid steps of the samudraka still passing. They had to hurry or they would be left behind. "Tilvy!" he yelled.

"Over here," Darnu called.

Garjae ran to where he thought Darnu must be. Pasith arrived at the same time. Darnu was walking back with Tilvy. She had a strange expression on her face, a mix of horror and excitement. Garjae couldn't make out what it meant.

"Where did you go?" Pasith asked.

Tilvy shook her head.

"Are you all right?"

She nodded.

"We'd better hurry," Garjae urged.

"Yes," agreed Tilvy and started running.

She took them all by surprise with her speed. Garjae pushed himself harder to catch up with her. "What is it?"

"Have to see the king," she answered and ran faster.

The top of the hill was littered with bodies. Samudraka dead outnumbered the humans. At this rate, Garjae thought, they won't have any warriors left when they get wherever it was Theseo was leading them. They ran on in the rain.

At the bottom of the next valley they found the samudraka

congregating, the hurried advance had come to a halt. Tilvy started pushing the large warriors aside, trying to make her way through. Darnu, Garjae and Pasith did their best to keep up.

Tilvy's way was barred by a group of lime-green samudraka.

"I have to see the king," she told them and tried to push her way past. She was pushed back.

"We all want to see the king," one of the warriors told her, "doesn't mean it's going to happen."

Spying a group of the dark-green Marr warriors beyond those blocking her, Tilvy called out, "Can you take me to Polyphemo? It's important."

The warriors pushed their way through and shouldered the lime-green samudraka aside.

"What's this about?" Darnu asked her.

Tilvy shook her head.

The Marr warriors, being of the samtaana of the king, held precedence over the others and space was quickly made for them to pass.

Polyphemo turned in surprise when the warriors called for him.

"I have to see the king," Tilvy told him.

"He's busy."

"It's important."

"What is?"

"There's something he has to see."

Polyphemo looked doubtful.

"Just take me to him, he'll want to see this."

"Wait here," Polyphemo said at last.

"What is it?" Darnu asked again.

"Just something the king has to see," Tilvy answered. She pressed her lips together, obviously not intending to say anything more.

"Why have we stopped?" Garjae asked one of the warriors.

"The king says we must recover our strength for the next push."

"What happened to delay serves the enemy?"

The warrior scowled at him. "We are still waiting for all our forces to come together."

Polyphemo returned with Theseo.

"Yes," the king asked impatiently.

His expression didn't encourage familiarity, but still Tilvy went to him. A warrior lowered a spear to stop her getting too close.

"Please," Tilvy said, "you need to know this."

Theseo pushed the spear away and Tilvy closed the distance. She stretched up to whisper in his ear.

Confusion spread across his features and he stared down at Tilvy in disbelief.

"You need to see this," she repeated.

Lightning flashed somewhere above the trees and thunder followed quickly. The heavy rain rattled the leaves above and fell about them in dribbles and splatters.

There was some sort of war going on behind Theseo's face. Abruptly, he looked away from Tilvy. "There is time. We can't move now. I can see this. I must see this." The interior argument over, he turned to Polyphemo. "But not alone."

Polyphemo nodded his approval.

Tilvy didn't argue, in fact she seemed pleased.

"Which way?"

Tilvy pointed.

Theseo walked quickly, warriors scattered left and right to make way for him. Polyphemo pointed to several of his warriors and they herded Tilvy and the others after Theseo. Once they were outside the assembly Theseo turned to Tilvy again for directions. She led them on through the trees, away from the army of samudraka.

"It's not far," she said brightly.

- - -

<I'm sorry, Asha. I'm so sorry,> Peren kept repeating.

"My dear little sister, what did I tell you?"

<I'm sorry,> Peren whispered quickly and then withdrew from Asha's mind.

"She means well," Jaimee said, "but she just doesn't understand the big picture."

"What big picture?" Sarva asked.

Jaimee glanced at him but returned his concentration to Asha. "I must say, you are looking very good tonight. A bit of intrigue and excitement seems to agree with you. Were you thinking of going somewhere?"

Asha shook her head.

"So this is just for me? I'm flattered." He looked across at John and grimaced. "But I'm forgetting, you already knew he was here, didn't you? Got yourself all spruced up for him, maybe? Seems a waste."

"Is he always like this?" Sarva asked.

Jaimee ignored Sarva and continued, "I'm afraid your friends' joy ride ran into a bit of a snag, well, an army truck. Did nasty things to our car."

"Are they hurt?" Asha asked.

"Bruises mostly, or so I'm told. Helix has gone to collect them all now."

"You promised she wouldn't—"

"And you promised to cooperate."

"You don't need them, let them go," Asha pleaded.

"You should be thankful we're bringing them back at all. I almost decided not to, but as it happens Helix had to go down there anyway, so it's all working out."

Asha felt John come closer and put his arm around her, so she knew she wasn't managing to hide the devastation she felt at this failure. Jaimee's face twitched slightly.

<John's not helping,> Peren's voice came through as the lightest of whispers and vanished again.

Asha straightened herself and tried to subtly urge John to stand clear. He removed his arm but didn't move away.

"Why won't you let Peren speak with me? What harm can it do now?"

"I think you've been a bad influence on my sister. She has always been the tender one of our family, and you've confused her."

"I thought you'd be pleased that there was *one* in your family I actually liked," Asha retorted.

Jaimee stiffened and turned from her, directing his gaze at Sarva. After a few moments he asked, "What is it that you do?"

"Much the same as anyone else. I talk, I walk."

"Too much and in the wrong direction," Jaimee said. "Let's see if we can help with that."

He stepped back into the corridor and Reyndani appeared beside him carrying a ray-gun. Asha felt John stiffen at her side, but he didn't say anything.

"You'll appreciate that my friend here can't be as precise with this

528

as we might like, so you'll understand if I keep behind him while we move. Come on."

"Where is the king?" Sarva asked as he exited the room ahead of Asha and John.

"Would you believe it?" Jaimee answered in tones of feigned incredulity. "He escaped."

Sarva didn't respond except with a tightening of his lips.

Warming to his subject, Jaimee continued, "The courageous king is now once more among his people, waving his pretty blue sword and leading their murderous rampage. There's just no stopping some people. He's so enthusiastic that we had to ask him to slow down a little. We can't have him getting ahead of schedule."

They were directed through the house and out into the courtyard to stand beneath the three great oak trees. Sando was already waiting there. The storm had renewed its intensity and even the thick foliage of the trees couldn't completely block the heavy rain.

John stayed close by Asha, holding Ellie carefully and trying to keep the water off her face. Sarva stood apart from them, and Asha was surprised by the expression on his face.

- - -

Sarva had all the senses of a narun, so the scene beneath these beautiful oak trees was clear to him. Their lush life attracted him and reminded him that it had been days since he last had a chance to merge and recover his strength. But none of that was what disturbed him.

These weren't ordinary oak trees, Sarva had seen that as they approached. Connections, like fine lightening, glimmered out from its branches. There was something here. Something that frightened Sarva badly. Asha was afraid of Jaimee, that much was obvious. It was a feeling Sarva could relate to, he had spent the last three years living in fear of meeting Helix again. He had done all he could to fight her, but the fear of what she was, what she represented, was always present. But what he felt here was raw terror. He felt like screaming.

Asha touched his arm. "It's okay," she reassured him.

He frowned, puzzled. He hadn't been listening. He couldn't tell how long he had been standing in dread of the power that surrounded him.

"We can force you," Jaimee said.

"Go on," Asha urged him. "There's nothing to fear from Peren."

Sarva took a reluctant step forward. Nothing to fear? If only the others could see what was here. Asha was beside him, guiding him to the trunk of one of the trees.

"She gets inside your head," Asha told him softly, "but it's okay. She's not malicious like the others. She's gentle. She doesn't push."

Sarva's eyes met Asha's and pleaded that she not make him do this. There was no room inside his head for anyone else, there was barely room for him.

Asha kissed his cheek and whispered in his ear, "I have missed you. I'm sorry we had to meet like this, but we need to do this. We need to keep pushing ahead until our chance comes to stop it. I think Peren might help. Listen to her."

Sarva reluctantly let his head fall back against the trunk. A rivulet of water broke across his head and flowed down his neck. Asha didn't know what she was asking. Sarva closed his eyes and waited.

Thunder rolled over them from distant lightning. The constant heavy drumming of the rain on the leaves was interspersed with splashes and spatters as the leaves shed their load. Trickling past his ear was the delicate whisper of water washing down the trunk. It was that sound that broke and made him tense. A warmth, fingers, gently touched his head and withdrew.

Something changed. He only noticed it because he was expecting something. A flicker, as if lightning had lit the sky, but there was no corresponding flash from outside his closed eyes. He trembled, waiting for the power to overwhelm him.

He remembered Helix's touch. He remembered the compulsion to abase himself before her. He remembered the overwhelming and helpless love he felt for the beautiful monster. He had broken that connection, but he still had nightmares about the helplessness, and it shamed him that it was this he remembered before Karya and what Helix had done to his beloved.

<Don't you see that it's the same memory? The same fear?>

No, he answered this strange thought silently.

<It is,> the thought insisted. *<You were helpless to save Karya. If you had not broken the connection you would have been more than helpless, you wouldn't have even tried. You fear being that*

helpless again.>

I wanted to save her, Sarva pleaded.

<I know you did.>

There was nothing I could do. No choice that would have saved her life. Helix gave me no choice.

<I know that. I can see that as I've never seen it before.>

There was water running down Sarva's face, mixing with the tears leaking from beneath his eyelids. I loved her.

<I know.>

"Peren!" a voice intruded. Jaimee.

<In a minute, brother,> the thought said irritably.

Brother? Sarva pulled himself away from the trunk and spun around. There was only the wet trunk of the oak tree.

<Sarva, I won't hurt you.>

Sarva stepped further back.

<Please. There's nothing to be frightened of.>

"You're Helix's sister," Sarva called aloud.

<Yes.>

He remembered now, Asha's words, "She gets inside your head," but still he had not recognised her arrival. Her words came like memories of a soft girl-woman's voice. Gentle, reassuring, comforting. But this was Helix's sister.

<But I'm not her.>

No. You're worse.

<No!>

You're much more powerful.

<No.>

You are, I can see it. Sarva's retreat was halted when he bumped into Asha. He turned. She was looking at him with a worried face. She should be worried. Couldn't she tell what insidious power this creature had?

<I'm not a creature.> The voice was weak now, it trembled as if it was upset, as if it had something to fear.

John was beside Asha, watching Sarva with open concern. Sarva could see the bond between this couple, it was strong and clear between them. It glowed in the ether. The same sort of bond had once existed between himself and Karya.

<You're the one!> Peren cried out.

It should have been loud, but it came to Sarva as if from a distance. Another flicker across his senses and he knew that his body had rejected another connection. All he could feel was relief.

- - -

"I think we're close," Tilvy said, and slowed. "Just here somewhere."

Theseo stepped past her. Lightning lit up the forest but showed no sign of anything unexpected. Theseo's question to Tilvy was lost in the thunder.

Darnu pointed. A figure approached them through the trees. Garjae had trouble making it out. It was carrying a spear, but didn't seem large enough for a samudraka. Perhaps a dhumraka.

"You?" Theseo exclaimed.

Lightning flashed and thunder rolled over them.

As the noise died away, the figure said in a smug tone, "I couldn't have timed it better if I'd tried. Aren't you pleased to see me?"

"Andrei," Darnu said.

"You're dead," Theseo said.

"It's a common mistake," Andrei answered. "Tilvy thought so too."

Another flash of lightning and then another and a third. The thunder that followed went on for a long time.

"Enough already," Andrei complained as the sound died away. "I've done my entrance bit. It's hard to get good help these days."

"But you're dead," Theseo repeated.

"You sound disappointed. I thought we were friends."

Theseo drew the zakti, it glowed in his hand.

"You're wondering about Zak?"

Theseo nodded.

"Tricky that, isn't it?" Andrei said, smiling.

"Sarva?" Theseo guessed.

"So you know?"

"He told me, yes."

Andrei held his free hand out, palm up. "We didn't mean anything by it, it just seemed the best way."

Garjae listened to all this in a daze. It turned everything upside down. And he wasn't the only one stunned by Andrei's reappearance. For a time the only sound was the rain and distant thunder.

"Why are you here?" Polyphemo called loudly.

"I'm sorry to tell you that the king is not quite himself. He's been touched."

"You lie," called one of the other warriors. "He has fought with us, killed humans with us. He is our king."

"And all the time leading you the wrong way. The papayamala lie that way." Andrei pointed behind him.

"Why would we believe you?" Polyphemo asked.

"Good question," Andrei acknowledged. "King Theseo, would you care to comment?"

Theseo took a fresh grip on the zakti and tilted the tip to Andrei.

"I thought not. You were followed, Theseo, from the time you left the lovely Helix. Very chummy with the dhumraka you were too."

Theseo swung his blade and Andrei skipped back out of the way.

"Ironic really, isn't it?" Andrei said cheerfully. "I don't have Zak any more, and *now* I'm going to fight you."

"Give him a chance to prove what he says," Garjae called to Polyphemo. The warrior looked worried and confused.

"You must," Darnu insisted. "The lives of your people may depend on it. Why would he make this up?"

"King Theseo?" Polyphemo called.

Theseo turned angrily. "You would listen to these lies?"

"My king, as he was, would have listened to this one." Polyphemo indicated Andrei.

"Do you want proof?" Andrei called. "Theseo, King of the Agadharastra, say these words after me: Helix is a fat bitch that gets off with squids."

An incoherent roar rose from Theseo and he bore down on Andrei with rapid swipes of the zakti. Andrei used his spear to try and divert the blade, stepping back each time another part of the spear was chopped away.

Darnu and Garjae rushed to try and help.

"Stay back," Andrei yelled. "I've got him." He waved his length of spear-shaft at Theseo and another piece was cut from the end.

Garjae pressed forward, but without a weapon there was nothing he could do. And now it was too late. Andrei had backed himself against a tree. He had nowhere to go.

"Say it!" Andrei yelled at Theseo.

"My queen!" Theseo screamed back at him.

Theseo raised his blade. A flash of lightning showed a branch swinging down from the tree. Thunder boomed over them and Theseo fell to the ground, the blade glowing dully as it fell from his hand. Rain washed the golden gash on the side of his head.

Senna dropped out of the tree and landed beside Andrei. He showed her the short stub of the spear left in his hand. "I could have had him with this."

Senna punched his shoulder. "Gets off with squids?"

"Ow. I was improvising."

The others formed a ring around Senna, Andrei and the king.

"Do you believe me now?" Andrei asked Polyphemo.

In answer Polyphemo raised his spear and prepared to drive it through the king's chest.

"No!" Andrei stepped over the king's body and pushed the spear away.

"No?"

"We don't need to kill him. Find Helix. Kill *her* and you can have your king back."

"You know this?"

Andrei shrugged. "Makes sense, doesn't it? Or would you rather have a Raktana for king?"

Senna knelt and pulled the zakti from Theseo's hand. "Just in case he wakes up."

"Don't," Andrei said in panic.

"It's all right," Senna assured him. "The king is not dead, it's still his." She passed it to Andrei.

He pulled his hands away. "It took me too long to get rid of it last time. Give it to him." Andrei pointed to Polyphemo.

"No," Polyphemo said. "She is right. You must mind Zamayitar. It is your place."

"I don't know how you work that out," Andrei grumbled, but took the sword anyway. He was relieved when it failed to react to him.

"What happens now?" Garjae asked. "There's an army of samudraka warriors in battle lust looking for their king."

Andrei put on a pained expression. "Can't you at least let me have my moment of glory before you ask awkward questions?"

534

- - -

Jaimee directed them back into the house, out of the worsening storm. They settled in the large front room. Reyndani, seated not far from Jaimee and Sando, remained alert with the ray-gun directed over the prisoners. Asha had seen enough of Helix's influence to know he would use the weapon without hesitation, despite the affection that once existed between himself and John.

"You can include Asha in our conversation," Jaimee said, "but no private asides."

<Thank you,> Peren answered meekly.

"It's good to hear you, my friend," Asha said.

"None of that shit!" Jaimee snapped at her.

Asha received a disapproving look from Sarva and puzzlement from John. "I can hear Peren in my mind," she explained.

"The sister of Helix and these," Sarva added, casting his hand toward Jaimee and Sando.

"Will you shut up?" Jaimee said. "I'm trying to think."

Sarva opened his mouth to retort, but Asha placed her hand on his arm and squeezed. He closed his mouth again. They were seated together on a wide sofa. On Asha's other side sat John, holding her hand, and with Ellie resting on his lap.

"Say it again, slowly this time," Jaimee said.

<Sarva can see the connections of life. He can help Asha to heal Mama.>

"Are you sure of this? Can you see them now?"

< ... No. I've lost him. I can't talk to him any more, I can't see.>

"Lost him how?"

<I don't know.>

"Has this ever happened before?"

<No.>

Jaimee stared unhappily across at Sarva. "Can you explain this?"

Sarva shrugged and held his palms out. "I guess it didn't take."

There were so many things Asha wanted to ask Sarva, but now wasn't the time. Given the smug expression that Sarva was trying unsuccessfully to hide, she assumed that he knew exactly what had happened to the connection.

"And you would trust this man with our mother?" Jaimee asked.

<I trust Asha,> Peren answered promptly.

Jaimee wasn't satisfied.

"Without help your mother will die," Asha said quietly. "What do you have to lose by trusting my brother?"

Jaimee started to answer, then stopped and grinned past the sofa to the door. "Ah, sister, I'm glad you're back."

Asha felt Sarva stiffen at her side. She turned her head to watch Helix and Stephenson walk into the room.

Jaimee frowned. "Where are the others?"

"I locked the humans in one of the cells, the aaranya got away before my dhumraka could get there," Helix answered.

"The aaranya won't get far. But why lock up the humans? Didn't you take them?"

"Peren said you didn't want that."

"That's a step too fucking far, sister!" Jaimee shouted into the air.

<You don't need them like that,> Peren responded weakly. Asha could feel her cringing under the intense anger of her brother.

"That's for me to say!"

"I can do it now," Helix offered.

Jaimee sat rigid for a moment, then slowly relaxed. "No, sister, there's no need for that. We've got something else on our minds right now." He pointed across at Sarva. "Asha's brother has presented us with an unexpected opportunity."

Helix turned to look at the figures on the sofa. Her eyes widened in shock.

"Hello again," Sarva said. He raised one hand, as if greeting a friend.

"It's him! He's the one," Helix said. She looked suddenly smaller and less confident.

"The one what?" Jaimee said.

"He can break connections. He's dangerous, Jaimee. Kill him! Kill him now!" Helix was almost screaming. When Jaimee didn't react she turned to Stephenson and pointed to Sarva. "Kill him!"

Sarva stood. "It's good to see you again too, Helix."

"Sit down!" Jaimee snapped at him. "Walt, put that down. Helix, relax. He's not going to do anything where he is."

Helix made her way carefully around the room to stand between her brothers, her eyes never left Sarva. It was only now that Asha saw that Reyndani had dropped the ray-gun, his hands were rubbing at the sides of his head.

"You didn't damage him did you, brother?" Jaimee asked.

Sando shook his head. Asha understood. Reyndani belonged to Helix, he would have tried to obey her. Only Sando's intervention had stopped her brother being killed. That left an open question about Stephenson, perhaps he didn't belong to Helix, just to Jaimee.

"Why the panic, sister?" Jaimee asked.

"A couple of years ago—" Helix started.

"Three," Sarva interrupted.

Jaimee flicked his fingers and a cut appeared on Sarva's cheek. "Shut up."

Asha lightly wiped the cut away.

"I told you," Helix started again, "a couple of years ago there was a man that broke the connection I made to him and another."

"You said he was dead."

"I thought he must have been."

"I wasn't," Sarva put in. Jaimee glared at him and Sarva wisely decided not to say the rest of what he had in mind.

"That complicates things," Jaimee admitted. "You see, sister, not only can he break connections, he can see them."

"So?"

"So between the two of them over there we might actually be able to heal Mother."

"He can't be allowed to live," Helix said firmly.

<We need him,> Peren said.

"I don't want to hear from you," Jaimee told her in an angry burst. "Sando?"

"Heal Mother and then kill him."

"Do you think you can force it from him? Helix can't."

Sando studied Sarva. Eventually he shook his head. "I can't be certain ... maybe if I could see what he sees."

"And then we wouldn't need him."

"Do we even know if it can be done?" Sando asked.

"Good question," Jaimee agreed.

Asha saw his eyes move to John and Ellie. Her hopes began to rise. According to Ulvanya they couldn't save Ellie, her mind would remain hidden, but perhaps she could save John. Jaimee's expression lightened and a smile grew on his face. Her hopes faltered but didn't fade.

"The preta would make a good test," Jaimee announced.

"Or John," Asha urged.

"No, he is not the same thing at all. The preta is the one I would like to see healed."

"It would be a start," John said softly. "I know it's not everything, but ..."

Asha nodded. "It might give us time."

"Don't do this, Asha."

She turned to Sarva in shock. "What?"

"You shouldn't do this. Can't you see what he's doing?"

Asha shook her head.

"His hold over you has weakened, he can see that. This is his way of bringing you back under control. He might even go so far as to allow us to heal John, though I wouldn't bet on it. Once they are healed they are new threats he can hold over you."

Asha looked across at Jaimee. The pale face held its familiar confident smile. Sarva was right, but so was Jaimee. This was not an opportunity she could reject.

"I want to heal John," she said to Jaimee.

"The preta first, then we'll see."

John lifted Ellie over to Asha. She met his eyes, there was no doubt there. She glanced back to Jaimee.

"Yes, now," he confirmed. "While we're all here to witness the miracle."

Asha couldn't tell what he meant by that. Was he being sincere or sarcastic?

<They plan to kill Sarva as soon as Mama is healed,> Peren whispered.

Asha concentrated on Ellie, trying not to give away her awareness of Peren. Won't Jaimee know you're here? Asha asked silently.

<He doesn't want to hear from me,> she answered petulantly. In a more serious tone she added, *<He's not listening for me. He doesn't know where I am.>*

What do I do?

<Try. Helix is scared of your brother. You have to give them some reason to keep him alive for now, after that ...>

What?

538

Peren didn't respond.

"Will you help me?" Asha asked Sarva. For a time she was certain he was going to shake his head. Instead, he leaned in and whispered in her ear.

"You're listening to the other one, aren't you?"

<He's still scared of me,> Peren whispered in disbelief.

Asha tilted her head in confirmation.

Sarva sat back and eyed John before concentrating on Asha again. "You're willing to accept what this might mean?"

Asha nodded.

"Tell her to go," he mouthed.

You saw that? Asha asked Peren.

<Yes.>

Just until we're done. Asha waited until Peren withdrew and nodded to Sarva.

"Can I do anything?" John asked.

"Keep them away," Sarva indicated the siblings on the other side of the room.

They were watching and waiting, Jaimee and Sando with curiosity, Helix with a mix of fear and anticipation. Asha noticed that Reyndani was still dazed but already picking up the ray-gun, she hoped Helix wouldn't make him use it.

"How do we start?" Asha asked, trying to put those concerns out of her mind.

"You're the healer."

Asha thought for a time and then smiled sadly at her brother. "Harihara?"

Sarva's stern expression softened and he nodded.

It was something they had played in childhood, though it wasn't precisely a game. They had been aware of the expectations of the stand – that as twins they might show special powers. They had started this as a way of trying to find their powers, but it had evolved into the way they comforted each other in times of need. Harihara, the conjoined gods of ancient human mythology. As children they had tried various forms but had finally settled on just one.

Asha lifted Ellie from her knees and turned on the sofa so that her body was facing Sarva. Her brother neatly mirrored her movements.

Their bodies remembered what Asha's mind had long forgotten. Their legs folded together, neatly interlocking, until they were sitting cross legged with their faces close.

"It still works," Asha said.

Sarva smiled.

Asha lowered Ellie onto the bed of legs between them and then leaned forward until her head was resting on Sarva's shoulder. Sarva mirrored her movements and they gently rested their heads together. All those years ago other children had tried to emulate them, but none could hold it long. Asha and Sarva could sit like this for hours. They had not found their powers like this, but at times it was like they could share their thoughts, that they could know each other's troubles without speaking them.

"Do you remember this?" Asha whispered.

"Yes."

"You stopped wanting to do it when we got older."

No response.

"Why did you leave?"

"Not now."

"You really can see the connections of life?"

"Yes ... and break them."

"Just break?"

"No. Sometimes I can sort of tie them off. It is what I did for John. I was there when his body died and the connection tore away. I tied off the break. It's not perfect, but it reduces the damage and slows down the loss."

"Thank you."

"You are very distracting like this. So intense. So female." Sarva's tone reflected his discomfort.

"I didn't plan this!"

"Your temper hasn't improved."

"Ellie," Asha whispered.

"Yes."

They drew their heads back from each other's shoulders until their temples were resting together. Their arms were draped between them, their hands touching Ellie. Asha had to concentrate to recognise which hands were hers.

"What now?" Sarva asked.

540

"Can you see it?"

"Yes. It's sort of shrivelled. That's probably what kept the leak so small all this time. ... But I think it sort of dries out and starts to open up again."

"Where?"

Sarva's fingers moved to the centre of Ellie's chest. "It's here ... but ... the connection starts further in. I can't see that clearly."

Asha started exploring with her finger tips, searching for flows that felt wrong.

I can see that. It's like your fingers have grown longer. I can see where you're touching. Sarva's thought appeared in her mind, almost as one of her own.

Asha kept exploring. The flows were sluggish and weak, but nothing here felt wrong. What if this doesn't work?

Deeper.

Asha reached further in. It was warmer, the flows subtly stronger.

There.

Yes, I feel something. ... No.

Over a bit.

It's like a draft against my fingers, Asha acknowledged, suddenly excited. I can feel the leak.

Can you heal it?

Asha tried to force some energy from her fingers as she would with an ordinary cut, but the life was simply drawn away and lost to that intangible void. Her hopes started to plummet.

You didn't get this far by quitting early.

No. But what do I do?

Cut it.

What?

Cut it. Make a wound you can heal.

Asha pushed her panic aside. She could sense he was right, but she also knew that this could kill Ellie.

She's dying anyway.

Asha started with the smallest cut she could and then quickly healed it.

Too fast.

I can see that!

She tried again.

Better, but not done yet.

The leak was almost too subtle to feel now. Asha felt around carefully trying to determine its limits. It was tiny. One more cut and she quickly drew at the edges, knitting them together with life from her finger tips. Was that it? She couldn't feel any more disruption to the normal flows. Sarva?

No response.

Sarva?

I think that's it. The shrivelled end fell away and vanished.

How do we know if it's enough?

Feed her again, see what happens.

Not yet. I don't want to put too much pressure on the scar until it's had time to strengthen.

Will she last?

Asha ran her hands over Ellie's head and chest. If the leak really has stopped then she has some time.

A pause. A sigh. Do we return to the real world now?

I suppose we must.

Reluctantly Asha lifted her head back. Their eyes met and held. They smiled.

"Did it work?" Jaimee asked.

Asha lifted Ellie and disentangled her legs from Sarva's, it didn't go as smoothly as their melding had. She turned around to John and answered the question on his face, "We think so." The sudden brightening of his expression made her doubt whether she should have raised his hopes. "I can't be sure yet."

"Be careful, Jaimee," Helix said.

Jaimee had crossed the room to stand near the sofa, he waved a dismissive hand at his sister. "When will you be sure?"

Asha shrugged.

"What are you doing up, Mother?" Sando said.

Everyone looked around. Angel had come into the room. She looked curiously at the figures on the sofa.

"Did you do this, Peren?" Jaimee asked, his voice tight.

<So many of the things we have done you said we were doing for Mama. Sometimes I think you forget that.>

Jaimee's hands drew into fists, but he restrained his anger in front of his mother. "You should be resting, Mother."

"I can't sleep." Angel went to an empty chair and drew herself up into it, obviously intending to stay.

"Jaimee!" Helix called. "The dhumraka are under attack."

"Peren, what's the king doing?"

<I don't know. You told me to stay with you, remember?>

"I didn't— What is he doing now?"

< ... I don't know. I can't see him.>

Jaimee turned to Sarva. "Did you do this?" he accused.

"I haven't been near him."

<It's not like that, Jaimee. It's like he's asleep or something.>

"You must have contact with some dhumraka out there," Jaimee insisted. "Tell me what's happening?"

<You want me to go now?>

"Yes!"

Asha tried to hide the joy she felt at Peren's small rebellion and Jaimee's discomfort. A glance at Sarva showed that he wasn't bothering to try. She wished she could share Peren's side of it, it might convince him that she was on their side – as much as she could be.

<It's the samudraka,> Peren reported.

"Of course it is!" Jaimee snapped at her. "Walt, alert Point Angel and then wake up the pilot, tell him we might be leaving after all."

27. Rage

Barma glanced back. Tracey was being assisted out of the crumpled car by a human soldier, other soldiers stood with their guns trained on Ray and Paul. There was nothing he could do here other than get caught himself. He rubbed his stomach, the seat belt had left it bruised after the sudden stop when they'd hit the truck, but it could have been worse. Movement on the edge of his senses told him someone was coming, a narun. That wasn't likely to be anyone they wanted to meet, so he turned away and ran to catch up with Beenae and Taiza.

It hadn't taken any effort to convince Beenae that they should return, and Taiza had already started walking. Asha had insisted that they leave with Tracey. However much they had argued, Asha had remained adamant and, finally, they had relented and agreed to go. When they found her again they could say they had tried.

They made a wide circle back to the destroyed gates. There was a human soldier still on guard here, but no dhumraka. They slipped quietly past the guard. Trickling water from the softly falling rain covered any sounds they made, the only risk would be if the guard noticed their forms interrupting the rain. He didn't.

When they were safely past the two fences they moved quickly into the trees. They hadn't gone far when a car came racing down the driveway. Barma bid Beenae and Taiza stay where they were and crept closer to the driveway to watch. A while later the car returned, this time at a more sedate pace, and Barma guessed his human friends were inside.

Barma crept back to the others and they made their way to the house, sensing ahead and behind as best they could in the rain. As far as they could tell there was no one watching for them and no one following.

The garage door had been left open and they went inside. It was difficult to see in here, no light and no life. Barma had to feel his way around the cars, Beenae and Taiza kept close behind. At the door to the interior of the house he looked back.

"Do we go in?"

Taiza looked at him. There was no obvious expression to his face, but his eyes seemed to be asking why Barma had stopped. Beenae grinned, no question there, he looked excited – maybe he was scared too. Barma didn't want to be the only one frightened out of his mind.

The door opened with a slight creak and they slipped through. Back along the corridor they came to the extent of what was familiar.

Barma tried to think. He didn't know this house, how was he going to find the others without getting caught himself? Should he go out and check the cages? Somehow he didn't think that was likely.

Taiza started walking again.

"Where are you going?" Barma whispered.

Beenae pointed to the floor. It was wet. The humans had come through here dripping water as they went.

- - -

Senna wormed her way through some undergrowth and slowly pushed her head through the foliage. The dhumraka were all still where they had been. She flicked her hand behind her. She cringed when she heard the others trying to come up quietly behind. It had been one thing to bring just Andrei through the dhumraka without being noticed, twice, but this wasn't going to work. There were too many of them and the samudraka were hopeless. They had only made it this far because of the rain, and because no one expected subtlety from the samudraka.

But the rain had slowed and the only thunder was distant. She risked pushing her head further out from the leaves. They were almost in the middle of the loose line of dhumraka now. It was as dangerous to go back as it was to go forward.

There was a groan. Theseo, carried across Polyphemo's back, was

545

waking. A wooden thunk and the groaning stopped. Not much noise, but enough.

Senna sensed movement from two of the dhumraka. She waved her hand to get the attention of the samudraka, then held up two fingers and pointed. They crouched, ready to stand. Senna indicated they should hold still.

The dhumraka approached the source of the noise, not noticing Senna's cloaked figure exposed just a short distance further up the slope. At the last moment Senna dropped her hand. The samudraka came out quickly, their spears slashing. The two dhumraka were dead before they could defend themselves, but not before the woman could scream.

Shouts erupted around them. Senna pushed the rest of the way out, there was no point trying to hide now. With Andrei at her side they broke into a run. A dhumraka man came from behind a tree. Andrei slid past the spear thrust and drove the zakti through the man's chest. They ran on.

More dhumraka. Andrei pulled Senna behind him and the samudraka warriors came up on either side. The shouting spread. It sounded to Senna like everyone was coming for them.

"My people are coming," Polyphemo announced.

Two of his warriors had been sent back to tell the samudraka army that their king had been abducted by the dhumraka, and to lead them this way. Now the trick was to get through the dhumraka and stay ahead of the samudraka.

The dhumraka glanced to the side, at their companions running past to confront the samudraka. The warriors near Senna took advantage of their distraction and attacked. Andrei stayed with Senna. The dhumraka fell quickly. One of the samudraka received a cut to one leg but kept up well enough when they again broke into a run.

No more dhumraka confronted them as they approached the top of the slope. They dropped down the other side and the sounds of the battle became obscured. They kept running, there was no way to know how quickly the samudraka might follow. Senna had little doubt that they would prevail.

They stopped briefly at the next crest and looked back. There was no sign of pursuit. Polyphemo used the break to swing the unconscious Theseo to his other shoulder. Tilvy was prodding Andrei, as if checking he was real. It seemed incongruous that Tilvy was smiling so broadly, though Senna could understand well enough. Senna had thought Andrei was dead for only a few minutes, it must have been much worse for the others.

They ran on in two distinct groups, Pasith and the aaranya to the front, with Senna continuing to lead, the samudraka came a short distance behind them.

"So Sarva wasn't as clever as he thought," Garjae observed.

"What?" Andrei asked.

"He didn't manage to kill you."

Andrei laughed. "Just you wait till we see him next, Garjae. It'll be a race to see who kisses him first, me or Senna."

Senna and Andrei exchanged grins.

"You mean ...?"

"He wasn't trying to kill me. Don't get me wrong, I thought he was, and it hurt like he had. Have you ever been stuck with a blunt sword?"

"It's not blunt."

"It was to me, remember? Then. It's plenty sharp again now, and not nearly as easy to use."

"But the zakti?" Darnu objected.

Andrei laughed again. "Sarva's been holding out on us. Like Asha, he can do some tricks of his own. Theseo's mum guessed it first, and together they planned my great escape. He couldn't tell Theseo. The king would have called him papayamala and killed him, and probably the rest of us too."

"But Lantea knows?"

"Sure. She was great, wasn't she Sen'?"

Senna said, "Yes," but with less enthusiasm. The king's mother made her uncomfortable, or maybe it was Andrei's reaction to her that Senna didn't like.

Andrei continued, "She took us down to one of those pools of life while I got over the worst of it. But we couldn't stay long, we might have been seen, so she brought us to the beach. I still wasn't feeling great, so Sen' made me stay merged with a tree for a few days while she kept watch over the soldiers."

They ran on in silence for a while.

547

"Why was Lantea staying away from the army?" Tilvy asked.

"Sarva told her something that disturbed her," Senna answered. "I'm not sure I understood exactly what."

"And how do you know where Asha is?" Garjae asked.

"I've got Cassey. She was leading us this way when we saw Theseo with Helix and decided we should find out what was going on."

They had to stop at the next ridge, Polyphemo needed a break. He refused to give up the king to any of the other warriors. The rain had stopped now, though water was still dripping from the trees. The forest here was changing to mostly tall, straight pines and there was less undergrowth to slow them down.

They got moving again and it wasn't much later that they reached a double fence at the bottom of a gentle slope.

One of the samudraka started to climb the fence but Darnu called him down. Pointing to the second fence, he said, "You can't climb that one, it burns, and in the middle there's no cover. We'll have to find another way."

Senna pointed. "That way."

- - -

Garjae was still trying to get used to the idea that Sarva had managed to save Andrei when the rest of them had been unable to do anything. He could understand why Sarva hadn't told them, they had to react as if Sarva really had done it, but it still rankled. A glance at Darnu suggested he was having trouble with the idea too.

Risking the cleared area alongside the fence, they made better time than they had through the forest. They came over a rise and saw breaks in the fences and the tangle of gates to one side. Human soldiers and their equipment filled the area between and outside the gateways. Bright lights lit the area, and from where they stood they could feel the slight hum of a detector field.

The detector field faded when they entered the trees and they risked getting closer to see what was happening.

"Could your skills get you past the detector?" Polyphemo asked Senna.

She shrugged. "I don't know. Maybe."

"Even if Senna could, I doubt the rest of us could," Darnu said.

Garjae peered through a gap in the trees. The soldiers looked alert, they were still moving things around. He got the impression they hadn't been there for long. Senna had said that Cassey had been trying to come this way, so Asha must be inside that fence somewhere. They were so close. There had to be a way through.

"Even cloaked they will still see us coming and be ready," Garjae muttered aloud.

"Maybe if they were distracted," Pasith offered.

"We can't wait for the samudraka to arrive," Andrei said. "They won't be happy that we stole their king."

Even Polyphemo and his friends weren't that happy about it, though they understood the need. As if responding to Garjae's gaze, the king started to move slowly on the ground where Polyphemo had placed him. Polyphemo swung his fist and the king fell silent again.

Andrei shook his head sadly. "Poor Theseo, he's going to have one hell of a headache when he wakes up."

"If he gets to wake up," Garjae said.

Polyphemo glanced at him unhappily but didn't say anything.

"We do what Pasith suggested," Darnu said. "We split up. Senna can lead Andrei, Garjae and me around the side, see if we can find a way to get closer without being seen. You all spread out and rush forward as if you're attacking, but stay among the trees and don't get too close until you feel the detector stop. While they're concentrating on you they might not notice our cloaked figures show up."

"Might not?" Andrei asked.

Darnu shrugged.

"You said it yourself," Garjae reminded Andrei, "we can't just sit here."

- - -

Tilvy smiled weakly at Pasith. He smiled back. He looked remarkably calm.

"You didn't have to be here," she reminded him. "This wasn't your fight."

"It involves all the narun. I just happened to be here."

"There. You were on your way back to Neso." Tilvy regretted bringing up her name when she saw the sadness it brought to Pasith's face.

"I'm afraid my disappearance will confirm her bad opinion of the aaranya."

"You can tell her that we're okay really when we get home."

Another smile from Pasith, slower and less certain.

"I think that's long enough," Polyphemo announced. "Spread out. When we run forward try to move around between the trees, we want to make it look like there are many of us."

Tilvy looked at their small group, eight if you didn't count the unconscious Theseo being lifted onto Polyphemo's back. How did you make eight look like an army?

A loud bang followed by a roaring sound came from the direction of the gates and they all turned in surprise. Something burning rose quickly into the sky. More explosions and more burning objects rose behind the first. The flames passed over the trees heading west.

- - -

Little had been said in the room that wasn't vague reports of the battle. Despite being outnumbered, the samudraka were forcing the dhumraka back. Asha saw the distress showing on Helix as more of her people were lost, the beautiful woman flinching as she paced the far side of the room. Jaimee and Sando were bent over the table, studying the map as if they could will everything into position just by moving the markers. Angel watched her children with concern, but said nothing.

Asha remained sitting between John and Sarva on the sofa, Ellie resting silently on John's lap, no better but no worse. The unwavering attention of the ray-gun in Reyndani's hand kept them still. They held hands and waited, sharing a confusing mix of excitement and dread. The samudraka were winning. The samudraka would kill them.

Stephenson called the human contingents back from their now useless decoy position and they attacked the samudraka from behind. But the detectors didn't distinguish the targets, the soldiers were killing more dhumraka than samudraka.

Jaimee drew back from the table. He cast angry eyes around the room before turning to Helix. "Launch the missiles while the humans mark the target area."

Helix stopped her pacing and stared at her brother.

Sarva started to stand.

"Sit down!" Jaimee yelled at him and glared.

Asha tugged at Sarva's arm until he reluctantly subsided. There

550

was nothing they could do that wouldn't be a futile gesture.

"Take the lot," Jaimee told Helix, his frustration seeping out through every movement and word. "We can start again if we have to."

Helix hesitated.

"Just do it!" he yelled and threw himself in a chair.

Helix closed her eyes.

There was a long moment of silence, and then the radio crackled in Stephenson's hand.

Stephenson passed on reports from the radio in a flat monologue. There were fights and shooting among the soldiers when some objected to firing on their own men. The trouble was subdued. "The missiles have fired," Stephenson said.

Seconds later Helix cried out in pain. Sando rushed to her and gently helped her to a chair.

<I don't know what's happening there any more,> Peren said in a quiet voice. *<All my contacts are dead.>*

- - -

They were still staring, stunned, at where the rockets had passed over them when they felt the ground vibrate and heard the sound of distant explosions.

"What was that?" Senna asked.

"I think they're blowing up everyone, dhumraka and samudraka together," Darnu said.

"Maybe humans too," said Andrei. "The humans that the samudraka were following must still be out there somewhere."

Rapid gunshots pulled their attention back to the gates. Senna had found them a gully that let them get close to the camp without feeling the detector. They were all cloaked, ready to go forward when the distraction started, but now that it had they were slow to react.

With his mind on the thought that Asha wasn't far away, Garjae leapt to his feet and started toward the camp. Darnu wasn't far behind and pulled at Garjae's arm.

"Not too fast," Darnu warned, "that will only attract attention."

Garjae forced himself back to a slow jog.

When they came out from the trees and onto the road they could feel the full blast of the detector field, and were dazzled by the glare of the lights, but no one was shooting their way. As they got closer, they could see the camp was in confusion. There appeared to have been a struggle among the humans, some were lying on the ground. To one side they could see the detector and its accompanying circle of soldiers firing into the forest.

Tilvy threw herself behind a tree. A barrage of shots had torn up the ground not far from her feet. When it cleared she forced herself to move again. Another tree. And then moving again. Splintering wood warned her of gunfire sweeping toward her and she dropped to the ground. When it passed over she stood and ran for cover.

At the end of a burst of gunfire Tilvy heard a cry of pain.

"Pasith!" she called.

There was no answer. Tilvy ran to where she thought it had come from. Another burst of gunfire forced her to the ground. She jumped up and ran again. Bark from a tree flew out at her, she had no time and nowhere to go. She felt the air stir in front of her face. The burst stopped. Tilvy kept going.

She found Pasith flat on his back and dreaded the worst. She knelt next to him, a fine graze had scored one side of his head, it glowed a pale gold. Bullets struck the ground to one side and came at them. She dragged Pasith behind a tree. She felt the dull vibrations of bullets hitting the tree. She felt like screaming.

Pasith groaned and moved in her arms, and she hugged him tighter.

The radio crackled again. "Point Angel is under attack," reported Stephenson.

"How the fuck did they get there?" Jaimee stood up and glared around the room. No one could answer him.

"We have to leave now," Sando reminded him.

Jaimee spun around and seemed about to yell at his brother. Then his shoulders sagged and he nodded.

"You promised to bring my friends," Asha told him.

Jaimee went rigid, stared at Asha, then snapped at Reyndani, "Get them from the cells and join us on the roof. If they don't come quietly, kill them."

Reyndani nodded.

<I'm going to need help,> Peren said.

Jaimee nodded absently. "Walt, keep your eye on these. If any of them step out of line, kill them." He pointed at Sarva. "Particularly him. Keep him right away from us."

- - -

They were almost on the group of soldiers surrounding the detector when the closest of them turned with his gun still firing. Garjae knew he was reacting too slowly but found himself mesmerised by the light flickering from the end of the barrel. He was flung to the ground by Darnu.

"Duck," Darnu whispered in his ear.

Garjae laughed and they rolled to their feet.

The soldier was reloading his weapon. The magazine was in. He was lifting it. And then Garjae was there, punching at the man's face. As the soldier fell back his gun fired into the sky.

Andrei slipped past as Darnu was knocking down another soldier, and ran the zakti along the cables behind the detector. The screen went black.

The soldiers were all looking around. Garjae ducked down as one of them started shooting in his direction. Beneath the table holding the screen was the black dome that generated the detector field. Garjae realised it was still going. He pushed himself between the legs of two of the soldiers and pushed the device out the other side of the table. A soldier on that side, seeing unexpected movement, fired down and the device exploded into pieces. A ricochet nicked one of Garjae's ears. The buzzing of the detector stopped.

Someone was pulling at one of his legs. A soldier. Garjae kicked out with his free leg but only hurt his foot. Then the soldier was falling away and Darnu bent down and pulled Garjae free of the tangle of bodies.

"Where—?" Garjae started.

Darnu pointed. Senna and Andrei were already working their way through the group of soldiers. It looked dangerous, but Garjae realised it made sense. The soldiers were trying not to shoot into their own group.

Darnu and Garjae had almost caught up to Andrei when a soldier turned unexpectedly and Senna, caught by surprise, bumped into him, stumbled, and fell to her knees. The soldier clutched at his sidearm. Andrei thrust out the zakti and stabbed him in the throat. As the man fell, Andrei threw himself over Senna. Other soldiers started shooting blindly. Darnu and Garjae dropped to the ground. Men yelled orders and the gunfire stopped.

They helped each other to their feet and carefully moved on. Equipment lay all around and cables ran to the many lights. There were groans from wounded soldiers, officers shouting orders, and men running back and forth. It was difficult to stay out of their way.

They had made it through the first gateway when Darnu looked back. "Garjae," he called, and pointed.

The soldiers had brought out another detector field generator and were setting it up. Garjae could see Tilvy, Pasith, Polyphemo with Theseo still over his back, and two other samudraka warriors coming out from the forest. There was no sign of the other warriors.

"You two go ahead," Darnu told Senna and Andrei.

Darnu and Garjae made their way back through the soldiers again. Not far from the group assembling the detector, Garjae pulled Darnu to a stop. There was a dead soldier near them, unattended while the others dealt with the wounded. Darnu nodded.

They knelt by the soldier's corpse, waiting to see if Tilvy and the others could make it past before the new detector came on. There was a short delay when the soldiers realised that not only was the device broken but the cables had been cut. Tilvy and Pasith came through, Darnu waved them on. Then Polyphemo and the others. Darnu and Garjae waited where they were while their friends traversed the still busy area between the gates. Senna and Andrei were already beyond the encampment, Garjae could see them waiting at the edge of the trees inside the fence line.

The buzz of the detector ran through Garjae's body, and a few moments later he saw the screen come to life. One soldier and then another turned from the screen and looked through the gates. Garjae picked up the dead soldier's rifle, pointed it at the detector and pulled the trigger. The rifle danced in his hands and men and equipment fell. The buzzing of the detector stopped.

Garjae tossed the rifle at the soldiers, Darnu was already pulling at his arm. They ran to the side of the road and threw themselves flat on the ground beneath the trees there. Several shots were fired, but officers shouted and order was quick to return.

They stood up. There was a young soldier a short distance from them, standing not far from the fence. He was staring in their direction, his eyes squinting. Garjae realised the soldier must have seen movement in the debris beneath the trees. Garjae reached behind him, and touched Darnu, telling him to be still. The soldier started to relax.

It was just a gentle gust of wind, a final puff from the departing storm. Drops of water fell from the branches above. Garjae felt them land on him and run over his body. They were gone almost as fast as they had arrived, but for that brief moment they had outlined his shape, glinting in the lights of the camp.

"There's—" the young soldier started. He didn't bother to finish. He drew his handgun and fired. Just once. Garjae felt the bullet tug at his arm.

"Cease firing!" an officer yelled.

The young soldier slowly lowered his gun, then turned to acknowledge the officer approaching him.

Garjae touched the wound on his arm, prana wet on his fingers. "That was close," he said lightly and turned back to Darnu.

Darnu was on the ground, the golden fluid of his life spilling from his chest. Nuttachen was on the ground next to Darnu's head, nuzzling at his ear. Darnu reached his hand up to Garjae.

Garjae rushed to his side, all thoughts of the nearby soldiers gone from his mind. With one hand he held Darnu's, with the other he tried to stem the flow of prana, but it was useless. Darnu shook his head. He was trying to say something. Garjae put his head down closer.

"I have always loved you, my friend," Darnu whispered.

"I know," Garjae said. "Best friends always."

"More ... more than that. You had Asha, and I ... I always had you. It was hopeless for both of us."

Garjae gripped Darnu's hand even tighter and stared into his friend's eyes. How could he have known? How could he have missed it? This was his best friend.

"I will ... miss ..." Darnu whispered.

Shouted commands made Garjae glance up briefly. When he looked back down Darnu was gone. There was just this fading shell, covered in the gold of life, and shrouded in its evaporating mists.

"Garjae!" Andrei called.

Garjae could see Andrei was coming back, already among the first of the soldiers on the far side of the gates. "Go back!" Garjae yelled. "Just go back!"

Rage overtook him then, he didn't wait to see if Andrei obeyed. He launched himself at the nearest soldier, knocked him out and grabbed at the rifle. At first it didn't fire. His rage subsided long enough to let him see the button. He pressed it. He lifted the rifle and began walking toward the thickest concentration of soldiers, firing as he went. When that rifle ran out he grabbed another from a fallen soldier and kept firing. Soldiers all around him were shooting now. Bullets tore past him. He felt their wind, even a sting on his leg and at his side. But none went deeper. Life wasn't that fair. He threw down the empty rifle and reached for another.

- - -

Asha and the others were swept in front of the siblings by Stephenson with his ray-gun. Asha tried to think of something, anything, that could let her achieve what she had promised to herself – that tonight would be an end to it, whatever the cost. She couldn't let Jaimee and the others escape. She had been willing to sacrifice herself, and even John and Ellie who were so soon to die anyway. But it wasn't that simple any more. Everything Asha thought of trying seemed destined to result in the senseless death or enslavement of everyone she loved, and still without stopping Jaimee and Helix.

They were directed back out to the oak trees. A dozen of Helix's personal guard came from inside the house and formed a circle around their group, each had a spear held ready.

"Okay, sister, we're here," Jaimee said.

<Asha. I want Asha,> Peren said.

Jaimee waved Asha ahead.

"What is it, Peren?" Asha asked, puzzled. "What do you need?"

<When Helix makes a new connection with someone she gains strength from that somehow.>

Asha nodded.

<I don't. It's the other way for me. The power your brother felt here doesn't come from me, not directly. It comes from these trees. They sustain me. They give me the strength to endure the load. I

haven't left them for years. Jaimee brings people to me because I can't go to them.>

"Hurry up," Jaimee called.

Asha ignored him. Can you leave?

<I don't know. I'm scared, Asha.>

Asha looked back at Jaimee.

"What?" he asked impatiently.

Does he realise? Asha asked Peren.

<Does he care?> Peren returned bitterly.

Angel came to Asha's side. "You're going to see my Daisy darling," she said.

<That's what Mama calls me,> Peren admitted.

"She's always been my Daisy darling," Angel continued. "She called me back from the darkness and saved us all."

Asha didn't know what that meant.

<I don't either. It was before we were born, when Mama's human body was dying. Mama always says it was me that saved her, I don't know how.>

"We don't have all night," Jaimee called to them.

What do you want me to do? Asha asked Peren.

- - -

Paul rubbed Tracey's shoulders and back vigorously, but still she shivered – it was definitely from the cold now, she felt too miserable to be frightened. Their clothes were no longer dripping wet, but they were still damp and this room was cold.

Tracey glanced across at Ray. He was sitting quite still, his arms wrapped around his chest and his face was pale. He'd come out worst from the crash. He'd tried to steer around the truck but lost control in the wet, and the car had hit on his side. The impact had aggravated his still healing chest wounds.

"Ray?" she said softly. Her chattering teeth distorted the word.

He looked across.

"Are you okay?"

He pulled one hand from his chest and rubbed his neck. "Think I got whiplash."

"Sue 'em, boss," Paul said. "The army's got plenty of money."

Ray smiled weakly.

Tracey pulled herself out of Paul's embrace and stood up. She paced around the small room stamping her feet, trying to get some feeling back in her toes. She wasn't as unhappy about being back here as she probably should be. It had felt so wrong to be deserting Asha, but there had been no good way to argue with her. So they were back. What now?

She sat back down and Paul put his arm around her. She huddled against his chest.

How much time passed like that she didn't know, but when they heard noises at the door they all came alert. The door swung open.

"We are going," Reyndani announced, and he waved the antenna of the gun, indicating they should move.

"Where?" Paul asked.

"Roof. Helicopter." Reyndani's words were clipped and emotionless.

"How lethal are those ray things, Tracey?" Ray asked.

"I don't know," she admitted, "but I don't think you want to find out."

Another gesture from Reyndani. "You are to hurry."

Tracey stood, her joints felt stiff from having been curled up so tightly against the cold.

Reyndani backed into the corridor to let them come out. He started to turn, a puzzled expression on his face as he sensed someone behind him, then he collapsed like a puppet with its strings cut. Moments later Tracey felt Barma at her side. She hugged him in welcome.

Paul knelt down next to Reyndani and lifted one shoulder. He drew out the antenna of the ray-gun, but it was broken, the main shaft dangling from the handle by a few wires.

"Pity," Ray acknowledged. "Did you have a plan from here?" He spoke into the air past Tracey's shoulder. Tracey felt a double tap on her hand and shook her head at Ray. Ray looked to Paul in question.

"You're the boss, boss."

"And I will remember to say how helpful you've been on your next review. Get him locked in," Ray pointed to Reyndani.

When that was done Ray appeared to have made up his mind what he wanted to do.

- - -

"No," Sarva whispered, "that's not possible."

558

A figure emerged from the tree, reaching out to the supporting arms of Asha and Angel. She glowed an intense gold, kaleidoscopic patterns swirling beneath the transparent skin. The woman was naked, although details of her form were difficult to make out beneath the dazzling patterns. Her hair, a delicate and pale shade of gold that was almost white, splayed out around her head. She looked young, frail and very weak. She appeared to be speaking to Asha and Angel, but John couldn't hear what she was saying.

John had seen something like this before. When his current form had first emerged from his human body he had seen similar golden patterns within his hand, but they weren't this bright, and his skin had thickened and covered them over. He remembered the weakness he had felt when his own body had looked like that and wondered how this woman could stand, even with help from her mother and Asha.

"Remember what I said, Walt," Jaimee said, pointing at Sarva. "Keep this one away from us. Come on, time we were gone."

Several dhumraka guards preceded them inside, the others followed at the back. John, carrying Ellie, walked with Sarva in front of Stephenson. Asha and Angel supported Peren in front of the other siblings. They were led back into the house and up the stairs.

They were approaching the door to the roof when there was a distant bang of a door below them somewhere. A few moments later someone shouted, "Hello! Are we in time for the party?"

Sarva grinned at John. "I told you Andrei wasn't dead."

They were hustled out onto the roof at spear point. Most of the dhumraka then ran back inside.

"Keep them back," Jaimee called after them before he slammed the door and slid the bolt across.

"Frazer," Stephenson called out from behind John and Sarva. "Get that damn thing going!"

The helicopter was silent. John could sense four humans in it.

Stephenson waved them closer. "Frazer?"

John was astonished to see Tracey and two men leap from the gaping helicopter door. Sarva pulled him out of their way. Shouts came from behind him.

- - -

Ray and Paul went directly for Stephenson, the only one they

559

could see. Tracey felt a sweeping blast from the ray-gun. Beside her, Paul was stumbling, falling in pain, but still reaching out. His hands fell against the antenna of the gun, pushing it back and away. Ray thudded into Stephenson, trying to force the huge man to the ground.

Tracey ran on, not knowing what she could do, but determined to try. Pain seared across her temples and she knew that Sando must be close. She tripped over her own feet and landed painfully on her knees. Her head felt like it would explode. She knew this pain, she knew its cause. She knew what Sando could do. Had done. She forced herself up. The pain flared again and she screamed. His presence was near. She flung herself at it. The light figure fell back. She knew this was him. She didn't know how she knew, but there was no doubt.

- - -

Sando struggled with the mad woman now clawing at his face. It was all he could do to keep her from scratching his eyes out. He tried to concentrate, to cause her pain, to kill her if he could, but she writhed in his arms and he stumbled. Her weight took him off balance and they fell to the ground.

<Jaimee!> he called in his mind, but his brother wasn't listening.

Sando's head banged against the rough tarmac of the roof, and pain seared across the back of his head.

<Jaimee, no!> he heard Peren's scream.

Pain rang through in his head as it struck the ground again. The woman was shaking him by the throat. He stopped trying to tear her hands away and struck out at her head.

- - -

Barma, Taiza and Beenae had hidden on the roof behind the door. No one was expecting them, no one was looking for them. When Tracey and the others came out of the helicopter, Barma yelled out a battle cry to cover his fear, and they leapt out to attack the two dhumraka that had remained on this side of the door.

One fell to a swipe of the long metal handle that Barma had found in the helicopter. The other was too fast, the sweeping point of the spear struck Beenae not far below his neck and the boy fell back, clutching at the wound and dropping the lump of wood he had been trying to wield. In the same movement, the warrior brought the spear across and knocked the wrench from Taiza's hand.

Barma swung his metal handle low, catching the dhumraka on the leg, but the blow lacked strength. In a blindingly fast swirl, the warrior fell Taiza with a blow to the head from the butt of his spear and struck out with the point at Barma. Barma jumped back and stumbled. He lost his grip on the slippery handle and it clattered away from him.

The dhumraka warrior smiled and came at Barma quickly.

- - -

Asha was only a few steps behind Stephenson when he fell beneath Ray.

Jaimee thrust out, cutting at the struggling humans.

Angel, confused by the events, stepped in front of him.

<Jaimee, no!> Peren cried, her voice deafening in Asha's mind.

Angel fell away to the side, clutching at the gushing wound in her neck. The ray-gun, still clutched in Stephenson's hand, his finger still squeezing on the trigger, swept its ray over Angel.

<Mama! Mama!> Peren called.

Paul grabbed at Stephenson's hand and smashed it against the ground. The antenna broke. Stephenson forced his hand up and smashed at Paul's head with what was left of the gun. Ray had his hands around Stephenson's neck, but the massive man's other hand was pounding at Ray's injured chest, and Ray's grip was weakening.

Peren pulled herself from Asha's grip and fell to the ground next to her mother.

Asha turned to face Jaimee. His expression was an ugly mix of a grin and a snarl. His fingers slashed out and a cut appeared on her shoulder. She ignored it. He pulled his hand back to strike again. John stepped in front of her. She felt him flinch as he was cut.

"Shirt," she said.

There was no hesitation, the shirt vanished.

Asha placed one hand on John's back, with the other she reached around him and ran her fingers over the cut on his chest. The power she had taken from the tree flowed through both her hands. When the next cut struck at John's neck it was healed before it could open.

Another cut, and another. With each one John flinched but made no sound. He took a step closer to Jaimee and Asha was forced to follow.

561

Andrei led the way up the stairs. A human appearing in a doorway was slain by a samudraka as they rushed past. At the last flight, the stairs leading to the roof, they were forced to stop. Ten dhumraka were arrayed on the stairs, their spears thrust forward aggressively.

Polyphemo dropped Theseo unceremoniously against the wall of the hallway and came up beside Andrei. Senna, Tilvy and Pasith, unarmed, were forced to the back. Andrei realised that the limited space was a good thing, given they were outnumbered, but that still left the problem of getting past the dhumraka.

A dhumraka woman danced lightly down and thrust her spear at Andrei. He brought Zak up just in time. It cut through the spear, taking the tip. The woman stared at it in surprise and then threw the shaft at Polyphemo who brushed it away. Andrei looked at the zakti. He'd been making it work for him, but it wasn't easy, not like it had been when it was his.

"Go back," Polyphemo told him.

Andrei nodded reluctantly.

One of the remaining samudraka warriors took his place beside Polyphemo and they made a tentative push up the stairs.

A spear was thrown by one of the dhumraka and Polyphemo brushed it away. Two more came in quick succession. The warrior beside Polyphemo avoided one, but the next took him in the eye. He fell back at Andrei's feet and the last of Polyphemo's companions took his place.

- - -

At first Sarva thought John was running out, but saw him quickly deposit Ellie inside the helicopter before rushing back to Asha. Satisfied, Sarva sought his own target.

Sarva's fear of Peren had dropped away when he saw how weak she was outside her trees. He could deal with her later. He moved directly at Helix. She saw him coming and backed away.

"I've been looking forward to this," he called to her. It was both a lie and the truth. He had feared it, but he had dreamt of it and anticipated it with a relish he knew wasn't rational.

Helix eyes flickered over to her brothers, torn between their need and her own. Movement caught her eye and she saw one of her warriors. He turned immediately, abandoning his target, and came rushing to his queen's aid.

Sarva was forced back by the point of the spear.

The warrior didn't pursue Sarva, but stayed close to Helix, guarding her.

Sarva rushed in. Helix stepped back, but the warrior stood his ground and swiped the spear across, almost slicing into Sarva's stomach.

Helix edged across toward Sando.

- - -

Tracey reeled from the blow to her head and her body started to drop to one side. She felt Sando moving. Her grip on his neck slackened. She was losing it. The pain started again.

- - -

Barma took a moment to realise that the warrior had turned away from him. Beenae was sitting next to the unconscious Taiza, still holding the wound below his neck. There was nothing Barma could do for them. There was banging on the door, the slide bolt was rattling as someone tried to come through. Was it friend or foe?

He saw the fallen spear and picked it up. When he looked out at the scene in front of him, he couldn't tell who needed him most. Asha and John were in a face-off with Jaimee. Ray and Paul were still struggling with Stephenson. Tracey was falling on her side, her hands clutching at her head. Barma went there first.

Helix and her warrior saw him coming and tried to intercept, but Sarva pressed from the other side and they were forced to defend themselves.

Barma tried to swing the butt of the spear at Sando's head, fearing that he might hurt Tracey if he used the point. He managed only a lightly glancing blow before he was forced to step back when the dhumraka warrior reached out and swiped his spear at Barma's head.

- - -

John knew he was weakening. It was getting harder to keep himself upright between Asha and Jaimee. He couldn't keep silent when the next cut ripped across his stomach, a cry of pain escaped his lips before he could bite down on them. This was where he was supposed to be. "You, she has named zaravarana, the shield", Ulvanya had told him. He forced himself straighter.

John could feel Asha's power radiating through his body, passing directly from her hand on his back to each wound as it appeared, closing them even as they opened. It felt like her hand was part of him, that he truly was a shield held before her.

But Asha was weakening too. The cut to his stomach was slower to heal. The surge of power through his body was weaker. And they were closer now. Every cut that Jaimee made went deeper. Another step and Jaimee would be able to touch him.

John took that step.

Jaimee grinned and reached out.

There was confusion among the dhumraka, some turning to try and get through the door behind them.

Polyphemo and his companion pressed their advantage. A dhumraka man fell to a thrust from Polyphemo's companion. Polyphemo let a spear slide past him, it left a gash across his chest, he grabbed the shaft and pulled the dhumraka down onto Polyphemo's spear. Now with a spear in each hand, Polyphemo pushed harder and more dhumraka fell.

Those knocking at the door returned their attention to the attack. Polyphemo's companion took a spear to the stomach, but pulled the dhumraka down with him. Andrei killed the dhumraka and moved up beside Polyphemo.

"I'm back," Andrei announced.

Behind Andrei, Tilvy, Pasith and Senna picked up fallen spears and prepared to fight.

Frustrated in his attempts to get to Helix, Sarva looked at Peren sitting on the ground next to her mother, weeping. Three connections were clearly visible, brighter and stronger than anything he had ever seen. A fourth, rapidly withering, had been as bright, but now her mother was dead. Those remaining were the bonds to her siblings. He had been wrong. These weren't two sets of twins, these were quadruplets.

Sarva hoped Barma could manage on his own. With a brief look of apology, Sarva turned away from Helix and went to Peren. The girl-woman didn't even look up when he got close.

He swept his eyes over the siblings and then back to this girl. He was puzzled for a moment, thinking that the connections were wrong. But they weren't wrong, he was. The siblings weren't connected to each other. They were all connected to this one. It was this weak, golden, glowing girl that linked them all.

Sarva reached out with both hands. He scooped the connections together, tightened his fists and tore them apart.

Barma felt the graze of the spear touch his cheek as he pulled his head back. He pulled his spear up higher, hoping to at least block the return stroke.

A scream came from Helix and she dropped to her knees. Barma gaped and the dhumraka whirled back to his queen to see what was wrong.

Barma felt only the slightest twinges of guilt as he plunged his spear point into the dhumraka warrior's back. He couldn't expect a third reprieve, it was take this opportunity or die. Somewhere behind him, Barma heard noises at the door. Andrei's voice?

The pain had fallen away briefly and Tracey fought for her life. She knew she had to keep him distracted, stop him from bringing his power against her, but against an enemy she couldn't see it was hopeless. Clutching and striking at one another, they had struggled their way to their knees.

Tracey had hold of one of Sando's wrists, her other hand she had at his neck, squeezing tight and shaking it in desperation. The pain returned and kept building in her head. A weak blow from Sando's free hand made her senses real, but she refused to release her hold, fearing that she would never regain it. Something burning hot was twisting and bending through her brain. Her hands couldn't maintain their pressure, he was sliding from her grasp.

And then the pain vanished, leaving just the dull thud of her pulse thumping in her head.

The figure beside her was moving. Sando was still alive. Did he think she was dead? She clutched at him again, but the strength was gone from her fingers. He was slipping away. No!

Sando tried to pull away from her. Something was horribly wrong. He was calling to his brother but there was no one there. No

565

Helix. No Peren. They had vanished. His mind was in a panic. Such emptiness, as if the entire world had receded from him. He could still see it, but he couldn't feel it. Where was his brother? He tried to strike away the fingers clutching at his hand.

Pain.

He looked down. A spear shaft protruded from his chest, and prana pumped out around it. Was it his?

Movement. His eyes followed it. Two women holding one another. The human and the aaranya called Tilvy. The one that had escaped. It made no sense.

Sando closed his eyes. Where was his brother?

- - -

John felt the cut start. This one piercing right through his shoulder. Jaimee's hand moved across. It was too deep, it could never be healed fast enough.

Jaimee jerked his hand back, a look of shock and pain spread across his face. His lips formed a word. No.

John felt Asha's body press against his back. One arm wrapped around John and held him still, the other reached out to Jaimee. Her slender fingers hesitated over his chest. Then touched.

Her hand pulled back and Jaimee's life gushed from the wound in his chest. It splashed out in a hot golden stream over John. Asha pulled him away from it.

Jaimee's face distorted in pain, then slowly changed to a puzzled hurt, as if he couldn't understand what he had done wrong. He dropped to his knees, then onto his face. His body lay still.

- - -

Peren collapsed, unconscious, when Sarva tore the links. He stared at her delicate golden form for a time and wondered if all those churning patterns beneath her skin meant something. Sarva couldn't bring himself to harm her further. It wasn't pity. Perhaps it was the affection that Asha had for this strange being, or perhaps it was something in his own heart.

He turned his attention back to Helix. She was kneeling, tears flooding down her face. Even in this distressed state she was still compellingly beautiful.

It was only then that he noticed the others. Andrei, Pasith and Polyphemo. Tilvy was kneeling next to Tracey. Sando was lying,

566

obviously dead, next to them. Asha had her arms around John and they stood over the still figure of Jaimee.

That only left Helix. She paid no attention to those around her, she seemed unaware they were there. She made no effort to defend herself against what she must know was coming. Sarva took a step closer. He wasn't sure what he intended to do, but the rage he had kept hidden for three years was boiling its way through.

A desperate, howling yell came from the doorway, "No!" Theseo rushed out, raising a spear.

Andrei swung his sword back. Sarva felt a pang of regret that Andrei must, after all, kill the samudraka king. But when the sword swung around it was to Helix that he swept the blade. Her head parted from her shoulders, and a fountain of gold erupted from her neck.

Polyphemo knocked the king aside before he could reach Andrei, who still had his back turned to his friend the king.

Sarva stopped. The once beautiful head was lying at his feet, the white-blond hair now stained with streaks of gold. The once elegant and self-confident face was slack and expressionless. The power was gone. All at once his rage was meaningless. It bubbled away for a few moments, he considered kicking the head, but before he could move his foot, the impulse and the rage evaporated. When he looked up it was at a brand new world.

28. Departure

Garjae found himself resting under a tree. He tried to remember why he was there. He remembered Darnu's death. He remembered walking among the human soldiers shooting, emptying rifle after rifle and yet never being hit in return. And then he was hit, but not by a bullet.

The samudraka had come. Not many, but enough to overrun the few remaining humans. Some of them had recognised Garjae. They did what they thought was the merciful thing. They weren't to know.

Nuttachen twittered in Garjae's ear. He turned and tried to smile at the little creature.

"He's gone, Nuttachen. He's gone," he whispered hoarsely.

The pale fur shivered and it began nuzzling at Garjae's shoulder like it wanted to merge.

"No," Garjae said firmly. He didn't think he could stand that.

There were still some lights working over the soldiers' encampment. They showed only dead bodies. He could see where Darnu's body must still lie, though its form was hidden from Garjae by the rise of the road. He wouldn't go back there. The body would be fading quickly and there was nothing more that Garjae needed to see.

He turned his head to look through the gateways and up the slope to where the house must be. It was possible that Asha was up there. It was possible she was dead. It was possible she was living but with John. It was even possible she was living but John was dead. However it had turned out, it had already happened. And however it had turned out, there was nothing there for him.

Garjae lifted Nuttachen in his hand and whispered a message into its ear. The brevi twittered back at him for a moment, as if questioning him.

"Go," Garjae told it gently.

It twittered again and jumped from his hand. He watched its pale form scuttle across onto the road and through the gates. He lost sight of it when it entered the trees on the other side.

He took another sad look around him and then pushed himself painfully to his feet. He hurt in a lot of places, but none of it was fatal. He had thought to pick a direction at random, but it was simpler than that. He wouldn't return to the ocean, the fence blocked him the other way, and he wouldn't walk back past Darnu.

"Goodbye, my friend," he said quietly in the direction of Darnu's body, then he turned and disappeared into the forest.

- - -

John stood beside Asha near the helicopter, his arm held protectively around her waist. She smiled at him. She would have to feed him soon, the struggle with Jaimee had taken a lot out of him. She turned back to his daughter in her arms and studied the small grey figure. Ellie hadn't weakened any further yet, perhaps the healing had worked. More than that, an idea was pushing at the back of her mind, they might yet find a way to bring Ellie back. She turned to look at Peren and saw Sarva crouching over her.

"Don't hurt her!"

"I can see it now," Sarva replied. "Every one of these connections is a load on her system. I need to reduce that load if she is to survive."

Asha and John watched over him. Sarva's fingers moved rapidly around Peren's head and torso. At each place he would rub his thumb over his fingers and move on to the next.

"You wanted to know why I left," Sarva said without looking up.

Asha didn't say anything.

Sarva continued to work. "There are hundreds of these," he said, "maybe thousands. And this is after so many of the dhumraka are gone. She must have touched so many others." His fingers paused and held still, as if showing them something. "Human? Aaranya? I can't tell." His fingers continued their work. "They're too fine to do in groups, this is the only way."

Asha glanced at the fading body of Angel lying next to her

daughter. She could never accept the decisions the woman had made in order to survive, but she was sorry that Angel had died like this.

"I killed our mother," Sarva said flatly.

It took a moment for Asha to realise that Sarva was no longer talking about the connections he was breaking, and longer still to understand what he had said. "A truck hit her," Asha finally responded.

Sarva nodded but kept working. "I came by my *gift*," Sarva gave the word a bitter edge, "when we were still in our youth. But I didn't know what it was. One day, when I was with Dad, I broke a connection. I didn't know what it was. I didn't know what it meant."

John squeezed Asha against him. She glanced at his face. She could see that Sarva had already told him this.

"That's when our dad started getting restless and wanting to move north," Sarva continued. "Though I didn't ... I didn't understand, then, that it was my fault. I had broken his connection to our Glade. It was fine, not like his connection to our mother. I hadn't touched that."

Sarva rolled Peren onto her side and continued working.

"It led to arguments. Our mother got upset. Mum and I were together, out on the other side of that road, and Mum was talking about it. How she was torn between wanting to be with Dad and wanting to stay near her home – and with us.

"I can't tell you exactly how I knew, but I could see that one particular connection on her body was bothering her ... so I broke it."

Sarva let Peren fall gently back. Asha thought it looked like Peren might be waking.

He had stopped breaking connections, but Sarva's fingers were still moving in front of him, rubbing at nothing. "It was her connection to Dad. When it parted, it hurt her so much that she screamed. She grew confused and ran – just ran ... without looking."

Sarva stood, glanced at Asha, then turned away. "I saw it hit."

Asha handed Ellie to John and went to her brother. She tugged on his shoulder until he turned. She put her arms around him and pulled him close. There was a long hesitation before he responded. His body shook against hers as he cried.

"Is it over?" Tracey asked. Her head was still aching, her mind was hazy and her thoughts slow, as if they had to travel a long way.

Tilvy tapped her hand once.

"Did it come out … okay?"

Another single tap.

Tracey glanced around. Ray and Paul were sitting to one side, looking lost and uncertain.

"I'd better go to them, let them know."

Tilvy led her by a circuitous route, Tracey could guess why. Ray and Paul looked at her hopefully. Tracey nodded and tried to smile.

Paul held out his hand hesitantly. Tracey took it, pulled it around her and hugged him. She pulled back and kissed him and then hugged him again. When he winced she released him hurriedly.

"Just a few bruises," he explained.

Tracey touched near a gash on the side of his head, then she looked to Ray. "And you?"

"I'll live. I'm afraid he didn't make it." Ray pointed to the large figure of Stephenson lying on the ground.

Tracey glanced at the corpse and looked away.

"We should get out of here," Ray said. He pointed to the helicopter. "We made sure that's not going anywhere, even if we still had a pilot. I doubt we'll get far by car, but it's worth a try. I'd rather not have to spend years explaining what happened."

"Some evidence to destroy first, boss," Paul said.

Ray nodded. "Can you get us downstairs to get started?" he asked Tracey.

"Would you like to kill me now or later?" Andrei asked Theseo.

The king was conscious but far from happy. It was obvious that his head must hurt a lot, and he was still trying to come to terms with what had happened, and what he himself had done, or tried to do.

"Polyphemo?" Theseo queried.

"My king."

Theseo shook his head, but regretted it and winced. "You know that those two over there are papayamala?" He pointed to Sarva and Asha.

"I know they are of the same birth," Polyphemo answered carefully.

"You would let them live, despite what they are?"

"I would speak with your mother."

Theseo looked unconvinced.

"She must have had her reasons."

"Mothers often have good advice for their children," Andrei said.

"How would you know? You never listened." Tilvy poked at him.

"I listened." Andrei grinned. "I just didn't think it applied to me."

"Samudraka," Senna called and pointed.

Theseo made his way to the edge of the roof and called down to say he would meet them down there. When he turned back he looked over the scene on the rooftop.

"Don't forget this." Andrei handed the zakti over.

The blade flared when Theseo grasped the hilt. He eyed Andrei warily.

Andrei grinned back. He wasn't completely certain the king wouldn't choose to use the blade, but by placing himself first in line he hoped he might at least make him think twice.

"You are a strange one," Theseo said. He put the zakti away at his side.

"But never boring."

"No. ... We must go." Theseo turned away.

"See you around," Andrei said.

Theseo looked back in surprise.

Senna elbowed Andrei. "He's joking."

As the two samudraka disappeared through the doorway, Andrei called out, "Thanks for the lessons, Polyphemo. They really came in handy." The large man raised a hand but didn't look back.

A moment later the tiny pale figure of Nuttachen bounded out of the doorway and raced up to Andrei. On his shoulder the brevi whispered in Andrei's ear with Garjae's voice, "I'm not coming home."

* * *

Flames were leaping from the windows of the estate as they drove away, and the eastern sky was starting to brighten with the start of a new day.

"Why does every place you visit end up going up in flames?"

572

Barma asked Andrei.

"Just ask Sen', I'm too hot for my own good. Ow." Andrei rubbed his side and kissed Senna. "I know you love me," he told her. To Barma he added, "Anyway, Taiza started the first one."

"Helped here too," Taiza put in from the other side of Senna.

"And me," added Beenae. He kept touching at the place below his neck where Asha had healed the deep cut.

There was a solemn silence when they drove slowly past the dead soldiers and the place where Darnu had been killed.

With Reyndani included, it was a tight fit for them all in one car, but no one wanted to separate. Ray expressed relieved surprise that the place wasn't already crawling with the military coming to see what had happened to their men. Whatever the reasons, presumably something that Jaimee had arranged, they got away from the area without being intercepted.

John and Asha and the other narun were left in a patch of forest not far from the city. Ray would arrange transport with people he knew and come back for them in a few days.

Most of them now sat in a secluded clearing. Pasith had found a stream and stayed there to refresh himself. Asha had taken some time to merge with a tree, rebuilding her strength after briefly feeding Ellie and John. John thought she had seemed a little distracted and secretive when she left him. Nuttachen and Casseta were tumbling together between Andrei and Senna. John watched on with a smile while he nursed Ellie.

"How long until the Glade opens again?" Tilvy asked of no one in particular.

"It will be so glad to see us get home, it will probably open straight back up," Andrei announced.

"At least it will be able to open now," said Barma.

Tilvy cuddled up to his side. "And the wait will be easier with company."

"You missed one," Peren said to Sarva after he leaned back from breaking connections.

Peren's golden glow was already fading and her skin was taking on a more natural hue, though some patterns were still visible. The pair of them sat very close.

"I can't see it, but I can feel it," Peren continued. Sarva reached out, but Peren intercepted his hand and held it. "Leave it. It's Lantea. I like her. Anyway, she was my first, I want to keep her."

Asha returned from somewhere behind John. She touched his shoulder as she walked past to kneel in front of Peren. "Would it be too much to ask you to make one new connection?"

Peren smiled widely. "I'd love to have you back."

Asha smiled. "I'd like that too, but that's not what I had in mind."

"Who?" Sarva asked defensively.

Asha waved to John. "Bring Ellie. Peren, your mother said you drew her back from the darkness. Maybe you can find Ellie too."

"I don't remember anything about that," Peren said.

"Can we try?"

Peren nodded nervously.

Asha took Ellie from John's arms and placed her gently on Peren's lap. Peren looked at Asha and John, then rested her eyes on Sarva. He nodded.

Peren stroked Ellie's head. She gently closed the lids over the sunken white orbs and then closed her own eyes. No one spoke. There were birds calling, and the sound of the nearby river, but for long minutes that was all.

"She's there," Peren whispered.

Asha clutched tightly at John's hand.

"Eloise," Peren whispered. "Ellie."

The small grey form began to change. The grey faded slowly to white. The limbs and torso altered subtly and her head sprouted fine white hair. A short time later the white skin took on a subtle pink hue.

"Ellie," Peren whispered again.

"Ellie," John whispered.

The child opened her eyes. They were a brilliant bright blue.

John grinned fit to burst. "Ellie," he called quietly.

"Dad?" It was almost inaudible, but to John it was the brightest of music.

"Yes, beautiful?"

"'m tired."

"Of course you are. It's been a long journey."

"Mum?"

John couldn't answer, couldn't make himself speak.

"Asha?"

"I'm here, my darling," Asha answered softly.

"Good." Ellie's eyelids drooped and then closed.

"She's asleep," Peren whispered.

"Just asleep?" John asked.

Peren nodded.

John sat back, speechless. He had his daughter back. Asha was beaming at his side. John reached for her and they squeezed each other tightly.

Asha pulled back before he was ready to let go. She stood quickly and pulled John to his feet.

"Are we going somewhere?"

Her eyes were bright and her smile wide. She had one hand resting across her belly. "It's not too late," she whispered, apparently to herself.

"What?" John asked.

"I have a job for you, but I think you'll like this one. I know I will."

"Anything."

Asha smiled. "There is one more life for you to save."

Epilogue

5 Years Later

It was a chilly morning. The fog had not long cleared and the sun had not yet had time to warm the ground. Traffic sounds growled in the distance – people of the city on their way to work. The noise was an intrusion into this quiet space, the grey headstones stood sombre and silent around them.

"I can still remember her," Asha said softly. She leant her head against his chest. "I can still remember her life slipping through my fingers."

John kissed her hair and held her tightly.

"If I had known then what I know now ... I might have saved her."

There was no way to answer that. It was probably true, but it couldn't be changed.

"Do you think I'm being morbid?"

"No," John whispered.

"I'm glad Ray found her at last. I don't know why. I know it doesn't make any real difference."

"It does to you."

John stared down at the headstone of the young girl he had never known. Asha had described her: dark and brash and loud. A girl very different to Ellie, but one that had been through the same ordeal. A girl whose life had flowed past Asha's fingers in Karlin's prison.

They stood quietly for a while in this small circle of peace within the city. John imagined that Asha's thoughts, like his own, were memories of what had happened since this girl's life was lost.

A human woman approached them, walking slowly with her head down, knowing her way without looking. At first John thought she was old, but as she got closer he realised it was just the way she held herself.

John and Asha stepped back, expecting the woman to pass on by. But she stopped at the same grave and gently removed the old flowers and replaced them with new.

"Time we went," John suggested.

Asha nodded. "Goodbye, Katarina," she whispered.

They returned to where Tracey and Tilvy were waiting in the car.

"Home?" Tracey asked after they got into the back seat.

"Yes," John jotted on the tablet computer in the back.

The message was reflected on a similar computer at the front, and Tracey started the car.

"Is Beenae coming back with us?" Asha asked Tilvy.

"No. He says Taiza has some project he doesn't want to leave, but I think it's just that Taiza doesn't like crowds."

Taiza's speech had never returned to exactly what it had been, but in most other respects he had fully recovered. The main difference was that he now had an almost constant companion in Beenae – leading Andrei to dub Beenae as "the apprentice". The downside to that, for Taiza, was that Beenae had grown popular, which meant that Taiza now saw more of others than he had in the past. But that didn't mean he was about to volunteer for an event like this one.

"Did you catch up with Pasith?" John asked.

Tilvy nodded. "He's doing fine. Neso is pregnant."

"So she finally forgave him for his extended absence?"

Tilvy grinned and nodded.

They chatted easily on the long drive back to John's house – except that it was Tracey's house now. The new Mrs Aldercott, with the enthusiastic support of her husband, Paul, had decided to leave the city and take up life in the country. Their own finances, supplemented by John's bequest, had allowed them to rebuild; a job that had driven the contractors to distraction with all the special provisions for how they worked and what they produced. The result was quite beautiful and very comfortable for the many aaranya visitors that they welcomed into their home.

When they arrived Paul was coming out of the house with Jason and his young son. Tracey got out and greeted them warmly. John thought his old friend looked to be doing well.

"You miss him," Asha said.

John nodded. There were parts of his old life that he still missed. There were, even now, times when he felt guilty for having found such happiness with Asha, as if he was somehow being disloyal to Samantha. He knew that was silly, Samantha wouldn't have expected him to spend the rest of his life pining for her. Perhaps it was just that he didn't feel worthy of this second chance.

When Jason was gone they were able to get out of the car without raising questions. There was a new garden setting out the back of the house and they settled there for a time chatting. Both Tracey and Paul were still having trouble adapting to the more conservative mores of their country life. Things worked differently here than they did in the city. Slower and more personal. Often this was a pleasant relief, but at other times it could be very frustrating. John remembered going through the same thing with Samantha.

Barma came out of the forest, his expression brightening when he saw that Tilvy was back. The two young couples started a conversation about Tracey's plans for a garden. Asha and John sat quietly listening for a time, then Asha caught John's attention with a gentle squeeze of his hand.

In unspoken agreement, John and Asha stood and went inside. They climbed the stairs to the bathroom. This was a human luxury that he hadn't had to forgo, thanks to the generosity of Paul and Tracey in sharing their house.

Asha leaned her back against him in the hot water. John let his hands wander gently over her skin as they talked.

"Are you looking forward to it?" John asked.

There was a pause before she answered, "Oh, that."

He could hear the smile in her voice. "Yes, that," he said. He moved his hand to a less suggestive position. Asha moved it back.

"Very much ... but I am a bit nervous."

"You think it mightn't happen?"

"No. I'm sure it's time. It's just ... what if you're disappointed?"

John didn't think that needed a serious response, so instead he held her body more tightly against his and asked, "Do I feel disappointed?"

They took their time returning through the forest, taking more days than they really needed. There was no fear of being late. Even if Asha wasn't certain of the timing, Peren kept her up to date with any changes.

Tilvy and Barma made their own way back, leaving John and Asha to spend their journey as they wished. Asha had made a habit of feeding John often. This was not through any feeling of desperation, as it had been once before, but because it had become another form of intimacy, as natural to them as their lovemaking.

As they got close they were joined by Tilvy and Barma again, and shortly after that a small welcoming committee approached them.

"Dad!" Ellie called and ran to him, her long blond hair bouncing out behind her.

John knelt down and scooped her into his arms. "Hello, beautiful. Have you been good?"

Ellie nodded earnestly. "Andrei's been teaching me tricks."

John looked at Andrei and raised an eyebrow.

"Kids' ones," Andrei said in offended innocence. Then he grinned. "Mostly."

"I warned you about leaving your children with Andrei," Tilvy said.

Ellie reached out for Asha and John handed her over. Ellie was still smaller than she had been when her human body had died, but she looked strong and healthy and showed no ill effects from her extended time as a preta. No one thought of her as a preta any more, now she was simply one of the aaranya. Perhaps it was because she had come to this life so young, Ellie had learned to merge with the trees. This was something that John could not do, he was reliant on Asha to sustain him.

A tiny figure flew down to Senna. She kissed him and then turned to direct the boy's gaze to John and Asha.

"Mum! Dad!" The boy leapt from Senna's arm and flew directly at John.

The small boy that landed in John's arms was still a wonder to him. Light brown hair like his mother, but his eyes were a dark blue, like John's. He was tiny and finely built, but incredibly agile and strong for his size. And the impossible wings. Covered in a fine brown hair that looked shiny and smooth like feathers from even a short distance. The wings changed shape as needed for different types of flight, and tucked away neatly against his back when not in use. And he glowed. His son was like a figure from a fairy tale.

"Guyen, have you been good for Andrei and Senna?"

The boy nodded.

Guyen called out to another child, beyond their welcoming committee, and jumped from John's arms to fly after him. Asha's eyes followed his flight.

"He might at least have said hello," she whispered.

John put his arm around her and squeezed. He understood. Guyen normally went to Asha first, and John had found himself ignored more than once. It was not always easy to accept the sometimes fickle turns of a child's attention.

They greeted the others. Sarva and Peren were there. Anyone that had met Helix would have recognised the similarities in what Peren had become, though Peren was smaller and her natural expression was meek and shy. There was also a sense of sadness and loneliness that surrounded her. It was less obvious when she was with Sarva, as she was most of the time.

The forest through here was all new growth, but already the trees were tall, and the feeling of life was so intense that the whole area seemed to be humming with it, vibrating just beyond John's ability to feel the movement. Here and there were blackened trunks still decomposing into the soil, remnants of the fire that had been through, but these, too, were part of the life here now.

The group of them walked on through the forest, chatting quietly. The talk faded when they reached their destination. The few children settled with their parents. Guyen sat on John's shoulder, one hand resting on John's head for balance, he looked around in contained excitement but didn't speak. There were other aaranya here. Some had come from the city with Ceeda and Nacee, or had followed later, and some had been left outside when the Glade closed.

Asha passed Ellie to John, then took his free hand and led him to where Ceeda stood with Nacee. With help from Asha and Peren, Nacee had recovered her legs and a little of her confidence, though she still clung to Ceeda whenever she could, and he still kept a protective and reassuring arm wrapped around her. Asha squeezed Nacee's hand in greeting. Nacee gave a small smile in return.

Andrei and Senna came up beside John, Barma and Tilvy next to them. Beyond was a space, as if acknowledging the absence of Darnu and Garjae. John looked behind him. Sarva and Peren were there, in the background where Peren preferred to remain. When John turned back he saw that Nuttachen and Casseta had emerged from Andrei and Senna, where they spent most of their time now, and were sitting quietly on adjacent shoulders. No one spoke.

Asha squeezed John's hand and they exchanged smiles.

There were two trees here that were taller and thicker than the others. They weren't yet the immense monuments that had stood here previously, but one day they would be. The sun was high in the sky, the day warm and clear. A perfect day and a perfect setting, John thought, for what was to come.

A faint glint caught John's eye, like a line of cobweb caught in the sunlight. The birds that had been calling fell quiet, the hum of insects faded, and the slight breeze that had been rustling the leaves subsided. Silence descended around them. Another glint. And another. These grew clearer and longer until they stretched between the two trees. More lines appeared between the first. The surface formed by the lines fluttered as if in a breeze, but the air was still. Fine lines continued to fill out the surface until a pale silver-white and translucent sheet was hanging in the air.

It stayed like that for some minutes before a shallow wave started from the top, and as it descended the surface went clear. When the wave reached the bottom, a glittering shimmer revealed the entire surface for a moment, then vanished. John wondered if something had gone wrong until he saw the faintly glistening arcs that showed that the surface was still rippling between the trees. He blinked.

Kaia was standing there.

"Wow," Andrei said quietly.

Asha went forward first and hugged her grandmother. She turned and beckoned John forward. Kaia seemed unsurprised to find John as he was, no longer exactly human. She kissed him on the cheek and rested her hand on his chest for a moment. She was about to say something to him when Ellie reached out and touched her arm.

"Yes, we know each other already, don't we, Ellie?" Kaia said.

"Welcome home." She turned to Guyen. "And you, my grandson. You bring joy to this old woman's heart."

More aaranya emerged from the Glade and greeted those on the outside. There was a lot of talk and quite a lot of confusion. Those that had been trapped inside wanted to explore the forest outside, those that had been outside wanted to visit their home.

John saw most of his friends go in through the Way, but he stayed with Asha, his children quiet in his arms.

Milla put his hand on John's shoulder. "We have a lot to talk about," he said in his deep voice. He glanced at Asha and Kaia briefly. "But not now." He went to Kaia and steered her away to the forest.

Asha, John and their children were alone now, though they could still hear the voices of the aaranya exploring the forest around them.

Asha lifted Guyen from John's shoulder. "Are you ready for this?" she asked. The small boy nodded seriously. John thought he looked almost as awed and nervous as John felt.

"And you?" John asked Ellie. She nodded vigorously. There was no fear there.

Asha took John's hand. "We made it," she said softly.

"We did."

Holding tight to each other, they stepped through the Way and the surface closed over them. A small ripple, glinting in the sunlight as it spread, was all that remained of their passing, and soon even that was gone.

Appendix

Glossary

Some of the words and phrases used in this story are my own invention, specifically for this story. Words such as *brevi*, *narun* and *spret*. Some words are normal English words with some particular emphasis or variation relevant to the story. Words such as *Glade* and *stand*. And many words have been borrowed or adapted from Sanskrit (an ancient language of India). Words such as *prana*, *preta*, *aaranya* and more. This glossary provides a reference to explain how these words are used in the story.

I started to use some Sanskrit words when I discovered that *prana* had meaning in Sanskrit very close to what I wanted, and it was a simple word that expressed the concept for which I had found no elegant expression in English. The Internet can be a wonderful place and soon I found the Spoken Sanskrit website that supplied even more beautifully expressive words. The words *aaranya* and *preta* soon found their way into my writing and established a tradition. But, *please*, any misuse or poor interpretation of these words as used here is probably due to my ignorance of languages in general and Sanskrit in particular. This glossary is provided to define the way these words are used in this story. Please *don't* try to use this story or this glossary as a way to learn Sanskrit. Consider the words to be part of a language with common roots to Sanskrit, rather than as Sanskrit itself.

The pronunciations offered here are simply how I hear these words in my head, if you hear them differently that's fine with me.

References used below include:

[s] = Spoken Sanskrit - spokensanskrit.de
[w] = Wikipedia - www.wikipedia.org
[d] = Dictionary.com - dictionary.reference.com

aaranya

[ah-run-ya] – noun, plural aaranya.

From the Sanskrit meaning forest-born[s]. It is the name used by the narun of the forest (the dryads or tree-folk) for their own people. Asha and Andrei are both aaranya.

acintya

[ack-int-yah] – noun / adjective.

From the Sanskrit adjective meaning unthinkable, incomprehensible or beyond thought[s]. Here it is the name used by the narun for the process of creating a *preta* – because the action is considered abhorrent by most narun.

Afflic

[Af-lik] proper noun

A samtaana (samudraka community). These samudraka have pale yellow skin, mottled with faded brown, and their tails are a darker brown with pale mottling.

Agadharastra

[Ah-gad-hah-ra-stra] – proper noun.

From the Sanskrit words: agAdha, meaning deep, profound, abyss, chasm[s]; and rASTra, meaning nation, people, empire, kingdom[s]. The name used by the samudraka for their kingdom in the Pacific Ocean. Translates as roughly "Kingdom of the Abyss".

Andama

[And-ah-mah] proper noun

The samtaana (samudraka community) of the Andaman sea (off Burma and Thailand). These samudraka have olive-green skin and tails with a similar colour, but with a silvery cast. The Andama and a few other samtaana of that region have long been associated with the Agadharastra, despite their location on the edge of another kingdom.

andhakara-nitya
[and-ha-kar-rah-nit-yia] noun

From the Sanskrit words: andhakAra, meaning darkness[s]; and nitya, meaning eternal, fixed, constant, sea, ocean[s]. Used by the samudraka as the name of the ocean depths (where the sun doesn't reach), translated as "eternal dark ocean". They have the saying: "Everything, eventually, falls into the andhakara-nitya."

baijika
[bay-ji-kah] – noun.

From the Sanskrit adjective meaning original, source, soul or spirit[s]. Here it is the name used by the aaranya for the massive tree that is the centre and core of the Glade, the tree that supports the Way inside the Glade. Every aaranya Glade (as opposed to jalaja or samudraka zarana) has such a central tree.

brevi
[bre-vee] noun, plural brevis

A small *praanin* creature (made of *prana*). They have the size and general appearance quite similar to a small sugar glider (Petaurus breviceps[w]), hence the name, but their colouring varies. These creatures are praanin, like *spret,* but are of and from the Glade. They are more intense in their prana and they seem to glow when happy. Unlike spret, or narun, these creatures can merge with animals, with humans, and even with narun. Brevi are as close as the aaranya have to pets. They have a homing instinct and also have greater intelligence than a spret. They can be trained to a certain extent. They can repeat messages given to them to pass on – the message is repeated exactly as it was given by the sender (same voice and tone etc.).

daiva
[day-va] – noun.

Sanskrit for: from the gods, sacred to the gods, divine, celestial, divine power or will, fate or depending on fate, attendants of a deity[s].

dhumraka

[doom-rah-ka] – noun, plural dhumraka.

Adapted from the Sanskrit for grey (dhuumra[s]). This is the name used by the grey-narun for their own kind. At the time of this book the origin of the dhumraka is not understood by others.

Eadie

[ee-di] proper noun

The samtaana (samudraka community) south west of Hawaii.

Gayatri

[Gah-yat-ree] – noun.

Gaia, mother nature, the earth as a living thing. Gayatri is something real to all narun, life that they can feel around them and beneath their feet. In Sanskrit this word is a feminine derivation of the word for song or hymn[s], and also for the goddess of education[w].

Glade

[Glay-d] proper noun, plural Glades

As described by Andrei: "The Glade is the heart of our stand," and "The Glade is our meeting place, a place where we can raise and protect our children, a place where our people come together to talk, sometimes to celebrate." Sometimes also called Aranyavaasa (Forest Residence in Sanskrit[s].) A Glade is a form of *zarana* that is specific to the aaranya.

Harihara

[Hari-har-rah] noun

From the Sanskrit name of the combined deity form of both Vishnu (Hari) and Shiva (Hara) from the Hindu traditions[w]. Is the name of a game played between Sarva and Asha when they were children.

Hartdarika

[Hart-dah-rik-ah] noun

Adapted from the Sanskrit, bhartRdArikA, princess, mistress[s].

Title used by samudraka for a woman courted by the king, or a king's son – one that has not yet born him a child. In some respects this position holds greater respect than comes later when the woman has produced the heir.

jalaja
[Jah-lah-jah] noun, plural jalaja
From the Sanskrit meaning born (or living) in water[s]. It is the name used by the narun of fresh water systems (the naiads or river-folk) for their own people.

jaluda
[Jal-oo-da] noun, plural jaluda
From the Sanskrit, jalUkA, meaning leech[s]. The samudraka name for the leech-like praanin creatures of the sarasi-jilvana.

Jatarupa
[Jat-ah-oo-pa] noun, plural Jatarupa
From the Sanskrit meaning golden[s]. Is the name used by the leaders of the evil narun of ancient times, those that started the Aeonian War – sometimes called kalpaanta for the devastation it caused.

kalpaanta
[Kal-pahn-ta] noun
From the Sanskrit meaning end of the world[s].

kravyada
[krah-vee-ar-dah] noun, plural kravyada
From the Sanskrit, kravyAda, meaning consuming flesh or corpses, predator, goblin[s]. The samudraka name for the piranha-like praanin creatures that inhabit the sarasi-jilvana.

Mahasarpa
[mar-ha-sar-pah] proper noun
From the Sanskrit for great serpent[s]. What the samudraka call the adult serpents, the dominant praanin predators of the ocean deeps.

Marr

[marh] proper noun

The samtaana (samudraka community) of the Mariana Trench. These samudraka have deep jade green skin and glossy black tails. Most have dark hair and dark eyes.

matsya

[matt-syah] noun, plural matsya

Fish-like creatures of the jalaja zarana. From the Sanskrit for fish[s].

Mieten

[mi-eh-ten] proper noun

The samtaana (samudraka community) south east of Hawaii. These samudraka have deep tan coloured skin and darker shiny brown tails. Most have dark hair and dark eyes.

nadi

[Nah-dee] noun, plural nadis

From Sanskrit. A channel (tube or pipe) along which vital energies (see prana) flow, connecting at special points of intensity called chakras. The literal meaning of nadi is 'flow'[w] so this word can be used for both the channel and the flow.

nikasa

[Nik-ah-sah] noun, plural nikasa

From Sanskrit nikasa, meaning touchstone, test[s]. A special stone obtained by the King of the Agadharastra from the zarana of the nirarkta. Obtaining the stone is a test in itself, and the stone is said to give the king the ability to detect truth and wise council. "Zamayitar is his power, nikasa is his wisdom."

nirarkta

[Near-ark-tah] noun, plural nirarkta

Adapted from the Sanskrit nirAkRti, meaning ugly, impeding, obstructing, deformed, shapeless, formless[s]. Used by the samudraka for the strange jellyfish like creatures of the zarana beneath Myanmar – the place that the King of the Agadharastra goes to find his touchstone, nikasa.

narun
[nah-run] – noun, plural narun.
Intelligent beings made of prana (vital energy, see below). We are human (made of flesh-and-blood), they are narun (made of prana). There are different variations (races) of narun, including: aaranya (tree-folk), samudraka (sea-folk), jalaja (lake-folk and river-folk), dhumraka (grey-narun) and yaayaavara (nomads).

papayamala
[pa-pa-yam-ah-lah] – noun.
From the Sanskrit words: papa, meaning vicious, villain, evil, bad, wretched, boding evil[s]; and yamala, meaning twin, brace, couple, pair[s]. Used by the samudraka to describe twins – who they consider to be perversions of nature.

paurakanya
[pour-a-kan-ya] – noun.
From the Sanskrit meaning maiden of the city[s]. A name in fun and endearment used by Andrei for Senna.

pazuka
[pah-zoo-kah] – noun, plural pazuka.
Creatures of the aaranya Glade. Brevi are a special/specific type of pazuka. From the Sanskrit for any small animal[s].

potamo
[poh-ta-moe] – noun, plural potamoes.
What the jalaja call their equivalent to the brevi, a sort of cross between a sting-ray shape and a seal. Small like the brevi but with short fur and a narrow tail. Borrowed from potamotrygonidae – which is the name for river sting-rays[w].

prana
[prah-nuh] – noun, plural prana.
From Sanskrit[s][w]. The vital principle. The breath of life.

According to ancient belief: prana suffuses all living forms but is not itself the soul or spirit; prana is what gives life to all things; in at least some contexts it is also considered the carrier of thought; the sun is a source of prana.

In this story prana is considered to be the carrier of the true-self and the spirit. Prana suffuses all living things, and this includes the soil and each tree and water system as individual living presences.

In animals, including humans, the prana is more dense than that of trees or rivers etc. The additional density makes it possible for the true-self (and spirit) to pull free of the material body and exist outside it – as a fragile, energy-like entity. The process of forcing this to happen through violence is called *acintya* and such violent expulsion produces *preta*.

Narun, spret, brevi and even preta are all praanin (see below), beings made entirely of prana, beings that have no material body.

There are certain traits peculiar to prana: an attraction and an ability to detect and affect nearby prana. The narun generally explain these traits as simply "life calls to life".

Another trait of prana is its special affinity with water. This is mostly seen as just another aspect of the close association between life and water.

praanin

[prah-nin] – noun, plural praanin.

Any living creature that consists only of prana: narun, spret, brevi, preta and others. Strictly speaking the Sanskrit definition is just *living creature*[s], but in this story the word describes only living creatures that are made only of prana – those that have no material body.

The prana of praanin (in this story) is sufficiently dense that they can interact well with the material world, the prana-skin acts as a sort of energy force-field. Such creatures, mostly, remain more fragile than their material counterparts but not (necessarily) exceptionally so.

Lack of material existence can make some material interactions difficult. If an object contains life, or once contained life, then the prana or nadis of the object can provide the equivalent of friction and allow fairly normal interactions. If an object was manufactured and carries no life, nor any nadis, then it will feel strange and often very slippery to a praanin.

preta
[preh-tuh] – noun, plural preta.

From the Sanskrit meaning dead, ghost[s] and Hindu mythology for a disturbed ghost[d], often referred to as a hungry ghost[w]. In this story it is defined as "hungry ghost" and used to describe the praanin bodies that were violently pushed from living animals or humans. They look like insubstantial narun and generally don't live very long. (See also *acintya*, *prana*, and *praanin*.)

When first pushed from the material body the preta closely resembles the body that it came from. Usually: if it lives very long (most don't) then the pain, psychological torment and the inability to feed properly all interact to distort the body and it gradually shrinks and fades until the being eventually dies.

Raktana
[Rark-tarna] proper noun

A samtaana (samudraka community). These samudraka have skin the colour of diluted dark (blood) red colour, their tails are similar but deeper in colour and glossy.

saardha
[sar-dhah] noun/proper-noun, plural saardha

Adapted from the Sanskrit word, sardha, meaning one half, joined with a half, increased by one half etc.[s]. Here it is the word for the physical body left over when the praanin body (saarvaya) has separated. Used as both a title for a material body (proper case: Saardha Ben), and as a noun to refer to such bodies generically (those saardha).

saarvaya
[sar-va-ya] noun/proper-noun, plural saarvaya

Adapted from the Sanskrit words: sardha and samavaaya[s], used here to mean one half. In this case the other half. ie. The praanin body. Used as both a title for an individual that has separated from its saardha (proper case, Saarvaya Ben), and as a noun to refer to such individuals generically.

Samgha
[sam-gha] noun, plural Samgha

Taken from the Sanskrit word samgha, meaning brotherhood or community[s]. Is the name used by the people (mostly-human) in northern Myanmar, for the central community of samvaya. The word is used both for the place where these people live (within the cliffs), and also for the group of samvaya that make up this central community.

samtaana
[sam-tah-nah] noun, plural samtaana

Adapted from the Sanskrit word samtana[s], meaning: race, family, offspring, continuance, continuity. This is the samudraka word for their communities, equivalent to how the aaranya use the word "stand". A community, samtaana, reside in a zarana. Different communities of samudraka have different traits, both in appearance and in their culture. See Marr, Andama, Raktana and Yezova.

samudraka
[sam-oo-drah-ka] noun, plural samudraka

Meaning "of the ocean". (Adapted from the Sanskrit word samudra for ocean or sea[s], I added "ka" to distinguish it with my own meaning for this book.) It is the name used by the narun of the oceans (the nereid or sea-folk) for their own people.

Samvaya
[sam-va-ya] noun/proper-noun, plural samvaya

Adapted from the Sanskrit word samavaaya[s], meaning: collection, conjunction, combination, aggregate, union. Samvaya is used in this story as both a title for an individual that can separate their praanin body from their material body (proper case), and as a noun to refer to such individuals generically. See Saardha and Saarvaya.

sarasa
[sar-as-ah] – noun, plural sarasa.

From the Sanskrit sarasa meaning bird[s], but used by the jalaja for all above-water creatures (land and air) inside their zarana.

sarasi-jilvana
[sar-as-ee-jill-vah-nah] – noun, plural sarasi-jilvana
From the Sanskrit words: sarasi, meaning pool, pond, lake[s]; and jilvana, meaning life, giving life, enlivening[s]. Used by the samudraka as the name for the "pools of life", concentrated accumulations of prana at the bottom of the sea.

spret
[spret] noun, plural spret
A creature made of prana (see above). Similar in the nature of their existence to narun, but not intelligent. These are effectively the animal version of the narun. Spret is the word used by aaranya, other narun have their own words they use for such creatures in their own environment.

stand
[stand] noun, plural stands
A community of aaranya (tree-folk). (Sometimes also *tarusanda*.)

tarusanda
[tar-oo-san-dah] noun, plural tarusanda
From the Sanskrit for grove, group of trees[s]. A community of aaranya (dryads, tree-folk). (Sometimes also *stand*.)

tiirtha
[ter-tha] noun
From the Sanskrit for sacred place, way, passage, ford, road[s]. This is the door/pathway into a *zarana*: like the *Way* into a *Glade* but describes an entry into a zarana as used by the jalaja and samudraka.

upapaurnamasi
[oo-pap-or-nam-ah-si] noun
From the Sanskrit meaning: At the time of the full moon[s]. In this story meaning "time of the full moon".

vanadevatas

[vah-nah-dev-ah-tas] noun

Adapted from the Sanskrit "vanadevataa" for silvan deity, wood-nymph[s]. This word is interpreted in the story as meaning forest-gods. This word is used by Waldron Stephenson for the name of his company that manages many forestry related enterprises.

vedana

[veh-dah-na] noun

From the Sanskrit meaning: Perception – also proclaiming, announcing, knowledge[s], traditionally related to "feeling" or "sensation"[w]. This word is used by the narun in this story to describe their life-sense, their ability to feel life (prana) around them, sometimes at great distances. "Life calls to life."

videzaka

[vid-eh-zark-ah] noun

From the Sanskrit meaning: foreign land, another place[s]. Used by the samudraka as an insult for foreigners like the aaranya – calling them foreign, and creatures of the land.

Way

[whey] noun

The gate-way into a *Glade*. This is the aaranya equivalent to the more general word: *tiirtha*.

yaayaavara

[yah-yah-vah-ra] noun, plural yaayaavara

From the Sanskrit meaning nomad[s]. Is the name used by the (land-based) nomadic narun, for their kind.

Yezova

[yeh-zoh-vah] proper noun

The samtaana (samudraka community) on the edge of the Sea of Okhotsk. These samudraka have cream coloured skin and glossy silver tails.

zakti

[zark-ti] noun, plural zakti

From the Sanskrit for sword, strength, power, lance[s]. It is the name of special weapons created by the narun inside their zarana (or Glade). The weapons carry life of their own, and sustain themselves through their connection to the one that possesses them. Zakti can be carried through the tiirtha (or Way), and used effectively inside or outside the zarana.

Zamayitar

[zam-ah-yee-tah] noun

Adapted from the Sanskrit zamayitR meaning slayer, killer, extinguisher, destroyer[s]. It is the name of the zakti sword that is the sword of the King of the Agadharastra. "Zamayitar is his power, nikasa is his wisdom."

zarana

[zah-rah-na] noun, plural zarana

From the Sanskrit meaning help, protection, house, dwelling, refuge, shelter, succour[s]. It is the name used by the samudraka for the place of sanctuary that forms in their communities. The aaranya use the word *Glade* for their zarana but it is the same thing, albeit with attributes better suited to the forest than the ocean.

A zarana is a place where life has grown to such strength and power that it extends into its own dimension creating a separate "place" that only praanin, not material beings, may enter.

zaravarana

[zar-ra-var-an-ah] noun

From the Sanskrit meaning shield, warder off of arrow[s].

9 780987 458346